Nora Roberts is the number author of more than one hu 300 million copies of her bo *York Times* bestsellers to dat the most celebrated women's

Visit her website at www.nora-roberts.co.uk

Nora Roberts Omnibus

KEY OF LIGHT
MORRIGAN'S CROSS

NORA ROBERTS

piatkus

PIATKUS

This omnibus edition first published in Great Britain in 2010 by Piatkus

Copyright © 2010 by Nora Roberts

Previously published separately:
Key of Light first published in the United States in 2003 by Berkley Publishing Group,
A division of Penguin Group (USA) Inc., New York
First published in Great Britain in 2004 by Piatkus Books
Reprinted 2005, 2006 (twice), 2007, 2008 (twice), 2009
Copyright © 2003 by Nora Roberts
Morrigans' Cross first published in the United States in 2003 by G. P. Putnam's Sons,
A member of Penguin Group (USA) Inc., New York
First published in Great Britain in 2006 by Piatkus Books
Reprinted 2008, 2009
Copyright © 2006 by Nora Roberts

A CIP catalogue record for this book
is available from the British Library.

ISBN 978-0-7499-5376-8

Printed in Great Britain by Clays Ltd, St Ives plc

Papers used by Piatkus are natural, renewable and recyclable
products sourced from well-managed forests and certified
in accordance with the rules of the Forest Stewardship Council.

 Mixed Sources
Product group from well-managed
forests and other controlled sources
www.fsc.org Cert no. SGS-COC-004081
© 1996 Forest Stewardship Council
FSC

Piatkus
An imprint of
Little, Brown Book Group
100 Victoria Embankment
London EC4Y 0DY

An Hachette UK Company
www.hachette.co.uk

www.piatkus.co.uk

key of light

key of light

For Kathy Onorato,
for being my keeper

'Tis to create, and in creating live
A being more intense, that we endow
With what form our fancy, gaining as we give
The life we image.

BYRON

Chapter One

THE storm ripped over the mountains, gushing torrents of rain that struck the ground with the sharp ring of metal on stone. Lightning strikes spat down, angry artillery fire that slammed against the cannon roar of thunder.

There was a gleeful kind of mean in the air, a sizzle of temper and spite that boiled with power.

It suited Malory Price's mood perfectly.

Hadn't she asked herself what else could go wrong? Now in answer to that weary, and completely rhetorical, question, nature—in all her maternal wrath—was showing her just how bad things could get.

There was an ominous rattling somewhere in the dash of her sweet little Mazda, and she still had nineteen payments to go on it. In order to make those payments, she had to keep her job.

She hated her job.

That wasn't part of the Malory Price Life Plan, which she had begun to outline at the age of eight. Twenty years later, that outline had become a detailed and organized checklist, complete with headings, subheadings, and cross-references. She revised it meticulously on the first day of each year.

She was supposed to *love* her job. It said so, quite clearly, under the heading of CAREER.

She'd worked at The Gallery for seven years, the last three of those as manager, which was right on schedule. And she had loved it—being surrounded by art, having an almost free hand in the displaying, the acquiring, the promotion, and the setup for showings and events.

The fact was, she'd begun to think of The Gallery as hers, and knew full well that the rest of the staff, the clients, the artists and craftsmen felt very much the same.

James P. Horace might have owned the smart little gallery, but he never questioned Malory's decisions, and on his increasingly rare visits he complimented her, always, on the acquisitions, the ambience, the sales.

It had been perfect, which was exactly what Malory intended her life to be. After all, if it wasn't perfect, what was the point?

Everything had changed when James ditched fifty-three years of comfortable bachelorhood and acquired himself a young, sexy wife. A wife, Malory thought with her blue-steel eyes narrowing in resentment, who'd decided to make The Gallery her personal pet.

It didn't matter that the new Mrs. Horace knew next to nothing about art, about business, about public relations, or about managing employees. James doted on his Pamela, and Malory's dream job had become a daily nightmare.

But she'd been dealing with it, Malory thought as she scowled through her dark, drenched windshield. She had determined her strategy: she would simply wait Pamela out. She would remain calm and self-possessed until this nasty little bump was past and the road smoothed out again.

Now that excellent strategy was out the window. She'd lost her temper when Pamela countermanded her orders on a display of art glass and turned the perfectly and beautifully organized gallery upside down with clutter and ugly fabrics.

There were some things she could tolerate, Malory told herself, but being slapped in the face with hideous taste in her own space wasn't one of them.

Then again, blowing up at the owner's wife was not the path to job security. Particularly when the words *myopic, plebeian bimbo* were employed.

Lightning split the sky over the rise ahead, and Malory winced as much in memory of her temper as from the flash. A very bad move on her part, which only showed what happened when you gave in to temper and impulse.

To top it off, she'd spilled latte on Pamela's Escada suit. But that *had* been an accident.

Almost.

However fond James was of her, Malory knew her livelihood was hanging by a very slim thread. And when the thread broke, she would be sunk. Art galleries weren't a dime a dozen in a pretty, picturesque town like Pleasant Valley. She would either have to find another area of work as a stopgap or relocate.

Neither option put a smile on her face.

She loved Pleasant Valley, loved being surrounded by the mountains of western Pennsylvania. She loved the small-town feel, the mix of quaint and sophisticated that drew the tourists, and the getaway crowds that spilled out of neighboring Pittsburgh for impulsive weekends.

Even when she was a child growing up in the suburbs of Pittsburgh, Pleasant Valley was exactly the sort of place she'd imagined living in. She craved the hills, with their shadows and textures, and the tidy streets of a valley town, the simplicity of the pace, the friendliness of neighbors.

The decision to someday fold herself into the fabric of

Pleasant Valley had been made when she was fourteen and spent a long holiday weekend there with her parents.

Just as she'd decided, when she wandered through The Gallery that long-ago autumn, that she would one day be part of that space.

Of course, at the time she had thought her paintings would hang there, but that was one item on her checklist that she'd been forced to delete rather than tick off when it was accomplished.

She would never be an artist. But she had to be, *needed* to be, involved with and surrounded by art.

Still, she didn't want to move back to the city. She wanted to keep her gorgeous, roomy apartment two blocks from The Gallery, with its views of the Appalachians, its creaky old floors, and its walls that she'd covered with carefully selected artwork.

But the hope of that was looking as dim as the stormy sky.

So she hadn't been smart with her money, Malory admitted with a windy sigh. She didn't see the point of letting it lie in some bank when it could be turned into something lovely to look at or to wear. Until it was used, money was just paper. Malory tended to use a great deal of paper.

She was overdrawn at the bank. Again. She'd maxed out her credit cards. Ditto. But, she reminded herself, she had a great wardrobe. And the start of a very impressive art collection. Which she would have to sell, piece by piece and most likely at a loss, to keep a roof over her head if Pamela brought the axe down.

But maybe tonight would buy her some time and good-will. She hadn't wanted to attend the cocktail reception at Warrior's Peak. A fanciful name for a spooky old place, she thought. Another time she would've been thrilled at the opportunity to see the inside of the great old house so high on the ridge. And to rub elbows with people who might be patrons of the arts.

But the invitation had been odd—written in an elegant hand on heavy, stone-colored paper, with a logo of an ornate gold key in lieu of letterhead. Though it was tucked in her evening bag now along with her compact, her lipstick, her cell phone, her glasses, a fresh pen, business cards, and ten dollars, Malory remembered the wording.

> *The pleasure of your company is desired*
> *for cocktails and conversation*
> *Eight P.M., September 4*
> *Warrior's Peak*
> *You are the key. The lock awaits.*

Now how weird was that? Malory asked herself, and gritted her teeth as the car shimmied in a sudden gust of wind. The way her luck was going, it was probably a scam for a pyramid scheme.

The house had been empty for years. She knew it had been purchased recently, but the details were sparse. An outfit called Triad, she recalled. She assumed it was some sort of corporation looking to turn the place into a hotel or a mini resort.

Which didn't explain why they'd invited the manager of The Gallery but not the owner and his interfering wife. Pamela had been pretty peeved about the slight—so that was something.

Still, Malory would have passed on the evening. She didn't have a date—just another aspect of her life that currently sucked—and driving alone into the mountains to a house straight out of Hollywood horror on the strength of an invitation that made her uneasy wasn't on her list of fun things to do in the middle of the workweek.

There hadn't even been a number or a contact for an R.S.V.P. And that, she felt, was arrogant and rude. Her intended response of ignoring the invitation would have been equally arrogant and rude, but James had spotted the envelope on her desk.

He'd been so excited, so pleased by the idea of her going, had pressed her to relay all the details of the house's interior to him. And he'd reminded her that if she could discreetly drop the name of The Gallery into conversation from time to time, it would be good for business.

If she could score a few clients, it might offset the Escada mishap and the bimbo comment.

Her car chugged up the narrowing road that cut through the dense, dark forest. She'd always thought of those hills and woods as a kind of Sleepy Hollow effect that ringed her pretty valley. But just now, with the wind and rain and dark, the less serene aspects of that old tale were a little too much in evidence for her peace of mind.

If whatever was rattling in her dash was serious, she could end up broken down on the side of the road, huddled in the car listening to the moans and lashes of the storm and imagining headless horsemen while she waited for a tow truck she couldn't afford.

Obviously, the answer was not to break down.

She thought she caught glimpses of lights beaming through the rain and trees, but her windshield wipers were whipping at the highest speed and were still barely able to shove aside the flood of rain.

As lightning snapped again, she gripped the wheel tighter. She liked a good hellcat storm as much as anyone, but she wanted to enjoy this one from someplace inside, anyplace, while drinking a nice glass of wine.

She had to be close. How far could any single road climb before it just had to start falling down the other side of the mountain? She knew Warrior's Peak stood atop the ridge, guarding the valley below. Or lording itself over the valley, depending on your viewpoint. She hadn't passed another car for miles.

Which only proved that anyone with half a brain wasn't out driving in this mess, she thought.

The road forked, and the bend on the right streamed between enormous stone pillars. Malory slowed, gawked at the life-size warriors standing on each pillar. Perhaps it was the storm, the night, or her own jittery mood, but they looked more human than stone, with hair flying around their fierce faces, their hands gripping the hilts of their swords. In the shimmer of lightning she could almost see muscles rippling in their arms, over their broad, bare chests.

She had to fight the temptation to get out of the car for a closer look. But the chill that tripped down her spine as she turned through the open iron gates had her glancing back up at the warriors with as much wariness as appreciation for the skill of the sculptor.

Then she hit the brakes and fishtailed on the crushed stone of the roadbed. Her heart jammed into her throat as she stared at the stunning buck standing arrogantly a foot in front of the bumper, with the sprawling, eccentric lines of the house behind him.

For a moment she took the deer for a sculpture as well, though why any sane person would set a sculpture in the center of a driveway was beyond her. Then again, *sane* didn't seem to be the operative word for anyone who would choose to live in the house on the ridge.

But the deer's eyes gleamed, a sharp sapphire blue in the beam of her headlights, and his head with the great crowning rack turned slightly. Regally, Malory mused, mesmerized. Rain streamed off his coat, and in the next flash of light that coat seemed as white as the moon.

He stared at her, but there was nothing of fear, nothing of surprise in those glinting eyes. There was, if such things were possible, a kind of amused disdain. Then he simply walked away, through the curtain of rain, the rivers of fog, and was gone.

"Wow." She let out a long breath, shivered in the warmth of her car. "And one more wow," she murmured as she stared at the house.

She'd seen pictures of it, and paintings. She'd seen its silhouette hulking on the ridge above the valley. But it was an entirely different matter to see it up close with a storm raging.

Something between a castle, a fortress, and a house of horrors, she decided.

Its stone was obsidian black, with juts and towers, peaks and battlements stacked and spread as if some very clever, very wicked child had placed them at his whim. Against that rain-slicked black, long, narrow windows, perhaps hundreds of them, all glowed with gilded light.

Someone wasn't worried about his electric bill.

Fog drifted around its base, like a moat of mist.

In the next shock of lightning, she caught a glimpse of a white banner with the gold key madly waving from one of the topmost spires.

She inched the car closer. Gargoyles hunched along the walls, crawled over the eaves. Rainwater spewed out of their grinning mouths, spilled from clawed hands as they grinned down at her.

She stopped the car in front of the stone skirt of a wide portico and considered, very seriously, turning back into the storm and driving away.

She called herself a coward, a childish idiot. She asked herself where she'd lost her sense of adventure and fun.

The insults worked well enough that she soon was tapping her fingers on the car's door handle. At the quick rap on her window, a scream shot out of her throat.

The bony white face surrounded by a black hood that peered in at her turned the scream into a kind of breathless keening.

Gargoyles do not come to life, she assured herself, repeating the words over and over in her head as she rolled the window down a cautious half inch.

"Welcome to Warrior's Peak." His voice boomed over the rain, and his welcoming smile showed a great many teeth. "If you'll just leave your keys in the car, miss, I'll see to it for you."

Before she could think to slap down the locks, he'd

pulled her door open. He blocked the sweep of wind and rain with his body and the biggest umbrella she'd ever seen.

"I'll see you safe and dry to the door."

What was that accent? English? Irish? Scots?

"Thank you." She started to climb out, felt herself pinned back. Panic dribbled into embarrassment as she realized she had yet to unhook her seat belt.

Freed, she huddled under the umbrella, struggling to regulate her breathing as he walked her to the double entrance doors. They were wide enough to accommodate a semi and boasted dull silver knockers, big as turkey platters, fashioned into dragons' heads.

Some welcome, Malory thought an instant before one of the doors opened, and light and warmth poured out.

The woman had a straight and gorgeous stream of flame-colored hair—it spilled around a pale face of perfect angles and curves. Her green eyes danced as if at some private joke. She was tall and slim, garbed in a long gown of fluid black. A silver amulet holding a fat, clear stone hung between her breasts.

Her lips, as red as her hair, curved as she held out a hand sparkling with rings.

She looked, Malory thought, like someone out of a very sexy faerie tale.

"Miss Price. Welcome. Such a thrilling storm, but distressing, I'm sure, to be out in it. Come in."

The hand was warm and strong, and stayed clasped over Malory's as the woman drew her into the entrance hall.

The light showered down from a chandelier of crystal so fine that it resembled spun sugar sparkling over the twists and curves of silver.

The floor was mosaic, depicting the warriors from the gate and what seemed to be a number of mythological figures. She couldn't kneel down and study it as she might have liked and was already struggling to hold back an orgasmic moan at the paintings that crowded walls the color of melted butter.

"I'm so glad you could join us tonight," the woman continued. "I'm Rowena. Please, let me take you into the parlor. There's a lovely fire. Early in the year for one, but the storm seemed to call for it. Was the drive difficult?"

"Challenging. Miss—"

"Rowena. Just Rowena."

"Rowena. I wonder if I could take a moment to freshen up before joining the other guests?"

"Of course. Powder room." She gestured to a door tucked under the long sweep of the front stairs. "The parlor is the first door on your right. Take your time."

"Thank you." Malory slipped inside and immediately decided that "powder room" was a very poor label for the plush, spacious area.

The half dozen candles on the marble counter streamed out light and scent. Burgundy hand towels edged in ecru lace were arranged beside the generous pool of the sink. The faucet gleamed gold in the fanciful shape of a swan.

Here the floor mosaic showed a mermaid, sitting on a rock, smiling out at a blue sea as she combed her flame-colored hair.

This time, after double-checking to make certain that she'd locked the door, Malory did kneel down to study the craftsmanship.

Gorgeous, she thought, running her fingertips over the tiles. Old, certainly, and brilliantly executed.

Was there anything more powerful than the ability to create beauty?

She straightened, washed her hands with soap that smelled faintly of rosemary. She took a moment to admire the collection of Waterhouse's nymphs and sirens framed on the walls before digging out her compact.

There was little she could do for her hair. Though she'd drawn it back and anchored it at her nape with a rhinestone clip, the weather had played havoc with the dark blond curls. It was a look, she thought, as she dusted her nose. Sort of arty and carefree. Not elegant like the redhead, but it suited her well enough. She reapplied her lipstick, satisfied that the pale rose had been a good investment. Subtle worked best with her milkmaid coloring.

She'd paid too much for the cocktail suit. Of course. But a woman was entitled to a few weaknesses, she reminded herself as she straightened the slim satin lapels. Besides, the slate blue was right for her eyes, and the tailored lines pulled it all together into a style both professional and elegant. She closed her bag, lifted her chin.

"Okay, Mal, let's go drum up some business."

She stepped out, forced herself not to tiptoe back down the hall to drool over the paintings.

Her heels clicked briskly on the tile. She always enjoyed the sound of it. Powerful. Female.

And when she stepped through the first arch to the right, the thrilled gasp escaped before she could block it.

She'd never seen its like, in or out of a museum. Antiques so lovingly tended that their surfaces gleamed like mirrors; the rich, deep colors that demonstrated an artist's flair; rugs, pillows, and draperies that were as much art forms as the paintings and statuary were. On the far wall was a fireplace she could have stood in with her arms stretched out at her sides. Framed in malachite, it held enormous logs that snapped with tongues of red and gold fire.

This was the perfect setting for a woman who looked like she'd stepped out of a faerie tale.

She wanted to spend hours there, to wallow in all that marvelous color and light. The uneasy woman who had huddled in her car in the rain was long forgotten.

"It took five minutes for my eyes to stop bugging out of my head after I walked in."

Malory jolted, then turned and stared at the woman who stood framed in the side window.

This one was a brunette, with dense brown hair skim-

ming between her jawline and shoulders in a stylish
swing. She was perhaps six full inches taller than Malory's compact five-four, and had the lush curves to match
the height. Both were set off with trim black pants and a
knee-length jacket worn over a snug white top.

She held a champagne flute in one hand and extended
the other as she walked across the room. Malory saw that
her eyes were deep, dark brown and direct. Her nose was
narrow and straight, her mouth wide and unpainted. The
faintest hint of dimples fluttered in her cheek when she
smiled.

"I'm Dana. Dana Steele."

"Malory Price. Nice to meet you. Great jacket."

"Thanks. I was pretty relieved when I saw you drive
up. It's a hell of a place, but I was getting a little spooked
rattling around by myself. It's nearly quarter after." She
tapped the face of her watch. "You'd think some of the
other guests would be here by now."

"Where's the woman who met me at the door? Rowena?"

Dana pursed her lips as she glanced back toward the
archway. "She glides in and out, looking gorgeous and
mysterious. I'm told our host will be joining us shortly."

"Who is our host?"

"Your guess is as good as mine. Haven't I seen you?"
Dana added. "In the Valley?"

"Possibly. I manage The Gallery." For the time being,
she thought.

"That's it. I've come to a couple of showings there.
And sometimes I just wander in and look around avari-
ciously. I'm at the library. A reference librarian."

They both turned as Rowena walked in. Though glided
in, Malory thought, was a better description.

"I see you've introduced yourselves. Lovely. What can
I get you to drink, Miss Price?"

"I'll have what she's having."

"Perfect." Even as she spoke, a uniformed maid came

in bearing two flutes on a silver tray. "Please help yourselves to the canapés and make yourselves at home."

"I hope the weather isn't keeping your other guests
away," Dana put in.

Rowena merely smiled. "I'm sure everyone who's expected will be here shortly. If you'll excuse me just another moment."

"Okay, this is just weird." Dana picked a canapé at
random, discovered it was a lobster puff. "Delicious, but
weird."

"Fascinating." Malory sipped her champagne and
trailed her fingers over a bronze sculpture of a reclining
faerie.

"I'm still trying to figure out why I got an invitation."
Since they were there, and so was she, Dana sampled
another canapé. "No one else at the library got one. No
one else I know got one, for that matter. I'm starting to
wish I'd talked my brother into coming with me after all.
He's got a good bullshit barometer."

Malory found herself grinning. "You don't sound like
any librarian I've ever known. You don't look like one
either."

"I burned all my Laura Ashley ten years ago." Dana
gave a little shrug. Restless, moving toward irritated, she
tapped her fingers on the crystal flute. "I'm going to give
this about ten more minutes, then I'm booking."

"If you go, I go. I'd feel better heading back into that
storm if I drove to the Valley behind someone else."

"Same goes." Dana frowned toward the window,
watched the rain beat on the other side of the glass.
"Crappy night. And it was an extremely crappy day. Driving all the way here and back in this mess for a couple
of glasses of wine and some canapés just about caps it."

"You too?" Malory wandered toward a wonderful
painting of a masked ball. It made her think of Paris,
though she'd never been there except in her dreams. "I
only came tonight in hopes of making some contacts for

The Gallery. Job insurance," she added, lifting her glass in a mock toast. "As my job is currently in a very precarious state."

"Mine too. Between budget cuts and nepotism, my position was 'adjusted,' my hours trimmed back to twenty-five a week. How the hell am I supposed to live on that? And my landlord just announced that my rent's going up first of next month."

"There's a rattle in my car—and I spent my auto-maintenance budget on these shoes."

Dana looked down, pursed her lips. "Terrific shoes. My computer crashed this morning."

Enjoying herself, Malory turned away from the painting and raised a brow at Dana. "I called my boss's new wife a bimbo and then spilled latte on her designer suit."

"Okay, you win." In the spirit of good fellowship, Dana stepped over and clinked her glass against Malory's. "What do you say we hunt up the Welsh goddess and find out what's going on around here?"

"Is that what the accent is? Welsh?"

"Gorgeous, isn't it? But be that as it may, I think . . ."

She trailed off as they heard that distinctive click of high heels on tile.

The first thing Malory noticed was the hair. It was black and short, with thick bangs cut so blunt they might have required a ruler. Beneath them, the tawny eyes were large and long, making her think of Waterhouse again, and his faeries. She had a triangular face, glowing with what might have been excitement, nerves, or excellent cosmetics.

The way her fingers kneaded at her little black bag, Malory went with the nerves.

She wore red, stoplight red, in an abbreviated dress that clung to her curvy body and showed off terrific legs. The heels that had clicked along the tile were a good four inches high and sharp as stilettos.

"Hi." Her voice was breathy and her gaze was already

flicking around the room. "Um. She said I should come right in."

"Join the party. Such as it is. Dana Steele, and my equally baffled companion this evening, Malory Price."

"I'm Zoe. McCourt." She took another cautious step into the room, as if she was waiting for someone to tell her there'd been a mistake and boot her out again. "Holy cow. This place, it's like a movie. It's, um, beautiful and all, but I keep expecting that scary guy in the smoking jacket to come in."

"Vincent Price? No relation," Malory said with a grin. "I take it you don't know any more about what's going on than we do."

"No. I think I got invited by mistake, but—" She broke off, ogling a bit when a servant entered with another flute on a tray. "Ah . . . thanks." She took the crystal gingerly, then just smiled down at the bubbling wine. "Champagne. It *has* to be a mistake. But I couldn't pass up the chance to come. Where is everybody else?"

"Good question." Dana angled her head, charmed and amused as Zoe took a small, testing sip of champagne. "Are you from the Valley?"

"Yes. Well, for the last couple years."

"Three for three," Malory murmured. "Do you know anyone else who got an invitation for tonight?"

"No. In fact, I asked around, which is probably why I got fired today. Is that food just to take?"

"You got fired?" Malory exchanged a look with Dana. "Three for three."

"Carly—she owns the salon where I work. Worked," Zoe corrected herself and walked toward a tray of canapés. "She heard me talking about it with one of my customers and got bent out of shape. Boy, these are terrific."

Her voice had lost its breathiness now, and as she appeared to relax, Malory detected the faintest hint of twang.

"Anyway, Carly's been gunning for me for months. I guess the invite, seeing as she didn't get one, put her nose out of joint. Next thing I know, she's saying there's twenty missing from the till. I never stole anything in my life. Bitch."

She took another, more enthusiastic gulp of champagne. "And then *bam!* I'm out on my ear. Doesn't matter. It's not going to matter. I'll get another job. I hated working there anyway. God."

It mattered, Malory thought. The sparkle in Zoe's eyes that had as much fear to it as anger said it mattered a great deal. "You're a hairdresser."

"Yeah. Hair and skin consultant, if you want to get snooty. I'm not the type who gets invited to fancy parties at fancy places, so I guess it's a mistake."

Considering, Malory shook her head. "I don't think someone like Rowena makes mistakes. Ever."

"Well, I don't know. I wasn't going to come, then I thought it would cheer me up. Then my car wouldn't start, again. I had to borrow the baby-sitter's."

"You have a baby?" Dana asked.

"He's not a baby anymore. Simon's nine. He's great. I wouldn't worry about the job, but I've got a kid to support. And I didn't steal any goddamn twenty dollars— or twenty cents, for that matter. I'm not a thief."

She caught herself, flushed scarlet. "Sorry. I'm sorry. Bubbles loosening my tongue, I guess."

"Don't worry about it." Dana rubbed a hand up and down Zoe's arm. "You want to hear something strange? My job, and my paycheck, just got cut to the bone. I don't know what the hell I'm going to do. And Malory thinks she's about to get the axe at her job."

"Really?" Zoe looked from one face to the other. "That's just weird."

"And nobody we know was invited here tonight." With a wary glance toward the doorway, Malory lowered her voice. "From the looks of things, we're it."

"I'm a librarian, you're a hairdresser, she runs an art gallery. What do we have in common?"

"We're all out of work." Malory frowned. "Or the next thing to it. That alone is strange when you consider the Valley's got a population of about five thousand. What are the odds of three women hitting a professional wall the same day in the same little town? Next, we're all from the Valley. We're all female, about the same age? Twenty-eight."

"Twenty-seven," Dana said.

"Twenty-six—twenty-seven in December." Zoe shivered. "This is just too strange." Her eyes widened as she looked at her half-empty glass, and she set it hastily aside. "You don't think there's anything in there that shouldn't be, do you?"

"I don't think we're going to be drugged and sold into white slavery." Dana's tone was dry, but she set her glass down as well. "People know we're here, right? My brother knows where I am, and people at work."

"My boss, his wife. Your ex-boss," Malory said to Zoe. "Your baby-sitter. Anyway, this is Pennsylvania, for God's sake, not, I don't know, Zimbabwe."

"I say we go find the mysterious Rowena and get some answers. We stick together, right?" Dana nodded at Malory, then Zoe.

Zoe swallowed. "Honey, I'm your new best friend." To seal it, she took Dana's hand, then Malory's.

"How lovely to see you."

Their hands were still joined as they turned and looked at the man who stood in the archway.

He smiled, stepped inside the room. "Welcome to Warrior's Peak."

Chapter Two

FOR a moment Malory thought one of the warriors from the gate had come to life. He had the same fierce male beauty in his face, the same powerful build. His hair, black as the storm, waved back in wings from that strong, sculpted face.

His eyes were midnight blue. She felt the power of them, a flash of heat along her skin, when they met hers.

She wasn't a fanciful woman. Anything but, she told herself. But the storm, the house, the sheer ferocity of that gaze made her feel as though he could see everything in her mind. Everything that had ever been in her mind.

Then his gaze left hers, and the moment passed.

"I am Pitte. Thank you for gracing what is, for now, our home."

He took Malory's free hand, lifted it to his lips. His touch was cool, the gesture both courtly and dignified. "Miss Price." She felt Zoe's fingers go lax on hers, then Pitte was moving to her, lifting her fingers in turn. "Miss McCourt." And Dana's. "Miss Steele."

A boom of thunder had Malory jolting, and her hand groped for Zoe's again. He was just a man, she assured herself. It was just a house. And someone had to get everything back on an even keel.

"You have an interesting home, Mr. Pitte," she managed.

"Yes. Won't you sit? Ah, Rowena. You've met my companion." He took Rowena's arm when she came to his side.

They fit, Malory decided, like two halves of a coin.

"By the fire, I think," Rowena said, gesturing toward the fireplace. "Such a fierce night. Let's be comfortable."

"I think we'd be more comfortable if we understood what's going on." Dana planted her high-heeled boots and stood her ground. "Why we were asked here."

"Certainly. But the fire's so lovely. There's nothing quite like good champagne, good fellowship, and a nice fire on a stormy night. Tell me, Miss Price, what do you think of what you've seen of our art collection?"

"Impressive. Eclectic." With a glance back at Dana, Malory let Rowena lead her toward a chair near the fire. "You must have spent considerable time on it."

Rowena's laugh rippled like fog over water. "Oh, considerable. Pitte and I appreciate beauty, in all its forms. In fact, you could say we revere it. As you must, given your choice of profession."

"Art is its own reason."

"Yes. It's the light in every shadow. And Pitte, we must make certain Miss Steele sees the library before the evening's over. I hope you'll approve." She gestured absently at the servant who entered with a crystal champagne bucket. "What would the world be without books?"

"Books are the world." Curious, cautious, Dana sat.

"I think there's been a mistake." Zoe hung back, looking from face to face. "I don't know anything about art. Not real art. And books—I mean, I read, but—"

"Please, sit." Pitte nudged her gently into a chair. "Be at home. I trust your son is well."

She stiffened, and those tawny eyes went tiger-bright. "Simon's fine."

"Motherhood's a kind of art, don't you think, Miss McCourt? A work in progress of the most essential, most vital kind. One that requires valor and heart."

"Do you have children?"

"No. I haven't been given that gift." His hand brushed Rowena's as he spoke, then he lifted his glass. "To life. And all its mysteries." His eyes gleamed over the rim of the glass. "There's no need to fear. No one here wishes you anything but health, happiness, and success."

"Why?" Dana demanded. "You don't know us, though you seem to know a great deal more about us than we do about you."

"You're a seeker, Miss Steele. An intelligent, straight-forward woman who looks for answers."

"I'm not getting any."

He smiled. "It's my fondest hope that you'll find all the answers. To begin, I'd like to tell you a story. It seems a night for stories."

He settled back. Like Rowena's, his voice was musical and strong, faintly exotic. The sort, Malory thought, de-signed for telling tales on stormy nights.

Because of it, she relaxed a little. What else did she have to do, after all, besides sit in a fantastic house by a roaring fire and listen to a strange, handsome man weave a tale while she sipped champagne?

It beat eating takeout while reconciling her checkbook hands down.

And if she could wheedle a tour of the place, and nudge Pitte toward The Gallery as a vehicle to expand his art collection, she might just save her job.

So she settled back as well and prepared to enjoy her-self.

"Long ago, in a land of great mountains and rich forests, lived a young god. He was his parents' only child, and well beloved. He was gifted with a handsome face and strength of heart and muscle. He was destined to rule one day, as his father before him, and so he was reared to be the god-king, cool in judgment, swift in action.

"There was peace in this world, since gods had walked there. Beauty, music and art, stories and dance were everywhere. For as long as memory—and a god's memory is infinite—there had been harmony and balance in this place."

He paused to sip his wine, his gaze tracking slowly from face to face. "From behind the Curtain of Power, through the veil of the Curtain of Dreams, they would look on the world of mortals. Lesser gods were permitted to mix and mate with those of the mortal realm at their whim, and so became the faeries and sprites, the sylphs and other creatures of magic. Some found the mortal world more to their tastes and peopled it. Some, of course, were corrupted by the powers, by the world of mortals, and turned to darker ways. Such is the way of nature, even of gods."

Pitte eased forward to top a thin cracker with caviar. "You've heard stories of magic and sorcery, the faerie tales and fantasies. As one of the guardians of stories and books, Miss Steele, do you consider how such tales become part of the culture, what root of truth they spring from?

"To give someone, or something, a power greater than our own. To feed our need for heroes and villains and romance." Dana shrugged, though she was already fascinated. "If, for instance, Arthur of the Celts existed as a warrior king, as many scholars and scientists believe, how much more enthralling, more potent, is his image if we see him in Camelot, with Merlin. If he was conceived with the aid of sorcery, and crowned high king as a young boy who pulled a magic sword out of a stone."

"I love that story," Zoe put in. "Well, except for the end. It seemed so unfair. But I think . . ."

"Please," Pitte said, "go on."

"Well, I sort of think that maybe magic did exist once, before we educated ourselves out of it. I don't mean education's bad," she said quickly, squirming as everyone's attention focused on her. "I just mean maybe we, um, locked it away because we started needing logical and scientific answers for everything."

"Well said." Rowena nodded. "A child often tucks his toys in the back of the closet, forgetting the wonder of them as he grows to manhood. Do you believe in wonder, Miss McCourt?"

"I have a nine-year-old son," Zoe replied. "All I have to do is look at him to believe in wonder. I wish you'd call me Zoe."

Rowena's face lit with warmth. "Thank you. Pitte?"

"Ah, yes, to continue the tale. As was the tradition, upon reaching his majority the young god was sent beyond the Curtain for one week, to walk among the mortals, to learn their ways, to study their weaknesses and strengths, their virtues and flaws. It happened that he saw a young woman, a maid of great beauty and virtue. And seeing, loved, and loving, wanted. And though she was denied to him by the rules of his world, he pined for her. He grew listless, restless, unhappy. He would not eat or drink, nor did he find any appeal in all the young goddesses offered to him. His parents, disturbed at seeing their son so distressed, weakened. They would not give their son to the mortal world, but they brought the maid to theirs."

"They kidnapped her?" Malory interrupted.

"They could have done." Rowena filled the flutes again. "But love cannot be stolen. It's a choice. And the young god wished for love."

"Did he get it?" Zoe wondered.

"The mortal maid chose, and loved, and gave up her

world for his." Pitte rested his hands on his knees. "There was anger in the worlds of gods, of mortals, and in that mystical half-world of the faeries. No mortal was to pass through the Curtain. Yet that most essential rule was now broken. A mortal woman had been taken from her world and into theirs, married to and bedded by their future king for no reason more important than love."

"What's more important than love?" Malory asked and earned a slow, quiet look from Pitte.

"Some would say nothing, others would say honor, truth, loyalty. Others did, and for the first time in the memory of the gods, there was dissension, rebellion. The balance was shaken. The young god-king, crowned now, was strong and withstood this. And the mortal maid was beautiful and true. Some were swayed to accept her, and others plotted in secret."

There was a whip of outrage in his voice, and a sudden cold fierceness that made Malory think of the stone warriors again.

"Battles fought in the open could be quelled, but others were devised in secret chambers, and these ate at the foundation of the world.

"It came to pass that the god-king's wife bore three children, three daughters, demigoddesses with mortal souls. On their birth, their father gifted each with a jeweled amulet, for protection. They learned the ways of their father's world, and of their mother's. Their beauty, their innocence, softened many hearts, turned many minds. For some years there was peace again. And the daughters grew to young women, devoted to each other, each with a talent that enhanced and completed those of her sisters."

He paused again, as if gathering himself. "They harmed no one, brought only light and beauty to both sides of the Curtain. But there remained shadows. One coveted what they had that no god could claim. Through sorcery, through envy, despite all precautions, they were taken into the half-world. The spell cast plunged them into eternal sleep, a living death. And sleeping, they were sent back through the Curtain, their mortal souls locked in a box that has three keys. Not even their father's power can break the locks. Until the keys turn, one, by two, by three, the daughters are trapped in an enchanted sleep and their souls weep in a prison of glass."

"Where are the keys?" Malory asked. "And why can't the box be opened by enchantment since it was locked by it?"

"Where they are is a puzzle. Many magicks and spells have been cast to unlock the box, all have failed—but there are clues. The souls are mortal, and only mortal hands can turn the keys."

"My invitation said I was the key." Malory glanced at Dana and Zoe, got nods of confirmation. "What do we have to do with some mythological legend?"

"I have something to show you." Pitte rose, gestured toward the archway. "I hope it interests you."

"The storm's getting worse." Zoe sent a wary look toward the windows. "I need to start home."

"Please, indulge me."

"We'll all leave together." Malory gave Zoe's arm a reassuring squeeze. "Let's just see what it is he wants to show us first. I hope you'll invite me back at some point," she continued as she walked to the doorway to join Pitte and Rowena. "I'd very much like to see more of your art collection, and perhaps repay the favor by giving you a private tour of The Gallery."

"You'll certainly be welcome back." Pitte took her arm lightly and led her down the wide hall. "It would be a pleasure for Rowena and me to discuss our collection with someone who understands and appreciates it."

He turned toward another archway. "I hope you'll understand and appreciate this particular piece of it."

Over another fireplace that roared with flame was a painting that towered to the ceiling.

The colors were so vivid, so rich, the style so bold and

strong, that Malory's art lover's heart took one fast leap.
The portrait was of three women, young, beautiful, in
flowing gowns of sapphire, of ruby, of emerald. The one
in blue, with golden curls rioting to her waist, sat on a
bench that circled a pool. She held a small gold harp.

Seated on the silver tiles at her feet, the girl in red had
a scroll and quill in her lap and her hand on her sister's—
for surely they were sisters—knee. Beside them, the girl
in green stood, a chubby black puppy in the crook of her
arm and a short silver sword at her hip. A heartbreak of
flowers spilled around them.

There were trees with jeweled fruit dripping from the
branches, and in the cerulean sky both birds and faeries
were on the wing.

Enthralled, Malory was halfway across the room for a
closer look when her heart gave another, harder knock.
The girl in blue had her face.

Younger, she thought as she came to an abrupt halt.
Certainly more beautiful. The skin was luminous, the eyes
deeper, bluer, the hair more luxurious and romantic. But
there was no mistaking the power of the resemblance, nor,
she saw as she steadied herself, the resemblance between
the others in the portrait and the other two guests at Warrior's Peak.

"Magnificent work. A master's work," Malory said,
and was amazed at how calm her voice sounded through
the buzzing in her ears.

"They look like us." There was wonder in the words
as Zoe moved beside Malory. "How can they?"

"Good question." And suspicion in Dana's. "How did
the three of us come to be used as models for what is,
obviously, a portrait of the three sisters in the story you
just told us?"

"It was painted before you were born. Before your parents, your grandparents, and those who sired them were
born." Rowena walked toward the portrait, stood below it

with her hands folded at her waist. "Its age can be verified through tests. Isn't that so, Malory?"

"Yes. Its approximate age can be authenticated, but whatever its age, you haven't answered Zoe's question."

The smile that spread on Rowena's face seemed to hold both approval and amusement. "No, I haven't. What else do you see in the painting?"

Malory reached in her purse, took out a pair of black-framed, rectangular glasses. She slipped them on and made a more thorough study.

"A key, in the right corner of the sky. It seems to be a bird until you look closely. A second one there, on the branch of a tree, almost hidden by the leaves and fruit. And the third, just visible under the surface of the pool. There's a shadow there, in the trees. In the form of a man, maybe a woman. Just the hint of something dark watching them. Another shadow, just sliding onto the silver tile at the edge. A snake. Ah, and here, in the far background."

She lost herself in the painting, forgot herself and stepped up onto the hearth. "There's a couple—a man and a woman—embracing. The woman is robed, richly, with the purple symbolizing a woman of rank. And the man is garbed like a soldier. A warrior. There's a raven in the tree just above them. A symbol of impending doom. Just as the sky here is darker, with storm lights. A threat. The sisters are unaware of the threat. They look forward, grouped together, the crown of their ranks glinting in the sunlight that washes this area of the foreground. There's a sense of companionship and affection between them, and the white dove here, on the edge of the pool, is their purity. Each wears an amulet, the same shape and size, with the jewel reflecting the color of their gown. They are a unit, yet individuals. It's magnificent work. You can almost see them breathe."

"You have a discerning eye." Pitte touched Rowena's arm as he nodded at Malory. "It's the prize of the collection."

"And still," Dana pointed out, "you haven't answered the question."

"Magick couldn't break the spell that locked the souls of the king's daughters in a box of glass. Sorcerers were called, and wizards and witches from all the worlds. But no magicks could unbind the curse. So another was cast. In this world, in every generation, three women are born who will come together in one place, at one time. They are not sisters, they are not gods, but mortal women. And they are the only ones who can release the innocents."

"And you want us to believe that we're those women?" Dana's brows arched. There was a tickle in her throat, but it didn't feel like laughter. "That we just happen to look like the women in this painting?"

"Nothing just happens. And whether you believe or not changes little." Pitte held out his hands toward them. "You are the chosen, and I am charged to tell you."

"Well, you've told us, so now—"

"And to make you this offer," he continued before Dana could finish. "You will each have, in turn, one phase of the moon to find one of the three keys. If within the twenty-eight days the first fails, the matter is done. If the first succeeds, the second's time begins. But if the second fails within her time, the matter is done. If all three keys are brought to this place, before the end of the third moon, you will be given a boon."

"What sort of boon?" Zoe asked.

"One million dollars. Each."

"Get out of town!" Dana snorted, then stared at her two companions. "Oh, come on, ladies. This is just screwy. Easy for him to toss money around like confetti when we'd be off on some wild-goose chase for a trio of keys that don't exist in the first place."

"And if they did—" Her eyes brilliant, Zoe turned toward Dana. "If they did, wouldn't you want a chance to find them? The chance for that kind of money?"

"What chance? It's a great big world out there. How do you expect to find a little gold key?"

"You will be given, each in turn, a guide." Rowena gestured to a small chest. "This we can do, if all agree. You may work together. In fact, we hope that you will. You must all agree. If one refuses the challenge, it's done. If all accept the challenge and the terms, you'll each be given twenty-five thousand dollars. It remains yours whether you fail or succeed."

"Wait a minute, wait a minute." Malory held up a hand, then pulled off her glasses. "Wait a minute," she repeated. "You're saying if we agree to look for these keys, just to look for them, we get twenty-five K? Free and clear?"

"The amount will be deposited in an account of your choosing. Immediately," Pitte stated.

"Oh, my God!" Zoe clasped her hands. "Oh, my God," she repeated and sat down heavily. "This has got to be a dream."

"A scam, you mean. What's the catch?" Dana questioned. "What's the fine print?"

"If you fail, any one of you, the penalty for all will be a year of your lives."

"What, like in jail?" Malory demanded.

"No." Rowena motioned to a servant to enter with a coffee cart. "A year of your life will not exist."

"Poof!" Dana snapped her fingers. "Like magic."

"The keys exist. Not in this house," Rowena murmured, "but in this world, this place. This we are able to do. More we are not allowed to say, although we may offer a little guidance. The quest isn't simple, so you will be rewarded for the attempt. Should you succeed, the reward is greater. Should you fail, there is penalty. Please, take this time to discuss it. Pitte and I will give you some privacy."

They walked out of the room, and Rowena turned back to slide the wide pocket doors shut.

"This," Dana said as she plucked a tiny cream puff from the dessert tray, "is a nuthouse. And if either of you is actually considering playing along with these fruitcakes, you belong in this nuthouse."

"Let me just say one thing." Malory poured a cup of coffee, stirred in two lumps of sugar. "Twenty-five thousand dollars. Each."

"You don't really believe they're going to plunk down seventy-five large because we say, oh, sure, we'll look for the keys. The ones that unlock the box holding the souls of a trio of demigoddesses."

Malory debated over a mini éclair. "Only one way to find out."

"They look like us." Ignoring the coffee and pastries, Zoe stood beneath the painting, staring up. "So much like us."

"Yes, they do, and that's just creepy." Dana nodded when Malory held up the coffeepot. "Why paint the three of us together that way? We've never met before tonight. And the idea of somebody watching us, taking pictures or sketches or whatever so they could put this portrait together, spooks me."

"It wasn't something painted on a whim, or quickly." Malory handed Dana the coffee cup. "It's a masterpiece— the skill, the scope, the detail. Someone poured himself or herself into that piece, someone with incredible talent. And it took an incredible amount of work. If this is a scam, it's an elaborate one. Plus, what's the point? I'm broke. You?"

Dana puffed out her cheeks. "Close enough."

"I've got some savings," Zoe put in. "But I'm going to go through them pretty quick if I don't get another job, and fast. I don't know a lot about it, but it doesn't look like these people would be after the little bit of money we've got."

"Agreed. You want some coffee?"

"Thanks." She turned back to them and spread her

hands. "Look, you all don't know me, and you've got no reason to care, but I could really use this money." Zoe came forward. "Twenty-five thousand would be like a miracle. Security for my son, a chance maybe to do what I've always wanted. Have my own little salon. All we have to do is say yes. So we look for some keys. It's not illegal."

"There are no keys," Dana insisted.

"What if there are?" Zoe put her cup down without drinking. "I have to say, the idea of twenty-five thousand dollars really helps open my mind to possibilities. And a million?" She gave a quick, baffled laugh. "I can't even think about it. It makes my stomach hurt."

"It'd be like a treasure hunt," Malory murmured. "It could be fun. God knows, it could be profitable. Twenty-five thousand would really close the gap for me, and that's a very practical priority just now. I might be able to have my own place, too. Not like The Gallery, but just a little place that spotlights artists and craftspeople."

It was a full ten years before that was due in the order of her life plan, but she could be flexible.

"Nothing's that simple. Nobody hands you money because you say you'll do something." Dana shook her head. "There's got to be more under all this."

"Maybe they believe it. The story," Malory added. "If you believed it, twenty-five thousand would be chump change. We're talking souls here." Unable to help herself, she looked back at the portrait. "A soul's worth more than twenty-five thousand dollars."

Excitement bounced inside her like a bright red ball. She'd never had an adventure, certainly not a paying adventure. "They've got money, they're eccentric, and they believe it. The fact is, going along with it sort of feels like we're the ones pulling the scam. But I'm going to get over that."

"You'll do it?" Zoe grabbed her arm. "You're going to do it?"

"It's not every day you get paid to work for the gods. Come on, Dana, loosen up."

Dana's brows drew together, her forehead forming a stubborn, vertical line between them. "It's asking for trouble. I don't know where or how, but it just feels like trouble."

"What would you do with twenty-five thousand?" Malory purred it, then offered another cream puff.

"Invest what I could so I could have my own little bookstore." Her sigh was wistful, and a sign that she was weakening. "I'd serve tea in the afternoons, wine in the evenings. Have readings. Oh, boy."

"It's strange how we're all having a job crisis, and that the thing we all want is to have our own place?" Zoe sent a wary look at the portrait again. "Don't you think it's strange?"

"No more strange than being here in this fortress and talking about going on a treasure hunt. Well, I'm in a fix," Dana muttered. "I say no, it kills it for both of you. Saying yes makes me feel like an idiot. I guess I'm an idiot."

"Yes?" With a hoot of laughter, Zoe threw her arms around Dana. "This is great! This is amazing!"

"Take it easy." Chuckling, Dana patted Zoe on the back. "I guess this is the time to pull out the right quote. 'One for all, and all for one.' "

"I got a better one." Malory picked up her cup again, lifted it in a toast. " 'Show me the money.' "

As if on cue, the doors opened. Rowena entered first. "Shall we sit?"

"We've decided to accept the . . ." Zoe trailed off, looked at Dana.

"The challenge."

"Yes." Rowena crossed her legs. "You'll want to look over the contracts."

"Contracts?" Malory echoed.

"Naturally. A name has power. The writing of one's

name, the promise of it, is necessary for all. Once you're satisfied, we'll select for the first key."

Pitte took papers out of a desk, handed one set to each woman. "They're simple, I believe, and cover the terms already discussed. If you'll write in where you wish the money to be sent, it will be done."

"Doesn't it matter to you that we don't believe in them?" Malory lifted a hand toward the portrait.

"You'll give your word that you'll accept the terms. That's enough for now," Rowena told her.

"Pretty straightforward for such an odd business," Dana commented. And promised herself she would take the contract to a lawyer the next day to see if it was binding.

Pitte handed her a pen. "As you are straightforward. If and when your turn comes, I know you'll do all you can."

Lightning sizzled along the window glass as the contracts were signed, then countersigned.

"You are the chosen," Rowena said as she rose again. "Now it's in your hands. Pitte?"

He walked back to the desk, picked up a carved box. "Inside are three disks. One has a figure of a key. The one who chooses that disk begins the quest."

"I hope it's not me." With a shaky laugh, Zoe wiped her damp palms on her skirt. "I'm sorry, I'm just really nervous." She closed her eyes, reached into the box. Keeping the disk clutched in her fist, she looked at Malory and Dana. "Let's all look at the same time. Okay?"

"Fine. Here goes." Dana reached in, kept the disk palmed against her side as Malory reached for the final one.

"Okay."

They stood in a circle, facing each other. Then held out the disks. "Wow." Malory cleared her throat. "Lucky me," she whispered as she saw the gold key etched into the white disk she had selected.

"You are the first," Rowena said, walking to her. "Your

time starts at sunrise tomorrow and ends at midnight on the twenty-eighth day thereafter."

"But I get a guide, right. A map or something?"

Rowena opened the small chest and withdrew a paper, which she offered to Malory. She then spoke the words written on it.

"You must seek beauty, and truth and courage. One alone will never stand. Two without the third is incomplete. Search within and know what you have yet to know. Find what the dark covets most. Search without, where the light conquers shadows, as love conquers sorrow. Silver tears fall for the song she makes there, for it springs from souls. Look beyond and between, see where beauty blooms and the goddess sings. There may be fear, there may be grief, but the true heart vanquishes both. When you find what you seek, love will break the spell, and the heart will forge the key and bring it to light."

Malory waited a beat. "That's it? That's supposed to be a clue?"

"I'm so glad I didn't have to go first," Zoe said.

"Wait—can't you tell me anything else? You and Pitte already know where the keys are, right?"

"This is all we are allowed to give you, but you have all you need to have." Rowena laid her hands on Malory's shoulders, then kissed her cheeks. "Blessings on you."

LATER Rowena stood, letting the fire warm her hands as she stared up at the painting. She felt Pitte come in to stand behind her, turned her face into his hand when he touched her cheek.

"I had higher hopes before they came," he told her.

"They're bright, resourceful. None are chosen who aren't capable."

"Yet we remain in this place, year by century by millennium."

"Don't." She turned, slid her arms around his waist,

pressed herself to him. "Don't despair, my dearest love, before it really begins."

"So many beginnings, but never an end." He bent his head, touched his lips to her brow. "How this place crowds me."

"We've done all that can be done." She laid her cheek on his chest, comforted by the steady sound of his heartbeat. "Have a little faith. I liked them," she added, and took his hand as they started toward the doors.

"They're interesting enough. For mortals," he replied.

As they passed through the archway, the roaring fire vanished and the lights snapped off, leaving behind a trail of gold in the dark.

Chapter Three

SHE couldn't say she hadn't seen it coming. And James was certainly gentle, even paternal. But the boot was the boot however it was administered.

Being prepared, even having the miraculous cushion of the twenty-five thousand dollars now tucked away in her account—a fact that she had confirmed that morning—didn't make being fired any less horrible and humiliating.

"Things change." James P. Horace, natty as always in his bow tie and rimless glasses, spoke in modulated tones.

In all the years Malory had known him, she'd never heard him raise his voice. He could be absentminded, occasionally negligent about practicalities when it came to business, but he was unfailingly kind.

Even now his face held a patient and serene expression. A little like an aged cherub, Malory thought.

Though the office door was closed, the rest of The Gallery's staff would know, very shortly, the outcome of the meeting.

"I like to think of myself as a kind of surrogate father, and as such I want only the best for you."

"Yes, James. But—"

"If we don't move in some direction, we stand still. I feel that though this may be difficult for you initially, Malory, you'll soon see it's the best thing that could happen."

How many clichés, Malory wondered, could one man use when lowering the boom?

"James, I know Pamela and I haven't seen eye to eye." I'll see your cliché, and raise you. "As the new kid on the block, she's bound to be a bit defensive, while I tend to be territorial. I'm so terribly sorry I lost my temper. Spilling the coffee was an accident. You know I'd never—"

"Now, now." He waved his hands in the air. "I'm sure it was. I don't want you to give that another thought. Water under the bridge. But the point is, Malory, Pamela wants to take a more active role in the business, to shake things up a bit."

Desperation slithered into her belly. "James, she moved everything in the main room, jumbled pieces in from the salon. She brought fabric in—gold lamé, James—and draped it over the Deco nude like a sarong. Not only was the flow interrupted by the placements, but the result was, well, just tacky. She doesn't understand art, and space. She—"

"Yes, yes." His voice never changed pitch, his face never altered its placid expression. "But she'll learn. And I believe that teaching her will be enjoyable. I appreciate her interest in my business, and her enthusiasm—just as I've always appreciated yours, Malory. But the fact is, I really think you've outgrown us here. It's time for you to stretch yourself. Broaden your horizons. Take some risks."

Her throat closed, and her voice sounded thick when she managed to speak. "I love The Gallery, James."

"I know you do. And you're always welcome here. I feel it's time for me to give you a nudge out of the nest.

Naturally, I want you to be comfortable while you're deciding what you'd like to do next." He took a check out of his breast pocket. "A month's severance should help keep the wolf from the door."

What will I do? Where will I go? Frantic questions flew around her brain like terrified birds. "This is the only place I've ever worked."

"Which makes my point." He set the check on the desk. "I hope you know how fond I am of you, and that you can come to me anytime, anytime at all, for advice. Though it would probably be best if we kept that between ourselves. Pamela is a little annoyed with you just now."

He gave her an avuncular peck on the cheek, a pat on the head, then strolled out.

PATIENT and placid he might be, but he was also weak. Weak, and though she hated to admit it—hated to realize it after all these years—selfish. It took a selfish weakness to fire an efficient, creative, loyal employee on the whim of his wife.

She knew it was useless to cry, but she cried a little anyway as she stood in the small office that she'd decorated herself and boxed up her personal things. Her lifetime, career-wise, fit into a single storage box.

That was efficient again, practical. And, Malory decided, pathetic.

Everything was going to be different now, and she wasn't ready. She had no plan, no outline, no list for what came next. She wouldn't be getting up tomorrow, eating a light, sensible breakfast, dressing for work in the outfit carefully selected tonight.

Day after day without purpose, without plan, stretched out in front of her like some bottomless canyon. And the precious order of her life was strewn somewhere down there in the void.

It terrified her, but marching along with the fear was

pride. So, she repaired her makeup and kept her chin up, her shoulders back, as she carried the box out of the office and down the stairs. She did her best to muster up a smile when Tod Grist rushed to the base of the stairs.

He was short and trim, clad in his signature black shirt and pants. Two tiny gold hoops glinted in his left earlobe. His hair was a shoulder-length streaky-blond, which Malory had always envied. The angelic face that it framed drew middle-aged and elderly ladies like the sirens' song drew sailors.

He'd started at The Gallery the year after Malory arrived and had been her friend, confidant, and bitching partner ever since.

"Don't go. We'll kill the bimbo. A little arsenic in her morning latte and she's history." He grabbed at the storage box. "Mal, love of my life, you can't leave me here."

"I got the boot. A month's severance, a pat on the head, and a pack of homilies." She fought to keep the tears from blurring her vision as she looked around the lovely, wide foyer, the streams of filtered light spilling over the glossy oak floor. "God, what am I going to do tomorrow when I can't come here?"

"Aw, baby. Here, give me that." He took the box, gave her a little nudge with it. "Outside, so we can blubber."

"I'm not going to blubber anymore." But she had to bite her lip when it quivered.

"I am," he promised and kept nudging until she was out the door. He set the box down on one of the iron tables on the pretty covered porch, then flung his arms around her. "I can't stand it! Nothing's going to be the same without you here. Who will I gossip with, who'll soothe my broken heart when some bastard breaks it? You notice this is all about me."

He made her laugh. "You'll still be my best bud, right?"

"Sure I will. You're not going to do something crazy, like move to the city?" He eased back to study her face.

"Or fall in with bad companions and work in a strip mall gift shop?"

A lead weight landed—*ka-boom*—in her stomach. Those were the only two reasonable choices she had if she was going to make a living. But because he looked as if he might cry, she waved them away to bolster him. "Perish the thought. I don't know what I'm going to do, exactly. But I've got this thing—" She thought of her odd evening, and the key. "I'll tell you about it later. I've got something to keep me occupied for a while, then . . . I don't know, Tod. Everything's out of kilter."

Maybe she was going to blubber a little after all. "Nothing's the way it's supposed to be, so I can't see how it *will* be. Getting fired was not in the Malory Price Life Plan."

"It's just a blip," he assured her. "James is in some sort of sexual haze. He could still come to his senses. You could sleep with him," he added, inspired. "I could sleep with him."

"I have one thing to say to both of those suggestions. Ick."

"Profound, and true. How about if I come by tonight, bring you Chinese and a cheap bottle of wine?"

"You're a pal."

"We'll plot Putrid Pamela's demise and plan your future. Want me to walk you home, sweetie pie?"

"Thanks, but I'll be fine. Give me time to clear my head. Say good-bye to . . . everybody. I just can't face it now."

"Don't you worry."

She tried not to worry as she walked home. She tried to ignore the panic that dogged her with every step she took away from routine and closer to that wide, wide canyon.

She was young, educated, hardworking. She had money in the bank. Her whole life was ahead of her, like blank canvas. All she had to do was choose her paints and get on with it.

But right now, she needed to think of something else. Anything else. She had a month to decide. And an intriguing task to perform in the meantime. It wasn't every day you were asked to find a mysterious key and play a part in saving souls.

She would play along with that until she figured out the rest of her life. She'd given her word, after all, so she'd best get started on keeping it. Somehow. Right after she went home and buried her sorrows in a pint of Ben and Jerry's.

As she came to the corner, she looked back, mistily, miserably, toward The Gallery. Who was she kidding? That had been home.

On a long sigh, she took a step. And landed hard on her butt.

Whatever had collided with her sent her box of possessions flying, then fell on top of her. She heard a grunt, and what sounded like a yip. With the breath knocked out of her, and what felt like a minor mountain pressing on her chest, she stared up into a hairy black face.

Even as she fought for the breath to scream, an enormous tongue rolled out and slurped her face.

"Moe! Stop, heel, get the hell off! Jeez. Jesus, I'm sorry."

Malory heard the voice, the light panic in it, as she gagged and turned her head to try to avoid the tongue. Abruptly, the huge black mass pinning her down grew arms. Then a second head.

This one was human, a great deal more attractive than the first, despite the sunglasses that slid down a sharp, straight nose and the grim set to the mouth.

"Are you all right? Are you hurt?"

He shoved the massive weight away, then squeezed his body between them, like a defensive wall. "Can you sit up?"

The question was moot, as he was already pulling her

from her ungainly sprawl to a sitting position. The dog tried to nose in but was elbowed back. "You lie down, you big sloppy idiot. Not you," he added with a quick, charming grin as he brushed Malory's hair back from her face. "I'm sorry. He's harmless, just clumsy and stupid."

"What . . . what is it?"

"Moe's a dog, or that's the rumor. We think he's a cross between a cocker spaniel and a woolly mammoth. I'm really sorry. My fault. I wasn't paying enough attention, and he got away from me."

She slid her gaze to the right, where the dog, if it *was* a dog, was hunkered down, thumping a tail as thick as her arm and looking as innocent as anything that homely could manage.

"You didn't hit your head, did you?"

"I don't think so." She found Moe's owner staring at her with a quiet intensity that made heat rush over her skin. "What?"

She was as pretty as a bakery-shop pastry. All that tumbled blond hair, the top-cream skin, the rosy, bottom-heavy mouth that was in a sexy little sulk. Her eyes were big, blue, and beautiful, despite the temper flames shooting out of them.

He nearly licked his lips when she scowled at him and lifted her hand to shove it through that terrific tangle of hair. "What are you staring at?"

"Just making sure you don't have little X's in your eyes. You went down pretty hard. Great eyes, by the way. I'm Flynn."

"And I'm tired of sitting on the sidewalk. Do you mind?"

"Oh. Yeah." He stood, took both her hands in both of his, and pulled her to her feet.

He was taller than she'd realized, and she automatically stepped back so she didn't have to tip her face up to keep an eye on him. The sun was streaming over his hair—a lot of thick, wavy brown hair with hints of chestnut. His hands were still clasping hers, firmly enough that she felt the ridge of callus on them.

"You sure you're all right? Steady? You went down pretty hard."

"I'm aware of that." Painfully aware in the portion of her anatomy that had hit the sidewalk first. She crouched and began gathering what had spilled out of the box.

"I'll get this stuff." He crouched beside her, then stabbed a finger at the dog who was trying to inch his way toward them with the same stealth as an elephant tiptoeing across the African plain. "Stay, or there's no treat for you."

"Just get your dog. I don't need any help here." She snatched up her emergency cosmetic bag, tossed it in the box. And when she saw that she'd chipped a nail, she wanted to curl into a ball of self-pity and wail. Instead, she selected the temper button.

"You have no business being out on a public street with a dog of that size if you can't control him. He's just a dog, he doesn't know any better, but you're supposed to."

"You're right. You're absolutely right. Um . . . this must be yours."

He held out a strapless black bra.

Mortified, Malory grabbed it out of his hand, stuffed it in the box. "Go away now. Go very, very far away."

"Listen, why don't you let me carry that—"

"Carry your silly dog," she snapped and, hefting the box, strode away with as much dignity as she could muster.

Flynn watched her go as Moe lumbered over to press his considerable weight against his master's side. Absently, Flynn patted the massive head and enjoyed the indignant sway of feminine hips in a short skirt. He doubted that run in her stocking had been there before her encounter with Moe, but from his perspective it did nothing to detract from a pair of great legs.

"Pretty," he said aloud as she slammed into a building halfway down the block. "And pretty steamed." He glanced down at the hopefully grinning Moe. "Nice job, jerk-face."

AFTER a hot shower, a change of clothes, and a medicinal bowl of cookie dough ice cream, Malory headed for the library. She hadn't made any firm arrangements with her—she supposed they were her partners—the night before. As she was the first, she would have to be in charge.

They needed to have some sort of meeting, to go over the clue, to plot out a plan of action. She didn't hold out any real hope of winning a million dollars, but she wasn't going to shrug it off or go back on her word.

She couldn't remember the last time she'd actually been in the library. For some reason, going in made her feel like a student again, full of naïveté, hope, and an eagerness to learn.

The main area wasn't large, and the tables were mostly unoccupied. She saw an older man reading the newspaper, a few people wandering the stacks, a woman with a toddler in tow at the checkout counter.

The place was so hushed, the ringing of a phone was like a shout. She glanced toward the sound, and the central island of counter. Dana sat there, a phone at her ear while her fingers clicked on a keyboard.

Pleased that she wouldn't have to search the building to find her, Malory walked over. She wagged her fingers as Dana nodded at her and finished the call.

"I was hoping you'd come by. Didn't expect you this soon."

"I'm now a woman of leisure."

"Oh." Sympathy softened Dana's face. "You got canned?"

"Canned, booted, axed, then knocked on my ass by an

idiot and his dog on the way home. All in all, it's been a lousy day, even with the expansion of my bank account."

"I have to say, I didn't believe it. Those two up on the Peak are certifiable."

"Lucky for us. But still, we have to earn it. I'm first up, so I figure I need to get started. Somewhere."

"I'm ahead of you. Jan? Will you take the desk?" As she rose, Dana gathered a stack of books from under the counter. "Come with me," she told Malory. "There's a nice table by the window where you can work."

"Work at what?"

"Research. I've got several books on Celtic mythology, gods and goddesses, lore and legend. I'm going with the Celts since Rowena's from Wales and Pitte's Irish."

"How do you know he's Irish?"

"I don't. He sounded Irish. At this point I know little or nothing about Celtic myths, and I figure it's the same for you and Zoe."

"I don't have a clue."

Dana set the books down with a muffled thud. "So, we need to get one. I'm off in a few hours, then I can give you a hand. And I can call Zoe in if you like."

Malory stared at the stack of books. "Maybe that's a good idea. I don't know where to start."

"Pick one. I'll get you a notebook."

After an hour Malory needed an aspirin as well. When Zoe rushed up to sit at the table beside her, she took off her glasses and rubbed her tired eyes. "Good. Reinforcements." She shoved a book across the table.

"I'm sorry it took me so long. I was running errands. I bought Simon this video game he's been wanting. I know I probably shouldn't have spent the money, but I wanted to get him something, just for fun. I've never had so much money in my life," she whispered. "I know I have to be careful with it, but if you can't do a little something fun, what's the point?"

"You don't have to sell me. And after you've been at

this for a while, you'll know you earned it. Welcome to the wacky world of the Celts. Dana's probably got another notebook."

"I brought my own." Out of an enormous bag, Zoe pulled a fresh notebook, thick as a brick, and a pack of pencils already sharpened to saber points. "It's sort of like going back to school."

Zoe's eager optimism cut through Malory's foul mood. "Want to pass notes and talk about boys?"

Zoe just grinned and opened a book. "We're going to find that key. I just know it."

By the time Dana joined them, Malory had written reams of notes in the modified shorthand she'd developed in college, had drained her pen and borrowed two of Zoe's pencils.

"Why don't we move this to my brother's place?" Dana suggested. "It's right around the corner. He's at work, so he won't be in the way. We can spread out a little, and you can give me the highlights."

"Fine with me." Stiff from sitting, Malory got to her feet.

"I can only stay for about an hour. I like to be there when Simon gets home from school, when I can."

"Then let's get started. These books are on me," Dana said as she began gathering some up. "Anybody takes one home for personal research, I need it back in a timely fashion and in the same condition it was in when you took it."

"She really is a librarian." Malory tucked books under her arm.

"Bet your ass." Dana led the way out. "I'm going to see what I can get off the Net, and through interlibrary loan."

"I don't know how much we're going to get out of books."

Dana slipped on her sunglasses, then tipped them down

and peered at Malory over the tops. "Anything worth any-thing can be found in books."

"Okay, now you're heading toward Scary Library Lady. What we need to do is figure out the clue."

"Without information on the story, the characters in it, we've got no base."

"We've got four whole weeks," Zoe put in, and dragged sunglasses out of her shoulder bag. "That's enough time to find out a lot of stuff, look in a lot of places. Pitte said the keys were around here. So it's not like we have the whole world to worry about."

"Around here could mean the Valley, or the highlands. It could mean the entire state of Pennsylvania." Malory shook her head at the sheer scope and disorder. "Pitte and pal left it pretty wide open. Even if it's close by, it could be in someone's dusty drawer, on the bottom of the river, in a bank vault, or buried under a rock."

"If it was easy, somebody else would have found it by now," Zoe pointed out. "And the grand prize wouldn't be three million dollars."

"Don't be sensible while I'm crabbing."

"Sorry, but there's one other thing I was wondering. I couldn't sleep last night, going over and over the whole evening in my head. It's all so unreal. But even if you set all that aside for a minute, even if we're optimistic and say you find the key, how do we know it's *your* key, and not one of the other two?"

"Interesting." Malory shifted her load of books as they turned the corner. "How come the Weird Twins didn't think of that?"

"I figure they did. See, first you have to say it's all real."

Dana shrugged. "We've all got money in the bank, and we're walking along with a load of books on Celtic myths. That's real enough for me."

"If it's all real, then Malory can only find the first key. Even if the other two were right in front of her, she wouldn't find them. And we wouldn't either, not before it's our turn to look."

Dana stopped, angling her head as she studied Zoe. "Do you really believe all this?"

Zoe flushed but gave a careless shrug. "I'd like to. It's so fantastic and important. I've never done anything fantastic or important." She looked up at the narrow three-story Victorian painted a soft slate blue with creamy gingerbread trim. "Is this your brother's house? I've always thought it was so pretty."

"He's been fixing it up bit by bit. Kind of a hobby."

They started up the brick walk. The grass was green and trim on either side, but it needed flowers, Malory thought. Color and shape and texture. And an old bench on the porch, next to a big copper pot full of interesting sticks and grasses.

The house looked lonely without them, like a perfectly attractive woman, she thought, who'd been stood up for a date.

Dana took out a key, unlocked the door. "The best I can say about the inside is it'll be quiet." She stepped in, and her voice echoed. "And private."

The foyer was empty but for a few boxes shoved into a corner. The stairway leading up was a lovely, fanciful curve with a griffin head as its newel post.

The foyer spilled into a parlor, where the walls were painted a rich, shady-river green that went well with the warm honey-toned pine of the floor. But the walls, like the yard, were naked.

There was a huge sofa in the middle of the floor, the sort that shouted to Malory, A man bought me! Despite the fact that some of the green in it matched the walls, it was a hideous plaid, clunky of style and too large for the charm potential of the room.

Some sort of crate stood in as a table.

There were more boxes, one of which sat on the hearth of a delightful little fireplace with an ornately carved man-

tel that she could envision dressing up with a fabulous
painting.

"So . . ." Zoe turned in a circle. "I guess he's just moving in."

"Oh, yeah. For the last year and a half." Dana laid her
books on the crate.

"He's lived here for over a year?" It hurt, simply hurt
Malory's heart. "And his single piece of furniture is this
really ugly couch?"

"Hey, you should've seen his room at home. At least
this is neat. Anyway, he's got some halfway decent stuff
upstairs. That's where he lives. There's probably not any
food, but there'll be coffee, beer, Coke. Anybody?"

"Diet Coke?" Malory asked.

Dana sneered. "He's a guy."

"Right. I'll live dangerously and have the real thing."

"Coke's fine," Zoe agreed.

"Coming up. Go ahead and sit. The couch is an eyesore
but it's comfortable."

"All this wonderful space wasted," Malory decided,
"on a man who would actually pay money for something
like this." She dropped down on the couch. "Okay, it's
comfortable. But it's still ugly."

"Can you imagine living in a place like this?" Zoe
turned a quick circle. "It's like a doll's house. Well, a
really big doll's house, but just as sweet. I'd spend all my
free time playing with it, hunting for treasures to put in
it, fussing with paint and fabric."

"So would I." Malory tilted her head. At her very best,
she thought, she would never look as hip and exotic as
Zoe managed to do in simple jeans and a cotton shirt.
And she'd done the math, calculating how old Zoe had
been when she'd had her baby. At that same age, Malory
had been shopping for the perfect prom dress and preparing for college.

And yet, here they were, together in a largely empty

room of a stranger's house and having nearly identical thoughts.

"It's strange how much we have in common. Strange, too, that we live in a relatively small town and never met before last night."

Zoe sat on the opposite end of the couch. "Where do you get your hair done?"

"Carmine's, out at the mall."

"That's a good salon. Hair Today, here in town, where I worked? It's mostly women who want the same do week after week after week." She rolled her big, tawny eyes. "Can't blame you for heading out of town. You've got great hair. Did your stylist ever suggest that you take a couple inches off?"

"Cut?" Instinctively Malory's hand went to her hair. "Cut?"

"Just a couple inches, take some of the weight off. It's a terrific color."

"It's mine. Well, I get it punched up a bit." She laughed and dropped her hand. "I get the feeling you're looking at my hair the way I'm looking at this room. Wondering just what I could do with it if I had a free hand."

"Cokes *and* cookies." Dana brought in a trio of cans and a bag of store-bought chocolate chip cookies. "So, what have we got so far?"

"I didn't find anything that mentions three daughters of a young god and a mortal woman." Malory popped the top and sipped, though she would have preferred a glass and some ice. "Jesus, this stuff is so sweet when you're not used to it. I also didn't find anything about trapped souls or keys. A lot of strange-looking names like Lug and Rhianna, Anu, Danu. Tales of battles—victories and death."

She took out her notebook, flipped it open to the first neatly arranged page. One look at it had Dana's dimples popping out.

"I bet you were an A student all the way through school. Honor roll, Dean's list. Fucking the curve for the rest of the class."

"Why?"

"You're too organized not to be. You made an outline and everything." She snatched the notebook, turned pages. "And time lines! Charts."

"Shut up." Laughing at herself, Malory grabbed the notebook back. "As I was saying before being snickered at for my organized research style, Celtic gods die—they appear to pop back, but they can actually be killed. And unlike what I know about the gods in Greek and Roman mythology, these don't live on some magic mountaintop. They inhabit the earth, live among people. Lots of politics and protocol."

Dana sat on the floor. "Anything that could be a metaphor for the keys?"

"If there was, it was over my head."

"Artists were gods, and warriors," Zoe added. "Or the other way around. I mean art—music, storytelling, all that—was important. And there were mother-goddesses. Motherhood was important. And the number three. So, it's like, Malory's the artist—"

It was a quick and painful twist in Malory's heart. "No, I sell art."

"You know art," Zoe said. "Like Dana knows books. I know about being a mother."

"That's good." Dana beamed at her. "That gives each of us our role in this. Pitte said beauty, truth, courage. In the painting, Malory—let's simplify by calling them by our names for now—Malory was playing an instrument. Music-art-beauty. I was holding a scroll and quill—book-knowledge-truth. And Zoe had the sword and the puppy. Innocence-protection-courage."

"Which means?" Malory demanded.

"We could say the first key, your key, is somewhere

that has to do with art and/or beauty. That goes along with the clue."

"Great. I'll pick it up on my way home." Malory nudged a book with her toe. "What if they just made it up? The whole story?"

"I refuse to believe they made the whole thing up just to have us scrambling around looking for keys." Thoughtfully, Dana bit into a cookie. "No matter what we believe, *they* believe it's true. So there's got to be some root, some basis for this legend or myth or story they told us last night. If there's a root, it's in a book. Somewhere."

"Actually . . ." Zoe hesitated, then went on, "the book I was reading talked about how a lot of the Celtic mythology and legends didn't get written down. They were passed orally."

"Those damn bards," Dana muttered. "Look, Pitte and Rowena heard it somewhere, and whoever told them heard it from someone else. The information is out there, and information is my god."

"Maybe what we have to do is get information on Pitte and Rowena. Who the hell are they?" Malory spread her hands. "Where do they come from? Where do they get the kind of money that allows them to pass it out like cupcakes?"

"You're right." Annoyed with herself, Dana blew out a breath. "You're absolutely right, and I should've thought of that before. It happens I know somebody who can help us with that while we're looking into the myth." She glanced toward the doorway as she heard the front door open. "And here he comes now."

They heard a thud, a slam, a scramble, and a curse.

It was just familiar enough to have Malory pressing her fingers to her temples. "Holy Mother of God."

Even as she spoke, the huge black dog raced in. His tail swung like a demolition ball, his tongue lolled. And his eyes went bright as stars as he spotted Malory.

He let out a series of ear-shattering barks, then leaped into her lap.

Chapter Four

FLYNN saw three things when he charged into the room after his dog: his sister sitting on the floor laughing like a lunatic; a sharp-looking brunette standing at the end of the couch heroically trying to dislodge Moe; and, to his surprise and delight, the woman he'd been thinking about for the better part of the day, mostly buried under Moe's bulk and insane affections.

"Okay, Moe, down. I mean it. That's enough." He didn't expect the dog to listen. He always tried; Moe never listened. But it seemed the right thing to do as he gripped the dog around the barrel of his belly.

He had to lean down—well, maybe not quite as far as he did. But she had the prettiest blue eyes, even when they were shooting daggers at him. "Hi. Nice to see you again."

Muscles jumped in her jaw when she clenched it. "Get him off!"

"Working on it."

"Hey, Moe!" Dana shouted. "Cookie!"

That did the trick. Moe leaped over the crate, nipped the cookie out of the hand Dana held in the air, then landed. It might have been a graceful landing if he hadn't skidded several feet over the uncarpeted floor.

"Works like a charm." Dana lifted her arm. Moe loped back, the cookie already history, and insinuated his bulk under it.

"Wow. He's really a big dog." Zoe eased over, held out a hand, then grinned when Moe licked it lavishly. "Friendly."

"Pathologically friendly." Malory brushed at the dog hair that had transferred itself to her once pristine linen shirt. "That's the second time today he's landed on me."

"He likes girls." Flynn took off his sunglasses, tossed them on the crate. "You never told me your name."

"Oh, so you're the idiot and his dog. Should've known. This is Malory Price," Dana said. "And Zoe McCourt. My brother, Flynn."

"Are you Michael Flynn Hennessy?" Zoe crouched to stroke Moe's ear, looked up at Flynn under her bangs. "M. F. Hennessy, with the *Valley Dispatch*?"

"Guilty."

"I've read a lot of your articles, and I never miss your column. I liked the one last week on the proposed ski lift up on Lone Ridge and the environmental impact."

"Thanks." He reached down for a cookie. "Is this a book club meeting, and will there be cake?"

"No. But if you've got a minute, maybe you could sit down." Dana patted the floor. "We'll tell you what it is."

"Sure." But he sat on the couch. "Malory Price? The Gallery, right?"

"Not anymore," she grimaced.

"I've been in a couple times, must've missed you. I don't cover arts and entertainment. I see the error of my ways."

His eyes, she noted, were the same color as the walls.

That lazy-river green. "I doubt we have anything to offer that could complement your decor."

"You hate the couch, right?"

"'Hate' is much too mild a word."

"It's very comfortable."

He glanced over at Zoe's comment and smiled. "It's a napping couch. You nap, your eyes are closed, so you don't care what it looks like. *Celtic Mythology*," he read, angling his head to read the titles on the books scattered over the crate. "*Myths and Legends of the Celts*." He picked one up, turned it in his hands as he studied his sister. "What gives?"

"I told you I was going to that cocktail party at Warrior's Peak?"

His face went hard the instant the affable smile faded. "I thought you weren't going because I said there had to be something off about that since nobody I talked to got an invitation."

Dana picked up her Coke can, gave him a mildly interested look. "Do you actually think I listen to you?"

"No."

"Okay, then. Here's what happened."

She'd barely begun when he turned away from her and those green eyes sharpened on Malory's face. "You got an invitation?"

"Yes."

"And you." He nodded at Zoe. "What do you do, Zoe?"

"Right now I'm an unemployed hairdresser, but—"

"Married?"

"No."

"Neither are you," he said as he looked at Malory again. "No ring. No 'I'm married' vibe. How long have the three of you known each other?"

"Flynn, stop doing a damn interview. Just let me tell you what happened."

Dana started again, and this time he boosted a hip off

the couch, took a notebook out of his back pocket. Doing her best to appear as if she wasn't the least bit interested in what he was doing, Malory slid her gaze to the left and down.

He used shorthand, she realized. And *real* shorthand, not any sort of bastardized version, as she did.

She tried to decipher it as Dana spoke, but it made her a little dizzy.

" 'The Daughters of Glass,' " Flynn muttered and kept scribbling.

"What?" Without thinking, Malory reached over and clamped her fingers on his wrist. "You know this story?"

"A version of it, anyway." Since he had her attention, he shifted toward her. His knee bumped hers. "My Irish granny told me lots of stories."

"Why didn't you recognize it?" Malory asked Dana.

"She didn't have my Irish granny."

"Actually, we're steps," Dana explained. "My father married his mother when I was eight."

"Or my mother married her father when I was eleven. It's all point of view." He reached up to toy with the ends of Malory's hair, grinned easily when she batted his fingers aside. "Sorry. There's just so much of it, it's irresistible. Anyway, my granny liked to tell stories, so I heard plenty of them. This one sounds like 'The Daughters of Glass.' Which doesn't explain why the three of you were invited up to the Peak to listen to a faerie tale."

"We're supposed to find the keys," Zoe put in, and snuck a peek at her watch.

"You're supposed to find the keys to unlock their souls? Cool." He stretched out to prop his feet on the crate, crossed his ankles. "Now it's my duty to ask how, when, and why."

"If you'd shut up for five minutes, I'd tell you." Dana reached for her Coke and drained it. "Malory goes first. She has twenty-eight days, starting today, to find the first key. When she does, either Zoe or I goes next. Same drill. Then the last of us gets her shot."

"Where's the box? The Box of Souls?"

Dana frowned as Moe deserted her to sniff Malory's toes. "I don't know. They must have it. Pitte and Rowena. If they don't the keys won't do them any good."

"You're telling me you're buying this? Miss Steeped-in-Reality? And you're going to spend the next few weeks looking for keys that open a magic glass box that holds the souls of three goddesses."

"Demigoddesses." Malory nudged Moe with her foot to discourage him. "And it isn't a matter of what we believe. It's a business deal."

"They paid us twenty-five thousand each." Dana offered. "In advance."

"Twenty-five thousand *dollars*? Get out!"

"The money's been deposited in our bank accounts. It's been verified." Forgetting herself, Malory reached for a cookie. Moe immediately dropped his heavy head on her knee. "Could you call off your dog?"

"Not as long as you've got cookies. These two people, whom you don't know, gave each of you twenty-five grand to look for magic keys? Did they have any beans for sale? A golden goose, maybe?"

"The money's real," Malory said stiffly.

"And what if you don't deliver? What's the penalty?"

"We lose a year."

"You're, what, indentured to them for a year?"

"A year gets taken away from us." Zoe looked at her watch again. She really had to go.

"What year?"

She gave him a blank look. "Well, I . . . The last year, I guess. When we're old."

"Or this year," he said and pushed to his feet. "Or next. Or ten years back, if we're being weird, which we sure as hell are."

"No, that can't be." Pale now, Zoe shook her head. "It

can't be from before. That would change everything. What if it's the year I had Simon, or the year I got pregnant? That can't be."

"No, it can't, because none of this can be." He shook his head and looked down at his sister. "Where's your head, Dana? Didn't it occur to you that when you don't come up with the goods these people might hurt you? Nobody dumps that kind of money on strangers. Which means you're not strangers to them. For whatever reason, they know you. They've looked into you."

"You weren't there," Dana said. "Eccentric is definitely apt in their case. Psychotic isn't."

"Besides, there's no motive for them to hurt us."

He spun back to Malory. No, he wasn't affable now, she realized, but annoyed. And working his way rapidly to irate. "And there is one for them to dump big gobs of money on you?"

"I've got to go." Zoe's voice shook as she grabbed her bag. "I have to get to Simon. My son."

She streaked out, and Dana leaped to her feet. "Nice job, Flynn. Very nice job scaring the single mother witless." She bolted after Zoe, hoping to calm her.

He jammed his hands in his pockets, stared hard at Malory. "You scared?"

"No, but I don't have a nine-year-old boy to worry about. And I don't believe Pitte or Rowena wants to hurt us. Besides, I can take care of myself."

"Why do women always say that after they've gotten themselves in a really big jam?"

"Because men usually come along and make things worse. I'm going to look for the key, as I agreed to do. We all are. So would you."

She had him there. He jingled the change in his pocket, considered. Cooled off. "What did they tell you would happen if you found the keys?"

"The souls would be unlocked. And we'd each get a

million dollars. And yes, I know how ridiculous that sounds. You had to be there."

"When you add that these three goddesses are currently sleeping in crystal beds in a castle behind the Curtain of Dreams, I guess you did have to be there."

"They have a painting of the Daughters of Glass. They look like us. It's a brilliant painting. I know art, Hennessy, and this is no paint-by-numbers deal. It's a goddamn masterpiece. It has to mean something."

His face sharpened with interest. "Who painted it?"

"It wasn't signed, not that I could see."

"Then how do you know it's a masterpiece?"

"Because I *know*. It's what I do. Whoever painted it has an amazing talent, and a great love and respect for the subject matter. That sort of thing shows. And if they'd wanted to hurt us, why didn't they do something last night, when we were all there? Dana was there, alone with them, before I arrived. Why not bash her over the head and chain her in the dungeon, then do the same with me, with Zoe. Or drug the wine? I've already thought about all that, already asked myself all the questions. And I'll tell you why. Because they believe everything they told us."

"And this eases your mind? Okay, who are they? Where do they come from? How did they get here? Why did they come here? This isn't exactly Mystic Central."

"Why don't you find out instead of scaring people?" Dana demanded as she returned.

"Is Zoe okay?" Malory asked her.

"Sure, she's just great now that she has visions of somebody using her kid as a human sacrifice." She punched Flynn in the shoulder.

"Hey, if you didn't want somebody to point out the flaws in the plan, you shouldn't have had your party at my place. So, tell me everything you know about this Rowena and Pitte."

He took more notes, managing to hold back any scathing comments on the lack of information.

"Anybody still got the invitation?"

He took the one Malory pulled out of her bag. "I'll see what I can find out."

"Did your grandmother's story say anything about where the keys were hidden?"

"No, just that they couldn't be turned by the hand of the gods. Which leaves a pretty open field."

Flynn waited until Malory left, then crooked a finger so Dana would follow him into the kitchen.

As rooms went it was a sad statement, with its ancient coppertone appliances, white-with-gold-speckled countertops and fake-brick linoleum floor.

"When are you going to do something about this room? It's awful."

"All in good time, my pretty, all in good time." He got a beer out of the fridge, wagged it at her.

"Yeah, why not?"

He got out a second, popped the tops on the wall opener that was in the shape of a bikini-clad blonde with a toothy grin.

"Now, tell me what you know about the very sexy Malory Price of the big blue eyes."

"I just met her last night."

"Uh-uh." He held back the beer. "Women know stuff about women. Like telepathically. The more a woman likes or dislikes another woman, the more she knows. There have been several scientific studies to verify this phenomenon. Give, or no beer for you."

She hadn't particularly wanted the beer, until he'd used it as a hammer. "Why do you want to know about her specifically? Why not Zoe?"

"My interest in Zoe is more academic. I can hardly start the wild and passionate affair I have in mind with Malory until I know all her secrets and desires."

"You're going to make me sick, Flynn."

He merely tipped up his beer, took a long, slow sip, while holding hers out of reach.

"I'm not your silly dog who'll beg for cookies. I'm only going to tell you so I can sit back and laugh derisively when she blows you off. I do like her," she added and held out a hand for the beer. "She strikes me as smart, ambitious, open-minded without being naive. She worked at The Gallery, just got canned over a dispute with the owner's new trophy wife. Since Malory called the new wife a bimbo, to her face, I'd say she doesn't always rate high on the tact and diplomacy scale, but calls 'em like she sees 'em. She likes good clothes and knows how to wear them—spends too much on them, which is why she was broke before this morning's windfall. She's not currently in a relationship and would like to own her own business."

"You really buried the lead." He took a long, slow sip. "So, she's not dating anyone. And she's gutsy. Not only does she tell off the boss's wife, but she drives alone, at night, to the spookiest house in western Pennsylvania."

"So did I."

"I can't have a mad, passionate affair with you, sweetie. It would just be wrong."

"Now, there, you have made me sick."

But she smiled when he leaned over and kissed her cheek. "Why don't you move in here for a couple weeks?"

Her dark chocolate eyes went baleful. "Stop looking out for me, Flynn."

"Can't do it."

"If I wouldn't move in when I was broke, why would I now that I'm flush? You know I like my own space, and you do too. Such as it is. And the goblins of Warrior's Peak are not going to come down and spirit me away in the night."

"If they were goblins, they wouldn't worry me." But because he knew her, he eased off. "How about telling your new pal Malory what an amazing man I am. All brainy and sensitive and buff."

"You want me to lie to her?"

"You're mean, Dana." He gulped down more beer. "You're just mean."

W H E N he was alone, Flynn settled down in his upstairs study. He preferred the term "study" to "office," as an office meant work. No way around it. In a study, you could, well, study, or nap or read, or stare into space thinking long thoughts. You could certainly work, but it wasn't a requirement.

He'd outfitted the room with a big, brawny desk and a couple of wide leather chairs that he thought felt as if you might sink into them until you disappeared.

He had files as well, but he disguised them with manly-looking chests. One wall was covered with framed prints of pinup girls from the forties and fifties.

If all else failed, he could kick back, study them, and pass an enjoyable hour in solitude.

He booted up his computer, stepped over Moe, who had already flopped in the middle of the floor, and pulled a second beer out of the mini fridge he'd installed under a work counter.

He'd considered that idea pretty damn clever.

Then he sat, rolled his head as a boxer might before a round, and got down to some serious surfing.

If there was anything in the cyberworld about the new residents of Warrior's Peak, he would find it.

As always, he got sucked into the sirens' song of information. His beer went warm. One hour passed into two, two headed toward three, before Moe solved the matter by giving the desk chair a push that shot it and Flynn halfway across the room.

"Damn it, you know I hate that. I just need a few more minutes."

But Moe had heard that one before, and he protested by plopping massive paws and a great deal of body weight onto Flynn's thighs. "So, maybe we'll take a walk. And if we happen to wander by a certain blonde's door, we could just stop in and share currently gathered information. And if that doesn't work, we'll pick up some pizza so it won't be a complete loss."

The word "pizza" had Moe tearing to the doorway. By the time Flynn made it downstairs, the dog was by the front door, his leash clamped between his teeth.

It was a nice evening for a walk. Quiet, balmy, with his little postcard town basking under the late-summer sun. At such moments, when the air was soft, the breeze fragrant, he was glad he'd made the decision to take over the *Dispatch* from his mother rather than heading out to make his mark at some big-city paper.

A lot of his friends had gone to the city, and the woman he'd thought he loved had chosen New York over him.

Or he'd chosen the Valley over her.

It depended, he supposed, on your point of view.

Maybe the news here didn't have the scope or the edge of the news in Philly or New York, but there was still plenty of it. And what happened in the Valley, in the hills and mountains that surrounded it, mattered.

And just now he scented a story that would be bigger and juicier than anything the *Dispatch* had reported in the sixty-eight years since its presses began to run.

If he could help three women, one of whom was a sister he loved very much, flirt with an incredibly attractive blonde, *and* expose a major con . . . well, that would be a hell of a hat trick.

"You have to be charming," he told Moe as they approached the trim brick building that he'd watched Malory enter that morning. "You act like a dog, we'll never get through the door."

As a precaution, Flynn wrapped the leash twice around

his fist before going into the twelve-unit building.

He considered it good luck that M. Price was on the ground floor. Not only would he not have to drag Moe up steps or pull him into an elevator, but the building's ground level had little patios.

That gave him the option of bribing Moe with the cookie he'd stuffed in his pocket and staking him outside.

"Charming," he said again, sotto voce, giving Moe a narrow stare before he knocked on Malory's door.

Her greeting, when she answered, wasn't what he could call flattering.

She took one look at him and Moe. "Oh, my God. You've got to be kidding."

"I can put him outside," Flynn said quickly. "But we really need to talk."

"He'll dig up my flowers."

"He doesn't dig." Please God, don't dig. "I've got a—I can't say the C word, or he'll get excited. But I've got one in my pocket. I'll just put him out there, out of the way."

"I don't—" Moe's nose arrowed straight into her crotch. "Christ." In defense she skipped back, which was all the invitation Moe required.

He was through the door, dragging Flynn merrily over an antique Turkish carpet, barely missing slapping his lethal tail into a Deco vase filled with late-summer lilies.

Terrified, Malory made a dash for her patio door, yanked it open. "Out, out, straight out."

It was a word Moe knew. And he objected to going out when he'd just come in to so many fascinating scents. He simply dropped his wide butt on the floor and dug in.

With dignity no longer an option, Flynn hooked both hands in Moe's collar and dragged him bodily across the room and out the door.

"Oh, yeah, that was charming." Out of breath, Flynn looped the leash around the trunk of a tree. And as Moe began to howl, he dropped to his knees. "Stop it. Have

you no pride? Have you no sense of masculine solidarity?
How am I going to get my hands on that woman if she
hates us?"

He pushed his face into Moe's. "Lie down and be
quiet. Do this for me, and the world is yours. Starting
with this."

He pulled out the cookie. The howling stopped instantly, and the tail began to thump.

"Screw this up and next time I leave you home."

He stood up and sent what he hoped was an easy smile
toward Malory, who stood warily on the other side of the
door.

He figured it was a major victory when she opened it
and let him in.

"Have you tried obedience school?" she demanded.

"Ah, well, yeah, but there was an incident. We don't
like to talk about it. This is a great place."

Stylish, arty, and female, he decided. Not delicate-
little-trinket female but bold-unique-fascinating female.

The walls were a deep, rich rose, a strong background
for the paintings. She favored antiques, or reproductions
that looked enough like the real thing to pass. Soft fabrics
and sleek sculpture.

And everything tidy as a shiny new pin.

It smelled female, classily so, from the lilies and the
dried flower petals that women were forever putting in
bowls. And, he supposed, from the woman herself.

She had music on low. What was that . . . Annie Len-
nox, crooning slyly about sweet dreams.

It seemed to Flynn that the entire place spoke of very
specific, very high-toned taste.

He wandered over to a painting of a woman rising up
out of a dark blue pool. There was a sense of speed about
it, of sexuality, and of power.

"She's beautiful. Does she live in the sea or on the
land?"

Malory arched her brow. At least he'd asked an intelligent question.

"I think she has yet to choose." She pondered him as
he wandered around. He seemed more . . . well, male, she
supposed, here in her place than he had on the sidewalk
or stalking around the largely unfurnished room in his
own house.

"What are you doing here?"

"First, I came because I wanted to see you again."

"Why?"

"You're really pretty." Because he found it both relaxing and entertaining to look at her, he hooked his thumbs
in his front pockets and did just that. "You might think
that's a shallow reason, but I like to think it's simply
basic. If people didn't like looking at attractive things, we
wouldn't have any art."

"How long did it take you to think of that one?"

His grin was fast and appreciative. "Not long at all.
I'm pretty quick. Have you had dinner?"

"No, but I have plans. Why else are you here?"

"Let's do this part first. You haven't had dinner tomorrow night yet. Would you like to have dinner with
me?"

"I don't think that's a good idea."

"Because you're annoyed with me? Or because you're
not interested?"

"You're pretty annoying."

Those lazy-river eyes flirted. "Not once you get to
know me. Ask anybody."

No, she had a feeling he wouldn't stay annoying. He'd
be entertaining and interesting. And trouble. Plus, however attractive he was, he was anything but her type. "I've
got enough on my plate without dating a man who has
terrible taste in furniture and questionable taste in pets."

She glanced toward the patio as she said it, then
couldn't stop the laugh as she saw Moe's ugly face
pressed hopefully against the glass.

"You don't really hate dogs."

"Of course I don't hate dogs. I like dogs." She angled her head to study the furry face. "I don't think that is a dog."

"They swore he was when I got him from the pound."

Her eyes went soft. "You got him from the pound."

Aha, a chink in the defensive wall. He stepped over so they could study Moe together. "He was a lot smaller then. I went in to do a story on the shelter, and he sort of came, well, gamboling up to me, looked at me like he was saying, Okay, I've been waiting for you to show. Let's go home. I was a goner."

"What's does 'Moe' stand for? 'Mountain'?"

"He looks like Moe. You know, Moe Howard." When her face stayed blank, Flynn sighed. "Women, they don't know what they're missing when it comes to the courageous comedy and wit of The Three Stooges."

"Yes, yes, we do know what we're missing. We miss it on purpose." Realizing they were standing close, she took a deliberate step back. "Was there something else?"

"I started running down these people you guys are tangled up with. Liam Pitte, Rowena O'Meara. At least those are the names they're using."

"Why shouldn't those *be* their names?"

"Because when I used my incredible skills and talents, I found no record of anyone under those names that jibes with the new owners of Warrior's Peak. No social security numbers, no passport numbers, no driver's licenses, business licenses. No corporate paper trail for this Triad. At least none that connects to them."

"They're not American," she began, then blew out a breath. "Okay, no passport numbers. Maybe you didn't find it yet, or maybe they've used different names to buy the house."

"Maybe. It'll be interesting to find out, because right now it's looking like they popped out of thin air."

"I'd like to know more about the Daughters of Glass.

The more I know about them, the better chance I have of finding the key."

"I'll call my grandmother, get more details of the legend. I can fill you in over dinner tomorrow."

She considered him, then looked back toward the dog. He was willing to help, and she only had four weeks. On a personal front, she would keep it simple. Friendly, but simple. At least until she'd decided what to do about him.

"Would that be a table for two or for three?"

"Two."

"All right. You can pick me up at seven."

"Great."

"And you can go out that way." She pointed toward the patio door.

"No problem." He walked to the door, glanced back. "You really are pretty," he said, then eased the door open just enough to squeeze out.

She watched him unhook the dog, watched him stagger under the weight when Moe leaped up to lavishly kiss his face. She waited until they'd trotted off before she chuckled.

Chapter Five

MALORY found Zoe's little house easily enough. It was a tiny box on a narrow stamp of lawn. But it had been painted a cheerful yellow with bright white trim. A colorful patch of flowers bloomed vigorously along either side of the door.

Even if Malory hadn't been sure of the address, hadn't recognized Zoe's car parked at the curb, she'd have known the house by the boy in the yard, tossing a ball high in the air, then racing to catch it.

He looked almost eerily like his mother. The dark hair, the long-lidded eyes in a pixie face. He had a slight build clad in ripped jeans and a Pittsburgh Pirates T-shirt.

When he spotted Malory, he stood, legs apart, flipping the ball lightly into the pocket of his glove.

He had the cautious and somewhat arrogant stance of a boy who'd had "don't talk to strangers" drummed into his head, and thought he was old enough, smart enough, to handle himself with one anyway.

"You must be Simon. I'm Malory Price, a friend of

your mother's." She kept a smile on her face as the boy sized her up—and she wished she knew more about base-ball than that it involved a number of men throwing, hit-ting, and trying to catch a ball and running around a field.

"She's in the house. I can get her." His way of doing so was to trot toward the door and shout, "Mom! There's a lady out here to see you!"

Moments later, Zoe opened the screen door, stood there wiping her hands on a dish towel. Somehow, despite the baggy shorts, old shirt, and bare feet, she still managed to look exotic.

"Oh. Malory." She lifted a hand to fiddle with one of the buttons of her shirt. "I wasn't expecting . . ."

"If this is a bad time—"

"No, no, of course not. Simon, this is Miss Price. One of the ladies I'm going to be working with for a while."

"Okay. Hi. Can I go over to Scott's now? I finished mowing the lawn."

"Looks great. Do you want a snack first?"

"Nuh-uh." At her arch look, he grinned, showing a missing tooth and sudden, dazzling charm. "I mean, no thanks."

"Go ahead, then. Have a good time."

"Yes!" He started to race off, then skidded to a halt when she spoke his name in a tone that Malory assumed mothers developed through hormonal changes during ges-tation.

He rolled his eyes, but made sure his back was to Zoe as he did. Then he gave Malory a quick and easy smile. "Nice to meet you, and all."

"Nice to meet you, and all too, Simon."

He dashed off, like an inmate escaping the prison walls.

"He's gorgeous."

At Malory's statement, Zoe's face lit up with pride and pleasure. "He really is, isn't he? Sometimes I'll sneak to the window while he's out in the yard and just look at him. He's my whole world."

"I could see that. And now you're worried that what we've done could hurt him somehow."

"Worrying about Simon is part of my job description. Listen, I'm sorry, come in. I used to spend Saturdays at the salon, so I thought I'd take advantage of having this one off and dig in around here."

"You've got a pretty house." She stepped inside the door, looked around. "A *very* pretty house."

"Thanks." Zoe looked around as well, grateful that she'd finished buffing up the living room. The pillows were plumped on the bright and cheery blue slipcovers of the sofa, and the old coffee table she'd antiqued was free of dust and held a trio of bottles filled with late-summer daisies snipped from her own little flower bed. The rug her grandmother had hooked when Zoe herself was a child was freshly vacuumed.

"These are great." Malory wandered over to look at the framed prints of foreign locales grouped on a wall.

"They're just postcards I matted and framed. I always ask customers to pick me up a postcard when they go on a trip."

"They're really clever, and fun."

"I like to, you know, put things together. Find stuff at yard sales or flea markets and haul it home, fix it up. It makes it yours that way, plus it doesn't cost a lot of money. Ah, would you like something to drink?"

"I would, if I'm not holding you up."

"No. I don't think I've had a Saturday off in . . ." She skimmed her fingers through her hair. "Ever," She decided. "It's nice to be home, and to have company."

Malory had a feeling that she was about to be invited to sit down while Zoe went back to the kitchen. To avoid that, she walked over and angled herself toward the doorway. "Did you plant the flowers yourself?"

"Simon and I did." With no choice, Zoe led the way

into the kitchen. "I don't have any soft drinks. Sorry, but I can't keep them around with Simon. I've got some lemonade."

"That's great."

She'd obviously caught Zoe in the midst of a major kitchen cleaning, but still the room exuded the same casual charm as the living area.

"I love this." She trailed a finger over the mint-green paint of a cupboard. "It really shows what someone can do with imagination, taste, and time."

"Wow." Zoe took a squat glass pitcher out of the refrigerator. "That's quite a compliment coming from somebody like you. I mean, somebody who knows art. I wanted to have pretty things but still make a place where Simon could run around like a boy. And it's just the right size for us. I don't care about the million dollars."

She set her company glasses on the counter, shook her head. "Boy, does that sound stupid. Of course I *care* about the million dollars. What I mean is I don't need a million. I just want enough so we're secure. I only got into this because it seemed so interesting, and because the twenty-five thousand was like a miracle."

"And because that night, up at Warrior's Peak, was so compelling, so dramatic? Like we were all the stars of our own movie."

"Yes." Zoe let out a laugh as she poured. "I got caught up in the idea of it all, but I never considered, not for a minute, that we'd be taking any kind of risk."

"I don't know that we are. I'm not going to worry about that until we know more. But I don't have a child to consider. I wanted to come by and say that if you want to back out, I understand."

"I've been thinking about it. One of the advantages of serious cleaning is it's good thinking time. Do you want to take these out in the back? I've got some chairs out there. It's kind of a nice spot."

They walked out, and it was a nice spot—that tidy little

yard, the two Adirondack chairs painted the same sunny yellow as the house, and a big, shady maple tree.

Once they were seated, Zoe took a deep breath. "If Pitte and Rowena are some kind of lunatics who've targeted us for some reason, there's no backing out. It won't matter. And if they are, doing whatever we can to find the keys makes the most sense. If they're not, then we should keep our word."

"It sounds like we're on the same track. I'm toying with going back up there to talk to them again, get another impression. In a day or two," Malory nodded, "after we—I hope—find out a little more. I know Dana will be zeroing in on the books, and Flynn's already heating up the Internet. If he finds anything, he'll tell me at dinner tonight."

"Dinner? You're going out with Flynn?"

"Apparently." Malory frowned into her lemonade. "Five minutes after he left my apartment I was wondering how he talked me into it."

"He's awfully cute."

"Any guy would look cute beside that big, ugly dog."

"And he was flirting with you." Zoe gestured with her glass so that the ice clinked. "Big time."

"That I got. Flirting isn't on the agenda for the next few weeks if I'm going to focus on finding the first key."

"Flirting with a cute guy's a nice side benefit." Zoe sighed, sat back and wiggled toes that she'd painted poppy pink. "Or at least I seem to recall it was, from the dim, dark past."

"Are you kidding?" Surprised, Malory looked back at Zoe's sexy faerie face. "Men must hit on you all the time."

"The initial sortie usually stops dead when they find out I've got a kid." She shrugged. "And I'm not interested in the let's-get-naked-and-keep-it-casual deal. I've been there."

"Right now, I'm not interested in the let's-get-naked-

and-make-it-serious deal. I have to figure out what I'm going to do with the rest of my life. My current windfall isn't going to last forever, but it does give me time to decide if I really want my own business, and how to go about it if I do."

"That's something else I was thinking about today. I'm going to have to get back to work. But the thought of starting a new job, with new people, out at the mall . . ." Zoe puffed out her cheeks and blew a hard breath. "And the last thing I want is to try to run a salon out of the house. Nobody takes you seriously when you do that. They start thinking hair's your hobby instead of your job. Plus, where you live isn't home anymore, and I'm not taking that away from Simon the way it was taken away from me."

"Your mother did hair out of your house?"

"Trailer." Zoe shrugged. "She did the best she could, considering we lived a couple miles outside Nowhere, West Virginia. My daddy took off when I was twelve, and I was the oldest of four."

"That's rough. I'm sorry."

"Rough on all of us, but like I said, she did the best she could. I'm just hoping to do better."

"I'd say making a pretty house and home for you and your son means you're doing absolutely fine."

Color washed into her face. "Thanks. Anyway, I thought I'd start scouting around, see if I could find a place for rent that I could outfit for a salon."

"If you find one, see if you can find a nice storefront for me and my artworks shop." With a laugh, Malory set her glass aside. "Or maybe we should just combine the two and go into business together. Art and beauty, one-stop shopping. I've got to go."

She rose. "I'm going to swing by and see Dana, then go home and see if I get a brainstorm over that stupid clue. You want to plan for the three of as to get together one day early next week? A powwow."

"Fine with me, as long as we can work around Simon's schedule."

"We can do that. I'll call you."

SHE didn't know if it qualified as a brainstorm, but it was at least a direction.

Malory studied the clue line by line, searching for metaphors and hidden meanings, double entendres, loose connections. Then she stepped back again to look at it as a whole.

There were mentions of the goddess. And the keys themselves were reputed to unlock imprisoned souls. Put all that together, she decided, and you had a sort of religious reference.

With that in mind, she spent the rest of the day going through every church and temple in the Valley.

She came home empty-handed, but she felt she'd done something positive with her day.

She dressed for dinner, keeping it simple with a sleeveless black top and black cropped pants, topped with a tailored jacket the color of strawberries.

At exactly seven, she was sliding into heeled sandals and preparing to wait. In her experience she was the only one who habitually made it a point to be on time.

So it was a surprise, a pleasant one, to hear the knock on her door even as she was checking the contents of her purse.

"You're prompt," she said to Flynn when she opened the door.

"Actually, I was here ten minutes ago, but I didn't want to seem anxious." He handed her a small bouquet of baby roses, nearly the same color as her jacket. "You look amazing."

"Thanks." She eyed him as she sniffed the rosebuds. He *was* cute, she thought. Dog or no dog. "I'll put these in water. Very nice touch, by the way."

"I thought so. Moe wanted to go for candy, but I held out for flowers."

She stopped. "He's not out there, is he?"

"No, no, he's home, making do with kibble and the Bugs Bunny marathon on the Cartoon Network. Moe's nuts about Bugs."

"I bet." She arranged the flowers in a clear glass vase. "Do you want a drink before we go?"

"Depends. Can you walk three blocks in those shoes or would you rather drive it?"

"I can walk three miles in heels. I'm a professional female."

"Can't argue with that. And because I can't, I'd like to do what I've been thinking about doing since I landed on top of you."

He moved in. That's what Malory would think later, when her brain started to function normally again. He simply moved into her, ran his hands up the sides of her body, over her shoulders, along her throat, then cupped her face in them.

It was all very slow, all very smooth. Then his mouth was on hers, taking its own sweet time. Somehow she was backed against the counter, pressed snugly between it and his body. Somehow her hands were gripping his hips, her fingers digging in.

And somehow she was sliding into the kiss without a single murmur of protest.

His fingers threaded back into her hair, and he nipped, not so playfully, at her bottom lip. When her breath caught, the tone of the kiss changed from flirty warmth to flashing heat.

"Whoa. Wait." She managed to catch the fading echo of warning bells ringing in her head, but her body stayed plastered against his.

"Okay. In a minute."

He needed another minute of her, of the taste of her,

and the feel of her. There was more here than he'd expected, and he'd expected quite a punch.

There was something erotically sharp about the flavor of her, as if her mouth was a rare delicacy that he'd only just been allowed to sample. And something so soft about her texture, all those clouds of gilded hair, all those lovely curves and dips.

He gave her lips one last rub with his, then eased back.

She stared at him, those blue eyes he'd decided were irresistible, now wide and wary.

"Maybe . . ." She hoped the long, slow breath would level her voice again. "Maybe we should just start walking now."

"Sure." He offered a hand, and found himself flattered when she not only evaded it, but skirted around him to get her purse. "I figured if I kissed you now, I wouldn't be thinking about it all during dinner and lose track of the conversation."

He went to the door, opened it for her. "The trouble is, now that I have kissed you, I'm probably going to be thinking about kissing you again all during dinner and lose track of the conversation. So if you notice that my mind wanders, you'll know where and why."

"You think I don't know why you just said that." She walked out into the shimmering evening light with him. "By saying that, you'll plant the seed in my head so I'll be thinking about you kissing me all through dinner. Or that's the plan."

"Damn, you're good. If you're quick enough to unravel the dastardly plots of men regarding sex, the puzzle of the key ought to be child's play to you."

"You'd think so, wouldn't you? But the simple fact is I've had more experience with the dastardly plots of men regarding sex than I have with puzzles regarding goddesses and mythological spells."

"I don't know why"—he caught her hand in his, grinned at the sidelong look she sent him—"but I find that very exciting. If I ply you with wine at dinner, will you tell me about those experiences? There may be some plots I've missed along the way."

"You're going to buy me a martini, then we'll see."

He'd chosen one of the town's prettiest restaurants and had arranged for a table on the back terrace with a view of the mountains.

By the time she was sipping her martini, she was relaxed again. "I'd like to discuss the key. If I find your attention wandering, I'll kick you under the table."

"So noted. I'd just like to say one thing first."

"Go ahead."

He leaned toward her, breathed deep. "You smell terrific."

She leaned toward him. "I know. Now, would you like to know what I did today?" She waited a beat, then kicked him lightly on the ankle.

"What? Yes. Sorry."

She lifted her glass for another sip to hide her amusement. "First I went to see Zoe."

She relayed the gist of their conversation, pausing when the first course was served.

"The little yellow house." Flynn nodded as he brought the look of it into his mind. "Used to be dog-shit brown. She's really fixed it up. I've seen the kid in the yard, now that I think about it."

"Simon. He looks just like her. It's almost spooky."

"Now that you mention it, I would've put that together when I met her if I'd been able to take my eyes off you for two minutes."

Her lips twitched, and damn it, she was flattered. "You've very good at that—both timing and delivery."

"Yeah, it's a gift."

"Then I went to see Dana at her apartment. She was buried in books and brooding."

"Two of her best things."

"She hasn't been able to track down a version of the

Daughters of Glass story yet, but she's working on it. Then I got this idea. Goddesses equal worship. All the reading I've been doing indicates that a lot of churches were built on pagan worship sites. Most Christian holy days coincide with the early pagan holy days, which were based on seasons, agriculture, that sort of thing. So I went to church. In fact I went to every church and temple in a twenty-mile radius."

"That's an interesting connection. Good, clear thinking."

"That's one of my major skills. I kept going over and over the clue. Look within, look without, singing goddess, and so on. So I went looking. Didn't expect to walk in and see the key waiting for me on a pew. But I thought maybe I'd see the symbol of it, you know? Something worked into a stained-glass window or a molding. But I didn't."

"It was still a good idea."

"A better one might be to go back to that house and talk to Rowena and Pitte again."

"Maybe. Want to know what I found out?"

"I do."

He waited while their entrées were served, then studied her fish and his steak. "How do you feel about surf and turf?"

"Amenable." They cut off portions, passed them.

"You know, this could develop into a serious deal. You and me? A lot of people are fussy about sharing food. I never get that." He sampled the steak. "I mean, it's food. You're supposed to eat it. What's the difference if it was on somebody else's plate first?"

"That's an interesting element to factor into a potential relationship. Now, what did you find out?"

"I talked to my grandmother about the story. There were some details I didn't remember clearly. First, there was dissension in the ranks over the god-king making a mortal his queen. It was okay to fool around with mortals, but he brought her behind the Curtain of Power—or the Curtain of Dreams. It's called both. And he took her as his wife. Because of this, some of the gods set themselves apart from the young king and his mortal wife, established their own rule."

"Politics."

"Can't get away from it. Naturally, this didn't sit too well with the king. There are other stories, full of war and intrigue and heroics, and that brings us to the daughters. Beloved by their parents, and by those loyal to the king and his wife. Each had beauty, as you'd expect, and each had power—a talent. One was an artist, one a bard, and one a warrior. Devoted to each other, they grew up in the kingdom, taught by a young goddess of magic, guarded by the king's most trusted warrior god. Either the teacher or the guard was to be with them at all times, to keep them safe from the plots surrounding them."

"In the painting there were two figures, a man and a woman, in the background. They seemed to be in an embrace."

Flynn gestured with his fork, then speared more steak. "That fits with what's coming. The king's advisers were campaigning to have the daughters marry three gods of rank from the opposing faction. To unite the kingdom again. But the self-proclaimed king of the opposing faction didn't like the idea of giving up his throne. Power had corrupted him, and his thirst for more, for complete dominance of this, let's say, netherworld, and the mortal one, consumed him. He wanted to kill the daughters, but he knew that if he did, all but his most devoted followers would turn against him. So he devised a plot, and the two who were closest to the daughters aided him, by falling in love."

"They betrayed the daughters?"

"Not purposely." He tipped more wine into their glasses. "By distraction. By looking at each other rather than looking after their charges. And as the daughters were young women, fond of their keepers, they made it easy for the lovers to slip away from time to time. And one day when they were unprotected, the spell was cast."

"Their souls were stolen."

"It's more than that. Are you going to eat the rest of that steak?"

"Hmm." She glanced down at her plate. "No. Do you want it?"

"For Moe. I go back empty-handed, he'll sulk." He asked the waiter to box up the leftovers, then smiled at Malory. "Dessert?"

"No, just coffee. Tell me the rest."

"Two coffees, a crème brûlée, and two spoons. You'll never hold out against the crème brûlée," he said to Malory, then leaned forward to finish the tale. "The bad king's a clever guy, and a sorcerer. He doesn't take heat for slaying innocents, and he turns the good king's choices and policy against him. If a mortal is fit to be queen, if three half-mortals are worthy of rank, then let the mortals prove it. Only mortals can break the spell. Until that's done, the daughters will sleep—unharmed. If mortal women, one to represent each daughter, can find each of the three keys, then the Box of Souls will be unlocked, the daughters' souls restored, and the kingdoms united."

"And if they fail?"

"The most popular version, according to my granny, has the bad king setting a time limit. Three thousand years—one millennium for each daughter. If the keys aren't found and the box unlocked within that time, he alone rules, both the god-world and the mortal."

"I never understand why anyone wants to rule the world. Seems like one big headache to me." She pursed her lips when the dish of crème brûlée was set between them. Flynn was right, she decided. She wasn't going to be able to hold out against it. "What happened to the lovers?"

"A couple of versions of that, too." He dipped his spoon in at one end of the dish while Malory dipped into the other. "My grandmother's pick is the one that has the grieving king sentencing the lovers to death, but his wife intervened, asking for mercy. Instead of execution, banishment. They were cast out through the Curtain of Dreams, forbidden to return until they found the three mortal women who would unlock the box of souls. And so they wander the earth, gods living as mortals, in search of the triad who will release not only the souls of the daughters but their own as well."

"Rowena and Pitte think they're the teacher and the warrior?"

It pleased him that their conclusions meshed. "That would be my take. You've got a couple of weirdos on your hands, Malory. It's a nice faerie tale. Romantic, colorful. But when people start casting themselves and others in the roles, you're edging into psychoville."

"You're forgetting the money."

"No, I'm not. The money worries me. Seventy-five thousand means it's not a game to them, not a little role-playing entertainment. They're serious. Either they actually believe the myth or they're seeding the ground for a con."

She toyed with another spoonful of the crème brûlée. "With the twenty-five thousand, I now have approximately twenty-five thousand, two hundred and five dollars, which includes the twenty I found in a jacket pocket this morning. My parents are fairly average middle-class people. They're not rich or influential. I don't have any rich or influential friends or lovers. I've got nothing worth conning."

"Maybe they're looking for something else, something you haven't thought of. But back to those lovers for a minute. Do you have any poor ones?"

She sipped her coffee, measuring him over the rim. The sun had set while they'd had dinner. Now it was candlelight that flickered between them. "Not at the moment."

"Here's a coincidence. Neither do I."

"I'm in the market for a key, Flynn, not a lover."

"You're assuming the key exists."

"Yes, I am. If I didn't assume that, I wouldn't bother to look for it. And I gave my word I would."

"I'll help you find it."

She set her cup down again. "Why?"

"A lot of reasons. One, I'm just a naturally curious guy, and however this thing works out, it's an interesting story." He skimmed a fingertip over the back of her hand, and the little thrill danced straight up her arm. "Two, my sister's involved. Three, I'll get to be around you. The way I figure it, you won't be able to hold out against me any more than you could hold out against the crème brûlée."

"Is that confidence or conceit?"

"Just fate, sweetie. Look, why don't we go back to my place and . . . Well, hell, I wasn't thinking about kissing you again until you gave me that snotty look. Now I've lost my train of thought."

"I'm not having any trouble following that train."

"Okay, that wasn't my track, but I'm willing to jump on board. What I was going to say was we could go back and do some research. I can show you what I've got so far, which is basically nothing. I can't dig up any data on your benefactors, at least not under the names they used to buy the Peak, or any variations of those names."

"I'll leave the research to you and Dana for now." She shrugged. "I've got some other trails to follow."

"Such as?"

"Logic. Goddesses. There are a couple of New Age shops in the area. I'm going to check them out. Then there's the painting. I'm going to find out who painted that portrait, see what else he or she has done, and where those paintings might be. Who owns them, how they acquired them. I need to take another trip up to Warrior's Peak, have another talk with Pitte and Rowena, and get another look at that painting. A better look."

"I'll go with you. There's a story here, Malory. This could be a huge scam, which would make it big news and my duty to report it."

She stiffened up. "You don't have any proof that Rowena and Pitte aren't legitimate—possibly loony, yes, but not crooks."

"Easy." He held up a hand for peace. "I'm not writing anything until I have all the facts. I can't get all the facts until I meet all the players. I need an entrée to that house. You're it. In exchange you get the benefit of my keen investigative skills and dogged reporter's determination. I go with you, or I talk Dana into taking me up there."

She tapped a finger on the table while she considered her options. "They might not talk to you. In fact, they may not like it that we've brought you into this, even on a peripheral level."

"Leave that part to me. Getting into places where I'm not wanted is part of my job description."

"Is that how you got into my apartment last night?"

"Ouch. Why don't we run up there tomorrow morning? I can pick you up at ten."

"All right." What harm could it do to have him along?

"THERE'S no need to walk me all the way to the door," Malory said as they approached her apartment building.

"Sure there is. I'm just an old-fashioned guy."

"No, you're not." She muttered it as she opened her purse for her key. "I'm not asking you in."

"Okay."

She slanted him a look as they stepped up to the door. "You say that like you're an affable, easygoing man. You're not that, either. It's a ploy."

He grinned. "It is?"

"Yes. You're stubborn and pushy and more than a little arrogant. You get away with it because you put on that big, charming smile and that I-wouldn't-hurt-a-fly demeanor. But they're just tools to help you get what you want."

"God, you see right through me." Watching her, he twirled a lock of her hair around his finger. "Now I either have to kill you or marry you."

"And being appealing on some screwy level doesn't make you less annoying. Therein lies the flaw."

At those words he caught her face in his hands and crushed his lips enthusiastically to hers. The heat shot straight up from her belly and seemed to burst out the top of her head.

"Neither does that," she managed. She shoved her key in the lock, pushed the door open. Then shut it in his face. Half a beat later, she yanked it open. "Thanks for dinner."

He rocked gently on his heels when the door shut in his face a second time. When he strolled away, he was whistling, and thinking Malory Price was the kind of woman who made a man's life really interesting.

Chapter Six

⬤

DANA gulped down her first cup of coffee while standing naked in her tiny kitchen, eyes closed, brain dead. She drained it, hot, black, and strong, before letting out a soft whimper of relief.

She downed half the second cup on the way to the shower.

She didn't mind mornings, mainly because she was never awake enough to object to them. Her routine rarely varied. Her alarm buzzed, she slapped it off, then rolled out of bed and stumbled into the kitchen, where the automatic coffeemaker already had the first pot ready.

One and a half cups later, her vision was clear enough for a shower.

By the time she was done, her circuits were up and running, and she was too awake to sulk about being awake. She drank the second half of the second cup and listened to the morning news report while she dressed for the day.

With a toasted bagel and her third cup of coffee, she

settled down with her current breakfast book.

She'd turned only the second page when the knock on her door interrupted her most sacred of rituals.

"Damn it."

She marked her place. Her annoyance faded, a little, when she opened the door to Malory.

"Aren't you the bright-and-early girl?"

"Sorry. You said you were working this morning, so I thought you'd be up and around by now."

"Up, anyway." She leaned on the jamb a moment and studied the minute green checks of the soft cotton shirt that precisely matched the color of Malory's pleated trousers. Just as the dove-gray slides she wore exactly matched the tone and texture of her shoulder bag.

"Do you always dress like that?" Dana wondered.

"Like what?"

"Perfect."

With a little laugh, Malory looked down at herself. "I'm afraid so. It's a compulsion."

"Looks good on you, too. I'll probably end up hating you for it. Come on in anyway."

The room was a compact, informal library. Books stood or were stacked on the shelves that ran along two walls from floor to ceiling, sat on the tables like knick-knacks, trooped around the room like soldiers. They struck Malory as more than knowledge or entertainment, even more than stories and information. They were color and texture, in a haphazard yet somehow intricate decorating scheme.

The short leg of the L-shaped room boasted still more books, as well as a small table that held the remains of Dana's breakfast.

With her hands on her hips, Dana watched Malory's perusal of her space. She'd seen the reaction before. "No, I haven't read them all, but I will. And no, I don't know how many I have. Want coffee?"

"Let me just ask this. Do you ever actually use the services of the library?"

"Sure, but I need to own them. If I don't have twenty or thirty books right here, waiting to be read, I start jonesing. That's my compulsion."

"Okay. I'll pass on the coffee, thanks. I already had a cup. Two, and I'm wired."

"Two, and I can just manage to form complete sentences. Bagel?"

"No, but go ahead. I wanted to catch you before you left for work. Fill you in."

"Fill away." Dana gestured to the second chair at the table, then sat to finish her breakfast.

"I'm going back up to Warrior's Peak this morning. With Flynn."

Dana's lip curled. "I figured he'd horn in. And hit on you."

"Are either of those things a problem for you?"

"No. He's smarter than he comes across. That's one of the ways he gets people to spill their guts to him. If he hadn't horned in, I'd have baited him until he helped out. As for hitting on you, I had to figure he'd go for either you or Zoe. Flynn really likes women, and they really like him."

Malory thought of the way he'd moved in on her in her kitchen, the way she'd gone pliant as putty when he had. "There's a definite chemical reaction there, but I haven't decided if I like him or not."

Dana crunched on her bagel. "Might as well give in to it. He'll just wear you down, which is another thing he's really good at. He's like a damn Border collie."

"Excuse me?"

"You know how they herd sheep?" She used her free hand, zagging it right and left to demonstrate. "How they keep heading them off, working them around until the sheep end up going where the collie wants them to go? That's Flynn. You'll think, nope, I want to go over here, and he's thinking, well, you'll be better off over there. So you end up over there before you realize you've been herded."

She licked cream cheese off her finger. "And the hell of it is, when you find yourself there you almost always realize you *are* better off. He stays alive by never saying I told you so."

She'd gone to dinner with him, hadn't she? Malory considered. Kissed him—twice. Three times if she was going to be technical. And he was not only coming with her to Warrior's Peak, he was driving her. Huh.

"I don't like being maneuvered."

Dana's expression was a combination of pity and amusement. "Well, we'll see how it goes." She rose, gathering her dishes. "What are you hoping for with Rowena and Pitte?"

"I don't expect to get much from them. It's the painting." Malory followed Dana into the little kitchen. It didn't surprise her to find books here as well, stacked in an open-fronted pantry where the average cook would have stored food staples.

"The painting's important somehow," she continued while Dana rinsed off the dishes. "What it says, and who said it."

She took a moment to explain the rest of the tale as Flynn had relayed it to her over dinner.

"So they're taking on the roles of the teacher and the guard."

"That's the theory," Malory confirmed. "I'm interested in how they'll react when I broach it. And I can use Flynn to distract them long enough to give me time to get another look at the painting and take a couple of pictures of it. That could lead to other paintings with similar themes. It might be helpful."

"I'll do a search on mythological art this morning." Dana checked her watch. "I've got to go. The three of us should get together on this as soon as we can."

"Let's see what we come up with today."

They walked out together, and Malory stopped on the sidewalk. "Dana. Is it just crazy to do all this?"

"Damn right. Call me when you get back from the Peak."

I T was a more pleasant, if less atmospheric, drive on a sunny morning. As a passenger, Malory could indulge herself with the scenery and wonder what it was like to live high on a ridge where the sky seemed only a hand span away and the world was spread out like a painting below.

A fitting view for gods, she supposed. Lofty and dramatic. She had no doubt Rowena and Pitte had chosen it for its power as much as for the privacy.

In another few weeks, when those elegantly rolling hills felt the chill of fall, the colors would stun the eye and catch the breath.

Mists would hover in the morning, sliding into those folds and dips between the hills, spreading like sparkling pools until the sun dissolved them.

And still the house would stand, black as midnight, with its fanciful lines etched against the sky. Guarding the valley. Or watching it. What did it see, she wondered, year after year across the decades?

What did it know?

The question brought on a shudder, a sudden sharp sense of dread.

"Cold?"

She shook her head, and rolled down her window. All at once the car seemed hot and stuffy. "No. I'm spooking myself, that's all."

"If you don't want to do this now—"

"I want to do it. I'm not afraid of a couple of rich eccentrics. In fact, I liked them. And I want to see the painting again. I can't stop thinking about it. Whatever direction my mind goes off in, I keep coming back to the painting."

She glanced out her window, into the deep, leafy woods. "Would you want to live up here?"

"Nope."

Intrigued, she looked back at him. "That was fast."

"I'm a social animal. I like having people around. Moe might like it." He gazed into the rearview mirror to see Moe, nose jammed into the narrow window opening, floppy ears flying.

"I can't believe you brought the dog."

"He likes to ride in the car."

She angled around, studied Moe's blissful expression. "Obviously. Have you ever considered getting him clipped so his hair isn't in his eyes?"

"Don't say clipped." Flynn winced as he muttered the word. "We're still not over the whole neutering deal."

He slowed as they drove along the wall that edged the estate. Then stopped to study the twin warriors who flanked the iron gate.

"They don't look friendly. I camped up here a couple of times with some friends when I was in high school. The house was empty then, so we climbed over the wall."

"Did you go into the house?"

"There wasn't enough courage in a six-pack of beer for that, but we had a hell of a time freaking ourselves out. Jordan claimed he saw a woman walking on the parapet or whatever you call it. Swore he did. He wrote a book about her later, so I guess he saw something. Jordan Hawke," Flynn added. "You might've heard of him."

"Jordan Hawke wrote about Warrior's Peak?"

"He called it—"

"*Phantom Watch*. I read that book." As a ripple of fascination raced up her spine, she stared through the bars of the gates. "Of course. He described it all perfectly, but then he's a wonderful writer." She looked back at Flynn, suspiciously. "You're friends with Jordan Hawke?"

"Since we were kids. He grew up in the Valley. I guess we were sixteen—me, Jordan, and Brad—sucking down beers in the woods, slapping mosquitoes the size of sparrows, and telling very inventive lies about our sexual prowess."

"It's illegal to drink at sixteen," Malory said primly.

He shifted, and even through the shaded lenses of his sunglasses, she could see his eyes laughing. "Really? What were we thinking? Anyway, ten years later, Jordan's got his first bestseller, and Brad's off running the family empire—that would be lumber and the HomeMakers chain for Bradley Charles Vane IV, and I'm planning on heading to New York to be a hotshot reporter for the *Times*."

Her eyebrows winged up. "You worked for the *New York Times*?"

"No, I never went. One thing and another," he said with a shrug. "Let's see what I can do about getting us through this gate."

Even as he started to step out of the car, the gate opened with a kind of otherworldly silence that sent a chill dancing along the nape of his neck. "Must really keep it lubed," he murmured. "And I guess somebody knows we're out here."

He slid back behind the wheel and drove through.

The house looked just as strange and stark and stunning in daylight as it had in a night storm. There was no magnificent stag to greet her, but the flag with its key emblem flew high and white, and rivers of flowers ran below. Gargoyles clung to the stone, and looked, to Malory's mind, as if they were considering leaping, not so playfully, on any visitor.

"I never got this close in the daylight." Slowly Flynn stepped out of the car.

"It's spooky."

"Yeah, but in a good way. It's terrific, like something you expect to see on a cliff above a raging sea. Too bad there's no moat. That would really top it off."

"Wait until you see the inside." Malory moved up beside him, and didn't object in the least when Flynn took her hand. The tickle at the back of her throat made her feel foolish and female.

"I don't know why I'm so nervous." She caught herself whispering it, then her hand jerked in Flynn's when the big entrance door opened.

Rowena stood framed in the towering doorway. She wore simple gray pants with a roomy shirt the color of the forest. Her hair spilled over her shoulders, her lips were unpainted, her feet bare. But however casual the outfit, she managed to look exotic, like some foreign queen on a quiet holiday.

Malory caught the glint of diamonds at her ears.

"How lovely." Rowena held out a hand on which rings sparkled elegantly. "How nice to see you again, Malory. And you've brought me such a handsome surprise."

"Flynn Hennessy. He's Dana's brother."

"Welcome. Pitte will be right along. He's just finishing up a call." She gestured them inside.

Flynn had to resist gawking at the foyer. "It doesn't seem like the kind of place you'd find telephones."

Rowena's chuckle was low, almost a purr. "We enjoy the advantages of technology. Come, we'll have tea."

"We don't want to put you to any trouble," Malory began, but Rowena waved her off.

"Guests are never any trouble."

"How did you find out about Warrior's Peak, Miss . . ."

"Rowena." She slid an arm silkily through Flynn's as she walked them to the parlor. "You must call me Rowena. Pitte always has an ear to the ground for an interesting spot."

"You travel a lot?"

"We do, yes."

"For work or pleasure?"

"Without pleasure, there's little point in work." She

trailed a fingertip playfully down his arm. "Won't you sit? Ah, here's the tea."

Malory recognized the servant from her first visit. She brought the tea cart in silently, and left the same way.

"What business are you in?" Flynn asked.

"Oh, we do a bit of this and that, and some of the other. Milk?" she asked Malory as she poured. "Honey, lemon?"

"A little lemon, thank you. I have a lot of questions."

"I'm sure you do, as does your very attractive companion. How do you like your tea, Flynn?"

"Black's fine."

"So American. And what is your business, Flynn?"

He took the delicate cup she offered. His gaze was direct, and suddenly very cool. "I'm sure you already know. You didn't pick my sister's name out of a hat. You know everything you need to know about her, and that would include me."

"Yes." Rowena added both milk and honey to her own tea. Rather than looking insulted or chagrined, she looked pleased. "The newspaper business must be very interesting. So much information to be gathered, and dispersed. I imagine it takes a clever mind to know how to do both well. And here is Pitte."

He entered a room, Flynn thought, like a general. Measuring the field, gauging his ground, outlining his approach. However genial his smile, Flynn was certain there was a steely soldier behind it.

"Miss Price. What a pleasure to see you again." He took her hand, brought it to within an inch of his lips in a gesture that seemed too fluid not to be natural.

"Thanks for seeing us. This is Flynn—"

"Yes. Mr. Hennessy." He inclined his head. "How do you do?"

"Well enough."

"Our friends have questions and concerns," Rowena

told him as she passed the cup of tea she'd already prepared.

"Naturally." Pitte took a seat. "You're wondering, I imagine, if we're . . ." He turned that mildly curious look to Rowena.

"Lunatics," she supplied, then lifted a plate. "Scones?"

"Ah, yes, lunatics." Pitte helped himself to a scone and a generous dollop of clotted cream. "I can assure you we're not, but then again, so would I if we were. So that's very little help to you. Tell me, Miss Price, are you having second thoughts about our arrangement?"

"I took your money and gave you my word."

His expression softened, very slightly. "Yes. To some that would make little difference."

"It makes all the difference to me."

"That could change," Flynn put in. "Depending on where the money comes from."

"Are you implying we could be criminals?" Now temper showed in the flush that swept Rowena's ice-edged cheekbones. "It shows considerable lack of courtesy to come into our home and accuse us of being thieves."

"Reporters aren't known for their courtesy, and neither are brothers when they're looking out for their sisters."

Pitte murmured something quiet and foreign, skimmed his long fingers over the back of Rowena's hand, the way a man might soothe a cat who was about to spit and claw. "Understood. It happens I've some skill in monetary matters. The money comes to us through perfectly legal means. We're neither lunatics nor criminals."

"Who are you?" Malory demanded before Flynn could speak again. "Where do you come from?"

"What do you think?" Pitte challenged softly.

"I don't know. But I think you believe you represent the teacher and the warrior who failed to protect the Daughters of Glass."

An eyebrow arched slightly. "You've learned more since you were here last. Will you learn more yet?"

"I intend to. You could help me."

"We're not free to help in that way. But I will tell you this. Not only teacher and warrior but companions and friends to those precious ones, and so only more responsible."

"It's only a legend."

The intensity in his eyes dimmed, and he leaned back again. "It must be, as such things are beyond the limits of your mind and the boundaries of your world. Still, I can promise you the keys exist."

"Where is the Box of Souls?" Flynn asked him.

"Safe."

"Could I see the painting again?" Now Malory turned to Rowena. "I'd like Flynn to see it."

"Of course." She rose and led the way into the room dominated by the portrait of the Daughters of Glass.

Malory heard Flynn catch his breath, then they were moving together closer to the painting. "It's even more magnificent than I remembered. Can you tell me who painted this?"

"Someone," Rowena said quietly, "who knew love, and grief."

"Someone who knows Malory. And my sister, and Zoe McCourt."

Rowena let out a sigh. "You're a cynic, Flynn, and a suspicious one. But as you've put yourself in the role of protector, I'll forgive you for it. We don't wish Malory, Dana, or Zoe any harm. Quite the opposite."

Something in her tone made him want to believe her. "It's pretty disconcerting to see my sister's face up there."

"You'd do whatever needed to be done to keep her safe and well. I understand that kind of loyalty and love. I admire and respect it. She's in no danger from me or Pitte. I can swear that to you."

He turned now, zeroing in on what hadn't been said. "But from someone else?"

"Life's a gamble," was all Rowena said. "Your tea's getting cold."

She turned toward the door just as Pitte stepped to it. "There seems to be a very large, very unhappy dog of some sort outside."

The temper and sharp words hadn't ruffled Flynn a bit, but that single statement made him wince. "He's mine."

"You have a dog?" The change in Rowena's tone was almost girlish. Everything about her seemed to go light and bright, then bubble out as she gripped Flynn's hand.

"He calls it a dog," Malory said under her breath.

Flynn merely gave her a sorrowful look before speaking to Rowena. "You like dogs?"

"Yes, very much. Could I meet him?"

"Sure."

"Ah, while you're introducing Rowena and Pitte to Moe, at their peril, could I take a minute to freshen up?" Casually, Malory gestured toward the powder room. "I remember where it is."

"Of course." For the first time since Malory had met her, Rowena seemed distracted. She already had a hand on Flynn's arm as they started down the hall. "What kind of a dog is he?"

"That's debatable."

Malory slipped into the powder room and counted to five. Slowly. Heart pounding, she opened the door a crack and did her best to peer up and down the corridor. Moving quickly now, she dashed back to the portrait, dragging out the little digital camera in her purse as she ran.

She took half a dozen full-length shots, then some of smaller details. With a guilty look over her shoulder, she shoved the camera back into the purse and pulled out her glasses, a plastic bag, and a small palette knife.

With her ears buzzing, she stepped up on the hearth and carefully, gently, scraped flakes of paint into the bag.

The entire process took less than three minutes, but her palms were slick with sweat, her legs loose and wobbly by the time she'd finished. She took another moment to compose herself, then strolled—with what she hoped was casual ease—out of the room and out of the house.

The instant she stepped outside, she stopped dead. There was the regal and magnificent Rowena sitting on the ground with a mountain of dog sprawled over her lap.

And she was giggling.

"Oh, he's wonderful. Such a big sweetheart. What a good boy you are." She bent her head and nuzzled Moe's fur. His tail beat like a jackhammer. "What a kind, pretty boy." She looked up at Flynn and beamed. "Did he find you or did you find him?"

"It was sort of mutual." One dog lover recognized another. Tucking his thumbs in his pockets, Flynn scanned the expansive lawns, the slices of woods. "Big place like this, lots of room to run. You could have a pack of dogs."

"Yes. Well." Rowena lowered her head again and rubbed Moe's belly.

"We travel considerably." Pitte laid a hand on Rowena's hair, stroked it.

"How long do you plan to stay here?"

"When the three months is up, we'll move on."

"To?"

"That will depend. *A ghra*."

"Yes. Yes." Rowena cuddled Moe another moment, then with a wistful sigh got to her feet. "You're very lucky to have such goodness in your life. I hope you treasure him."

"I do."

"I see you do, yes. You may be cynical and suspicious, but a dog like this knows a good heart."

"Yeah," Flynn agreed. "I believe that."

"I hope you'll bring him if you come back. He can run. Good-bye, Moe."

Moe sat up and lifted one massive paw with unaccustomed dignity.

"Wow. That's a new one." Flynn blinked as Moe politely allowed Rowena to shake his paw. "Hey, Mal! Did you see—"

As he said her name, Moe's head swiveled, and he was off at a sprint in Malory's direction, bringing a distressed yip to her throat as she braced for the onslaught.

Rowena called out, a single indecipherable word in a calm, brisk tone. Moe skidded to a halt inches from Malory's feet, plopped onto his butt. And once more lifted his paw.

"Well." Malory expelled a relieved breath. "That's more like it." She reached down, obligingly shook the offered paw. "Good for you, Moe."

"How the hell'd you do that?" Flynn wanted to know.

"I have a way with animals."

"I'll say. What was that, Gaelic?"

"Mmmm."

"Funny that Moe would understand a command in Gaelic when he mostly ignores them in plain English."

"Dogs understand more than words." She held out a hand for Flynn's. "I hope you'll all come back. We enjoy company."

"Thanks for your time." Malory walked to the car with Moe trotting happily beside her. The minute she sat, she tucked her purse on the floor like a guilty secret.

Rowena laughed, but the sound was a bit watery as Moe stuck his head out of the backseat window. She lifted a hand in a wave, then leaned against Pitte as Flynn drove away.

"I have real hope," she murmured. "I can't remember the last time I felt real hope. I—it frightens me. It actually frightens me to feel it."

Pitte wrapped an arm around her, drew her tighter to his side. "Don't weep, my heart."

"Foolish." She dashed a tear away. "To cry over a stranger's dog. When we get home . . ."

He shifted her, cupped her face in his hands. His tone

was gentle, yet somehow urgent. "When we get home, you'll have a hundred dogs. A thousand."

"One will do." She rose on her toes to brush her lips across his.

IN the car Malory let out a long, long breath.

"I take that sound of relief to mean you got the pictures."

"I did. I felt like an international art thief. I guess I have to give Moe points for being the main distraction. So, tell me what you thought of them."

"They're slick, smart, and full of secrets. But they don't seem crazy. They're used to money—real money. Used to drinking tea out of antique cups brought in by a servant. They're educated, cultured, and a little snobby with it. The place is full of stuff—fancy stuff. They've only been here a few weeks, so they didn't furnish those rooms locally. They had it shipped in. I should be able to track that."

Frowning, he tapped his fingers on the steering wheel. "She went goony on Moe."

"What?"

"She turned into a puddle the minute she saw him. I mean, he's got a lot of charm, but she melted. I have this impression of her from inside. Cool, confident, aloof. The kind of woman who's sexy because she knows she's in charge. Strolling up Madison Avenue with a Prada bag on her arm, or running a board meeting in L.A. Power, money, brains, and looks all wrapped up in sex."

"I get it. You thought she was sexy."

"Last checkup, I had a pulse, so, yeah. But you should've seen her face when Moe jumped out of the car. All that polish, that sheen just vanished. She lit up like Christmas morning."

"So, she likes dogs."

"No, it was more. It wasn't the coochee-coo that some

fancy women do with dogs. It was fall down on the ground, roll in the grass, and gut-laugh. So why doesn't she have one?"

"Maybe Pitte won't have one around."

Flynn shook his head. "You're more observant than that. The guy would slice open a vein for her if she asked him to. Something strange about the way she got Moe to shake hands. Something strange about the whole deal."

"No argument. I'm going to concentrate on the painting, at least until one of us comes up with a different angle. I'll leave you to try to pin down Rowena and Pitte."

"I've got to cover a town hall meeting tonight. How about we get together tomorrow?"

He maneuvers. He herds. She remembered Dana's words and shot him a quick, suspicious look. "Define 'get together.' "

"I'll adjust the definition any way you want."

"I've got four weeks—less now—to find this key. I'm currently unemployed and have to figure out what I'm going to do, at least professionally, for the rest of my life. I recently ended a relationship that was going nowhere. Add up all the above, and it's very clear I don't have time for dating and exploring a new personal relationship."

"Hold on a minute." He pulled off to the side of the windy road, unhooked his seat belt. He leaned over, took her shoulders, and eased her over as far as her own belt would allow while his mouth ravished hers.

A rocket of heat shot up her spine and left its edgy afterburn in her belly.

"You've, ah, really got a knack for that," she managed when she could breathe again.

"I practice as often as possible." To prove it, he kissed her again. Slower this time. Deeper. Until he felt her quiver. "I just wanted you to add that to your equation."

"I was an art major. Math isn't my strong suit. Come back here a minute." She grabbed his shirt, yanked him to her, and let herself go.

Everything inside her sparked. Blood and bone and brain.

If this was what it meant to be herded, she thought dimly, she could be flexible about her direction.

When his hands clenched in her hair, she felt a stir of power and anxiety that was as potent as a drug.

"We really can't do this." But she was tugging his shirt out of his waistband, desperate to get her hands on flesh.

"I know. Can't." He fumbled with the buckle of her seat belt. "We'll stop in a minute."

"Okay, but first . . ." She brought his hand to her breast, then moaned as her heart seemed to tip into his palm.

He shifted her, cursed when he rapped his elbow on the steering wheel. And Moe, delighted with the prospect of a wrestling match, squeezed his head between the seats and slathered both of them with sloppy kisses.

"Oh, God!" Torn between laughter and shock, Malory scrubbed at her mouth. "I really, *really* hope that was your tongue."

"Ditto." Struggling to get his breath back, Flynn stared down at her. Her hair was sexily tousled, her face flushed, her mouth just a little swollen from the assault of his.

With the flat of his hand, he shoved Moe's face away and snapped out a curt order to sit. The dog flopped back on his seat and whined as if he'd been beaten with a club.

"I wasn't planning on moving this fast."

Malory shook her head. "I wasn't planning on moving at all. And I've *always* got a plan."

"Been a while since I tried this in a car parked on the side of the road."

"Me, too." She slid her gaze toward the pathetic sounds coming from the backseat. "Under the circumstances . . ."

"Yeah. Better not. I want to make love with you." He drew her up. "To touch you. To feel you move under my hands. I want that, Malory."

"I need to think. Everything about this is complicated,

so I have to think about it." She certainly had to think about the fact that she'd nearly torn the man's clothes off in the front seat of a car, on the side of a public road, in broad daylight.

"My life's a mess, Flynn." The thought depressed her enough to have her pulse calming again. "Whatever the equation, I've screwed things up, and I have to get back on track. I don't do well with messy situations. So, let's slow this down a little."

He hooked a finger in the V of her blouse. "How much is a little?"

"I don't know yet. Oh, I can't stand it." She scooted around, leaned over the seat. "Don't cry, you big baby." She ruffled the fur between Moe's ears. "Nobody's mad at you."

"Speak for yourself," Flynn grumbled.

Chapter Seven

I feel the sun, warm and somehow fluid like a quiet wa-terfall gliding from a golden river. It pours over me in a kind of baptism. I smell roses, and lilies, and some spicier flower that cuts the sweetness. I hear water, a playful trickle and plop as it rises up, then falls back into itself.

All these things slide over me, or I slide into them, but I see nothing but a dense white. Like a curtain I can't part.

Why am I not afraid?

Laughter floats toward me. Bright and easy and fe-male. There's a youthful cheer in it that makes me smile, that brings a tickle of laughter to my own throat. I want to find the source of that laughter and join in.

Voices now, that quick bird-chatter that is again youth and female.

The sounds come and go, ebb and flow. Am I drifting toward it or away?

Slowly, slowly, the curtain thins. Only a mist now, soft as silken rain with sunlight sparkling through it. And through it, I see color. Such bold, rich color it sears through that thinning mist and stuns my eyes.

Tiles are gleaming silver and explode with sunlight in blinding flashes where the thick green leaves and hot-pink blossoms of trees don't shade or shelter. Flowers swim in pools or dance in swirling beds.

There are three women, girls, really, gathered around the fountain that plays its happy tune. It's their laughter I hear. One has a small harp in her lap, and the other a quill. But they're laughing at the wriggling puppy the third holds in her arms.

They're so lovely. There is about them a touching innocence that's so perfectly suited to the garden where they spend this bright afternoon. Then I see the sword sheathed at one's hip.

Innocent perhaps, but strong. There is power here; I can feel the tingle of it now sparking on the air.

And still I'm not afraid.

They call the puppy Diarmait, and set it down so it can romp around the fountain. Its excited yaps ring like bells. I see one girl slide her arm around the waist of another, and the third rest her head on the second's shoulder. There, they become a unit. A kind of triad. A whole of three parts that chatter about their new puppy, and laugh as he rolls gleefully in the flowers.

I hear them say names I know, somehow know, and look as they look. In the distance, in the shade of a tree that drips down with graceful branches heavy with jeweled fruit, are a couple caught in a passionate embrace.

He's tall and dark, and there's a strength to him I can sense might be terrible if roused. She's beautiful, and very slender. But there is about her, too, a sense of more.

They're desperately in love. I can feel that need, that heat inside me, throbbing like a wound.

Is love so painful?

The girls sigh over it. And they wish. Someday, they hope. Someday they will love like that—desire and ro-

mance, fear and joy all tied into one consuming entity. They will know the taste of a lover's lips, the thrill of a lover's touch.

Someday.

We are, all of us, caught in that urgent embrace, absorbed with our envy and our dreams. The sky darkens. The colors dim. I feel the wind now. Cold, cold as it spins around and around. The sudden roar of it screams in my ears. Blossoms tear from branches, petals fly like bright bullets.

Now I'm afraid. Now I'm terrified even before I see the sly black shape of the snake slither over those silver tiles, before I see the shadow slink out of the trees and lift high the glass box it holds in its black arms.

Words boom out. Though I press my hands to my ears to block them, I hear them inside my head.

Mark this time and mark this hour when I wield my awful power. Mortal souls of daughters three forever will belong to me. Their bodies lie in eternal sleep, their souls imprisoned in this glass. The spell will hold sure and deep unless these things come to pass. Three keys to find, to fit, only by mortal hands to turn. Three thousand years in which to learn. An instant more and souls will burn.

This test, this quest, to prove a mortal's worthiness. With these words I wind them, and with my art I bind them. These locks I seal and forge these keys, and here hurl them to the hand of destiny.

The wind dies, and the air goes still. There on those sunwashed tiles, the three girls lie, their eyes closed as if in sleep, their hands clasped. Three parts of one whole.

Beside them is a glass box, its clear panels leaded at the seams, its trio of locks glinting gold. Warm blue lights dance frantically inside it, seem to beat against the glass walls like trapped wings.

Three keys lie scattered around it.
And seeing them, I weep.

Malory was still shaky when she opened the door to
Zoe.

"I got here as soon as I could. I had to get Simon off
to school. You sounded so upset on the phone. What—"

"Dana's not here yet. I'd rather just go through this
once. I made coffee."

"Great." Zoe put a hand on Malory's shoulder and simply lowered her into a chair. "I'll get it. You look like
you still need to catch your breath. Kitchen that way?"

"Yeah." Grateful, Malory leaned back, rubbed her
hands over her face.

"Why don't you tell me how your date with Flynn
went the other night?"

"What? Oh. Good. Fine." She dropped her hands, then
stared at them as if they belonged to someone else. "He
seems almost normal without his dog. That must be
Dana."

"I'll get it. Just sit." Zoe hurried out from the kitchen,
heading Malory off before she could rise.

"Okay, where's the fire?" Dana demanded. Then
stopped, sniffed. "Coffee. Don't make me beg for it."

"I'm getting it. Go sit with Malory," Zoe added under
her breath.

Dana plopped down in a chair, pursed her lips, and
gave Malory a long, hard stare. "You look terrible."

"Thanks so much."

"Hey, don't expect hugs and kisses when you get me
out of bed and over here within twenty minutes and on
one cup of coffee. Besides, it's reassuring to know you
don't roll out of bed looking perfect. What's up?"

Malory glanced over as Zoe came back with three thick
white mugs of coffee on a tray. "I had a dream."

"I was having a damn good one myself. I think it involved Spike from *Buffy the Vampire Slayer* and a really

big vat of dark chocolate, and then you called and interrupted it."

"Dana." Zoe shook her head, then sat on the arm of
Malory's chair. "A nightmare?"

"No. At least . . . no. As soon as I woke up, I typed it
out." She rose now and picked up papers from the table.
"I've never had a dream with so much detail before. At
least I've never remembered details so clearly after I woke
up. I wrote it down because I wanted to make sure I didn't
forget anything. But I'm not going to. Anyway, it'll be
easier if you both just read it."

She handed them the typed pages, then took her own
coffee and paced to the patio doors.

It was going to be another beautiful day, she mused.
Another beautiful late-summer day with clear skies and
warm breezes. People would walk around town, enjoying
the weather, going about their business. Their normal,
everyday chores in the normal, everyday world.

And she would never forget the sound of that dream-
wind, the feel of that sudden, bitter cold.

"Wow. I can see why this shook you up." Dana set the
pages aside. "But it's pretty clear where it came from.
Flynn told me you guys went up to see the painting again
yesterday. All of this is on your mind, and your subcon-
scious just flipped you into it."

"It's scary." Zoe rushed to finish the last few sentences
before she got up. Walking over, she rubbed her hands
on Malory's shoulders. "No wonder you were so upset.
I'm glad you called us."

"It wasn't just a dream. I was there." She warmed her
chilled hands on the coffee mug as she turned. "I walked
into that painting."

"Okay, honey, take it down a notch or two." Dana held
up a hand. "You're overidentifying, that's all. A strong,
vivid dream can really suck you in."

"I don't expect you to believe me, but I'm going to
say out loud what's been in my head since I woke up."

Woke up, she remembered, shaking with cold, with the sound of that terrible wind still ringing in her ears.

"I was there. I could smell the flowers and feel the heat. Then the cold and the wind. I heard them screaming." She closed her eyes and fought a fresh surge of panic.

She could still hear them screaming.

"And I felt this, this charge in the air, this pressure. When I woke, my ears were still ringing from it. They were speaking Gaelic, but I understood them. How could I?"

"You just thought—"

"No!" She shook her head fiercely at Zoe. "I *knew*. When the storm came, when everything went crazy, I heard them calling out for their father. *Chi athair sinn*. Father, help us. I looked it up this morning, but I knew. How could I know?"

She took a steadying breath. "Their names were Venora, Niniane, and Kyna. How would I know?"

She walked back to sit. The relief of saying it all calmed her. Her pulse leveled, as did her voice. "They were so afraid. One minute they were just young girls playing with their puppy in a world that seemed so perfect and peaceful. And the next, what made them human was being torn out of them. It hurt them, and there was nothing I could do."

"I don't know what to think about this," Dana said after a moment. "I'm trying to be logical here. The painting's drawn you from the first, and we know the legend is Celtic in origin. We look like the girls in the painting, so we identify with them."

"How did I know the Gaelic? How do I know their names?"

Dana frowned into her coffee. "I can't explain that."

"I'll tell you something else I know. Whatever locked those souls away is dark, and it's powerful, and it's greedy. It won't want us to win."

"The box and the keys," Zoe interrupted. "You saw them. You know what they look like."

"The box is very simple, very beautiful. Leaded glass, a high, domed lid, three locks across the front. The keys are like the logo in the invitations, like the emblem on the flag flying on the house. They're small. Only about three inches long, I'd say."

"It still doesn't make sense," Dana insisted. "If they had the keys, why hide them? Why not just hand them to the right people, and game over?"

"I don't know." Malory rubbed her temples. "There must be a reason."

"You said you knew the names they called the couple making out under the tree," Dana reminded her.

"Rowena and Pitte." Malory dropped her hands. "Rowena and Pitte," she repeated. "They couldn't stop it either. It happened so quickly, so violently."

She took a long, long breath. "Here's the kicker. I believe it all. I don't care how crazy it sounds, I believe it all. It happened. I was taken into that painting, through the Curtain of Dreams, and I watched it happen. I have to find that key. Whatever it takes, I have to find it."

A F T E R a morning staff meeting that included jelly doughnuts and a pissed-off reporter who'd had her article on fall fashion cut by two inches, Flynn escaped to his office.

As his staff consisted of fewer than thirty people, including the eager sixteen-year-old he paid to write a weekly column from the teenage perspective, having one reporter in a snit was a major staff glitch.

He flipped through his messages, punched up a feature on Valley nightlife, approved a couple of photos for the next day's edition, and checked the accounting on ads.

He could hear the occasional ring of a phone, and even with his door shut, the muffled clatter of fingers on keyboards. The police radio on top of his file cabinet beeped and hummed, the television squeezed between books on a shelf was set on mute.

He had the window open and could hear the light whoosh of morning traffic, the sporadic thump of bass from a car stereo playing too loud.

Now and then he heard a door or drawer slam from the room beyond. Rhoda, the society/fashion/gossip reporter, was still making her annoyance known. Without looking through the glass, he could see her in his mind, spitting darts at him.

She, along with more than half the staff, had worked for the paper since he'd been a boy. And plenty of them, he knew, continued to see the *Dispatch* as his mother's paper.

If not his grandfather's.

There were times when he resented it, times when he despaired of it, and times when it simply amused him.

He couldn't decide which reaction he was having at the moment. All he could think was that Rhoda scared the hell out of him.

The best he could do was not think about it, or her, and settle in to polish his article on the meeting he'd attended the night before. A proposed stoplight at Market and Spruce, a debate over the budget and the need to repair the sidewalks on Main. And a rather spirited argument regarding the highly controversial notion of installing parking meters on Main to help pay for those repairs.

Flynn did what he could to inject a little energy into the subject matter and still stay true to the reporter's code of objectivity.

The *Dispatch* wasn't exactly the *Daily Planet*, he reflected. But then again, he wasn't exactly Perry White. Nobody around here would ever call him Chief. Even without Rhoda's periodic snits, he wasn't certain that anyone, including himself, really believed he was in charge.

His mother cast a very long shadow. Elizabeth Flynn Hennessy Steele. Even her name cast a very long shadow.

He loved her. Of course he did. Most of the time he even liked her. They'd butted heads plenty when he was growing up, but he'd always respected her. You had to respect a woman who ran her life and her business with equal fervor, and expected everyone else to do the same.

Just as you had to give her credit for stepping out of that business when necessity demanded it. Even if she had dumped it in her reluctant son's lap.

She'd dumped it all, including, he thought with a wary glance toward Rhoda's desk, surly reporters.

She was filing her nails instead of working, he noted. Baiting him. File away, he thought. Today's not the day we square off, you cranky old bat.

But that day soon will come.

He was deep into adjusting the layout on page 1 of section B when Dana walked in.

"Not even a cursory knock. No flirtatious little head peek in the door. Just stomp right in."

"I didn't stomp. I've got to talk to you, Flynn." She threw herself into a chair, then glanced around. "Where's Moe?"

"It's backyard day for the Moe."

"Oh, right."

"And maybe you could go by, hang out with him for a while this afternoon. Then maybe you could throw together some dinner, so I'd come home to a hot meal."

"Sure, that'll happen."

"Listen, I've had a rough morning, I've got a goddamn headache, and I've got to finish this layout."

Dana pursed her lips as she studied him. "Rhoda sniping at you again?"

"Don't look," Flynn snapped before Dana could turn around. "You'll just encourage her."

"Flynn, why don't you just fire her ass? You take entirely too much crap off her."

"She's been with the *Dispatch* since she was eighteen. That's a long time. Now, while I appreciate you dropping in to tell me how to handle my employee problems, I need to finish this."

Dana just stretched out her endless legs. "She really stirred you up this time, huh?"

"Fuck it." He blew out a breath, then yanked open his desk drawer to hunt up a bottle of aspirin.

"You do a good job here, Flynn."

"Yeah, yeah," he muttered as he dug a bottle of water out of another drawer.

"Shut up. I'm serious. You're good at what you do. As good as Liz was. Maybe better at some areas of it because you're more approachable. Plus you're a better writer than anybody you've got on staff."

He eyed her while he washed the aspirin down. "What brought this on?"

"You look really bummed." She couldn't stand to see him seriously unhappy. Irritated, confused, pissed off, or surly was fine. But it hurt her heart to see misery etched on his face. "Pleasant Valley needs the *Dispatch*, and the *Dispatch* needs you. It doesn't need Rhoda. And I bet knowing that just sticks in her craw."

"You think?" The idea of that smoothed out the raw edges. "The sticking-in-the-craw part, I mean."

"You bet. Feel better?"

"Yeah." He capped the water bottle, dropped it back in the drawer. "Thanks."

"My second good deed for the day. I've just spent an hour at Malory's, and another twenty minutes wandering around trying to decide if I should dump on you or just keep it between us girls."

"If it has to do with hairstyles, monthly cycles, or the upcoming Red Tag sale at the mall, keep it between you girls."

"That's so incredibly sexist, I'm not even going to . . . what Red Tag sale?"

"Watch for the ad in tomorrow's *Dispatch*. Is something wrong with Malory?"

"Good question. She had a dream, only she doesn't believe it was a dream."

Dana related the discussion before digging in her bag for the typed account Malory had given her. "I'm worried about her, Flynn, and I'm starting to worry about me, because she's got me half convinced that she's right."

"Quiet a minute." He read it through twice, then sat back in his chair, staring at the ceiling. "What if she is right?"

Exasperation spiked into her voice. "Do I have to start playing Scully to your Mulder? We're talking about gods and sorcery and the capture of souls."

"We're talking about magic, about possibilities. And possibilities should always be explored. Where is she now?"

"She said she was going to The Gallery, to do some research on the painting."

"Good. Then she's sticking with the plan."

"You didn't see her."

"No, but I will. What about you? Dig anything up?"

"I'm tugging a few lines."

"Okay, let's all meet at my place tonight. Let Zoe know, I'll tell Mal." When Dana frowned at him, he only smiled. "You came to me, honey. I'm in it now."

"I really owe you for this. . . ."

"Oh, sweetheart, any day I can do something behind the bimbo-nazi's back is a day of celebration."

Still, Tod cast a cautious look right and left before he opened the door to what had once been Malory's office and was now Pamela's domain.

"Oh, God, what has she done to my space?"

"Hideous, isn't it?" Tod actually shuddered. "It's like the walls vomited Louis XIV. My only satisfaction is that she actually has to look at this when she comes in."

The room was jammed full. The curvy desk, the tables, the chairs, and two tasseled ottomans all vied for space on a rug that screamed with red and gold. The walls were covered with paintings overpowered by thick, ornate gold frames, and statuary, ornamental bowls and boxes, glassware and whatnots crowded every flat surface.

Each piece, Malory noted, was a small treasure in itself. But packing it all together in this limited space made it look like someone's very expensive garage sale.

"How does she manage to get anything done?"

"She has her slaves and minions—meaning me, Ernestine, Julia, and Franco. Simone Legree sits up here on her throne and gives orders. You had a lucky escape, Mal."

"Maybe I did." But still, it had been a wrench to come through the front door again, knowing she no longer belonged.

Not knowing where she belonged.

"Where is she now?"

"Lunch at the club." Tod checked his watch. "You've got two hours."

"I won't need that much. I need the client list," she said as she headed for the computer on the desk.

"Oooh, are you going to steal clients from under her rhinoplasty?"

"No. Hmm, happy thought, but no. I'm trying to pin down the artist on a particular painting. I need to see who we have that buys in that style. Then I need our files on paintings with mythological themes. Damn it, she's changed the password."

"It's mine."

"She uses your password?"

"No—M-I-N-E." He shook his head. "She wrote it down so she wouldn't forget it—after she forgot two other passwords. I happened to, ah, come across the note."

"I love you, Tod," Malory exclaimed as she keyed it in.

"Enough to tell me what this is all about?"

"More than enough, but I'm in kind of a bind about that. A couple of people I'd have to talk to first." She worked fast, locating the detailed client list, copying it to the disk she'd brought with her. "I swear I'm not using this for anything illegal or unethical."

"That's a damn shame."

She chuckled at that, then opened her bag to offer him a look at the printout she'd made from the digital photo. "Do you recognize this painting?"

"Hmm, no. But something about the style."

"Exactly. Something about the style. I can't quite place it, but it's nagging at me. I've seen this artist's work before, somewhere." When the file was copied, she switched to another, put in a fresh disk. "If you remember, give me a call. Day or night."

"Sounds urgent."

"If I'm not having a psychotic episode, it may very well be."

"Does this have anything to do with M. F. Hennessy? Are you working on a story for the paper?"

She goggled. "Where did that come from?"

"You were seen having dinner with him the other night. I hear everything," Tod added.

"It doesn't have anything to do with him, not directly. And no, I'm not writing a story. Do you know Flynn?"

"Only in my dreams. He's very hot."

"Well . . . I think I might be dating him. I wasn't going to, but I seem to be."

"Lip lock?"

"Several of them."

"Rating?"

"Top of the scale."

"Sex?"

"Almost, but cooler heads prevailed."

"Damn."

"Plus he's funny and interesting and sweet. Pretty bossy in a really clever way so you barely notice until you've been bossed. Smart, and I think tenacious."

"Sounds perfect. Can I have him?"

"Sorry, pal, but I may have to keep him." She snatched out the disk, then carefully closed documents and shut down. "Mission accomplished with no loss of life. Thanks, Tod." She threw her arms around him, gave him a big, noisy kiss. "I've got to get to work on this."

S H E hunkered down in her apartment, systematically going through the data, cross-referencing, eliminating, until she had a workable list. By the time she left for Flynn's, she'd winnowed The Gallery's client list by seventy percent.

Dana was already there when she arrived.

"Had dinner?"

"No." Malory looked, cautiously, for Moe. "I forgot."

"Good. We've got pizza coming. Flynn's out back with Moe for their daily romp. You're okay that I told him about your dream?"

"Yeah. We seem to have brought him into this."

"Okay. Go in and flop. We'll have some wine."

She'd barely done so when Zoe arrived with Simon in tow. "I hope it's all right. I couldn't get a sitter."

"I don't *need* a sitter," Simon declared.

"I need a sitter." Zoe hooked an arm around his neck. "He's got homework, so if there's a corner he can use. I brought the shackles."

Dana winked at him. "We'll use the dungeon. Can we torture him, then feed him pizza?"

"We've already had—"

"I could eat pizza," Simon interrupted. Then he let out a whoop as Moe charged in from the back of the house. "Wow! That's some dog!"

"Simon, don't—"

But boy and dog were already rushing together, caught in the throes of mutual love at first sight.

"Hey, Flynn, look what Zoe brought us. We get to make him do homework."

"I've always wanted to do that with somebody. You must be Simon."

"Uh-huh. This is a great dog, mister."

"The dog's Moe, I'm Flynn. Zoe, can Simon take Moe back out so they can run around like maniacs for a while?"

"Sure. Twenty minutes, Simon, then you hit the books."

"Sweet!"

"Straight out the back," Flynn told him. "There's a ball out there with toothmarks and drool all over it. He likes you to chase it and fetch it back to him."

"You're funny," Simon decided. "Let's go, Moe!"

"Pizza," Dana announced when the bell rang. "Want to call him back?"

"No, he's fine. He just finished eating three helpings of spaghetti."

"Flynn, be a man. Pay for the pizza."

"Why do I always have to be the man?" Then he ze-roed in on Malory and grinned. "Oh, yeah. That's why."

Dana sat on the floor with a fresh notebook in her lap. "Let's be organized about this. The librarian in me de-mands it. Zoe, pour yourself some wine. We can each report what we've found or thought or speculated on since the last time we got together."

"I haven't found much." Zoe took a folder out of her canvas bag. "I typed up all my notes, though."

"Aren't you a good girl?" Delighted, Dana took the folder, then pounced on the first box of pizza when Flynn dropped two of them on the coffee table. "I'm *starving*."

"There's news." He sat on the sofa beside Malory,

turned her face toward him with his hand, then kissed her long and firm. "Hi."

"Gee, don't I get one of those?"

At Zoe's question, he shifted and leaned toward her, but she laughed and gave him a light shove. "I'd better settle for the wine."

"If Flynn's finished kissing girls," Dana began.

"Which won't be until I've drawn my last, gasping breath."

"Settle down," Dana ordered. "We know about Mal's experience. I have the typed report of it here, which I'll add to the collection of notes and other data."

"I've got more." Since it was there, Malory took a slice of pizza from the box and dropped it onto a paper plate. "I have a list of people—clients through The Gallery—who've purchased or shown interest in classical and/or mythological subject matter in art. I've also started a search of like styles, but that's going to take some time. I intend to start making phone inquiries tomorrow."

"I could help," Zoe offered. "I was thinking that maybe we should do a search for paintings that include the element of a key. Like a theme."

"That's good," Malory acknowledged, and tore a sheet off the roll of paper towels that stood in for napkins. "I've got some appointments tomorrow, but I'll work around them."

"I've been working on the clue itself." Dana picked up her wineglass. "I'm wondering if we should take some of the key phrases and do a search on place names. Like restaurants or shops. Take the Singing Goddess, for example. I didn't find anything on that, but it's the sort of thing that could be the name of a shop or a restaurant or a site."

"Not bad," Flynn said and helped himself to another slice of pizza.

"I've got some more." Still she said nothing as she reached into the box herself, topped off her wine. "I put in some Internet time running the three names Malory heard in her . . . in her dream. "Niniane" comes up a few times. Some legends have her as the sorceress who enchanted Arthur's Merlin and trapped him in the cave of crystal. There's another that has her as Merlin's mother. But when I put her together with the other two, I found one hit from this esoteric little site on goddess worship. It gives a variation on the Daughters of Glass—and calls them by those names."

"Those are their names. You can't think it's a coincidence that I dreamed those names and you found them today."

"No," Dana said carefully. "But isn't it possible you came across the same site and the names stuck in your head?"

"No. I would've written it down. I would've remembered. I never heard them before the dream."

"Okay." Flynn patted her knee. "First, I'll tell you I haven't found any record of a shipping or moving company that serviced Warrior's Peak. And no record of any company shipping furniture here for clients under Triad."

"They had to get all that stuff in there somehow," Dana protested. "They didn't just click the heels of their ruby slippers together."

"Just giving you the facts. The real-estate company didn't make the arrangements for them, either. At this point, I haven't found any trail leading Rowena or Pitte to the Peak. Not saying there isn't one," he continued before Dana could protest. "Just saying I haven't found one through the logical sources."

"I guess we have to look at the illogical ones."

He shifted to beam at Zoe. "There you go. But I've got one more logical step to take. Who do I know who collects art seriously, someone I could use as a source? The Vanes. So I gave my old pal Brad a call. It so happens he's heading back here in a couple of days."

"Brad's coming back to the Valley?" Dana asked.

"He's taking over the local headquarters for Home-Makers. Brad's got the Vanes' passion for art. I described the painting to him, or started to. I wasn't close to being finished when he gave me the title. *The Daughters of Glass.*"

"No, that can't be. I'd have heard of it." Malory pushed herself to her feet and began to pace. "Who's the artist?"

"Nobody seems to be sure."

"Just not possible," Malory continued. "A major talent like that, I'd have heard. I'd have seen more of the artist's work."

"Maybe not. According to Brad, nobody seems to know much about the artist. *The Daughters of Glass* was last seen in a private home in London. Where it was, by all accounts, destroyed during the Blitz. In 1942."

Chapter Eight

MALORY closed herself in her apartment for two days. She submerged herself in books, telephone calls, E-mail. It was foolish, she'd decided, to run around chasing a dozen different angles and suppositions. Better— far better—to conduct the search with technology and systematic logic.

She couldn't function, simply couldn't *think*, in disorder. Which was why, she admitted as she carefully labeled yet another file, she'd failed as an artist.

Art, the creation of true art, required some mysterious, innate ability to thrive in chaos. Or that was her opinion. To be able to see and understand and *feel* dozens of shapes and textures of emotions at one time.

Then, of course, there was the little matter of possessing the talent to transfer those emotions onto a canvas.

She lacked the gift, on all levels, while the artist of *The Daughters of Glass* had it in spades.

The painting at Warrior's Peak, or one done by the same artist, was the path. She was sure of that now. Why else did she keep coming back to it? Why had she some-how in her dreams walked into it?

Why had she been chosen to find the first key, she thought, if not for her knowledge of and contacts in the art world?

She'd been told to look within and without. Within the painting, or another by the same artist? Did "without" mean to look at what surrounded the painting?

Opening a file folder, she studied the printout of the painting again. What surrounded the daughters? Peace and beauty, love and passion—and the threat to destroy it. As well as, she mused, the method to restore it.

A key in the air, in the trees, in the water.

She was damn sure she wasn't about to pluck a magic key out of the air or from a tree branch, so what did it *mean*? And which of those three was hers?

Too literal? Perhaps. Maybe "within" meant she was to look inside herself to her feelings about the painting, both the emotional and the intellectual response.

Where the goddess sings, she reflected as she rose from her piles of research to pace. No one had been singing in the dream. But the fountain had reminded her of music. Maybe it had something to do with the fountain.

Maybe water was her key.

And, she thought in frustration, she might not have left her apartment, but she was still running in circles.

There were only three weeks left.

Her heart jumped at the quick *rat-a-tat* on her glass patio doors. There stood the man and his dog on the other side. Instinctively she ran a hand over the hair she'd yanked back into a ponytail sometime that morning. She hadn't bothered with makeup or with changing out of the baggy cotton pants and tank she'd slept in.

Not only was she not looking her best, but she was pretty sure she'd dipped below her personal worst.

When she opened the door, she decided Flynn verified

that when he took a good, hard look at her and said, "Honey, you need to get out."

She felt, actually felt, her face arrange itself in a sulk. "I'm busy. I'm working."

"Yeah." He glanced at the neat stacks of research materials on her dining room table, the pretty coffee carafe and china cup. There were small containers, all in matching red plastic, that held pencils, paper clips, Post-its.

A glass paperweight swirling with ribbons of color anchored a few typed pages. A storage box was tucked under the table, and he imagined she placed everything that related to her project inside it every night and took it out again every morning.

It was amazing to him, and oddly charming. Even alone and at work she kept things tidy.

Moe bumped her leg with his snout, then gathered himself to leap. Recognizing the signal now, Malory stuck out a hand. "No jumping," she ordered and had Moe quivering in his desire to obey.

As a reward she gave him a congratulatory pat on the head. "I don't have any—"

"Don't say it," Flynn warned. "Don't say any food words. He loses his head. Come on, it's great out." He caught Malory's hand in his. "We'll go for a walk."

"I'm working. Why aren't you?"

"Because it's after six, and I like to pretend I have a life outside of the newspaper."

"After six?" She glanced down at her watch, remembered she hadn't put it on that morning. It was just another sign that the efficient train of her life had jumped its tracks. "I didn't realize it was so late."

"Which is why you need to go for a walk. Fresh air and exercise."

"Maybe, but I can't go out like this."

"Why not?"

"I'm in my pajamas."

"They don't look like pajamas."

"Well, they are, and I'm not going out in them, and with my hair all horrible and no makeup on."

"There's no dress code for walking the dog." Still, he was a man who had a mother and a sister, and he knew the rules. "But if you want to change, we'll wait."

HE'D dealt with enough women to know the wait could be anywhere from ten minutes to the rest of his life. Since he'd learned to think of the female grooming process as a kind of ritual, he didn't mind. It gave him a chance to sit out on the patio, with Moe flopped over his feet, and scribble ideas for articles in his notebook. In his opinion, time was only wasted if you didn't do something with it. If the something was staring off into space and letting the mind drift on whatever current was the strongest at that moment, that was fine.

But since that current was how he might get his hands on Malory again, he figured it would be more productive all around to channel his energies into work.

Since Brad was coming back to the Valley, the *Dispatch* would need a solid feature on him, on the Vanes, on HomeMakers. The history of the family and their business, the face of that business in today's economic climate, and any plans for the future.

He would handle that one himself, and combine his professional and personal interests. Just as he was doing with Malory. So he began to note down various aspects that described her.

"Blond, brainy, beautiful" headed his list.

"Hey, it's a start," he said to Moe. "She was picked for a reason, and the reason has to have something to do with who or what she is. Or isn't."

Organized. Arty.

He had never met anyone who managed to be both.

Single. Unemployed.

Huh. Maybe they should do an article on twenty- and

thirtysomething singles in the Valley. The dating scene in small-town USA. If he gave that to Rhoda, she might start speaking to him again.

He glanced up when he caught a movement out of the corner of his eye, and watched Malory walk to the patio door. It hadn't taken her as long to transform herself as he'd figured it would.

He got to his feet, hooking a hand in Moe's collar before the dog could leap on Malory. "You look great. Smell even better."

"And I'd like to keep it that way." She leaned down, tapped a finger lightly on Moe's nose. "So, no jumping."

"Why don't we take a drive down to the river? Then he can run around like crazy."

SHE had to give him points. He'd managed to turn walking the dog into a date and had done it smoothly. So smoothly, she didn't realize she was on a date until they were sitting on a blanket by the river eating fried chicken while Moe raced around barking hopefully at squirrels.

But it was hard to complain when the air was cool and fresh, and the light softening as the sun sank lower in the west. When it dropped beneath those peaks, everything would go soft and gray and it would be cooler yet. She would need the light jacket she'd brought along—at least she would if they stayed to watch the stars come out.

And how long had it been since she'd watched the stars come out?

Now that she was here, she wondered if the enforced hibernation, however brief, had accomplished anything more than creating a logjam in her mind.

She wasn't an isolationist. She needed contact with people. Conversations, stimuli, sound and movement. And realizing that only made her understand how much she needed to be part of the workforce again.

If she grabbed the million dollars at the end of this

strange rainbow, she would still need to work. Just for the day-to-day energy.

"I have to admit, I'm glad you got me out."

"You're not a cave dweller." He dug in the bucket for another drumstick when she frowned at him. "You're a social animal. Take Dana, she's more cave dweller than social animal. If you left her alone, she'd be perfectly happy holed up with mountains of books and a vat of coffee. At least for a few weeks. Then she'd need to come up for air. Me, I'd go nuts after a day or two. I need the charge. So do you."

"You're right. And I'm not sure how I feel about you figuring that out so soon."

"Soon's relative. I've spent, oh, about a year thinking about you in the past week. Given time and energy ratios. It's been a while since I've given that much thought to a woman, in case you're wondering."

"I don't know what I'm wondering. Yes, I do," she corrected. "Why haven't you brought up the key, or asked me what I'm doing about finding it?"

"Because you've had enough of that for now. If you'd wanted to get into it, you'd have brought it up. You're not shy."

"You're right. Why did you bring me out here, away from town?"

"It's quiet. Nice view. Moe likes it. There's the slim chance I can get you naked on this blanket—"

"Try slim to none."

"Slim's enough to keep me going." He dipped a plastic fork into the fast-food potato salad. "And I wanted to see if Brad's moving in yet." He looked across the ribbon of water to the rambling two-story frame house on the opposite bank. "Doesn't look like it."

"You miss him."

"You got that right."

She plucked a blade of grass, ran it idly through her fingers. "I have some friends from college. We were so close, and I guess we all thought we'd be close forever. Now we're all scattered and hardly see each other. Once or twice a year if we can all manage it. We talk on the phone or through E-mail now and then, but it's not the same. I miss them. I miss who we were when we were friends, and that telepathy you develop so that you know what the other's thinking, or what she'd do in some situation. Is it that way for you?"

"Pretty much." He reached over, toyed with the ends of her hair in the same absent way she toyed with the blade of grass. "But we go back to being kids together. None of us are big on phone calls. Maybe because Brad and I end up on the phone through most of our workday. E-mail does the job. Jordan, he's the E-mail king."

"I met him for about ninety seconds at a book signing, in Pittsburgh, about four years ago. All dark and handsome, with a dangerous gleam in his eye."

"You want dangerous?"

It made her laugh. He was sitting on a ratty blanket eating bucket chicken while his big, silly dog barked at a squirrel that was ten feet up a tree.

Then she was flat on her back, his body pressed to hers, and the laugh died in her throat.

His mouth *was* dangerous. Foolish of her to have forgotten that. However affable and easy he appeared on the surface, there were storms inside him. Hot, whippy storms that could crash over the unwary before they could think about taking shelter.

So she didn't think at all, but let it rage. And let that secret part of herself, that part she'd never risked exposing, slide out. And take, even as it was taken.

"How's this working for you?" he murmured as he fixed that amazing mouth on her throat.

"So far, so good."

He lifted his head, looked down at her. And his heart shuddered in his chest. "Something here. Some big something here."

"I don't think—"

"Yes, you do." Impatience, potent and unexpected, snapped out. "You may not want to think—I'm not real keen on it myself, but you do. I really hate using the obvious metaphor, but this is like turning a key in a lock. I can hear the goddamn click."

He pushed up, dragged an unsteady hand through his hair. "I'm not ready to hear any goddamn click."

She sat up quickly, brushed fussily at the front of her shirt. It threw her off balance that she could find his temper both irritating and arousing at the same time. "You think *I* want to hear one? I've got enough on my mind right now without you clicking around in my head. I need to find the first key. I've got to work this out. I need to find a job. And I don't even want a stupid job. I want . . ."

"What? What do you want?"

"I don't *know*." She scrambled to her feet. There was a fury inside her. She didn't know where it came from or where it needed to go. Turning away, she stared at the house across the river, folded her arms firmly over her chest. "And I always know what I want."

"You're one up on me there." He rose, but didn't go to her. Whatever was pumping inside him—anger, need, fear—was too unstable to risk touching her.

The breeze was playing with the ends of her hair, as he had. All those tumbling clouds the color of old gold, like something out of a painting. She looked so slim, so perfect, standing there, half turned away from him while the dying sun shot a thin line of fire along the rise of western hills.

"The only thing I've been absolutely sure I wanted . . . ever," he realized, "is you."

She glanced back as nervous wings began to stir in her belly. "I don't imagine I'm the only woman you've wanted to sleep with."

"No. Actually, the first was Joley Ridenbecker. We

were thirteen. And that particular desire was never ful-filled."

"Now you're making a joke of it."

"I'm not. Not really." He stepped toward her and his voice was gentle. "I wanted Joley, as much as I knew what that meant at thirteen. It was intense, even painful, and kind of sweet. Eventually I found out what that meant. I wanted other women along the way. I even loved one, which is why I know the difference between wanting a woman, and wanting you. If it was just sex, it wouldn't piss me off."

"It's hardly my fault you're pissed off." She scowled at him. "And you don't look or sound as if you are."

"I tend to get really reasonable when I'm seriously an-noyed. It's a curse." He picked up the ball Moe spat at his feet, then threw it with a strong whiplash of arm. "And if you think it's a joy to be able to see both sides of an argument, to see the validity on each end, let me tell you, it's a pain in the ass."

"Who was she?"

He shrugged, then picked up the ball Moe returned, threw it again. "Doesn't matter."

"I'd say it does. And that she still does."

"It just didn't work out."

"Fine. I should be getting back now." She walked back to kneel on the blanket and tidy the remains of their im-promptu picnic.

"That's a skill I admire, and nobody does it like a woman. The implied 'fuck you,' " he explained, then shot the ball in the air for Moe once more. "She left me. Or I didn't go with her. Depends on your point of view. We were together the best part of a year. She was a reporter for the local station, moved up to weekend anchor, then evening anchor. She was good, and we got to have all these arguments and discussions over the impact and value of our particular news medium. Which is sexier than it may sound. Anyway, we planned to get married, move to New York. Eventually, on the moving part. Then she got an offer from an affiliate up there. She went. I stayed."

"Why did you stay?"

"Because I'm George fucking Bailey." The ball burst out of his hand again like a rocket.

"I don't understand."

"George Bailey, giving up his dreams of travel and adventure to stay in his hometown and rescue the old savings and loan. I'm no Jimmy Stewart, but the *Dispatch* sure as hell turned out to be my savings and loan. My stepfather, Dana's dad, had been ill. My mother shifted some of the responsibilities of editor in chief to me. I assumed it was temporary, until Joe got back on his feet. But the doctors, and my mother, wanted him out of the cold winters. And they wanted, deserved, to enjoy a retirement period. She threatened that if I didn't take over for her at the paper, she would shut it down. My mother doesn't make idle threats."

With a humorless laugh, he tossed the ball again. "You can bet your ass she doesn't. A Flynn runs the *Valley Dispatch* or there is no *Dispatch*."

Michael Flynn Hennessy, she thought. So Flynn was a family name *and* a legacy. "If she knew you wanted something different . . ."

He managed to smile. "She didn't want something different. I could've gone, just kicked the dust off my heels and gone with Lily to New York. And all the people who work at the paper would've been out of a job. Half of them, maybe more, wouldn't have been picked up by whoever started another paper. She knew I wouldn't go."

He studied the ball in his hand, turned it slowly, spoke softly. "She never did like Lily anyway."

"Flynn—"

He gave in to Moe's desperate excitement and heaved the ball. "Before I make it sound pitiful and pathetic—I did want to go, then. I loved Lily, then. But I didn't love her enough to pack up and go when she gave me the ultimatum. She didn't love me enough to stay, or to give me the time to work things out here and meet up with her."

Then you didn't love each other at all, Malory thought, but she remained silent.

"Less than a month after she'd landed in New York, she called and broke our engagement. She needed to concentrate on her career, couldn't handle the stress of a relationship, much less a long-distance one. I should be free to see other people and make a life, while she was going to be married to her job.

"And in six months she was married to an NBC news exec and moving steadily up the ladder. She got what she wanted, and in the end so did I."

He turned back to Malory. His face was calm again, the deep green eyes clear as if the fury had never been behind them. "My mother was right—and I really hate that part. But she was right. This is my place, and I'm doing exactly what I want to do."

"The fact that you see that says a lot more about you than about either one of them."

He threw the ball one last time. "I made you feel sorry for me."

"No." Though he had. "You made me respect you." She rose, walked to him and kissed his cheek. "I think I remember this Lily from the local news. Redhead, right? Lots of teeth."

"That'd be Lily."

"Her voice was entirely too nasal, and she had a weak chin."

He leaned over, kissed her cheek in turn. "That's a really nice thing to say. Thanks."

Moe raced back and spat out the ball on the ground between them. "How long will he do that?" Malory asked.

"For all eternity, or until my arm falls off."

She gave the ball a good boot with her foot. "It's getting dark," she said as Moe raced happily off. "You should take me home."

"Or I could take Moe home and we could—ah, I see by the way your eyebrows have arched and your lip has curled that your mind is in the gutter. I was going to say we could go to the movies."

"You were not."

"I certainly was. In fact, it so happens I have the movie section in the car, for your perusal."

They were all right again, she realized, and wanted to kiss him—this time in friendship. Instead, she fell into the rhythm and played the game out. "You have the entire paper in the car, because it's your paper."

"Be that as it may, I'll still let you pick the flick."

"What if it's an art film with subtitles?"

"Then I'll suffer in silence."

"You already know there aren't any such films playing at the local multiplex, don't you?"

"That's neither here nor there. Come on, Moe, let's go for a ride."

I T had done her good, Malory decided, to step away from the puzzle and the problems for an evening. She felt fresher this morning, and more optimistic. And it felt good to be interested in and attracted to a complicated man.

He *was* complicated, she thought. Only more so because he gave the impression, at least initially, of being simple. And so that made him yet another puzzle to solve.

She couldn't deny that *click* he'd spoken of. Why should she? She wasn't a game player when it came to relationships—she was cautious. It meant she needed to find out if the click was merely sexual or tangled around something more.

Puzzle number three, she decided as she hunkered down to continue her research.

Her first phone call of the morning left her stunned.

Moments after hanging up, she was tearing through her old college textbooks on art history.

T H E door of the Vane house was wide open. A number of burly men were hauling furniture and boxes in, or hauling furniture and boxes out. Just watching them gave Flynn a backache.

He recalled the weekend years before when he and Jordan had moved into an apartment. How they, with Brad's help, had carted a secondhand sofa that weighed as much as a Honda up three flights of stairs.

Those were the days, Flynn reminisced. Thank God they were over.

Moe leaped out of the car behind him and without waiting for an invitation raced straight into the house. There was a crash, a curse. Flynn could only pray that one of the Vane family antiques hadn't bit the dust as he hurriedly followed.

"Jesus Christ. You call this a puppy?"

"He was a puppy—a year ago." Flynn looked at his oldest friend, currently being greeted by and slobbered on by his dog. And his heart simply sang.

"Sorry about the . . . was that a lamp?"

Brad glanced at the broken china scattered in the foyer. "It was a minute ago. All right, big guy. Down."

"Outside, Moe. Chase the rabbit!"

In response, Moe let out a series of barks and bombed out the door.

"What rabbit?"

"The one that lives in his dreams. Hey." Flynn stepped forward, crunching broken shards under his feet, and caught Brad in one hard hug. "Looking good. For a suit."

"Who's a suit?"

He couldn't have looked less like one in worn jeans and a denim work shirt. He looked, Flynn thought, tall and lean and fit. The Vanes' golden child, the family prince, who was as happy running a construction crew as he was a board meeting.

Maybe happier.

"I came by last evening, but the place was deserted. When did you get in?"

"Late. Let's get out of the way," Brad suggested as the movers carried in another load. He jerked a thumb and led the way to the kitchen.

The house was always furnished, and made available to execs or visiting brass from the Vane corporation. Once it had been their home in the Valley, a place Flynn had known as well as his own.

The kitchen had been redone since the days when he'd begged cookies there, but the view out the windows, off the surrounding deck, was the same. Woods and water, and the rising hills beyond.

Some of the best parts of his childhood were tied up in this house. Just as they were tied up in the man who now owned it.

Brad poured coffee, then led Flynn out on the deck.

"How's it feel to be back?" Flynn asked him.

"Don't know yet. Odd, mostly." He leaned on the rail, looked out beyond.

Everything was the same. Nothing was the same.

He turned back, a man comfortable in his frame. He had a layer or two of big city on him, and was comfortable with that as well.

His hair was blond that had darkened with the years, just as the dimples in his cheeks were closer to creases now. Much to his relief. His eyes were a stone gray under straight brows. They tended to look intense, even when the rest of his face smiled.

Flynn knew it wasn't the mouth that showed Brad's mood. It was the eyes. When they smiled, he meant it.

They did so now. "Son of a bitch. It's good to see you."

"I never figured you for coming back, not for any length of time."

"Neither did I. Things change, Flynn. They're meant to, I guess. I've been itchy the last few years. I finally figured out I was itchy for home. How are things with you, Mr. Editor in Chief?"

"They're okay. I assume you'll be subscribing to our paper. I'll make arrangements for that," he added with a grin. "We put up a nice red box next to the mailbox on the road. Morning delivery out here usually hits by seven."

"Sign me up."

"I will. And I'm going to want to interview Bradley Charles Vane IV at his earliest convenience."

"Shit. Give me a while to settle in before I have to put on my corporate hat."

"How about next Monday? I'll come to you."

"Christ, you've become Clark Kent. No, worse, Lois Lane—without the great legs. I don't know what I've got going on Monday, but I'll have my assistant set it up."

"Great. How about we grab some beer and catch up tonight?"

"I can get behind that. How's your family?"

"Mom and Joe are doing fine out in Phoenix."

"Actually, I was thinking more about the delicious Dana."

"You're not going to start hitting on my sister again? It's embarrassing."

"She hooked up with anybody?"

"No, she's not hooked up with anybody."

"She still built?"

Flynn winced. "Shut up, Vane."

"I love yanking your chain over that one." And with a sigh, Brad was home. "Though it's entertaining, that's not why I asked you to come out. There's something I think you're going to want to see. I did some thinking when you told me about this deal Dana and her friends got themselves into."

"You know something about these people up at Warrior's Peak?"

"No. But I know something about art. Come on. I had them put it in the great room. I'd just finished uncrating it personally when I heard you drive up."

He walked along the deck, around the corner of the house to the double glass doors bordered by etched panels.

The great room boasted a towering ceiling with a circling balcony, a generous fireplace with hearth and mantel of hunter-green granite framed in golden oak. There was space for two sofas, one in the center of the room, the other tucked into a cozy conversation area along the far wall.

More space spilled through a wide arch, where the piano stood and where Brad had spent countless tedious hours practicing.

There, propped against the hearth of a second fireplace, was the painting.

The muscles in Flynn's belly went loose. "Jesus. Oh, Jesus."

"It's called *After the Spell*. I got it at an auction about three years ago. Do you remember I mentioned I'd bought a painting because one of the figures in it looked like Dana?"

"I didn't pay any attention. You were always razzing me about Dana." He crouched down now, stared hard at the painting. He didn't know art, but even with his limited eye, he'd have bet the farm that the same hand had painted this that had created the painting at Warrior's Peak.

There was no joy or innocence here, however. The tone was dark, a kind of grieving, with the only light, pale, pale light, glowing from the three glass coffins where three women seemed to sleep.

His sister's face, and Malory's, and Zoe's.

"I have to make a phone call." Flynn straightened and dug out his cell phone. "There's someone who has to see this right away."

Chapter Nine

SHE didn't like to be told to hurry, especially when she wasn't given a good reason why. So, on principle, Malory took her time driving to the Vane house.

She had a lot on her mind, and a little drive in the country was just the ticket, she decided, to line those thoughts up in some organized fashion.

And she liked tooling along in her little car over the windy road that followed the river, and the way the sun sprinkled through the leaves overhead to splatter patterns of light on the roadbed.

If she could paint, she would do a study of that—just the way light and shadow played on something as simple and ordinary as a country road. If she could paint, she thought again—which she couldn't, despite all the desire, all the study, all the years of trying.

But someone sure as hell could.

She should've tried to track down Dana and Zoe before driving out here. Really, she was supposed to be working with them, not with Flynn. He was . . . like an accessory, she told herself. A really attractive, sexy, interesting accessory.

Boy, she loved accessories.

Not a productive train of thought.

She switched the car radio off, steeped herself in silence. What she needed to do was find Dana and Zoe, tell them what she'd discovered. Maybe if she said it all out loud she, or they, could decipher what it meant.

Because at the moment she didn't have a clue.

All she knew, in her gut, was that it was important. Even vital. If not the answer, it was one of the bread crumbs that would lead to the answer.

She turned off the road and onto the private lane. No gates here. No circling walls. The Vanes were certainly wealthy enough to rate them. She wondered why they hadn't chosen to buy Warrior's Peak instead of building by the river, closer to town.

Then the house came into view and answered her question. It was beautiful, and it was wood. A lumber baron would hardly build or buy in stone or brick. He would, as he had, build to illustrate the art of his product.

The wood was honey gold, set off by copper trim that had gone dreamy green with age and weather. There was a complex arrangement of decks and terraces, skirting or jutting from both stories. Half a dozen rooflines peaked or sloped, all with a kind of artful symmetry that brought harmony to the whole.

The grounds were informal, as suited the site and the style, but she imagined that the placement of every shrub, every tree, every flower bed had been meticulously selected and designed.

Malory approved of meticulous design and execution.

She pulled up beside a moving van and was about to step out when she heard the wild, delighted barking.

"Oh, no, not this time. I've got your number, buddy." She reached into the box on the floor beside her and pulled out a large dog biscuit.

Even as Moe's homely face smooshed against the car window, she rolled it down. "Moe! Get the cookie!" And threw the dog biscuit as far as she could manage.

As he raced in pursuit, she nipped out of the car and made a dash for the house.

"Nice job." Flynn met her at the door.

"I'm a quick study."

"Counting on that. Malory Price, Brad Vane. Already called it," Flynn added in subtle warning as he saw the interest light in Brad's eye.

"Oh? Well, can't blame you." Brad smiled at Malory. "It's still nice to meet you, Malory."

"What are you talking about?"

"It's guy-speak," Flynn told her, and dipped his head to kiss her. "Just bringing Brad up-to-date. Dana and Zoe on the way?"

"No. Dana's working, and I couldn't reach Zoe. I left messages for both of them. What's this all about?"

"You're going to want to see it for yourself."

"See what? You drag me out here—no offense," she added to Brad, "you have a beautiful house—without any explanation. And I was busy. The time factor—"

"I'm starting to think time's a real factor." Flynn tugged her along toward the great room.

"Excuse the disorder. I've got a lot going out, a lot coming in today." Brad kicked aside a chunk of broken lamp. "Flynn tells me you managed the art gallery in town."

"Yes, until recently. Oh, what a fabulous room." She stopped, absorbed the space. It needed paintings, sculpture, more color, more texture. Such a wonderful space deserved art.

If she'd had a free hand and an unlimited budget she could've made this room a showcase.

"You must be eager to unpack your things, settle in, and . . . oh, my God."

The shock struck the instant she saw the painting. The

stunning blast of discovery pumped straight into her blood, had her fumbling her glasses out of her purse and going down to her knees in front of it for a closer study.

The colors, the brushstrokes, the technique, even the medium. The same. The same, she thought, as the other. The three main subjects, the same.

"After the theft of the souls," she stated. "They're here, in this box on the pedestal in the foreground. My God, look at how the light and color seem to pulse inside the glass. It's genius. There, in the background, the two figures from the first painting, with their backs turned here. They're leaving. Banished. About to walk through that mist. The Curtain of Dreams. The keys."

She scooped her hair back, held the mass of it in one hand as she peered more closely. "Where are the keys? There! You can just see them, on a chain the female figure holds in her hand. Three keys. She's the keeper."

Wanting to see more detail, she fished a small silver-handled magnifying glass out of a felt bag in her purse.

"She carries a magnifying glass in her purse," Brad uttered in amazement.

"Yeah." Flynn grinned like a fool. "Isn't she great?"

Focused on the painting, she shut out the comments behind her and peered through the glass. "Yes, yes, it's the same design of key. They're not worked into the background the way they are in the other painting. Not symbolism this time, but fact. She has the keys."

She lowered the glass, eased back slightly for an overview. "The shadow's still in the trees, but farther back now. You can barely see his shape. His work's done, but still he watches. Gloats?"

"Who is *he*?" Brad wanted to know.

"Quiet. She's working."

Malory slipped the glass back into its pouch, then returned it to her purse. "Such a sad painting, such grief in the light, in the body language of the two as they step toward that curtain of mist. The main subjects in their

crystal coffins look serene, but they're not. It's not seren-
ity, it's emptiness. And there's such desperation in that
light inside the box. It's painful, and it's brilliant."

"Is it the same artist?" Flynn asked her.

"Of course. This is no student, no mimic, no homage.
But that's opinion." She sat back on her heels. "I'm not
an authority."

Could've fooled me, he thought. "Between you and
Brad, I figure we've got all the authority we need."

She'd forgotten Brad, and flushed a bit with embarrassment. She'd all but lapped the painting up, kneeling
before it like a supplicant. "Sorry." Still kneeling, she
looked up at him. "I got carried away. Could you tell me
where you acquired this?"

"At auction, in New York. A small house. Banderby's."

"I've heard of them. The artist?"

"Unknown. You can just make out a partial signature—
an initial, really. Might be an *R,* or a *P,* followed by the
key symbol."

Malory bent lower to study the lower left corner. "You
had it dated, authenticated?"

"Of course. Seventeenth century. Though the style has
a more contemporary feel, the painting was tested exten-
sively. If you know Banderby's you know it's both meticulous and reputable."

"Yes. Yes, I know."

"And I had it tested independently. Just a little habit
of mine," Brad added. "The results coincided."

"I have a theory," Flynn began, but Malory waved him
off.

"Can I ask you why you bought it? Banderby's isn't
known for its bargains, and it's an unknown artist."

"One reason is I was struck how much the middle figure resembled Dana." It was true enough, Brad thought,
if not the whole truth. "The overall painting, the power
of it, caught me first, then that detail drew me in. And . . ."

He hesitated, his gaze tracking across the painting. Then, feeling foolish, he shrugged. "You could say it spoke to me. I wanted it."

"Yes, I understand that." She took her glasses off, folded them and, slipped them carefully back in their case, then slid the case into her purse. "Flynn must have told you about the painting at Warrior's Peak."

"Sure, I told him. And when I saw this, I figured—"

"Ssh." Malory tapped him on the knee, then held up a hand for him to help her to her feet. "It has to be a series. There's another painting that comes before or after or in between. But there have to be three. It's consistently three. Three keys, three daughters. The three of us."

"Well, there are five of us now," Brad put in. "But, yeah, I follow you."

"You followed me when I said the same damn thing a half hour ago," Flynn complained. "My theory."

"Sorry." This time Malory patted him on the arm. "It's all tumbling around in my head. I can almost make out the pieces, but I can't quite see the shape, or where they go. What they mean. Do you mind if we sit down?"

"Sure. Sorry." Immediately, Brad took her arm, led her to a sofa. "Can I get you something to drink?"

"Got any brandy? I know it's early, but I could really use just a little brandy."

"I'll find some."

Flynn sat beside her as Brad left the room. "What is it, Mal? You look a little pale all of a sudden."

"It hurts me." She looked toward the painting again, then closed her eyes as tears gathered in them. "Even as it dazzles my mind and my spirit, it hurts to look at it. I saw this happen, Flynn. I felt this happen to them."

"I'll put it away."

"No, no." She caught his hand, and the contact comforted her. "Art's supposed to touch you in some way. That's its power. What will the third be? And when?"

"When?"

She shook her head. "How flexible is your mind, I wonder? I'm just starting to find out how flexible mine is. You've told Brad all of it?"

"Yeah." Something here, he realized as he watched her. Something she wasn't quite sure she could say. "You can trust him, Malory. You can trust me."

"The question will be if either of you will trust me after I tell you both what I found out this morning and what I think it means. Your old friend might politely nudge me out the door and bolt it behind me."

"I never lock beautiful women out of the house." Brad walked back in with a snifter of brandy. He handed it to her, then sat on the coffee table, facing her. "Go ahead, knock it back."

She did just that, downing the brandy as she might a quick dose of medicine. It slid smoothly down her throat and soothed her jittery stomach. "It's a crime to treat a Napoleon that carelessly. Thanks."

"Knows her brandy," he said to Flynn. Color was seeping back into her cheeks. To give her a chance to recover more fully, he rapped Flynn with his elbow. "How the hell did you manage to get a woman with taste and class to look twice at you?"

"I had Moe knock her down, pin her to the ground. Better, Mal?"

"Yes." She blew out a breath. "Yes. Your painting's seventeenth century. That's absolutely conclusive?"

"That's right."

"I found out this morning that the painting at Warrior's Peak is twelfth century, possibly earlier but no later."

"If you got that from Pitte or Rowena—" Flynn began.

"No. I got that from Dr. Stanley Bower, of Philadelphia. He's an expert, and a personal acquaintance. I sent him scrapings of the painting."

"How'd you get scrapings?" Flynn wanted to know.

More color rose in her cheeks, but it wasn't the brandy that caused it. She cleared her throat, fussed with the clasp of her purse. "I took them when you went up there with me last week. When you and Moe distracted them. It was completely inappropriate, absolutely unethical. I did it anyway."

"Cool." Pure admiration shone in Flynn's tone. "So that means either Brad's experts or yours is off, or you're wrong about both being done by one artist. Or . . ."

"Or, the experts are right and so am I." Malory set her purse aside, folded her hands tight in her lap. "Dr. Bower would have to run more complex and in-depth tests to verify the date, but he wouldn't be off by centuries. I've seen both paintings, up close. Everything I know tells me they were done by the same hand. I know it sounds crazy. It *feels* crazy, but I believe it. Whoever created the portrait at Warrior's Peak did so in the twelfth century, and that same artist painted Brad's five hundred years later."

Brad slid his gaze toward Flynn, surprised that his friend wasn't goggling, or grinning. Instead, Flynn's face was sober and considering. "You want to believe that my painting was executed by a five-hundred-year-old artist?"

"Older, I think. Much older than that. And I think the artist painted both from memory. Rethinking bolting the door?" Malory asked him.

"I'm thinking both of you have gotten caught up in a fantasy. A romantic and tragic story that has no basis in reality."

"You haven't seen the painting. You haven't seen *The Daughters of Glass*."

"No, but I've heard about it. All accounts place it in London, during the Blitz. Where it was destroyed. Most likely answer is that the one at the Peak is a copy."

"It's not. You think I'm being stubborn. I can be," Malory admitted, "but this isn't one of those times. I'm not a fanciful person either—or I haven't been."

She shifted her attention to Flynn, and her voice grew urgent. "Flynn, everything they told me, everything they told me and Dana and Zoe that first night was absolutely true. Even more amazing is what they didn't tell us. Rowena and Pitte—teacher and warrior—they're the figures in the background of each painting. They were there, in reality. And one of them painted both those portraits."

"I believe you."

Her breath shuddered out in relief at Flynn's simple faith. "I don't know what it means, or how it helps, but learning this—and believing it—is why I was picked. If I don't find the key, and Dana and Zoe don't find theirs after me, those souls will keep screaming inside that box. Forever."

He reached out, ran a hand over her hair. "We won't let that happen."

"Excuse me." Zoe hesitated at the entrance to the room. She was hard-pressed not to rub her hands over the satiny trim, or kick off her shoes to slide barefoot across the glossy floors.

She wanted to rush to the windows and study every view.

"The men outside said I should come right in. Um, Flynn? Moe's out there rolling around in something that looks a lot like dead fish."

"Shit. Be right back. Zoe, Brad." And he ran outside.

Brad got to his feet. He wasn't sure how he managed it when his knees had dissolved. He heard his own voice, a bit cooler than normal, a bit stilted, over the roar of blood in his head.

"Come in, please. Sit down. Can I get you something?"

"No, thanks. Sorry. Malory, I got your message and came right out. Is something wrong?"

"I don't know. Brad here thinks I've slipped a few gears, and I don't blame him."

"That's ridiculous." In her instant leap to defend, she forgot the charm of the house, the aloof charm of the man. Her cautious and apologetic smile turned into a chilly scowl as she strode across the room to Malory's side.

"And if you said any such thing, you're not only wrong, you're rude."

"Actually, I didn't get around to saying it yet. And as you don't know the circumstances—"

"I don't have to. I know Malory. And if you're a friend of Flynn's, you should know better than to upset her."

"I beg your pardon." Where had that stiff, superior tone come from? How had his father's voice popped out of his mouth?

"It's not his fault, Zoe. Really. As to being upset, I don't know what I am." Malory shoved back her hair and, rising, gestured toward the painting. "You should take a look at this."

Zoe moved closer. Then clutched her throat. "Oh. Oh." And her eyes filled with hot tears. "It's so beautiful. It's so sad. But it belongs with the other. How did it get here?"

Malory slipped an arm around her waist so they stood joined together. "Why do you think it belongs with the other?"

"It's the Daughters of Glass, after the . . . the spell or the curse. The box, with the blue lights. It's just the way you described it, from your dream. And it's the same— the same . . . I don't know how to say it. It's like a set, or part of a set, painted by the same person."

Malory glanced over her shoulder at Brad, cocked a brow.

"Are you an art expert?" Brad asked Zoe.

"No." She didn't bother to look at him, and her tone was flat. "I'm a hairdresser, but I'm not stupid."

"I didn't mean to imply—"

"No, you meant to *say*. Will it help you find the key, Malory?"

"I don't know. But it means something. I have a digital camera out in the car. Can I take some pictures of it?"

"Be my guest." Brad jammed his hands into his pockets as Malory hurried out and left him alone with Zoe. "Are you sure I can't get you something? Coffee?"

"No, I'm fine. Thank you."

"I, ah, came in on this after the first reel," he began. "You might give me a little time to catch up."

"I'm sure Flynn will tell you everything you need to know." She crossed the room, using the excuse of looking out for Malory as a chance to see the lovely river view.

What would it be like, she wondered, to be able to stand here whenever you wanted, to see the water and the light, the hills? Liberating, she imagined. And peaceful.

"Malory just told me she believes the Daughters of Glass exist, in reality. In some reality. And that the people you met at Warrior's Peak are several thousand years old."

She turned back, didn't so much as blink. "If she believes that, she has good reason. And I trust her enough to believe it too. Now would you like to tell me I've slipped a couple of gears?"

Irritation flickered over his face. "I never said that to her. I thought it, but I didn't say it. I'm not saying it to you either."

"But you're thinking it."

"You know, I only have two feet, but I'm managing to stay on the wrong one with you."

"Since I doubt we're going dancing anytime soon, I'm not really worried about your feet. I like your house."

"Thanks, so do I. Zoe—"

"I've done a lot of business at HomeMakers. I've found good values and excellent customer service in the local store."

"Good to know."

"I hope you're not planning on making any major changes there, but I wouldn't mind a little more variety on the seasonal stuff. You know, bedding plants, snow shovels, outdoor furniture."

His lips twitched. "I'll keep that in mind."

"And it wouldn't hurt to add a couple more cashiers on Saturdays. There's always a wait at the checkout."

"So noted."

"I'm starting my own business, so I pay attention to how things run."

"Are you opening your own salon?"

"Yes." She said it firmly, despite the way her stomach muscles clutched. "I was looking at space before I got Mallory's message to come out here."

And why didn't Mallory come back in? She was running out of steam now that her temper had leveled off. She didn't know what to talk about with a man who lived in a house like this, one who helped run an enormous national conglomerate. If "conglomerate" was the word for it.

"In the Valley?"

"What? Oh, yes, I'm looking for a place in town. I'm not interested in a mall space. I think it's important to maintain a good downtown, and I want to be close to home so I can be more available to my son."

"You have a son?" His gaze zeroed in on her left hand, and he nearly sighed with relief at the lack of a wedding ring.

All Zoe saw was the quick look. She straightened her shoulders, stiffened them. "Yes. Simon's nine."

"Sorry it took me so long," Mallory apologized as she came back in. "Flynn's got Moe tied to a tree in the side yard. He's hosing him down, for all the good that's going to do. He'll just be a wet incredibly smelly dog instead of only an incredibly smelly one. He said to ask if you had any shampoo or soap you could spare."

"I can come up with something. Go ahead and take your pictures."

Mallory aimed the camera, waited until Brad's footsteps receded. "Talk about gods," she murmured to Zoe.

"What?"

"Bradley Charles Vane IV. His kind of looks just smack a woman right in the hormones."

"Looks are genetic." Zoe very nearly sniffed. "Personality and manners are developed."

"It was one fine day in the gene pool when he was made." She lowered the camera. "I gave you the impression he was giving me a hard time. Really, he wasn't."

"Maybe, maybe not. But he's an arrogant snob."

"Wow." Malory blinked at the vehemence in Zoe's voice. "I didn't get that. I can't imagine Flynn being friends with anyone who fits the snob category. Arrogant is debatable."

Zoe jerked a shoulder. "I've run into his type before. They're more interested in looking good than in being human. Anyway, he's not important. The painting is."

"I think it is. And what you said about them being a set, part of a set. I think that's true, and there's at least one more. I have to find it. Something in them, or about them, is going to point me toward the key. I'd better hit the books."

"Want some help?"

"All I can get."

"I'll head back now. There are a couple of things I need to do, then I'll swing by your place."

ABOUT the time Brad unearthed a bottle of shampoo he heard a car start. He went to the window, cursed under his breath as he watched Zoe and Malory head down his lane.

As far as first impressions went, he'd made a complete mess of it. He didn't usually alienate women on sight. But then again, the sight of a woman didn't usually slam into him like a hard, sweaty fist. Considering that, he supposed he could be excused for not being at his best.

He went downstairs, then detoured back into the great room instead of continuing to the outside. He stood staring at the painting as he had the first time he'd seen it at the auction house. The way he'd stared at it countless times since he'd acquired it.

He'd have paid any price for it.

It was true enough what he'd told Malory and Flynn. He'd bought it because it was magnificent, powerful, compelling. He'd been intrigued by the one figure's face, its resemblance to his childhood friend.

But it had been another face in the painting that had dazzled him, consumed him. Undone him. One look at that face, Zoe's face, and he'd fallen unreasonably in love.

Strange enough, he thought, when the woman had simply been a figure in a painting. How much more complicated and impossible was it now that he knew she was real?

H E thought about it while he put some of his house in order. He continued to think about it later when he and Flynn climbed up to sit on the wall surrounding Warrior's Peak.

They each opened a beer and studied the exotic silhouette etched against a gloomy sky.

Lights glowed against the windows here and there, but as they drank their beers in silence, they saw no figure pass behind the glass.

"They probably know we're out here," Flynn said after a time.

"If we take your girlfriend's theory to heart, and label them Celtic gods with a few thousand years under their belts, yeah, pretty safe bet they know we're out here."

"You used to be more open-minded," Flynn noted.

"Ah, no. Not really. Jordan would be the one inclined to bite on this kind of a story line and run with it."

"You see him lately?"

"A couple months ago. He's been doing a lot of traveling, so we don't manage to get together as often as we used to. Fuck it, Flynn." Brad flung an arm around

Flynn's shoulder. "I've missed you assholes."

"Same goes. You going to tell me what you thought of Malory?"

"Classy, intellectual, and very, very hot—despite her dubious taste in men."

Flynn tapped the heels of his ancient tennis shoes against the stone of the wall. "I'm about half crazy about her."

"Serious crazy, or let's mambo crazy?"

"I don't know. Haven't figured it yet." He studied the house, and the quarter slice of moon that drifted over it. "I'm hoping it's door number two, because I'd just as soon not get serious crazy at this point."

"Lily was a social-climbing opportunist with a great rack."

"Jesus, Vane." He wasn't sure whether to laugh or give his friend a hard shove off the seven-foot wall. So he did neither and only brooded instead. "I was in love with her. I was going to marry her."

"Now you're not and you didn't. Lucky break for you. She wasn't worthy, Flynn."

Flynn shifted. He couldn't see Brad's eyes clearly. Their color blended into the night. "Worthy of what?"

"Of you."

"That's a hell of a thing to say."

"You'll feel better about the whole thing once you admit I'm right. Now back to current affairs. I liked her—your Malory—if you're keeping score."

"Even though you think she's whacked."

Boggy ground, Brad mused, even when you were walking it with a friend. "I think she's found herself in extraordinary circumstances and she's caught up in the mystique. Why wouldn't she be?"

Flynn had to smile. "That's just a diplomatic, bullshit way of saying she's whacked."

"You once punched me in the face for saying Joley

Ridenbecker had beaver teeth. I'm not heading meetings on Monday with a black eye."

"See, you are a suit. If I admit that Joley did indeed have teeth like a beaver, will you believe me if I tell you I've never known anyone with less of a whack quotient than Malory Price?"

"Okay, I'll take your word. And I'll admit the whole thing about the paintings is intriguing." Brad gestured with the beer, then drank again. "I'd like to get a look at the one in there myself."

"We can go up, knock on the door."

"In the daylight," Brad decided. "When we haven't been drinking."

"Probably better."

"Meanwhile, why don't you tell me more about this Zoe?"

"Haven't known her long, but I did some background checking. On her and Mal. Just in case Dana was getting sucked into some weird-ass scam. She moved to the Valley three years ago, with her kid."

"Husband?"

"Nope. Single parent. Looks like a good one to me. I met the kid. He's bright, normal, appealing. She worked at Hair Today, girly hair place on Market. Word is she's good at her profession, personable with customers, reliable. Got canned the same time Malory did, and around the same time they cut Dana's hours at the library to the bone. Another weird coincidence. She bought this little cardboard box of a house when she moved here. Apparently she's done most of the fixing-up work herself."

"Boyfriend?"

"Not that I know of. She . . . wait a minute. You ask two questions. Husband, boyfriend. My razor-sharp reporter's instinct leads me to the conclusion that you're thinking of the mambo."

"Or something. I should get back. I've got a hell of a lot to do in the next couple of days. But there's this one thing." Brad took another pull on the bottle. "How the hell are we going to get off this wall?"

"Good question." Flynn pursed his lips, studied the ground. "We could just sit here and keep drinking until we fall off."

Brad sighed, drained the bottle. "There's a plan."

Chapter Ten

MALORY was barely out of the shower when she heard the knock on her front door. She belted her robe, snagged a towel, and wound it around her hair as she hurried to answer.

"Tod. You're up and about early."

"On my way to the coffee shop to ogle the nine-to-fivers before heading to work." He peered over her right shoulder, her left, then gave her a leer. "Got company?"

Malory swung the door wider in invitation. "No. All alone."

"Ah, too bad."

"You're telling me." She tucked up the ends of the towel more securely. "Want coffee here? I've already put the pot on."

"Not unless you can offer me a skinny mocha latte and a hazelnut muffin."

"Sorry, fresh out."

"Well, maybe I should just give you the good news, then be on my way." Still, he flopped into a chair.

"Oh! New boots?"

"Fabulous, aren't they?" He stretched out his legs, turned his feet right and left to admire them. "They're killing me, of course, but I couldn't resist them. I made a quick run through Nordstrom's on Saturday. Darling, you've got to go." He sat up, grabbed her hand as she curled on the end of the sofa. "The cashmere! There's a cowl neck in periwinkle that's calling your name."

"Periwinkle?" She sighed, long and deep, like a woman under the hands of a skilled lover. "Don't say periwinkle cashmere when I'm in the middle of a shopping moratorium."

"Mal, if you don't treat yourself, who will?"

"That's true. That's so true." She bit her lip. "Nordstrom's?"

"And there's a twinset in a strong peachy pink that was made for you."

"You know I have no defense against twinsets, Tod. You're killing me."

"I'll stop, I'll stop." He held up his hands. "But on to our morning bulletin. The Pamela has stepped in deep and stinky doo-doo."

"Oh, boy." Malory wiggled into the cushions. "Tell me everything. Don't spare the details."

"As if. Okay. We got in a Deco bronze—female figure wearing a flapper-style dress, feathered headband, pearls, gorgeous open-toed shoes, trailing a long scarf. She's absolutely charming. Witty, terrific details, with this sly 'let's you and me Charleston, big boy' smirk on her face. I fell in love."

"Did you call Mrs. Karterfield in Pittsburgh?"

"Ah, see!" He shot a finger in the air, as if proving a point. "Naturally you would assume that, or would have done so personally had you still been in charge. Which you should be."

"Goes without saying."

"I did, of course, call Mrs. Karterfield, who, as expected, asked us to hold it for her until she could come down personally to see it. Next week. And what happens when our darling Mrs. Karterfield from Pittsburgh comes into The Gallery to see a Deco figure?"

"She buys it. And often at least one other piece. If she comes in with a friend, which is usually the case, she harangues her companion until she buys something too. It's a good day when Mrs. Karterfield comes to town."

"Pamela sold it out from under her."

It took Malory ten seconds to find her voice. "What? What? How? Why? Mrs. K's one of our best customers. She *always* gets first look at Deco bronzes."

His lips folded into a thin, derisive smile. "A bird in the hand. That's what the twit told me when I found out. And how did I find out? I'll tell you," he said with a triumphant ring in his voice. "I found out when Mrs. K came in unexpectedly yesterday afternoon to see it. Just couldn't wait, she told me. And she brought *two* friends. Two, Mal. I could cry."

"What happened? What did she say?"

"I took her over to see it, and there's a Sold sign tucked under the base. I assumed it was a mistake, but I went to check. Pamela sold it that morning, apparently while I was in the back on the phone trying to soothe Alfred because Pamela the Putrid had accused him of overcharging for the crating for the marble nudes."

"Alfred? Overcharging?" Malory pressed her hands to her temples. "I can't keep up."

"It was horrible, just horrible. It took me twenty minutes to talk him down, and even then I wasn't sure he wouldn't stomp in and beat her with his hammer. Maybe I should've let him," Tod considered, then waved the thought away with both hands. "Anyway, while I was busy with Alfred, Pamela sold Mrs. K's Deco to a *stranger*. To some fly-by-night, some wanderer in off the street!"

He flopped back, splaying a hand over his chest. "I

still can't believe it. Mrs. K was, naturally, very upset, and demanded to see you. Then I had to tell her you weren't with us any longer. And the doo-doo hit the fan. Big time."

"She asked for me? That's so sweet."

"It gets sweeter. Pamela came down. And they got into it. Boy, did they. Mrs. K asking how an item on hold for her could be sold. Pamela getting snippy and says how it's not gallery policy to hold a piece without a cash deposit. Can you *imagine*?"

"Cash deposit?" Horrified, Malory could only goggle. "From one of our oldest and most reliable clients?"

"Exactly! Then Mrs. K's all, Well, I've been patronizing The Gallery for fifteen years, and my word has always been good enough. And where is James? And Pamela's, I beg your pardon, but I'm in charge here. And Mrs. K shoots back that if James has put a moron in charge he's obviously gone senile."

"Oh, go, Mrs. K!"

"Meanwhile, Julia runs into the back and calls James to let him know there's a big, fat problem. Pamela and Mrs. K are practically coming to blows over the bronze when he comes rushing in. He's trying to calm them both down, but they're too into it. Mrs. K's saying she won't deal with *this woman*. I loved the way she said it. *This woman*. It sang. And Pamela's saying The Gallery's a business and can hardly run on one customer's whim."

"Oh, my God."

"James is frantic, promising Mrs. K he'll sort all this out, but she's furious. Her face is positively puce. She tells him she won't set foot in the place again as long as *that woman* is associated with The Gallery. And, you'll love this—if he let a jewel like Malory Price slip through his fingers he deserves to go out of business. And with that she sails out the door."

"She called me a jewel." Delighted, Malory hugged

herself. "I love her. This is good stuff, Tod. It's really started my day off on a high note."

"There's even more. James is pissed. When's the last time you've seen James pissed?"

"Um. Never."

"Bingo." Tod punched a finger in the air. "He was pale as a sheet, his mouth was all tight and grim. And he told Pamela between clenched teeth"—Tod clamped his together to demonstrate—"'I need to speak with you, Pamela. Upstairs.'"

"What did she say?"

"Well, she stormed up, and he went behind her. Then he closed the door, which was very disappointing. I couldn't hear much of what he said, even though I went up and lurked around hoping to. But you could hear her clearly enough when she started raging. I'm making something out of this place, she tells him. You said I was in charge. I'm tired of having Malory Price thrown in my face every time I turn around. Why the hell didn't you marry her instead of me?"

"Oh." Malory thought about that scenario for a couple of seconds. "Eeuuw."

"Then she started crying, saying she was working so hard and nobody appreciated her. And she ran out. I barely scrambled away in time. It was all so exhausting, yet oddly exhilarating."

"Crying? Damn it." A little worm of sympathy crawled into Malory's chest. "Were they I'm-really-hurt-and-sad tears, or were they just I'm-really-pissed-off tears?"

"Pissed-off tears."

"Okay, then." She squashed the worm without mercy. "I'm probably going to hell, right, for getting such a charge out of all this?"

"We'll get a nice little condo together. But while we're still shuffling on this mortal coil, I think James is going to ask you to come back. In fact, Mal, I'm sure of it."

"Really?" Her heart gave a quick leap. "What did he say?"

"It's not so much what he said, as what he didn't say. He didn't go running after the weeping Pamela to dry her beady eyes. In fact, he stayed for the rest of the day, going over accounts. And he looked grim when he left. Absolutely grim. I'd say Pamela's reign of terror is at an end."

"This is a good day." Malory let out a long sigh. "A really good day."

"And I've got to get started on it. Not to worry," he said as he got up. "I'll keep you updated with bulletins. Meanwhile, the painting you were wondering about? The portrait?"

"The what? Oh, yes. What about it?"

"Remember how we both thought there was something familiar about it? It came to me. Do you remember, about five years ago, the oil on canvas, unsigned? Young Arthur of Britain, on the verge of drawing Excalibur from an altar of stone?"

Chilly fingers brushed the nape of her neck as the painting floated into her mind. "My God. I remember. Of course I remember. The color, the intensity, the way the light pulsed around the sword."

"Definitely the same style and school as the one you showed me. Might be the same artist."

"Yes . . . yes, it might. How did we acquire it? Through an estate, wasn't it? In Ireland. James went to Europe for several weeks to acquire. That was the best piece he brought back with him. Who bought it?"

"Even my razor-sharp memory has its limits, but I looked it up. Julia sold it to Jordan Hawke. The writer? Local boy, or was. Lives in New York now, I think."

Her stomach did a long, slow roll. "Jordan Hawke."

"Maybe you can contact him through his publisher if you want to talk to him about the painting. Well, got to run, sugarplum." He leaned down to give her a kiss. "Let me know the minute James calls you to grovel. I want all the deets."

THERE were half a dozen people at keyboards and phones when Malory reached the third level of the *Dispatch*, where Flynn had his office. She saw him immediately, through the glass walls.

He paced back and forth in front of a desk, tipping a bright silver Slinky from one hand to the other. And appeared to be holding a conversation with himself.

She wondered how he could stand the lack of privacy while he worked, that constant sensation of being on display. And the noise, she thought. With all the clacking, ringing, talking, and beeping, she would go mad trying to formulate a single creative thought.

She wasn't sure whom to speak with. No one looked particularly like an assistant or secretary. And despite the retro toy that Flynn was currently playing with, it suddenly dawned on Malory that he was a busy man. An important man. Not a man she should pop in on without notice.

As she stood, undecided, Flynn sat on the corner of his desk, pouring the Slinky from right hand to left and back again. His hair was mussed, as if he'd spent some time playing with it before he'd gotten hold of the toy.

He wore a dark green shirt tucked into casual khakis and very possibly the oldest athletic shoes she'd ever seen.

There was a quick tingle in her belly, followed by a helpless little thud just under her heart.

It was all right to be attracted to him, she told herself. That was acceptable. But she couldn't let this move to the level it was headed for so quickly. That wasn't smart, it wasn't safe. It wasn't even . . .

Then he looked out through the glass, his eyes meeting hers for one fast, hot beat before he smiled. And the tingle, the thud, became more intense.

He flicked his wrist and the Slinky fell back into itself, then he gave her a come-ahead gesture with his free hand.

She wound her way through the desks and the din. When she stepped through the open office door, she saw with some relief that he hadn't been talking to himself, but on a speakerphone.

Out of habit, she closed the door behind her, then looked toward the sound of heroic snoring to see Moe sprawled belly-up between two filing cabinets.

What did you do about a man who brought his big, silly dog to work with him? she wondered. Maybe more to the point, how did you resist such a man?

Flynn held up a finger to signal one more minute, so she took the time to study his work area. There was a huge corkboard on one wall, jammed with notes, articles, photographs, and phone numbers. Her fingers itched to organize it, as well as the maze of papers on his desk.

Shelves were full of books, several of which seemed to be law and medical journals. There were phone books for a number of Pennsylvania counties, books of famous quotations, movie and music guides.

In addition to the Slinky, he had a yo-yo and a number of warlike action figures. There were several plaques and awards—to the paper and to Flynn personally, stacked together as if he hadn't gotten around to hanging them. She didn't know where she would have hung them either, as what little wall space he had was taken up by the corkboard and an equally large wall calendar for the month of September.

She turned around when he ended the call. Then stepped back as he moved toward her.

He stopped. "Problem?"

"No. Maybe. Yes."

"Pick one," he suggested.

"I got a tingle in my stomach when I saw you in here."

His grin spread. "Thanks."

"No. No. I don't know if I'm ready for that. I have a

lot on my mind. I didn't come here to talk about that, but see—I'm already distracted."

"Hold that thought," he told her when his phone rang again. "Hennessy. Uh-huh. Uh-huh. When? No, that's no problem," he continued and scribbled on a pad that he unearthed from the rubble. "I'll take care of it."

He hung up, then unplugged the phone. "It's the only way to kill the beast. Tell me more about this tingle."

"No. I don't know why I told you in the first place. I'm here about Jordan Hawke."

"What about him?"

"He bought a painting from The Gallery about five years ago—"

"A painting? Are we talking about the same Jordan Hawke?"

"Yes. It's of young Arthur about to draw the sword from the stone. I think—I'm nearly sure—it's by the same artist as the painting at Warrior's Peak and the one your other friend owns. I need to see it again. It was years ago, and I want to be sure I'm remembering the details of it correctly and not just adding them in because it's convenient."

"If you're right, it's an awfully big coincidence."

"If I'm right, it's not a coincidence at all. There's a purpose to it. To all of it. Can you get in touch with him?"

Because his mind was racing through the details and possibilities, Flynn filled his hands with the Slinky again. "Yeah. If he's traveling, it might take a while, but I'll track him down. I didn't know Jordan had ever been in The Gallery."

"His name's not on our client list, so I'm assuming this was a one-shot deal. To my mind, that only makes it more important."

Excitement rose in her throat and bubbled out in her voice. "Flynn, I nearly bought that painting myself. It was beyond my budget at the time, but I was doing some creative math to justify the purchase. It was sold on my morning off, just before I was planning to go to James to ask him if I could buy it on a payment plan. I have to believe all this means something."

"I'll get in touch with Jordan. My take would be he bought it for somebody. He's not much on stuff, unlike Brad. He tends to travel light and keep the acquisitions to a minimum."

"I need to see the painting again."

"Got that. I'm on it. I'll find out what I can today and fill you in over dinner tonight."

"No, that's not a good idea. It's a really, really bad idea."

"Dinner's a bad idea? People have embraced the concept of the evening meal throughout history. There's documentation."

"Us having dinner is the bad part. I need to slow things down."

He set the toy down. He shifted his body, and when she would have countered to keep that distance between them, he grabbed her hand, tugged her forward. "Somebody rushing you?"

"More like something." Her pulse began to skip—in her wrists, in her throat, even at the back of her suddenly shaky knees. There was something about that cool calculation that came into his eyes, the sort that reminded her he tended to think two or three steps ahead. "Look, this is my problem, not yours, and . . . Stop," she ordered when his free hand cupped the back of her neck. "This is hardly the place for—"

"They're reporters." He inclined his head toward the glass wall between his office and the newsroom. "As such, they're aware that I kiss women."

"I think I'm in love with you."

She felt his hand jerk, then go limp. She saw the amusement and purpose on his face slide into blank shock. And twin demons of hurt and temper stabbed at her heart.

"There. Now I've made it your problem too." She

pushed back from him—a simple matter, as he was no longer touching her.

"Malory—"

"I don't want to hear it. I don't need to hear you tell me it's too soon, too fast, you're not looking for this level of a relationship. I'm not stupid. I know all the brush-off lines. And I wouldn't be in this position right now if you'd taken no for an answer in the first place."

"Wait a minute now." Panic washed over his face, into his voice. "Let's take a second here."

"Take a second." Mortification was quickly outweighing the hurt and the anger. "Take a week. Take the rest of your life. Just take it someplace where I'm not."

She stormed out of his office. Since bloodcurdling terror still had a grip on him, he didn't consider going after her.

In love with him? She wasn't supposed to fall in love with him. She was supposed to let him seduce her into bed, be sensible enough to keep things simple. She was supposed to be careful and practical and smart enough to keep *him* from falling in love with *her*.

He'd worked it all out, and now she was messing up the plan. He'd made himself very specific promises when his engagement had fallen apart. The first of which was to be sure he didn't put himself in that position again—a position where he was vulnerable to someone else's whims and wishes. To the point that his own ended up shattered around him.

His life was nothing like he'd thought it would be. Women—his mother, Lily—had shifted the lines on him. But damn it, he *liked* his life now.

"Women." Disgusted, he dropped into the chair behind his desk. "There's no figuring them."

"M E N. They want everything their way."

Dana lifted her glass of wine in Malory's direction. "Sing it, sister."

Hours after she'd stalked out of Flynn's office, Malory was soothing her wounded pride with a nice Pinot Grigio, female companionship, and salon treatments in the comfort of her own home.

There were a number of things to discuss, but she couldn't think about paintings and keys and destiny until she'd vented her spleen.

"I don't care if he is your brother. He's still a man."

"He is." Dana looked mournfully into her wine. "I'm sorry to say, but he is. Have some more potato chips."

"I will." With her hair pulled back from a face coated with a green-clay refining mask, Malory sipped and munched. She studied the folds of tinfoil Zoe was layering in Dana's hair. "Maybe I should have highlights too."

"You don't need them," Zoe told her and painted another section of Dana's hair. "You need shaping."

"Shaping involves scissors."

"You won't even know I've cut it, except it'll look and feel better."

"Let me drink a little more first. And see how it looks after you've whacked at Dana's."

"Don't say 'whack' in a sentence about my hair," Dana cautioned. "Are you going to tell us what you and Flynn fought about?"

Malory sniffed. "He just wants sex. Typical."

"Pig." Dana reached into the chip bowl. "I really miss sex."

"Me too." Zoe set another square of foil. "Not just the sex part, but the leading up to it and the coming down from it parts. The excitement and the nerves and the anticipation beforehand. Then all that skin and movement and discovery during, and the full and floating feeling after. I miss that a lot."

"I need another drink." Malory reached for the bottle. "I haven't had sex in four months."

"Got that beat." Dana raised her hand. "Seven and a half and counting."

"Sluts," Zoe said with a laugh. "Try a year and a half."

"Oh, ouch." Dana took the bottle, topped off her glass and Zoe's. "No, thanks all the same, but I don't think I want to try a year and a half of celibacy."

"It's not so bad if you keep busy. You're set for a while." Zoe patted Dana on the shoulder. "Just relax while I take off Malory's mask."

"Whatever you do to me, make sure I'm gorgeous. I want Flynn to suffer the next time he sees me."

"Guaranteed."

"It's really sweet of you to do all this."

"I like it. It's good practice."

"Don't say 'practice' when I've got a headful of tin-foil," Dana complained around a mouthful of chips.

"It's going to be great," Zoe assured her. "I want to have a full-service salon, and I need to be sure I can handle all the treatments I want to offer. I looked at this wonderful building today."

Her face went wistful as she cleaned and blotted Malory's skin. "It's way too big for what I need, but it was just great. Two stories with a big attic space. A frame house right on the border of business and residential on Oak Leaf Drive. It's got a wonderful covered porch, even a garden in the back where you could set tables and benches. High ceilings, solid hardwood floors that need work. The rooms all sort of tumble into each other on the first floor. A really nice flow of space that keeps it all intimate."

"I didn't know you were looking at houses," Malory said.

"I'm just looking. This is the first place I've seen that caught at me. You know?"

"Yeah, I know. If it's too big, and you really love it, maybe you could get somebody to take part of it for another business."

With the mask removed, Zoe began to stroke on a moisturizer. "I thought of that. Actually, I have this wild idea. Don't tell me I'm crazy until I finish. Each of us said what we really wanted was to have our own place."

"Oh, but—"

"Not till I'm finished." Zoe cut Malory off as she dabbed on eye cream. "The lower floor has two wonderful bow windows. Perfect for displays. There's a central hall, and on each side are those nice rooms. If someone was interested in opening a tasteful gallery for art and local crafts, she couldn't find a better place. At the same time, on the other side of that hall there's a wonderful set of parlors that would make a terrific bookstore, with room for a hip little bistro or tearoom."

"I didn't hear anything about a salon in there," Dana pointed out, but she was listening.

"Upstairs. When someone comes in to get her hair or nails done, or enjoy any number of our wonderful treatments and services, she'll have to pass by the gallery and the bookstore, coming and going. Perfect time to select that lovely gift for Aunt Mary, or pick up a book to read while she's being combed out. Maybe even have a nice glass of wine or cup of tea before heading home. It's all there, in one fabulous setting."

"You really have been thinking," Malory murmured.

"I sure have. I even have a name for it. 'Indulgence.' People need to indulge themselves from time to time. We could do packages and cross-promotions. I know it's a big idea, especially when we haven't known each other very long. But I think it could work. I think it could be great. Just look at it before you say no."

"I'd like to see it," Dana said. "I'm miserable at work. And what's the point of being miserable?"

Malory could almost see the energy and enthusiasm for the idea pumping off Zoe in waves. There were a dozen rational comments she could make to point out why it wasn't just a big idea but a messy one.

She didn't have the heart to do that, but she felt obliged to ease carefully back. "I don't want to muck things up, but I'm pretty sure I'm going to be asked to come back to The Gallery. In fact, my old boss called this afternoon and asked if I'd come in and speak with him tomorrow."

"Oh. Well. That's great." Zoe stepped behind Malory's chair, began to run her fingers through Malory's hair to get a feel for the weight and the lines. "I know you love working there."

"It was like home." Malory lifted a hand, covered one of Zoe's. "I'm sorry. It did sound like a good idea. A fun one, but—"

"Don't worry about it."

"Hey." Dana waved a hand. "Remember me? I'm still interested. I can take a look at the place tomorrow. Maybe we can make it work between the two of us."

"Great. Mal, let's wet down your hair."

She felt too guilty to argue, and with her hair dampened, she sat stoically while Zoe snipped.

"I'd better tell you both why I went by the newspaper this morning to see Flynn, to whom I'm no longer speaking."

Zoe continued to snip as she told them about the painting in The Gallery and her belief that it was done by the same artist.

"You'll never guess who bought it," she continued. "Jordan Hawke."

"Jordan Hawke?" Dana all but squeaked. "Goddamn it, now I want chocolate. You must have some."

"Emergency supply, deli drawer of the fridge. What's the problem?"

"We were semi-involved a million years ago. Damn it, damn it, damn it," Dana repeated as she yanked open the drawer and found two bars of Godiva. "Godiva's your emergency chocolate?"

"Why not have the best when you're feeling your worst?"

"Good point."

"You were involved with Jordan Hawke?" Zoe wanted to know. "Romantically?"

"It was years ago, when I was still young and stupid." Dana unwrapped the bar, took a big bite. "Bad breakup, he took off. End of story. Bastard, creep, asshole." She took another bite. "Okay, I'm done."

"I'm sorry, Dana. If I'd known . . . Well, I don't know what I'd have done. I need to see the painting."

"Doesn't matter. I'm over him. I'm so over him." But she picked up the chocolate bar again, had another bite.

"I have to say something, and you might want the second emergency bar after I do. I can't buy coincidence on this. I can't rationalize it all. The three of us—and Flynn, your brother. Now Flynn's two best friends. And one of those friends is a former lover of yours. That makes a very tight circle."

Dana stared at her. "Just let me go on record as saying I really hate that part. Do you have another bottle of this wine?"

"I do. Rack above the fridge."

"I'll either walk home or call Flynn to pick me up. But I'm planning on being toasted by the time I leave."

"I'll drive you home," Zoe offered. "Go ahead and get toasted—as long as you're ready to leave by ten."

"YOUR hair looks fabulous." Swaying a little from trying to keep Dana company with wine consumption, Mallory waved her fingers at Dana's new hair.

The subtle blond highlights accented Dana's dusky skin tone and dark eyes. And as a result of whatever else Zoe's magic fingers had done, the long, straight sweep looked sleeker, glossier.

"I'll have to take your word. I'm pretty blind."

"Mine looks fabulous too. Zoe, you're a genius."

"Yes, I am." Flushed with success, Zoe nodded at both of them. "Use that night cream sample I gave you for the next couple of days," she told Malory. "Let me know what you think. Come on, Dana, let's see if I can pour you into the car."

" 'kay. I really like you guys." With a drunk and sentimental smile, Dana threw her arms around each of them. "I can't think of anybody I'd rather be in the big mess with. And when it's over, we should have hair and drinking nights once a month. Like a book club."

"Good idea. 'Night, Mal."

"You want some help with her?"

"Nope." Zoe wrapped a supporting arm around Dana's waist. "I've got her. I'm stronger than I look. I'll call you tomorrow."

"Me too! Did I tell you Jordan Hawke is a jerk?"

"Only about five hundred times." Zoe guided Dana toward the car. "You can tell me again on the drive home."

Malory closed the door, carefully locked it, then wove her way to the bedroom. Unable to resist, she stood in front of the mirror and experimented with the new cut, tossing her hair, tilting her head at different angles.

She couldn't tell, not exactly, what Zoe had done, but whatever it was, it was right. Could be, she mused, it paid to keep her mouth shut for a change instead of directing the hairdresser's every snip.

Maybe she should feel guilty and drink wine every time she visited the salon.

She could try the combination in other areas of her life. The dentist, ordering in restaurants, men. No, no, not men. She scowled at herself in the mirror. If you didn't direct men, they directed you.

Besides, she wasn't going to think about men. She didn't need men. She didn't even like men at the moment.

In the morning, she would spend an hour working on the puzzle of the key. Then she would dress, very carefully, very professionally. A suit, she decided. The dove gray with the white shell. No, no, the red. Yes, the red suit. Powerful *and* professional.

She raced to the closet, scanned her wardrobe, which was arranged precisely according to function and color. With the red suit in hand, she danced back to the mirror, held it in front of her.

"James," she began, trying out a sympathetic yet aloof expression, "I'm so sorry to hear that The Gallery is going to hell in a handbasket without me. Come back? Well, I don't know if that's possible. I have several other offers. Oh, please, please, don't grovel. It's embarrassing."

She fluffed her hair. "Yes, I know Pamela is the devil. We all know that. Well, I suppose if things are *that* bad, I'll have to help you out. Now, now, don't cry. Everything's going to be fine. Everything's going to be perfect again. Just as it should be."

She snickered and, pleased that all would soon be right with her world again, turned away to prepare for bed.

She undressed and lectured herself into putting her clothes away instead of just throwing them around the room. When she heard the knock on her front door, she was wearing only a white silk sleep shirt. Assuming it was one of her friends who'd forgotten something, she turned off the locks and opened the door.

And blinked at a grim-faced Flynn.

"I want to talk to you."

"Maybe I don't want to talk to you," she responded, trying to enunciate each word instead of slurring them together.

"We need to work this out if we're going to . . ." He took a good look at her, the wonderfully tumbled hair, the glowing face, the slim curves under clingy white silk. And the vague and glassy look of her eyes.

"What? You're drunk?"

"I'm only half drunk, which is completely my business and my right. Your sister is fully drunk, but you've no cause for concern as Zoe, who is not in any way drunk, is driving her home."

"It takes countless beers or an entire bottle of wine to get Dana completely drunk."

"That seems to be correct, and in this case it was wine. Now that we've established that, I'll remind you I'm only half drunk. Come in and take advantage of me."

He let out what might've been a laugh and decided the best place for his hands—well, not the best but the smartest—was his pockets. "That's a delightful invitation, sweetie, but—"

She solved the problem by gripping his shirt firmly and giving a good yank. "Come on in," she repeated, then fixed her mouth on his.

Chapter Eleven

FLYNN found himself shoved back against the door, tripping over his own feet as it swung shut behind him. Most of the blood had drained out of his head by the time she'd gone to work on his throat with lips and teeth.

"Whoa, wait. Mal."

"Don't wanna wait." Her hands got as busy as her mouth. Had she actually thought she didn't like men? She certainly liked this one. So much that she wanted to gobble him up in quick and greedy bites.

"How come people always say you gotta wait? I want you to . . ." She clamped her teeth on his earlobe, then whispered a creative demand.

"Oh, God."

He wasn't entirely sure if it was a prayer of thanks or a plea for help. But he was sure his willpower had a very specific limit, and he was fast approaching it.

"Okay, okay, let's just calm down here a minute. Malory." She slid her body over his, and when her eager fingers danced down, down, he felt his eyes do a slow roll to the back of his head. "Now hold on."

"I am." She tipped her head back to send him a wicked grin.

"Ha, ha. Yeah, you are." He closed his hands over her wrists and with no little regret lifted her busy hands to his shoulders.

He was out of breath and hard as stone. "We've got a choice here. You can hate me in the morning, or I can." Her eyes sparkled up at him, and her lips were curved in a feline smile that had his throat going dry. "God, you're pretty when you're half plowed. You should go lie down now."

"Okay." She pressed herself against him, gave her hips a suggestive little grind. "Let's."

Slippery knots of lust tied and tangled in his belly. "I'm just going to back away from the beautiful drunk woman."

"Uh-uh." She rose on her toes to rub her lips over his again, felt the desperate plunge of his heart. "You'll never make it out the door. I know what I'm doing, and I know what I want. Does that scare you?"

"Pretty much, yeah. Honey, I came by to talk to you, about something I'm currently incapable of remembering. Why don't I make us some coffee and we'll . . ."

"I guess I have to do everything." In one fluid motion, she slid the sleep shirt over her head and tossed it aside.

"Oh, sweet Jesus."

Her body was pink and white—delicious—with that elegant cloud of hair tumbling down to tease her breasts. Her eyes, deeply blue and suddenly full of knowledge, fixed on his as she stepped close to him again.

Her arms had wound around his neck, and her mouth was a hot, silky temptation on his. "Don't be afraid," she whispered. "I'll take very good care of you."

"I bet." Somehow his hands had gotten lost in the sexy mass of her hair. His body was a maze of aches and needs, and reason couldn't find the exit. "Malory, I'm no hero."

"Who wants one?" With a laugh, she nipped at his jaw. "Let's be bad, Flynn. Let's be really bad."

"Since you put it that way." He swung her around, reversing their position so she was trapped between the door and his body. "I hope to God you remember whose idea this was, and that I tried to—"

"Shut up, and take me."

If he was going to hell, he'd make damn sure it was worth the trip. With his hands on her hips, he jerked her up to her toes, and caught the light of triumph on her face an instant before his mouth crushed hers.

It was like holding a lit fuse, all sizzle and spark, a dangerous woman who knew her own power. Who was testing his. Her skin was already flushed and hot, and as he took his hands over her the soft sounds she made in her throat weren't whimpers but urgings. Already desperate, he buried his face in her hair, pressed his hand between her thighs.

She erupted. A throaty cry, a bite of nails on his back, a lightning surge of hips. Then she was dragging his shirt over his head, scraping her teeth over his shoulder as her quick hands yanked at his jeans.

"In bed." Though he had wild, erotic visions of taking her against the door, the pleasure would end too soon that way. Instead he circled her, prying off his shoes as they bumped into a corner of the wall.

She didn't care where. She only wanted to go on feeling this wild whiplash of power, having these wonderful pulsing aches continue to dominate her body. She was spinning in some mad world of exquisite sensations, and every touch, every taste, added more.

She wanted to feel his muscles quiver, to feel the heat pumping out of his pores. And to know, deep inside, that she had caused it.

They fell on the bed, breathless and insane, and rolled, an erotic tangle of limbs on the pretty pastel covers.

She laughed when he clamped his hands on hers and yanked her arms over her head.

"Gotta slow down a little," he managed.

She arched up to him. "Why?"

"Because I'm going to do things to you, and that takes time."

She ran her tongue over her top lip. "Where would you like to start?"

His belly tightened to the edge of pain. He lowered his head to start with her mouth. Plump and soft, hot and wet. He drugged himself with her until they both trembled. He slid his tongue over the hollow of her throat, where her pulse hammered. Then down, slowly, until he could taste the delicate, scented breasts. And when he caught her nipple between his teeth and tugged, she began to moan.

She gave herself over to the pleasure, the sheer bliss of being savored and exploited. Her body was open to him, to that ravenous mouth, those questing hands. When he took her up, she flew free, riding the hot punch of air, tumbling down again to draw him closer.

She could see him in the light that spilled from the hallway, and her heart leaped at the intensity on his face as he watched her. Love and delight raced through her. Here was an answer, the answer to at least one question.

He was for her. And she rose up, wrapping herself around him with a kind of giddy glee.

Their mouths met again in a deep, shuddering kiss that had his heart flipping over inside his chest.

She smelled of something secret, of seduction. Those quick, catchy gasps coming from her sliced through him like tiny silver knives. He wanted to bury himself inside her until the world ended. And when her hands cruised over him, when those soft sounds of approval hummed in her throat as she explored him, he wondered if it already had.

She scraped her nails over his belly and had him quiv-

ering like a stallion. "I want you. I want you inside me.
Tell me you want me."

"I do. I want you." He lowered his mouth to hers once
more. "Malory. From the first minute."

Her lips curved under his. "I know." She arched her
hips. "Now."

He braced himself, then a sliver of sanity cut through
the madness. "Oh, Christ. Condom. Wallet. Pants. Where
are my pants?"

"Mmm. It's okay." She rolled over him, nipping at his
shoulder as she pulled open the nightstand drawer. "Condom. Drawer. Nightstand."

"Have I mentioned that I love practical, prepared
women?"

"Why don't I help you on with this?"

She took her sweet time so that he had to fist his hands
in the tangled spread to keep himself from flying to the
ceiling.

The woman had wicked hands, he thought and bit back
a groan.

Wonderful, wicked hands.

She rose over him, shook her hair back. And smiled.
"Now," she said.

He moved fast, flipping her onto her back, pinning her
body with his. "Now," he repeated and drove deep inside
her.

He watched the shock race over her face, felt the waves
of it vibrate through him. They trembled there, each
caught on some fine edge.

And with her eyes locked on his, she began to move.
A rising up, a falling away, so smooth, so fluid it was like
sliding through silk. Her name echoed in his head, like a
song, or a prayer. He clung to the echo of it, clung to the
frayed threads of control as she shattered around him.

She fell apart. Oh, God, the most wonderful sensation.
A losing of self, then a gathering back. Her mind hazed.

And with one last liquid sigh, she rode the final crest.

Locking him close, she took him with her.

HE didn't want to think. Thinking under the current circumstances couldn't be productive. It would be much better for all involved if he kept his mind a solid blank and just enjoyed the superior sensation of having a soft, sexy woman under him.

If he didn't think, he might be able to keep her there long enough to make love with her again. Then there'd be another period of not-thinking.

Who knew how long he could keep up that pattern? Maybe indefinitely.

When she moved under him, a lazy kind of stretch, it seemed a very good possibility.

"I want some water." She stroked a hand down his back. "You thirsty?"

"Not if it means moving for the next five or ten years."

She gave his ass a light pinch. "*I'm* thirsty. So you have to move."

"Okay." But he nuzzled her hair a moment longer. "I'll get it."

"That's all right." She gave him a little shove and wiggled out from under him. "I'll get it."

She stopped by the closet on the way out, and he had a glimpse of something thin and silky billowing out over that gorgeous body before she strolled out the door.

"Maybe I'm dreaming. Maybe this is just some wish-fulfillment fantasy, and I'm really in my own bed with Moe snoring on the floor."

Or maybe not.

He sat up, scrubbed his hands over his face. And unfortunately, began to think. He'd come over because he'd been churned up, pissed off, and generally confused by the scene they'd had in his office that morning.

And now he was in her bed, naked, and they'd just

had incredible sex. When she'd been drunk. Well, maybe
not drunk, but impaired.

He should've walked away. He should've found the
moral fortitude to walk away from a naked, willing
woman when that naked, willing woman's inhibitions had
been erased by alcohol.

And what was he, a saint?

When she walked back in wearing nothing but a short
red robe, he scowled at her.

"I'm a human being. I'm a man."

"Yes. I think we've established that beyond doubt."
She sat on the side of the bed, offered him the glass she'd
brought in.

"You were naked." He took the glass, gulped down
water. "You were all over me."

She cocked her head. "And your point is?"

"If you regret this—"

"Why should I?" She took the glass back, swallowed
the stingy sip he'd left behind. "I got you where I wanted
you. I'd been drinking, Flynn, but I knew what I was
doing."

"Okay, then. Okay. It's just that, after what you said
this morning . . ."

"That I'm in love with you?" She set the glass on the
coaster she kept on her nightstand. "I am in love with
you."

Emotions ran through him, all too hot and fast to decipher. But layered over all of them was sheer, sweaty
fear. "Malory." When she only continued to study him
with a quiet patience, the fear began to trickle into his
throat. "Listen, I don't want to hurt you."

"Then don't." She gave his hand a comforting little
squeeze. "Actually, you've got a lot more to worry about
than I do."

"I do?"

"Yes, you do. I love you, which means, naturally, I
want you to love me back. I don't always get what I want,

but I usually find a way to get it. Almost always, in fact. So to my way of thinking, you'll end up in love with me. Since the idea of that scares you, you've got more to worry about than I do."

She trailed a hand over his chest. "You're in really good shape for somebody who works at a desk."

He grabbed her hand before it could head south. "Let's stay focused here. The whole love deal just isn't in the cards for me."

"You had a bad experience." She leaned in to give him a light kiss. "That sort of thing's bound to leave a mark. Lucky for you, I can be patient. And gentle," she added as she shifted, then straddled him. "And very, very determined."

"Oh, boy. Malory—"

"Why don't you just lie back and enjoy the fringe benefits of being courted?"

Aroused, flustered, grateful, he let her nudge him back. "Sort of hard to argue with that."

"As well as a waste of time." She unbelted her robe, let it slide from her shoulders. She ran her hands up his chest, then caught his face in them before she kissed him senseless. "I'm going to marry you," she murmured. And laughed when his body jerked in shock. "Don't worry. You'll get used to the idea."

Still laughing, she smothered his unintelligible protest with her mouth.

S H E felt so *good*. Not just the sex, Malory thought as she sang in the shower. Though that could hardly be discounted. She always felt good, confident, directed, when she had a clear, well-defined purpose.

The quest for the key was so nebulous that it confused as much as it energized. But convincing Flynn that they belonged together was crystal clear. A goal she could get her teeth into.

She hadn't a clue why she'd fallen in love with him, and that's what told her it was real.

He certainly didn't fit her image of her dream man. He didn't cook gourmet meals or speak fluent French (or Italian) or love spending his free time in museums. He didn't wear tailored suits or read poetry.

At least, she didn't think he read poetry.

She'd always planned to fall in love with a man who had some of those attributes. And, naturally, in her outline the right man would court her, charm her, seduce her, then pledge his undying love at the perfect romantic moment.

Before Flynn she had analyzed and dissected every relationship, picked at every flaw until she'd worked a dozen holes into the cloth of it.

And in the end, that hadn't mattered, because none of them had been right.

She had no desire to worry about the flaws with Flynn. She only knew her heart had gone splat when she'd least expected it. And she liked it.

She had to admit she also liked the idea that he was spooked. It was intriguing, and it was challenging to be the pursuer for a change. To be the aggressor, and to keep a man slightly off balance with honesty.

When he'd finally managed to stumble out of bed sometime around three in the morning, she'd sensed his fear and confusion just as much as she'd sensed his desire to stay.

Let him stew about it for a while, she decided.

She amused herself by calling the local florist and ordering a dozen red roses to be delivered to his office. She almost danced out of her apartment to keep her appointment with James.

"Well, aren't we bright and sassy this morning," Tod commented when she swung into The Gallery.

"Aren't we just." She caught his face in her hand and gave him a noisy kiss. "Is he in?"

"Upstairs. He's expecting you. Sugarpie, you look fab-ulous. Good enough to eat."

"I feel good enough to eat." She patted his cheek, then glided up the steps. She knocked on the office door, stepped in. "Hello, James."

"Malory." He rose from the desk, both hands extended. "Thank you so much for coming in."

"Of course." She took the chair he gestured toward. "How are things?"

With a pained expression on his face, he sat. "I'm sure you've heard about the difficulty Pamela had with Mrs. K. A terrible misunderstanding, which I'm afraid may have cost The Gallery a valued client."

Malory forced herself to appear concerned even while her mind jumped with glee. "Yes, I'm so sorry that things have . . ." Don't say gone to hell in a handbasket, she ordered herself, and continued without missing a beat. "Been a bit difficult during this transition."

"Yes. Difficult. Pamela's very enthusiastic about The Gallery, but I'm afraid she's still learning. I see now that I gave her too much autonomy too quickly."

To keep from punching her fists in the air, Malory sedately folded her hands on her knee. "She has a very precisely defined vision."

"Yes. Yes." He worried his gold pen, fiddled with his tie. "I think her strengths may lie in a more peripheral area than actual client-staff relations. I realize there's fric-tion between the two of you."

Cool, she reminded herself. "I also had a very precisely defined vision, which unfortunately clashed with hers. So, yes, there was considerable friction."

"Well." He cleared his throat. "Perhaps I let Pamela influence me in that regard. I felt, sincerely, that it might be time for you to explore your talents, to experiment. However, I see I didn't take into consideration your af-fection and loyalty to The Gallery, or how being nudged out of the nest, as it were, might upset you."

"I admit it did." But she tempered her statement with the sweetest of smiles.

"I have considered all of this over the last couple of weeks. I'd very much like you to come back, Malory. To resume your managerial duties. At a ten percent increase in salary."

"This is so unexpected." She had to imagine her butt glued to the chair so she couldn't leap up and do a victory dance. "And I'm flattered. But . . . can I be frank?"

"Of course."

"The friction we spoke of is still going to be there. I have to admit I hadn't been happy here the last several months. Your . . . nudging me out of the nest," she said, "was painful and frightening. But once I was out, I had the opportunity to look back and realize that the nest had become . . . let's say a little crowded."

"I understand." He held up his hands, then clasped then together under his chin. "I can promise that Pamela won't interfere with your authority, or with the policies that have long been in effect here. You'll have the last word, barring mine, of course, on acquisitions and displays, on featured artists and so on. Just as before."

It was exactly what she'd wanted. More than, she realized when she calculated the bonus in salary. She would be back doing what she did best, and with considerable financial reward, and she would have the personal, if unattractive, satisfaction of putting Pamela's nose out of joint.

She would have won, without firing a shot.

"Thank you, James. I can't tell you how much it means to me to know you want me back, that you have confidence in me."

"Wonderful, wonderful." He beamed at her. "You can start right away, today if that's good for you. It'll be like the last two weeks never even happened."

Like they never even happened.

Her stomach gave a mighty pitch. Then, suddenly, it

was as if sensible Malory stepped to the side and listened
in shock as reckless Malory took charge.

"But I can't come back. I'll always be grateful for
everything you taught me, all the opportunities you gave
me—the last being pushing me out the door so I'd have
to leave my comfort zone. I'm going to open my own
business."

Oh, my God, she thought. I'm going to open my own
business.

"It won't be anything as grand as The Gallery. Smaller,
more . . ." She nearly said "accessible," then managed to
backtrack. "Low-key," she continued. "I'm going to focus
primarily on local artists and craftspeople."

"Malory, you must be aware how much time and energy that sort of thing consumes. And more, the financial
risk involved." There was no doubt about it, James was
panicking.

"I know. I don't seem to be as worried about taking
risks as I used to be. In fact, I'm excited by the prospect
of taking them. But thank you, thank you so much for all
you've done for me. I really have to go now."

She got up quickly, afraid she would change her mind.
Here was her safety net, spread out, ready to catch her.
And she was swinging out beyond it to where the ground
was very hard, and very far away.

"Malory, I wish you'd take some time to think this
through."

"Do you know what happens when you always look
before you leap?" She reached out and touched his hand
before hurrying toward the door. "You hardly ever make
the jump."

S H E didn't waste time. Malory hunted down the address
Zoe had relayed, and pulled into a double driveway behind Dana's car.

Good location, she decided, sliding practical Malory

back into place. There would be some pedestrian traffic, and reasonable parking for people who needed it.

The house was charming. Homey, she thought. And the three of them working together could certainly perk it up. Paint the porch, plant some trailing vines. Zoe probably already had a horde of ideas on that.

The walkway needed to be repaired or replaced. She noted that detail down on the clipboard she'd brought with her. Window boxes? Yes, planted seasonally.

And wouldn't it snazz up the entrance to have a stained-glass window replace the clear one over the front door? Something designed specifically for them. She had some contacts in that area.

Still making notes, she opened the front door.

The foyer could be a showcase for all three businesses. Yes, there was a way to do that with clever placement and displays, keeping it friendly and informal while advertising their goods and services.

The light was good, the floors a treasure once they were refinished. The walls, well, paint would solve that.

She wandered through, delighted with the rooms. They did seem to tumble together, she thought. Just as Zoe had said.

An excellent way to blend businesses.

After filling pages with notes she strolled back, just as Dana and Zoe came down the stairs.

"Eventually, I'd like to refit the master bath with a Swedish shower and aromatherapy station," Zoe was saying. "But for now . . . Malory, hi."

"Hi." Malory lowered her clipboard. "I'm in."

"I knew it!" With a whoop, Zoe flew down the stairs and grabbed her. "I just knew it. Did you see? Have you been through? Isn't it great? Isn't it perfect?"

"Yes, yes, and yes. I haven't been upstairs yet, but down here . . . I love it," she said.

Dana stood on the stairs, her lips pursed in speculation. "Why'd you change your mind?"

"I don't know. At least I don't know in any reasonable, logical sense. When James offered me my job back, with a raise, I thought, thank God, everything'll be back to normal now."

She let out a breath and, hugging the clipboard to her chest, spun in a circle. "Then, I don't know, I heard myself telling him I couldn't come back, I was starting my own business. I guess I realized I don't want everything to be back to normal. I want to do this, and I want to do it with both of you. That's all I know."

"We've all got to be really sure. Zoe, tell her what you told me. About the house."

"Well, the owner's willing to rent it, but they're looking for a buyer. The fact is, it makes more financial sense to buy it."

"Buy it?" The gorge she was leaping across suddenly widened. "How much?"

Zoe named a price, then hurried on when Malory paled. "But that's just the asking price. Plus, I've been doing some figuring, and if you compare the mortgage payment at current interest rates over a thirty-year term to the proposed monthly rent, it's not that much more. And it's equity. It's an investment. Then there's the tax break."

"Don't get her started on the tax break," Dana warned. "Your brains will start leaking out of your ears. Just take my word for it, she's got it covered."

"We need a lawyer to draw up a legal partnership," Zoe continued. "Then we pool our money. We have enough for the down payment, especially once we negotiate the asking price down. And still there's enough left over to hold us. We'll take a loan for the property and the start-up costs. We can do it."

"I believe you. I think that's why my stomach hurts." Malory pressed a hand to it, then looked at Dana. "Buy?"

"God help us. Buy," she agreed.

"I guess we should shake or something." Zoe held out a hand.

"Wait, before we do, I should tell you something." Malory cleared her throat. "I had sex with Flynn last night. Three times."

"Three?" Dana abruptly sat down on the stairs. "Ah, go, Flynn?"

"You're okay with that?"

"I'm his sister, not his mother." But she rubbed at her temple. "Weren't you drunk last night?"

"No, you were. I was just buzzed. I'll add that being aware I was buzzed, he attempted, pretty strongly, to be a gentleman and step back."

"That's so sweet," Zoe offered.

"Even after I got naked and jumped him."

"That's . . . Wow!"

With a laugh, Malory patted Zoe's shoulder. But Dana remained silent. "I didn't get naked and jump him just because I was buzzed and well, horny. I'm in love with him. I don't have the whys on that any more than I know why I want to own this house with the two of you. It just is, from somewhere deep inside me. It just is. I'm in love with him, and I'm going to marry him."

"Malory! This is wonderful." Leading with her romantic heart, Zoe flung her arms around her friend. "I'm so happy for you."

"Don't hand out the orange blossoms yet. I still have to convince him he can't live without me." She stepped forward. "I'm in love with him, Dana."

"I'm getting that."

"I know this might complicate our friendship, and any business relationship we might plan on having."

"And if it does?"

"Then I'm sorry. I'll back out of the friendship. I'll back out of the business plans. But I'm going to keep Flynn, whether he likes it or not."

Dana's lips twitched as she got to her feet. "I guess he's toast. We going to shake hands on this deal and get us a lawyer or what?"

Chapter Twelve

SHE didn't know what she was feeling. She wasn't sure what she was doing. But little snags like that had never stopped Dana before.

The minute she could manage it, she tracked down Flynn.

She missed him at the paper, followed his trail to the vet's, where she was told she'd missed him and Moe by fifteen minutes. The irritation of that had her deciding she was angry with him, though she had no concrete reason to be.

But by the time she arrived at his house, she was enjoying her temper.

She slammed the door and stalked into the living room, where both her brother and his dog were sprawled out like the dead.

"I need to talk to you, Casanova."

"Don't yell." Flynn remained on the sofa. On the floor beside him Moe whimpered. "Moe needed his shots. We've both been traumatized. Go away. Come back tomorrow."

"Now, right now, before I find a sharp implement to stick in your rump. What's the idea of banging Malory when you know perfectly well she has to keep her mind on the goal?"

"I don't know. Might've had something to do with my tripping and falling over her naked body. And it wasn't banging. I object to the term 'banging,' which is beside the fact that it's none of your goddamn business."

"It's my business when she's just become my business partner. When prior to that we were partners of another sort, and it's my business because I like her a lot, and she's in love with you. This shows a remarkable lack of taste, but is nonetheless the way it is."

Guilt crept slyly into his belly. "It's not my fault she thinks she's in love with me."

"I didn't say 'thinks.' She's not an idiot, despite her lousy taste in men. She knows her own mind and heart. And if you're not taking her feelings into consideration before you unzip your fly—"

"For Christ's sake, give me a break." He sat up now, dropped his head in his hands. "She won't listen to me. And she did the unzipping."

"You were just an innocent bystander."

"There's no point in blasting me about this. I've spent considerable time blasting myself, for all the good that's done. I don't know what the hell to do."

She sat on the table, leaned toward him. "What do you want to do?"

"I don't know. She sent me flowers."

"Excuse me?"

"She sent me a dozen red roses this morning. The card said, 'Think of me.' How the hell could I *not* think of her?"

"Roses?" The idea just tickled her. "Where are they?"

He squirmed. "Um. I put them up in the bedroom. Goofy. This role reversal, it's just not right. It's not natural. I think it flies in the face of countless rules of scientific order.

I need to put things back on track. Somehow. Back on track. Stop grinning at me."

"You're hooked."

"I am not hooked. And that's another term I object to. Someone with a degree in library science should be able to find more appropriate terms."

"She's perfect for you." She kissed his cheek. "Congratulations. I'm not mad at you anymore."

"I don't care who you're mad at. And it's not a matter of who's perfect for me. I'm not perfect for anyone. I'm a slob. I'm inconsiderate and selfish. I like having my life loose and unstructured."

"You're a slob, no question. But you're neither inconsiderate nor selfish. It's that inconsiderate and selfish bitch Lily who put that in your head. If you buy that, you're just stupid."

"So, are you wishing a stupid slob on your new pal?"

"Maybe. I love you, Flynn."

"Man, I'm getting a lot of that lately." He tapped a finger on her nose. "Love you, too."

"No. Say: 'I love you.' "

"Come on."

"All three words, Flynn. Choke them out."

"I love you. Now go away."

"I'm not finished."

He groaned and fell back on the couch. "We're trying to take a nap here, for our mental health."

"She never loved you, Flynn. She liked who you were in the Valley. She liked being seen with you, and she liked picking your brain. You may be stupid, but you're pretty smart in some areas. She used you."

"And that's supposed to make me feel better. Knowing I let myself be used?"

"It's supposed to make you stop blaming yourself for what happened with Lily."

"I'm not blaming myself. I hate women." He showed

his teeth in a vicious smile. "I just want to bang them. Now will you go away?"

"You've got red roses in your bedroom."

"Oh, man."

"Hooked," she repeated and drilled a finger in his belly.

He took the sisterly poke like a man. "Let me ask you something. Did anybody like Lily?"

"No."

He hissed out a breath, stared up at the ceiling. "Just checking."

The knock on the door had him cursing and her bounding up. "I'll get it." She sang it out. "Maybe it's more flowers."

Amused, she pulled open the door. And it was her turn to curse, with more imagination and viciousness than Flynn had managed.

"Hey, nice mouth, Stretch."

Jordan Hawke, handsome as the devil and to Dana's mind twice as evil, gave her a wink and strolled back into her life.

She considered, for one brief, heady moment, tripping him. She grabbed his arm instead, imagined twisting it into cartoon taffy. "Hey. Nobody asked you in."

"You living here now?" He shifted his body in a slow, easy move. He'd always had moves. At six three he had five inches on her. She'd once found that fact exciting, but now it was simply irritating.

He hadn't gotten fat, or ugly, or fallen victim to male-pattern baldness. And wasn't that just too damn bad? No, he was still lanky and gorgeous, and all that thick black hair remained sexily rumpled around a tanned, rawboned face set off by sizzling blue eyes. His mouth was full and sculpted and, she had reason to know, very inventive.

It curved now in a lazy, mocking smile that made her want to bloody it.

"Looking good, Dane." He smoothed a hand over her

hair, and had her head jerking back before she could stop herself.

"Hands off. And no, I'm not living here. What do you want?"

"A date with Julia Roberts, a chance to jam with Bruce Springsteen and the E Street Band, and a really cold beer. How about you?"

"To read the details of your slow, painful death. What are you doing here?"

"Annoying you, apparently. But that's just a side benefit. Flynn home?"

He didn't wait for an answer, but stepped away from her and headed for the living room. Moe roused himself, sent out a halfhearted growl.

"That's it, Moe," Dana said cheerfully. "Sic 'im."

Obviously unconcerned about being attacked by an enormous mass of canine, Jordan crouched down. "So this is the famous Moe."

Veterinary trauma forgotten, Moe scrambled up. He charged, flopped both front paws on Jordan's shoulders, and gave him a welcoming kiss.

Dana could only grind her teeth as Jordan's laugh joined Moe's happy bark.

"You're a big guy, aren't you? Look at that face." He rumpled Moe's fur, scratched his ears, then glanced over at Flynn. "How's it going?"

"Okay. Didn't know you were coming so soon."

"Had some time. Got a beer?"

"Sure."

"I hate to interrupt this emotional, heartfelt reunion." Dana's voice was an ice pick aimed at the nape of Jordan's neck. "But what the hell's he doing here?"

"Spending some time with friends, in my hometown." Jordan got to his feet. "Still okay to bunk here?"

"Absolutely." Flynn unfolded himself from the couch. "Man, it's good to see you."

"Same here. Big house. Great dog. Bad couch."

With a laugh, Flynn swung his arms around his oldest friend. "Really good to see you."

For a moment, just an instant, as she watched the two grown men hug, Dana's heart softened. Whatever else she could say about Jordan Hawke—and the list was long— he was and had always been Flynn's. As much brother, she supposed, as friend.

Then those hot blue eyes met hers and baked her heart hard again.

"How about that beer, Stretch? We can play catch-up and you can tell me how you got roped into looking for imaginary keys."

She shot her brother one accusatory look, then jerked her chin up. "Unlike the two of you, I actually have things to do."

"Don't you want to see the painting?"

That nearly stopped her, but giving in to curiosity would've spoiled her exit. She continued to the door and strode out without a backward glance.

She had things to do, all right. The first of which was to carve a wax doll in Jordan's image and stick pins in sensitive areas.

"Did you have to piss her off?" Flynn demanded.

"My breathing pisses her off." And knowing that put a little hole in his gut. "How come she's not living here? The house is big enough."

"She won't." With a shrug, Flynn led the way back to the kitchen. "Wants her own space and blah-blah. You know Dana. Once her mind's set you can't move her with a forklift."

"Tell me about it."

Because Moe was dancing around, Flynn dug out a dog biscuit and flipped it to him before getting the beers. "You brought the painting?"

"Yeah. I don't know what it's going to tell you."

"Me either. I'm hoping it tells Malory something."

"So when am I going to meet this Malory?" Jordan leaned back against the counter.

"I don't know. Soon."

"I thought there was a deadline on this deal," Jordan said.

"Yeah, yeah. We've still got a couple weeks."

"Problem, pal?"

"No. Maybe. We've gotten tangled up, and it's getting really serious really fast. I can't think."

"What's she like?"

"Smart, funny, sexy."

"You put sexy third." Jordan gestured with his beer. "That's serious. What else?"

"Goal-oriented, I'd say." He began to pace. "With a kind of tidy nature. Honest. Not much game-playing there. Grounded. You could say she's grounded, which is why her getting wound up in this key business makes it all seem possible. She's got blue eyes. Big blue eyes," Flynn sighed.

"Again, the physical falls well down the list. You're stuck on her."

Uneasy, Flynn lifted his beer. "There are degrees of being stuck."

"True enough, but if she's got you this worried I'd say you're already in to your knees, and sinking. Why don't you give her a call? She can come get a look at the painting, and I can get a look at her."

"Let's give it till tomorrow."

"You're scared of her. Make that up to your waist and sinking."

"Shut up. I just think it'd be smart for Brad to bring his painting over, let the three of us give them both a good look. See what we come up with, without the female element."

"Works for me. You got any food around here?"

"Not really. But I've got all the takeout and delivery places on speed dial. Take your pick."

"Surprise me. I'll go get my stuff."

*   *   *

IT wasn't so different from their youth, unless you considered that the living room where they sprawled belonged
to one of them rather than to a parent.

Since the choice had been left to Flynn, they were eating Italian, but the beer had been upgraded to a bottle of
Johnnie Walker Blue that Brad had brought with him.

The paintings were propped side by side against the
wall while the three of them sat on the floor. Moe took
the couch.

"I don't know much about art," Flynn began.

"But you know what you like," Brad finished.

"I wasn't going to stoop to a cliché."

"Actually, it's a valid statement." Jordan agreed. "Art,
by its very nature, is subjective. Warhol's *Campbell's
Soup Can*, Dalí's *Melting Watch*, da Vinci's *Mona Lisa*.
It's all in the eye of the beholder."

"As impossible to compare Monet's *Water Lilies* with
Picasso's *Lady in Blue* as it is to compare Dashiell Ham-
mett and Steinbeck. It's all in the style, purpose, and perception."

Flynn rolled his eyes toward Brad. "What I was going
to say before the two of you went off on that little intellectual riff is that it seems to me that the same person
painted both of these. Or if it was two different people,
one was emulating the other's style."

"Oh." Brad swirled the liquor in his glass and grinned.
"Okay, then. I'll go along with that. And what does that
tell us?"

"It'll tell us a lot if we have Jordan's painting tested.
We already know the one at Warrior's Peak and Brad's
were done more than five hundred years apart. We need
to know where Jordan's fits in."

"Fifteenth century."

Flynn turned his head, stared at Jordan. "You had it
dated already?"

"A couple years after I bought it. I needed to get some stuff insured. Turned out it was worth several times what I paid for it. Kinda weird when you think of it, as The Gallery's got a rep for being pricey."

"Why'd you buy it?" Brad asked him.

"I don't know how many times I've asked myself that. I don't even know why I went in there that day. It wasn't one of my usual stops. Then I saw it, and it just grabbed me. That moment, that breath just before destiny, between innocence and power. He'll pull the sword free. You know it. And in that moment, the world changes. Camelot's born, Arthur's fate is sealed. He'll unite a people, be betrayed by a woman and a friend, and sire the man who'll kill him. In this moment, he's a boy. In the next, he'll be a king."

"Some would argue that he was born a king."

Jordan shook his head at Brad's statement. "Not until he put his hands on the hilt of the sword. He could have walked away from it. I wonder if he would have if he'd known what was coming. Glory and grandeur, sure, and a slice of peace, but then deceit, deception, war. And an early death."

"Well, that's cheerful." Flynn started to pour another drink. Then he stopped, looked back at the paintings. "Wait a minute. Maybe you're on to something. In the other, you've got the results after that moment of destiny you were talking about. Would the god-king have married the mortal, conceived three daughters, if he'd known their fate? Is it about choices, which direction we take?"

"And if it is?" Brad put in. "It doesn't tell us much."

"It gives us a theme. And if we make the leap that the paintings are clues to the location of the keys, then we have to follow the theme. Maybe the first is in a place where a decision was made, one that changed the course of lives."

"Flynn." Jordan hesitated, swirled his drink. "You seriously believe these keys exist?"

"That's right. And if you guys had been around since the beginning of this, you'd have come around to that by now. There's no way to explain it, Jordan, no more than you can explain why that boy was the only person in the world who could pull Excalibur from the stone."

"How about you?" Jordan asked Brad.

"I'm trying to keep an open mind. You've got to add up the coincidences, or what appear to be coincidences. You and I own those paintings. We're all back in the Valley, and so are they. Flynn's involved, personally involved with two of the women who were invited to Warrior's Peak. Jordan and Dana used to be an item. And I bought the painting because I was caught by that face— Zoe's face. It just about knocked me on my ass. And let's keep that little tidbit among the three of us."

"You're interested in Zoe?" Flynn asked.

"Yeah, which is dandy, since she appears to have taken an instant dislike to me. Which I don't get," he added with some heat. "Women don't dislike me right off the bat."

"No, it usually takes a little time," Jordan agreed. "Then they dislike you."

"On the contrary. I'm a very smooth operator. Usually."

"Yeah, I remember how smooth you were with Marsha Kent."

"I was seventeen," Brad argued. "Fuck you."

"Do you still have her footprint on your ass?" Jordan wanted to know.

"You still got Dana's on your balls?"

Jordan winced. "Tit for tat there. Question. Does that painting look as much like the other two as it does like Dana?"

"Oh, yeah," Flynn told him. "Different dos, but the faces are dead on."

"No question as to the age on it, Brad?"

"None."

Jordan sat silent a moment, nursing his drink, studying Dana's face. So still, so pale, so empty. "Okay, I'll take a side step out of logic and into the zone. There are six of us and three keys. And what, just over two weeks left to find the first one?" He reached for the bottle again. "It'll be a snap."

BEYOND the puzzle to be solved, Flynn thought, it was good to have his friends back. Good to know even as he crawled into bed in the early hours of the morning that Jordan was crawling onto the mattress in the spare room. And Brad was already zonked out on the sofa downstairs, guarded by Moe.

It had always seemed to him that there'd been nothing they couldn't do together. Whether it had been fighting off imaginary alien invaders, learning how to unhook a girl's bra one-handed, or driving cross-country in a secondhand Buick. They'd always come through for each other.

When Jordan's mother had died, both he and Brad had been there, holding vigil during those endless nights at the hospital.

When Lily had dumped him, the one constant Flynn had been sure of was his friends.

Through good times and not so good times, he thought sentimentally, they'd been there for each other. Physical distance never meant a damn.

But it was better, a hell of a lot better, to have them here. Since they were, the first key was practically in the lock.

He closed his eyes and instantly fell asleep.

THE house was dark, and bitterly cold. He could see his breath puff out in thin white vapors as he wandered aimlessly down dark corridors that turned, that twisted. There was a storm blasting, a crash and boom that shook the air and shot out fast, angry light, zigzagging in the dark.

In the dream he knew he walked the halls of Warrior's Peak. Though he could barely see, he recognized it and knew the turn of the corridor, the feel of the wall under his trailing fingers. Though he had never walked there before.

He could see the rain whipping outside the second-story window, could see the way it glowed blue in the lightning strikes. And he saw the ghost of his own face blurry in the glass.

He called out, and his voice echoed. On and on, like a rolling wave. There was no one to answer. And yet he knew he wasn't alone.

Something walked those halls with him. Lurking just behind. Out of sight, out of reach. Something dark that pushed him on, up the stairs.

Fear tripped into his heart.

Doors lined the corridor, but all of them were locked. He tried each one, turning, tugging the knob with fingers gone stiff with cold.

Whatever stalked him crept closer. He could hear it breathe now, horrible, somehow liquid pulls on the air that merged with his own rapid panting.

He had to get out, get away. So he began to run, loping through the storm-slashed dark while what pursued him followed, with rapid clicks on the wood like eager claws.

He burst out onto a parapet, into the storm where lightning speared down and set the stone to smoking. The air burned and froze, and the rain pelted him like shards of glass.

With nowhere left to run, with fear a cold snake crawling in his belly, he turned to fight.

But the shadow was so huge, so close. It covered him before he could raise his fists. The cold tore through him, drove him to his knees.

He felt something ripped from him—wild, unspeakable pain, dull, shocking horror. And knew it was his soul.

FLYNN woke, shuddering with cold, clammy with the dregs of terror, and with the sun pouring in onto his face.

Struggling for breath, he sat up. He'd had his share of nightmares, but never one this intense. Never one where he'd actually felt pain.

Could still feel it, he thought as he gritted his teeth against the sharp stabs in his chest and belly.

He tried to tell himself it was the combination of pizza and whiskey and late night. But he didn't believe it.

As the pain dulled, he slid gingerly out of bed, walked as cautiously as an old man to the bathroom, and turned the shower on hot. He was freezing.

He reached up to swing open the mirrored medicine cabinet for aspirin and caught a glimpse of his face.

The pallor of his skin, the glassy edge of shock in his eyes, were bad enough. But they were nothing compared to the rest.

He was soaking wet. His hair was drenched, his skin beaded with water. Like a man who'd been out in a storm, he thought, and lowered himself to the seat of the toilet as his legs gave way.

Not just a nightmare. He'd been inside Warrior's Peak. He'd been out on the parapet. And he hadn't been alone.

This was more than a quest for magic keys. More than a puzzle to be solved with the promise of a pot of gold at the end.

There was something else here. Something powerful. Dark and powerful.

He was going to find out what the hell was going on before any of them got in any deeper.

He stepped into the shower and let the hot water beat on him until it penetrated the chill in his bones. Then, calmer, he downed some aspirin, pulled his sweatpants on.

He would go down and make coffee, then he'd be able to think. Once his head was clear, he would roust both of his friends and get their take.

Maybe it was time for the three of them to go up to Warrior's Peak and get the truth out of Rowena and Pitte.

He was halfway down when the bell rang, and Moe raced out barking like the hounds of hell on speed.

"Okay, okay. Shut up." Johnnie Walker hadn't given Flynn a hangover, but the nightmare had stepped up to the plate and knocked one home. He grabbed Moe by the collar, yanked back as he pulled the door open with his other hand.

She looked like a sunbeam. It was his only clear thought as he stared at Malory. Dressed in a pretty blue suit that showed off her legs, she smiled at him. Then stepped forward, wrapped her arms around him.

"Good morning," she said, and by pressing her lips to his drained even that single thought out of his mind.

His fingers went limp on Moe's collar, then fell away from it to lift up, dive into her hair. The aches and dread he'd awakened with fell away as well.

In that one moment he felt as if nothing would ever be beyond his reach again.

Moe gave up trying to shoehorn himself between them, and settled on leaping and barking for attention.

"Christ Jesus, Hennessy, can't you get your dog to . . ." At the top of the stairs, Jordan trailed off. Below him stood his friend and the woman, bathed in morning sunlight. And drowning in each other.

The fact was, even when Flynn eased back from the embrace and glanced up, he had the look of a man going under for the third time. Blissfully.

"Morning. Sorry to interrupt. You must be Malory."

"Yes, I must be." Her brain was a bit muddled from the kiss, but she was pretty sure she was staring up at a great-looking guy wearing nothing but black boxer shorts. "I'm sorry. I didn't realize Flynn had company . . . oh." Her brain cleared. "You're Jordan Hawke. I'm a big fan."

"Thanks."

"Hold it." Flynn held up a hand as Jordan started down. "Maybe you could go put some pants on."

"Sure."

"Come on back. I need to let Moe out." Giving her hand a tug, Flynn managed to dislodge her from the spot she'd frozen in to stare at Jordan. But she dug in again at the living room entrance.

Brad was facedown on the couch, with one arm and one leg drooping off. He was dressed like Jordan, though his boxers were white.

It was interesting to note, Malory thought, that the scion of the Vane empire had an excellent butt.

"Slumber party?" she ventured.

"Guys don't have slumber parties. We just hang out. Moe!" Flynn called the dog, who'd wandered in to lick the portion of Brad's face that wasn't smashed into the cushions. "Brad's always been able to sleep through anything."

"So it would seem. It's nice to have your friends back in town."

"Yeah." He pulled her back to the kitchen. Moe beat them to it, and stood dancing at the back door as if he'd been waiting for hours. He streaked out the instant Flynn opened it.

"Why don't I make some coffee?" Malory offered.

"Yeah? You'll make it?"

"Just part of the service." Since the coffee can was already on the counter, she measured enough for a full pot. "If you marry me, I'd make the coffee every morning. Of course, I'd expect you to take out the trash every day." She tossed a grin over her shoulder. "I believe in sharing household chores."

"Uh-huh."

"And there's the unlimited access to sex."

"That's a big plus."

She laughed as she measured the water. "I like making you nervous. I don't think I've ever made a man nervous before. Then again . . ." She switched the pot on, turned around. "I've never been in love with one before. Not like this."

"Malory—"

"I'm a very determined woman, Flynn."

"Oh, yeah, that's coming through loud and clear." He stepped back even as she moved in on him. "I just think we should . . ."

"What?" She trailed her hands up his chest.

"See? I can't remember once you start looking at me."

"I take that as a good sign." She touched her lips lightly to his.

"I'm already making a habit of this," Jordan said as he came in. "Sorry."

"It's all right." Malory brushed her hair back as she turned away to find clean coffee mugs. "I just stopped in to ask Flynn to marry me. It's nice to meet another of his friends. Are you in town for long?"

"Depends. What did he say when you asked him?"

"Oh, he has trouble making complete sentences when I bring up love and marriage. Odd, isn't it, seeing as he's a journalist."

"You know, I'm standing right here," Flynn pointed out.

"Is that coffee?" Brad stumbled in, blinked when he spotted Malory, then stumbled back out again. "Sorry."

Amused, she wiped out the mugs. "This house is full of attractive men, and I've seen all of them without their clothes on. My life has certainly changed. How do you take your coffee, Jordan?"

"Black's fine." He leaned a hip on the counter while she poured. "Flynn said you were smart, funny, and sexy. He was right."

"Thanks. I've got to run. I've got an appointment to sign papers."

"For what?" Flynn asked.

"The partnership papers with Dana and Zoe. I thought Dana told you."

"Told me what?"

"That we're buying the house, going into business."

"What house? What business?"

"The house on Oak Leaf. And our business. Businesses, I suppose. My gallery, Dana's bookstore, Zoe's salon. We're calling it Indulgence."

"Catchy," Jordan decided.

"I can't believe I'm jumping in like this." She pressed a hand to her stomach. "So unlike me. I'm terrified. Well, I don't want to be late." She stepped over, caught Flynn's baffled face in her hands and kissed him again. "I'll call you later. We're hoping you'll do a story on our new enterprise. Nice meeting you, Jordan."

"Really nice meeting you." He watched her walk down the hall. "Nice legs, killer eyes, and bright enough to light up a cave. You got yourself a live wire there, buddy."

His lips were still vibrating from hers. "Now that I've got her, what am I going to do with her?"

"You'll figure it out." He moved over to top off his coffee. "Or she will."

"Yeah." Flynn rubbed a hand over his heart. There was a flutter in it. Maybe that's what came from handling a live wire. "I need more coffee, then I need to talk to you and Brad. You guys aren't going to believe the dream I had last night."

Chapter Thirteen

"I can't believe they didn't show it to you." Dana dug the key to Flynn's house out of her purse.

"Neither can I. I didn't even think," Malory added, as annoyance propelled her from the car to Flynn's front door. "I just assumed Jordan was having it shipped. Plus the three of them were half naked. It was distracting."

"Don't blame yourself." Zoe gave her a bolstering pat on the back. "And anyway, you'll get to see it now."

"They're up to something," Dana muttered. "I can just feel it. When the three of them get together, they're *always* up to something." She unlocked the door, pushed it open. Waited a beat.

"Nobody's home."

"They were just getting up when I was here a couple of hours ago." Malory walked inside without a qualm. "And now that I think about it, Flynn did look like he was up to something."

"They'll try to cut us out." Ready and willing to work herself into a rant on men in general, Dana tossed her keys back in her purse. "It's typical behavior for their species. Oh, we know better, don't you worry your pretty head, little lady."

"I hate that." Firing up, Zoe hissed a breath between her teeth. "You know how an auto mechanic always gives you that smirk and says he'll explain the problem to your husband?"

Dana sucked air through her nose. "That burns my ass."

"If you ask me, that Bradley Vane's at the bottom of it." Zoe set her fists on her hips. "He's just the type to try to run everything and everyone. I pegged him from the get-go."

"No, it'll be Jordan." Dana kicked a shoe out of her way. "He's an instigator."

"It's Flynn's responsibility," Malory disagreed. "It's his house, they're his friends, and . . . oh, my God."

Light slanted across both paintings as they stood propped carelessly against the wall just where Flynn had left them. Her heart squeezed with admiration and envy at the sight.

She walked toward them slowly, as she might a lover who both dazzled and titillated. Her throat ached as she knelt on the floor in front of them.

"They're beautiful," Zoe said from behind her.

"They're more." Gently, Malory lifted the portrait of Arthur, tilting it toward the light. "It's not just talent. Talent can be technical, achieve a kind of perfection of balance and proportion."

She came close to that, she thought, when she painted. Fell just short of technical perfection. And miles away from the magic that made an image art.

"It's genius when you're able to take that talent beyond technique and into emotion," she continued. "To message, or just to simple beauty. When you have that, you light up the world. Can't you feel his heart pounding?" she asked as she studied the young Arthur. "His muscles quivering as he takes the hilt? That's the power of the artist. I'd give anything—anything—to be able to create like this."

A shiver ran through her, twin snakes of hot and cold. For a heartbeat her fingers seemed to burn. And for that heartbeat something inside her opened, and lit, and she saw how it could be done. Must be done. How she could explode on canvas into art.

The knowledge filled her to bursting, left her breathless.

Then was gone in an instant.

"Mal? Malory?" Zoe crouched down, took her shoulders. "What's wrong?"

"What? Nothing. I got dizzy for a second."

"Your eyes went funny. They went huge and dark."

"It must've been the light." But she felt strangely queasy as she pulled her purse over and took out her magnifying glass.

Using the natural light, she began a slow, careful study of each painting.

There was the shadow, just the hint of a form lurking deep, deep in the green of the forest. And two figures—a man and a woman—watching the boy, the sword, the stone, from the far background. From a chain at the woman's waist hung three gold keys.

"What do you think?" Dana demanded.

"I think we've got a couple of choices." Considering them, Malory sat back, rolled her shoulders. "We can convince Brad and Jordan to have these sent to experts for verification of whether or not it's the same artist. And by doing so, we risk this entire business getting out."

"What's the other choice?" Zoe asked her.

"We can take my word for it. Everything I know, everything I've studied and learned tells me the same person painted both of these. The same person who painted the portrait at Warrior's Peak."

"If we go with that, what do we do with it?" Dana demanded.

"We figure out what the paintings are telling us. And we go back up to Warrior's Peak. We ask Rowena and Pitte how at least two of these works were done more than a century apart."

"There's another part that goes with that," Zoe said quietly. "We accept the magic. We believe."

" I always have time to entertain three handsome men." Rowena all but purred it as she showed Flynn, Brad, and Jordan into the parlor where the portrait of the Daughters of Glass dominated.

She paused, waiting until all attention was focused on it. "I assume the painting interests you, Mr. Vane. Your family has quite an extensive and eclectic art collection, I'm told."

He stared at the portrait, at the figure carrying both a short sword and a little dog. Zoe's eyes stared back at him. "Yes, we do."

"And has the interest passed down to you?"

"It has. As a matter of fact, I believe I own another painting by this artist."

She sat, a secret smile playing around her mouth as she spread the long skirts of her white dress. "Is that so? What a small world."

"It gets smaller," Jordan put in. "I seem to have another painting that may be by this artist."

"Fascinating. Ah." She gestured as a servant rolled a cart in. "Coffee? I assumed you'd prefer it to tea. American men aren't much on tea, are they?"

"You don't ask about the subject of the other paintings." Flynn sat beside her.

"I'm sure you'll tell me. Cream, sugar?"

"Black. Seems a waste of time when I'm pretty sure you already know. Who's the artist, Rowena?"

She poured the coffee with a steady hand, taking the liquid to within a half inch of the rim while her gaze stayed level with Flynn's. "Did Malory ask you to come here today?"

"No. Why?"

"The quest is hers, as are the questions. Such matters have rules. If she asked you to represent her, that's a different thing altogether. Did you bring your dog?"

"Yeah, he's outside."

Her face went wistful. "I don't mind if he comes in."

"White dress, big black dog. You might want to rethink that. Rowena, Malory didn't ask us to come, but she and the others know we're helping them look into things. It's okay with them."

"But you didn't tell them you were coming to speak with me. Men often make the mistake of assuming that a woman wishes to be relieved of responsibilities and details." Her face was open and friendly, her voice carrying the lilt of a laugh. "Why is that?"

"We didn't come here to discuss male-female dynamics," Jordan began.

"What else is there, really? Man to man, woman to woman, certainly," Rowena continued with an elegant spread of her hands. "But it all comes down to people, what they are to each other. What they'll do for and to one another. Even art is only a representation of that, in one form or another. If Malory has concerns or questions about the painting or paintings she must ask. You won't find the key for her, Flynn. It's not for you."

"I dreamed I was in this house last night. Only it wasn't a dream. It was more."

He watched her eyes change, go dark with shock. Or something else, something bigger.

"Such a dream isn't unusual under the circumstances."

"I've only been in the foyer and in two rooms in this place. Or had been until last night. I can tell you how many rooms are on the second floor, and that there's a

staircase on the east side leading to the third that has a
newel post carved like a dragon. I couldn't see it well in
the dark, but I felt it."

"Wait. Please."

She rose quickly and hurried from the room.

"This is some strange deal you've got going here,
Flynn." Jordan poked at the pretty cookies arranged on a
glass plate. "There's something familiar about that
woman. I've seen her somewhere before."

"Where?" Brad demanded.

"I don't know. It'll come to me. Hell of a looker. A
face like that, you don't forget. And why should she freak
over you having a dream? Because freak's just what she
did, in her own classy way."

"She's afraid." Brad walked closer to the portrait. "She
went from sly to scared in a heartbeat. She knows the
answer to the paintings, and she was having a good time
toying with us about that until Flynn dropped his dream
adventure on her."

"And I didn't even get to the best part." Flynn got to
his feet to explore the room before Rowena got back.
"Something's off here."

"You just getting that, son?"

Flynn spared a glance at Jordan as he opened a lacquered cabinet. "Not just the already established 'off.'
That's a woman in control," he said with a jerk of his
thumb toward the doorway. "Cool, confident, sure of herself. The woman who just took a flyer out of here wasn't
any of those things. Man, there's some high-class booze
in here."

"Would you care for a drink, Mr. Hennessy?"

Though he winced a little, Flynn turned toward the
doorway and spoke equably to Pitte. "No, thanks. A little
early for me yet." He closed the cabinet. "How's it going?"

Rowena laid a hand on Pitte's arm before he could

respond. "Finish it," she ordered Flynn. "Finish the dream."

"Let's talk quid pro quo." Inclining his head, Flynn walked back to sit on the sofa. "You want to hear about the rest of the dream, and we want to know about the paintings. I show you mine, you show me yours."

"You bargain with us?"

Flynn was amazed at the stunned outrage in Pitte's voice. "Yeah."

"It's not permitted." Again Rowena laid a hand on Pitte's arm. But from the hot, impatient look he sent her, Flynn didn't bank on her restraining him for long. "We can't give you answers just because you ask. There are limits. There are paths. It's important that we know what happened to you."

"Give me something back."

Pitte snapped something out, and though the language was a mystery to Flynn, he recognized an oath when he heard one. Following it was a bright flash, an electric slice through the air. Warily, Flynn looked down at his lap, and the banded stacks of hundred-dollar bills that now rested there.

"Ah. Nice trick."

"You've got to be kidding." Jordan had already leaped forward and now reached down and plucked up a stack of bills. He fanned them, then patted them against his palm as he stared at Pitte. "Definitely time for some answers."

"Do you require more?" Pitte demanded, and Rowena turned on him with a kind of stunning female fury.

The words they hurled at each other were unintelligible. Gaelic, Flynn thought. Maybe Welsh. But the gist was clear enough. Their temper rocked the room.

"Okay, take five." With three determined strides, Brad moved forward, stepped between them. "This isn't getting us anywhere." His voice was calm and controlled, and had both of them snarling at him. Still, he stayed where he was and glanced back at Flynn. "Our host just pulled . . . how much?"

"Looks like about five thousand."

"Five grand out of thin air—and boy, have I got some stockholders who'd like to talk to you. He seems to think you want cash for information. Do you?"

"Tough as it is to turn down five thousand magic dollars, no." It stung, he could admit it, but Flynn set the stack on the table. "I'm worried about three women who haven't hurt anyone, and I'm a little worried about myself. I want to know what's going on."

"Tell us the rest, and we'll tell you what we can. Tell us freely," Rowena added as she moved back to Flynn. "I'd prefer not to make you tell us."

Irritated now, Flynn leaned forward. "Make me?"

Her voice was winter cool against the heat of his when she spoke. "My dear, I could make you quack like a duck, but as I imagine your brave and sensible friend would say, such an incident wouldn't accomplish anything. You think we wish harm to you, or to your women? We don't. We wish harm to none. That I can tell you freely. Pitte." She shifted, angled her head. "You've insulted our guest with this crass display. Apologize."

"Apologize?"

"Yes." She sat again, brushed at her skirts. Waited.

Pitte bared his teeth. He tapped his fingers restlessly on his thighs. "Women are a plague to man."

"Aren't they just?" Jordan agreed.

"I'm sorry to have offended you." Then he flicked a wrist. The money vanished. "Better?"

"There's no reasonable way to answer that question, so I'll ask one instead. Who the hell are you people?" Flynn demanded.

"We're not here to answer your questions." Pitte walked over to the silver pot, poured coffee into a Dresden cup. "Even a journalist—which I warned you would be an annoyance," he added as an aside to Rowena—

"should be aware of certain rules of behavior when invited into someone's home."

"Why don't I just tell you who you are," Flynn began, then broke off as the delighted bark banged into the room seconds before Moe arrived. "Oh, shit."

"There he is!" Rowena simply spread her arms in welcome, and had them full of dog when the women walked into the room. "How nice, how lovely. It's like a party."

"Sorry to burst in on you this way." Malory scanned the room, then zeroed in on Flynn. "But there's an issue of certain people thinking they should take over from the womenfolk."

"That's not exactly true."

"Really? And what would be exactly true?"

"Just following a lead, that's all. You were busy rushing into business partnerships, buying houses."

"I've been rushing into a lot of things lately. Maybe we should debate the fact that I rushed you into bed."

The twin claws of embarrassment and annoyance pricked him as he got to his feet. "Sure, we can do that. Maybe we can find a more appropriate time and place for it."

"You want to talk about appropriate when you and your testosterone team try to take over my responsibilities, my business? Just because I'm in love with you, just because I sleep with you, doesn't mean I'll sit back and let you run my life."

"Who's running whose life?" Frustration had him flinging out his arms. "You're the one who has mine mapped out. I'm in this, Malory, whether I want to be or not. And I'm here to find out what that means. And if it's heading where I think it is, you're out. All of you." He shot scathing looks at Dana and Zoe. "Out."

"Who made you boss?" Dana demanded. "You couldn't tell me what to do when I was ten. You sure as hell can't pull it off now."

"Oh, you watch me. You made it seem like a game."

He shot the accusation at Rowena. "Even some sort of romantic quest. But you didn't tell them what might be at stake."

"What are you talking about?" Malory jabbed at his shoulder.

"The dreams." Ignoring Malory, Flynn continued to speak to Rowena. "They're warnings, aren't they?"

"You never finished telling us. Perhaps everyone should sit down, and you can start from the beginning."

"You had a dream? Like mine?" Malory jabbed at him again. "Why didn't you tell me?"

"Just shut it down a damn minute." Out of patience, he nudged her onto the couch. "Just be quiet," he ordered. "I don't want to hear anything out of you until I'm finished."

He started at the beginning, with him wandering the house, with the sensation of being watched, stalked. He related the experience on the parapet, the fear and pain, and ended with his waking in his own bed, drenched with rain.

"He—it—wanted my soul, was letting me know that that could be the price for being in this."

"This isn't the way." Pitte clamped a hand on Rowena's and spoke to her as if no one else was in the room. "This can't be the way. They aren't to be harmed. That was the first and most sacred promise."

"We can't know. If we're not allowed behind the Curtain, we can't know what situation now exists. If he's broken the vow, he must believe he can escape the consequences. He must believe . . . they are the ones," she said in a whisper. "It can be done, and they can succeed. He's opened the Curtain to stop them. He's come through."

"If they fail—"

"They cannot fail." She spun around, her face set with purpose. "We'll protect you."

"Will you?" Shaken, Malory folded her hands on her

lap, squeezing her fingers until the pain cleared her head. "The way you protected the Daughters of Glass? Teacher and warrior. Somehow, you are." She got up, walked to the portrait. "You're here," she said, gesturing to the couple in the background. "And here, in this room. In this place. And you think that what's there, in the shadows of the trees is here too. You don't show his face."

"He has more than one." Rowena spoke in a matter-of-fact tone that was utterly chilling.

"You painted this, and the two that we have."

"Painting is one of my passions," Rowena confirmed. "One of my constants. Pitte." She turned to him. "They know this much."

"I don't know a damn thing," Dana declared.

"Step over here, to the cynical side of the room," Jordan invited.

"It's what Malory knows that matters now." Rowena held out a hand. "All that I have will be used to keep you safe."

"Not good enough." Flynn shook his head. "She's out of it. They're all out of it. You want your money back, we'll—"

"Excuse me, I can speak for myself. This isn't a matter of a refund, is it?" she asked Rowena. "There's no turning back, no saying, uh-oh, the stakes are higher than I realized, game over."

"The agreement was made."

"Without full disclosure," Brad put in. "Whatever sort of contract these women signed with you won't hold up legally."

"The issue isn't legal," Malory said impatiently. "It's moral. And more than that, it's destiny. As long as I am, as long as I know, I'm part of it. Until the four weeks are up. And if I find the first key, one of them is next." She looked at Dana and Zoe. "One of them will be at risk for the next phase of the moon."

"Yes."

"You know where the keys are," Flynn exploded. "Just hand them over. End this."

"Do you think, if that were possible, we would remain in this prison?" In a gesture that mirrored both disgust and bitterness Pitte flung out his arms. "Year by century by millennium, trapped in a world not our own. Do you think we live with you out of *choice*? That we place our fates, the fates of those in our charge, in your hands because we wish it? We are bound here, bound by this single task. And now so are you."

"You can't go home." After the boom of Pitte's, Zoe's quiet voice was like a hammer blow. "We are home. You had no right to trick us into being part of this without telling us the risks."

"We didn't know." Rowena spread her hands.

"For a couple of gods, there's a hell of a lot you don't know and can't do."

Pitte's eyes went to smoke as he rounded on Flynn. "Perhaps you'd like a demonstration of what we can do."

Fists already clenched, Flynn stepped forward. "Bring it on."

"Gentlemen." Rowena's heavy sigh was like a flood of cool water, designed to lower the rising temperature of the room. "The male, regardless of his origins, remains woefully predictable in some areas. Your pride and manhood aren't at risk here, in either case. Flynn, whatever the world, there are laws woven through the fabric of it."

"Rip the fabric. Break the law."

"If it were within my power to hand out the keys at this moment, it would solve nothing."

"They wouldn't work," Malory stated and earned a nod of approval from Rowena.

"You understand."

"I think I do. If this spell . . . is it a spell?"

"That's the simplest word for it," Rowena agreed.

"If it's to be broken, it has to be by us. Women. Mortal women. Using our brains, our wits and energies, our resources in our world. Otherwise, no key opens the box. Because . . . we're the real keys. The answer's in us."

"You're so close to where you need to be." Emotions storming across her face, Rowena rose, laid her hands on Malory's arms. "Closer than any have come before."

"But not close enough, not yet. And half my time is gone. I need to ask you some questions. In private."

"Hey, one for all here," Dana reminded her. Malory sent her a silent plea. "Okay, okay. We'll wait outside."

"I'll stay with you." Flynn laid a hand on Malory's shoulder, but she shrugged it off.

"I said this was private. I don't want you here."

His face went blank and cold. "Fine, then, I'll get out of your way."

With obvious regret, Rowena gave Moe a little nudge to send him along. She frowned at the sharp slam of the door behind Flynn. "Your man has a sensitive heart. More easily bruised than yours."

"Is he my man?" Before Rowena could speak, Malory shook her head. "First things first. Why was I taken behind the Curtain?"

"He wanted to show you his power."

"Who is he?"

Rowena hesitated, then when Pitte nodded, continued. "He is Kane, a sorcerer. The dark one."

"The one in the shadows, the one I saw in my dream. The stealer of souls."

"He showed himself to you so you would be frightened. There's no need to frighten you unless you can succeed."

"Why did he hurt Flynn?"

"Because you love him."

"Do I?" Malory's voice thickened with emotion. "Or have I been made to think I do? Is that just one more trick?"

"Ah." Rowena let out a soft breath. "Perhaps you're

not as close as I thought. Don't you know your own heart, Malory?"

"I've known him two weeks, and I feel as if my life will never be quite right if he's not in it. But is it real? At the end of my four weeks, will I still feel that way?" She pressed a hand to her heart. "Or will it be taken away from me? Is it any worse to have your soul taken from you than your heart?"

"I think not, for one feeds the other. And I can't give you the answer, because you already have it. If you choose to look."

"Then tell me this. Will he be safe if I step away from him? If I close my heart to him, will he be safe?"

"You'd give him up to protect him?" Pitte asked.

"Yes."

Thoughtful, he walked to the lacquered cabinet, opened it to take out a bottle of brandy. "And you'd tell him this?"

"No, he'd never—"

"Ah, so you would deceive him." With a small smile, Pitte poured brandy into a snifter. "And justify the lie by saying that it was for his own good. Women, whatever their world, are predictable," he said, with a mocking bow to Rowena.

"Love," she corrected, "is a constant force in any universe. Your decisions, your choices, must be yours," she told Malory. "But your man won't thank you for any sacrifice you make to protect him." She gave Pitte a mocking bow in turn. "They never do. Go now." She touched a hand to Malory's cheek. "Rest your mind a while, until you can think clearly with it. And you have my word, whatever can be done to keep you, your man, your friends safe will be done."

"I don't know them." She pointed to the portrait. "But I know those people outside. You should know, if it comes down to a choice, I'll choose those I know."

Pitte waited until they were alone before bringing

Rowena a second snifter. "I have loved you through time and through worlds."

"And I you, my heart."

"But I've never understood you. You could have answered her question about love and eased her mind."

"She'll be the wiser, and the happier, for finding the answer herself. How much can we do for them?"

He leaned down, pressed his lips to her brow. "Our best."

Chapter Fourteen

$\int$ H E needed time, Malory admitted. She'd been on a roller coaster since the first of the month, and though there'd been a thrill in riding those fast dips and sharp turns, she needed a break.

Nothing in her life was the same as it had been, she thought as she let herself into her apartment. She'd always counted on consistency, and that single element had slipped through her fingers.

Or been tossed aside on impulse.

She didn't have The Gallery. She wasn't completely certain she had her sanity. On one of those dips and turns, she'd stopped being sensible, dependable Malory Price and had become irrational, emotional, fanciful Malory Price—a woman who believed in magic, in love at first sight.

All right, maybe third sight, she corrected as she closed her curtains and crawled onto her bed. But it was the same thing, essentially.

She'd taken money that could have seen her through

several lean months and invested it in an enterprise with
two women she'd known for less than four weeks.

And trusted implicitly, she decided. Without reserva-
tion.

She was about to embark on a business of her own,
without any stock, any solid plan, any safety net. Against
all logic, the idea of it made her happy.

And still her head was pounding, her stomach churning. Over the thought that she might not be in love at all.
That the blissful confidence and pleasure she felt in Flynn
was only an illusion.

If the illusion shattered, she was afraid she would
grieve for the rest of her life.

She bunched the pillow under her head, curled into a
ball, and begged for sleep.

IT was sunny and warm when she woke, and the air
smelled like summer roses. She snuggled in for a moment.
Warm sheets carrying the faint scent of her man, the soft
drift of silence.

She rolled over lazily, blinked. Something odd hung
over her mind. Not really unpleasant, just odd.

The dream. The strangest dream.

She sat up and stretched, feeling the healthy pull of
muscles. Naked, and easy with it, she slid out of bed,
sniffed the butter-yellow roses on the dresser before picking up her robe. She paused by the window to admire her
garden, draw in the fragrant air. She pushed the window
open wider and let the sound of birdsong follow her out
of the room.

The odd feeling was already fading—as a dream does
on waking—as she glided down the stairs, trailing a hand
over the silky wood of the banister. Jewel lights from the
window over the door played on the floor. More flowers,
exotic sprays of white orchids, speared out of the antique
vase on the entrance table.

His keys were tossed beside them, in the little mosaic bowl she'd bought just for that purpose.

She wound her way through the house to the kitchen, then grinned. He was at the stove, sliding a battered slice of bread into the skillet. There was a tray beside him, already topped with a flute of sparkling juice, a single rose in a bud vase, her pretty coffee cup.

The back door was open. Through it, she could hear the birds continuing to sing and the dog's occasional happy barks. Blissful, she crept forward, then wrapped her arms around his waist, pressed a kiss to the nape of his neck.

"Watch it. My wife could wake up any minute."

"Let's risk it."

He turned, caught her up in a long, hard kiss. Her heart leaped, her blood fired, even as she thought, Perfect. It's all so perfect.

"I was going to surprise you." Flynn ran his hands over her back as he eased her away. "Breakfast in bed. The Hennessy Special."

"Make it a better surprise, and have breakfast in bed with me."

"I could probably be persuaded. Hold on." He grabbed a spatula, flipped the bread over.

"Mmm. It's after eight. You shouldn't have let me sleep so late."

"I didn't let you get much sleep last night." He winked at her. "Seemed only fair to let you catch a little this morning. You've been working so hard, Mal, getting ready for your show."

"I'm nearly done."

"And when it's over, I'm going to take my incredibly beautiful and talented wife on a well-deserved vacation. Do you remember that week we spent in Florence?"

Sun-drenched days, love-drenched nights. "How could I forget? Are you sure you can take the time off? I'm not the only one who's been busy around here."

"We'll make time." He flipped the French toast onto a plate. "Why don't you grab the paper, and we'll crawl back into bed for an hour . . . or two."

Sleepy cries began to sound from the baby monitor on the counter. Flynn glanced toward it. "Or maybe not."

"I'll get him. Meet me upstairs."

She hurried up, part of her mind acknowledging the paintings lining the walls. The street scene she'd done in Florence, the seascape from the Outer Banks, the portrait of Flynn sitting at his desk in his office.

She turned toward the nursery. The walls there were decorated with her paintings as well. The bright faerie-tale scenes she'd done the entire time she'd been pregnant.

And in the crib with its glossy spindle bars, her little boy cried impatiently for attention.

"There now, sweetheart. Mama's right here." She picked him up, cuddled him close.

He would have his father's hair, she thought, as she cooed and swayed. It was already coming in dark, with those hints of chestnut shining through when the light caught it.

He was so perfect. So absolutely perfect.

But as she carried him toward the changing table, her legs went weak.

What was his name? What was her baby's name? Panicked, she clutched him close, then whirled as she heard Flynn come to the door.

"You look so beautiful, Malory. I love you."

"Flynn." Something was wrong with her eyes. It was as if she could see through him, as if he were fading away. "Something's wrong."

"Nothing's wrong. Everything's exactly right. Everything's just the way you wanted it to be."

"It's not real, is it?" Tears began to sting her eyes. "It's not real."

"It could be."

A light flashed, and she was standing in a studio awash

with light. Canvases were stacked against the walls or rested on easels. She faced another, brilliant with color and shape. A brush was in her hand, and she was already daubing it on her palette.

"I've done this," she whispered as she stared at the canvas. It was a forest, misty with green light. The figure walking on the path was alone. Not lonely, she thought, but solitary. There was home at the end of the path, and a bit of time yet to enjoy the quiet and the magic of the woods.

Her hand had done that. Her mind, her heart. She could feel it, just as she could feel and remember every brushstroke on every canvas in the room.

The power of that, the glory of it with all its pain and pleasure.

"I can do this." With a kind of frantic glee, she continued to paint. "I have to do this."

The joy was like a drug, and she was greedy for it. She knew how to mix just the right tone of color, when to sweep it on, when to switch for the fine, fine details.

How to create that light, that shadow so one might feel as if he or she could slip inside, walk that path, and find home at the end of it.

But even as she painted, tears began to run down her cheeks. "It's not real."

"It could be."

The brush clattered to the floor, splattering paint, as she whirled.

He stood beside her, with the sun's rays flooding over him. And still he was dark. His hair, black and glossy, spread like wings to his shoulders. His eyes were a strong stone gray. Sharp, high cheekbones hollowed his cheeks, and his mouth was full, appealingly wicked.

Beautiful, she thought. How could he be beautiful?

"Did you think I'd look like a demon? Like something out of a nightmare?" His amusement only added charm.

"Why should I? They've made you think poorly of me, haven't they?"

"You're Kane." Fear was alive in her, with its cold hands closing around her throat. "You stole the souls from the Daughters of Glass."

"It needn't concern you." His voice was beautiful as well. Melodic, soothing. "You're an ordinary woman in an ordinary world. You know nothing of me or mine. I wish you no harm. The opposite, in fact." With a dancer's grace, he wandered the room, his soft boots silent on the paint-splattered floor. "This is your work."

"No."

"Oh, yes, you know it." He lifted a canvas, studied the sinuous lines of a mermaid lounging on a rock. "You remember painting this, and the others. You know now how it feels to have that power. Art makes gods out of men." He set the canvas down again. "Or women. What are we, in my world, but artists and bards, magicians and warriors? You want to keep the power, Malory?"

She swiped at the tears, saw her work through them. "Yes."

"You can have it, all of it, and more. The man you want, the life, the family. I'll give them to you. The child you held in your arms? It can all be real, it can all belong to you."

"At what price?"

"So little." He slid a finger over her damp cheek, and the tear he stole flamed on its tip. "So very little. You've only to stay within this dream. To wake and sleep within it, to walk, to speak, to eat, to love. All you can wish for will be here for you. Perfection—without pain, without death."

She let out a shuddering breath. "There are no keys in this dream."

"You're a clever woman. Why care about keys, about bastard goddesses who have nothing to do with you? Why risk yourself and those you love for foolish girls who should never have been born? Would you give up your own dream for strangers?"

"I don't want a dream. I want my life. I won't trade my life for your illusions."

His skin went white, his eyes black. "Then lose all!"

She screamed as he reached for her, and again when the cold speared through her. Then she was pulled clear, tumbled free, to wake gasping in her own bed.

She heard the banging on the door, the shouting. Terror leaped out of bed with her. She made it to the living room at a stumbling run and spotted Flynn on the other side of her patio doors, about to smash one of her chairs through the glass.

He tossed it aside as she unlocked the door, shoved it open.

"Who's in here?" He grabbed her shoulders, lifted her right off her feet, and set her out of his way. "Who hurt you?"

"Nobody's here."

"You were screaming. I heard you screaming." He strode into the bedroom, fists ready.

"I had a nightmare. It was just a bad dream. No one's here but me. I have to sit down." She braced a hand on the couch, lowered herself.

His own legs felt a little shaky. She'd screamed as if something was tearing her to pieces. He'd had a good taste of terror the night before, but it had been nothing compared to what had pumped into him on the other side of that glass door.

He marched into the kitchen, poured a glass of water. "Here, drink some. Take it slow."

"I'll be okay in a minute. I woke up, and you were pounding and shouting. Everything's still confused."

"You're trembling." He glanced around, spotted a chenille throw. Wrapping it around her shoulders, he sat on the couch beside her. "Tell me about the dream."

She shook her head. "No. I don't want to talk about

it, or think about it right now. I just want to be alone for a while. I don't want you here."

"That's the second time today you've said that to me. But this time you're not getting your way. In fact, I'm calling Jordan and letting him know I'm staying here tonight."

"This is my apartment. Nobody stays here unless I invite them."

"Wrong again. Get undressed, get in bed. I'll make you some soup or something."

"I don't want soup, I don't want you. And I certainly don't want to be coddled."

"Then what the hell do you want?" He lunged to his feet, vibrating with fury and frustration. "One minute you're all over me, telling me you're in love with me, you want to spend your life with me. Then the next you want me to hit the road. I'm sick to death of women and their mixed signals and capricious minds and their goddamn expectations of me. Right now, you're going to do what I want, and that's getting into bed while I make you something to eat."

She stared at him. A dozen vile and vicious words leaped into her throat. And she lost them all in a burst of tears.

"Oh, Christ." Flynn scrubbed his hands over his face. "Nice job. Take a bow, Hennessy."

He stalked to the window, stared out while she wept wildly behind him. "I'm sorry. I don't know what to do about you. I can't keep up. You don't want me here, fine. I'll call Dana. But I don't want you to be alone."

"I don't know what to do about me either." She reached in the drawer for a pack of tissues. "If I've sent you mixed signals, it hasn't been deliberately." She mopped at her face, but the tears simply wouldn't stop. "I don't have a capricious mind—at least I never used to. And I don't know what my goddamn expectations of you are. I don't even know what my goddamn expectations are of me anymore. I used to. I'm scared. I'm scared of what's happening around me and inside me. And I'm scared because I don't know what's real. I don't know if you're actually standing over there."

He came back, sat beside her again. "I'm here," he said as he took her hand firmly in his. "This is real."

"Flynn." She steadied herself by staring at their joined hands. "All my life I've wanted certain things. I wanted to paint. For as long as I can remember, I wanted to be an artist. A wonderful artist. I studied, and I worked. And I never came close. I don't have the gift."

She closed her eyes. "It hurt, more than I can tell you, to accept that." Steadier, she let out a breath, looked at him. "The best I could do was work with art, to be around it, to find some purpose for this love." She fisted a hand on her heart. "And that I was good at."

"Don't you think there's something noble about doing what we're really good at, even if it wasn't our first choice?"

"That's a nice thought. But it's hard to set a dream aside. I guess you know that."

"Yeah, I know that."

"The other thing I wanted was to love someone, to be loved by him. Absolutely. To know when I went to bed at night, woke in the morning, that this someone was with me. Understood me and wanted me. I never had much luck with that one either. I might meet someone, and we'd seem to click. But it never got inside me. I never felt that leap, or the burn that eases into that wonderful, spreading warmth. When you just know this is the one you were waiting for. Until you. Don't say anything," she said quickly. "I need to finish."

She picked up the water again, soothed her throat. "When you wait all your life for something and then you find it, it's like a miracle. All the parts inside you that've been on hold, they open up and start beating. You were okay before, you were good. You had purpose and direction, and everything was just fine. But now it's more. You can't explain what that more is, but you know, if you lose it, you'll never be able to fill those empty spaces in just the same way again. Not ever. That's terrifying. I'm afraid that what's inside me is just a trick. That I'll wake up tomorrow and what's beating in here will have stopped. It'll be quiet again. I won't feel this way. I won't feel the way I've waited all my life to feel."

Her eyes were dry again, her hand steady as she set the water down. "I can stand you not loving me back. There's always the hope that you will. But I don't know if I can stand not loving you. It would be like . . . like having something stolen from inside me. I don't know if I can handle going back to the way I was."

He brushed a hand down her hair, then drew her close to his side so her head rested on his shoulder. "Nobody's ever loved me, not the way you're talking about. I don't know what to do about it, Malory, but I don't want to lose it either."

"I saw the way things could be, but it wasn't true. Just an ordinary day that was so perfect it was like a jewel in the palm of my hand. He made me see it and feel it. And want it."

He eased back, turning her to face him. "The dream?"

She nodded. "It hurt more than anything I've ever known to let it go. It's a hard price, Flynn."

"Can you tell me?"

"I think I have to. I was tired. I felt like I'd been through this emotional wringer. I just wanted to lie down, have it go away for a while."

She took him through it, the waking with that sensation of absolute well-being, of moving through a house that was full of love, finding him in the kitchen making her breakfast.

"That should've clued you in. Me, cooking? An obvious delusion."

"You were making me French toast. It's my favorite

lazy-morning treat. We talked about going on vacation, and I remembered all the other places we'd gone, what we'd done. Those memories were inside me. Then the baby woke up."

"Baby?" He went icy pale. "We had—there was . . . a baby?"

"I went up to get him out of the crib."

"Him?"

"Yes, him. Along the walls on the way were paintings I'd done. They were wonderful, and I could remember painting them. Just as I could remember painting the ones in the nursery. I picked the baby up, out of the crib, and this love, this terrible love for him. I was full of it. And then . . . and then I didn't know his name. I had no name for him. I could feel the shape of him in my arms, and how soft and warm his skin was, but I didn't know his name. You came to the door, and I could see through you. I knew it wasn't real. None of it was real."

She had to stand up, to move. She walked over to open the curtains again. "Even as I started to hurt, I was in a studio. My studio, surrounded by my work. I could smell the paint and the turpentine. I had a brush in my hand, and I knew how to use it. I knew all the things I'd always wanted to know. It was powerful, like having the child who had come from me in my arms. And just as false. And he was there."

"Who was there?"

She drew in a sharp breath, turned back. "His name is Kane. The stealer of souls. He spoke to me. I could have it all—the life, the love, the talent. It could be real. If I just stayed inside it, I'd never have to give it up. We would love each other. We'd have a son. I'd paint. It would all be perfect. Just live inside the dream, and the dream's real."

"Did he touch you?" He rushed to her to run his hands over her as if to check for wounds. "Did he hurt you?"

"This world or that," she said, steady again. "My

choice. I wanted to stay, but I couldn't. I don't want a dream, Flynn, no matter how perfect it is. If it's not real, it means nothing. And if I'd stayed, isn't that just another way of giving him my soul?"

"You were screaming." Undone, Flynn laid his forehead on hers. "You were screaming."

"He tried to take it, but I heard you shouting for me. Why did you come here?"

"You were upset, with me. I didn't want you to be."

"Annoyed," she corrected and slid her arms around him. "I still am, but it's a little hard to get through everything else to my irritation. I want you to stay. I'm afraid to sleep, afraid I might go back and this time I won't be strong enough to come out again."

"You're strong enough. And if you need it, I'll help pull you out."

"This might not be real either." She lifted her mouth to his. "But I need you."

"It's real." He lifted her hands, kissed each one in turn. "That's the only thing I'm sure of in this whole damn mess. Whatever I'm feeling for you, Malory, it's real."

"If you can't tell me what you feel, then show me." She drew him to her. "Show me now."

All the conflicting emotions, the needs and doubts and wants, poured into the kiss. And as she accepted them, accepted him, he felt himself settle. Tenderness spread through him as he picked her up, cradled her in his arms.

"I want to keep you safe. I don't care if it irritates you." He carried her to her room and laid her on the bed, began to undress her. "I'll keep getting in the way, if that's what it takes."

"I don't need someone to look out for me." She lifted a hand to his cheek. "I just need you to look at me."

"Malory, I've been looking at you from the beginning, even when you're not around."

She smiled, arched up so he could slip off her blouse.

"That's a strange thing to say, but it's nice. Lie down with me."

They were side by side, faces close. "I feel pretty safe right now, and it's not particularly irritating."

"Maybe you're feeling a little too safe." He skimmed a fingertip over the swell of her breast.

"Maybe." She sighed when he began to nuzzle the side of her neck. "That doesn't scare me a bit. You're going to have to try a lot harder."

He rolled over, pinned her, then plundered her mouth with his.

"Oh. Nice work," she managed.

She was trembling, just enough to arouse him, and her skin was flushing warm. He could steep himself in her, in the tastes and textures. He could lose himself in that low, driving urge to give her pleasure.

He was tied to her. Perhaps he had been even before he'd met her. Could it be that all the mistakes he'd made, all the changes in direction, had been only to lead him to this time, and this woman?

Was there never any choice?

She sensed him drawing back. "Don't. Don't go away," she begged. "Let me love you. I need to love you."

She wound her arms around him, used her mouth to seduce. For now, she would trade pride for power without a qualm. As her body moved sinuously under his, she felt his quiver.

Hands stroked. Lips took. Breathy moans slid into air that had gone dim and thick. Long, lazy kisses built in intensity and ended on gasps of greed.

He was with her now, locked in a rhythm too primal to resist. The hammer blows of his heart threatened to shatter his chest, and still it wasn't enough.

He wanted to gorge on the flavors of her, to drown in that sea of needs. One moment she was pliant, yielding; the next, as taut as a bunched fist. When her breath sobbed out his name, he thought he might go mad.

She rose over him. Locking her hands in his, she took him into her, a slow, slow slide that tied his frantic system into knots.

"Malory."

She shook her head, leaning down to rub her lips over his. "Want me."

"I do."

"Let me take you. Watch me take you."

She arched back, stroking her hands up her torso, over her breasts, into her hair. And she began to ride.

Heat slapped him back, a furnace blast that had his muscles going to jelly, that scorched his bones. She rose above him, slim and strong, white and gold. She surrounded him, possessed him. Spurred him toward madness.

The power and pleasure consumed her. She drove them both faster, harder, until her vision was a blur of colors. Alive, was all she could think. They were alive. Blood burned in her veins, pumped in her frenzied heart. Good healthy sweat slicked her skin. She could taste him in her mouth, feel him pounding in the very core of her.

This was life.

She clung to it, clung even when the glory climbed toward the unbearable. Until his body plunged, and she let go.

H E made good on the soup, though he could tell it amused her to have him stirring a pot at her stove. He put on music, kept the lights low. Not for seduction, but because he desperately wanted to keep her relaxed.

He had questions, a great many more questions, about her dream. The part of him that felt that asking questions was a human obligation warred with the part that wanted to tuck her up safe and quiet for a while.

"I could run out," he suggested, "grab some videos. We can veg out."

"Don't go anywhere." She snuggled closer to him on the couch. "You don't have to distract me, Flynn. We have to talk about it eventually."

"Doesn't have to be now."

"I thought a newspaperman dug for all the facts fit to print, and then some."

"Since the *Dispatch* isn't going to be running a story on Celtic myths in the Valley until all of this is finished, there's no rush."

"And if you were working for the *New York Times*?"

"That'd be different." He stroked her hair, sipped his wine. "I'd be hard-boiled and cynical and skewer you or anybody else for the story. And I'd probably be strung out and stressed. Maybe have a drinking problem. Be working toward my second divorce. I think I'd like bourbon, and I'd have a redhead on the side."

"What do you *really* think it'd be like if you'd gone to New York?"

"I don't know. I like to think I'd have done good work. Important work."

"You don't think your work here's important?"

"It serves a purpose."

"An important purpose. Not only keeping people informed and entertained, giving them the continuity of tradition, but keeping a lot of them employed. The people who work on the paper, deliver it, their families. Where would they have gone if you'd left?"

"I wasn't the only one who could run it."

"Maybe you were the only one who was supposed to run it. Would you go now, if you could?"

He thought about it. "No. I made the choice. Most of the time I'm glad I chose as I did. Just every once in a while, I wonder."

"I couldn't paint. Nobody told me I couldn't or made me give it up. I just wasn't good enough. It's different when you're good enough, but someone tells you you can't."

"It wasn't exactly like that."

"What was it like?"

"You have to understand my mother. She makes very definite plans. When my father died, well, that must've really messed up Plan A."

"Flynn."

"I'm not saying she didn't love him, or didn't mourn. She did. We did. He made her laugh. He could always make her laugh. I don't think I heard her laugh, not really, for a year after we lost him."

"Flynn." It broke her heart. "I'm so sorry."

"She's tough. One thing you can say about Elizabeth Flynn Hennessy Steele, she's no wimp."

"You love her." Malory brushed at his hair. "I wondered."

"Sure I do, but you won't hear me say she was easy to live with. Anyway, when she pulled herself out of it, it was time for Plan B. Big chunk of that was passing the paper to me when the time came. No problem for me there, since I figured that was way, way down the road. And that I would deal with it, and her, when I had to. I liked working for the *Dispatch*, learning not just about reporting but about publishing too."

"But you wanted to do that in New York."

"I was too big for a podunk town like Pleasant Valley. Too much to say, too much to do. Pulitzers to win. Then my mother married Joe. He's a great guy. Dana's dad."

"Can he make your mother laugh?"

"Yeah. Yeah, he can. We made a good family, the four of us. I don't know that I appreciated that at the time. With Joe around, I figured some of the pressure on me was off. I guess we all figured they'd work the paper together for decades."

"Joe's a reporter?"

"Yeah, worked for the paper for years. Used to joke that he'd married the boss. They made a good team too, so it looked like everything was going to work out fine and dandy. After college, I figured to build up another couple years' experience here, then give New York a break and offer my invaluable skills and services. I met Lily, and that seemed to be the icing on the cake."

"What happened?"

"Joe got sick. Looking back, I imagine my mother was frantic at the idea that she might lose somebody else she loved. She's not big on emotional displays. She's sort of contained and straightforward, but I can see it, hindsight-wise. And I can't imagine what it was like for her. They had to move. He had a better chance of copping more time if they got out of this climate, and away from stress. So either I stayed, or the paper closed."

"She expected you to stay."

He remembered what he'd said about expectations. "Yeah. Do my duty. I was pissed off at her for a year, then irritated for another. Somewhere in year three I hit resigned. I don't know exactly when that became . . . I guess you could say contentment. But around the time I bumped into contentment, I bought the house. Then I got Moe."

"I'd say you're off your mother's plan and on your own."

He let out a half laugh. "Son of a bitch. I guess I am."

Chapter Fifteen

T HERE was very little that Dana dragged herself out of bed for. Work, of course, was the primary incentive. But when she had the morning off, her main choice for entertainment was sleep.

Giving that up at Flynn's request demonstrated, in her opinion, extreme sisterly affection. And should earn her major points, to be redeemed in any future necessity.

She knocked on Malory's door at seven-thirty, wearing a Groucho Marx T-shirt, ripped jeans, and a pair of Oakleys.

Because he knew his sister, Flynn opened the door and shoved a steaming cup of coffee into her hands.

"You're a peach. You're a jewel. You are my personal treasure chest."

"Stuff it." She strode in, sat on the couch, and began to inhale the coffee. "Where's Mal?"

"Still sleeping."

"Got bagels?"

"I don't know. I didn't look. I should've looked," he

said instantly. "I'm a selfish bastard, thinking only of my-self."

"Excuse me, but I'd have liked to say that."

"Just saving you the time and energy. I've got to go. I need to be at the paper in . . . shit, twenty-six minutes," he said when he looked at his watch.

"Just tell me why I'm in Malory's apartment, drinking coffee and hoping there are bagels, when she's asleep."

"I don't have time to get into it. She had a rough one, and I don't want her to be alone. At all, Dana."

"Jesus, Flynn, what? Did somebody beat her up?"

"You could say that. Emotionally speaking. And it wasn't me," he added as he headed for the door. "Just stick with her, will you? I'll shake loose as soon as I can, but I've got a full slate today. Let her sleep, then, I don't know, keep her busy. I'll call."

He was out the patio door and loping away while Dana scowled after him. "For a reporter, you're sure stingy with the deets." Deciding to make the best of it, she got up to raid Malory's kitchen.

She was taking the first enthusiastic bite of a poppy-seed bagel when Malory came in.

Heavy-eyed, Dana noted. A little pale. Considerably rumpled. She imagined the rumpled part was on Flynn. "Hi. Want the other half?"

Obviously groggy, Malory just blinked. "Hi, yourself. Where's Flynn?"

"He had to run. Go stand for journalism and all that. Want some coffee instead?"

"Yes." She rubbed her eyes and tried to think. "What're you doing here, Dana?"

"Don't have a clue. Flynn called me, at the ungodly hour of about forty minutes ago, and asked me to come over. He was short on details but long on pleading, so I hauled my ass over here. What's up?"

"I guess he's worried about me." She considered it,

then decided she didn't mind very much. "That's sort of sweet."

"Yeah, he's sugar. Why is he worried about you?"

"I think we'd better sit down."

She told Dana everything.

"What did he look like?" Dana demanded.

"Well . . . strong face, leaning toward the ascetic side. Wait a minute—I think I can sketch it."

She got up to take a pad and pencil from a drawer, then sat down again. "He had very well-defined features, so it won't be too hard. But more than how he looked was the way he felt. Compelling. Even charismatic."

"What about the house you were in?" Dana pressed while Malory worked.

"I just got impressions. It seemed so familiar in the dream, the way your home does. So you don't notice a lot of details. Two-story with a lawn in the back, a pretty garden. Sunny kitchen."

"It wasn't Flynn's house?"

Malory looked up then. "No," she said slowly. "No, it wasn't. I didn't think of that. Wouldn't you assume it would be? If it's my fantasy, why weren't we living in his house? It's a great house, it's already in my head."

"Maybe he couldn't use Flynn's house because it's already occupied, and . . . I don't know. It's probably not important."

"I think everything's important. Everything I saw and felt and heard. I just don't know how yet. Here . . ." She turned the pad around. "It's rough, but that's the best I can do. It's a pretty decent impression of him anyway."

"Wow!" Dana pursed her lips, whistled. "So Kane the sorcerer's a hottie."

"He scares me, Dana."

"He couldn't hurt you, not really. Not when it came right down to it."

"Not this time. But he was in my head. It was like an invasion." She pressed her lips together. "A kind of rape.

He knows what I feel, and what I wish for."

"I'll tell you what he didn't know. He didn't know you'd tell him to kiss your ass."

Malory sat back. "You're right. He didn't know I'd refuse, or that I'd understand—even in the dream—that he wanted me trapped somewhere, however wonderful, where I couldn't find the key. Both of those things surprised and irritated him. And that means he doesn't know everything."

WITH considerable reluctance, Dana tagged along when Malory decided to work at Flynn's house. It made sense, as the two paintings were there. But so was Jordan Hawke.

Her hopes that he would be out somewhere were quashed when she saw the vintage Thunderbird in Flynn's driveway.

"Always had a thing about cars," she muttered, and though she sniffed at the T-Bird, she secretly admired its lines, the sweep of tail fins and the sparkle of chrome.

She'd have paid money to get behind the wheel and open that engine up on a straightaway.

"Don't know why the jerk has to have a car when he lives in Manhattan."

Malory recognized the tone, both the sulkiness and the bitterness, and paused at the door. "Is this going to be a problem for you? Maybe we can make arrangements to see the paintings again when Jordan's not here."

"No problem for me. He doesn't exist in my reality. I long ago drowned him in a vat of ebola. It was a messy, yet oddly satisfying, task."

"Okay, then." Malory lifted a hand to knock, but Dana nudged her aside.

"I do *not* knock on my brother's door." She shot her key into the lock. "No matter what morons he might have staying with him."

She strode in, prepared for a confrontation. Unwilling to be so easily deflated when she didn't see him, she slammed the door.

"Dana."

"Oops. Slipped." Hooking her thumbs in her pockets, she strolled into the living room. "Just where we left them," she said with a nod at the paintings. "And you know what, I don't see anything different about them either. Job's done for today. Let's go shopping or something."

"I want to do a more thorough study of them, and I want to go through all the research notes. But there's no reason for you to hang around."

"I promised Flynn."

"Flynn's a worrywart."

"Well, yeah, but I promised." Sensing movement in the doorway behind her, she stiffened. "And unlike some, I keep my promises."

"And hold a grudge with equal fervor," Jordan commented. "Hello, ladies. What can I do for you?"

"I'd like to go over the paintings and my notes again," Malory told him. "I hope you don't mind."

"Who's he to mind? It's not his house."

"True enough." Jordan, tall and tough in black jeans and black T-shirt, leaned against the doorjamb. "Help yourself."

"Haven't you got something better to do than lurk?" Dana tossed out. "A book to pretend to write, a publisher to skin."

"You know us commercial fiction hacks. We just knock 'em out in a couple weeks, then lounge around on our royalties."

"I don't mind if the two of you want to fight, really, I don't." Malory dumped her briefcase, fat with notes, on the crate. "But maybe you could take it to another room."

"We're not fighting." Jordan replied. "This is foreplay."

"In your dreams."

"Stretch, in my dreams you're usually wearing a lot less. Let me know if I can help you out with anything, Malory." He straightened, then strolled away.

"Be right back." Dana was after him like a rocket. "In the kitchen, hotshot." She streamed by, then gritted her teeth while she waited for him to catch up.

He moved at his own pace, she thought, and always had. Her temper sparked as he wandered in. She was readying the first salvo when he stepped right up, gripped her hips, and covered her shocked mouth with his.

The blast of heat blew straight through her.

That had always been, as well.

Fire and flash and promise all balled together in some sort of molten comet that exploded in the brain and left the system wrecked.

Not this time, not this time. Not ever again.

With considerable force she shoved him back a step. She wouldn't slap. Too predictable and female. But she very nearly punched.

"Sorry. I thought that was what you called me out here for."

"Try that again, and you'll be bleeding from various fatal wounds."

He shrugged, sauntered over to the coffeepot. "My mistake."

"Damn right. Any rights you had to touch me expired a long time ago. You may be part of this thing because you happened to buy that damn painting, and I'll tolerate you because of that. And because you're Flynn's friend. But as long as you're here, you'll abide by the rules."

He poured two mugs of coffee, set hers on the counter. "Spell them out for me."

"You don't ever touch me. If I'm about to step in front of a damn bus, you don't so much as reach out to pull me back to the curb."

"Okay. You'd rather be run over by a bus than have me touch you. Check. Next?"

"You're a son of a bitch."

Something that might have been regret flashed across his face. "I know it. Look, let's step back a minute. Flynn's important to both of us, and this is important to Flynn. That woman out there's important to him, and she's important to you. We're all connected here, whether we want to be or not. So let's try to figure it out. He was in and out of here in about three minutes flat this morning. I didn't get much more out of him then, or when he called last night, than that Malory's in trouble. Fill me in."

"If Malory wants you to know, she'll tell you."

Hand her an olive branch, he thought, and she rams it down your throat. "Still a hard-ass."

"It's private stuff," she snapped. "Intimate stuff. She doesn't know you." Despite a thousand vows, she felt her eyes fill. "Neither do I."

That single tearful look punched a hole in his heart. "Dana."

When he stepped toward her, she snatched a bread knife off the counter. "Put your hands on me again, I'll hack them off at the wrist."

He stayed where he was, slid his hands into his pockets. "Why don't you just stick it in my heart and get it over with?"

"Just stay away from me. Flynn doesn't want Malory left alone. You can consider this your shift, because I'm leaving."

"If I'm going to be guard dog, it would help to know what I'm guarding against."

"Big, bad sorcerers." She yanked open the back door. "Anything happens to her, I'll not only jam that knife in your heart, I'll cut it out and feed it to the dog."

"Always were good with imagery," he drawled after she'd slammed out.

He rubbed a hand over his stomach. She'd tied it in

knots—something else she was damn good at. He looked at the coffee she hadn't touched. Though he knew it was foolishly symbolic, he picked up the cup and poured the coffee down the sink.

"Down the drain, Stretch. Just like us."

MALORY studied the paintings until her vision blurred. She made more notes, then stretched out on the floor to stare at the ceiling. She jumbled what she knew in her head, hoping it would form a new, clearer pattern.

A singing goddess, shadows and light, what was within herself and outside herself. To look and see what she hadn't seen. Love forged the key.

Hell.

Three paintings, three keys. Did that mean there was a clue, a sign, a direction in each painting for each key? Or was there a compilation in the three paintings for the first key? For hers?

Either way, she was missing it.

There were common elements in each portrait. The legendary subject matter, of course. The use of forest and shadows. The figure cloaked by them.

That would be Kane.

Why was Kane in the portrait of Arthur? Had he actually been there at the event, or was his inclusion, and Rowena's and Pitte's, symbolic?

But still, even with those common elements, the Arthurian portrait didn't seem part of what she was certain was a set. Was there another painting, to complete the triad, of the Daughters of Glass?

Where would she find it, and what would it tell her when she did?

She rolled over, examined the portrait of young Arthur once more. The white dove at the right top. A symbol for Guinevere? The beginning of the end of that shining moment?

Betrayal by love. The consequences of love.

Wasn't she dealing with consequences of love now, within herself? The soul was as much a symbol of love and beauty as the heart was. Emotions, poetry, art, music. Magic. Soulful elements.

Without a soul, there were no consequences, and no beauty.

If the goddess could sing, didn't that mean she still had her soul?

The key might be in a place where there was art, or love. Beauty or music. Or where the choice to keep them or discard them was made.

A museum, then? A gallery? The Gallery, she thought and bolted to her feet.

"Dana!"

She dashed toward the kitchen, pulling up short when she saw Jordan sitting at the scarred table working on a small, sleek laptop.

"Sorry. I thought Dana was in here."

"She took off hours ago."

"Hours?" Malory passed a hand over her face as if coming out of a dream. "I lost track of time."

"Happens to me regularly. Want some coffee?" He glanced toward the empty pot on the counter. "All you have to do is make it."

"No, I really need to . . . You're working. I'm sorry to interrupt."

"No problem. I'm having one of those days where I fantasize about having an alternate profession. Like being a lumberjack in the Yukon or a bartender at a tropical resort."

"Pretty disparate choices."

"Either of which seems like more fun than what I'm doing."

She noted the empty coffee cup, the half-full ashtray set beside the jazzy laptop on a secondhand picnic table in a stupendously ugly kitchen.

"Could be the ambience isn't particularly conducive to creativity."

"When things are going well, you can be in a sewer with a notebook and a Ticonderoga."

"I suppose that's true, but I'm wondering if you're set up in this . . . unfortunate room because you're watching out for me."

"Depends." He eased back, fiddled with his dwindling pack of cigarettes. "If that's okay with you, sure. If it's going to piss you off, then I'm afraid I don't know what you're talking about."

She cocked her head. "And if I said I had to leave now, that there's something I want to check out?"

He gave her an easy smile, one she thought might pass for innocent on a less wicked face. "I'd say, is it okay if I tag along? It might do me good to get out of the house for a while. Where are we going?"

"The Gallery. It occurred to me that the key must be attached to art, to beauty, to the paintings. It's the most logical place in the area to look."

"Uh-huh. So, you're going to walk into a public place of business, during business hours, and nobody's going to mind if you go on a scavenger hunt through the stock and/or office areas."

"Well, when you put it that way." Deflated, she sat across from him. "Do you think this whole thing is just some kind of lunacy?"

Jordan recalled watching several thousand dollars appear and disappear. "Not necessarily."

"And if I said I might have a way to get into The Gallery *after* business hours?"

"I'd say you wouldn't have been picked to be a part of this unless you were a creative woman with a flexible mind who's willing to take some chances."

"I like that description. I don't know if it always applied, but it does now. I need to make some phone calls. And, Jordan? I think it shows a strong sense of character and loyalty for a man to waste his day looking after a stranger because a friend asked him to."

MALORY took the keys from Tod and gave him a huge hug in return. "I owe you big."

"I'll say, but I'll settle for any sort of an explanation."

"As soon as I can. I promise."

"Honeybun, this is all getting really weird. You get fired, then you hack into Pamela's files. You turn down the invitation to come back to home and hearth with a substantial raise. And now you're going to skulk around the place after closing."

"You know what?" She jingled the keys in her hand. "That's not the really weird part. All I can tell you is I'm doing something important, and with the best intentions. I'm not going to do The Gallery or James, or most especially you, any harm."

"I'd never think you would."

"I'll have these back to you tonight. First thing in the morning at the latest."

Tod glanced out the window to see Flynn loitering on the sidewalk. "This doesn't have anything to do with sexual fetishes or fantasies?"

"No."

"Well, that's a shame. I'm walking away. I'm going to have a lovely martini, maybe two, and put all this completely out of my mind."

"Do just that."

He started out, then stopped and looked back at her. "Whatever you're doing, Mal, be careful."

"I will. Promise."

She waited, watched Tod stop to speak to Flynn before sauntering off. She opened the door, gestured Flynn in, then locked it, set the security code. "What did Tod say to you?"

"That if I got you into any sort of trouble he'd hang

me up by my balls and then snip off various other body parts with manicure scissors."

"Ouch. Good one."

"You bet." He peered out the window to make sure Tod was gone. "And let me tell you, if I was thinking about getting you into any sort of trouble, that image would be a very strong deterrent."

"I guess, when it comes down to it, I'm the one who could be getting you in trouble. There's the legal angle, the criminal angle, and your reputation as publisher and editor in chief of the *Dispatch* on the line here. You don't have to do this."

"I'm in. Manicure scissors are those little pointy ones that curve, right?"

"That's right."

He hissed out a breath. "Yeah, I was afraid of that. Where do we start?"

"Upstairs, I think. We can work our way down. Assuming the keys in the painting are in proportion, it'll be about three inches long."

"Little key."

"Yes, a fairly little key. The business end is a single, simple drop," she continued and handed him a small sketch. "The other end is decorative, this complex pattern. It's a Celtic design, a triple spiral called a *triskeles*. Zoe found the pattern in one of Dana's books."

"You three make a good team."

"It feels like it. It's gold, probably solid gold. I can't imagine we won't recognize it when we see it."

He glanced toward the main showroom with its vaulted ceilings and generous space. There were the paintings, of course, and the sculpture and other artworks. Display cases and tables. Drawers and chests and counters with infinite cubbyholes.

"A lot of places a key might hide in here."

"Wait until we get into the storage and shipping areas."

They started in the offices. Malory set aside her guilt

at going through drawers, riffling through personal items. This wasn't any time for delicacy, she told herself. She crawled around James's desk, searching under it.

"Do you really think people like Rowena and Pitte, or whatever god's in charge of hiding the keys, would tape the secret key to the bottom of a desk drawer?"

She sent him a sulky look as she slid the drawer back in place. "I don't think we can afford to overlook any possibility."

She looked so cute, he thought, sitting on the floor with her hair tied back from her face and her mouth all pouty. He wondered if she'd worn black because she felt it suited the circumstances.

It would be just like her.

"Fair enough, but we'd get through those possibilities faster if we called the whole team in."

"I can't have a pack of people running around here. It's just not right." And the guilt of what she was doing scraped her conscience like ragged fingernails. "It's bad enough you're here. You can't use anything you see here in a story."

He crouched down with her, stared into her face with eyes that had gone winter cool. "Is that what you think?"

"It doesn't seem unreasonable that the thought crossed my mind." She rose to take a painting off the wall. "You're a journalist," she continued as she checked the frame, tested the backing. "I owe something to this place, to James. I'm just saying that I don't want him involved."

She rehung the painting, chose another.

"Maybe you should write up a list of what is and isn't appropriate for me to write about. In your opinion."

"There's no need to get testy."

"Oh, yeah, there is. I've invested a lot of my time and energy in this, and I haven't printed a word. Don't question my ethics, Malory, just because you're questioning your own. And don't ever tell me what I can or can't write."

"It's just a matter of saying this is off the record."

"No, it's not. It's a matter of you trusting and respecting someone you claim to love. I'm going to start in the next room. I think we'll do better separately."

Just how, she wondered, had she managed to screw that one up so completely? She took the last painting off the wall, ordered herself to concentrate.

Obviously Flynn was oversensitive. She'd made a perfectly reasonable request, and if he wanted to get huffy about it, it was his problem.

She spent the next twenty minutes going over every inch of the room, and comforting herself with her conviction that he'd overreacted.

They didn't speak for the next hour, and though they were two people performing the same task in the same space, they managed to avoid contact.

By the time they started on the main level, they'd developed a rhythm, but they still weren't speaking.

It was tedious, frustrating work. Checking every painting, every sculpture, every pedestal and objet d'art. Going over the stairs tread by tread, crawling along the trim.

Malory took herself off to the storeroom. It was both painful and thrilling to come across newly acquired pieces, or to see others that had been sold since she'd left The Gallery and were waiting to be crated and shipped.

Once she'd been privy to every step and stage, and had been granted the right to acquire items and negotiate a price. In her heart The Gallery had been hers. She couldn't count the times she'd been inside it after hours like this. No one would have questioned her presence then. There would have been no need to beg the keys from a friend, or to feel guilt.

To question her ethics, she admitted.

She wouldn't have felt this awful grief, she realized. Grief that this part of her life had been taken away from her. Maybe she was crazy for refusing the offer to take it back. Maybe she was making a huge mistake by deviating from the sensible, the *tangible*. She could go back and speak to James, tell him she'd changed her mind. She could slide back into routine again, have what she'd always had.

And it would never be the same.

That was the grief. Her life was changed, irrevocably. And she hadn't taken the time to mourn the loss. She did so now, with every piece she touched, every minute she spent in the space that had once been the most important part of her life.

She revisited a thousand memories, so many of them part of the day-to-day routine that had meant nothing at the time. And everything once it had been taken away.

Flynn pulled open the door. "Where do you want to—" He broke off when she turned toward him. Her eyes were dry, but devastated. She held a rough stone sculpture in her arms as she might a child.

"What is it?"

"I miss this place so much. It's like something's died." Very gently, she replaced the sculpture on a shelf. "I acquired this piece, about four months ago. It's a new artist. He's young, with all the fire and temperament you'd expect from the feel of his work. He's from a small town in Maryland, and he's had a little local luck, but no major gallery showed any interest. It felt good to give him his first real break, and to think of what he might do, what *we* might do in the future."

She ran a fingertip over the stone. "Someone bought this. I didn't have anything to do with that part, don't even recognize the name on the invoice. It's not mine anymore."

"It wouldn't have been here or have been sold if it wasn't for you."

"Maybe, but those days are over. I don't have a place here anymore. I'm sorry for what I said before. Very sorry I hurt your feelings."

"Forget it."

"No." She drew a breath. "I'm not going to say I didn't have some concerns about how you might handle this whole thing eventually. I can't claim that I have absolute trust in you. That conflicts with loving you, and I can't explain it. No more than I can explain how I know the key's not here. How I knew that the minute I walked in to get the keys from Tod. I still have to look, have to finish what I started. But it's not here, Flynn. There's nothing here for me now."

Chapter Sixteen

FLYNN closed the door of his office, a signal that he was writing and was not to be disturbed. Not that anybody paid a great deal of attention to the signal, but it was the principle of the thing.

He let the idea for the column simply flow out initially, a kind of serpentine river of thought that he would channel into a more disciplined form on the second pass.

What defined the artist? Were artists only those who created what was perceived as the beautiful or the shocking, those who formed some piece of work that delivered a visceral punch? In painting, in music, in literature or theater?

If so, did that make the rest of the world nothing more than the audience? Passive observers whose only contribution was applause or criticism?

What became of the artist without the audience?

Not his usual sort of column, Flynn mused, but it had been kicking around in his head since the night he and Malory had searched The Gallery. It was time to let it out.

He could still see the way she'd looked in that store-room. A stone figure in her arms and grief swimming in her eyes. In the three days since, she'd kept him and everyone else at arm's length. Oh, she paid lip service to being busy, to following different angles on her quest, to putting her life back in order.

Though from his point of view there'd never been any real disorder to it.

Still, she refused to come out. And she wouldn't let him in.

Maybe the column was a kind of message to her.

He rolled his shoulders, tapped his fingers on the edge of his desk until his mind shifted back and found the words.

Wasn't the child who first learned to form his own name with letters a kind of artist? One who was exploring intellect, coordination, and ego. When the child held that fat pencil or bright crayon in his fist, then drew those letters on paper, wasn't he creating a symbol of himself with lines and curves? This is who I am, and no one else is quite the same.

There is art in the statement, and in the accomplishment.

What about the woman who managed to put a hot meal on the table in the evening? To a Cordon Bleu chef, this might be a pedestrian feat, but to those who were baffled by the directions on a can of condensed soup, having that meat loaf, mashed potatoes, and string beans hit the table in unison was a great and mysterious art.

"Flynn?"

"Working," he snapped without looking up.

"You're not the only one." Rhoda shut the door at her back, marched over and sat in a chair. She folded her arms across her chest and stared holes at Flynn through her square-framed glasses.

But without the audience, ready and willing to consume

the art, it becomes congealed leftovers to be dumped . . .
"Damn it."

He shoved back from his keyboard. "What?"

"You cut an inch from my feature."

His hands itched to pick up his Slinky. And wrap its
coils around Rhoda's skinny throat. "And?"

"You said it was running a full twelve inches."

"And what you had was eleven solid inches, and an
inch of fill. I cut the fill. It was a good piece, Rhoda. Now
it's a better piece."

"I want to know why you're always picking on me,
why you're always cutting my pieces. You barely put a
mark on John's or Carla's, and they're all over my work."

"John handles sports. He's been handling sports for
over a decade. He's got it down to a science."

Art and science, Flynn thought and made a quick shorthand note to remind himself to work it into the column.
And sports . . . If anyone watched the way a pitcher
sculpted the dirt on the mound with his feet until it was
exactly the shape, the texture, the slope he—

"Flynn!"

"What? What?" He snapped back, rewound the tape in
his mind. "And I do edit Carla when and if she needs it.
Rhoda, I'm on a deadline myself here. If you want to get
into this, let's schedule some time tomorrow."

Her mouth pruned. "If we don't resolve this now, I
won't be coming in tomorrow."

Instead of reaching for his action figure of Luke Skywalker and imagining the Jedi knight drawing his light
saber and blasting the superior smirk off Rhoda's face,
Flynn sat back.

The time had come, he decided, to do the blasting himself.

"Okay. First, I'm going to tell you I'm tired of you
threatening to walk. If you're not happy here, not happy
with the way I run the paper, then go."

KEY OF LIGHT 257

She flushed scarlet. "Your mother never—"

"I'm not my mother. Deal. I run the *Dispatch*. I've been running it for nearly four years now, and I intend to run it for a long time. Get used to it."

Now her eyes filled, and since Flynn considered tears fighting dirty, he struggled to ignore them. "Anything else?" he asked coolly.

"I've been working here since before you could read the damn paper."

"Which may be our problem. It suited you better when my mother was in charge. Now it suits you better to continue to think of me as a temporary annoyance, and an incompetent one at that."

Rhoda's mouth dropped open in what appeared to be sincere shock. "I don't think you're incompetent. I just think—"

"That I should stay out of your work." The genial tone was back in his voice, but his expression remained frigid. "That I should do what you tell me instead of the other way around. That's not going to happen."

"If you don't think I do good work, then—"

"Sit down," he ordered as she started to rise. He knew the drill. She would storm out, slam things around, glare at him through the glass, then make sure her next piece slid in only minutes before deadline.

"It so happens I think you do good work. Not that it matters a hell of a lot coming from me because you don't have any confidence in or respect for my skill or my authority. I guess that makes it tough for you because you're a journalist, we're the only game in town, and I'm in charge. I don't see any of those factors changing. Next time I ask for twelve inches, give me a solid twelve and we won't have a problem." He tapped the tip of his pencil against the desk while she gaped at him.

Perry White, he mused, might've handled it better, but he figured he was in the ballpark. "Anything else?"

"I'm going to take the rest of the day off."

"No, you're not." He swiveled back to his keyboard. "Have that piece on the elementary school expansion on my desk by two. Close the door on your way out."

Flynn went back to typing, pleased when he heard the door click closed instead of slam. He waited thirty seconds, then shifted in his chair enough to look through the glass wall. Rhoda was sitting at her desk as if paralyzed.

He hated confrontations like that. The woman used to sneak him gumdrops when he would come into the offices after school. It was hell, he decided, rubbing his temple and pretending to concentrate on his work. Just hell being a grown-up.

HE escaped for an hour in the afternoon to meet Brad and Jordan at the Main Street Diner. It hadn't changed much since the three of them had gathered there regularly after football games or for late-night bullshit sessions that had revolved around girls and life plans.

The air was still ripe with the smell of the diner's signature chicken-fried steak, and the counter still held a four-tiered display rack of that day's pies. As Flynn looked down at the burger he'd ordered out of habit, he wondered if it was the diner that had gotten stuck in the past, or himself.

He frowned at Brad's club sandwich. "Trade me."

"You want my sandwich?"

"I want your sandwich. Trade me." To solve the matter, Flynn switched the plates himself.

"If you didn't want a burger, why'd you order one?"

"Because. I'm a victim of habit and tradition."

"And eating my sandwich is going to solve that?"

"It's a start. I also started breaking habit by reaming Rhoda out at the paper this morning. Once she comes out of shock, I'm pretty sure she'll start planning my demise."

"How come you wanted his sandwich instead of mine?" Jordan asked.

"I don't like Reubens."

Jordan considered, then switched his plate with Brad's.

"Jesus, are we finished playing musical plates now?" Brad scowled at the Reuben, then decided it actually looked pretty good.

Though he was already wishing he had his burger back, Flynn picked at the club sandwich. "Do you think staying in your hometown all your life keeps you too attached to the past, too resistant to change and growth, and thereby inhibits your ability to function as a mature adult?"

"I didn't know this was going to be a philosophical discussion." But willing to play, Jordan considered the question as he squeezed ketchup on the burger. "It could be said that staying in your hometown means you're comfortable there and have created strong roots and ties. Or that you're just too lazy and complacent to get your ass out."

"I like it here. Took me a while to come to that. Up until recently I'd been pretty complacent about how things were going. Complacency's taken a backseat since around the first of the month."

"Because of the keys?" Brad asked. "Or Malory?"

"One goes with the other. The keys, that's an adventure, right? Sir Galahad and the Holy Grail, Indiana Jones and the Lost Ark."

"Elmer Fudd and Bugs Bunny," Jordan put in.

"Right, same deal." You could always count on Jordan to get your drift, Flynn thought. "None of our lives are going to suffer if we don't find them. Not really."

"One year," Brad said. "That's a pretty stiff penalty clause to my way of thinking."

"Okay, yeah." Flynn plucked a potato chip from the little mound beside his sandwich. "But I'm having a hard time seeing either Rowena or Pitte punishing these women."

"They may not be the ones who do the messing," Jordan commented. "They may simply be the conduit, so to speak, to reward or punishment. Why do we assume they have a choice either?"

"Trying to think positive here," Flynn replied. "And the idea that we will find the keys, and what happens then, is compelling."

"Besides the fact that it's a puzzle, and it's damn hard to walk away from a puzzle."

Flynn nodded at Brad, shifted in his seat. "Then there's the magic. The acceptance that magic, some kinds of magic, are real. Not an illusion, but an actual kick in the ass of the natural order. I mean, how cool is that? That's the kind of thing we give up when we become adults. The casual belief in magic. This has given it back."

"You want to look at it as a gift or a burden?" Jordan wondered. "Could go either way."

"Thanks again, Mr. Bright Side. But yes, I know that too. We're coming up on deadline here. A little more than a week. If we don't find it, maybe we'll pay, maybe we won't. But we'll never *know*."

"You can't dismiss the potential consequences of failure," Brad pointed out.

"I'm trying to believe that nobody's going to screw up the lives of three innocent women because they tried and failed."

"You go back to the beginning of this, and the lives of three innocent women—demigoddesses or not—were screwed up simply because they existed." Jordan dashed salt on what had been Flynn's fries. "Sorry, pal."

"Add in that the women in the portrait look like the women we know." Brad drummed his fingers on the table. "There's a reason for that, and the reason puts them at the core of it all."

"I'm not letting anything happen to Malory. Or any of them," Flynn responded.

Jordan picked up his glass of iced tea. "Just how stuck on her are you?"

"That's another question. I haven't figured it out."

"Well, we'll help you there." Jordan winked at Brad. "What're friends for? How's the sex?"

"Why's that always first with you?" Flynn demanded. "That's a lifelong pattern."

"Because I'm a guy. And if you don't think women rate sex high on the list, you're a sad and pitiful fool."

"It's great." Flynn met Jordan sneer for sneer. "You only wish you were having this level of sex with a beautiful woman. But it's not like that's the only thing going on between us. We have actual conversations, with and without clothes on."

"Including phone conversations?" Brad asked. "That last over five minutes?"

"Yeah, so?"

"Just making the list. Have you cooked her anything? Not just nuking something, but using an actual stove."

"I just made her some soup when—"

"That counts. Take her to any chick flicks?"

Frowning, Flynn picked up a triangle of sandwich. "I don't know that it qualified as a chick flick." He set it down again. "Okay, yes. Once, but it was—"

"No explanations, this part of the quiz is true or false. We can move on to our essay section," Jordan assured him. "Picture your life in, let's say five years. That work?" he asked Brad.

"Some require ten, but I think we can be more lenient. Five works for me."

"Okay, picture your life in five years. Can you structure the visual without her being in it?"

"I don't know how I'm supposed to picture five years from now when I'm not sure what I'll be doing in five days."

But he could, he could see his house, with some of the long-term plans he had for it in place. He could see himself at the paper, walking Moe, hanging out with Dana. And he could see Malory at every angle. Walking down the stairs in the house, coming by the paper to meet him, chasing Moe out of the kitchen.

He went a little pale. "Oh, man."

"She's in there, isn't she?" Jordan asked.

"She's in there all right."

"Congratulations, son." Jordan slapped him on the shoulder. "You're in love."

"Wait a minute. What if I'm not ready?"

"Tough luck," Brad replied.

B R A D knew all about luck and decided his was in when he stepped out of the diner and spotted Zoe stopped at the traffic light.

She was wearing dark wraparound sunglasses and moving her lips in a way that made him assume she was singing along with the car stereo.

It wasn't stalking, exactly, if he just happened to hop in his car, zip out into traffic and follow. The fact that he cut off a pickup truck was completely incidental.

It was reasonable, even important, that they get to know each other better. He could hardly help Flynn if he didn't know the women Flynn was connected to.

That made sense.

It had nothing to do with obsession. Just because he'd bought a painting with her face in it, just because he couldn't get that face out of his mind, all that didn't mean he was obsessed.

He was merely interested.

And if he was practicing various opening lines under his breath, it was only because he understood the value of communication. He certainly wasn't nervous about speaking to a woman. He spoke to women all the time.

Women spoke to *him* all the time, if it came to that. He was considered one of the top eligible bachelors—and God, did he hate that term—in the country. Women went out of their way to talk to him.

If Zoe McCourt couldn't spare five minutes for some polite conversation, well, that was her loss.

By the time she pulled into a driveway, he'd worked himself into a mass of nerves and irritation. The vaguely annoyed glance she sent him when he pulled up behind her put a cap on it.

Feeling foolish and insulted, he climbed out.

"Are you following me?" she demanded.

"Excuse me?" In defense, his voice was flat and cold. "I think you're overestimating your charms. Flynn's worried about Malory. I saw you and thought you'd be able to tell me how she's doing."

Zoe continued to observe him warily as she unlocked her trunk. Her jeans were tight enough to afford him an intriguing view of firm female butt. She wore a short, snug red jacket with an equally snug striped top that stopped a full inch above the waistband of the jeans.

He noted, with some fascination that her belly button was pierced and sported a tiny silver bar. He actually felt his fingertips grow warm with the urge to touch it.

"I stopped by to see her before."

."Huh? Who? Oh, Malory." Now the back of his neck grew warm and he cursed himself. "How is she?"

"She looks tired, and a little down on herself."

"I'm sorry." He stepped forward as she began to unload the trunk. "Let me give you a hand."

"I can get it."

"I'm sure you can." He solved the matter by taking the two heavy sample books of wallpaper from her. "But I don't see any reason you should. Redecorating?"

She took out a paint sample book, a small toolbox—which he pulled away from her—a notebook, and some tile chips. "We contracted for this house. We're going to open the business here. It needs work."

He walked ahead, leaving her to slam the trunk. Yes, it did need work, but it had a sturdy look, and the lot was nicely established. Solid location, decent parking.

"Looks like it has good bones," he commented. "You have the foundation checked out?"

"Yes."

"Wiring up to code?"

She dug out the keys she'd picked up from the realtor. "Just because I'm a woman doesn't mean I don't know how to buy a house. I looked at a number of properties, and this was the best value, with the best location. Most of the work it needs is cosmetic."

She shoved open the door. "You can just dump them on the floor. Thanks. I'll tell Malory you asked about her."

Brad just kept walking so that she had to step back. Though it took some effort, he refused to let his gaze drift down to her navel again. "Are you always irritated when someone tries to help you?"

"I'm irritated when someone thinks I can't handle myself. Look, I don't have that much time to do what I'm here to do. I need to get started."

"Then I'll stay out of your way."

He studied the ceiling, the floor, the walls as he wandered through the entrance area. "Nice space."

He didn't detect any damp, but there was a definite chill. He wasn't sure if it was a faulty furnace or the woman who was blowing cold. "Which part are you taking?"

"Upstairs."

"Okay." He started up, nearly amused now by her impatient indrawn breath. "Nice stairs. Can't go wrong with white pine."

Some of the trim needed to be replaced, he noted. And the double-hung window at the top of the steps had yet to be upgraded. She'd need to see to that, get herself a double-glazed for insulation.

The walls had gone dingy, and there were a few cracks from settling. But that was easily seen to.

He liked the way the rooms split off and ran together, and wondered if she would remove some of the hollow-core doors altogether or replace them with something more solid and in tune with the feel of the house.

And what was she going to do about lighting? He didn't know anything about salons, but it seemed logical that good, strong lighting would be essential.

"Excuse me. I need my toolbox."

"What? Oh, sorry." He handed it to her, then ran his fingers over the chipped and peeling window trim. "You know, you could go with cherry for contrast here. Different woods, leaving the natural grain, going with warm tones. You're not going to cover these floors, are you?"

She took out her measuring tape. "No."

Why didn't he go away? She had work to do, thinking to do. And most of all she'd wanted to be alone in her wonderful building, planning and deciding and dreaming about how it was all going to be when she'd finished.

The colors, the textures, the tones, the smells. Everything.

And here he was, in her way, wandering around. All male and gorgeous and distracting in his perfect suit and his expensive shoes. He smelled, oh so subtly, of high-end soap and aftershave.

He probably paid more for a cake of soap then she had for the jeans and shirt she was wearing. And he thought he could just mill around, wafting in *her* air, making her feel clumsy and inferior.

"What are your plans for this room?"

She wrote down her measurements and kept her back to him. "This is the main salon. It's for hair, manicures, and makeup." When he didn't respond, she was compelled to look over her shoulder. He was staring contemplatively at her ceiling. "What?"

"We have these mini track lights. Very practical, but with a fun look. They have the advantage of being able to be set in a number of directions. You going for fun or elegant in here?"

"I don't see why it can't be both."

"Good point. Soft colors or bold?"

"Bold here, soft in the treatment rooms. Look, Bradley—"

"Ouch. That sounded like my mother." He'd already crouched down to flip through a sample book, and cast her a quick grin. "Do you guys have like a training center where you learn how to develop that withering tone?"

"Men aren't allowed to have that information. If I told you, I'd have to kill you. And I just don't have the time. We're going to close on the property in a month, and I want to have my plans outlined so I can start on them the minute we do."

"I can help you."

"I know what I'm doing and how I want to do it. I don't know why you assume—"

"Hold on. Boy, are you touchy." Wouldn't you think a woman who wore skintight jeans and decorated her navel would be a little more approachable? "I'm in the business, remember?" He tapped the HomeMakers logo on the sample book. "Not only that, but I like helping a building meet its potential. I can give you a hand with some labor and material."

"I'm not looking for a handout."

He set the book aside, slowly got to his feet. "I said a hand, not a handout. What is it about me that puts your back up?"

"Everything. That's unfair." She shrugged. "But it's true. I don't understand people like you, so I tend to distrust them."

"People like me?"

"Rich, privileged people who run American empires. I'm sorry, I'm sure you have some very nice qualities or you wouldn't be Flynn's friend. But you and I have nothing in common. Plus, I have a lot on my plate right now and no time to play games. So let's clear this up, then we can move on. I'm not going to have sex with you."

"Okay, well, obviously my life is no longer worth living."

She wanted to smile at that, nearly did. But she had reason to know his sort was very tricky. "Are you going to tell me that you're not hoping to sleep with me?"

He took a careful breath before speaking. She'd hooked the earpiece of her sunglasses in the V of her shirt, and those long, tawny eyes were staring very directly into his. "You and I both know there's no way for me to answer that question correctly. It's the mother of trick questions. Others in this category are, Do I look fat in this? Do you think she's pretty? And if you don't know, I'm certainly not going to tell you."

Now she had to bite the inside of her lip to hold back the laughter. "The last isn't a question."

"It's still a mystery and a trap. So why don't I just say I find you very attractive. And we have more in common than you seem to think, starting with a circle of friends. I'm willing to help you, Malory, and Dana with this place. None of you has to have sex with me in return. Though if the three of you wanted to get together and organize a nice tasteful orgy I wouldn't say no. Meanwhile, I'll let you get back to work."

He started out, then said casually as he walked down the stairs, "By the way, HomeMakers is having a sale on wall treatments—paper and paint—next month. Fifteen to thirty percent off all stock."

Zoe hurried to the top of the steps. "When next month?"

"I'll let you know."

So, she wasn't going to have sex with him. Brad shook his head as he walked to his car. That had been an unfortunate statement on her part. Obviously, she wasn't aware that the one thing no Vane could resist was a direct challenge.

His only plan had been to ask her out to dinner. Now, he decided as he studied the windows on the second level, he'd have to take a little time and work out a strategy.

Zoe McCourt was about to go under siege.

ZOE had other things on her mind. She was running late, but that was nothing new. There always seemed to be another flood of things to do or remember or fix right before she walked out the door.

"You give those cookies to Chuck's mother. She'll divvy them up." Zoe turned the car into the driveway two blocks from her own house, then sent her son a stern look. "I mean it, Simon. I don't have time to take them in myself. If I go to the door she'll keep me there for twenty minutes, and I'm already late."

"Okay, okay. I coulda walked."

"Yeah, but then I wouldn't've been able to do this." She grabbed him, dug her fingers into his ribs to make him squeal.

"Mom!"

"Simon!" she said in the same exasperated tone.

He was laughing as he got out and dragged his duffel from the backseat.

"You mind Chuck's mother, and don't keep everybody up all night. You've got Malory's number?"

"Yes, I've got Malory's number. And I know how to dial nine-one-one, and to run out of the house if I set it on fire when I play with matches."

"Smart guy. Come over here and give me a kiss."

He made a show of dragging his feet, keeping his head dipped to hide his grin as he approached her car window. "Make it quick. Somebody might see us."

"Just tell them I wasn't kissing you. I was yelling at you." She gave him a kiss, resisted hugging him. "See you tomorrow. Have a good time, baby."

"You, too, baby." He snickered, then raced for the house.

With a mother's skill, she backed out of the drive while watching her boy until he was safely inside.

Then she headed off to Malory's, and her first grown-up sleepover.

Chapter Seventeen

MALORY knew what was going on. Nobody wanted her to be alone, and her new friends were worried about her. Zoe had been so enthusiastic about the brainstorm of an all-girl sleepover that Malory hadn't been able to refuse.

The very fact that she'd wanted to refuse, had wanted to burrow into her cave alone, forced her to admit she needed a change.

She'd never been a loner, nor had she been much of a brooder in the past. When she was troubled, she went out, saw people. Bought things, gave a party.

Zoe's request for an all-nighter gave Malory the push to do all of that. She bought food and pretty new candles with citrusy scents. And fragrant soaps and fussy new guest towels, then some good wine.

She cleaned the apartment she'd been neglecting, spilled spicy potpourri into bowls. And groomed herself in the meticulous way that women groomed for other women.

By the time Dana arrived, she had cheese and fruit and fancy crackers set out, the candles lit and music set on low.

"Wow, pretty elegant around here. I should've dressed up some."

"You look great." Determined to be cheerful, Malory leaned in to kiss Dana's cheek. "I appreciate you guys doing this."

"Doing what?"

"Hanging out with me, giving me a boost. I've been feeling down the last couple of days."

"None of us figured on the energy drain this deal would be." She passed Malory a grocery bag, then set down her overnight case. "I bought extra supplies. Wine, Cheez-Its, chocolate truffles, and popcorn. You know, the four basic food groups." Dana flipped through the movie selection next to the entertainment center. "Did you rent every chick flick ever made?"

"Every one currently available on DVD. How about some wine?"

"You don't have to twist my arm. New perfume?"

"No, must be the candles."

"Nice. That's Zoe. Better pour another glass."

Zoe came in through the patio doors, loaded down with bags. "Cookies," she said a little breathlessly. "Videos, aromatherapy, and coffee cake for the morning."

"Nice job." Dana took one of the bags from her and handed her a glass of wine. Then she leaned closer and said, "How do you get your lashes to look like that? All sooty and spiky?"

"I'll show you. This is fun. I went by the house today to do some measuring and to look at some samples there in the space and light. I've got wallpaper books and paint chips in the car if we want to look later. Bradley Vane caught me while I was there. What's his story?"

"Golden boy with a social conscience." Dana attacked the Brie. "Star athlete, high school and college. Track a specialty. Honor student but not a nerd. Semi-engaged a couple of times, but always managed to wiggle out before it stuck. Been friends with Flynn just about from birth. Excellent body, which I've been fortunate enough to see through various stages. Interested in seeing it yourself?"

"Not that way. I haven't had much luck with men, so the only one who's going to be in my life for the time being is Simon. Oh, I love this song." She slipped out of her shoes to dance. "So, Mal, how's it going with Flynn?"

"Well, I love him, so it's pretty irritating. I wish I could dance like that."

"Like what?"

"All long legs and loose hips."

"Come on, then." Zoe set her wine down, held out her hands. "We'll work on it. You do one of two things. Pretend nobody's watching or pretend that this guy, this incredibly sexy guy, is watching. Either way, depending on your mood, you just let go."

"How come girls always end up dancing with girls?" Malory wondered as she tried to get her hips to move independent of the rest of her body, as Zoe's seemed to do.

"Because we're better at it."

"Actually," Dana said, helping herself to a little tree of green grapes, "it's a kind of social, sexual ritual. The female performs, tempts, and teases, the male observes, fantasizes, and selects. Or is selected. Jungle drums or the Dave Matthews Band, it comes down to the same thing."

"Are you going to dance?" Malory asked her.

"Sure." Popping one more grape, Dana got up. Hips and shoulders went into a sinuous rhythm as she moved toward Zoe. They slithered into a dance that was, to Malory's mind, both sexy and free.

"Now I'm totally outclassed."

"You're doing fine. Loosen your knees. And speaking of rituals, I have some ideas. But . . ." Zoe grabbed her wine again. "I think we should have some more wine before I bring it up."

"You can't do that," Dana complained. "I hate that. What's the idea?" She took Zoe's glass, had a hurried sip. "Look, I drank more. Tell me."

"Okay. Let's sit down."

Remembering her role as hostess, Malory brought the wine and the tray of food to the coffee table. "If this ritual has anything to do with leg waxing, I need much more wine first."

"No." Zoe laughed. "But I have an almost painless technique with hot wax. I can give you a Brazilian without anyone shedding a tear."

"A Brazilian?"

"Tidy up the bikini area. It leaves just a neat little strip so you can wear the tiniest thong without looking, well, unkempt."

"Oh." Instinctively Malory folded her hands over her crotch. "Not even if you use morphine and shackles."

"Honest, it's all in the wrist." Zoe explained. "Well, so . . . back to what I was saying," she continued. "I know we've all been reading and researching and trying to come up with theories and ideas to help Malory find the first key."

"And you've both been great. Really. I just feel like I'm missing something, some little thing that could open it all up."

"Maybe we've all missed something," Zoe countered. "The legend itself. Mortal woman mates with Celtic god and becomes queen. Female power. She has three daughters. Female again. One of their guardians is a female."

"Well, it is a fifty-fifty shot," Dana pointed out. "Even for gods."

"Wait. So when their souls are stolen and trapped *by a man*, it's said that three mortals, mortal *women*, have to find and turn the keys."

"Sorry, Zoe, I'm not following you. We already know

all this." Malory reached halfheartedly for a grape.

"Let's take it a little further. Gods, in Celtic lore, are, well, earthier than say the Greek or Roman ones. They're more like wizards and sorcerers than . . . what's the word? Um, omniscient beings. Is that right?" she asked Dana.

"Yeah."

"They have ties to the earth, to nature. Like, well, witches. There's black magic and white, but they both use natural elements and forces. And here's where you sort of have to step out of the box."

"We haven't been in the box since September the fourth," Dana pointed out.

"What if we were chosen because we're . . . well, because we're witches?"

Malory frowned at the level of wine in Zoe's glass. "How much did you have to drink before you got here?"

"No, just think about it. We look like them. Maybe we're somehow related to that . . . bloodline or something. Maybe we have power, but we just never knew it."

"The legend says mortal women," Malory reminded her.

"Witches aren't necessarily immortal. They're just people with more. I've been reading up. In Wicca the female witch has three stages. The maiden, the mother, the crone. And they pay homage to the goddess. They—"

"Wicca is a young religion, Zoe," Dana said.

"But its roots are old. And three, that's a magic number. There are three of us."

"I really think I'd know if I were a witch." Malory considered it as she sipped her wine. "And if this has somehow escaped my notice for nearly thirty years, what am I supposed to do about it now? Conjure something, cast a spell?"

"Turn Jordan into a horse's ass. Sorry," Dana shrugged when Malory stared at her. "Just daydreaming."

"We could try it. Together. I bought some things." Zoe jumped up, pulled open her bag. "Ritual candles," she said, digging through. "Incense. Table salt."

"Table salt?" Baffled, Malory picked up the dark blue box of Morton's and studied the cheerful girl with her umbrella.

"You can make a protective circle with it. It wards off evil spirits. Ash wands. Sort of wands. I bought a baseball bat and cut it up to make them."

"Martha Stewart meets Glenda the Good Witch." Dana picked up the thin wooden wand, waved it. "Shouldn't it sprinkle fairy dust?"

"Drink more wine," Zoe ordered. "Crystals. Amethyst and rose quartz and this really great ball." She held up the globe.

"Where'd you get all this loot?" Malory demanded.

"New Age shop at the mall. Tarot cards—Celtic ones because it seemed right. And—"

"A Ouija board!" Dana pounced on it. "Man, oh, man, I haven't seen one of these since I was a kid."

"I found it at the toy store. They don't carry them in the New Age place."

"We had this pj party when I was a kid. Got all toked up on Pepsi and M&Ms and lit candles. Everybody asked the name of the guy they'd marry. Mine came up PTZBAH." Dana gave a sentimental sigh. "It was really sweet. Let's do the Ouija first," Dana suggested. "For old times' sake."

"Okay, but we've got to do it right. Take it seriously." Zoe rose to turn off the lights and music.

"I wonder if Ptzbah is still out there." Dana slid to the floor, opened the box.

"Wait. We have to set up the ritual. I got a book."

They sat in a circle on the floor.

"We have to cleanse our minds," Zoe instructed. "Visualize opening our chakras."

"I never open my chakras in public." Dana giggled, unrepentant, until Malory slapped her knee.

"And we light the ritual candles. White for purity. Yel-

NORA ROBERTS

276

low for memory. Purple for power." Zoe bit her lip as she carefully ignited the tapers. "Place the crystals. Amethyst for . . . shoot." She reached for her book, flipped pages. "Here. Amethyst for intuition. And the incense. Rose quartz for psychic power and divination."

"It's pretty," Malory decided. "Soothing."

"I think we should all take turns with the Tarot cards, and maybe try some chants, but let's make Dana happy and do this first." Zoe set the board between them and placed the pointer in its center.

"We have to concentrate," she said. "Focus our minds and our powers on one question."

"Can it be about the love of my life? I pine for Ptzbah."

"No." Zoe swallowed a laugh and tried to look stern. "This is serious business. We want the location of the first key. Malory should do the asking, but you and I need to think it."

"We should close our eyes." Malory rubbed her fingers on her pants, took a deep breath. "Ready?"

They laid fingertips on the pointer, sat in silence.

"Should we call on the Otherworld or something?" Malory whispered. "Pay our respects, ask for guidance? What?"

Zoe opened one eye. "Maybe you should call on the ones behind the Curtain of Dreams."

"Denizens," Dana suggested. "That's a good word. Call on the denizens behind the Curtain of Dreams for guidance."

"Okay, here goes. Everybody quiet, everyone be calm. Concentrate." Malory waited ten seconds in silence. "We call on the denizens behind the Curtain of Dreams, to aid and to guide us in our, um, in our quest."

"Tell them you're one of the chosen ones," Zoe said out of the corner of her mouth and was shushed by Dana.

"I am one of the chosen, one of the seekers of the keys. Time is short. I ask you to show me the way to the key so that we can free the souls of . . . Dana, no pushing the pointer."

"I'm not. Really."

Mouth dry, Malory opened her eyes and watched the pointer shudder under their fingertips.

"The candles," Zoe whispered. "Oh, jeez, look at the candles."

The flames shot up, a trio of slim gold edged with red. Light began to throb, like a pulse. Something blew cold through the room and set those flames dancing.

"This is wild!" Dana exclaimed. "I mean seriously wild."

"It's moving." The pointer jerked, with Malory's fingers trembling on it. She heard nothing but the roar of blood in her own head as she watched it slide from letter to letter.

YOUR DEATH

Her gasp was still strangled in her throat when the room suddenly burst with light and wind. She heard someone scream, threw up an arm to shield her eyes as a form coalesced out of a whirlpool of air.

The board shattered as if made of glass.

"What are you playing at?" Rowena stood in the center of them, the sharp heel of her shoe digging into a shard of the board. "Have you no more sense than to open a door to such things as you cannot understand or defend against?"

With an annoyed sigh, she stepped gracefully out of the circle and picked up the wine. "I'd like a glass, please."

"How did you get here? How did you know?" Malory pushed herself up on rubbery legs.

"It's fortunate for you that I did both." She picked up the salt, and upended the box over the remains of the board.

"Oh, now, just a damn minute."

"Sweep it up together," Rowena ordered Zoe. "Then burn it. I'd very much appreciate a glass of wine." She handed the bottle to Malory, then sat on the sofa.

Outraged, Malory stalked into the kitchen, yanked a wineglass from the cupboard. She marched back and shoved the glass into Rowena's hand. "I didn't invite you into my home."

"On the contrary, you invited me and whoever else chose to come through the opening."

"Then we are witches."

Rowena's expression changed as she looked over at Zoe's rapt face. "No, not the way you mean." Her tone was more gentle now, patient teacher to eager student. "Though every woman has some magic. Still, together your powers are trebled, and you had just enough skill, just enough desire to issue an invitation. I'm not the only one who answered it. You felt him," she said to Malory. "You've felt him before."

"Kane." She cupped her elbows and shuddered as the memory of the cold seeped into her. "He moved the pointer, not us. He was playing with us."

"He threatened Malory." The thrill forgotten, Zoe was on her feet now. "What are you going to do about it?"

"All I can."

"Maybe that's not good enough." Dana reached up to link her hand with Malory's. "I heard you scream. I saw your face when you did. You felt something Zoe and I didn't, and it was real terror. It was real pain."

"It's the cold. It's . . . I can't describe it."

"The absence of all warmth," Rowena murmured. "All hope, all life. But he can't touch you unless you allow it."

"Allow it? How the hell did she . . ." Zoe broke off, looked down at the broken board at her feet. "Oh, God. I'm so sorry. Mal, I'm so sorry."

"It's not your fault. It's not." She took Zoe's hand, so for a moment the three of them were linked.

Seeing them, Rowena smiled into her wine.

"We were looking for answers, and you had an idea. Which is more than I've had the last couple of days. We tried something. Maybe it was the wrong something," she added as she whipped back to Rowena, "but that doesn't give you the right to slap at us for it."

"You're absolutely right. I apologize." She leaned forward to spread Brie on a cracker, then tapped a finger against the Tarot deck. Light flickered over them, then was gone. "These will do you no harm. You may develop a skill for readings, or even find you have a gift for them."

"You . . ." Zoe pressed her lips together. "If you hadn't come when you did . . ."

"It's my duty, and my wish, to keep you from harm. When and how I can. Now I should go, leave you to your evening." Rowena rose, looked around the room. "You have a pretty home, Malory. It suits you."

Feeling ungracious and childish, Malory huffed out a breath. "Why don't you stay, finish your wine?"

Surprise ran across Rowena's face. "That's very kind of you. I'd like that. It's been a very long time since I've sat in the company of women. I've missed it."

It wasn't very strange, after the initial awkwardness, to have a woman who'd lived for thousands of years sitting in her living room drinking her wine.

And it became apparent by the time they started on the truffles that women—goddess or mortal—were the same under the skin.

"I rarely fuss with it," Rowena said while Zoe worked her mane of hair into an elegant upsweep. "It's not one of my talents, so I tend to wear it down. I've cut it occasionally, but I always regret it."

"Not everyone can wear it simply as you do, and still look regal."

Rowena studied herself in the hand mirror as Zoe worked, then tilted the glass to study her stylist. "I'd love to have your hair. It's so striking."

"Couldn't you? I mean if you wanted to look a certain way, couldn't you just . . ." Zoe fluttered her fingers and made Rowena laugh.

"That isn't my gift."

"What about Pitte?" Dana rolled over on the couch. "What's his deal?"

"He's a warrior, full of pride and arrogance and will. He's maddening and exciting." She lowered the mirror.

"Zoe, you're an artist."

"Oh, I just like playing with hair." She stepped in front of Rowena and released a few tendrils around her face. "A great look for that important board meeting or the after-Oscars bash. Sexy, female, and powerful. Well, you give that off no matter what the do."

"Excuse me, but I just have to ask," said Dana, "what's it like to be with the same guy for, well, basically forever?"

"He's the only man I want," Rowena answered.

"Oh, come on, come, on. You've got to have had a few hundred fantasies about other men in the last couple of millennia."

"Of course." Rowena set the mirror down, and her lips bowed into a dreamy smile. "There was a young waiter once, in Rome. Such a face and form. With eyes so dark it seemed I could see worlds drowning in them. And he served me coffee and a bun. He called me *bella donna* with such a knowing smile. While I ate my bun I imagined biting into his tasty bottom lip."

She pressed her own together, then laughed. "I painted him in my studio, and let him flirt with me outrageously. And when I nudged him along after a session, I would drag Pitte away from whatever he might be doing and seduce him."

"You never cheated."

"I love my man," Rowena said simply. "We're bound, body, heart, soul. There's magic in that, more potent than any spell, more wicked than any curse." She reached up, laid a hand over Zoe's. "You loved a boy, and he gave you a son. For that, you'll always love him, even though he was weak and betrayed you."

"Simon's my world."

"And you've made it a bright and loving world. I so envy you your child. You." She rose, stepped closer to trail her fingers over Dana's hair. "You loved one who was no longer a boy, yet not quite a man. For that, you've never forgiven him."

"Why should I?"

"There's a question," Rowena replied.

"What about me?" Malory asked, and Rowena sat on the arm of the sofa, touched a hand to her shoulder.

"You love the man so much, so fast and fierce, it makes you doubt your own heart. For that, you can't trust him."

"How can I trust what doesn't make sense?"

"As long as you need to ask, you won't have the answer." She leaned down, pressed her lips to Malory's brow. "Thank you for having me in your home, for sharing yourselves with me. Here, take this."

She held out her hand, offered Malory the pale blue stone in the palm. "What is it?"

"A small charm. Put it under your pillow tonight. You'll sleep well. I must go." She smiled a little, lifting her hand to her hair as she rose and crossed to the glass door. "I wonder what Pitte will think of my hair. Good night." She opened the door and slipped into the night.

Zoe waited three seconds, then scurried to the door. Framing her face with her hands, she pressed it close to the glass. "Shoot. I thought she'd go poof or something, but she's just walking. Like a normal person."

"She seems pretty normal." Dana shifted around to reach the popcorn. "You know, for a goddess with a few thousand years under her belt."

"But sad." Malory turned the blue stone over in her hand. "There's all that sophistication and cool amusement on the surface, but there's this terrible sadness under it. She meant it when she said she was envious of you for having Simon, Zoe."

"It's funny to think about." Zoe wandered back, chose a brush, a rat-tail comb, and pins, then moved behind the sofa. "She lives in that big, well, castle, really, with all those beautiful things." She began to brush Dana's hair. "And she's beautiful, even wise, I think. She's rich and has a man she loves. She's traveled and she can paint those wonderful pictures."

Dividing sections of Dana's hair, she began to braid. "But she envies someone like me because I have a kid. Do you think she can't have children? I didn't want to ask, it's so personal. But I wonder why she couldn't. If she can do all the things she can do, why couldn't she have a baby?"

"Maybe Pitte doesn't want to have kids." Dana shrugged her shoulders. "Some people don't. What're you doing back there, Zoe?"

"New do. I'm mixing some skinny braids in. It should be young and kicky. Do you?"

"Do I what?"

"Want to have kids?"

Dana munched popcorn and considered. "Yeah. I'd like to have a couple. I figure if I don't find a guy I can stand being with for the long term in the next few years, I'll just do it on my own. You know, make love with medical science."

"You'd do that?" Fascinated, Malory reached into the bowl. "Raise a child on your own. I mean, on purpose," she added, looking up at Zoe. "You know what I mean."

"Sure, I would." Dana settled the bowl between them. "Why not? I'm healthy. I think I'd be good at the parenting thing, that I have a lot to offer a kid. I'd want to make sure I had solid financial security first, but if I'm cruising toward say, thirty-five and there's no guy in the picture, I'd do the deed."

"Sort of takes the romance out of it," Malory commented.

"Maybe, but it gets results. You've got to look at the big picture. If there's something you want, deep down want, you can't let anything stop you from getting it."

Malory thought of her dream, of the child she'd held in her arms. Of the light filling her world, her heart. "Even if you really, really want something, there are lines."

"Well, murder and a certain amount of mayhem are discouraged. I'm talking about making important choices, then going the distance and dealing with the results. What about you, Zoe? Would you do it again? The raise-a-kid-on-your-own part?" Dana asked.

"I don't think I'd set out to do it again. It's hard. There's nobody to share the load with, and sometimes the load seems impossible for one person. But more, there's nobody who looks at the child and feels what you feel. Nobody to share that love and pride and, I don't know, surprise with."

"Were you scared?" Malory asked her.

"Yeah. Oh, yeah. I still get scared. I think it's supposed to be scary because it's so important. Do you want babies, Mal?"

"I do." She rubbed the stone gently between her fingers. "More than I realized."

B Y three, Dana and Zoe were sleeping in her bed, and Malory was picking up the worst of the debris, too restless to settle in on the sofa. There were too many thoughts, too many images flitting around in her mind.

She studied the little blue stone again. Maybe it would work. She'd accepted bigger things than having a piece of rock under her pillow as the cure for the insomnia that was plaguing her.

Or maybe she hadn't. Maybe she really hadn't accepted any of it, not in that deep-down way Dana spoke of. She was exhausted, yet she wasn't putting the stone under her pillow and letting herself try.

She claimed to love Flynn, yet she was waiting, tucking a small part of herself safely away and waiting for the feeling to pass. And at the same time, she was annoyed and hurt that he didn't simply fall over in love with her and even things out.

After all, how could she keep her balance, outline plans, and keep it all tidy if everything between them wasn't equal?

Everything belongs in its place, doesn't it? Everything has its slot. And if it doesn't fit just right, well, you're not the one who's going to change. That's up to the other guy.

With a sigh, she dropped down on the couch. She'd pursued a career in art like a demon because while fate hadn't cooperated by giving her talent, she wasn't about to admit that all those years of study and work had been wasted.

She made it fit.

She'd stayed at The Gallery because it was comfortable, because it was sensible and convenient. She'd made noise about striking out on her own one day. But she hadn't meant it. Too big a risk, too messy. If Pamela hadn't come along, she would still be at The Gallery.

And why did she resent Pamela with every fiber of her being? All right, the woman was pushy and had all the taste of overcooked trout, but a more flexible woman than Malory Price would've found a way around that. She resented Pamela primarily because she'd shifted the balance, she'd changed the lines.

She just hadn't fit.

Now there was the business she and Dana and Zoe were starting. She'd been the one to drag her feet on that. Oh, she'd come through in the end, but how many times had she questioned that decision since? How many times had she considered backing out because it was too hard to see how it could all be neatly done?

And she hadn't moved forward on it. Hadn't gone back to the property or made any plans, put out any feelers for artists and craftspeople.

Hell, she hadn't even mailed off the application for her business license. Because once she did, she was committed.

She was using the key as an excuse not to take the final step. Oh, she was looking for it, giving the quest her time and her energy. One thing she took seriously was responsibility.

But here and now, alone and awake at three in the morning, it was time to admit one undeniable fact. Her life may have changed in a dozen strange and fascinating ways in three weeks' time, but she hadn't changed at all.

She put the stone under her pillow. "There's still time," she murmured, and curled up to sleep.

Chapter Eighteen

WHEN she woke, the apartment was silent as a
tomb. She lay still a moment, studying the lance
of light that sneaked through the chink in the patio drapes
and onto her floor.

Morning, she thought. Full morning. She didn't remember falling asleep. Better, much, much better, she
didn't remember tossing and turning and worrying about
sleep.

Slowly, she slid a hand under her pillow, feeling for
the stone. She frowned, groping now, then sat up to lift
the pillow. There was no stone under it. She searched
under the cushions, on the floor, under the couch, before
sitting down again with a huff of confusion.

Stones didn't just disappear.

Or maybe they did. When they'd served their purpose.
She'd slept and slept well, hadn't she? Just as promised.
In fact, she felt wonderful. As if she'd had a nice, relaxing
vacation.

"Okay, thanks, Rowena."

She stretched out her arms, took a deep breath. And drew in the unmistakable scent of coffee.

Unless the gift included morning coffee, someone else was up.

She walked into the kitchen and found a pleasant surprise.

Zoe's coffee cake was on the counter, set on a pretty plate and protected with Saran Wrap. The coffeepot was on warm and was three-quarters full, and the morning paper was neatly folded and placed between.

Malory picked up the note tucked under the cake plate and read Zoe's somewhat exotic mix of cursive and printing.

Good morning! Had to get going—have a teacher's conference at ten.

Ten, Malory thought with an absent glance at the kitchen clock. Her mouth fell open when she saw that it was nearly eleven.

"That can't be right. Can it?"

Didn't want to wake either of you, tried to be quiet.

"You must move like a ghost," Malory said aloud.

Dana's got to be at work at two. Just in case, I set the alarm clock in your room for her. Set it for noon so she wouldn't have to rush and would have time for breakfast.

I had the best *time. Just wanted to tell you, both of you, that whatever happens I'm so glad I found you. Or we found each other. However it worked, I'm just really grateful you're my friends.*

Maybe next time we can get together at my place.

Love, Zoe.

"Looks like it's a day for gifts." Smiling, Malory set the note down where Dana would find it, too. Hoping to extend her good mood, she cut a sliver of cake, poured the coffee. She arranged them on a tray, added the paper and a small glass of juice, then carried it all out to her patio.

Fall was teasing the air. She'd always enjoyed the faint,

smoky scent that autumn brought with it when the leaves began to take on hints of the vibrant colors to come.

She needed to pick up some potted mums, she noted as she broke off a piece of coffee cake. She was behind schedule on that. And some pumpkins and gourds for festive arrangements. She would gather some leaves, the maple ones once they'd turned scarlet.

She could pick up some extra things and do something fun for Flynn's front porch.

She sipped coffee while she skimmed the front page. Reading the morning paper was a different experience now that she'd met Flynn. She liked wondering how he decided what went where and how he juggled it all— stories, ads, pictures, typeface, tone—and made it one cohesive whole.

She nibbled and sipped her way through, then felt her heart give a quick jolt when she came to his column.

Odd, wasn't it, that she'd seen it before. Week after week. What had she thought? she wondered. Cute guy, nice eyes, or something just that casual and forgettable. She'd read his column, had either agreed or disagreed. She hadn't taken any notice of the work and effort he put into it, what turned his mind to whatever subject he wrote about that week.

It was different now that she knew him, now that she could hear his voice speaking the words she read. She could envision his face, its expressions. And have some insight into the workings of his very flexible mind.

What defines the artist? she read.

By the time she'd finished the column and was going back to read it through a second time, she'd fallen in love with him all over again.

FLYNN sat on the corner of a desk and listened while one of his reporters pitched him an idea for an article about a local man who collected clowns.

Stuffed clown dolls, clown statues, clown pictures. Porcelain clowns, plastic clowns, clowns with dogs. Clowns that danced or sang or drove little clown cars.

"He's got more than five thousand clowns, not including clown memorabilia."

Flynn tuned out for a moment, as the very idea of five thousand clowns in one place at one time was slightly terrifying. He imagined them banding together in a clown army and waging war with seltzer bottles and rubber bats.

All those big red noses, all that maniacal laughter. All those huge, scary smiles.

"Why?" Flynn asked.

"Why?"

"Why does he have five thousand clowns?"

"Oh." Tim, a young reporter who habitually wore suspenders and too much hair gel, creaked back in his chair. "See, his father started the collection back in the twenties or something. It's like this generational deal. He started adding to it himself, you know, like in the fifties, then the whole bunch of them got passed to him when his father died. Some of his collection is like museum quality. This stuff goes for real bucks on eBay."

"Okay, give it a run. Take a photographer. I want a shot of the whole collection with the guy in it. And him with a couple of the more interesting pieces. Get him to give you the history or significance of specific pieces. Play up the father-son connection, but lead off with the numbers and a couple of pieces from each end of the money scale. It could work for the Weekender section. And Tim, try to edit out the 'you knows' and 'likes' when you interview him."

"Got it."

Flynn looked over to see Malory standing between the desks holding an enormous pot of rust-colored mums. Something about the sparkle in her eye made the rest of the room fade away.

"Hi. Doing some gardening?"

"Maybe. Is this a bad time?"

"No. Come on back. How do you feel about clowns?"

"Wrathful when they're painted on black velvet."

"Good one. Tim?" he called back. "Get some shots of any clown paintings on black velvet. Sublime to ridiculous and back again," Flynn added. "It could be good."

She stepped into the office ahead of him, continuing on to set the flowers on his window ledge. "I wanted to—"

"Wait." He held up a finger while he tuned in to the call coming out of his police scanner. "Hold that thought," he told her, and poked his head back out the door. "Shelly, there's a TA, five hundred block of Crescent. Local PD and EMTs responding. Take Mark."

"TA?" Malory repeated when he turned back to her.

"Traffic accident."

"Oh. I was thinking just this morning how much you have to juggle and weigh and shape to put out the paper every day." She bent down to pat the snoring Moe. "And you manage to have a life at the same time."

"In a manner of speaking."

"No, you have a very good life. Friends, family, work that satisfies you, a house, a silly dog. I admire that." She straightened. "I admire you."

"Wow. You must've had a really good time last night."

"I did. I'll tell you about that, but I don't want to—what is it—smother my lead."

"Bury the lead."

"Right." She stepped over the dog, laid her hands on Flynn's shoulders. And leaning in, kissed him. Long, long and warm. "Thank you."

His skin had started to hum. "What for? Because if it was really good, maybe you should thank me again."

"Okay." This time she linked her hands behind his head and added a bit of heat to the warmth.

Outside the office, applause broke out.

"Jesus, I've got to get blinds for this place." He tried

the psychological angle of shutting the door. "I don't mind being the hero, but maybe you should tell me what dragon I slayed."

"I read your column this morning."

"Yeah? Usually if somebody likes my column they just say 'Nice job, Hennessy.' I like your way better."

" 'It isn't only the artist holding brush and vision who paints the picture,' " she quoted. " 'It's those who look and see the power and the beauty, the strength and the passion, who bring brushstroke and color to life.' Thank you."

"You're welcome."

"Every time I start feeling sorry for myself because I'm not living in Paris and setting the art world on its ear, I'm going to take out your column and remind myself what I've got. What I am."

"I think you're extraordinary."

"Today, so do I. I woke up feeling better than I have in days. Amazing what a good night's sleep will do—or a little blue stone under the pillow."

"You lost me."

"It's not important. Just something Rowena gave me. She joined our little sleepover last night."

"Yeah? What was she wearing?"

Laughing, she sat on the edge of his desk. "She didn't stay long enough for the pajama section of the night's entertainment, but you could say she arrived in the nick. The three of us were fooling around with a Ouija board."

"You've got to be kidding."

"No. Zoe had this theory that maybe the three of us were witches but didn't know it. Which is why we were chosen . . . and really, it made some sense at the time. In any case, things got very strange. Candle flames rising, wind blowing. And Kane, he got in. Rowena said we'd opened a door, like an invitation."

"Damn it, Malory. Goddamn it! What're you doing playing around with—with mystical forces? He's already had a shot at you. You could've been hurt."

He had such a face, she thought. Such a great face. It could change from interested to amused to furious in a split second. "That's something Rowena made very clear last night. There's no point in being angry with me about it now."

"I didn't have the option of being angry with you before now."

"True enough." She grunted when Moe, awakened by the temper in Flynn's voice, tried to jump in her lap. "You're absolutely right that we shouldn't have played with something we didn't understand. I'm sorry, believe me, and it isn't something I plan on trying again."

He reached over to give her hair a quick tug. "I'm trying to have an argument here. The least you could do is cooperate."

"I'm too happy with you to argue today. Let's pencil something in for next week. Besides, I just came by to bring you the flowers. I've interrupted your day long enough."

He glanced at the mums—the second bunch of flowers she'd brought to him. "You're sure cheerful today."

"Why shouldn't I be? I'm a woman in love, who's made what I feel are very good decisions about . . ."

"About?" he prompted when her eyes went blank.

"Choices," she mumbled. "Moments of decision, moments of truth. Why didn't I think of that before? Maybe it was your house, but my dream perception of perfection turned it around. Made it all fit. More mine than yours. Or maybe that has nothing to do with it. And it's just you."

"What is?"

"The key. I need to search your house. Is that going to be a problem?"

"Ah . . ."

Impatient now, she waved away his hesitation. "Look, if you have anything personal or embarrassing tucked away like skin magazines or adventurous sex toys, I'll give you a chance to get them out. Or promise to ignore them."

"The skin mags and adventurous sex toys are all locked in the vault. I'm afraid I can't give you the combination."

She moved into him, trailed her hands up his chest. "I know it's a lot to ask. I wouldn't like anyone poking through my place when I wasn't there."

"Not that much to poke through. But I don't want any grief about how I should spring for new underwear and use what I've got as dustrags."

"I'm not your mother. Will you let Jordan know I'm coming?"

"He's off somewhere today." Flynn pulled his keys out of his pocket, worked the house key off the chain. "You think you'll still be there when I get home?"

"Why don't I make sure I'm there when you get home?"

"Why don't you? Then I'll call Jordan, tell him to stay away. He can bunk with Brad tonight, and I can have you all to myself."

She took the key, bumped her lips lightly on his. "I'll look forward to being had."

The wicked gleam in her eye kept him grinning for an hour after she'd gone.

MALORY jogged up the steps to Flynn's front door. She was going to be systematic, slow and thorough, she told herself.

She should have thought of this before. It was like connecting the dots.

The paintings reflected moments of change, of destiny. Certainly her life had changed when she'd fallen for Flynn. And this was Flynn's house, she thought as she stepped inside. Hadn't he said he'd bought it when he'd accepted *his* destiny?

Looking within and without, she remembered as she merely stood and tried to absorb the feel of the place. Inside the house, outside in the yard?

Or was it more metaphorical, in that she'd begun to see herself inside this space?

Light and shadows. The house was full of both.

She could only be grateful it wasn't full of things. Flynn's spartan style was going to make the search simpler.

She started in the living room, automatically wincing at the couch. She looked under the cushions, found eighty-nine cents in loose change, a Bic lighter, a paperback edition of a Robert Parker novel, and cookie crumbs.

Unable to stand it, she hunted up the vacuum cleaner and a dustrag and began to clean as she went.

This two-for-one process kept her in the kitchen for more than an hour. At the end of it she was sweaty and the kitchen sparkled, but she hadn't turned up anything resembling a key.

She switched gears and headed upstairs. She'd begun and ended her dream upstairs, she recalled. Maybe that was symbolic. And certainly there couldn't be anything up here in as deplorable shape as the kitchen.

One glance at the bathroom disabused her of that notion. Even love—of a man and of order—had its limits, she decided, and shut the door without going inside.

She stepped into his office and was immediately charmed. All the dark thoughts that had damned him for a pig vanished.

It wasn't neat. God knew, it needed a good dusting, and there was enough dog hair balled in the corners to knit an afghan. But the walls were sunny, the desk was a beauty, and the framed posters showed an eye for art and style that she hadn't given him credit for.

"You've got all these wonderful sides to you, don't you?" She trailed her fingers over the desk, impressed by the stack of files, amused by the action figures.

It was a good work space. A good thinking space, she imagined. He didn't give a damn about the state of his kitchen. His sofa was just a place to take a nap or stretch out and read a book. But he took care with his surroundings when it was important to him.

Beauty, knowledge, courage. She'd been told she would need all three. In the dream there had been beauty—love, home, art. Then the knowledge that it was illusion. And finally the courage to break that illusion.

Maybe that was a part of it.

And love would forge the key.

Well, she loved Flynn. She accepted that she loved Flynn. So where was the damn key?

She turned a circle, then wandered over to take a closer look at his art collection. Pinup girls. He was such a . . . guy, she decided. A very clever guy.

There was a sexual punch to the photographs, but an innocence underlying that. Betty Grable's legs, Rita Hayworth's mane of hair, Monroe's unforgettable face.

Legends, as much for their beauty as their talent. Goddesses of the screen.

Goddesses.

Her fingers shook as she took the first print from the wall.

She had to be right. This had to be it.

But she examined every print, every frame, then every inch of the room, and found nothing.

Refusing to be discouraged, she sat at his desk. She was close. A step off, one way or the other, but close. The pieces were all there, she was certain of it now. She just needed to find the right pattern and make them fit.

She needed to get out in the air for a while, let it turn over in her mind.

She would do something ordinary while it brewed in there.

No, not something ordinary. Something inspired. Something artful.

*   *   *

FLYNN decided it was time to reverse the roles back to where they had started, and so he stopped off on the way home to buy her flowers. There was a bite of fall in the air, and its nip had already teased color into the trees. The surrounding hills were hazed with reds and golds and umbers over the green.

Over those hills, a three-quarter moon would rise to-night.

Did she think of that, he wondered, and worry?

Of course she did. It would be impossible for a woman like Malory to do otherwise. Still, she'd been happy when she came to his office. He meant to keep her that way.

He would take her out to dinner. Maybe drive into Pittsburgh for a change of scene. A long drive, a fancy dinner—that would appeal to her, keep her mind off . . .

The minute he stepped in the front door, he knew something was off.

It smelled . . . good.

A little lemony, he thought as he approached the living room. A little spicy. With female undertones. Did women just sort of exude scent when they'd been in a place for a few hours?

"Mal?"

"Back here! In the kitchen!"

The dog beat him by a mile and was already being given a biscuit, a stroke, and a firm nudge out the back door. Flynn wasn't sure what made his mouth water, the scents pumping out of the stove or the woman wearing a white bib apron.

God, who knew an apron could be sexy?

"Hi. What're you doing?"

"Cooking." She shut the back door. "I know it's an eccentric use for a kitchen, but call me crazy. Flowers?" Her eyes went soft, almost dewy. "They're pretty."

"You are too. Cooking?" He tossed his embryonic

plans for the evening aside without a qualm. "Would that involve anything resembling dinner?"

"It would." She took the flowers, kissed him over them. "I decided to dazzle you with my culinary talents, so I went to the grocery store. You didn't have anything in here that qualified as actual food."

"Cereal. I have a lot of cereal."

"I noticed." Because he didn't own a vase, she filled a plastic pitcher with water for the flowers. The fact that she didn't cringe while doing so made her very proud of herself. "You also didn't appear to own any of the usual implements used in preparing actual food. Not a single wooden spoon."

"I don't understand why they make spoons out of wood. Haven't we progressed beyond carving tools out of trees?" He picked one up off the counter, then frowned. "Something's different in here. Something changed."

"It's clean."

Shock registered on his face as he stared around the room. "It *is* clean. What did you do, hire a brigade of elves? What do they charge by the hour?"

"They work for flowers." She sniffed at them, and decided they looked very sweet in the plastic pitcher after all. "You're paid in full."

"You cleaned. That's so . . . weird."

"Presumptuous, but I got carried away."

"No, 'presumptuous' isn't the word that springs to mind." He took her hand, kissed her fingers. "The word's 'wow.' Should I be really embarrassed?"

"I won't if you won't."

"Deal." He drew her close, rubbed his cheek against hers. "And you're cooking. In the oven."

"I wanted to take my mind off things for a while."

"So did I. I was going to play the let's-go-out-to-a-fancy-dinner card, but you trumped my ace."

"You can tuck the ace up your sleeve and play it any-time. Putting things in order helps clear my mind, and there was a lot to put in order around here. I didn't find the key."

"Yeah, I got that. I'm sorry."

"I'm close." She stared at the steam puffing out of a pot as if the answer might appear in it. "I feel like I'm just missing a step somewhere. Well, we'll talk about that. Dinner's about ready. Why don't you pour the wine. I think it'll complement the meat loaf."

"Sure." He picked up the wine she had breathing on the counter, then set it down again. "Meat loaf? You made meat loaf."

"Mashed potatoes too—shortly," she added as she set up the mixer she'd brought over from her own kitchen. "And green beans. It seemed harmonious, considering your column. And I assumed that since you used the meal, you must like meat loaf."

"I'm a guy. We live for meat loaf. Malory." Ridiculously moved, he caressed her cheek. "I should've brought you more flowers."

She laughed and got to work on the potatoes she'd boiled. "Those will do nicely, thanks. This is actually my first meat loaf. I'm more a toss-some-pasta-together or a sauté-some-chicken girl. But I got the recipe from Zoe, who swears it's foolproof and guy-friendly. She claims Simon inhales it."

"I'll try to remember to chew." Then he took her arm to turn her toward him and moved in, slowly, ran his hands up her body until his fingers skimmed her jaw. He laid his lips on hers, softly, sliding her into the kiss the way he might slide her into a feather bed.

Her heart did one long, lazy roll even as the mists shimmered over her brain. The rubber spatula she held slipped out of limp fingers as everything inside her melted against him, into him.

He felt it, that shudder and give, that surrender to self as much as to him. When he eased her back, her eyes were blue and blurry. It was woman, he realized, who had the power to make man feel like a god.

"Flynn."

His lips curved as he brushed them over her forehead. "Malory."

"I . . . I forgot what I was doing."

He bent down to retrieve the spatula. "I think you were mashing potatoes."

"Oh. Right. Potatoes." Feeling a bit drunk, she walked to the sink to wash the spatula.

"This has to be the nicest thing anyone's ever done for me."

"I love you." She pressed her lips together, stared out the window. "Don't say anything. I don't want to make things uncomfortable for either of us. I've been thinking about this a lot. I know I've rushed and I've pushed. Neither of which is much like me." She spoke briskly now as she went back to the mixer.

"Malory—"

"Really, you don't need to say anything. It'd be enough, more than enough for now, if you just accepted it, maybe enjoyed it a little. It seems to me love shouldn't be a weapon or a device or a weight. Its beauty is that it be a gift, with no strings attached to it. Just like this meal."

She smiled, though the steady way he watched her was unnerving. "So, why don't you pour the wine, then wash up? And we'll both just enjoy it."

"Okay."

It could wait, Flynn thought. Maybe it was meant to wait. In any case, the words in his head sounded off-key when compared with the simplicity of hers.

So they would enjoy each other, and the meal she'd prepared in the awkward, homely kitchen with fresh flowers arranged in a plastic pitcher.

As beginnings went, this one had elements of both of

them. Wasn't it interesting how one managed to complement the other?

"You know, if you made me a list of stuff I should have in here, I could pick it up."

She arched her brows, took the wine he offered, then pulled a little notepad out of her apron pocket. "This is already half full. I was planning to wait until you were lulled into complacency by meat and potatoes."

He flipped through the notebook and noted that items were listed under specific headings. Foodstuffs, Cleaning Supplies—with subheadings Kitchen, Bathroom, Laundry—Household Necessities.

Jesus, the woman was irresistible.

"Am I going to need to take out a loan?"

"Think of it as an investment." Taking the notebook from him, she tucked it into his shirt pocket, then concentrated on the potatoes. "Oh, by the way, I really like the art in your office upstairs."

"Art?" It took him a minute. "Oh, my girls. Really?"

"Clever, nostalgic, sexy, stylish. It's a great room altogether, which I admit was something of a relief to me, considering the rest of the house. Enough that I wasn't flattened by disappointment when my brainstorm about the key didn't pan out." She drained the beans that she'd dashed with basil into one of her serving bowls, handed it to him. "Monroe, Grable, Hayworth, and so on. Screen goddesses. Goddess, key."

"Good segue."

"Yeah, it seemed so, but no luck." She passed him the bowl of potatoes, then using the potholders she'd bought, took the meat loaf out of the oven. "Still, I think I'm on the right track, and it gave me the chance to see your thinking space."

She sat, scanned the table. "Hope you're hungry."

They dished up the meal. At the first bite of meat loaf, Flynn sighed. "Good thing you put Moe out. I'd hate to torment him with this, since he won't be getting much of it. My compliments to the artist."

There was pleasure, Malory discovered, in watching someone you loved eat what you'd prepared. Pleasure in sharing a simple meal at the kitchen table at the end of the day.

She'd never felt deprived eating dinner alone, or in the company of a friend. But now it was easy to see herself sharing this hour with him, night after night, year after year.

"Flynn, you said that when you accepted that you were meant to stay in the Valley, you bought this house. Did you—do you—have a vision for it? How you want it to look and feel?"

"I don't know if you'd call it a vision. I liked the look of it, the lines of it, and the big yard. Something about a big yard makes me feel prosperous and safe."

He went back for seconds. "I figure I'll have to gut this room sooner or later, rip it into the new millennium. Buy stuff for the rest of the place, eventually. But I never seem to get around to it. I guess because it's just me and Moe."

He poured more wine for both of them. "If you've got some ideas, I'm open to suggestions."

"I've always got ideas, and you should be careful before you get me started. But that wasn't why I asked. I had a vision for the property we bought—Dana and Zoe and I. As soon as I walked into that house I could see how it would work, what it needed from me, what I could bring to it. And I haven't been back since."

"You've been pretty busy."

"That's not it. I deliberately haven't been back. That's not like me. Usually when I have a project, I can't wait to get started, to start fiddling with things, lining them up, making lists. I took the step. I signed on the dotted line, but I haven't taken the next step."

"It's a big commitment, Mal."

"I'm not afraid of commitment. Hell, I thrive on it. But I've been a little afraid of this. I'm going to go over to-morrow, take a look at the place. Apparently the previous owners left a lot of stuff they didn't want in the attic. Zoe asked me to go through it before she started hauling things out."

"What kind of attic? A dark, spooky attic or a big, fun, Grandma's attic?"

"I have no idea. I haven't been up there." It shamed her to admit that. "I haven't been off the ground floor, which is ridiculous, as I own a third of the property. Or will. I'm going to change that. Change isn't my best thing."

"Want me to go with you? I'd like to see the place anyway."

"I was hoping you'd say that." She reached over to give his hand a squeeze. "Thanks. Now, since you asked about ideas on this house, I'd suggest you start in the living room, which by my definition is an area where you're supposed to live."

"You're going to insult my sofa again, aren't you?"

"I don't believe I have the skills to form the insult that sofa merits. But you might want to think about actual tables, lamps, area rugs, curtains."

"I was thinking I could just order a bunch of stuff out of a catalogue."

She sent him a very long, very dry stare. "You're try-ing to scare me, but it won't work. And since you've generously offered to help me out tomorrow, I'll return the favor. I'd be glad to give you a hand with turning that space into a room."

Since he'd all but licked his plate clean a second time, he resisted going for thirds. "Was that a trick, some clever ploy to drag me off to a furniture store?"

"It wasn't, but it sure circled around to it well, didn't it? I can give you some of my thoughts while we do the dishes."

She rose to stack dishes, but he put a hand over hers. "Let's just go in there now, and you can show me what's so wrong with my simple, minimalist approach."

"After the dishes."

"Uh-uh. Now." He began to pull her out of the room, amused at the struggle on her face as she glanced back at the table. "They'll still be there when we get back. Trust me. It's not going to hurt to do them out of the logical order."

"Yes, it does. A little. Five minutes, then. The condensed consultation. First, you did a good job with the walls. It's a good-sized room, and the strong color's a complement, which you could enhance with touches of other strong colors in curtains and . . . What're you doing?" she demanded when he began unbuttoning her shirt.

"Getting you naked."

"Excuse me." She tapped his fingers away. "I charge extra for naked decorating consults."

"Bill me." He swept her off her feet.

"This was just a trick, wasn't it? A ploy to get my clothes off and have your way with me."

"Sure circled around nicely, didn't it?" He dumped her on the couch and dived on top of her.

Chapter Nineteen

HE made her laugh as he nipped along her jawline, playfully wrestled her down when she tried to squirm away.

"You taste even better than meat loaf."

"If that's the best you can do, then *you're* the one who'll be washing dishes."

"Your threats don't scare me." He walked his fingers up her ribs toward her breast. "There's a dishwasher somewhere in that kitchen."

"Yes, there is. And you had a bag of dog food stored in it."

"Is that where that went to?" He nibbled at her earlobe.

"It's now in the utility closet, where it belongs." She turned her head slightly to give him easier access to her neck. "You're obviously unaware that there are very practical, even attractive, containers manufactured to store items such as dog food."

"No kidding? Looks like I've got my work cut out for me, getting these domestic worries out of your mind. But

I like a challenge after a good meal. Let's just get this off."

He tugged at her shirt, then made a throaty sound as he smoothed a finger over the salmon-colored lace of her bra. "I like this. We'll leave that on a while."

"We could take this upstairs, you know. I cleaned under the cushions and learned just what this monster can swallow. We could be next."

"I'll protect you."

He replaced his fingertips with his lips, skimmed them over lace and flesh.

The enormous cushions gave under their weight, cradled them together as he sampled her. She wiggled and squirmed in mock resistance, an erotic game that aroused them both.

Her mind began to fog as he scraped his teeth down her torso. "What do you think of Brazilians?"

Baffled, he lifted his head. "What? The people, or the nuts?"

She stared at him, amazed that she'd spoken out loud, delighted with his response. Laughter shook her, rolled straight up from her belly as she grabbed him and rained kisses over his face. "Nothing. Never mind. There." She dragged his shirt over his head. "Now we're even."

She loved the feel of his skin under her hands, the sturdy shoulders, the play of muscles. She loved, oh, yes, the feel of his hands on her. Gentle or rough, rushed or patient.

And as the evening light slipped through the windows, as he roamed down her body, she closed her eyes and let sensation rule.

Flutters and tugs, heat and chills. Each was a separate thrill blending into a single, steady ache. His fingers danced over her belly, made it quiver, before he drew her pants down her hips and legs.

Then his tongue slid over her, down her, into her, and flashed her to peak.

She moaned his name when her body went bowstring taut under his. Sighed his name as she seemed to dissolve under his hands.

He wanted, as he'd wanted in that stunning moment in his kitchen, to give her anything. Everything she wanted, all she needed, more than she could imagine.

He'd never known what it was to be offered unconditional love, to know it waited for him. He'd never felt deprived of it because he'd never known it existed.

And now he held the woman who'd given it to him.

She was his miracle, his magic. His key.

He pressed his lips to her shoulder, her throat, rode on the punch of these huge new emotions when her arms came around him.

Words tumbled through his mind, but none of them were enough. He found her mouth with his, cupped her hips, and filled her.

WARM and loose and sleepy, she curled into him. She was more than willing to cocoon herself in this lovely sexual haze, to drift in it to the sound of her own skin humming. Chores could wait, forever if need be. As long as she could snuggle here, feeling Flynn's heart pound against hers.

She wondered why they didn't just drift off to sleep this way, warm, naked, and tangled with the bloom of lovemaking covering them both like soft, silky clouds.

She stretched luxuriously under his hand when he stroked her back. "Mmmm. Let's just stay here all night, like a couple of bears in a cave."

"You're happy?"

She tipped her face up to smile at him. "Of course I am." She snuggled back in. "So happy I'm pretending there aren't dishes waiting to be washed or leftovers to put away."

"You haven't been happy the last few days."

"No, I guess I haven't." She settled her head more comfortably on his shoulder. "I felt like I'd lost my direction, and everything around me was shifting and changing so fast I couldn't keep up. Then it occurred to me that if I didn't change, at least open myself to changing, the direction didn't matter. Because I was going nowhere."

"There are some things I want to tell you, if you can handle some more changes."

Uneasy, as his tone was so serious, she braced herself. "All right."

"About Lily."

He felt her tense, an instant tightening of muscles, and could all but feel her will herself to relax again. "This may not be the best moment to tell me about another woman. Especially one you loved and planned to marry."

"I think it is. We knew each other casually for several months, then intimately for the best part of a year. We clicked on a number of levels. Professionally, socially, sexually—"

Her lovely cocoon was now in shreds, and she began to feel the cold. "Flynn—"

"Hear me out. It was the longest adult relationship I'd had with a woman. Serious relationship with long-term planning. I thought we were in love with each other."

"She hurt you, I know. I'm sorry, but—"

"Quiet." He tapped a finger on the top of her head. "She didn't love me, or if she did, that love had specific requirements. So you couldn't call it a gift."

He was silent for a moment, selecting his words carefully. "It isn't easy looking in the mirror and accepting that you were missing some element, some *thing* that kept a person you wanted from loving you."

She tried to keep steady. "No, it's not."

"And even when you come to terms with it, when you realize it just wasn't right, that there was something missing from the other person, too, something missing from the whole, it still breaks your stride. It makes you a lot more hesitant about taking that kind of chance again."

"I understand that."

"And you end up going nowhere," he stated, echoing her earlier statement. "Jordan said something to me the other day that had me thinking, and thinking back. I asked myself if I'd ever really imagined life with Lily. You know, pictured how we'd be together a few years down the road. I could see the immediate future, the moving-to-New-York thing. How we'd get jobs in our chosen fields, find a place to live, and then I realized that was pretty much it. That was all I'd been able to see. Not how we would live or what we'd do beyond that vague picture, not how we'd look together in a decade. It wasn't hard to picture my life without her in it, maybe harder to pick up my life at the point she dumped me. Lots of bruises on the pride and ego. Lots of anger and hurt. And the by-product of feeling like I probably wasn't cut out for the whole love-and-marriage thing."

Her heart was twisting, for both of them. "You don't have to explain."

"I'm not finished. I was bumping along pretty well. Had my life in order—not so you'd think so, but it suited me. Then Moe knocked you flat on the sidewalk, and things began to change. No secret I was attracted to you from the get-go, and hoped we'd end up naked on this sofa sooner or later. But, initially, that's as far as I could see things, regarding you and me."

This time he tipped her face up. He wanted her to look at him now. Wanted to see her face. "I've known you less than a month. On a lot of basic points we come at it from opposite angles. But I can see my life with you, the way you can look through a window and see your own little world spread out. I can see how it could be a year from now, or twenty years from now, with you and me and what we make."

He skimmed his fingers along her cheek, just to feel

the shape of it. "What I can't see is how I'd pick up my life from this point and make it without you."

He watched her eyes fill with tears, watched them spill over. "I love you." He brushed away a tear with his thumb. "I don't have a master plan for what happens next. I just know I love you."

Emotions surged through her, so bright and rich she wondered that they didn't burst out of her in colored light. Terrified that she was about to fall apart, she struggled to smile. "I have to ask you for something important."

"Anything."

"Promise me you'll never get rid of this couch."

He laughed, nuzzled her cheek. "You're going to regret that."

"No, I won't. I'm not going to regret a thing."

WITH the two women who had become her friends and partners, Malory sat on the front porch of the house that would be one-third hers.

The sky had clouded up since she'd arrived, clouds stacking on clouds to make a multilayered sweep of grays.

Storm brewing, she figured, and found herself pleased with the idea of being inside with rain pounding on the roof. But first she wanted to sit while the electricity gathered in the air and those first puffs of wind bent the trees.

More than anything she'd needed to share her joy and her nerves with her friends.

"He loves me." She didn't think she would ever tire of saying it aloud. "Flynn loves me."

"It's so romantic." Zoe dug a tissue out of her purse and sniffled into it.

"It was. You know, there was a time I wouldn't have thought so. I'd have had a very detailed outline in my mind. Candlelight, music, with me and the perfect man in some elegant room. Or outdoors, in some spectacular setting. It would all have had to be arranged, just so."

With a shake of her head, she laughed at herself. "That's why I know it's the real thing. Because it didn't have to be just so, and elegant and perfect. It just had to be. It had to be Flynn."

"Jeez. It's hard for me to equate the stars in your eyes with Flynn." Dana rested her chin on her fist. "Nice and all, because I love him too. But it's Flynn, my favorite moron. I've never pictured him as a romantic figure." She turned toward Zoe. "What the hell's in that meat loaf? Maybe I should get the recipe."

"I'm going to take another look at it myself." She patted Malory's knee. "I'm really happy for you. I liked the way you two looked together right from the start."

"Hey, you moving in with him?" Dana perked up. "That would set Jordan out on his butt that much sooner."

"Sorry, we didn't get to that stage yet. We're just basking in the we're-in-love moment for now. And that, friends and neighbors, is a real change for me. I'm not making schedules and lists. I'm just going with it. God, I feel like I could take on the world! Which brings me to the next part of this session. I'm sorry I haven't contributed to any of the plans for the house here or done anything about moving forward with ideas for fixing it up, putting it all together."

"I wondered if you were going to bail," Dana admitted.

"I was thinking about it. I'm sorry I didn't tell you. I guess I had to work out for myself what I was doing and why. Now I know. I'm starting my own business because the longer you put off dreams, the less chance you have of making them real. I'm going into a partnership with two women I like a lot. Not only am I not going to let them down, but I'm not going to let me down either."

She got to her feet, and with her hands planted on her hips, turned to look at the house. "I don't know if I'm ready for this, but I'm ready to try. I don't know if I'm going to find the key in the time I have left, but I know I've tried there, too."

"I know what I think." Zoe rose to join her. "If it weren't for the key, you wouldn't be with Flynn now. We wouldn't be together, and we wouldn't have this place. Because of that I've got a chance to make something special, for myself, for Simon. I wouldn't have had that without the two of you."

"Let me start off saying we can skip the group hug." Still, Dana walked over to them. "But I feel the same way. I wouldn't have had the chance for this without both of you. My idiot brother has a classy lady in love with him. All that starts with the key. I say you're going to find it."

She looked up as rain began to splatter. "Now let's get the hell in out of the rain."

Inside, they stood in a loose semicircle.

"Together or separate?" Malory asked.

"Together," Zoe answered.

"Top or bottom?"

"Top." Dana glanced over, got assenting nods. "You said Flynn was coming by?"

"Yeah, he's going to slip over for an hour."

"We can use him as a pack mule, then, for anything we want to haul out of the attic."

"Some of the stuff up there is great." Zoe's face shone with enthusiasm as they started up. "I know it looks like junk at first glance, but I think once we get to it, we'll be able to use some. There's an old wicker chair that could be rewoven and painted. It'd look good on the porch. And there's a couple of those pole lamps. The shades are trash, but the poles could be cleaned up and antiqued."

Her voice faded away as Malory climbed the steps. The window at the top was wet with rain, dull with dust. And her heart began to thud like a fist against her ribs.

"This is the place," she whispered.

"Yeah, it is. This is it." Dana set her hands on her hips as she looked around the second floor. "It'll be ours and the bank's in a few weeks."

"No, this is *the* place. From my dream. This is the

house. How could I be so stupid not to realize, not to understand?" Excitement pitched into her voice, rushing the words out. "It wasn't what was Flynn's, but what was mine. I'm the key. Isn't that what Rowena said?"

She whirled back to face them, her eyes brilliant and bright. "Beauty, knowledge, courage. That's the three of us, that's this place. And the dream, that was my fantasy, my idea of perfection. So it had to be my place."

She pressed a hand to her heart as if to keep it from leaping free. "The key's here. In this house."

In the next instant she was alone. The staircase behind her filled with a thin blue light. Like a mist, it rolled toward her, crawled along the floor at her feet until she stood ankle-deep in the damp chill of it. Rooted in shock, she called out, but her voice rang hollow in a mocking echo.

With her heart drumming, she looked at the rooms on either side of her. The eerie blue fog snaked and twined its way up the walls, over the windows, blocking even the gloomy light of the storm.

Run! It was a frantic whisper in her mind. Run. Get out now, before it's too late. This wasn't her fight. She was an ordinary woman leading an ordinary life.

She gripped the banister, took the first step down. She could still see the door through that sheer blue curtain that so quickly ate the true light. Through the door was the real world. Her world. She had only to open that door and walk out for normalcy to click back into place.

That was what she wanted, wasn't it? A normal life. Hadn't her dream shown her that? Marriage and family. French toast for breakfast and flowers on the dresser. A pretty life of simple pleasures built on love and affection.

It was waiting for her, outside the door.

She walked down the steps like a woman in a trance. She could see beyond the door, somehow *through* the door, where the day was perfect with autumn. Trees a wash of color gilded by sunlight, air brisk and tart. And though her heart continued to gallop inside her chest, her lips curved in a dreamy smile as she reached for the door.

"This is wrong." She heard her own voice, oddly flat and calm. "This is another trick." A part of her shuddered in shock as she turned away from the door, turned from the perfect life waiting outside. "What's out there isn't real, but this is. This is our place now."

Stunned that she'd nearly deserted her friends, she called out for Dana and Zoe again. Where had he put them? What illusion had separated them? Fear for them had her rushing back up the steps. Her flight tore the blue mists, only to have it gather back into nasty ribbons behind her.

To orient herself she went to the window at the top of the stairs and rubbed away those frigid mists. Her fingertips went numb, but she could see it was still storming. Rain whipped down out of a bruised sky. Her car was in the drive, just where she'd left it. Across the street a woman with a red umbrella and a bag of groceries dashed toward a house.

That was real, Malory told herself. That was life, messy and inconvenient. And she would get it back. She'd find her way back. But first she had a job to do.

Chills crawled along her skin as she turned to the right. She wished for a jacket, for a flashlight. For her friends. For Flynn. She forced herself not to run, not to rush blindly. The room was a maze of impossible corridors.

It didn't matter. Just another trick, one meant to confuse and frighten her. Somewhere in this house was the key, and her friends. She would find them.

Panic tickled her throat as she walked. The air was silent now, even her lonely footsteps were smothered by the blue mist. What was more frightening to the human heart than being cold and lost and alone? He was using that against her, playing her with her own instinct.

Because he couldn't touch her unless she allowed it.

"You're not going to make me run," she shouted. "I

know who I am and where I am, and you're not going to make me run."

She heard someone call her name, just the faintest ripple through the thick air. Using it as a guide, she turned again.

The cold intensified, and the mists swirled with wet. Her clothes were damp, her skin chilled. The call could have been another trick, she thought. She could hear nothing now but the blood beating inside her own head.

It hardly mattered which direction she chose. She could walk endlessly in circles or stand perfectly still. It wasn't a matter of finding her way, or being misdirected now. It was, she realized, nothing more than a battle of wills.

The key was here. She meant to find it; he meant to stop her.

"It must be lowering to pit yourself against a mortal woman. Wasting all your power and skill on someone like me. And still, the best you can do is this irritating blue-light special."

An angry red glow edged the mist. Though Malory's heart plunged, she gritted her teeth and kept moving. Maybe it wasn't wise to challenge a sorcerer, but aside from the risk she realized another side effect.

She could see another door now where the red and blue lights merged.

The attic, she thought. It had to be. Not illusionary corridors and turns, but the true substance of the house.

She focused on it as she walked forward. When the mists shifted, thickened, swirled, she ignored them and kept the image of the door in her head.

At last, her breath shallow, she plunged a hand through the fog and clamped her fingers around the old glass knob.

Warmth, a welcome flood of it, poured over her as she pulled the door open. She started up, into the dark, with the blue mist creeping behind her.

*　　*　　*

OUTSIDE, Flynn navigated through the mean-tempered storm, edging forward in the driver's seat to peer through the curtain of rain that his wipers could barely displace.

In the backseat, Moe whimpered like a baby.

"Come on, you coward, it's just a little rain." Lightning pitchforked through the black sky, followed by a boom of thunder like a cannon blast. "And some lightning."

Flynn cursed and muscled the wheel in position when the car bucked and shuddered. "And some wind," he added. With gusts approaching gale force.

It hadn't seemed like more than a quick thunderstorm when he'd left the office. But it worsened with every inch of road. As Moe's whimpers turned to pitiful howls, Flynn began to worry that Malory or Dana or Zoe, maybe all three of them, had gotten caught in the storm.

They should have been at the house by now, he reminded himself. But he would have sworn that the rage of the storm was worse, considerably worse, on this end of town. Fog had rolled down from the hills, blanketed them in gray as thick and dense as wool. His visibility decreased, forcing him to slow down. Even at a crawl, the car fishtailed madly on a turn.

"We'll just pull over," he said to Moe. "Pull over and wait it out."

Anxiety skated up his spine, but instead of easing when he nudged the car to the curb, it clamped on to the back of his neck like claws. The sound of the rain pounding like fists on the roof of the car seemed to hammer into his brain.

"Something's wrong."

He pulled out into the street again, his hands vising on the wheel as the wind buffeted the car. Sweat, born of effort and worry, snaked down his back. For the next three blocks he felt like a man fighting a war.

There was a trickle of relief when he spotted the cars

in the driveway. They were okay, he told himself. They were inside. No problem. He was an idiot.

"Told you there was nothing to worry about," he said to Moe. "Now you've got two choices. You can pull yourself together and come inside with me, or you can stay here, quaking and quivering. Up to you, pal."

Relief drained away when he parked at the curb and looked at the house.

If the storm had a heart, it was there. Black clouds boiled over the house, pumped the full force of their fury. Even as he watched, lightning lanced down, speared like a fiery arrow into the front lawn. The grass went black in a jagged patch.

"Malory."

He didn't know if he spoke it, shouted it, or his mind simply screamed it, but he shoved open the car door and leaped into the surreal violence of the storm.

The wind slapped him back, a back-handed blow so intense that he tasted blood in his mouth. Lightning blasted like a mortar directly in front of him, and the air stank with burning. Blind from the driving rain, he bent over and lurched toward the house.

He stumbled on the steps and was calling her name, over and over like a chant, when he saw the hard blue light leaking around the front door.

The knob burned with cold and refused to turn under his hand. Baring his teeth, Flynn reared back, then rammed the door with his shoulder. Once, twice, and on the third assault, he broke it in.

He leaped inside, into that blue mist.

"Malory!" He shoved his dripping hair out of his face. "Dana!"

He whirled when something brushed his leg, and lifted his fists, only to lower them on an oath when it turned out to be wet dog. "Goddamn it, Moe, I don't have time to—"

He broke off when Moe growled deep in his throat, let

out a vicious bark, and charged up the stairs.

Flynn sprinted after him. And stepped into his office.

"If I'm going to do a decent job covering the foliage festival, then I need the front page of the Weekender section and a sidebar on the related events." Rhoda folded her arms, her posture combative. "Tim's interview with Clown Guy should go on page two."

There was a vague ringing in his ears, and a cup of coffee in his hand. Flynn stared at Rhoda's irritated face. He could smell the coffee, and the White Shoulders fragrance that Rhoda habitually wore. Behind him, his scanner squawked and Moe snored like a steam engine.

"This is bullshit."

"You've got no business using that kind of language with me," Rhoda snapped.

"No, this is bullshit. I'm not here. Neither are you."

"It's about time I got treated with a little respect around here. You're only running this paper because your mother wanted to keep you from making a fool of yourself in New York. Big-city reporter, my butt. You're a small-time, small-town guy. Always have been, always will be."

"Kiss my ass," Flynn invited and threw the coffee, cup and all, in her face.

She let out one short scream, and he was back in the mist.

Shaken, he rounded once again toward the sound of Moe's barking.

Through that rolling mist, he saw Dana on her knees with her arms flung around Moe's neck.

"Oh, God, thank God. Flynn!" She sprang up, wrapped herself around him as she had the dog. "I can't find them. I can't find them. I was here, then I wasn't, now I am." Hysteria pitched and rocked in her voice. "We were together, right over there, then we weren't."

"Stop. Stop." He yanked her back, shook her. "Breathe."

"Sorry. I'm sorry." She shuddered, then scrubbed her

hands over her face. "I was at work, but I wasn't. I couldn't have been. It was like being in a daze, going through the motions and not being able to pinpoint what was wrong. Then I heard Moe barking. I heard him barking, and I remembered. We were here. Then I was back, standing here in this—whatever the hell this is—and I couldn't find them."

She fought for calm. "The key. Malory said the key's here. I think she must be right."

"Go. Get outside. Wait for me in the car."

She breathed deep, shuddered again. "I'm freaked, but I'm not leaving them here. Or you either. Jesus, Flynn, your mouth's bleeding."

He swiped the back of his hand over it. "It's nothing. Okay, we stick together." He took her hand, linked fingers.

They heard it at the same time, the hammering of fists on wood. With Moe once again in the lead, they rushed through the room.

Zoe stood at the attic door, beating on it. "Over here!" She called out. "She's up there, I know she's up there, but I can't get through."

"Get back," Flynn ordered.

"You're all right?" Dana gripped her arm. "Are you hurt?"

"No. I was home, Dana. Puttering around the kitchen with the radio on. Wondering what to fix for dinner. My God, how long? How long were we separated? How long has she been up there alone?"

Chapter Twenty

SHE was afraid. It helped to admit it, accept it. To know that she was more afraid than she'd ever been in her life, and to realize she was determined not to give in.

The warmth was already being eaten away as the light took on that harsh blue hue. Fingers of mist crawled along the exposed beams on the ceiling, down the unfinished walls, along the dusty floor.

Through it, she could see the pale white vapor of her own breath.

Real, she reminded herself. That was real, a sign of life. Proof of her own humanity.

The attic was a long, wide room with two stingy windows at either end and the ceiling rising to a narrow pitch. But she recognized it. In her dream there had been skylights and generous windows. Her paintings had been stacked against walls done in soft cream. The floor had been clean of dust, and speckled with a cheerful rainbow of paint drops and splatters.

The air had carried a summer warmth and the scent of turpentine.

It was dank now, and cold. Rather than canvases, cardboard boxes were stacked against the walls. Old chairs and lamps and the debris of other lives were stored there. But she could see—oh, so clearly see—how it could have been.

As she imagined it, it began to form.

Warm, washed with light, alive with color. There, on her worktable with her brushes and palette knives, was the little white vase filled with the pink snapdragons she'd picked from her own garden that morning.

She remembered going out after Flynn had left for work, remembered picking those sweet and tender flowers to keep her company while she worked.

Worked in her studio, she thought dreamily, where the blank canvas waited. And she knew, oh, yes, she knew how to fill it.

She walked to the canvas waiting on an easel, picked up her palette, and began to mix her paints.

Sun streamed through her windows. Several were open for the practical purpose of cross-ventilation, and for the simple pleasure of feeling the breeze. Music pumped passionately out of the stereo. What she intended to paint today required passion.

She could already see it in her mind, feel the power of it gathering in her like a storm.

She raised her brush, swirled it in color for the first stroke.

Her heart lifted. The magnitude of the joy was almost unbearable. She might burst from it if she didn't transfer it onto canvas.

The image was burned in her mind, like a scene etched on glass. With stroke after stroke, color blended on color, she began to bring it to life.

"You know this was always my deepest dream." She spoke conversationally as she worked. "For as long as I can remember I wanted to paint. To have the talent, the vision, the skill to be an important artist."

"Now you have it."

She switched brushes, glancing at Kane before she faced the canvas again. "Yes, I do."

"You were wise, making the right choice in the end. A shopkeeper?" He laughed, dismissed the idea with a wave of his hand. "Where is the power in that? Where is the glory in selling what others have created when you can create yourself? You can be and have whatever you choose here."

"Yes, I understand. You've shown me the way." She slid him a coy look. "What else can I have?"

"You want the man?" Kane shrugged elegantly. "He's bound to you here, a slave to love."

"And if I'd chosen otherwise?"

"Men are capricious creatures. How could you ever be sure of him? Now, you paint your world as you do that canvas. As you wish."

"Fame? Fortune?"

His lip curled. "So it is with mortals always. Love, they say, is what matters more than even life. But it's wealth and it's glory that they really crave. Take it all, then."

"And you, what will you take?"

"I have already taken it."

She nodded, switched brushes. "You'll have to excuse me. I need to concentrate."

She painted in the warm bath of sunlight while the music soared.

FLYNN hit the door with his shoulder, then gripped the knob and prepared to ram it again. The knob turned smoothly in his hand.

Zoe gave him a jittery smile. "I must've loosened it for you."

"Stay down here."

"Save your breath," Dana advised and pushed up behind him.

The light seemed to pulse now, thicker and somehow animate. Moe's growling became wet snarls.

Flynn saw Malory, standing at the far end of the attic. Relief was like a hammer blow to his heart.

"Malory! Thank God." He leaped forward, and hit the solid wall of mist.

"It's some sort of barrier." He spoke frantically now as he pushed and slammed against it. "She's trapped in there."

"I think we're trapped out here." Zoe pressed her hands against the mist. "She doesn't hear us."

"We have to make her hear us." Dana looked around for something to batter against the wall. "She must be somewhere else, in her head, the way we were. We have to make her hear us so she'll snap out of it."

Moe went wild, leaping up to tear and bite at the wall of mist. His barks echoed like gunshots, and still Malory stood like a statue, her back to them.

"There has to be another way." Zoe dropped to her knees, pressed her fingers along the mist. "It's freezing. You can see her trembling from the cold. We have to get her *out*."

"Malory!" Helpless rage had Flynn pummeling the wall until his hands bled. "I'm not going to let this happen. You have to hear me. I love you. Damn it, Malory, I love you. You listen to me."

"Wait!" Dana gripped his shoulder. "She moved. I saw her move. Keep talking to her, Flynn. Just keep talking to her."

Struggling for calm, he pressed his forehead to the wall. "I love you, Malory. You've got to give us a chance to see where we can go with it. I need you with me, so either come out or let me in."

Malory pursed her lips at the image taking shape on canvas. "Did you hear something?" she asked absently.

"There's nothing." Kane smiled at the three mortals on

the other side of the mist. "Nothing at all. What are you painting there?"

"Uh-uh-uh." She wagged a playful finger at him. "I'm temperamental. I don't like anyone looking at my work until it's done. My world," she reminded him and daubed on color. "My rules."

He gave a single, elegant shrug. "As you wish."

"Oh, don't pout. I'm nearly done." She worked quickly now, all but willing the image from her mind onto the canvas. It was, she thought, her masterpiece. Nothing she'd ever done would be so important.

"Art isn't just in the eye of the beholder," she said. "But in that, in the artist, in the subject, in the purpose, and in those who see."

Her pulse skipped and stumbled, but her hand remained steady and sure. For a timeless moment, she shut everything out of her mind but the colors, the textures, the shapes.

And when she stepped back, her eyes glittered with triumph.

"It's the finest thing I've ever done," she declared. "Perhaps the finest thing I will ever do. I wonder what you'll think of it."

She gestured in invitation.

"Light and shadow," she said as he stepped toward the easel. "In looking within, and without. From within me to without and onto the canvas. What my heart speaks. I call it *The Singing Goddess*."

It was her face she'd painted. Her face and the first Daughter of Glass. She stood in a forest, full of sparkling gold light, softened with green shadows, with the river sliding over rock like tears.

Her sisters sat on the ground behind her, their hands clasped.

Venora, for she knew it was Venora, carried her harp, and with her face lifted toward the sky you could almost hear the song she sang.

"Did you think I would settle for cold illusion when I have a chance for the real thing? Did you think I'd trade my life, and her soul, for a dream? You underestimate mortals, Kane."

As he spun toward her, fury leaping off him like flames, she prayed she hadn't overestimated herself, or Rowena.

"The first key is mine." As she spoke she reached toward the painting, reached into it. A stunning blast of heat shot up her arm as she closed her fingers around the key she'd painted at the feet of the goddess.

The key that gleamed in a beam of light that cut the shadows like a gilded sword.

She felt its shape, its substance, then with a cry of victory, she drew it free. "This is my choice. And you can go to hell."

The mists roiled as he cursed her. As he lifted his hand to strike, both Flynn and Moe burst through the wall. With a barrage of sharp, staccato barks, Moe leaped.

Kane faded like a shadow in the dark, and was gone.

As Flynn plucked Malory off her feet, sunlight shimmered in the tiny windows, and rain dripped musically from the eaves outside. The room was only an attic, filled with dust and clutter.

The painting she'd created out of love, knowledge, and courage was gone.

"I've got you." Flynn buried his face in her hair as Moe leaped on them. "You're all right. I've got you."

"I know. I know." She began to weep quietly as she looked down at the key still clutched in her fingers. "I painted it." She held it out to Dana and Zoe. "I have the key."

BECAUSE she insisted, Flynn drove her directly to Warrior's Peak, with Dana and Zoe following. He kept the heater on high, and had wrapped her in a blanket from his trunk that unfortunately smelled of Moe. And still she shivered.

"You need a hot bath or something. Tea. Soup." He dragged a hand that was still far from steady through his hair. "I don't know. Brandy."

"I'll take all of the above," she promised, "as soon as we get the key where it belongs. I won't be able to relax until it's out of my hand."

She clutched it in a fist held tight to her breast.

"I don't know how it can be in my hand."

"Neither do I. Maybe if you explain it to me, we'll both get it."

"He tried to confuse me, the way he separated us. To make me feel lost and alone and afraid. But he must have some limits. He couldn't keep all three of us, and you, in those illusions. Not all at once. We're connected, and we're stronger than he realized. At least that's what I think."

"I can go with that. To give him credit, he had Rhoda pretty much down pat."

"I made him mad, just mad enough, I guess. I knew the key was in the house." She pulled the blanket a little tighter, but couldn't find warmth. "I'm not telling this in good journalistic style."

"Don't worry about that. I'll edit it later. How did you know?"

"The attic's where I made the choice, when he showed me all the things I wanted so much. I realized that was the dream place once I went upstairs with Zoe and Dana. And the studio, the artist's studio, had been on the top floor. The attic. It had to be where I had that moment of decision—like in the paintings. At first I thought we would have to hunt through whatever was up there, and we'd find something that jibed with the clue. But it was more than that, and less."

She closed her eyes and sighed.

"You're tired. Just rest until we get there. We can talk later."

"No, I'm okay. It was so strange, Flynn. When I got up there and I realized it all. My place—in reality and in my dream. And how he brought the dream back, tried to slide me into it. I let him think he had. I thought about the clue and saw the painting in my head. I knew how to paint it, every stroke. The third painting of the set.

"The key wasn't in the world he created for me," she said as she turned to him. "But it was in what I created, if I had the courage to do it. If I could see the beauty of it, and make it real. He gave me the power to bring the key into the illusion."

To forge it, she thought, with love.

"I bet that burns his ass."

She laughed. "Yeah, that's a nice side benefit. I heard you."

"What?"

"I heard you calling to me. All of you, but especially you. I couldn't answer you. I'm sorry because I know you were afraid for me. But I couldn't let him know I heard."

He reached over to cover her hand with his. "I couldn't get to you. I didn't know what fear was until then, when I couldn't get to you."

"I was afraid at first that it was just another of his tricks. I was afraid that if I turned around and saw you, I'd break. Your poor hands." She lifted his hand, pressed her lips gently to the torn knuckles. "My hero. Heroes," she corrected, looking back at Moe.

She kept her hand in his as they drove through the gates at Warrior's Peak.

Rowena stepped out, her hands folded at the waist of a flame-red sweater. Malory could see the gleam of tears in her eyes as she walked across the portico to meet them.

"You're safe, and well?" She touched Malory's cheek, and the chill Malory had been unable to shake slid into blessed warmth.

"Yes, I'm fine. I have—"

"Not yet. Your hands." She laid her palms under Flynn's, lifted them. "This will scar," she said. "There, beneath the third knuckle of your left hand. A symbol, Flynn. Herald and warrior."

She opened the back door of the car herself so Moe could leap out and greet her with wags and licks. "Ah, there, the fierce and brave one." She hugged him, then leaned back on her heels, listening attentively as he barked and grumbled. "Yes, you had quite the adventure." She rose, resting a hand on Moe's head as she smiled at Dana and Zoe. "All of you did. Please come in."

Moe didn't need to be asked twice. He bounded across the stones and straight through the doorway where Pitte stood. Pitte raised an elegant eyebrow as the dog skidded over the foyer floor, then turned the look onto Rowena.

She only laughed and hooked an arm through Flynn's. "I have a gift for the loyal and courageous Moe, if you'll allow it."

"Sure. Look, we appreciate the hospitality, but Malory's pretty worn out, so—"

"I'm fine. Really."

"We won't keep you long." Pitte gestured them into what Malory thought of as the portrait room. "We're in your debt, more than can be paid. What you've done, whatever tomorrow brings, will never be forgotten." He tipped Malory's face up with one long finger and laid his lips on hers.

Zoe nudged Dana. "I think we're getting gypped in this one-for-all deal."

Pitte glanced over, and his sudden grin was alive with charm. "My woman is a jealous creature."

"No such thing," Rowena objected, then lifted a brightly woven collar from a table. "These symbols speak of valor, and a true heart. The colors are also symbolic. Red for courage, blue for friendship, black for protection."

She crouched to remove Moe's frayed and faded collar and replace it.

He sat through the business of it, Flynn thought, with the stalwart dignity of a soldier being awarded a medal.

"There. How handsome you are." Rowena kissed Moe's nose, then got to her feet. "Will you still bring him to see me, now and then?" she asked Flynn.

"Sure."

"Kane underestimated you. All of you—heart and spirit and spine."

"He's unlikely to do so again," Pitte pointed out, but Rowena shook her head.

"This is a time for joy. You are the first," she told Malory.

"I know. I wanted to get this to you right away." She started to hold out the key, then stopped. "Wait. Do you mean I'm the *first*? The first to ever find a key?"

Saying nothing, Rowena turned to Pitte. He walked to a carved chest beneath the window, lifted the lid. The blue light that spilled out made Malory's stomach clutch. But this was different from the mist, she realized. This was deeper, brighter.

Then he lifted from the chest a glass box alive with that light, and her throat filled with tears. "The Box of Souls."

"You are the first," Pitte repeated as he set the box on a marble pedestal. "The first mortal to turn the first key."

He turned, stood beside the box. He was the soldier now, Malory thought, the warrior at guard. Rowena stepped to the other side so they flanked the glass and the swirling blue lights inside it.

"It's for you to do," Rowena said quietly. "It was always for you to do."

Malory clutched the key tighter in her fist. Her chest was so full it hurt and still seemed incapable of containing the galloping racing of her heart. She tried to draw a calming breath, but it came out short and sharp. As she stepped closer, those lights seemed to fill her vision, then the room. Then the world.

Her fingers wanted to tremble, but she bore down. She would not do this thing with a shaking hand.

She slid the key into the first of the three locks worked into the glass. She saw the light spread up the metal and onto her fingers, bright as hope. And she turned the key in the lock.

There was a sound—she thought there was a sound. But it was no more than a quiet sigh. Even as it faded, the key dissolved in her fingers.

The first lock vanished, and there were two.

"It's gone. Just gone."

"A symbol again, for us," Rowena said and laid a hand gently on the box. "For them. Two are left."

"Do we . . ." They were weeping inside that glass, Dana thought. She could almost hear them, and it ripped at her heart. "Do we pick now, which one of us goes next?"

"Not today. You should rest your minds and hearts." Rowena turned to Pitte. "There should be champagne in the parlor. Would you see to our guests? I'd like a private word with Malory before we join you."

She lifted the glass box herself, carefully placed it back in the chest. When she was alone with Malory she turned. "Pitte said we owe you a debt we can never pay. That's true."

"I agreed to look for the key, and I *was* paid," Malory corrected. She looked at the chest, imagined the box within. "It seems wrong now to have taken the money."

"The money is nothing to us, I promise you. Others have taken it and done nothing. Others have tried and failed. And you've done something brave and interesting with the money."

She crossed over, took Malory's hands in hers. "That pleases me. But it isn't dollars and cents I speak of when I speak of debt. If not for me, there would be no Box of

Souls, no keys, no locks. You wouldn't have had to face what you faced today."

"You love them." Malory gestured toward the chest.

"As sisters. Young, sweet sisters. Well . . ." She walked over to look at the portrait. "I have hope to see them like this again. I can give you a gift, Malory. It's my right to do so. You refused what Kane offered you."

"It wasn't real."

"It can be." She turned back. "I can make it real. What you felt, what you knew, what you had inside you. I can give you the power you had in his illusion."

Dizzy, Malory groped for the arm of a chair, then slowly lowered herself into it. "You can give me painting."

"I understand the need—and the joys and pain of having that beauty inside you, feeling it leap out." She laughed. "Or fighting to get it out, which is every bit as brilliant. You can have it. My gift to you."

For a moment, the idea of it swarmed through Malory, intoxicating as wine, seductive as love. And she saw Rowena watching her, so calm, so steady, with a soft smile on her lips.

"You'd give me yours," Malory realized. "That's what you mean. You would give me your talent, your skill, your vision."

"It would be yours."

"No, it would never be mine. And I would always know it. I . . . painted them because I could see them. Just as I could see them in that first dream. As if I were there, in the painting. And I painted the key. I forged the key, was able to because I loved enough to give it up. I chose the light instead of the shadow. Isn't that right?"

"Yes."

"Having made that choice, knowing it was the right one, I can't take what's yours. But thank you," she said as she rose. "It's nice to know I can be happy doing what I do. I'm going to make a beautiful shop, and a successful business. And a damn good life," she added.

"I have no doubt. Will you take this, then?" Rowena gestured, smiling when Malory let out a shocked gasp.

"*The Singing Goddess*." She rushed to the framed canvas that rested on a table. "The painting I did when Kane . . ."

"You painted it." Rowena joined her, laid a hand on her shoulder. "Whatever his trick, this was your vision, and your heart that found the answer. But if having this, if seeing it is painful, I can put it away."

"No, it's not painful. It's a wonderful gift. Rowena, this was an illusion. You brought it into my reality. It's solid. It exists." Bracing herself, she stepped back, kept her eyes level with Rowena's. "Can you—have you done the same with emotions?"

"You question if your feelings for Flynn are real?"

"No. I know they are." She pressed a hand to her heart. "This is no illusion. But his for me—if that's some kind of reward . . . it's not fair to him, and I can't accept it."

"You would give him up."

"No." Her expression went combative. "Hell, no. I'd just deal with it, and him, until he fell in love with me. If I can find some mystical key, I can sure as hell make Michael Flynn Hennessy realize I'm the best thing that's ever happened to him. Which I am," she added. "Which I absolutely am."

"I like you, very much," Rowena said with a grin. "And I'll promise you this. When Flynn walks into this room again, whatever he feels or doesn't feel will be a true reflection of his heart. The rest is up to you. Wait here, I'll send him in."

"Rowena? When will we begin the second round?"

"Soon," Rowena called out as she left the room. "Very soon."

Which one of them would be next? Malory wondered as she studied the portrait. And what would the second one risk? What would she win or lose in the search?

She'd lost one love, she thought, lifting her painting. One love, so briefly tasted. And now, with Flynn, she had to risk another. The most vital love of her life.

"I brought you some of this very jazzy champagne," Flynn said, walking in with two brimming flutes. "You're missing the party. Pitte actually laughed. It was a moment."

"I just needed a couple of minutes first." She set the painting down and reached for a glass.

"What's this? One of Rowena's?" He hooked an arm companionably around Malory's shoulder, and she felt his body stiffen when he understood. "It's yours? This is what you did? The painting you did in the attic, with the key. It's here."

He brushed his fingers over the gold key, only painted now, at the feet of the goddess. "It's amazing."

"Even more when you're the one who reached into a painting and pulled out a magic key."

"No. I mean, yeah, that's out there. But I meant the whole thing. It's beautiful, Malory. Hell, it's stupendous. You gave this up." He spoke softly, then looked over at her. "You're the one who's amazing."

"I'll have this. Rowena clicked her heels together, twitched her nose, whatever she does, and brought it here for me. It means a lot to have it. Flynn . . ."

She had to take a drink, had to put some distance between them. Whatever she'd said to Rowena, she understood now that she was a about to do something much more wrenching than giving up a talent with paint and brush.

"This has been a strange month, for all of us."

"And then some," he agreed.

"Most of what's happened, it's beyond the scope of anything we could have imagined, anything we might have believed a few weeks ago. And what's happened, it's changed me. In a good way," she added, turning toward him. "I like to think it's a good way."

"If you're going to tell me you turned the key in that lock, and now you don't love me anymore, that's too damn bad for you. Because you're stuck."

"No, I'm . . . Stuck?" she repeated. "What do you mean *stuck*?"

"With me, my ugly couch and my sloppy dog. You're not wiggling your way out of it, Malory."

"Don't take that tone with me." She set the flute down. "And don't think for one minute you can stand there and tell me I'm stuck with you, because *you're* stuck with *me*."

He set his flute beside hers. "Is that right?"

"That's exactly right. I've just outwitted an evil Celtic god. You're child's play for me."

"You want to fight?"

"Maybe."

They both grabbed for each other. With his mouth on hers, she let out a strangled sigh. And held on for her life. She drew back, but kept her arms linked around his neck.

"I'm exactly right for you, Flynn."

"Then it's really handy that I'm in love with you. You're my key, Mal. The one key to all the locks."

"You know what I want right now? I want a hot bath, some soup, and a nap on an ugly couch."

"Today's your lucky day. I can arrange that for you." Taking her hand, he led her from the room.

Later, Rowena leaned her head against Pitte's shoulder as they watched the cars drive away.

"It's a good day," she told him. "I know it's not over, but today is a good day."

"We have a little time before we begin the next."

"A few days, then the four weeks. Kane will watch them more carefully now."

"So will we."

"Beauty prevailed. Now knowledge and courage will be tested. There's so little, really, that we can do to help. But these mortals are strong and clever."

"Odd creatures," Pitte commented.

"Yes." She smiled up at him. "Odd, and endlessly fascinating."

They stepped back into the house, closed the door. At the end of the drive, the iron gates quietly swung shut. The warriors that flanked them would stand vigil through the next phase of the moon.

morrigan's cross

For my brothers,
Jim, Buz, Don and Bill

None but the brave deserves the fair.
—DRYDEN

Finish, good lady; the bright day is done,
And we are for the dark.
—SHAKESPEARE

Prologue

It was the rain that made him think of the tale. The lash of it battered the windows, stormed the rooftops and blew its bitter breath under the doors.

The damp ached in his bones even as he settled by the fire. Age sat heavily on him in the long, wet nights of autumn— and would sit heavier still, he knew, in the dark winter to come.

The children were gathered, huddled on the floor, squeezed by twos and threes into chairs. Their faces were turned to his, expectant, for he'd promised them a story to chase boredom from a stormy day.

He hadn't intended to give them this one, not yet, for some were so young. And the tale was far from tender. But the rain whispered to him, hissing the words he'd yet to speak.

Even a storyteller, perhaps especially a storyteller, had to listen.

"I know a tale," he began, and several of the children squirmed in anticipation. "It's one of courage and cowardice, of blood and death, and of life. Of love and of loss."

"Are there monsters?" one of the youngest asked, with her blue eyes wide with gleeful fear.

"There are always monsters," the old man replied. "Just as there are always men who will join them, and men who will fight them."

"And women!" one of the older girls called out, and made him smile.

"And women. Brave and true, devious and deadly. I have known both in my time. Now, this tale I tell you is from long ago. It has many beginnings, but only one end."

As the wind howled, the old man picked up his tea to wet his throat. The fire crackled, shot light across his face in a wash like gilded blood.

"This is one beginning. In the last days of high summer, with lightning striking blue in a black sky, the sorcerer stood on a high cliff overlooking the raging sea."

Chapter 1

Eire, the region of Chiarrai
1128

There was a storm in him, as black and vicious as that which bullied its way across the sea. It whipped inside his blood, outside in the air, battling within and without as he stood on the rain-slickened rock.

The name of his storm was grief.

It was grief that flashed in his eyes, as bold and as blue as those lightning strikes. And the rage from it spit from his fingertips, jagged red that split the air with thunderclaps that echoed like a thousand cannon shots.

He thrust his staff high, shouted out the words of magic. The red bolts of his rage and the bitter blue of the storm clashed overhead in a war that sent those who could see scurrying into cottage and cave, latching door and window, gathering their children close to quake and quail as they prayed to the gods of their choosing.

And in their raths, even the faeries trembled.

Rock rang, and the water of the sea went black as the mouth of hell, and still he raged, and still he grieved. The rain that poured out of the wounded sky fell red as blood—and sizzled, burning on land, on sea so that the air smelled of its boiling.

It would be called, ever after, The Night of Sorrows, and those who dared speak of it spoke of the sorcerer who stood tall on the high cliff, with the bloody rain soaking his cloak, running down his lean face like death's tears as he dared both heaven and hell.

His name was Hoyt, and his family the *Mac Cionaoith,* who was said to be descended from Morrigan, faerie queen and goddess. His power was great, but still young as he was young. He wielded it now with a passion that gave no room to caution, to duty, to light. It was his sword and his lance.

What he called in that terrible storm was death.

While the wind shrieked, he turned, putting his back to the tumultuous sea. What he had called stood on the high ground. She—for she had been a woman once—smiled. Her beauty was impossible, and cold as winter. Her eyes were tenderly blue, her lips pink as rose petals, her skin milk white. When she spoke, her voice was music, a siren's who had already called countless men to their doom.

"You're rash to seek me out. Are you impatient, Mac Cionaoith, for my kiss?"

"You are what killed my brother?"

"Death is . . ." Heedless of the rain, she pushed back her hood. "Complex. You are too young to understand its glories. What I gave him is a gift. Precious and powerful."

"You damned him."

"Oh." She flicked a hand in the air. "Such a small price for eternity. The world is his now, and he takes whatever he wants. He knows more than you can dream of. He's mine now, more than he was ever yours."

"Demon, his blood is on your hands, and by the goddess, I will destroy you."

She laughed, gaily, like a child promised a particular treat. "On my hands, in my throat. As mine is in his. He is like me now, a child of night and shadow. Will you also seek to destroy your own brother? Your twin?"

The ground fog boiled black, folded away like silk as she waded through it. "I smell your power, and your grief, and your wonder. Now, on this place, I offer this gift to you. I will make you once more his twin, Hoyt of the Mac

Cionaoiths. I will give you the death that is unending life."

He lowered his staff, stared at her through the curtain of rain. "Give me your name."

She glided over the fog now, her red cloak billowing back. He could see the white swell of her breasts rounding ripely over the tightly laced bodice of her gown. He felt a terrible arousal even as he scented the stench of her power.

"I have so many," she countered, and touched his arm—how had she come so close?—with just the tip of her finger. "Do you want to say my name as we join? To taste it on your lips, as I taste you?"

His throat was dry, burning. Her eyes, blue and tender, were drawing him in, drawing him in to drown. "Aye. I want to know what my brother knows."

She laughed again, but this time there was a throatiness to it. A hunger that was an animal's hunger. And those soft blue eyes began to rim with red. "Jealous?"

She brushed her lips to his, and they were cold, bitter cold. And still, so tempting. His heart began to beat hard and fast in his chest. "I want to see what my brother sees."

He laid his hand on that lovely white breast, and felt nothing stir beneath it. "Give me your name."

She smiled, and now the white of her fangs gleamed against the awful night. "It is Lilith who takes you. It is Lilith who makes you. The power of your blood will mix with mine, and we will rule this world, and all the others."

She threw back her head, poised to strike. With all of his grief, with all of his rage, Hoyt struck at her heart with his staff.

The sound that ripped from her pierced the night, screamed up through the storm and joined it. It wasn't human, not even the howl of a beast. Here was the demon who had taken his brother, who hid her evil behind cold beauty. Who bled, he saw as a stream of blood spilled from the wound, without a heartbeat.

She flew back into the air, twisting, shrieking as lightning tore at the sky. The words he needed to say were lost in his horror as she writhed in the air, and the blood that fell steamed into filthy fog.

"You would dare!" Her voice gurgled with outrage, with pain. "You would use your puny, your pitiful magic on me? I have walked this world a *thousand* years." She slicked her hand over the wound, threw out her bloody hand.

And when the drops struck Hoyt's arm, they sliced like a knife.

"Lilith! You are cast out! Lilith, you are vanquished from this place. By my blood." He pulled a dagger from beneath his cloak, scored his palm. "By the blood of the gods that runs through it, by the power of my birth, I cast you back—"

What came at him seemed to fly across the ground, and struck with the feral force of fury. Tangled, they crashed over the cliff to the jagged ledge below. Through waves of pain and fear he saw the face of the thing that so closely mirrored his own. The face that had once been his brother's.

Hoyt could smell the death on him, and the blood, and could see in those red eyes the animal his brother had become. Still, a small flame of hope flickered in Hoyt's heart.

"Cian. Help me stop her. We still have a chance."

"Do you feel how strong I am?" Cian closed his hand around Hoyt's throat and squeezed. "It's only the beginning. I have forever now." He leaned down, licked blood from Hoyt's face, almost playfully. "She wants you for herself, but I'm hungry. So hungry. And the blood in you is mine, after all."

As he bared his fangs, pressed them to his brother's throat, Hoyt thrust the dagger into him.

With a howl, Cian reared back. Shock and pain rushed over his face. Even as he clutched at the wound, he fell. For an instant, Hoyt thought he saw his brother, his true brother. Then there was nothing but the screams of the storm and the slashing rain.

He crawled and clawed his way up the cliff. His hands, slippery with blood and sweat and rain, groped for any hold. Lightning illuminated his face, tight with pain, as he inched his way up rock, tore his fingers in the clawing. His neck, where the fangs had scraped, burned like a brand. Breath whistling, he clutched at the edge.

If she waited, he was dead. His power had waned with

exhaustion, drained with the ravages of his shock and grief. He had nothing but the dagger, still red with his brother's blood.

But when he pulled himself up, when he rolled to his back with the bitter rain washing over his face, he was alone.

Perhaps it had been enough, perhaps he'd sent the demon back to hell. As he had surely sent his own flesh and blood to damnation.

Rolling over, he gained his hands and knees, and was viciously ill. Magic was ashes in his mouth.

He crawled to his staff, used it to help him stand. Breath keening, he staggered away from the cliffs, along a path he'd have known had he been blinded. The power had gone out of the storm as it had gone out of him, and now was merely a soaking rain.

He smelled home—horse and hay, the herbs he'd used for protection, the smoke from the fire he'd left smoldering in the hearth. But there was no joy in it, no triumph.

As he limped toward his cottage, his breath whistled out, hisses of pain that were lost in the rise of the wind. He knew if the thing that had taken his brother came for him now, he was lost. Every shadow, every shape cast by the storm-tossed trees could be his death. Worse than his death. Fear of that slicked along his skin like dirty ice, so that he used what strength he had to murmur incantations that were more like prayers for whoever, or whatever, would listen.

His horse stirred in its shelter, let out a huff as it scented him. But Hoyt continued shakily to the small cottage, dragging himself to the door and through.

Inside was warmth, and the ripple from the spells he'd cast before he'd gone to the cliffs. He barred the door, leaving smears of his and Cian's blood on the wood. Would it keep her out? he wondered. If the lore he'd read was fact, she couldn't enter without an invitation. All he could do was have faith in that, and in the protection spell that surrounded his home.

He let his soaked cloak fall, let it lay in a sodden heap on the floor, and had to fight not to join it there. He would mix potions for healing, for strength. And would sit through the night, tending the fire. Waiting for dawn.

He'd done all he could for his parents, his sisters and their families. He had to believe it was enough.

Cian was dead, and what had come back with his face and form had been destroyed. He would not, could not, harm them now. But the thing that had made him could.

He would find something stronger to protect them. And he would hunt the demon again. His life, he swore it now, would be dedicated to her destruction.

His hands, long of finger, wide of palm, were tremulous as he chose his bottles and pots. His eyes, stormy blue, were glazed with pain—the aches of his body, of his heart. Guilt weighed on him like a shroud of lead. And those demons played inside him.

He hadn't saved his brother. Instead, he had damned and destroyed him, cast him out and away. How had he won that terrible victory? Cian had always been physically superior to him. And what his brother had become was viciously powerful.

So his magic had vanquished what he'd once loved. The half of him that was bright and impulsive where he himself was often dull and staid. More interested in his studies and his skills than society.

Cian had been the one for gaming and taverns, for wenches and sport.

"His love of life," Hoyt murmured as he worked. "His love of life killed him. I only destroyed that which trapped him in a beast."

He had to believe it.

Pain rippled up his ribs as he shucked off his tunic. Bruises were already spreading, creeping black over his skin the way grief and guilt crept black over his heart. It was time for practical matters, he told himself as he applied the balm. He fumbled considerably, cursed violently, in wrapping the bandage over his ribs. Two were broken, he knew, just as he knew the ride back home in the morning would be a study in sheer misery.

He took a potion, then limped to the fire. He added turf so the flames glowed red. Over them he brewed tea. Then wrapped himself in a blanket to sit, to drink, to brood.

He had been born with a gift, and from an early age had soberly, meticulously sought to honor it. He'd studied, often in solitude, practicing his art, learning its scope.

Cian's powers had been less, but, Hoyt remembered, Cian had never practiced so religiously nor studied so earnestly. And Cian had played with magic, after all. Amusing himself and others.

And Cian had sometimes drawn him in, lowered Hoyt's resistance until they'd done something foolish together. Once they'd turned the boy who'd pushed their younger sister in the mud into a braying, long-eared ass.

How Cian had laughed! It had taken Hoyt three days of work, sweat and panic to reverse the spell, but Cian had never worried a whit.

He was born an ass, after all. We've just given him his true form.

From the time they'd been twelve, Cian had been more interested in swords than spells. Just as well, Hoyt thought as he drank the bitter tea. He'd been irresponsible with magic, and a magician with a sword.

But, steel hadn't saved him, nor had magic, in the end.

He sat back, chilled to his bones despite the simmering turf. He could hear what was left of the storm blowing still, splattering on his roof, wailing through the forest that surrounded his cottage.

But he heard nothing else, not beast, not threat. So was left alone with his memories and regrets.

He should've gone with Cian into the village that evening. But he'd been working, and hadn't wanted ale, or the smells and sounds of a tavern, of people.

He hadn't wanted a woman, and Cian had never *not* wanted one.

But if he'd gone, if he'd put aside his work for one bloody night, Cian would be alive. Surely the demon couldn't have overpowered both of them. Surely his gift would have allowed him to sense what the creature was, despite her beauty, her allure.

Cian would never have gone with her had his brother been by his side. And their mother would not be grieving.

The grave would never have been dug, and by the gods, the thing they buried would never have risen.

If his powers could turn back time, he would give them up, abjure them, to have that one night to re-live that single moment when he'd chosen work over his brother's company.

"What good do they do me? What good are they now? To have been given magic and not be able to use it to save what matters most? Damn to them all then." He flung his cup across the little room. "Damn to them all, gods and faeries. He was the light of us, and you've cast him into the dark."

All of his life Hoyt had done what he was meant to do, what was expected of him. He had turned away from a hundred small pleasures to devote himself to his art. Now those who had given him this gift, this power, had stood back while his own brother was taken?

Not in battle, not even with the clean blade of magic, but through evil beyond imagination. This was his payment, this was his reward for all he had done?

He waved a hand toward the fire, and in the hearth flames leapt and roared. He threw up his arms, and overhead the storm doubled in power so that the wind screamed like a tortured woman. The cottage trembled under its might, and the skins pulled tight over the windows split. Cold gusts spilled into the room, toppling bottles, flapping the pages of his books. And in it he heard the throaty chuckle of the black.

Not once in all of his life had he turned from his purpose. Not once had he used his gift for ill, or touched upon the black arts.

Perhaps now, he thought, he would find the answers in them. Find his brother again. Fight the beast, evil against evil.

He shoved to his feet, ignoring the scream in his side. He whirled toward his cot and flung out both hands toward the trunk he'd locked by magic. When it flew open, he strode to it, reached in for the book he'd shut away years before.

In it were spells, dark and dangerous magicks. Spells that used human blood, human pain. Spells of vengeance and greed that spoke to a power that ignored all oaths, all vows.

It was hot and heavy in his hands, and he felt the seduction of it, those curling fingers that brushed the soul. Have all, have any. Are we not more than the rest? Living gods who take whatever is desired?

We have the right! We are beyond rules and reasons.

His breath came short for he knew what could be his if he accepted it, if he took in both hands what he'd sworn never to touch. Unnamed wealth, women, unspeakable powers, life eternal. Revenge.

He had only to say the words, to rebuke the white and embrace the black. Clammy snakes of sweat slithered down his back as he heard the whispers of voices from a thousand ages:

Take. Take. Take.

His vision shimmered, and through it he saw his brother as he'd found him in the muck on the side of the road. Blood pooled from the wounds in his throat, and more smeared his lips. Pale, Hoyt thought dimly. So very pale was his face against that wet, red blood.

Now Cian's eyes—vivid and blue—opened. There was such pain in them, such horror. They pleaded as they met Hoyt's.

"Save me. Only you can save me. It's not death I'm damned to. 'Tis beyond hell, beyond torment. Bring me back. For once don't count the cost. Would you have me burn for all eternity? For the sake of your own blood, Hoyt, help me."

He shook. It wasn't from the cold that blew through the split skins, or the damp that whirled in the air, but from the icy edge on which he stood.

"I would give my life for yours. I swear it on all I am, on all we were. I would take your fate, Cian, if that were the choice before me. But I can't do this. Not even for you."

The vision on the bed erupted in flames, and its screams were past human. On a howl of grief, Hoyt heaved the book back in the trunk. He used the strength left to him to charm the lock before he collapsed on the floor. There he curled up like a child beyond all comfort.

* * *

Perhaps he slept. Perhaps he dreamed. But when he came to, the storm had passed. Light seeped into the room and grew, bold and bright and white, to sear his eyes. He blinked against it, hissing as his ribs protested when he tried to sit up.

There were streams of pink and gold shimmering in the white, warmth radiating from it. He smelled earth, he realized, rich and loamy, and the smoke from the turf fire that was still shimmering in the hearth.

He could see the shape of her, female, and sensed a staggering beauty.

This was no demon come for blood.

Gritting his teeth, he got to his knees. Though there was still grief and anger in his voice, he bowed his head.

"My lady."

"Child."

The light seemed to part for her. Her hair was the fiery red of a warrior, and flowed over her shoulders in silky waves. Her eyes were green as the moss in the forest, and soft now with what might have been pity. She wore white robes trimmed in gold as was her right by rank. Though she was the goddess of battle, she wore no armor, and carried no sword.

She was called Morrigan.

"You have fought well."

"I have lost. I have lost my brother."

"Have you?" She stepped forward, offered him a hand so he would rise. "You stayed true to your oath, though the temptation was great."

"I might have saved him otherwise."

"No." She touched Hoyt's face, and he felt the heat of her. "You would have lost him, and yourself. I promise you. You would give your life for his, but you could not give your soul, or the souls of others. You have a great gift, Hoyt."

"What good is it if I cannot protect my own blood? Do the gods demand such sacrifice, to damn an innocent to such torment?"

"It was not the gods who damned him. Nor was it for you to save him. But there is sacrifice to be made, battles to be fought. Blood, innocent and otherwise, to be spilled. You have been chosen for a great task."

"You could ask anything of me now, Lady?"

"Aye. A great deal will be asked of you, and of others. There is a battle to be fought, the greatest ever waged. Good against evil. You must gather the forces."

"I am not able. I am not willing. I am . . . God, I am tired."

He dropped to the edge of his cot, dropped his head in his hands. "I must go see my mother. I must tell her I failed to save her son."

"You have not failed. Because you resisted the dark you are charged to bear this standard, to use the gift you've been given to face and to vanquish that which would destroy worlds. Shake off this self-pity!"

His head rose at the sharp tone. "Even the gods must grieve, Lady. I have killed my brother tonight."

"Your brother was killed by the beast, a week ago. What fell from the cliff was not your Cian. You know this. But he . . . continues."

Hoyt got shakily to his feet. "He lives."

"It is not life. It is without breath, without soul, without heart. It has a name that is not spoken yet in this world. It is vampyre. It feeds on blood," she said, moving toward him. "It hunts the human, takes life, or worse, much worse, turns that which it hunts and kills into itself. It breeds, Hoyt, like a pestilence. It has no face, and must hide from the sun. It is this you must fight, this and other demons that are gathering. You must meet this force in battle on the feast of Samhain. And you must be victorious or the world you know, the worlds you have yet to know, will be overcome."

"And how will I find them? How will I fight them? It was Cian who was the warrior."

"You must leave this place and go to another, and another still. Some will come to you, and some you will seek. The witch, the warrior, the scholar, the one of many forms, and the one you've lost."

"Only five more? Six against an army of demons? My lady—"

"A circle of six, as strong and true as the arm of a god. When that circle is formed, others may be formed. But the six will be my army, the six will make the ring. You will teach and you will learn, and you will be greater than the sum of you. A month to gather, and one to learn, and one to know. The battle comes on Samhain.

"You, child, are my first."

"You would ask me to leave the family I have left, when that thing that took my brother may come for them?"

"The thing that took your brother leads this force."

"I wounded her—it. I gave her pain." And the memory of that bubbled up in him like vengeance.

"You did, aye, you did. And this is only another step toward this time and this battle. She bears your mark now, and will, in time, seek you out."

"If I hunt her now, destroy her now."

"You cannot. She is beyond you at this time, and you, my child, are not ready to face her. Between these times and worlds, her thirst will grow insatiable until only the destruction of all humankind will satisfy it. You will have your revenge, Hoyt," she said as he got to his feet. "If you defeat her. You will travel far, and you will suffer. And I will suffer knowing your pain, for you are mine. Do you think your fate, your happiness is nothing to me? You are my child even as you are your mother's."

"And what of my mother, Lady? Of my father, my sisters, their families? Without me to protect them, they may be the first to die if this battle you speak of comes to pass."

"It will come to pass. But they will be beyond it." She spread her hands. "Your love for your blood is part of your power, and I will not ask you to turn from it. You will not think clearly until you have assurance they will be safe."

She tipped back her head, held her arms up, palms cupped. The ground shook lightly under his feet, and when Hoyt looked up, he saw stars shooting through the night sky. Those points of light streamed toward her hands, and there burst into flame.

His heart thumped against his bruised ribs as she spoke, as her fiery hair flew around her illuminated face.

"Forged by the gods, by the light and by the night. Symbol and shield, simple and true. For faith, for loyalty, these gifts for you. Their magic lives through blood shed, yours and mine."

Pain sliced over his palm. He watched the blood well in his, and in hers as the fire burned.

"And so it shall live for all time. Blessed be those who wear Morrigan's Cross."

The fire died, and in the goddess's hands were crosses of gleaming silver.

"These will protect them. They must wear the cross always—day and night—birth to death. You will know they are safe when you leave them."

"If I do this thing, will you spare my brother?"

"You would bargain with the gods?"

"Aye."

She smiled, an amused mother to a child. "You have been chosen, Hoyt, because you would think to do so. You will leave this place and gather those who are needed. You will prepare and you will train. The battle will be fought with sword and lance, with tooth and fang, with wit and treachery. If you are victorious, the worlds will balance and you will have all you wish to have."

"How do I fight a vampyre? I've already failed against her."

"Study and learn," she said. "And learn from one of her kind. One she made. One who was yours before she took him. You must first find your brother."

"Where?"

"Not only where, but when. Look into the fire, and see."

They were, he noted, in his cottage again, and he was standing in front of the hearth. The flames spiked up, became towers. Became a great city. There were voices and sounds such as he'd never heard. Thousands of people rushed along streets that were made of some kind of stone. And machines sped with them.

"What is this place?" He could barely whisper the words. "What world is it?"

"It is called New York, and its time is nearly a thousand

years from where we are. Evil still walks the world, Hoyt, as well as innocence, as well as good. Your brother has walked the world a long time now. Centuries have passed for him. You would do well to remember that."

"Is he a god now?"

"He is vampyre. He must teach you, and he must fight beside you. There can be no victory without him."

Such size, he thought. Buildings of silver and stone taller than any cathedral. "Will the war be in this place, in this New York?"

"You will be told where, you will be told how. And you will know. Now you must go, take what you need. Go to your family and give them their shields. You must leave them quickly, and go to the Dance of the Gods. You will need your skill, and my power, to pass through. Find your brother, Hoyt. It is time for the gathering."

He woke by the fire, the blanket wrapped around him. But he saw it hadn't been a dream. Not with the blood drying on the palm of his hand, and the silver crosses lying across his lap.

It was not yet dawn, but he packed books and potions, oatcakes and honey. And the precious crosses. He saddled his horse, and then, as a precaution, cast another protective circle around his cottage.

He would come back, he promised himself. He would find his brother, and this time, he would save him. Whatever it took.

As the sun cast its first light, he began the long ride to An Clar, and his family home.

Chapter 2

He traveled north on roads gone to mud from the storm. The horrors and the wonders of the night played through his mind as he hunched over his horse, favoring his aching ribs.

He swore, should he live long enough, he would practice healing magic more often, and with more attention.

He passed fields where men worked and cattle grazed in the soft morning sunlight. And lakes that picked up their blue from the late summer sky. He wound through forests where the waterfalls thundered and the shadows and mosses were the realm of the faerie folk.

He was known here, and caps were lifted when Hoyt the Sorcerer passed by. But he didn't stop to take hospitality in one of the cabins or cottages. Nor did he seek comfort in one of the great houses, or in the conversations of monks in their abbeys or round towers.

In this journey he was alone, and above battles and orders from gods, he would seek his family first. He would offer them all he could before he left them to do what he'd been charged to do.

As the miles passed, he struggled to straighten on his horse whenever he came to villages or outposts. His dignity cost him considerable discomfort until he was forced to take his ease by the side of a river where the water gurgled over rock.

Once, he thought, he had enjoyed this ride from his cottage to his family home, through the fields and the hills, or along the sea. In solitude, or in the company of his brother, he had ridden these same roads and paths, felt this same sun on his face. Had stopped to eat and rest his horse at this very same spot.

But now the sun seared his eyes, and the smell of the earth and grass couldn't reach his deadened senses.

Fever sweat slicked his skin, and the angles of his face were keener as he bore down against the unrelenting pain.

Though he had no appetite, he ate part of one of the oatcakes along with more of the medicine he'd packed. Despite the brew and the rest, his ribs continued to ache like a rotted tooth.

Just what good would he be in battle? he wondered. If he had to lift his sword now to save his life he would die with his hands empty.

Vampyre, he thought. The word fit. It was erotic, exotic, and somehow horrible. When he had both time and energy, he would write down more of what he knew. Though he was far from convinced he was about to save this world or any other from some demonic invasion, it was always best to gather knowledge.

He closed his eyes a moment, resting them against the headache that drummed behind them. A witch, he'd been told. He disliked dealing with witches. They were forever stirring odd bits of this and that in pots and rattling their charms.

Then a scholar. At least he might be useful.

Was the warrior Cian? That was his hope. Cian wielding sword and shield again, fighting alongside him. He could nearly believe he could fulfill the task he'd been given if his brother was with him.

The one with many shapes. Odd. A faerie perhaps, and

the gods knew just how reliable such creatures were. And this was somehow to be the front line in the battle for worlds?

He studied the hand he'd bandaged that morning. "Better for all if it had been dreaming. I'm sick and tired is what I am, and no soldier at the best of it."

Go back. The voice was a hissing whisper. Hoyt came to his feet, reaching for his dagger.

Nothing moved in the forest but the black wings of a raven that perched in shadows on a rock by the water.

Go back to your books and herbs, Hoyt the Sorcerer. Do you think you can defeat the Queen of the Demons? Go back, go back and live your pitiful life and she will spare you. Go forward, and she will feast on your flesh and drink of your blood.

"Does she fear to tell me so herself then? And so she should, for I will hunt her through this life and the next if need be. I will avenge my brother. And in the battle to come, I will cut out her heart and burn it."

You will die screaming, and she will make you her slave for eternity.

"It's an annoyance you are." Hoyt shifted his grip on the dagger. As the raven took wing he flipped it through the air. It missed, but the flash of fire he shot out with his free hand hit the mark. The raven shrieked, and what dropped to the ground was ashes.

In disgust Hoyt looked at the dagger. He'd been close, and would likely have done the job if he hadn't been wounded. At least Cian had taught him that much.

But now he had to go fetch the bloody thing.

Before he did, he took a handful of salt from his saddle-bags, poured it over the ashes of the harbinger. Then retrieving his dagger, he went to his horse and mounted with gritted teeth.

"Slave for all eternity," he muttered. "We'll see about that, won't we?"

He rode on, hemmed in by green fields, the rise of hills chased by cloud shadows in light soft as down. Knowing a gallop would have his ribs shrieking, he kept the horse to a plod. He dozed, and he dreamed that he was back on the cliffs struggling with Cian. But this time it was he who tumbled off, spiraling down into the black to crash against the unforgiving rocks.

He woke with a start, and with the pain. Surely this much pain meant death.

His horse had stopped to crop at the grass by the side of the road. There a man in a peaked cap built a wall from a pile of steely gray rock. His beard was pointed, yellow as the gorse that rambled over the low hill, his wrists thick as tree limbs.

"Good day to you, sir, now that you've waked to it." The man touched his cap in salute, then bent for another stone. "You've traveled far this day."

"I have, yes." Though he wasn't entirely sure where he was. There was a fever working in him; he could feel the sticky heat of it. "I'm to An Clar, and the Mac Cionaoith land. What is this place?"

"It's where you are," the man said cheerfully. "You'll not make your journey's end by nightfall."

"No." Hoyt looked down the road that seemed to stretch to forever. "No, not by nightfall."

"There'd be a cabin with a fire going beyond the field, but you've not time to bide here. Not when you've so far yet to go. And time shortens even as we speak. You're weary," the man said with some sympathy. "But you'll be wearier yet before it's done."

"Who are you?"

"Just a signpost on your way. When you come to the second fork, go west. When you hear the river, follow it. There be a holy well near a rowan tree, Briget's Well, that some now call saint. There you'll rest your aching bones for the night. Cast your circle there, Hoyt the Sorcerer, for they'll come hunting. They only wait for the sun to die. You must be at the well, in your circle, before it does."

"If they follow me, if they hunt me, I take them straight to my family."

"They're no strangers to yours. You bear Morrigan's Cross. It's that you'll leave behind with your blood. That and your faith." The man's eyes were pale and gray, and for a moment, it seemed worlds lived in them. "If you fail, more than your blood is lost by Samhain. Go now. The sun's in the west already."

What choice did he have? It all seemed a dream now, boiling in his fever. His brother's death, then his destruction. The thing on the cliffs that called herself Lilith. Had he been visited by the goddess, or was he simply trapped in some dream?

Maybe he was dead already, and this was merely a journey to the afterlife.

But he took the west fork, and when he heard the river, turned his horse toward it. Chills shook him now, from the fever and the knowledge that the light was fading.

He fell from his horse more than dismounted, and leaned breathlessly against its neck. The wound on his hand broke open and stained the bandage red. In the west, the sun was a low ball of dying fire.

The holy well was a low square of stone guarded by the rowan tree. Others who'd come to worship or rest had tied tokens, ribbons and charms, to the branches. Hoyt tethered his horse, then knelt to take the small ladle and sip the cool water. He poured drops on the ground for the god, murmured his thanks. He laid a copper penny on the stone, smearing it with blood from his wound.

His legs felt more full of water than bone, but as twilight crept in, he forced himself to focus. And began to cast his circle.

It was simple magic, one of the first that comes. But his power came now in fitful spurts, and made the task a misery. His own sweat chilled his skin as he struggled with the words, with the thoughts, and with the power that seemed a slippery eel wriggling in his hands.

He heard something stalking the woods, moving in the deepest shadows. And those shadows thickened as the last rays of sunlight eked through the cover of trees.

They were coming for him, waiting for that last flicker to die and leave him in the dark. He would die here, alone, leave his family unprotected. And all for the whim of the gods.

"Be damned if I will." He drew himself up. One chance more, he knew. One. And so he ripped the bandage from his hand, used his own blood to seal the circle.

"Within this ring the light remains. It burns through the night at *my* will. This magic is clean, and none but clean shall bide here. Fire kindle, fire rise, rise and burn with power bright."

Flames shimmered in the center of his circle, weak, but there. As it rose, the sun died. And what had been in the shadows leaped out. It came as a wolf, black pelt and bloody eyes. When it flung itself into the air, Hoyt pulled his dagger. But the beast struck the force of the circle, and was repelled.

It howled, snapped, snarled. Its fangs gleamed white as it paced back and forth as if looking for a weakness in the shield.

Another joined it, skulking out of the trees, then another, another yet, until Hoyt counted six. They lunged together, fell back together. Paced together like soldiers.

Each time they charged, his horse screamed and reared. He stepped toward his mount, his eyes on the wolves as he laid his hands upon it. This at least, he could do. He soothed, lulling his faithful mare into a trance. Then he drew his sword, plunged it into the ground by the fire.

He took what food he had left, water from the well, mixed more herbs—though the gods knew his self-medicating was having no good effect. He lowered to the ground by the fire, sword on one side, dagger on the other and his staff across his legs.

He huddled in his cloak shivering, and dousing an oat-cake with honey, forced it down. The wolves sat on their haunches, threw back their heads, and as one, howled at the rising moon.

"Hungry, are you?" Hoyt muttered through chattering teeth. "There's nothing here for you. Oh, what I wouldn't give for a bed, some decent tea." He sat, the fire dancing in his eyes until they began to close. As his chin drooped to his chest, he'd never felt so alone. Or so unsure of his path.

He thought it was Morrigan who came to him, for she was beautiful and her hair as bold as the fire. It fell straight as rain, its tips grazing her shoulders. She wore black, a strange garb, and immodest enough to leave her arms bare and allow the swell of her breasts to rise from the bodice. Around her neck she wore a pentagram with a moonstone in its center.

"This won't do," she said in a voice that was both foreign and impatient. Kneeling beside him, she laid her hand on his brow, her touch as cool and soothing as spring rain. She smelled of the forest, earthy and secret.

For one mad moment, he longed to simply lay his head upon her breast and sleep with that scent filling his senses.

"You're burning up. Well, let's see what you have here, and we'll make do."

She wavered in his vision a moment, then re-crystallized. Her eyes were as green as the goddess's, but her touch was human. "Who are you? How did you get within the circle?"

"Elderflower, yarrow. No cayenne? Well, I said we'd make do."

He watched as she busied herself, as women would, dipping water from the well, heating it with his fire. "Wolves," she murmured, shivered once. And in that shudder, he felt her fear. "Sometimes I dream of the black wolves, or ravens. Sometimes it's the woman. She's the worst. But this is the first time I've dreamed of you." She paused, and looked at him for a long time with eyes of deep and secret green. "And still, I know your face."

"This is my dream."

She gave a short laugh, then sprinkled herbs in the heated water. "Have it your way. Let's see if we can help you live through it."

She passed her hand over the cup. "Power of healing, herbs and water, brewed this night by Hecate's daughter. Cool his fever, ease his pain so that strength and sight remain. Stir magic in this simple tea. As I will, so mote it be."

"Gods save me." He managed to prop himself on an elbow. "You're a witch."

She smiled as she stepped to him with the cup. And sitting beside him, braced him with an arm around his back. "Of course. Aren't you?"

"I'm not." He had just enough energy for insult. "I'm

a bloody sorcerer. Get that poison away from me. Even the smell is foul."

"That may be, but it should cure what ails you." She simply cradled his head on her shoulder. Even as he tried to push free, she was pinching his nose closed and pouring the brew down his throat. "Men are such babies when they're sick. And look at your hand! Bloody and filthy. I've got something for that."

"Get away from me," he said weakly, though the smell of her, the feel of her was both seductive and comforting. "Let me die in peace."

"You're not going to die." But she gave the wolves a wary glance. "How strong is your circle?"

"Strong enough."

"Hope you're right."

Exhaustion—and the valerian she'd mixed in the tea—had his head drooping again. She shifted, so she could lay his head in her lap. And there she stroked his hair, kept her eyes on the fire. "You're not alone anymore," she said quietly. "And I guess, neither am I."

"The sun . . . How long till dawn?"

"I wish I knew. You should sleep now."

"Who are you?"

But if she answered, he didn't hear.

She was gone when he woke, and so was the fever. Dawn was a misty shimmer letting thin beams eke through the summer leaves.

Of the wolves there was only one, and it lay gored and bloody outside the circle. Its throat had been ripped open, Hoyt saw, and its belly. Even as he gained his feet to step closer, the sun beamed white through those leaves, struck the carcass.

It erupted into flame that left nothing behind but a scatter of ashes on blackened earth.

"To hell with you, and all like you."

Turning away, Hoyt busied himself, feeding his horse, brewing more tea. He was nearly done when he noticed his palm was healed. Only the faintest scar remained. He flexed his fingers, held his hand up to the light.

Curious, he lifted his tunic. Bruises still rained over his side, but they were fading. And when he tested he found he could move without pain.

If what had come to him in the night had been a vision rather than a product of a fever dream, he supposed he should be grateful.

Still, he'd never had a vision so vivid. Nor one who'd left so much of itself behind. He swore he could smell her still, and hear the flow and cadence of her voice.

She'd said she'd known his face. How strange that somewhere in the center of him, he felt he'd known hers.

He washed, and while his appetite had come back strong, he had to make do with berries and a heel of tough bread.

He closed the circle, salted the blackened earth outside it. Once he was in the saddle, he set off at a gallop.

With luck, he could be home by midday.

There were no signs, no harbingers, no beautiful witches on the rest of his journey. There were only the fields, rolling green, back to the shadow of mountains, and the secret depths of forest. He knew his way now, would have known it if a hundred years had passed. So he sent his mount on a leap over a low stone wall and raced across the last field toward home.

He could see the cook fire. He imagined his mother sitting in the parlor, tatting lace perhaps, or working on one of her tapestries. Waiting, hoping for news of her sons. He wished he brought her better.

His father might be with his man of business or out riding the land, and his married sisters in their own cottages, with young Nola in the stables playing with the pups from the new litter.

The house was tucked in the forest, because his grandmother—she who had passed power to him, and to a lesser extent, Cian—had wanted it so. It stood near a stream, a rise of stone with windows of real glass. And its gardens were his mother's great pride.

Her roses bloomed riotously.

One of the servants hurried out to take his horse. Hoyt merely shook his head at the question in the man's eyes. He walked to the door where the black banner of mourning still hung.

Inside, another servant was waiting to take his cloak. Here in the hall, his mother's, and her mother's tapestries hung, and one of his father's wolfhounds raced to greet him.

He could smell beeswax, and roses cut fresh from the garden. The turf fire simmering in the grate. He left them behind, walked up the stairs to his mother's sitting room.

She was waiting, as he'd known she would be. She was sitting in her chair, her hands in her lap, clasped so tightly the knuckles were white. Her face carried all the weight of her grief, and went heavier yet when she saw what was in his eyes.

"Mother—"

"You're alive. You're well." She got to her feet, held out her arms to him. "I've lost my youngest son, but here is my firstborn, home again. You'll want food and drink after your journey."

"I have much to tell you."

"And so you will."

"All of you, if you please, madam. I cannot stay long. I'm sorry." He kissed her brow. "I'm sorry to leave you."

There was food and there was drink, and the whole of his family—save Cian—around the table. But it was not a meal like so many he remembered, with laughter and shouted arguments, with joy or petty disagreements. Hoyt studied their faces, the beauties, the strengths and the sorrows as he told them what had passed.

"If there is to be a battle, I will come with you. Fight with you."

Hoyt looked at his brother-in-law Fearghus. His shoulders were broad, his fists ready.

"Where I go, you can't follow. You're not charged with this fight. It's for you and Eoin to stay here, to protect with my father, the family, the land. I would go with a heavier heart if I didn't know you and Eoin stand in my stead. You must wear these."

He took out the crosses. "Each of you, and all the children who come after. Day and night, night and day. This," he said and lifted one, "is Morrigan's Cross, forged by the gods in magic fire. The vampyre cannot turn any who wear it into its kind. This must be passed on to those who come after you, in song and story. You will swear an oath, each of you, that you will wear this cross until death."

He rose, draping a cross over each neck, waiting for the sworn oath before moving on.

Then he knelt by his father. His father's hands were old, Hoyt noted with a jolt. He was more farmer than warrior, and in a flash, he knew his father's death would come first, and before the Yule. Just as he knew he would never again look in the eyes of the man who'd given him life.

And his heart bled a little.

"I take my leave of you, sir. I ask your blessing."

"Avenge your brother, and come back to us."

"I will." Hoyt rose. "I must gather what I need."

He went up to the room he kept in the topmost tower, and there began to pack herbs and potions without any real sense of what would be needed.

"Where is your cross?"

He looked toward the doorway where Nola stood, her dark hair hanging to her waist. She was but eight, he thought, and held the softest spot in his heart.

"She didn't make me one," he said, briskly. "I have another sort of shield, and there's no need for you to be worrying. I know what I'm about."

"I won't cry when you go."

"Why would you? I've gone before, haven't I, and come back handily enough?"

"You'll come back. To the tower. She'll come with you."

He nestled bottles carefully in his case, then paused to study his sister. "Who will?"

"The woman with red hair. Not the goddess, but a mortal woman, one who wears the sign of the witch. I can't see Cian, and I can't see if you'll win. But I can see you, here with the witch. And you're afraid."

"Should a man go into battle without fear? Isn't fear something that helps keep him alive?"

"I don't know of battles. I wish I were a man, and a warrior." Her mouth, so young, so soft, went grim. "You wouldn't be stopping me from going with you the way you stopped Fearghus."

"How would I dare?" He closed his case, moved to her. "I am afraid. Don't tell the others."

"I won't."

Aye, the softest place in his heart, he thought, and lifting her cross, used his magic to scribe her name on the back in ogham script. "It makes it only yours," he told her.

"Mine, and the ones who'll have my name after me." Her eyes glimmered, but the tears didn't fall. "You'll see me again."

"I will, of course."

"When you do, the circle will be complete. I don't know how, or why."

"What else do you see, Nola?"

She only shook her head. "It's dark. I can't see. I'll light a candle for you, every night, until you return."

"I'll ride home by its light." He bent down to embrace her. "I'll miss you most of all." He kissed her gently, then set her aside. "Be safe."

"I will have daughters," she called after him.

It made him turn, and smile. So slight, he mused, and so fierce. "Will you now?"

"It is my lot," she told him with a resignation that made his lips twitch. "But they will not be weak. They will *not* sit and spin and knead and bake all the damn day."

Now he grinned fully, and knew this was a memory he would take with him happily. "Oh won't they? What then, young mother, will your daughters do?"

"They will be warriors. And the vampyre who fancies herself a queen will tremble before them."

She folded her hands, much as their mother was wont to do, but with none of that meekness. "Go with the gods, brother."

"Stay in the light, sister."

They watched him go—three sisters, the men who loved

them, the children they'd already made. His parents, even the servants and stable boys. He took one last long look at the house his grandfather, and his father before, had built of stone in this glade, by this stream, in this land he loved with the whole of his heart.

Then he raised his hand in farewell, and rode away from them and toward the Dance of the Gods.

It stood on a rise of rough grass that was thick with the sunny yellow of buttercups. Clouds had rolled to layer the sky so that light forced its way through in thin beams. The world was so still, so silent, he felt as though he rode through a painting. The gray of the sky, the green of the grass, the yellow flowers, and the ancient circle of stones that had risen in its dance since beyond time.

He felt its power, the hum of it, in the air, along his skin. Hoyt walked his horse around them, paused to read the ogham script carved into the king stone.

"Worlds wait," he translated. "Time flows. Gods watch."

He started to dismount when a shimmer of gold across the field caught his eye. There at the edge of it was a hind. The green of her eyes sparkled like the jeweled collar she wore. She walked toward him regally, and changed to the female form of the goddess.

"You are in good time, Hoyt."

"It was painful to bid my family farewell. Best done quickly then."

He slid off the horse, bowed. "My lady."

"Child. You have been ill."

"A fever, broken now. Did you send the witch to me?"

"There's no need to send what will come on its own. You'll find her again, and the others."

"My brother."

"He is first. The light will go soon. Here is the key to the portal." She opened her hand and offered a small crystal wand. "Keep it with you, keep it safe and whole." When he started to re-mount, she shook her head, took the reins. "No, you must go on foot. Your horse will get safely back home."

Resigned to the whimsy of gods, he took his case, his bag. He strapped on his sword, hefted his staff.

"How will I find him?"

"Through the portal, into the world yet to come. Into the Dance, lift the key, say the words. Your destiny lies beyond. Humankind is in your hands, from this point forward. Through the portal," she repeated. "Into the world yet to come. Into the Dance, lift the key, say the words. Through the portal . . ."

Her voice followed him in, between the great stones. He locked his fear inside him. If he'd been born for this, so be it. Life was long, he knew. It simply came in short bursts.

He lifted the stone. A single beam of light speared out of those thick clouds to strike its tip. Power shot down his arm like an arrow.

"Worlds wait. Time flows. Gods watch."

"Repeat," Morrigan told him, and joined him so that the words became a chant.

"Worlds wait. Time flows. Gods watch."

The air shook around him, came alive with wind, with light, with sound. The crystal in his uplifted hand shone like the sun and sang like a siren.

He heard his own voice come out in a roar, shouting the words now as if in challenge.

And so he flew. Through light and wind and sound. Beyond stars and moons and planets. Over water that made his sorcerer's belly roil with nausea. Faster, until the light was blinding, the sounds deafening and the wind so fierce he wondered it didn't flay the skin from his bones.

Then the light went dim, the wind died, and the world was silent.

He leaned on his staff, catching his breath, waiting for his eyes to adjust to the change of light. He smelled something—leather, he thought, and roses.

He was in a room of some sort, he realized, but like nothing he'd ever seen. It was fantastically furnished with long, low chairs in deep colors, and cloth for a floor. Paintings adorned some of the walls, and others were lined with books. Dozens of books bound in leather.

He stepped forward, charmed, when a movement to his left stopped him cold.

His brother sat behind some sort of table, where the lamp that lit the room glowed strangely. His hair was shorter than it had been, shorn to the jawline. His eyes were vivid with what seemed to be amusement.

In his hand was some sort of metal tool, which instinct told Hoyt was a weapon.

Cian pointed it at his brother's heart and tipped back in the chair, dropping his feet on the surface of the table. He smiled, broadly, and said, "Well now, look what the cat dragged in."

With some confusion, Hoyt frowned, scanning the room for the cat. "Do you know me?" Hoyt stepped forward, farther into the light. "It's Hoyt. It's your brother. I've come to . . ."

"Kill me? Too late. Already long dead. Why don't you just stay where you are for the moment. I see quite well in low light. You're looking . . . well, fairly ridiculous really. But I'm impressed nonetheless. How long did it take you to perfect time travel?"

"I . . ." Coming through the portal might have addled his brains, he thought. Or it might be simply seeing his dead brother, looking very much alive. "Cian."

"I'm not using that name these days. It's Keene, right at the moment. One syllable. Take off the cloak, Hoyt, and let's have a look at what's under it."

"You're a vampyre."

"I am, yes, certainly. The cloak, Hoyt."

Hoyt unhooked the brooch that held it in place, let it drop.

"Sword and dagger. A lot of weaponry for a sorcerer."

"There's to be a battle."

"Do you think so?" That amusement rippled again, coldly. "I can promise you'll lose. What I have here is called a gun. It's quite a good one, really. It fires out a projectile faster than you can blink. You'll be dead where you stand before you can draw that sword."

"I haven't come to fight you."

"Really? The last time we met—let me refresh my memory. Ah yes, you pushed me off a cliff."

"You pushed me off the bloody cliff first," Hoyt said with

some heat. "Broke my bloody ribs while you were about it. I thought you were gone. Oh merciful gods, Cian, I thought you were gone."

"I'm not, as you can plainly see. Go back where you came from, Hoyt. I've had a thousand years, give or take, to get over my annoyance with you."

"For me you died only a week ago." He lifted his tunic. "You gave me these bruises."

Cian's gaze drifted over them, then back to Hoyt's face. "They'll heal soon enough."

"I've come with a charge from Morrigan."

"Morrigan, is it." This time the amusement burst out in laughter. "There are no gods here. No God. No faerie queens. Your magic has no place in this time, and neither do you."

"But you do."

"Adjustment is survival. Money is god here, and power its partner. I have both. I've shed the likes of you a long time ago."

"This world will end, they will all end, by Samhain, unless you help me stop her."

"Stop who?"

"The one who made you. The one called Lilith."

Chapter 3

Lilith. The name brought Cian flashes of memories, a hundred lifetimes past. He could still see her, smell her, still feel that sudden, horrified thrill in the instant she'd taken his life.

He could still taste her blood, and what had come into him with it. The dark, dark gift.

His world had changed. And he'd been given the privilege—or the curse—of watching worlds change over countless decades.

Hadn't he known something was coming? Why else had he been sitting alone in the middle of the night, waiting?

What nasty little twist of fate had sent his brother—or the brother of the man he'd once been—across time to speak her name?

"Well, now you have my attention."

"You must come back with me, prepare for the battle."

"Back? To the twelfth century?" Cian let out a short laugh as he leaned back in his chair. "Nothing, I promise you, could tempt me. I like the conveniences of this time. The water runs hot here, Hoyt, and so do the women. I'm not interested in your politics and wars, and certainly not in your gods."

"The battle will be fought, with or without you, Cian."

"Without sounds perfectly fine."

"You've never turned from battle, never hidden from a fight."

"*Hiding* wouldn't be the term I'd use," Cian said easily. "And times change. Believe me."

"If Lilith defeats us, all you know will be lost in this time, for all time. Humankind will cease to be."

Cian angled his head. "I'm not human."

"Is that your answer?" Hoyt strode forward. "You'll sit and do nothing while she destroys? You'll stand by while she does to others what she did to you? While she kills your mother, your sisters? Will you sit there while she turns Nola into what you are?"

"They're dead. Long dead. They're dust." Hadn't he seen their graves? He hadn't been able to stop himself from going back and standing over their stones, and the stones of those who'd come after them.

"Have you forgotten all you were taught? Times change, you say. It's more than change. Could I be here now if time was solid? Their fate is not set, nor is yours. Even now our father is dying, yet I left him. I will never see him alive again."

Slowly Cian got to his feet. "You have no conception of what she is, what she is capable of. She was old, centuries old, when she took me. You think to stop her with swords and lightning bolts? You're more fool than I remember."

"I think to stop her with you. Help me. If not for humanity, then for yourself. Or would you join her? If there's nothing left of my brother in you, we'll end this between us now."

Hoyt drew his sword.

For a long moment, Cian studied the blade, considered the gun in his hand. Then he slipped the weapon back in his pocket. "Put your sword away. Christ, Hoyt, you couldn't take me one-on-one when I was alive."

Challenge, and simple irritation, rushed into Hoyt's eyes. "You didn't fare very well the last time we fought."

"True enough. It took me weeks to recover. Hiding around in caves by day, half starving. I looked for her then, you know. Lilith, who sired me. By night, while I struggled to hunt enough food to survive. She abandoned me. So I've a point to square with her. Put the damn sword away."

When Hoyt hesitated, Cian simply leaped. In the blink of an eye he was up, gliding over Hoyt's head and landing lightly at his back. He disarmed his brother with one careless twist of the wrist.

Hoyt turned slowly. The point of the sword was at his throat. "Well done," he managed.

"We're faster, and we're stronger. We have no conscience to bind us. We are driven to kill, to feed. To survive."

"Then why aren't I dead?"

Cian lifted a shoulder. "We'll put it down to curiosity, and a bit of old time's sake." He tossed the sword across the room. "Well then, let's have a drink."

He walked to a cabinet, opened it. Out of the corner of his eye he saw the sword fly across the room and into Hoyt's hand. "Well done on you," he said mildly and took out a bottle of wine. "You can't kill me with steel, but you could—if you were lucky enough—hack some part of me off that I'd rather keep. We don't regenerate limbs."

"I'll put my weapons aside, and you do the same."

"Fair enough." Cian took the gun out of his pocket, set it on a table. "Though a vampire always has his weapon." He offered a brief glimpse of fangs. "Nothing to be done about that." He poured two glasses while Hoyt laid down his sword and dagger. "Have a seat then, and you can tell me why I should get involved in saving the world. I'm a busy man these days. I have enterprises."

Hoyt took the glass offered, studied it, sniffed at it. "What is this?"

"A very nice Italian red. I've no need to poison you." To prove it, he sipped from his own glass. "I could snap your neck like a twig." Cian sat himself, stretched out his legs. Then he waved a hand at Hoyt. "In today's worlds, what we're having here could be called a meeting, and you're about to make your pitch. So . . . enlighten me."

"We must gather forces, beginning with a handful. There is a scholar and a witch, one of many forms and a warrior. That must be you."

"No. I'm no warrior. I'm a businessman." He continued to sit, at his ease, giving Hoyt a lazy smile. "So the gods, as usual, have given you pitifully little to work with, and an all but impossible task. With your handful, and whoever else is fool enough to join you, you're expected to defeat an army led by a powerful vampire, most likely with troops of her kind, and other manner of demon if she deigns to bother with them. Otherwise, the world is destroyed."

"Worlds," Hoyt corrected. "There are more than one."

"You're right about that anyway." Cian sipped, contemplated. He'd nearly run out of challenges in his current persona. This, at least, was interesting.

"And what do your gods tell you is my part in this?"

"You must come with me, teach me all that you can about her kind, and how to defeat them. What are their weaknesses? What are their powers? What weaponry and magic will work against them? We have until Samhain to master these and gather the first circle."

"That long?" Sarcasm dripped. "What would I gain from all this? I'm a wealthy man, with many interests to protect here and now."

"And would she allow you to keep that wealth, those interests, should she rule?"

Cian pursed his lips. Now there was a thought. "Possibly not. But it's more than possible if I help you I'll risk all that and my own existence. When you're young, as you are—"

"I'm the eldest."

"Not for the last nine hundred years and counting. In any case, when you're young you think you'll live forever, so you take all manner of foolish risks. But when you've lived as long as I, you're more careful. Because existence is imperative. I'm driven to survive, Hoyt. Humans and vampires have that in common."

"You survive sitting alone in the dark in this little house?"

"It's not a house," Cian said absently. "It's an office. A place of business. I have many houses, as it happens. That, too, is survival. There are taxes and records and all manner of things to be gotten around. Like most of my kind I rarely stay in one place for long. We're nomadic from nature and necessity."

He leaned forward now, resting his elbows on his knees. There were so few he could speak to about what he was. That was his choice, that was the life he'd made. "Hoyt, I've seen wars, countless wars, such as you could never imagine. No one wins them. If you do this thing, you'll die. Or become. It would be a feather in Lilith's cap to turn a sorcerer of your power."

"Do you think there is a choice here?"

"Oh yes." He sat back again. "There always is. I've made many in my lifetimes." He closed his eyes now, lazily swirling his wine. "Something's coming. There have been rumblings in the world under this one. In the dark places. If it's what you say, it's bigger than I assumed. I should've paid more attention. I don't socialize with vampires as a rule."

Baffled, as Cian had always been sociable, Hoyt frowned. "Why not?"

"Because as a rule they're liars and killers and bring too much attention to themselves. And those humans who socialize with them are usually mad or doomed. I pay my taxes, file my reports and keep a low profile. And every decade or so, I move, change my name and keep off the radar."

"I don't understand half of what you say."

"Imagine not," Cian replied. "She'll fuck this up for everyone. Bloodbaths always do, and those demons who go about thinking they want to destroy the world are ridiculously shortsighted. We have to live in it, don't we?"

He sat in silence. He could focus and hear each beat of his brother's heart, hear the faint electrical hum of the room's climate controls, the buzz of the lamp on his desk across the room. Or he could block them out, as he most often did with background noises.

He'd learned to do, and not do, a great deal over time.

A choice, he thought again. Well, why not?

"It comes down to blood," Cian said, and his eyes stayed closed. "First and last, it comes to blood. We both need it to live, your kind and mine. It's what we sacrifice, for the gods you worship, for countries, for women. And what we spill for the same reasons. My kind doesn't quibble about reasons."

He opened his eyes now, and showed Hoyt how they could burn red. "We just take it. We hunger for it, crave it. Without it, we cease to be. It's our nature to hunt, kill, feed. Some of us enjoy it more than others, just as humans do. Some of us enjoy causing pain, inciting fear, tormenting and torturing our prey. Just as humans do. We're not all of the same cloth, Hoyt."

"You murder."

"When you hunt the buck in the forest and take its life, is it murder? You're no more than that, less, often less, to us."

"I saw your death."

"The tumble off the cliffs wasn't—"

"No. I saw her kill you. I thought it a dream at first. I watched you come out of the tavern, go with her in her carriage. And couple with her as it drove out of the village. And I saw her eyes change, and how the fangs glinted in the dark before she sank them into your throat. I saw your face. The pain, the shock, and . . ."

"Arousal," Cian finished. "Ecstasy. It's a moment of some intensity."

"You tried to fight, but she was an animal on you, and I thought you were dead, but you weren't. Not quite."

"No, to feed you simply take, drain the prey dry if you choose. But to change a human, he must drink from the blood of his maker."

"She sliced her own breast, and pressed your mouth to her, and still you tried to fight until you began to suckle on her like a babe."

"The allure is powerful, as is the drive to survive. It was drink or die."

"When she was done, she threw you out into the road, left you there. It was there I found you." Hoyt drank deeply as his belly quivered. "There I found you, covered with blood and mud. And this is what you do to survive? The buck is given more respect."

"Do you want to lecture me?" Cian began as he rose to get the bottle again. "Or do you want to know?"

"I need to know."

"Some hunt in packs, some alone. At wakening we're most vulnerable—from the first when we wake in the grave, to every evening if we've slept through the day. We are night creatures. The sun is death."

"You burn in it."

"I see you know some things."

"I saw. They hunted me when I journeyed home. In the form of wolves."

"Only vampires of some age and power, or those under the protection of another powerful sire can shape shift. Most have to content themselves with the form in which they died. Still, we don't age, physically. A nice bonus feature."

"You look as you did," Hoyt replied. "Yet not. It's more than the garb you wear, or the hair. You move differently."

"I'm not what I was, and that you should remember. Our senses are heightened, and become more so the longer we survive. Fire, like the sun, will destroy us. Holy water, if it's been faithfully blessed, will burn us, as will the symbol of the cross, if held in faith. We are repelled by the symbol."

Crosses, Hoyt thought. Morrigan had given him crosses. Part of the weight eased from his shoulders.

"Metal is fairly useless," Cian continued, "unless you manage to cut off our heads. That would do the trick. But otherwise . . ."

He rose again, walked over and picked up Hoyt's dagger. He flipped it in the air, caught the hilt neatly, then plunged the blade into his chest.

Blood seeped out on the white of Cian's shirt even as Hoyt lunged to his feet.

"Forgot how much that hurts." Wincing, Cian yanked the blade free. "That's what I get for showing off. Do the same with wood, and we're dust. But it must pierce the heart. Our end is agonizing, or so I'm told."

He took out a handkerchief, wiped the blade clean. Then he pulled off his shirt. The wound was already closing.

"We've died once, and aren't easily dispatched a second time. And we'll fight viciously anyone who tries. Lilith is the oldest I've ever known. She'll fight more brutally than any."

He paused, brooded into his wine. "Your mother. How did you leave her?"

"Heartbroken. You were her favorite." Hoyt moved his shoulders as Cian looked up into his face. "We both know it. She asked me to try, to find a way. In her first grief, she could think of nothing else."

"I believe even your sorcery stops short of raising the dead. Or undead."

"I went to your grave that night, to ask the gods to give her heart some peace. I found you, covered with dirt."

"Clawing out of the grave's a messy business."

"You were devouring a rabbit."

"Probably the best I could find. Can't say I recall. The first hours after the Wakening are disjointed. There's only hunger."

"You ran from me. I saw what you were—there had been rumors of such things before—and you ran. I went to the cliffs the night I saw you again, at our mother's behest. She begged me to find a way to break the spell."

"It's not a spell."

"I thought, hoped, if I destroyed the thing that made you . . . Or failing that, I would kill what you'd become."

"And did neither," Cian reminded him. "Which shows you what you're up against. I was fresh and barely knew what I was or what I was capable of. Believe me, she'll have cannier on her side."

"Will I have yours on mine?"

"You haven't a prayer of winning this."

"You underestimate me. I have a great deal more than one prayer. Whether a year has passed or a millennium, you are my brother. My twin. My blood. You said yourself, it's blood, first and last."

Cian ran a finger down his wine glass. "I'll go with you." Then held the finger up before Hoyt could speak. "Because I'm curious, and a bit bored. I've been in this place for more than ten years now, so it's nearly time to move on in any case. I promise you nothing. Don't depend on me, Hoyt. I'll please myself first."

"You can't hunt humans."

"Orders already?" Cian's lips curved slightly. "Typical. As I said, I please myself first. It happens I haven't fed on human blood for eight hundred years. Well, seven hundred and fifty as there was some backsliding."

"Why?"

"To prove that I could resist. And because it's another way to survive—and well—in the world of humans, with their laws. If they're prey, it's impossible to look at them as anything more than a meal. Makes it awkward to do business. And death tends to leave a trail. Dawn's coming."

Distracted, Hoyt glanced around the windowless room. "How do you know?"

"I feel it. And I'm tired of questions. You'll have to stay with me, for now. You can't be trusted to go walking about the city. We may not be identical, but you look too much like me. And those clothes have to go."

"You expect me to wear—what are those?"

"They're called pants," Cian said dryly and moved across the room to a private elevator. "I keep an apartment here, it's simpler."

"You'll pack what you need, and we'll go."

"I don't travel by day, and I don't take orders. I give them now, and have for some time. I have a number of things to see to before I can leave. You need to step in here."

"What is it?" Hoyt poked at the elevator walls with his staff.

"A mode of transportation. It'll take us up to my apartment."

"How?"

Cian finally dragged a hand through his hair. "Look, I've books up there, and other educational matter. You can spend the next few hours boning up on twenty-first-century culture, fashion and technology."

"What is technology?"

Cian pulled his brother inside, pushed the button for the next floor. "It's another god."

* * *

This world, this time, was full of wonder. Hoyt wished he had time to learn it all, absorb it. There were no torches to light the room but instead something Cian called electricity. Food was kept in a box as tall as a man that kept it cold and fresh, and yet another box was used to warm and cook it. Water spilled out of a wand and into a bowl where it drained away again.

The house where Cian lived was built high up in the city, and such a city! The glimpse Morrigan had given him had been nothing compared to what he could see through the glass wall of Cian's quarters.

Hoyt thought even the gods would be stunned by the size and scope of this New York. He wanted to look out at it again, but Cian had demanded his oath that he would keep the glass walls covered, and he would not venture out of the house.

Apartment, Hoyt corrected. Cian had called it an apartment.

He had books, so many books, and the magic box Cian had called a television. Indeed the visions inside it were many, of people and places, of things, of animals. And though he spent only an hour playing with it, he grew weary of its constant chatter.

So he surrounded himself with books and read, and read until his eyes burned and his head was too full for more words or images.

He fell asleep on what Cian had called a sofa, surrounded by books.

He dreamed of the witch, and saw her in a circle of light. She wore nothing but the pendant, and her skin glowed milk-pale in the candlelight.

Her beauty simply flamed.

She held a ball of crystal aloft in both hands. He could hear the whisper of her voice, but not the words. Still, he knew it was an incantation, could feel the power of it, of her across the dream. And he knew she was seeking him out.

Even in sleep he felt the pull of her, and that same impatience he'd sensed from her within his circle, within his own time.

It seemed for an instant that their eyes met across the mists. And it was desire that pierced through him as much as power. In that instant, her lips curved, opened, as if she would speak to him.

"What the hell is that get-up?"

He came awake and found himself staring up into the face of a giant. The creature was tall as a tree, and every bit as thick. He had a face even a mother would weep over, black as a moor and scarred at the cheek, and surrounded by knotted hanks of hair.

He had one black eye and one gray. Both narrowed as he bared strong white teeth.

"You're not Cain."

Before Hoyt could react, he was hauled up by the scruff of the neck where he was shaken like a mouse by a very large, angry cat.

"Put him down, King, before he turns you into a small white man."

Cian strolled out of his bedroom, and continued lazily into the kitchen.

"How come he's got your face?"

"He's got his own," Cian retorted. "We don't look that much alike if you pay attention. He used to be my brother."

"That so? Son of a bitch." King dropped Hoyt unceremoniously back on the sofa. "How the hell did he get here?"

"Sorcery." As he spoke, Cian removed a clear packet of blood from a locked cold box. "Gods and battles, end of the world, blah blah."

King looked down at Hoyt with a grin. "I'll be damned. I always thought half of that crap you told me was, well, crap. He's not much for conversation before he's had his evening fix," he said to Hoyt. "You got a name, brother?"

"I am Hoyt of the Mac Cionaoith. And you will not lay hands on me again."

"That's a mouthful."

"Is he like you?" both Hoyt and King demanded in unison.

Wearily Cian poured the blood in a tall, thick glass, then set it in the microwave. "No, to both. King manages my club, the one downstairs. He's a friend."

Hoyt's lips peeled back in disgust. "Your human servant."

"I ain't nobody's servant."

"You've been reading." Cian took out the glass and drank. "Some vampires of rank have human servants. I prefer employees. Hoyt's come to enlist me in the army he hopes to raise to fight the big evil."

"The IRS?"

In better humor, Cian grinned. Hoyt saw something pass between them, something that had once only passed between himself and his brother.

"If only. No, I told you I've heard rumblings. Apparently for a reason. According to the gossip of the gods, Lilith of the Vampires is amassing her own army and plans to destroy humanity, take over the worlds. War, pestilence, plague."

"You can jest?" Hoyt said in barely suppressed fury.

"Christ Jesus, Hoyt, we're talking about vampire armies and time travel. Bloody right I can joke about it. Going with you is likely to kill me."

"Where are you going?"

Cian shrugged at King. "Back to my past, I suppose, to act in an advisory capacity, at least, for General Sobriety there."

"I don't know if we're to go back, or forward, or to the side." Hoyt shoved books over the table. "But we will go back to Ireland. We will be told where we travel next."

"Got a beer?" King asked.

Cian opened the refrigerator, took out a bottle of Harp and tossed it.

"So when do we leave?" King twisted off the cap, took a long slug.

"You don't. I told you before, when it was time for me to leave, I'll give you controlling interest in the club. Apparently, that time's come."

King simply turned to Hoyt. "You raising an army, General?"

"Hoyt. I am, yes."

"You just got your first recruit."

"Stop." Cian strode around the counter that separated the kitchen. "This isn't for you. You don't know anything about this."

"I know about you," King returned. "I know I like a good fight, and I haven't had one in a while. You're talking major battle, good against evil. I like to pick my side from the get."

"If he's a king, why should he take orders from you?" Hoyt put in, and the black giant laughed so hard and long, he had to sit on the sofa.

"Gotcha."

"Misplaced loyalty will get you killed."

"My choice, brother." King tipped the bottle toward Cian. Once again, something silent and strong passed between them with no more than a look. "And I don't figure my loyalty's misplaced."

"Hoyt, go somewhere else." Cian jerked a thumb toward his bedroom. "Go in there. I want a word in private with this idiot."

He cared, Hoyt thought as he obliged. Cian cared about this man, a human trait. Nothing he'd read had indicated vampires could have true feelings toward humans.

He frowned as he scanned the bedroom. Where was the coffin? The books had said the vampire slept in the earth of his grave, in a coffin, by day. What he saw here was an enormous bed, one with ticking as soft as clouds and covered with smooth cloth.

He heard the raised voices outside the door, but set about exploring his brother's personal room. Clothes enough for ten men, he decided when he found the closet. Well, Cian had always been vain.

But no looking glass. The books said the vampyre cast no reflection.

He wandered into the bathroom, and his jaw dropped. The expansive privy Cian had showed him before retiring had been amazing and was nothing to this. The tub was large enough for six, and there was a tall box of pale green glass. The walls were marble, as was the floor.

Fascinated, he stepped into the box, began to play with the silver knobs that jutted out of the marble. And yipped in shock when a shower of cold water spurted out of many flat-headed tubes.

"Around here, we take our clothes off before getting in the shower." Cian came in, shut the water off with one violent twist of the wrist. Then he sniffed the air. "On second thought, clothed or otherwise, you could sure as hell use one. You're fucking rank. Clean up," he ordered. "Put on the clothes I've tossed out on the bed. I'm going to work."

He strode out, leaving Hoyt to fumble through on his own.

He discovered, after some time and chill that the temperature of the water could be adjusted. He scalded himself, froze, but eventually found the happy medium.

His brother must have been telling pure truth when he spoke of his wealth, for here was luxury never imagined. The scent of the soap seemed a bit female, but there was nothing else.

Hoyt wallowed in his first twenty-first-century shower, and wondered if he might find a way to duplicate it, by science or magic, once he returned home.

The cloths hanging nearby were as soft as the bed had been. He felt decadent using one to dry his skin.

He didn't care for the clothes, but his own were soaked. He debated going out and getting the spare tunic out of his case, but it seemed best to follow Cian's advice in wardrobe.

It took him twice as long to dress as it would have. The strange fastenings nearly defeated him. The shoes had no laces, but simply slipped on the foot. He was forced to admit that they were quite comfortable.

But he wished there was a bloody looking glass so he could see himself. He stepped out, then came up short. The black king was still on the sofa, drinking from the glass bottle.

"That's an improvement," King observed. "You'll probably pass if you keep your mouth mostly shut."

"What is this fastening here?"

"It's a zipper. Ah, you're going to want to keep that closed, friend." He pushed to his feet. "Cian's gone on down to the club. It's after sunset. He fired me."

"You're burned? I have salve."

"No. Shit. He terminated my employment. He'll get over it. He goes, I go. He don't have to like it."

"He believes we'll all die."

"He's right—sooner or later. You ever see what a vamp can do to a man?"

"I saw what one did to my brother."

King's odd eyes went grim. "Yeah, yeah, that's right. Well, it's this way. I don't figure to sit around and wait for one to do it to me. He's right, there's been rumbling. There's going to be a fight, and I'm going to be in it."

A giant of a man, Hoyt thought, of fearsome face and great strength. "You are a warrior."

"Bet your ass. I'll kick some vampire ass in this, believe me. But not tonight. Why don't we go on down, see what's jumping. That'll piss him off."

"To his . . ." What had Cian called it. "His club?"

"You got it. He calls it Eternity. I guess he knows something about that."

Chapter 4

She was going to find him. If a man was going to drag her into his dreams, push her into out-of-body experiences and generally haunt her thoughts, she was going to track him down and find out why.

For days now she had felt as if she stood on the edge of some high, shaky cliff. On one side there was something bright and beautiful, and on the other a cold and terrifying void. But the cliff itself, while a little unstable, was the known.

Whatever was brewing inside her, he was part of it, that she knew. Not of this time, not of this place. Guys just didn't ride around on horses wearing cloaks and tunics in twenty-first-century New York as a rule.

But he was real; he was flesh and blood and as real as she was. She'd had that blood on her hands, hadn't she? She'd cooled that flesh and watched him sleep off the fever. His face, she thought, had been so familiar. Like something she remembered, or had caught a glimpse of in dreams.

Handsome, even in pain, she mused as she sketched it. Lean and angular, aristocratic. Long narrow nose, strong, sculpted mouth. Good, slashing cheekbones.

His image came true on paper as she worked, first in broad strokes, then in careful detail. Deep-set eyes, she remembered, vividly blue and intense with an almost dramatic arch of brows over them. And the contrast of that black hair, those black brows and wild blue eyes against his skin just added more drama.

Yes, she thought, she could see him, she could sketch him, but until she found him, she wouldn't know whether she should jump off the edge of that cliff or scramble back from it.

Glenna Ward was a woman who liked to know.

So, she knew his face, the shape and feel of his body, even the sound of his voice. She knew, without question, he had power. And she believed he had answers.

Whatever was coming, and every portent warned her it was major, he was tied to it. She had a part to play, had known almost since her first breath that she had a part to play. She had a feeling that she was about to take on the role of her lifetime. And the wounded hunk with the clouds of magic and trouble all around him was slated to co-star.

He'd spoken Gaelio, Irish Gaelic. She knew some of it, used the language occasionally in spells, and could even read some in a very rudimentary fashion.

But oddly enough, she'd not only understood everything he'd said in the dream—experience, vision, whatever—she'd been able to speak it herself, like a native.

So somewhere in the past—the good, long past, she determined. And possibly somewhere in Ireland.

She'd done scrying spells and locator spells, using the bloodied bandage she'd brought back with her from that strange and intense visit to . . . wherever she'd been. His blood and her own talent would lead her to him.

She'd expected it to be a great deal of work and effort. Doubled by whatever work and effort would be involved in transporting herself—or at least her essence—to his time and place.

She was prepared to do just that, or at least try. She sat within her circle, the candles lit, the herbs floating on the water in her bowl. Once more she searched for him, focusing on the sketch of his face and holding the cloth she'd brought back with her.

"I seek the man who bears this face, my quest to find his time, his place. I hold his blood within my hand, and with its power I demand. Search and find and show to me. As I will, so mote it be."

In her mind she saw him, brow furrowed as he buried himself in books. Focusing, she drew back, saw the room. Apartment? Dim light, just slanting over his face, his hands.

"Where are you?" she asked softly. "Show me."

And she saw the building, the street.

The thrill of success mixed with absolute bafflement.

The last thing she'd expected was to learn he was in New York, some sixty blocks away, and in the now.

The fates, Glenna decided, were in an all-fired hurry to get things started. Who was she to question them?

She closed the circle, put away her tools and tucked the sketch in her desk drawer. Then she dressed, puzzling over her choices for a bit. What exactly did a woman wear when she went to meet her destiny? Something flashy, subdued, businesslike? Something exotic?

In the end she settled on a little black dress she felt could handle anything.

She traveled uptown by subway, letting her mind clear. There was a drumming in her heart, an anticipation that had been building in her over the past weeks. This, she thought, was the next step to whatever was waiting.

And whatever it was, whatever was coming, whatever would happen next, she wanted to be open to it.

Then she'd make her decisions.

The train was crowded, so she stood, holding the overhead hook and swaying slightly with the movement of the car. She liked the rhythm of the city, its rapid pace, its eclectic musics. All the tones and hues of it.

She'd grown up in New York, but not in the city. The small town upstate had always seemed too limited to her, too closed-in. She'd wanted more, always. More color, more sound, more people. She'd spent the last four of her twenty-six years in the city.

And all of her life exploring her craft.

Something in her blood was humming now, as if it

knew—some part of her knew—she'd been preparing all of her life for these next hours.

At the next station, people filed on, people filed off. She let the sound of them flow over her as she brought the image of the man she sought back into her head.

Not the face of a martyr, she thought. There'd been too much power on him for that. And too much annoyance in him. She'd found it, she could admit, a very interesting mix.

The power of the circle he'd cast had been strong, and so had been whatever hunted him. They chased her dreams, too, those black wolves that were neither animal nor human, but something horribly of both.

Idly, she fingered the pendant she wore around her neck. Well, she was strong, too. She knew how to protect herself.

"She will feed on you."

The voice was a hiss rippling over the back of her throat, icing her skin. Then what spoke moved, seemed to glide and float in a circle around her, and the cold from it had the breath that trembled from between her lips frosting the air.

The other passengers continued to sit or stand, read or chat. Undisturbed. Unaware of the thing that slithered around their bodies like a snake.

Its eyes were red, its eye teeth long and sharp. Blood stained them, dripped obscenely from its mouth. Inside her chest, Glenna's heart tightened like a fist and began to beat, beat, beat against her ribs.

It had human form, and worse, somehow worse, wore a business suit. Blue pinstripes, she noted dully, crisp white shirt and paisley tie.

"We are forever." It swiped a bloody hand over the cheek of a woman who sat reading a paperback novel. Even while red stained her cheek, the woman turned the page and continued to read.

"We will herd you like cattle, ride you like horses, trap you like rats. Your powers are puny and pathetic, and when we're done with you, we'll dance on your bones."

"Then why are you afraid?"

It peeled back its lips in a snarl, and it leapt.

Glenna choked on a scream, stumbled back.

As the train streaked through a tunnel, the thing vanished.

"Watch it, lady." She got an impatient elbow and mutter from the man she'd fallen into.

"Sorry." She gripped the hook again with a hand gone slick with sweat.

She could still smell the blood as she rode the last blocks uptown.

For the first time in her life, Glenna actively feared the dark, the streets, the people who passed by. She had to struggle to not run when the train stopped. Had to suppress the urge to shove and push her way off and race across the platform to the steps leading up.

She walked quickly, and even with the city noises she heard the rapid clip of her heels on the sidewalk and the fearful wheeze of her own breath.

There was a line snaking out from the entrance of the club called Eternity. Couples and singles crammed together hoping to get the signal to go inside. Rather than wait, she walked up to the man on the door. She flashed a smile, did a quick charm.

He passed her through without checking his list or her ID.

Inside was music, blue light and the throb of excitement. For once the press of humanity, the pulse and beat didn't excite her.

Too many faces, she thought. Too many heartbeats. She wanted only one, and the prospect of finding him among so many suddenly seemed impossible. Every bump and jostle as she worked her way into the club jolted through her. And her own fear shamed her.

She wasn't defenseless; she wasn't weak. But she felt both. The thing on the train had been every nightmare. And that nightmare had been sent to her.

For her.

It had known her fear, she thought now. And it had played with it, taunted her until her knees were water and the screams inside her had slashed her mind like razors.

She'd been too shocked, too frightened to reach for the only weapon she held. Magic.

Now anger began to eke through the terror.

She'd told herself she was a seeker, a woman who took risks, valued knowledge. A woman who possessed defenses and skills most couldn't imagine. Yet here she was quivering at the first real whiff of danger. She stiffened her spine, evened her breathing, then headed straight for the huge circular bar.

Halfway across the silver span of the floor she saw him.

The flood of relief came first, then the pride that she'd succeeded in this initial task so quickly. A trickle of interest worked its way through as she veered in his direction.

The guy cleaned up very well.

His hair was carelessly styled rather than ragged, a shining black and shorter than it had been during their first meeting. Then again, he'd been wounded, troubled and in a hell of a fix. He wore black, and it suited him. Just as the watchful, slightly irritable look in those brilliant eyes suited him.

With a great deal of her confidence restored, she smiled and stepped into his path.

"I've been looking for you."

Cian paused. He was accustomed to women approaching him. Not that he couldn't get some enjoyment from it, particularly when the woman was exceptional as this one was. There was a spark in her eyes, jewel green, and a flirtatious hint of amusement. Her lips were full, sensuous and curved; her voice low and husky.

Her body was a good one, and poured into a little black dress that showed a great deal of milky skin and strong muscle tone. He might have amused himself with her for a few moments, but for the pendant she wore.

Witches, and worse, those who played at witchcraft, could be troublesome.

"I enjoy being looked for by beautiful women when I have time to be found." He would have left it at that, moved on, but she touched his arm.

He felt something. And apparently so did she, for her eyes narrowed, and the smile faded.

"You're not him. You only look like him." Her hand tightened on his arm, and he sensed power seeking. "But that's not completely true either. Damn it." She dropped her hand, shook back her hair. "I should've known it wouldn't be so easy."

This time he took her arm. "Let's get you a table." In a dark, quiet corner, Cian thought. Until he knew who or what she was.

"I need information. I need to find someone."

"You need a drink," Cian said pleasantly, and steered her quickly through the crowd.

"Look, I can get my own drink if I want one." Glenna considered causing a scene, but decided it would probably get her tossed out. She considered a push of power, but knew from experience that depending on magic for every irritation led to trouble.

She glanced around, gauging the situation. The place was stacked with people on every level. The music was a throb, heavy on the bass with the female singer purring out the lyrics in a sensual and feline voice.

Very public, very active, Glenna decided with a lot of chrome and blue lighting slicking class over sex. What could he possibly do to her under the circumstances?

"I'm looking for someone." Conversation, she told herself. Keep it conversational and friendly. "I thought you were him. The light in here isn't the best, but you look enough alike to be brothers. It's very important I find him."

"What's his name? Maybe I can help you."

"I don't know his name." And the fact that she didn't made her feel foolish. "And okay, I know how that sounds. But I was told he was here. I think he's in trouble. If you'd just—" She started to shove at his hand, found it hard as stone.

What could he do to her in these circumstances? she thought again. Almost any damn thing. With the first fresh flicker of panic tickling her throat, she closed her eyes and reached for power.

His hand flinched on her arm, then his grip tightened. "So, you're a real one," he murmured, and turned those eyes—as steely as his grip—on her. "I think we'll take this upstairs."

"I'm not going anywhere with you." Something kin to the fear she'd felt on the subway worked its way into her. "That was low wattage. Believe me, you don't want me to up the amps."

"Believe me." And his voice was silky. "You don't want to piss me off."

He pulled her behind the curve of open, spiral stairs. She planted her feet, prepared to defend herself by any and all means at her disposal. She brought the four-inch spike of her heel down on his instep, slammed a back-fist into his jaw. Rather than wasting her breath on a scream, she began an incantation.

Her breath whooshed out when he lifted her off her feet as if she weighed nothing. Her only satisfaction came from the fact that in thirty seconds, when she finished the spell, he'd be flat on his ass.

That didn't stop her from fighting. She reared back, elbows and feet, and sucked in a breath to add a scream after all.

And the doors on what she saw was a private elevator whisked open.

There he was, flesh and blood. And so like the man currently heaving her over his shoulder she decided she could hate him, too.

"Put me down, you son of a bitch, or I'll turn this place into a moon crater."

When the doors of the transportation box opened, Hoyt was assaulted with noise and smells and lights. They all slammed into his system, stunning his senses. He saw through dazzled eyes, his brother with his arms full of struggling woman.

His woman, he realized with yet another jolt. The witch from his dream was half-naked and using language he'd rarely heard even in the seediest public house.

"Is this how you pay someone back for helping you?" She shoved at the curtain of her hair and aimed those sharp green eyes at him. She shifted them, scanned them up and down King, snarled.

"Come on then," she demanded. "I can take all three of you."

As she was currently over Cian's shoulder like a sack of

potatoes, Hoyt wasn't certain how she intended to see the threat through. But witches were tricky.

"You're real then," he stated softly. "Did you follow me?"

"Don't flatter yourself, asshole."

Cian shifted her, effortlessly. "Yours?" he said to Hoyt.

"I couldn't say."

"Deal with it." Cian dropped Glenna back on her feet, caught the fist aimed at his face just before it connected. "Do your business," he told her. "Quietly. Then take off. Keep a lid on the magic. Both of you. King."

He walked off. After a grin and a shrug, King trailed after him.

Glenna smoothed down her dress, shook back her hair. "What the hell's wrong with you?"

"My ribs still pain me a little, but I'm largely healed. Thank you for your help."

She stared at him, then huffed out a breath. "Here's how this is going to work. We're going to sit down, you're going to buy me a drink. I need one."

"I . . . I have no coin in these pants."

"Typical. I'll buy." She hooked an arm through his to make sure she didn't lose him again, then began to wind through the crowd.

"Did my brother hurt you?"

"What?"

He had to shout. How could anyone have a conversation in such noise? There were too many people in this place. Was it some sort of festival?

There were women writhing in what must have been some sort of ritual dance, and wearing even less than the witch. Others sat at silver tables and watched or ignored, drank from clear tankards and cups.

The music, he thought, came from everywhere at once.

"I asked if my brother hurt you."

"Brother? That fits. Bruised my pride for the most part."

She chose the stairs, moving up where the noise wasn't quite so horrific. Still clinging to his arm, she looked right, left, then moved toward a low seat with a candle flickering on the table. Five people were jammed around it, and all seemed to be talking at once.

She smiled at them, and he felt her power hum. "Hi. You really need to get home now, don't you?"

They got up, still chattering, and left the table littered with those clear drinking vessels, some nearly full.

"Sorry to cut their evening short, but I think this takes precedence. Sit down, will you?" She dropped down, stretched out long, bare legs. "God, what a night." She waved a hand in the air, fingered her pendant with the other as she studied his face. "You look better than you did. Are you healed?"

"Well enough. What place are you from?"

"Right to business." She glanced over at the waitress who came to their table to clear it. "I'll have a Grey Goose martini, straight up, two olives. Dry as dust." She cocked a brow at Hoyt. When he said nothing, she held up two fingers.

She tucked her hair behind one ear as she leaned toward him. There were silver coils dangling from her ear in a Celtic knot pattern.

"I dreamed of you before that night. Twice before I think," she began. "I try to pay attention to my dreams, but I could never hold on to these, until the last one. I think in the first, you were in a graveyard, and you were grieving. My heart broke for you, I remember feeling that. Odd, I remember more clearly now. The next time I dreamed of you, I saw you on a cliff, over the sea. I saw a woman with you who wasn't a woman. Even in the dream I was afraid of her. So were you."

She sat back, shuddering once. "Oh yes, I remember that now. I remember I was terrified, and there was a storm. And you . . . you struck out at her. I pushed—I remember I pushed what I had toward you, to try to help. I knew she was . . . she was wrong. Horribly wrong. There was lightning and screams—" She wished actively for her drink. "I woke up, and for an instant, the fear woke with me. Then it all faded."

When he still said nothing, she drew in a breath. "Okay,

we'll stick with me for a while. I used my scrying mirror, I used my crystal, but I couldn't see clearly. Only in sleep. You brought me to that place in the woods, in the circle. Or something did. Why?"

"It was not my work."

"It wasn't mine." She tapped nails painted red as her lips on the table. "You have a name, handsome?"

"I'm Hoyt Mac Cionaoith."

Her smile turned her face into something that all but stopped his heart. "Not from around here, are you?"

"No."

"Ireland, I can hear that. And in the dream we spoke Gaelic, which I don't—not really. But I think it's more than where. It's when, too, isn't it? Don't worry about shocking me. I'm immune tonight."

He waged an internal debate. She'd been shown to him, and she had come within the circle. Nothing that meant harm to him should have been able to come within his protective ring. While he had been told to seek a witch, she was nothing, *nothing* that he'd expected.

Yet she'd worked to heal him, and had stayed with him while the wolves had stalked his ring. She'd come to him now for answers, and perhaps for help.

"I came through the Dance of the Gods, nearly a thousand years in time."

"Okay." She whistled out a breath. "Maybe not completely immune. That's a lot to take on faith, but with everything that's been going on, I'm willing to take the leap." She lifted the glass the waitress set down, drank immediately. "Especially with this to cushion the fall. Run a tab, will you?" Glenna asked and took a credit card out of her purse.

"Something's coming," she said when they were alone again. "Something bad. Big, fat evil."

"You don't know."

"I can't see it all. But I feel it, and I know I'm connected with you on this. Not thrilled about that at this point." She drank some more. "Not after what I saw on the subway."

"I don't understand you."

"Something very nasty in a designer suit," she explained.

"It said she would feed on me. She—the woman on the cliff, I think. I'm going out on a limb here, a really shaky one. Are we dealing with vampires?"

"What is the subway?"

Glenna pressed her hands to her eyes. "Okay, we'll spend some time later bringing you up to date on current events, modes of mass transportation and so on, but right now, I need to know what I'm facing. What's expected of me."

"I don't know your name."

"Sorry. Glenna. Glenna Ward." She held a hand out to him. After a brief hesitation, he took it. "Nice to meet you. Now, what the hell is going on?"

He began, and she continued to drink. Then she held up a hand, swallowed. "Excuse me. Are you saying your brother— the guy who manhandled me, is a vampire?"

"He doesn't feed on humans."

"Oh good. Great. Points for him. He died nine hundred and seventy-odd years ago, and you've come here and now from there and then to find him."

"I am charged by the gods to gather an army to fight and destroy the army the vampire Lilith is making."

"Oh God. I'm going to need another drink."

He started to offer her his, but she waved him away and signaled the waitress. "No, go ahead. You're going to need it, too, I imagine."

He took a testing sip, blinked rapidly. "What is this brew?"

"Vodka martini. You should like vodka," she said absently. "Seems to me they make it from potatoes."

She ordered another drink and some bar food to counteract the alcohol. Calmer now, she listened to the whole of it without interrupting.

"And I'm the witch."

There wasn't just beauty here, he realized. There wasn't just power. There was a seeking and a strength. Some he would seek, he remembered the goddess saying. And some would seek him.

So she had.

"I have to believe you are. You, my brother and I will find the others and begin."

"Begin what? Boot camp? Do I look like a soldier to you?"

"You don't, no."

She propped a chin on her fist. "I like being a witch, and I respect the gift. I know there's a reason this runs in my blood. A purpose. I didn't expect it to be this. But it is." She looked at him then, fully. "I know, the first time I dreamed of you that it was the next step in that purpose. I'm terrified. I'm so seriously terrified."

"I left my family to come here, to do this thing. I left them with only the silver crosses and the word of the goddess that they would be protected. You don't know fear."

"All right." She reached out, laid a hand on his in a kind of comfort he sensed was innate in her. "All right," she repeated. "You've got a lot at stake. But I've got a family, too. They're upstate. I need to make sure they're protected. I need to make sure I live to do what I'm meant to do. She knows where I am. She sent that thing to scare me off. I'm guessing she's a lot more prepared than we are."

"Then prepared is what we'll get. I have to see what you're capable of."

"You want me to audition? Listen, Hoyt, your army so far consists of three people. You don't want to insult me."

"We have four with the king."

"What king?"

"The black giant. And I don't like working with witches."

"Really?" She drew out the word as she leaned toward him. "They burned your kind just as hot as mine. We're kissing cousins, Merlin. And you need me."

"It may be that I do. The goddess didn't say I had to like it, did she? I have to know your strengths and your weaknesses."

"Fair enough," she said with a nod. "And I have to know yours. I already know you couldn't heal a lame horse."

"That's false." And this time insult edged his voice. "It happens I was wounded, and unable to—"

"Mend a couple of broken ribs and a gash on your own palm. So, you won't be in charge of injuries if and when we manage to build this army."

"It's welcome you are to the task," he snapped. "And building the army is what we'll do. It's my destiny."

"Let's hope it's my destiny to get home in one piece." She signed the check, picked up her purse.

"Where are you going?"

"Home. I have a lot to do."

"That's not the way. We must stay together now. She knows you, Glenna Ward. She knows all of us. It's safer we are, and stronger together."

"That may be, but I need things from my home. I have a lot to do."

"They're night creatures. You'll wait until sunrise."

"Orders already?" She tried for flip, but the image of what had circled her in the subway came to her, very clearly.

Now he gripped her hand, held her in her seat and felt the clash of their emotions in the heat that vibrated between their palms. "Is this a game to you then?"

"No. I'm scared. A few days ago I was just living my life. My terms. Now I'm being hunted, and I'm supposed to fight some apocalyptic battle. I want to go home. I need my own things. I need to think."

"It's fear that makes you vulnerable and foolish. Your things will be there in the morning just as they are now."

He was right, of course. Added to it, she wasn't sure she had the bravado or the courage to step back outside into the night. "And just where am I supposed to stay until sunrise?"

"My brother has an apartment upstairs."

"Your brother. The vampire." She flopped back against her seat. "Isn't that cozy?"

"He won't harm you. You have my word on it."

"I'd rather have his, if you don't mind. And if he tries . . ." She held her palm up on the table, focused on it. A small ball of flame kindled just above her hand. "If the books and movies have it right, his type doesn't do well with fire. If he tries to hurt me, I'll torch him, and your army's down by one."

Hoyt merely laid his hand over hers, and the flame became a ball of ice. "Don't pit your skills against mine, or threaten to harm my family."

"Nice trick." She dumped the ice in her empty glass. "Let's put it this way. I have a right to protect myself, from anyone or anything who tries to hurt me. Agreed?"

"Agreed. It will not be Cian." Now he rose, offered his hand. "I will pledge this to you, here and now. I will protect you, even from him, if he means you harm."

"Well then." She put her hand in his, got to her feet. She felt it, knew he did by the way his pupils dilated. The magic, yes, but more. "I guess we've got our first deal."

As they went down, turned toward the elevator, Cian cut across their path. "Hold it. Where do you think you're taking her?"

"I'm going with him," Glenna corrected, "not being taken."

"It's not safe for her to go out. Not until daylight. Lilith already sent a scout after her."

"Check the magic at the door," Cian told Glenna. "She can have the spare room tonight. Which means you get the couch, unless she wants to share."

"He can have the couch."

"Why do you insult her?" Temper sizzled in the words. "She's been sent; she's come here at risk."

"I don't know her," Cian said simply. "And from now on, I expect you to check with me before you invite anyone into my home." He punched in the code for the elevator. "Once you're up, you stay up. I'm locking the elevator behind you."

"What if there's a fire?" Glenna said sweetly, and Cian merely smiled.

"Then I guess you'd better open a window, and fly."

Glenna stepped into the elevator when the doors opened, then laid a hand on Hoyt's arm. Before the doors shut, she flashed Cian that smile again. "Better remember who you're dealing with," she told him. "We may do just that."

She sniffed when the doors shut. "I don't think I like your brother."

"I'm not very pleased with him myself at the moment."

"Anyway. Can you fly?"

"No." He glanced down at her. "Can you?"

"Not so far."

Chapter 5

The voices woke her. They were muted and muffled so that at first she feared she was having another vision. However much she might have prized her art, she also valued sleep—especially after a night of martinis and strange revelations.

Glenna groped for a pillow to put over her head.

Her attitude toward Cian had leveled a bit after she'd gotten a look at the guest room. It boasted a sumptuous bed with lovely soft sheets and enough pillows to satisfy even her love of luxury.

It hadn't hurt that the room was spacious, decked out with antiques and painted the soft, warm green of forest shadows. The bath had been a killer, too, she recalled as she snuggled in. An enormous jet tub in gleaming white dominated a room nearly half the size of her entire loft, with that same rich green for the acre of counters. But it was the wide bowl of sink in hammered copper that had made her purr with delight.

She'd nearly given in to the temptation to wallow in the tub, indulge herself with some of the bath salts and oils housed in heavy crystal jars and arranged with fat, glossy candles on the counter. But images of movie heroines attacked while bathing had her putting that idea on hold.

All in all, the vampire's pied-à-terre—she could hardly call such luxury a den—made mincemeat of her little loft in the West Village.

Though she admired the vampire's taste, it didn't stop her from putting a protective charm on the bedroom door in addition to turning the lock.

Now, she rolled over, shucked the pillow to stare at the ceiling in the dim light of the lamp she'd left on low through the night. She was sleeping in a vampire's guest room. She'd displaced a twelfth-century sorcerer to the sofa. A gorgeous and serious-minded type who was on a mission, and expected her to join in his battle against an ancient and powerful vampire queen.

She'd lived with magic all of her life, was gifted with skills and knowledge most people never dreamed existed in reality. And still, this was one for the books.

She liked her life the way it was. And knew, without a doubt, that she would never have it quite that way again. Knew, in fact, she might lose that life altogether.

But what were her choices? She couldn't very well do nothing, couldn't put a pillow over her head and hide for the rest of her life. It *knew* her, and had already sent an emissary.

If she stayed, pretended none of it had ever happened, it could come for her, any time, anywhere. And she'd be alone.

Would she fear the night now? Would she glance over her shoulder every time she was outside after sunset? Would she wonder if a vampire only she could see would slink onto the subway the next time she rode uptown?

No, that was no way to live at all. The only way to live— the only real choice—was to face the problem, and handle the fear. And to do just that along with joining her powers and resources to Hoyt's.

Knowing sleep was no longer possible, she glanced at the clock, rolled her eyes at the early hour. Then resigned, she climbed out of bed.

* * *

In the living room, Cian ended his night with a brandy, and an argument with his brother.

He had, on occasion, returned to his living quarters at dawn with the sensation of loneliness, a kind of hollowness. He took no woman in the daylight, even with the drapes closed. Sex was, in Cian's mind, a position of vulnerability as well as power. He didn't choose to share that vulnerability when the sun was up.

It was rare for him to have company after sunrise and before dusk. And those hours were often long and empty. But he'd discovered on stepping into his own apartment and finding his brother there, he preferred the long and empty to the crowded and demanding.

"You expect her to stay here until you decide your next move. And I'm telling you that isn't possible."

"How would she be safe otherwise?" Hoyt argued.

"I don't believe her safety is on my list of immediate concerns."

How much had his brother changed, Hoyt thought in disgust, that he wouldn't immediately stand for a woman, for an innocent? "We're all at risk now, everything's at risk now. We have no choice but to stay together."

"I have a choice, and it isn't sharing my quarters with a witch, or with you, for that matter," he added, gesturing with the snifter. "I don't allow anyone in here during the day."

"I was here through yesterday."

"An exception." Cian got to his feet. "And one I'm already regretting. You're asking far too much from one who cares far too little."

"I haven't begun to ask yet. I know what must be done. You spoke of survival. And it's yours at risk now, as much as hers. As mine."

"More, as your redhead might take it into her head to stake me while I sleep."

"She isn't my . . ." Frustrated, Hoyt waved that off. "I would never let her harm you. I swear it to you. In this place, at this time, you're my only family. My only blood."

Cian's face went blank as stone. "I have no family. No blood but my own. The sooner you come to that, Hoyt, accept that, the better you'll be for it. What I do, I do for myself, not for you. Not for your cause, but for me. I said I'd fight with you, and so I will. But for my own reasons."

"What are they then? Give me that at least."

"I like this world." Cian eased down on the arm of a chair as he sipped brandy. "I like what I've carved out of it, and I intend to keep it, and on my own terms—not on Lilith's whimsy. That's worth the fight to me. Added to it, a century of existence has its eras of boredom. I seem to be in one. But I have limits. Having your woman tucked up in my quarters goes beyond them."

"She's hardly my woman."

A lazy smile curved Cian's mouth. "If you don't make her so, you're even slower than I remember in that area."

"This isn't sport, Cian. It's a fight to the death."

"I know more of death than you will ever know. More of blood and pain and cruelty. For centuries I've watched mortals, again and again, teeter close to their own extinction, by their own hand. If Lilith were more patient, she could simply wait them out. Take your pleasures where you find them, brother, for life is long and often tedious."

He toasted with his glass. "Another reason I'll fight. It's something to do."

"Why not join with her then?" Hoyt spat out. "With the one who made you what you are."

"She made me a vampire. I made myself what I am. As for why I align with you and not with her? I can trust you. You'll keep your word, for that's the way you're made. She never will. It's not her nature."

"And what of your word?"

"Interesting question."

"I'd like the answer to it." Glenna spoke from the doorway. She wore the black silk robe she'd found hanging in the closet with a number of other pieces of intimate female attire. "You two can squabble all you like, it's what men do, and siblings. But since my life's on the line, I want to know who I can count on."

"I see you made yourself at home," Cian commented.

"Do you want it back?"

When she angled her head, reached for the tie, Cian grinned. Hoyt flushed.

"Don't be encouraging him," Hoyt said. "If you'd excuse us for a moment—"

"No, I won't. I want the answer to your question. And I want to know if your brother gets a little peckish, he's going to look to me as a snack."

"I don't feed on humans. Particularly witches."

"Because of your deep love of humanity."

"Because it's troublesome. If you feed, you have to kill or word gets around. If you change the prey, you're still risking exposure. Vampires gossip, too."

She thought it over. "Sensible. All right, I prefer sensible honesty to lies."

"I told you he wouldn't harm you."

"I wanted to hear it from him." She turned back to Cian. "If you're concerned about me going after you, I'd give you my word—by why should you trust it?"

"Sensible," Cian returned.

"But your brother's already told me he'd stop me if I tried. He may find that more difficult than he believes, but . . . it would be stupid of me to try to kill you, and alienate him, given the situation we're in. I'm afraid, but I'm not stupid."

"I'd have to take your word for that as well."

Idly, she fingered the sleeve of her robe and sent him a mildly flirtatious smile. "If I'd intended to kill you, I'd have already tried a spell. You'd know if I had. You'd feel it. And if there's no more trust than this between the three of us, we're doomed before we start."

"There you have a point."

"What I want now is a shower, and some breakfast. Then I'm going home."

"She stays." Hoyt stepped between them. When Glenna started to step forward, he merely lifted a hand, and the force of his will knocked her back to the doorway.

"Just one damn minute."

"Be silent. None of us leaves this place alone. None

of us. If we're to band together we start now. Our lives are in each other's hands, and a great deal more than our own lives."

"Don't flick your power at me again."

"Whatever I have to do, I'll do. Understand me." Hoyt shifted his gaze between them. "Both of you. Dress yourself," he ordered Glenna. "Then we'll go get whatever it is you think you need. Be quick about it."

In answer, she stepped back, slammed the door.

Cian let out a short laugh. "You certainly know how to charm the ladies. I'm going to bed."

Hoyt stood alone in the living room and wondered why the gods thought he could save worlds with two such creatures at his side.

She didn't speak, but a man who has sisters knows women often use silence as a weapon. And her silence flew around the room like barbs as she filled some sort of carafe with water from the silver pipe in Cian's kitchen.

Women's fashion might have changed radically in nine hundred years, but he believed their inner workings were very much the same.

And still, much of those remained a mystery to him.

She wore the same dress as the night before, but had yet to don her shoes. He wasn't certain what weakness it spoke to in him that the sight of her bare feet should bring on an unwelcomed tinge of arousal.

She shouldn't have flirted with his brother, he thought with considerable resentment. This was a time of war, not dalliance. And if she intended to stroll about with her legs and arms exposed, she'd just have to . . .

He caught himself. He had no business looking at her legs, did he? No business thinking of her as anything but a tool. It didn't matter that she was lovely. It didn't matter that when she smiled it started something like a low fire in the center of his heart.

It didn't matter—couldn't—that when he looked at her, he wanted to touch.

He busied himself with books, returned her silence with his own and lectured himself on proper behavior.

Then the air began to simmer with some seductive aroma. He shot her a glance, wondering if she was trying some of her women's magic. But her back was to him as she rose on the toes of those lovely bare feet to take a cup from a cupboard.

It was the carafe, he realized, filled now with black liquid, and steaming with an alluring scent.

He lost the war of silence. In Hoyt's experience, men always did.

"What are you brewing?"

She simply poured the black liquid from carafe to cup, then turned, watching him with chilly green eyes over the rim as she sipped.

To satisfy himself, he got up, walked into the kitchen and took a second cup down. He poured the liquid as she had, sniffed—detected no poisons—then sipped.

It was electric. Like a quick jolt of power, both strong and rich. Potent, like the drink—the martini—from the night before. But different.

"It's very good," he said then took a deeper drink.

In response, she skirted around him, crossed the room and went back through the doorway of the guest room.

Hoyt lifted his gaze to the gods. Would he be plagued by bad tempers and sulks from both this woman and his brother? "How?" he asked. "How am I to do what must be done if already we fight among ourselves?"

"While you're at it, why don't you ask your goddess to tell you what she thinks about you slapping at me that way." Glenna came back in, wearing the shoes, and carrying the satchel he'd seen her with the evening before.

"It's a defense against what seems to be your argumentative nature."

"I like to argue. And I don't expect you to flick at me whenever you don't like what I have to say. Do it again, and I'll hit back. I have a policy against using magic as a weapon. But I'll break it in your case."

She had the right of it, which was only more annoying. "What is this brew?"

She heaved a breath. "It's coffee. You've had coffee before, I imagine. The Egyptians had coffee. I think."

"Not the like of this," he replied.

And because she smiled, he assumed the worst of it was over. "I'm ready to go, as soon as you apologize."

He should have known better. Such was the way of females. "I'm sorry I was forced to use my will to stop you from arguing the morning away."

"So, you can be a smart-ass. This once, I'll accept that. Let's get moving." She walked to the elevator, pushed its button.

"Is it the fashion for women of this time to be aggressive and sharp-tongued, or is it only you?"

She glanced back at him over her shoulder. "I'm the only one you have to worry about right now." She stepped into the elevator, held the door. "Coming?"

She'd worked out a basic strategy. First, she was going to have to spring for a cab. Whatever the conversation, however strangely Hoyt might behave, a New York City cabbie would have seen and heard it all before.

Added to that, her courage wasn't quite back up to the level to let her ride the subway again.

As she'd anticipated, the minute they were out of the building, Hoyt stopped. And stared. He looked everywhere, up, down, right, left. He studied the traffic, the pedestrians, the buildings.

No one would pay any attention to him, and if they did, they'd mark him as a tourist.

When he opened his mouth to speak, she tapped a finger on her lips. "You're going to have a million questions. So why don't you just line them up and file them? We'll get to them all eventually. For now, I'm going to hail us a cab. Once we're inside, try not to say anything too outrageous."

Questions might have been scrambling in his mind like ants, but he cloaked himself in dignity. "I'm not a fool. I know very well I'm out of place here."

No, he wasn't a fool, Glenna thought as she stepped to the

curb, held up a hand. And he was no coward either. She'd expected him to gawk, but with having the rush and noise and crowds of the city thrust on him, she'd also expected to see some fear, and there was none. Just curiosity, a dose of fascination and a bit of disapproval.

"I don't like the way the air smells."

She nudged him back when he joined her at the curb. "You get used to it." When a cab cruised up to the curb, she whispered to Hoyt as she opened the door. "Get in the way I do, and just sit back and enjoy the ride."

Inside, she reached over him to pull the door shut and gave the cabbie her address. When the cabbie shot back out into traffic, Hoyt's eyes widened.

"I don't know that much about it," she said under the Indian music pumping from the cabbie's radio. "It's a cab, a kind of car. It runs on a combustible engine, fueled by gasoline, and oil."

She did her best to explain traffic lights, crosswalks, skyscrapers, department stores and whatever else came to mind. She realized it was like seeing the city for the first time herself, and began to enjoy it.

He listened. She could all but see him absorbing and tucking all the information, the sights, the sounds, the smells, away in some internal data bank.

"There are so many." He said it quietly, and the troubled tone had her looking over at him. "So many people," he repeated, staring out the side window. "And unaware of what's coming. How will we save so many?"

It struck her then, a sharp, weighted spear in the belly. So many people, yes. And this was just part of one city in just one state. "We can't. Not all. You never can." She reached for his hand, gripped it tight. "So you don't think of the many, or you'll go crazy. We just take it one at a time."

She took out the fare when the cab pulled over—which made her think of finances, and how she'd handle *that* little problem over the next few months. She reached for Hoyt's hand again when they were on the sidewalk.

"This is my building. If we see anyone inside, just smile

and look charming. They'll just think I'm bringing home a lover."

Shock rippled over his face. "Do you?"

"Now and again." She unlocked the door, then squeezed with him into the tiny anteroom to call for the elevator. With an even tighter squeeze, they started up.

"Do all buildings have these . . ."

"Elevators. No, but a lot of them do." When they reached her apartment, she pulled open the iron gate, stepped inside.

It was a small space, but the light was excellent. Her walls were covered with her paintings and her photographs, and were painted the green of minced onions to reflect the light. Rugs she'd woven herself dotted the floor with bold tones and patterns.

It was tidy, which suited her nature. Her convertible bed was made up as a sofa for the day, plumped with pillows. The kitchen alcove sparkled from a recent scrubbing.

"You live alone. With no one to help you."

"I can't afford help, and I like living alone. Staff and servants take money, and I don't have enough of it."

"Have you no men in your family, no stipend or allowance?"

"No allowance since I was ten," she said dryly. "I work. Women work just as men do. Ideally, we don't depend on a man to take care of us, financially or otherwise."

She tossed her purse aside. "I make my living such as it is selling paintings and photographs. Painting, for the most part for greeting cards like notes, letters, messages people send each other."

"Ah, you're an artist."

"That's right," she agreed, amused that her choice of employment, at least, seemed to meet with his approval. "The greeting cards, those pay the rent. But I sell some of the artwork outright now and then. I like working for myself, too. I make my own schedule, which is lucky for you. I don't have anyone to answer to, so I can take time to do, well, what has to be done."

"My mother is an artist, in her way. Her tapestries are beautiful." He stepped up to a painting of a mermaid, rising up out of a churning sea. There was power in the face, a kind of knowledge that he took as inherently female. "This is your work?"

"Yes."

"It shows skill, and that magic that moves into color and shape."

More than approval, she decided. Admiration now, and she let it warm her. "Thanks. Normally, that kind of thumbnail review would make my day. It's just that it's a very strange day. I need to change my clothes."

He nodded absently, moved to another painting.

Behind him, Glenna cocked her head, then shrugged. She went to the old armoire she used as a closet, chose what she wanted, then carried it into the bathroom.

She was used to men paying a little more attention, she realized as she stripped out of the dress. To the way she looked, the way she moved. It was lowering to be so easily dismissed, even if he did have more important things on his mind.

She changed into jeans and a white tank. Letting the subtle glamour she'd been vain enough to use that morning fade, she did her make-up, then tied her hair back into a short tail.

When she came back, Hoyt was in her kitchen, fiddling with her herbs.

"Don't touch my stuff." She slapped his hand away.

"I was only . . ." He trailed off, then looked deliberately over her shoulder. "Is this what you wear in public?"

"Yes." She turned, and just as deliberately invaded his space. "Problem?"

"No. You don't wear shoes?"

"Not around the house, necessarily." His eyes were so blue, she thought. So sharp and blue against those thick black lashes. "What do you feel when we're like this? Alone. Close."

"Unsettled."

"That's the nicest thing you've said to me so far. I mean, do you feel something? In here." She laid a fist on her belly, kept her eyes locked on his. "A kind of reaching. I've never felt it before."

He felt it, and a kind of burn in and under his heart as

well. "You haven't broken your fast," he managed, and stepped carefully back. "You must be hungry."

"Just me then," she murmured. She turned to open a cupboard. "I don't know what I'm going to need, so I'm going to take whatever feels right. I'm not traveling light. You and Cian have to deal with that. We should probably leave as soon as possible."

He'd lifted a hand, was on the point of touching her hair, something he'd wanted to do since he'd first seen her. Now he dropped it. "Leave?"

"You don't expect to sit around in New York and wait for the army to come to you? The portal's in Ireland, and we have to assume the battle's to take place in Ireland, or some mystical facet thereof. We need the portal, or at some point we will. So we need to go to Ireland."

He simply stared at her as she loaded bottles and vials into a case not dissimiliar from his own. "Aye, you're right. Of course, you're right. We need to start back. A voyage will take much of the time we have. Oh, Jesus, I'll be sick as six dogs sailing home."

She looked over. "Sailing? We don't have time for the *Queen Mary,* sweetie. We'll fly."

"You said you couldn't."

"I can, if it's in a plane. We'll have to figure out how to get you a ticket. You don't have ID, you don't have a passport. We can do a charm on the ticket agent, the custom's agent." She brushed it away. "I'll work it out."

"A plain what?"

She focused on him, then leaned back against the counter and laughed until her sides ached. "I'll explain later."

"It's not my purpose to amuse you."

"No, it wouldn't be. But it's a nice side pocket. Oh hell, I don't know what to take, what not to take." She stepped back, rubbed her hands over her face. "It's my first apocalypse."

"Herbs, flowers and roots grow in Ireland, and quite well."

"I like my own." Which was foolish, and childish. But still . . . "I'll just take what I consider absolutely essential in this area, then start on books, clothes, and so on. I have to make some calls, too. I've got some appointments that I need to cancel."

With some reluctance, she closed her already loaded case and left it on the counter. She crossed to a large wooden chest in the far corner of the room, and unlocked it with a charm.

Curiosity piqued, Hoyt moved over to study the contents over her shoulder. "What do you keep here?"

"Spell books, recipes, some of my more powerful crystals. Some were handed down to me."

"Ah, then, you're a hereditary witch."

"That's right. The only one of my generation who practices. My mother gave it up when she married. My father didn't like it. My grandparents taught me."

"How could she give up what's inside her?"

"A question I've asked her many times." She sat back on her heels, touching what she could take, and what she couldn't. "For love. My father wanted a simple life, she wanted my father. I couldn't do it. I don't think I could love enough to give up what I am. I'd need to be loved enough to be accepted for what I am."

"Strong magic."

"Yeah." She took out a velvet sack. "This is my prize." From it she lifted the ball of crystal he'd seen her with in the vision. "It's been in my family a long time. Over two hundred and fifty years. Chump change to a man of your years, but a hell of a run to me."

"Strong magic," he repeated, for when she held it in her hands, he could see it pulse, like a heart beating.

"You're right about that." She looked at him over the orb with eyes that had gone suddenly dark. "And isn't it time we used some? Isn't it time we do what we do, Hoyt? She knows who I am, where I am, what I am. It's likely she knows the same about you, about Cian. Let's make a move." She held the crystal aloft. "Lets find out where she's hiding."

"Here and now?"

"Can't think of a better time or place." She rose, jutted her chin toward the richly patterned rug in the room's center. "Roll that up, will you?"

"It's a dangerous step you're after taking here. We should take a moment to think."

"We can think while you're rolling up the rug. I have everything we need for a locator spell, everything we need for protection. We can blind her to us while we look."

He did as she asked and found the painted pentagram under the rug. He could admit that taking a step, any step, felt right and good. But he'd have preferred, very much, to take it alone.

"We don't know if she can be blinded. She's fed on magic blood, and likely more than once. She's very powerful, and very sly."

"So are we. You're talking about going into battle within three months. When do you intend to start?"

He looked at her, nodded. "Here and now then."

She laid the crystal in the center of the pentagram, and retrieved two athames from her chest. She placed these in the circle, then gathered candles, a silver bowl, crystal wands.

"I won't be needing all these tools."

"Fine for you, but I prefer using them. Let's work together, Merlin."

He lifted an athame to study its carving as she ringed the pentagram with candles. "Will it bother you if I work sky-clad?"

"Aye," he said without looking up.

"All right, in the spirit of compromise and teamwork, I'll keep my clothes on. But they're restricting."

She removed the band from her hair, filled the silver bowl with water from a vial and sprinkled herbs on it. "Generally I invoke the goddesses when casting the circle, and it seems most appropriate for this. Suit you?"

"Well enough."

"You're a real chatterbox, aren't you? Well. Ready?" At his nod she walked to the opposite curve from him. "Goddesses of the East, of the West, of the North of the South," she began, moving around the circle as she spoke. "We ask your blessing. We call to you to witness and to guard this circle, and all within it."

"Powers of Air, and Water, of Fire and of Earth," Hoyt chanted. "Travel with us now as we go between worlds."

"Night and day, day and night, we call you to this sacred rite. We cast this circle, one times three. As we will, so mote it be."

Witches, he thought. Always rhyming. But he felt the air stir, and the water in the bowl rippled as the candles leapt to flame.

"It should be Morrigan we call on," Glenna said. "She was the messenger."

He started to do so, then decided he wanted to see what the witch was made of. "This is your sacred place. Ask for guidance, and cast your spell."

"All right." She laid down the sacred knife, lifted her hands, palms up. "On this day and in this hour, I call upon the sacred power of Morrigan the goddess and pray she grant to us her grace and prowess. In your name, Mother, we seek the sight, ask you to guide us into the light."

She bent, lifted the crystal into her hands. "Within this ball we seek to find the beast who hunts all mankind, while her eyes to us are blind. Make keen our vision, our minds, our hearts so the clouds within this ball will part. Shield us and show us what we seek to see. As we will, so mote it be."

Mists and light swirled within the glass. For an instant he thought he could see worlds inside it. Colors, shapes, movement. He heard it beat, as his heart beat. As Glenna's heart beat.

He knelt as she did. And saw, as she did.

A dark place, mazed with tunnels and washed by red light. He thought he heard the sea, but couldn't be sure if it was within the glass or just the roaring of power in his own head.

There were bodies, bloodied and torn and stacked like cordwood. And cages where people wept or screamed, or simply sat with dull and deadened eyes. Things moved within the tunnels, dark things that barely stirred the air. Some crawled up the walls like bugs.

There was horrible laughter, high, hideous shrieking.

He traveled with Glenna through those tunnels where the

air stank of death and blood. Down, deep down in the earth, where the stone walls dripped with wet and worse. To a door scribed with ancient symbols of black magicks.

He felt the breath go cold in his body as they passed through.

She slept on a bed fit for a queen, four-posted and wide with sheets that had the sheen of silk and were white as ice. Droplets of blood stained them.

Her breasts were bare above the sheets, and the beauty of her face and form were undiminished since last he'd seen her.

Beside her was the body of a boy. So young, Hoyt thought with a terrible pity. No more than ten years, so pale in death with his cornsilk hair falling over his brow.

Candles were guttering, sending wavering light to flicker over her flesh, and his.

Hoyt gripped the athame, lifted it over his head.

And her eyes opened, stared into his. She screamed, but he heard no fear in it. Beside her the boy opened his eyes, bared fangs and leaped up to skuddle along the ceiling like a lizard.

"Closer," she crooned. "Come closer, sorcerer, and bring your witch. I'll make a pet of her once I drain you dry. Do you think you can *touch* me?"

As she leaped off the bed, Hoyt felt himself flying backward, tearing through air so cold it was shards of ice in his throat.

Then he was sitting within the circle, staring into Glenna's eyes. Hers were dark and wide. There was blood dripping from her nose.

She stanched it with a knuckle while she struggled to get her breath.

"First part worked," she managed. "The blinded part didn't take very well, obviously."

"She has power as well. She's not without skill."

"Have you ever felt anything like that?" she asked him.

"No."

"Neither have I." She allowed herself one hard shudder. "We're going to need a bigger circle."

Chapter 6

Before she packed, Glenna took the time to cleanse the entire loft. Hoyt didn't disagree. She wanted no trace of what they'd touched on, no echoes, no dregs of that darkness in her home.

In the end, she put her tools and books back in the chest. After what she'd seen, what she'd felt, she wasn't going to risk the pick and choose. She was taking the whole lot, along with her travel case, most of her crystals, some basic art supplies, cameras, and two suitcases.

She cast one longing look at the easel standing near the window, and the barely started painting resting on it. If she came back—no *when,* she corrected. When she came back, she would finish it.

She stood beside Hoyt, studying the pile of belongings as he did.

"No comments?" she asked. "No arguments or sarcastic remarks about how I intend to travel?"

"To what end?"

"A wise stand. Now there's the little matter of getting all this out of here, uptown and into your brother's place. At which time, I doubt he'll be as wise as you. But first things first." She toyed with her pendant as she considered. "Do we haul it all by hand, or try a transportation spell? I've never done anything of this scope."

He sent her a bland look. "We'd need three of your cabs and most of what we have left of the day to deal with all of this."

So, he considered the situation as well. "Visualize Cian's apartment," he ordered. "The room where you slept."

"All right."

"Concentrate. Bring it fully into your mind, the details, the shape, the structure."

She nodded, closed her eyes. "I am."

He chose the chest first as he sensed it held the most power. Its magic would aid him in the task. He circled it three times, then reversed, circled again while he said the words, while he opened himself to the power.

Glenna struggled to fix her focus. There was something deeper, richer about his voice, something erotic in the way it spoke the ancient tongue. She felt the heat of what he stirred on her skin, and in her blood. Then a swift and solid punch of air.

When she opened her eyes, the chest was gone.

"I'm impressed." More honestly, she was amazed. She was capable, with considerable preparation and effort, of transporting small, simple objects some distance. But he'd simply and efficiently *poofed* a two-hundred-pound chest.

She could picture him now, in billowing robes on the cliff he'd spoken of in Ireland. Challenging the storm, charging himself with it. And facing what no man should have to face, with faith and with magic.

Her belly tightened with sheer and simple lust.

"Was that Gaelic you were speaking?"

"Irish," he said, so obviously distracted, she didn't speak again.

Once more he circled, focusing now on the cases that contained her photography and art equipment. She nearly yipped a protest, then reminded herself to have faith. Calling on it, she closed her eyes again, brought the guest room back into her mind. Gave him what she could of her own gift.

It took him fifteen minutes to accomplish what she was forced to admit would have taken her hours, if she could have managed it at all.

"Well that was . . . that was something." The magic was still on him, turning his eyes opaque, rippling through the air between them. She felt it like a ribbon wound around both of them, tying them together. Her own arousal was so keen, she had to step back, deliberately break the bond between them.

"No offense, but are you sure they're where we want them?"

He continued to stare at her with those fathomless blue eyes until the heat in her belly grew so strong she wondered it didn't shoot fire from her fingertips.

It was nearly too much, this pressure, this need, the mad beat of it at every pulse. She started to step back again, but he simply lifted a hand and stopped her in her tracks.

She felt the pull, from him, to him, with just enough play for her to resist, to snap that lead and escape. Instead she stood, kept her eyes locked with his as he closed the distance between them with one easy stride.

Then there was nothing easy.

He yanked her to him so that her breath expelled on a quick hitching gasp, and that gasp ended on a moan when their mouths met. The hot, drugging kiss spun through her head, through her body, sizzling in her blood when she clung to him.

Candles she'd left in the room flashed into flame.

At once aggressive and desperate, she dug her hands into his shoulders and plunged headfirst into the storm of sensation. This, this was what she'd craved from the first moment she'd seen him in dreams.

She felt his hands on her hair, her body, her face, and everywhere he touched quivered. No dream now, just need and heat and flesh.

He couldn't stop himself. She was like a feast after the fast, and all he wanted was to gorge. Her mouth was full and soft, and fit so truly to his it was as if the gods had formed it for only that purpose. The power he'd wielded had snapped back on him, inciting an impossible hunger that ached in his belly, in his loins, in his heart and cried out to be sated.

Something burned between them. He'd known it from the first instant, even ill with fever and pain while the wolves stalked beyond his fire. And he feared it nearly as much as he feared what they were fated to face together.

He drew her back, shaken to the bone. What they'd stirred was alive on her face, sultry and tempting. If he accepted and took, what price would they both pay for it?

There was always a price.

"I apologize. I . . . I was caught on the tail of the spell."

"Don't apologize. It's insulting."

Women, was all he could think. "Touching you in that way isn't?"

"If I hadn't wanted you to touch me that way, I'd have stopped you. Oh, don't flatter yourself," she snapped out when she read the expression on his face. "You may be stronger, physically, magically, but I can handle myself. And when I want an apology, I'll ask for one."

"I can't find my balance in this place, or with you." Frustration rippled out from him now, as the magic had. "I'm not liking it, or what I'm feeling for you."

"That's your problem. It was just a kiss."

He caught her arm before she could turn away. "I don't believe, even in this world, that was just a kiss. You've seen what we have to face. Desire is a weakness, one we can't risk. Everything we have must be charged toward what we have to do. I won't risk your life or the fate of the world for a few moments of pleasure."

"I can promise it would be more than a few. But there's no point in arguing with a man who sees desire as a weakness. Let's chalk it up to the moment, and move on."

"I'm not after hurting you," he began with some regret, and she aimed a single, quelling look.

"Apologize again, and you're on your ass." She picked up her keys, her purse. "Put out the candles, would you, and let's go. I want to make sure my things arrived safely, and we've got to arrange for flights to Ireland. And figure out how to smuggle you out of the country."

She grabbed sunglasses from a table, put them on. A great deal of her irritation faded at the baffled expression on his face. "Shades," she explained. "They cut the glare of the sun, and in this case are a sexy fashion statement."

She opened the iron gate, then turned, looked back at her loft, her things. "I have to believe I'll come back here. I have to believe I'll see all this again."

She stepped inside, pushed the button for the ground floor. And left behind much that she loved.

When Cian came out of his room, Glenna was in the kitchen cooking. On their return, Hoyt had taken himself off to the study adjoining the living room, hauling his books with him. Now and again, she felt something ripple out, and assumed he was practicing some spells.

It kept him out of her hair. But it didn't keep him out of her head.

She was careful with men. Enjoying them, certainly, but she didn't share herself recklessly. Which is exactly what she'd done with Hoyt, and she couldn't deny it. It had been reckless, impulsive and apparently a mistake. And though she'd said it had been just a kiss, it had been as intimate an act as she'd ever experienced.

He wanted her, there was no question of that. But he didn't choose to want her. Glenna preferred to be chosen.

Desire wasn't a weakness, not in her mind—but it was a distraction. He was right in that they couldn't afford distractions. That strength of character and good solid sense were two of his appealing traits. But considering her own jumpy system, they were equally irritating ones.

So she cooked, because it kept her busy and settled her down.

When Cian came in looking sleek and sleepy, she was briskly chopping vegetables.

"*Mi casa* is, apparently, *su casa*."

She kept right on chopping. "I brought some perishables—among other things—from home. I don't know if you eat."

He looked dubiously at the raw carrots and leafy greens.

"One of the advantages of my fate is I don't have to eat my vegetables like a good lad." But he'd scented what was on the stove, and moved to it to sniff at the spicy tomato sauce simmering. "On the other hand, this looks appealing."

He leaned back on the counter to watch her work. "So do you."

"Don't waste your questionable charm on me. Not interested."

"I could work on that, just to get under Hoyt's skin. Might be entertaining. He tries not to watch you. He fails."

Her hand hesitated, then she brought down the knife again. "I'm sure he'll succeed eventually. He's a very determined man."

"Always was, if memory serves. Sober and serious, and as trapped by his gift as a rat in a cage."

"Do you see it that way?" She set down the knife, turned to him. "As a trap. It's not, not for him, not for me. It's a duty, yes. But it's a privilege and a joy as well."

"We'll see how joyful you are when you're in Lilith's path."

"Been there. We did a locator spell at my place. She's holed up in a cave with a series of tunnels. Near the sea, I think. Near, I think, that cliffside where Hoyt faced her. She gave us a good solid blast. We won't be so easy to push next time."

"You're mad as Fat Tuesday, the pair of you." He opened his cold box, took out a bag of blood. His face tightened at the small sound Glenna couldn't quite smother. "You'll have to get used to it."

"You're right. I will." She watched him pour the contents in a thick glass, then set it in the microwave to heat. This time it was a snicker she couldn't smother. "Sorry. But it's just so damn odd."

He studied her, obviously saw no rancor, and relaxed. "Want some wine?"

"Sure, thanks. We need to go to Ireland."

"So I'm told."

"No. Now. As soon as it can be arranged. I've got a passport, but we have to figure out how to get Hoyt out of this country and into another. And we'll need a place to set up, to stay and to, well, train and practice."

"Peas in a pod," Cian muttered, pouring her a glass of wine. "It's not a simple matter, you know, to delegate responsibilities for my businesses, particularly since the man I trust to run the club downstairs is bound and determined to join Hoyt's holy army."

"Look, I spent a lot of my time today packing, transferring my rather limited funds so I could pay the rent on my place through October, cancelling appointments, and handing off a couple of what would be fairly lucrative jobs to an associate. You'll just have to manage."

He retrieved his own glass. "And what is it you do? These fairly lucrative jobs?"

"Greeting card art, of the mystical variety. I paint. And do some photography."

"You any good?"

"No, I suck. Of course, I'm good. The paying photography is mostly weddings. More arty stuff for my own pleasure and the occasional sale. I'm adaptable at keeping the wolf from the door." She lifted her wine. "How about you?"

"Can't survive a millennium otherwise. So, we'll leave tonight."

"Tonight? We can't possibly—"

"Adapt," he said simply and drank.

"We need to check on flights, buy tickets—"

"I have my own plane. I'm a licensed pilot."

"Oh."

"A good one," he assured her. "I've several decades of air time, so you needn't worry on that score."

Vampires who drank blood out of pricey stemware and owned planes. No, what did she have to worry about? "Hoyt doesn't have any identification, no passport, no papers. I can work a charm to get him through Customs, but—"

"No need." He crossed the room, opened a panel on the wall she hadn't detected, and revealed a safe.

Once he'd unlocked it, he took out a lock box, and coming back set it on the counter and flipped the combination.

"He can take his choice," Cian said and pulled out a half a dozen passports.

"Well, wow." She plucked one, opened it, studied the picture. "Handy you look so much alike. The serious lack of mirrors in this place tells me the lore about no reflections hangs true. No problem being photographed?"

"If you're using a reflector camera, you'd have a moment, when the mirror engages when you'd be very puzzled. Then it disengages as you shoot—and there I am."

"Interesting. I brought my cameras. I'd like to try some pictures, when there's time."

"I'll think about it."

She tossed the passport down. "I hope that plane of yours has plenty of cargo space, because I'm loaded."

"We'll manage. I've calls to make, and packing of my own to see to."

"Wait. We don't have a place to stay."

"It won't be a problem," he said as he left the room. "I've something that will suit."

Glenna blew out a breath, looked back at the pot on the stove. "Well, at least we'll get in a good meal first."

It wasn't a simple matter, even with Cian's money and connections laying a path. The luggage and cargo had to be transported the ordinary and laborious way this time. She could see all three of the men she'd hooked her fate with looking for a way to cut down on her load. She cut that route off with a firm: "It all goes"—and left it at that.

She had no idea what Cian had in the single suitcase or the two large metal chests he packed.

She wasn't sure she wanted to know.

She couldn't imagine what they must have looked like, the two tall, dark men, the enormous black man, and the redhead with enough luggage to re-sink the *Titanic*.

She enjoyed the privilege of being female, and left it to the men to do the loading, while she explored Cian's sleek and elegantly appointed private jet.

He wasn't afraid of color, or of spending his money, she

had to give him credit for that. The seats were a deep, rich blue in buttery leather, and generous enough to be comfortable for even a man of King's proportions. The carpet was thick enough to sleep on.

It boasted a small, efficient conference room, two sophisticated bathrooms, and what she initially took to be a cozy bedroom. More than that, she realized when she noted it had no windows, no mirrors, and its own half bath. A safe room.

She wandered into the galley, approved it, and appreciated the fact that Cian had already called ahead to have it stocked. They wouldn't starve on the flight to Europe.

Europe. She trailed her finger over one of the fully reclining seats. She'd always planned to go, to spend as much as a month. Painting, taking photographs, exploring. Visiting the ancient sites, shopping.

Now she was going, and getting there well above the first-class level. But she wouldn't be wandering the hills and the sacred grounds at her leisure.

"Well, you wanted adventure in your life," she reminded herself. "Now you've got it." She closed a hand around the pendant she wore and prayed she'd have not only the strength but also the wits to survive it.

She was seated when the men boarded, and making a show out of enjoying a glass of champagne.

"I popped the cork," she said to Cian. "I hope you don't mind. It seemed appropriate."

"*Sláinte.*" He moved directly to the cockpit.

"Want the two-dollar tour?" she asked Hoyt. "Want to look around?" she explained. "I imagine King's flown in this little beauty before and is thoroughly jaded."

"Beats the hell out of commercial," King agreed, and got himself a beer in lieu of champagne. "The boss knows how to handle this bird." He gave Hoyt a slap on the shoulder. "No worries."

Because he looked far from convinced, Glenna rose and poured another glass of champagne. "Here, drink, relax. We're going to be in here all night."

"In a bird made out of metal and cloth. A flying machine." Hoyt nodded, and because it was in his hand, sipped the bubbling wine. "It's a matter of science and mechanics."

He'd spent two full hours reading of the history and technology of aircraft. "Aerodynamics."

"Exactly." King tapped the beer bottle to Hoyt's glass, then Glenna's. "Here's to kicking some ass."

"You look like you're looking forward to it," Glenna commented.

"Damn straight. Who wouldn't? We get to save the frigging world. The boss? He's been restless the last few weeks. He gets restless, I get restless. Ask me, this is just what the doctor ordered."

"And dying doesn't worry you?"

"Everybody dies." He glanced toward the cockpit. "One way or another. 'Sides, a big bastard like me doesn't go down easy."

Cian strolled in. "We're cleared, boys and girls. Have a seat, strap in."

"Got your back, Captain." King followed Cian back into the cockpit.

Glenna sat, offered a smile as she patted the seat beside hers. She was prepared to soothe Hoyt through his first flight. "You'll need your seat belt. Let me show you how it works."

"I know how it works. I read of it." He studied the metal for a moment, then locked the pieces together. "In the event there is turbulence. Pockets of air."

"You're not the least bit nervous."

"I came through a time portal," he reminded her. He began to play with the control panel, amusement crossing his face when the back reclined, came up again. "I think I'll be enjoying this trip. Bloody shame it's got to be done over water."

"Oh, I nearly forgot." She dug into her purse, pulled out a vial. "Drink this. It'll help. Drink it," she repeated when he frowned at the vial. "It's herbs and some powdered crystals. Nothing harmful. It may help the queasiness."

The reluctance was clear on his face, but he downed it. "You have a heavy hand with the cloves."

"You can thank me when you don't have to use the barf bag."

She heard the engines hum, felt the vibration beneath her. "Spirits of the night, give us wings to take this flight. Hold us safe within your hand until we touch upon the land." She slid her eyes to Hoyt. "It never hurts."

He wasn't ill, but she could see that her potion and his will were fighting a hard battle to keep his system steady. She made him tea, brought him a blanket, then reclined his seat, brought up the footrest herself.

"Try to sleep a little."

Too ill to argue, he nodded, closed his eyes. When she was sure he was as comfortable as she could make him, she moved forward to join the others in the cockpit.

There was music playing. Nine Inch Nails, she recognized. In the co-pilot's seat, King had kicked back and was snoring along with the beat. Glenna looked through the windscreen and felt her heart do a little dance of its own.

There was nothing but the black.

"I've never been in a cockpit before. Awesome view."

"I can kick that one out of here if you want his seat for a bit."

"No. I'm fine. Your brother's trying to sleep. He's not feeling very well."

"He used to turn green crossing the Shannon. I imagine he's sick as a dog by now."

"No, just queasy. I gave him something at takeoff, and he's got an iron will to add to it. Do you want anything?"

He glanced back. "Aren't you the helpful one?"

"I'm too revved up to sleep, too restless to sit. So, coffee, tea, milk?"

"I wouldn't mind the coffee. Thanks for that."

She brewed a short pot, brought him a mug of it. Then stood behind him, staring out into the night sky. "What was he like as a boy?"

"As I told you."

"Did he ever doubt his power? Ever wish he hadn't been given the gift?"

It was a strange sensation, having a woman question him

about another man. Generally if they weren't talking about themselves they were asking about him, trying to nudge aside what some of them saw as a curtain of mystery.

"Not that he ever told me. And he would have," Cian said after a moment. "We were close enough in those days."

"Was there someone—a woman, a girl—for him back there?"

"No. He looked, and he touched, and he had a few. He's a sorcerer not a priest. But he never told me of one special to him. I never saw him look at any of the girls as he looks at you. To your peril, Glenna, I'd be saying. But mortals are fools when it comes to love."

"And I'd say if you can't love when you're facing death, then death's not worth fighting. Lilith had a child with her. Did he tell you that?"

"He didn't, no. You need to understand there's no sentiment there, no softness. A child is just easy prey, and a sweet meal."

Her stomach turned, but she kept her voice even. "Eight or ten years old, I'd say," she continued. "In the bed with her, in those caves. She'd made him like her. She'd made that child like her."

"That shocks and angers you, well, that's fine then. Shock and anger can be strong weapons in the right hand. But remember this. If you see that child, or one like him, put your pity away, because he'll kill you without thought or mercy unless you kill him first."

She studied Cian now, that profile that was so like his brother's, yet so completely his own. She wanted to ask if he'd ever turned a child, or fed on one. But she was afraid the answer might be unforgivable, and she needed him.

"Could you do that, destroy a child whatever he'd become?"

"Without thought or mercy." He glanced at her, and she saw he'd known the other question running in her mind. "And you're not good to us or yourself if you can't do the same."

She left him then without a word and went back to stretch out beside Hoyt. Because the conversation with Cian had chilled her, she pulled her own blanket up to her throat, curled toward Hoyt's body heat.

And when she slept, finally slept, she dreamed of children, with sunny hair and bloody fangs.

She woke with a start to find Cian leaning over her. A scream clawed up to her throat until she realized he was shaking Hoyt awake.

She pushed at her hair, skimmed her fingers over her face for a quick glamour. They were speaking in low tones and, she realized, in Irish.

"English, please. I can't follow that much, especially with the accents."

Both turned vibrant blue eyes on her, and Cian straightened as she brought her chair up. "I'm telling him we've about an hour flight time left."

"Who's flying the plane?"

"King's got it for the moment. We'll be landing at dawn."

"Good. Great." She barely stifled a yawn. "I'll throw some coffee and breakfast together so . . . Dawn?"

"Aye, dawn. I need a good cloud cover. Rain would be a bonus. Can you do this? Otherwise King will land it. He's capable, and I'll be spending the rest of the flight and the day in the back of the plane."

"I said I could do it, and I will."

"We can do it," Glenna corrected.

"Well, be quick about it, will you? I've been singed a time or two and it's unpleasant."

"You're welcome," she muttered when he left them. "I'll get a few things from my travel case."

"I don't need them." Hoyt brushed her aside, got up to stand in the aisle. "This time, it'll be my way. He's my brother, after all."

"Your way then. How can I help?"

"Call the vision to your mind. Clouds and rain. Rain and clouds." He retrieved his staff. "See it, feel it, smell it. Thick and steady, with the sun trapped behind the gloom. Dusky light, light without power or harm. See it, feel it, smell it."

He held his staff in both hands, braced his legs apart for balance, then raised it.

"I call the rain, the black clouds that cover the sky. I call the clouds, fat with rain that streams from the heavens. Swirl and close and lay thick."

She felt it spin, spin out from him, spin out to the air. The plane shook, bucked, trembled, but he stood as if he stood on a floor of granite. The tip of the staff glowed blue.

He turned to her, nodded. "That should do it."

"Well. Okay then. I'll make coffee."

They landed in gloom with the rain like a gray curtain. A little overdone, in Glenna's opinion, and it was going to be a miserable drive from the airport to wherever the hell they were going.

But she stepped off the plane and onto Ireland, and there it was. A connection, instant and surprising even to her. She had a quick sense of memory of a farm—green hills, stone fences and a white house with clothes flapping on a line in a brisk wind. There was a garden in the dooryard with dahlias big as dinner plates and calla lilies white as wishes.

It was gone almost as quickly as it had come. She wondered if it was her memory from another time, another life, or simply a call through her blood. Her grandmother's mother had come from Ireland, from a farm in Kerry.

She had brought her linens and her best dishes—and her magic—to America with her.

She waited for Hoyt to deplane. This would always be home for him, she saw it now in the pleasure that ran over his face. Whether it was a busy airport or an empty field, this was his place. And part, very much a part, she understood now, that he would die to save.

"Welcome home."

"It looks nothing like it did."

"Parts of it will." She took his hand and squeezed. "Nice job with the weather, by the way."

"Well, that at least, is familiar."

King trotted over, wet as a seal. His thick dreads dripped rain. "Cian's arranging for most of the stuff to be delivered by truck. Take what you can carry, or have to have right now. The rest'll be along in a couple hours."

"Where are we going?" Glenna demanded.

"He's got a place here." King shrugged. "So that's where we're going."

They had a van, and even then it was a tight squeeze. And, Glenna discovered, another sort of adventure altogether to sweep along through the pouring rain on wet roads, many of which seemed as narrow as a willow stem.

She saw hedgerows ripe with fuchsia, and those hills of wet emerald rolling up and back into the dull gray sky. She saw houses with flowers blooming in dooryards. Not the one of her quick image, but close enough to make her smile.

Something here had belonged to her once. Now maybe it would again.

"I know this place," Hoyt murmured. "I know this land."

"See." Glenna patted his hand. "I knew some of it would be the same for you."

"No, this place, this land." He pushed up to grab Cian by the shoulder. "Cian."

"Mind the driver," Cian ordered and shook off his brother's hand before turning between the hedgerows and onto a narrow spit of a land that wound back through a dense forest.

"God," Hoyt breathed. "Sweet God."

The house was stone, alone among the trees, and quiet as a tomb. Old and wide, with the jut of a tower and the stone aprons of terraces. In the gloom, it looked deserted and out of its time.

And still there was a garden outside the door, of roses and lilies and the wide plates of dahlia. Foxglove sprang tall and purple among the trees.

"It's still here." Hoyt spoke in a voice thick with emotion. "It survived. It still stands."

Understanding now, Glenna gave his hand another squeeze. "It's your home."

"The one I left only days ago. The one I left nearly a thousand years ago. I've come home."

Chapter 7

I t wasn't the same. The furnishings, the colors, the light, even the sound his footsteps made crossing the floor had changed, turning the familiar into the foreign. He recognized a few pieces—some candlestands and a chest. But they were in the wrong places.

Logs had been set in the hearth, but were yet unlit. And there were no dogs curled up on the floor or thumping their tails in greeting.

Hoyt moved through the rooms like a ghost. Perhaps that's what he was. His life had begun in this house, and so much of it had been woven together under its roof or on its grounds. He had played here and worked here, eaten and slept here.

But that was hundreds of years in the past. So perhaps, in a very true sense, his life had ended here as well.

His initial joy in seeing the house dropped away with a weight of sadness for all that he'd lost.

Then he saw, encased in glass on the wall, one of his mother's tapestries. He moved to it, touched his fingers to the glass as she came winging back to him. Her face, her voice, her scent were as real as the air around him.

"It was the last she'd finished before . . ."

"I died," Cian finished. "I remember. I came across it in an auction. That, and a few other things over time. I was able to acquire the house oh, about four hundred years ago now, I suppose. Most of the land as well."

"But you don't live here any longer."

"It's a bit out of the way for me, and not convenient to my work or pleasures. I have a caretaker whom I've sent off until I order him back. And I generally come over once a year or so."

Hoyt dropped his hand, turned. "It's changed."

"Change is inevitable. The kitchen's been modernized. There's plumbing and electricity. Still it's drafty for all that. The bedrooms upstairs are furnished, so take your choices. I'm going up to get some sleep."

He started out, glanced back. "Oh, and you can stop the rain if you've a mind to. King, give me a hand will you, hauling some of this business up?"

"Sure. Very cool digs, if you don't mind a little spooky." King hauled up a chest the way another man might have picked up a briefcase, and headed up the main stairs.

"Are you all right?" Glenna asked Hoyt.

"I don't know what I am." He went to the window, drew back heavy drapes to look out on the rain-drenched forest. "It's here, this place, the stones set by my ancestors. I'm grateful for that."

"But they're not here. The family you left behind. It's hard what you're doing. Harder for you than the rest of us."

"We all share it."

"I left my loft. You left your life." She stepped to him, brushed a kiss over his cheek. She had thought to offer to fix a hot meal, but saw that what he needed most just then was solitude.

"I'm going up, grab a room, a shower and a bed."

He nodded, continued to stare out the window. The rain suited his mood, but it was best to close the spell. Even when he had, it continued to rain, but in a fine, misty drizzle. The fog crawled across the ground, twined around the feet of the rose bushes.

Could they be his mother's still? Unlikely, but they were roses, after all. That would have pleased her. He wondered if in some way having her sons here again, together, would please her as well.

How could he know? How would he ever know?

He flashed fire into the hearth. It seemed more like home with the fire snapping. He didn't choose to go up, not yet. Later, he thought, he'd take his case up to the tower. He'd make it his own again. Instead he dug out his cloak, swirled it on and stepped out into the thin summer rain.

He walked toward the stream first where the drenched foxgloves swayed their heavy bells and the wild orange lilies Nola had particularly loved spread like spears of flame. There should be flowers in the house, he thought. He'd have to gather some before dusk. There had always been flowers in the house.

He circled around, drawing in the scent of damp air, wet leaves, roses. His brother kept the place tended; Hoyt couldn't fault him for that. He saw the stables were still there—not the same, but in the same spot. They were larger than they'd been, with a jut to one side that boasted a wide door.

He found it locked, so opened it with a focused thought. It opened upward to reveal a stone floor and some sort of car. Not like the one in New York, he noted. Not like the cab, or the van they had traveled in from the airport. This was black and lower to the ground. On its hood was a shining silver panther. He ran his hands over it.

It puzzled him that there were so many different types of cars in this world. Different sizes and shapes and colors. If one was efficient and comfortable, why did they need so many other kinds?

There was a long bench in the area as well, and all manner of fascinating-looking tools hanging on the wall or layered in the drawers of a large red chest. He spent some time studying them, and the stack of timber that had been planed smooth and cut into long lengths.

Tools, he thought, wood, machines, but no life. No grooms, no horses, no cats slinking about hunting mice. No litter of wriggling pups for Nola to play with. He closed and locked the door behind him again, moved down the outside length of the stable.

He wandered into the tack room, comforted somewhat by the scents of leather and oil. It was well organized, he saw, just as the stall for the car had been. He ran his hands over a saddle, crouched to examine it, and found it not so different from the one he'd used.

He toyed with reins and bridles, and for a moment missed his mare as he might have missed a lover.

He passed through a door. The stone floor had a slight slope, with two stalls on one side, one on the other. Fewer than there had been, but larger, he noted. The wood was smooth and dark. He could smell hay and grain, and . . .

He moved, quickly now, down the stone floor.

A coal-black stallion stood in the last of three stalls. It gave Hoyt's heart a hard and happy leap to see it. There were still horses after all—and this one, he noted, was magnificent.

It pawed the ground, laid back its ears when Hoyt opened the stall door. But he held up both hands, began to croon softly in Irish.

In response, the horse kicked the rear of the stall and blew out a warning.

"That's all right then, that's fine. Who could blame you for being careful with a stranger? But I'm just here to admire you, to take in your great handsome self, is all I'm about. Here, have a sniff why don't you? See what you think. Ah, it's a sniff I said, not a nip." With a chuckle, Hoyt drew back his hand a fraction as the horse bared his teeth.

He continued to speak softly and stand very still with his hand out while the horse made a show of snorting and pawing. Deciding bribery was the best tack, Hoyt conjured an apple.

When he saw the interest in the horse's eye, he lifted it, took a healthy bite himself. "Delicious. Would you be wanting some?"

Now the horse stepped forward, sniffed, snorted, then nipped the apple from Hoyt's palm. As he chomped it, he graciously allowed himself to be stroked.

"I left a horse behind. A fine horse I'd had for eight years.

I called her Aster, for she had a star shape right here." He stroked two fingers down the stallion's head. "I miss her. I miss it all. For all the wonders of this world, it's hard to be away from what you know."

At length he stepped out of the stall, closed the door behind him. The rain had stopped so he could hear the murmur of the stream, and the plop of rain falling from leaf to ground.

Were there still faeries in the woods? he wondered. Playing and plotting and watching the foibles of man? He was too tired in his mind to search for them. Too tired in his heart to take the lonely walk to where he knew his family must be buried.

He went back to the house, retrieved his case, and walked up all the winding steps to the topmost tower.

There was a heavy door barring his way, one that was deeply scribed with symbols and words of magic. Hoyt ran his fingers over the carving, felt the hum and the heat. Whoever had done this had some power.

Well, he wouldn't be shut out of his own workroom. He set to work to break the locking spell, and used his own sense of insult and anger to heat it.

This was *his* home. And never in his life had a door here been locked to him.

"Open locks," he commanded. "It is my right to enter this place. It is my will that breaks this spell."

The door flew open on a blast of wind. Hoyt took himself and his resentment inside, letting the door slam shut behind him.

The room was empty but for dust and spider webs. Cold, too, he thought. Cold and stale and unused. Once it had carried the scent of his herbs and candlewax, the burn of his own power.

He would have this back at least, as it had been it would be again. There was work to do, and this was where he intended to do it.

So he cleaned the hearth and lit the fire. He dragged up from below whatever suited him—a chair, tables. There was no electricity here, and that pleased him. He'd make his own light.

He set out candles, touched their wicks to set them to burn. By their light he arranged his tools and supplies.

Settled in his heart, in his mind, for the first time in days, he stretched out on the floor in front of the fire, rolled up his cloak to pillow his head, and slept.

And dreamed.

He stood with Morrigan on a high hill. The ground sheered down in steep drops, slicing rolls with shadowy chasms all haunted by the distant blur of dark mountains. The grass was coarse and pocked with rock. Some rose up like spears, others jutted out in gray layers, flat as giant tables. The ground dipped up and down, up again to the mountains where the mists fell into pockets.

He could hear hisses in the mists, the panting breath of something older than time. There was an anger to this place. A wild violence waiting to happen.

But now, nothing stirred on the land as far as his eye could see.

"This is your battleground," she told him. "Your last stand. There will be others before you come here. But this is where you will draw her, and face her with all the worlds in the balance of that day."

"What is this place?"

"This is the Valley of Silence, in the Mountains of Mist, in the World of Geall. Blood will spill here, demon and human. What grows after will be determined by what you, and those with you do. But you must not stand upon this land until the battle."

"How will I come here again?"

"You will be shown."

"We are only four."

"More are coming. Sleep now, for when you wake, you must act."

While he slept the mists parted. He saw there was a maiden standing on that same high ground. She was slim and young with brown hair in a tumble down her back, loose as suited a maiden. She wore a gown of deep mourning, and her eyes showed the ravages of weeping.

But they were dry now, and fixed upon that desolate land,

as his had been. The goddess spoke to her, but the words were not for him.

Her name was Moira, and her land was Geall. Her land, and her heart and her duty. That land had been at peace since the gods had made it, and those of her blood had guarded that peace. Now, she knew, peace would be broken, just as her heart was broken.

She had buried her mother that morning.

"They slaughtered her like a spring lamb."

"I know your grief, child."

Her bruised eyes stared hard through the rain. "Do the gods grieve, my lady?"

"I know your anger."

"She harmed no one in her life. What manner of death is that for one who was so good, so kind?" Moira's hands bunched at her sides. "You cannot know my grief or my anger."

"Others will die even a worse death. Will you stand and do nothing?"

"What can I do? How do we defend against such creatures? Will you give me more power?" Moira held out her hands, hands that had never felt so small and empty. "More wisdom and cunning? What I have isn't enough."

"You've been given all you need. Use it, hone it. There are others, and they wait for you. You must leave now, today."

"Leave?" Stunned, Moira turned to face the goddess. "My people have lost their queen. How can I leave them, and how could you ask it of me? The test must be taken; the gods themselves deemed this so. If I'm not to be the one to stand in my mother's stead, take sword and crown, I still must bide here, to help the one who does."

"You help by going, and this the gods deem so. This is your charge, Moira of Geall. To travel from this world so you might save it."

"You would have me leave my home, my people, and on such a day? The flowers have not yet faded on my mother's grave."

"Would your mother wish you to stand and weep for her and watch your people die?"

"No."

"You must go, you and the one you trust most. Travel to the Dance of the Gods. There I will give you a key, and it will take you where you need to go. Find the others, form your army. And when you come here, to this land, on Samhain, you'll fight."

Fight, she thought. She had never been called to fight, had only known peace. "My lady, am I not needed here?"

"You will be. I tell you to go now where you're needed now. If you stay, you're lost. And your land is lost, as the worlds are. This was destined for you since before your birth. It is why you are.

"Go immediately. Make haste. They only wait for sunset."

Her mother's grave was here, Moira thought in despair. Her life was here, and all she knew. "I'm in mourning. A few days more, Mother, I beg you."

"Stay even one day longer, and this is what befalls your people, your land."

Morrigan waved an arm, parting the mists. Beyond them it was black night with only the silver ripple of light from the cold moon. Screams ripped through the air. Then there was smoke, and the shimmering orange glow of fires.

Moira saw the village overlooked by her own home. The shops and cottages were burning, and those screams were the screams of her friends, her neighbors. Men and women ripped to pieces, children being fed on by those horrible things that had taken her mother.

She watched her own uncle fight, slashing with his sword while blood stained his face and hands. But they leaped on him from above, from below, those creatures with fangs and eyes of feral red. They fell on him with howls that froze her bones. And while the blood washed the ground, a woman of great beauty glided over it. She wore red, a silk gown tightly laced at the bodice and bedecked with jewels. Her hair was uncovered and spilled gold as sunlight over her white shoulders.

In her arms was a babe still swaddled.

While the slaughter raged around her, the thing of great beauty bared fangs, and sank them into the babe's throat.

"No!"

"Hold your grief and your anger here, and this will come." The cold anger in Morrigan's voice pierced through Moira's terror. "All you know destroyed, ravaged, devoured."

"What are these demons? What hell loosed them on us?"

"Learn. Take what you have, what you are and seek your destiny. The battle will come. Arm yourself."

She woke beside her mother's grave, shaking from the horrors she'd seen. Her heart was as heavy as the stones used to make her mother's cairn.

"I couldn't save you. How can I save anyone? How can I stop this thing from coming here?"

To leave all she'd ever known, all she'd ever loved. Easy for gods to speak of destiny, she thought as she forced herself to her feet. She looked over the graves to the quiet green hills, the blue ribbon of the river. The sun was high and bright, sparkling over her world. She heard the song of a lark, and the distant lowing of cattle.

The gods had smiled on this land for hundreds of years. Now there was a price to be paid, of war and death and blood. And her duty to pay it.

"I'll miss you, every day," she said aloud, then looked over to her father's grave. "But now you're together. I'll do what needs to be done, to protect Geall. Because I'm all that's left of you. I swear it here, on this holy ground before those who made me. I'll go to strangers in a strange world, and give my life if my life is asked. It's all I can give you now."

She picked up the flowers she'd brought with her, and laid some on each grave. "Help me do this thing," she pleaded, then walked away.

He was waiting for her on the stone wall. He had his own grief, she knew, but had given her the time she'd needed alone. He was the one she trusted most. The son of her mother's brother—the uncle she'd seen cut down in the vision.

He jumped lightly to his feet when she approached, and simply held open his arms. Going into them, she rested her head on his chest. "Larkin."

"We'll hunt them. We'll find them and kill them. What-ever they are."

"I know what they are, and we will find them, kill them. But not here. Not now." She drew back. "Morrigan came to me, and told me what must be done."

"Morrigan?"

At the suspicion on his face she was able to smile a little. "I'll never understand how someone with your skills doubts the gods." She lifted a hand to his cheek. "But will you trust me?"

He framed her face, kissed her forehead. "You know I will."

As she told him what she'd been told, his face changed again. He sat on the ground, shoving a hand through his mane of tawny hair. She'd envied his hair as long as she'd lived, mourning the fact that she'd been given ordinary brown. His eyes were tawny as well, gilded she'd always thought, while hers were gray as rain.

He'd been gifted with more height, as well as other things she envied.

When she was finished, she drew a long breath. "Will you go with me?"

"I'd hardly let you go alone." His hand closed over hers, firm and steady. "Moira, how can you be sure this vision wasn't simply your heartbreak?"

"I know. I can only tell you that I know what I saw was real. But if it's nothing more than grief, we'll only have wasted the time it takes to go to the dance. Larkin, I need to try."

"Then we'll try."

"We tell no one."

"Moira—"

"Listen to me." Urgently, she gripped his wrists. "Your father would do his best to stop us. Or to come with us if he believed me. This isn't the way, it isn't my charge. One, the goddess told me. I was to take only one, the one I trusted most. It can only be you. We'll write it down for him. While we're gone, he'll rule Geall, and protect it."

"You'll take the sword—" Larkin began.

"No. The sword isn't to leave here. That was a sacred oath, and I won't be the one to break it. The sword remains until I return. I don't take my place until I lift it, I don't lift it until I've earned my place. There are other swords. Arm yourself, she said, so see that you do. Meet me in an hour. Tell no one."

She squeezed his hands now. "Swear to me on the blood we share. On the loss we share."

How could he deny her when tears were still on her cheeks? "I swear it to you. I'll tell no one." He gave her arms a quick rub in comfort. "We'll be back by supper, I wager, in any case."

She hurried home, across the field and up the hill to the castle where her blood had reigned over the land since it was created. Those she passed bowed their heads to her to show their sympathy, and she saw tears glimmer.

And she knew when they dried, many would look to her for guidance, for answers. Many would wonder how she would rule.

So did she.

She crossed the great hall. There was no laughter here now, no music. Gathering the burdensome skirts of her gown, she climbed the steps to her chamber.

There were women nearby, sewing, tending to children, speaking in low voices so it sounded like doves cooing.

Moira went quietly by, and slipped into her room. She exchanged her gown for riding clothes, laced on her boots. It felt wrong to put off her mourning garb so quickly, so easily, but she would travel more swiftly in the tunic and tewes. She bound her hair back in a braid and began to pack.

She would need little but what was on her back, she decided. She would think of this as a hunting trip—there, at least, she had some skill. And so she got out her quiver and her bow, a short sword and lay them on the bed while she sat to write a message to her uncle.

How did you tell a man who'd stood in as father for so many years that you were taking his son into a battle you didn't understand, to fight what was impossible to comprehend, in the company of men you didn't know?

The will of the gods, she thought, her mouth tight as she wrote. She wasn't certain if she followed that or simply her own rage. But go she would.

I must do this thing, she continued in a careful hand. *I pray you will forgive me for it, and that I go only for the sake of Geall. I ask that if I don't return by Samhain, you lift the sword and rule in my place. Know that I go for you, for Geall, and that I swear by my mother's blood, I will fight to the death to defend and protect what I love.*

Now I leave what I love in your hands.

She folded the letter, heated the wax and sealed it.

She put on the sword, shouldered her quiver and bow. One of the women bustled out as she left her chambers.

"My lady!"

"I wish to ride out alone." Her voice was so sharp, her manner so curt that there was nothing but a gasp behind her as she strode away.

Her belly shook, but she didn't pause. When she reached the stables, she waved the boy away and saddled her mount herself. She looked down at him, his soft, young face bursting with freckles.

"When the sun sets, you're to stay inside. This night and every night until I tell you. Do you heed me?"

"Aye, my lady."

She wheeled her horse, kicked her heels lightly at its flanks, riding off at a gallop.

She would not look back, Moria thought. She would not look back at home, but forward.

Larkin was waiting for her, sitting loose in the saddle while his horse cropped grass.

"I'm sorry, it took longer."

"Women always take longer."

"I'm asking so much of you. What if we never get back?"

He clicked to his horse, walking it beside hers. "Since I don't believe we're going anywhere, I'm not worried." He sent her an easy smile. "I'm just indulging you."

"I'd feel nothing but relief if this is nothing more than that." But once again she urged her horse to the gallop. Whatever was waiting, she wanted to meet it quickly.

He matched her pace as they rode, as they had so often, over the hills that sparkled in the sunlight. Buttercups dotted the fields with yellow, giving swarms of butterflies a reason to dance in the air. She watched a hawk circle overhead, and some of the heaviness lifted from her.

Her mother had loved to watch the hawk. She'd said it was Moira's father, there to look down on them while he flew free. Now she prayed her mother flew free as well.

The hawk circled over the ring of stones, and raised its cry.

Nerves made her queasy so she swallowed hard.

"Well, we made it this far." Larkin shook back his hair. "What do you suggest?"

"Are you cold? Do you feel the cold?"

"No. It's warm. The sun's strong today."

"Something's watching." She shivered even as she dismounted. "Something cold."

"There's nothing here but us." But when he jumped down from his horse, Larkin laid a hand on the hilt of his sword.

"It sees." There were voices in her head, whispers and murmurs. As if in a trance, she took her bag from the saddle. "Take what you need. Come with me."

"You're acting considerably strange, Moira." With a sigh, Larkin took his own bag, tossing it over his shoulder as he caught up with her.

"She can't enter here. Never. No matter what her power, she can never enter this circle, never touch these stones. If she tries she'll burn. She knows, she hates."

"Moira . . . your eyes."

She turned them on him. They were nearly black, and they were depthless. And when she opened her hand, there was a wand of crystal in it. "You are bound, as I am bound, to do this thing. You are my blood." She took her short sword, cut her palm, then reached for his.

"Well, bollocks." But he held out his hand, let her slice across the palm.

She sheathed the knife, gripped his bloody hand with hers. "Blood is life, and blood is death," she said. "And here it opens the way."

With his hand in hers, she stepped into the circle.

"Worlds wait," she began, chanting the words that swirled in her head. "Time flows. Gods watch. Speak the words with me."

Her hand throbbed in his as they repeated the words.

The wind swirled, whipping the long grass, snapping their cloaks. Instinctively, Larkin put his free arm around her, folding her into him as he tried to use his body as a shield. Light burst, blinding them.

She gripped his hand, and felt the world spin.

Then the dark. Damp grass, misty air.

They still stood within the circle, on that same rise. But not the same, she realized. The forest beyond wasn't quite the same.

"The horses are gone."

She shook her head. "No. We are."

He looked up. He could see the moon swimming behind the clouds. The dying wind was cold enough to reach his bones. "It's night. It was barely midday and now it's night. Where the bloody hell are we?"

"Where we're meant to be, that's all I know. We need to find the others."

He was baffled, and unnerved. And could admit that he hadn't thought beyond the moment. That would stop now, for now he had only one charge. To protect his cousin.

"What we're going to do is look for shelter and wait for sunrise." He tossed her his pack, then started to stride out of the circle. As he walked, he changed.

The shape of his body, the sinew, the bone. In place of skin a pelt, tawny as his hair, in place of hair a mane. Now a stallion stood where the man had been.

"Well, I suppose that would be quicker." Ignoring the knots in her belly, Moira mounted. "We'll ride the way that would be toward home. I think that makes the most sense—if any of this does. Best not gallop, in case that way is different from what we know."

He set off in a trot, while she scanned the trees and the moonstruck hills. So much the same, she thought, but with subtle differences.

There was a great oak where none had been before, and the murmur of a spring in the wrong direction. Nor was the road the same. She nudged Larkin off it, in the direction where home would be if this were her world.

They moved into the trees, picking their way now carefully, following instinct and a rough path.

He stopped, lifted his head as if scenting the air. His body shifted under her as he turned. She felt muscles bunch.

"What is it? What do you—"

He flew, risking low branches, hidden rocks as he broke into a strong gallop. Knowing only he'd sensed danger, she lowered her body, clung to his mane. But it came like lighting, flying out of the trees as if it had wings. She had time to shout, time to reach for her sword before Larkin reared up, striking the thing with both hooves.

It screamed, tumbled off into the dark.

She would have urged him back into a gallop, but he was already shaking her off, already turning back into a man. They stood back-to-back now, swords drawn.

"The circle," she whispered. "If we can get back to the circle."

He shook his head. "They've cut us off," he replied. "We're surrounded."

They came slowly now, slinking out of the shadows. Five, no six, Moira saw as her blood chilled. Their fangs gleamed in the shivering moonlight.

"Stay close," Larkin told her. "Don't let them draw you away from me."

One of the things laughed, a sound that was horribly human. "You've come a long way to die," it said.

And leaped.

Chapter 8

Too restless to sleep, Glenna wandered the house. It was big enough, she supposed, to accommodate an army—certainly large enough to keep four relative strangers comfortable and afford some privacy. There were high ceilings—gorgeous with ornate plaster work—and steps that spiraled or curved to more rooms. Some of those rooms were small as cells, others spacious and airy.

Chandeliers were iron, the style intricate and artful and leaning toward the Gothic. They suited the house more than anything contemporary, or even the elegance of crystal.

Intrigued by the look, she went back for a camera. While she wandered, she paused when the mood struck, framed in a portion of ceiling, or a light. She spent thirty minutes alone on the dragons carved into the black marble of the fireplace in the main parlor.

Wizards, vampires, warriors. Marble dragons and ancient houses secluded in deep woods. Plenty of fodder for her art, she thought. She could very well make up the hit to her income when she got back to New York.

Might as well think positive.

Cian must have spent a great deal of time and money re-furbishing, modernizing, decorating, she decided. But then, he had plenty of both. Rich colors, rich fabrics, gleaming antiques gave the house a sense of luxury and style. And yes, she thought, the place just sat here, year after year, empty and echoing.

A pity, really. A waste of beauty and history. She de-plored waste.

Still, it was lucky he had it. Its location, its size, and she supposed, its history made it the perfect base.

She found the library and nodded in approval. It boasted three staggered tiers of books, towering to the domed ceiling where another dragon—stained glass this time—breathed fire and light.

There were candlestands taller than a man, and lamps with jeweled shades. She didn't doubt the lake-sized Orien-tal rugs were the genuine articles and possibly hundreds of years old.

Not only a good base, she mused, but an extremely com-fortable one. With its generous library table, deep chairs and enormous fireplace, she deemed this the perfect war room.

She indulged herself by lighting the fire and the lamps to dispel the gloom of the gray day. From her own supply, she gathered crystals, books, candles, arranging them through-out the room.

Though she wished for flowers, it was a start. But more was needed. Life didn't run on style, on luck, or on magic alone.

"What're you up to, Red?"

She turned, saw King filling the doorway. "I guess we could call it nesting."

"Hell of a nest."

"I was thinking the same. And I'm glad you're here. You're just the man I need."

"You and every other woman. What've you got in mind?"

"Practicalities. You've been here before, right?"

"Yeah, a couple times."

"Where are the weapons?" When his eyebrows shot up, she spread her arms. "Those pesky items required for fight-ing wars—or so I've heard, since this would be my first war. I know I'd feel better if I had a couple of howitzers handy."

"Don't think the boss runs to those."

"What does he run to?"

He considered. "What you got going in here?"

She glanced toward the crystals. "Just some things I've set around for protection, courage, creativity and so on. This struck me as a good place to strategize. A war room. What?" she said when his lips curved in a wide grin.

"Guess you're on to something." He walked over to a wall of books, ran his big fingers along the carved trim.

"You're not going to tell me there's a . . . secret panel," she finished with a delighted laugh when the wall swiveled out.

"Place is full of 'em." King pushed the wall completely around before she could peek through the gap. "I don't know as he'd want you poking around in the passages. But you said weapons." He gestured. "You got weapons."

Swords, axes, maces, daggers, scythes. Every manner of blade hung gleaming on the exposed wall. There were crossbows, long bows, even what she thought was a trident.

"That's just a little bit scary," she declared, but stepped forward to take down a small dagger.

"Little advice," King began. "You use something like that, whatever's coming for you is going to have to get real close before it does you any good."

"Good point." She replaced the dagger, took down a sword. "Wow. Heavy." She replaced it, took down what she thought would be termed a foil. "Better."

"You got any idea how to use that?"

"Hack, hack, hack, jab, jab?" She gave it a testing swing, found herself surprised she liked the feel of it. "Okay, no. Not a clue. Someone will have to teach me."

"Do you think you could slice through flesh with that?" Cian spoke as he came in the room. "Strike bone, spill blood?"

"I don't know." She lowered the sword. "I'm afraid I'm going to have to find out. I saw what she was, what she did, what she has with her. I'm not going into this with only potions and spells. And I'm sure as hell not going to stand there and go *eek* if she tries to bite me."

"You can wound them with that, slow them down. But you won't kill, you won't stop them unless you use it to cut off the head."

With a grimace she studied the slender blade, then resigned, put it back, took down the heavier sword.

"Swinging that around takes a great deal of strength."

"Then I'll get strong, strong enough."

"Muscle's not the only kind of strength you'll need."

She kept her gaze level. "I'll get strong enough. You know how to use this. You and Hoyt, and you," she said to King. "If you think I'm going to sit back, stirring a cauldron when it comes time to fight, think again. I wasn't brought here so I could have men protect me. I wasn't given this gift to be a coward."

"Me," King said with that wide grin in place again, "I like a woman with grit."

Gripping the hilt with both hands, she sliced the air with the blade. "So. When's my first lesson?"

Hoyt descended the stairs. He tried not to mourn what was changed, what was gone. He would get back, back to his true home, back to his family, and his life.

He would see the torches flaming on the walls again, smell his mother's roses in the garden. And he would walk the cliffs beyond his own cottage in Chiarrai again, and know the world was free of the vermin that sought to destroy it.

He'd needed rest, that was all. Rest and solitude in a place he knew and understood. Now he would work, and he would plan. He was done with this sensation of being swept away into what he couldn't understand.

Darkness had fallen, and those lights—those strange, harsh lights that came from electricity rather than fire—illuminated the house.

It irritated him that he found no one about, and could scent no supper cooking from the direction of the kitchen. It was time to be busy, and time the rest understood it was necessary to take the next steps.

A sound made him pause, then hiss out a breath. He followed the sound of clashing steel at a run. Then he swung toward where a doorway had been and cursed when he found sheer wall. He sprinted around it, and burst into the library where he saw his brother slashing a sword toward Glenna.

He didn't think; didn't hesitate. He punched his power toward Cian, and sent his sword spinning away to clatter on the floor. With her forward motion unblocked, Glenna sliced Cian's shoulder.

"Well, shit." Cian flicked a hand at the sword even as Glenna pulled it back in horror.

"Oh God! Oh my God. Is it bad? How bad?" She dropped her sword to rush forward.

"Back!" With another sweep of power, Hoyt had Glenna tumbling back and landing on her ass. "You want blood?" Hoyt plucked up Glenna's discarded sword. "Come then, get mine."

King grabbed a sword from the wall, slapped the blade against Hoyt's. "Back off, magic boy. Now."

"Don't interfere," Cian said to King. "Step away." Slowly, Cian picked up his own sword, met Hoyt's eyes. "You tempt me."

"Stop it! Stop it this minute. What the hell's wrong with you?" Regardless of the blades, Glenna pushed between the brothers. "I've stabbed him, for God's sake. Let me see."

"He attacked you."

"He did not. He was giving me a lesson."

"It's nothing." With his gaze still burning into Hoyt's, Cian nudged Glenna aside. "Shirt's ruined, and it's the second I've trashed on your account. If I'd wanted her blood, I wouldn't take it with a sword, waste it. But for yours, I could make an exception."

Glenna's breath wanted to heave, the words wanted to babble. But if she knew anything about men, she knew it would take only a flick of a finger to have these two spilling each other's blood.

Instead she spoke sharply—annoyed female to foolish boys. "It was a mistake, an accident on all sides. I appreciate you coming to the rescue," she said to Hoyt. "But I didn't, and don't need the white horse. And you—." She jabbed a finger at Cian. "You know very well what it must have looked like to him, so take it down a little. And you." She rounded on King. "You can just stop standing over there adding to it."

"Hey! All I did was—"

"Add more trouble," she interrupted. "Now go, get some bandages."

"I don't need them." Cian walked back to replace his sword. "I heal quickly, which is something you need to bear in mind." He held out a hand for King's sword. The glance Cian gave him might have been affectionate, Glenna thought. Or proud. "Unlike our irritated witch, I appreciate the gesture."

"No big." King handed Cian the sword, then sent Glenna a kind of sheepish shrug.

Unarmed now, Cian turned back to his brother. "You couldn't beat me with a sword when I was human. You damn well couldn't take me now."

Glenna put a hand on Hoyt's arm, felt the muscles quiver. "Put it down," she said quietly. "This needs to stop." She ran her hand down his arm to his wrist, then took the sword.

"The blade needs cleaning," Cian commented.

"I'll take care of it." King stepped away from the wall. "I'll toss something together for dinner while I'm at it. Got my appetite worked up."

Even after he walked out, Glenna thought there was so much testosterone in the room she couldn't have hacked through it with one of Cian's battleaxes.

"Can we move on?" she said briskly. "I thought we could use the library for our war room. And considering the weapons in here, and the books on magic, warfare, vampires and demons, it seems appropriate. I've got some ideas—"

"I bet you do," Cian mumbled.

"The first . . ." She moved to the table, picked up her crystal ball.

"Did you learn nothing the first time?" Hoyt demanded.

"I don't want to look for her. We know where she is. Or was." She wanted to change the mood. If there had to be tension, she thought, at least they could use it constructively.

"Others are coming, that's what we keep being told. There will be others. I think it's time we find some of them."

He'd planned to do exactly that, but could hardly say so now without looking foolish. "Put that down. It's too soon to use it after the last time."

"I've cleansed and recharged it."

"Regardless." He turned to the fire. "We'll do this my way."

"A familiar refrain." Cian stepped over to a cabinet, took out a heavy decanter. "Have at it then, the pair of you. I'm having a brandy. Elsewhere."

"Please stay." Glenna offered a smile, and there was both apology and cajolery in it. "If we find someone, you should be here to see. We need to decide what to do. All of us need to decide. In fact, I should go get King, so the four of us can do this."

Hoyt ignored them, but found it wasn't quite as simple to ignore the little prick that might have been jealousy. Teaching her swordplay and her fretting over the slightest scratch.

He spread his hands, and began to focus on the fire, using his annoyance to mix the heat.

"A nice thought." Cian nodded toward Hoyt. "But it seems he's already started."

"Well, for— All right then, all right. But we should cast a circle."

"I don't need one for this. Witches are forever casting circles, spinning rhymes. That's why true sorcery eludes them."

When Glenna's mouth dropped open, Cian grinned at her, added a wink. "Always been full of himself. Brandy?"

"No." Glenna set down her ball, folded her arms. "Thank you."

The fire snapped, rose higher and began to snap greedily at the logs.

He used his own tongue, the language of his birth and blood to draw the fire into a dance. Some part of him knew he was showing off, drawing out the moment and the drama.

With a billow of smoke, a hiss of flame, the images began to form in the flames. Shadows and movement, shapes and silhouettes. Now he forgot all but the magic and the purpose, all but the need and the power.

He felt Glenna move closer—in body and in mind. In magic.

In the flames, the shapes and silhouettes became.

A woman on horseback, her hair in a long braid down her back, a quiver of arrows over her shoulder. The horse was gold and sleek, and moved at a powerful, even reckless gallop through the dark forest. There was fear on the woman's face, and a steely determination along with it as she rode low, one hand clutched in the flying mane.

The man that wasn't a man leapt out of the forest, and was struck away. More took shape, sliding out of the dark, moving to surround.

The horse quivered, and in a sudden shimmer of light was a man, tall and lean and young. He and the woman stood back-to-back, blades drawn. And the vampires came for them.

"It's the road leading to the dance." Cian sprang toward the weapons, grabbed a sword and a two-headed ax. "Go in with King," he ordered Glenna as he raced for the window. "Stay here. Let no one in. No one and nothing."

"But—"

He threw up the window and seemed . . . seemed to *fly* out of it.

"Hoyt—"

But he was already grabbing a sword, a dagger. "Do as he says."

He was out the window himself, nearly as quickly as his brother. Glenna didn't hesitate. She followed.

He made for the stables, throwing his power ahead of him to open the doors. When the stallion charged out, Hoyt held up his hands to stop him. It was no time for niceties.

"Go back," he shouted at Glenna.

"I'm going with you. Don't waste time arguing. I'm in this, too." When she grabbed a handful of mane and sprang onto the horse's back, she tossed back her head. "I'll follow on foot."

He cursed her, but held down his hand for her to grip. The horse reared as King charged the stables. "What the hell's going on?"

"Trouble," Glenna shouted back. "On the road to the dance." When the horse reared again, she wrapped her arms tight around Hoyt. "Go!"

In the clearing, Moira fought, but no longer for her life. There were too many, and they were too strong. She believed she would die here. She fought for time, each precious moment of breath.

There was no room or time for her bow, but she had her short sword. She could hurt them, *did* hurt them. If her blade pierced flesh, they shrieked, and some fell back. But they rose again and came again.

She couldn't count them, no longer knew how many Larkin battled. But she knew if she fell, they would have him. So she fought to stand, fought just to hold on.

Two came at her, and with her breath sobbing out she hacked at one. His blood gushed out in a horrible scream as those red eyes rolled back to white. To her horror one of his fellows fell on him and began to drink. But still another got past her guard and sent her flying. It pounced on her like a mad dog with greedy fangs and red eyes.

She heard Larkin shout her name, heard the terror in it as she struggled. Those fangs grazed her throat, and the burn was beyond belief.

Something came out of the night, some dark warrior with sword and axe. What was on her was hurled away. Her dazed eyes watched him cleave the axe down, behead the thing. It screamed and flashed, and turned to dust.

"Take their head," the warrior shouted to Larkin, then turned burning blue eyes on her. "Use your arrows. Wood through the heart."

Then his sword began to sing and slice.

She gained her feet, yanked an arrow out of her quiver. Tried to steady her blood-slicked hand to notch it on the bow. Rider coming, she thought dimly when she heard the thunder of hoofbeats.

Another came for her, a girl younger than herself. Moira shifted, but there was no time to shoot. The girl leaped, and the arrow impaled her. There was nothing left but dust.

The horseman jumped down, sword already swinging.

They would not die, Moira thought as sweat dripped into her eyes. They would not die tonight. She notched an arrow, let it fly.

The three men had formed a triangle, and were beating the things back. One slithered through, crouched to charge the horse where a woman sat watching the battle. Moira scrambled forward, trying to find a clear shot, but could only call out a warning.

The second warrior spun around, sword raised as he prepared to attack. But the woman reared back the horse, so its hooves flashed out to strike the thing down.

When the sword sliced through its neck, there was nothing left but blood and dust.

In the silence, Moira sank to her knees, fighting for breath and against a terrible sickness. Larkin dropped down beside her, running his hands over her body, her face. "You're hurt. You're bleeding."

"Not bad. Not bad." Her first battle, she thought. And she was alive. "You?"

"Nicks, scratches. Can you get up? I'll carry you."

"I can get up, yes, and no, you won't carry me." Still kneeling, she looked up at the man who'd come out of the dark. "You saved my life. Thank you. I think we've come to find you, but I'm grateful you found us instead. I'm Moira, and we've come through the dance from Geall."

He simply looked at her for what seemed like the longest moment. "We need to get back, and inside. It isn't safe here."

"Larkin is my name." He held out a hand. "You fight like a demon."

"True enough." Cian clasped hands briefly. "Let's get them back," he said to Hoyt, and glanced toward Glenna. "The two of you helped yourself to my horse. Good thinking as it turned out. She can ride up with Glenna."

"I can walk," Moira began only to find herself lifted off her feet and onto the horse.

"We need to move," Cian said briskly. "Hoyt, take point, and you stay beside the women. I'm behind you."

Hoyt laid a hand on the stallion's neck as he passed, and glanced up at Glenna. "You've a steady seat."

"I've been riding since I was four. Don't think about trying to leave me behind again." Then she turned on the horse to look over her shoulder at Moira. "I'm Glenna. Nice to meet you."

"It's the pure truth I can't think of anyone in my life it's been nicer to meet." As the horse moved forward, Moira risked a look back. She couldn't see the warrior. He seemed to have melted into the dark.

"What is his name? The one who came on foot?"

"That would be Cian. Hoyt's up ahead. They're brothers, and there's a great deal to explain on all sides. But one thing's for damn sure, we just survived our first battle. And we kicked some vampire ass."

Moira bided her time. Under normal circumstances she would have considered herself a guest, and behaved accordingly. But she knew that was far from the case. She and Larkin were soldiers now, in what was a very small army.

It may have been foolish, but she was relieved not to be the only woman.

Inside the manor house, she sat in a wondrous kitchen. A huge man with skin dark as coal worked at a stove, though she didn't think he was a servant.

He was called King, but she understood this wasn't his rank. He was a man, like the others. A soldier like her.

"We'll patch you up," Glenna told her. "If you want to clean up first, I can show you upstairs."

"Not until we're all here."

Glenna cocked her head. "All right then. I don't know about the rest of you, but I want a drink."

"I'd kill for one," Larkin said with a quick smile. "Actually, it seems I have. I didn't believe you, not really." He laid a hand on Moira's. "I'm sorry."

"It's all right, it's no matter. We're alive, and where we're meant to be. That's what matters." She looked up as the door opened. But it was Hoyt who came in, not the one called Cian. Still she got to her feet.

"We haven't thanked you properly for coming to help us. There were so many. We were losing until you came."

"We've been waiting for you."

"I know. Morrigan showed you to me. And you," she said to Glenna. "Is this Ireland?"

"It is, yes."

"But—"

Moira merely laid a hand on Larkin's shoulder. "My cousin believes Ireland is a fairy tale, even now. We come from Geall, that which was made by the gods from a handful of Ireland, to grow in peace and to be ruled by the descendent of the great Finn."

"You're the scholar."

"Well, she loves her books, that's for certain. Now this is fine," Larkin said after a sip of wine.

"And the one of many shapes," Hoyt added.

"That'd be me, all right."

When the door opened again, Moira felt relief rush through her like a tide.

Cian flicked a glance at her, then at Glenna. "She needs tending to."

"Wouldn't budge until the gang was all here. Why don't you finish your wine, Larkin? Moira, come on upstairs with me."

"I have so many questions."

"We all do. Let's talk over dinner." Glenna took Moira's hand, drew her out.

Cian poured himself a drink, dropped down at the table. There was blood soaked through his shirt. "Do you usually bring your woman into strange places?"

Larkin took another gulp of wine. "She wouldn't be my woman, but my cousin, and fact of it is, she brought me. Had a vision or a dream or something mystical or other—which isn't that unusual for her. Fanciful sort, she is. But she was bound and determined to do this thing, and I couldn't have stopped her. Those things out there, some came to Geall. They killed her mother."

He took another deep drink. "We buried her this morning, if time's the same here. Ripped her to pieces is what they did. Moira saw it."

"How did she survive to tell it?"

"She doesn't know. At least—well, she won't really speak of it. Not as yet."

Upstairs, Moira washed in the shower as Glenna had showed her. The sheer pleasure of it helped ease her aches and hurts, and she considered the heat of the water nothing short of miraculous.

When the blood and sweat had been washed away, she put on the robe Glenna left her, then came out to find her new friend waiting in the bedchamber.

"No wonder we speak of Ireland like a fairy tale. It seems like one."

"You look better. Some color in your cheeks. Let's have a look at that wound on your neck."

"It burns, considerable." Moira touched her fingers to it. "It's hardly more than a scratch."

"It's still a vampire bite." Examining it closely, Glenna pursed her lips. "Not a puncture though, or just barely, so that's good. I've got something that should help."

"How did you know where to find us?"

"We saw you in the fire." Glenna poked into her case for the right balm.

"You're the witch."

"Mmm-hmm. Here we are."

"And the one called Hoyt is the sorcerer."

"Yes. He's not from this world either—or not from this time. It looks like they're getting us from all over hell and back. How does that feel?"

"Cool." Moira let out a sigh as the balm eased the burn. She raised her eyes to Glenna's. "Lovely, thanks. And Cian, what manner of man is he?"

Glenna hesitated. Full disclosure, she decided. Honesty and trust had to be bywords of their little battalion. "He's a vampire."

Going pale again, Moira pushed to her feet. "Why would you say that? He fought them, he saved my life. He's even now down in the kitchen, inside the house. Why would you call him a monster, a demon?"

"I didn't, because I don't consider him either. He's a vampire, and has been one for over nine hundred years. The one who made him is called Lilith, and she's the one we need to worry about. He's Hoyt's brother, Moira, and he's pledged to fight just like the rest of us."

"If what you say . . . He isn't human."

"Your cousin changes into a horse. I'd say that makes him something more than human, too."

"It's not the same."

"Maybe not. I don't have the answers. I do know Cian didn't ask for what happened to him all those years ago. I know he's helped us get here, and he was the first one out of the house to fight for you when we saw you in the fire. I know how you're feeling."

In her mind Moira saw what had been done to her mother, heard the screams, smelled the blood. "You couldn't know."

"Well, I know I didn't trust him initially either. But I do now. Completely. And I know we need him to win this. Here. I brought you some clothes. I'm taller than you, but you can just roll up the pants until we get you something that fits better. We'll go down, have a meal, talk some of this through. And see what goes."

It seemed they would eat in the kitchen, like family or like servants. Moira wondered if she could eat at all, but found her appetite huge. The chicken was fried juicy and crisp with heaps of potatoes and snap beans.

The vampire ate little.

"We're gathered," Hoyt began, "and must gather more at some point yet to be known. But it was to start with us, and so it has. Tomorrow we'll begin to train, to learn. Cian, you know best how to fight them. You'll be in charge. Glenna and I will work on the magicks."

"I need to train, too."

"Then you'll be busy. We'll need to find our strengths, and our weaknesses. We need to be ready when the final battle takes place."

"In the world of Geall," Moira said, "in the Valley of Silence, in the Mountains of Mist. On the sabbot of Samhain." Avoiding Cian's eyes she looked at Hoyt. "Morrigan showed me."

"Aye." He nodded. "I saw you there."

"When the time comes, we'll go through the dance again, and march to the battleground. It's five days' walk, so we'll need to leave in good time."

"Are there those in Geall who'll fight with us?"

"Any and all will fight. Any and all would die to save our home, and the worlds." The burden of it weighed down on her. "I have only to ask."

"You have a lot of faith in your fellow man," Cian commented.

She looked at him now, forced herself to meet his eyes. Blue, she thought, and beautiful. Would they go demon-red when he fed?

"So I do. And in my countrymen, and in humankind. And if I did not, I would order it so. For when I return to Geall, I must go to the Royal Stone, and if I'm worthy, if I'm the one as there is no other, I will pull the sword from that sheath. And I will be queen of Geall. I won't see my people slaughtered by what made you what you are. Not like lambs. If they die, they'll die in battle."

"You should know that the little skirmish you came through tonight was nothing. It was nothing. What were there? Eight, ten of them? There'll be thousands." He got to his feet. "She's had nearly two thousand years to make her army. Your farmers will have to do more than beat their plowshares into swords to survive."

"Then they will."

He inclined his head. "Be ready to train hard, and not tomorrow. Starting tonight. You forget, brother, I sleep days."

He left them with that.

Chapter 9

Glenna signalled to Hoyt, and left the others to King. She glanced back toward the kitchen, down toward the hall. She had no idea where Cian had gone.

"We need to talk. In private."

"We need to work."

"I won't argue with that, but you and I need to go over some things. Alone."

He frowned at her, but nodded. If she wanted privacy, there was one place he could be sure of it. He lead the way up the stairs, wound his way up to his tower.

Glenna wandered the room, studied his work areas, his books and tools. She went to each narrow window, opened the glass that had been put there since his day, closed it again.

"Nice. Very nice. Are you going to share the wealth?"

"What is your meaning?"

"I need a place to work—more, I'd say you and I need a place to work together. Don't give me that look." She waved a hand at him as she walked over to shut the door.

"What look would that be?"

"The 'I'm a solitary sorcerer and don't care for witches'

look. We're stuck with each other, and with the rest. Somehow, God knows, we have to become a unit. Because Cian's right."

She walked back to one of the windows, looked out into the moonstruck dark. "He's right. She'll have thousands. I never looked that far, never thought that big—though, Jesus, what's bigger than an apocalypse? But of course, she'll have thousands. We have a handful."

"It's as it was told to us," he reminded her. "We're the first, the circle."

She turned back, and though her eyes stayed level, he saw the fear in them. And the doubt. "We're strangers, and far from ready to join hands in a circle and chant some unity spell. We're uneasy and suspicious of each other. Even resentful when it comes to you and your brother."

"I don't resent my brother."

"Of course, you do." She pushed at her hair, and now he saw frustration as well. "You drew a sword on him a couple of hours ago."

"I thought he—"

"Yes, yes, and more gratitude for rushing to my rescue."

Her dismissive tone insulted his chivalry, and put his back up. "You're bloody welcome."

"If you actually save my life at some point, my gratitude will be sincere, I promise you. But defending the damsel was only part of it, and answering that was only part of why he very nearly fought you. You know it, I know it, and so does he."

"That being the case, there's no need for you to babble on about it."

She stepped forward. He saw with some satisfaction his wasn't the only back up now. "You're angry with him for letting himself be killed, and worse, changed. He's angry with you for dragging him into this, and forcing him to remember what he was before Lilith got her fangs into him. All of that's a waste of time and energy. So, we either have to get past those emotions, or we have to use them. Because as it stands, as we stand, she's going to slaughter us, Hoyt. I don't want to die."

"If you're afraid—"

"Of course I'm afraid. Are you stupid? After what we've seen and dealt with tonight, we'd be morons not to be afraid." She pressed her hands to her face, struggled to even her breathing again. "I know what has to be done, but I don't know how to do it. And neither do you. None of us do."

She dropped her hands, went to him. "Let's you and I be honest here. We have to depend on each other, have to trust each other, so let's be honest. We're a handful—with power, yes, with skills—but a handful against untold numbers. How do we survive this, much less win?"

"We gather more."

"How?" She lifted her hands. "How? In this time, in this place, Hoyt, people don't believe. Anyone who goes around talking openly about vampires, sorcerers, apocalyptic battles and missions from gods is either considered eccentric—best case—or put in a padded cell."

Needing the contact, she brushed a hand down his arm. "We have to face it. There's no cavalry coming to the rescue here. We *are* the cavalry."

"You give me problems, but no solutions."

"Maybe." She sighed. "Maybe. But you can't find solutions until you outline the problems. We're ridiculously outnumbered. We're going up against creatures—for lack of a better word—that can only be killed in a limited number of ways. They are controlled or led or driven by a vampire of enormous power and, well, thirst. I don't know much about warfare, but I know when the odds aren't in my favor. So we have to even the odds."

She spoke the kind of cold-blooded sense he couldn't deny. The fact that she would say it was, in his mind, another kind of courage. "How?"

"Well, we can't go out and cut off thousands of heads, it's just not practical. So we find the way to cut off the head of the army. Hers."

"If it were so simple, it would already be done."

"If it were impossible, we wouldn't be here." Frustrated, she rapped a fist on his arm. "Work with me, will you?"

"I haven't a choice in that."

Now there was hurt, just the shadow of it in her eyes. "Is it really so distasteful to you? Am I?"

"No." And more than a shadow of shame in his. "I'm sorry. No not distasteful. Difficult. Distracting. You're distracting, the way you look, the way you smell, the way you are."

"Oh." Her lips curved up slowly. "That's interesting."

"I don't have time for you, in that way."

"What way? Be specific." It wasn't fair, she knew, to tease and to tempt. But it was a relief to simply be human.

"Lives are at stake."

"What's the point of living without feeling? I feel for you. You stir something in me. Yes, it's difficult, and it's distracting. But it tells me I'm here, and that being afraid isn't all there is. I need that, Hoyt. I need to feel more than afraid."

He lifted a hand to brush his fingers over her cheek. "I can't promise to protect you, but only to try."

"I'm not asking you to protect me. I'm not asking you for anything—yet—more than truth."

He kept his hand on her face, bringing his other up to join it in framing her as he lowered his lips. Hers parted for him, offering. So he took, needing as she did, to feel and to know.

To be human.

It was a slow simmering in the blood, a lazy tightening of muscle, a flutter of pulse—hers and his.

So easy, he thought, so easy to sink into the warm and the soft. To be surrounded by her in the dark and let himself forget, for a moment, for an hour, all that lay before them.

Her arms slid around him, linking his waist as she shifted up on her toes to meet his mouth more truly. He tasted her lips and her tongue, and the promise of them. This could be his. And he wanted to believe it more than he'd ever believed anything.

Her lips moved on his, forming his name—once, then twice. A sudden spark flared, simmer to sizzle. The heat of it rippled over his skin, burned into his heart.

Behind them, the fire that had gone to embers flared up like a dozen torches.

He drew her back, but his hands still lingered on her cheeks. He could see the fire dance in her eyes.

"There's truth in that," he whispered. "But I don't know what it is."

"Neither do I. But I feel better for it. Stronger." She looked toward the fire. "We're stronger together. That means something."

She stepped back. "I'm going to bring my things up here, and we'll work together and find out what it means."

"You think lying together is the answer?"

"It may be, or may be one of them. But I'm not ready to lie with you yet. My body is," she admitted. "But my mind isn't. When I give myself to someone, it's a commitment for me. A big one. Both of us have committed quite a bit already. We'll both have to be sure we're ready to give more."

"Then what was this?"

"Contact," she said quietly. "Comfort." She reached a hand for his. "Connection. We're going to make magic together, Hoyt, serious magic. That's as intimate to me as sex. I'm going to get what I need, bring it up."

Women, he thought, were powerful and mystical creatures even without witchcraft. Add that dose of power and a man was at a serious sort of disadvantage.

Wasn't her scent still wrapped around him, and the taste of her still on his lips? Women's weapons, he decided. Just as slipping away was a kind of weapon.

He'd do well to arm himself against that sort of thing.

She intended to work here in his tower, alongside him. There was good, strong sense in that. But how was a man supposed to work when his thoughts kept drifting to a woman's mouth, or her skin, her hair, her voice?

Perhaps he'd be wise to make use of a barrier, at least temporarily. He moved to his worktable and prepared to do just that.

"Your potions and spells will have to wait," Cian said from the doorway. "And so will romance."

"I don't follow your meaning." Hoyt continued to work.

"I passed Glenna on the stairs. I know when a woman's had a man's hands on her. I could smell you on her. Not that I blame you," Cian added lazily as he strolled into and around the room. "That's a very sexy witch you have there.

Desirable," he added at his brother's stony look. "Alluring. Bed her if you like, but later."

"Who I bed, and when, is nothing to you."

"Who, certainly not, but when's another matter. We'll use the great hall for combat training. King and I have already begun to set up. I don't intend to end up with a stake through my heart because you and the redhead are too busy to train."

"It won't be a problem."

"I don't intend to let it be. The newcomers are unknown entities. The man fights well enough with a sword, but he's protective of his cousin. If she can't stand up in battle, we need to find another use for her."

"It's your job to see that she can, and will, stand up in battle."

"I'll work her," Cian promised. "And the rest of you. But we'll need more than swords and stakes, more than muscle."

"We'll have it. Leave that to me. Cian," he said before his brother could leave the room. "Did you ever see them again? Do you know how they fared, what became of them?"

He didn't have to be told his brother spoke of their family. "They lived and they died, as humans will."

"Is that all they are to you?"

"Shadows are what they are."

"You loved them once."

"My heart beat once as well."

"Is that the measure of love? A heartbeat?"

"We can love, even we can love. But to love a human?" Cian shook his head. "Only misery and tragedy could follow. Your parents sired what I was. Lilith made what I am."

"And do you have love for her?"

"For Lilith." His smile was slow, thoughtful. And humorless. "In my fashion. But don't worry. It won't stop me from destroying her. Come down, and we'll see what you're made of."

"Two hours' hand-to-hand, every day," Cian announced when they were gathered. "Two hours' weapons training, every day. Two hours' endurance, and two on martial arts. I'll work you here at night. King will take over in the daylight when you can train outdoors."

"We need time for study and strategy as well," Moira pointed out.

"Then make it. They're stronger than you, and more vicious than you can imagine."

"I know what they are."

Cian merely looked at her. "You think you do."

"Had you ever killed one before tonight?" she demanded.

"I have, more than one."

"In my world those that would kill their own kind are villains and outcasts."

"If I hadn't, you'd be dead."

He moved so quickly no one had a chance to react. He was behind Moira's back, an arm around her waist. And a knife at her throat. "Of course, I wouldn't need the knife."

"You're not to touch her." Larkin laid a hand on the hilt of his own knife. "You're not to put your hands on her."

"Stop me," Cian invited, and tossed his knife aside. "I've just snapped her neck." He laid his hands on either side of Moira's head, then gave her a little nudge that sent her careening into Hoyt. "Avenge her. Attack me."

"I won't attack the man who fought at my back."

"I'm not at your back now, am I? Show some spine, or don't the men of Geall have any?"

"We've plenty." Larkin drew his knife, crouched. Began to circle.

"Don't play at it," Cian taunted. "I'm unarmed. You have the advantage. Use it—quickly."

Larkin lunged—feinted, then slashed. And found himself flat on his back, with his knife skittering over the floor.

"You never have the advantage over a vampire. First lesson."

Larkin shook back his hair and grinned. "You're better than they were."

"Considerably." Amused, Cian held down a hand, helped Larkin to his feet.

"We'll start with some basic maneuvers, see what you're made of. Choose an opponent. You have one minute to take that opponent down—bare-handed. When I call switch, choose another. Move fast, and hard. Now."

He watched his brother hesitate and the witch turn into him, using her body to shift him off-balance, then hooking her foot behind his to send him down.

"Self-defense training," Glenna announced. "I live in New York."

While she was grinning, Hoyt swept her feet out from under her. Her ass hit the floorboards, hard. "Ouch. First request, we get pads for the floor."

"Switch!"

They moved, they maneuvered, grappled. And it was more game and competition than training. Even so, Glenna thought, she was going to have her share of bruises. She faced off with Larkin, sensed he would hold back. So she sent him a flirtatious smile, and when the laugh lit his eyes, flipped him over her shoulder.

"Sorry. I like to win."

"Switch."

The bulk of King filled her vision, and she looked up, up, until she met his eyes. "Me, too," he told her.

She went with instinct, a movement of her hands, a rapid chant. When he smiled blankly, she touched his arm. "Why don't you sit down?"

"Sure."

When he obeyed, she glanced over, saw Cian watching her. And flushed a little. "That was probably against the rules—and it's unlikely I'd be able to pull it off in the heat of battle, but I think it should count."

"There are no rules. She's not the strongest," he called out. "She's not the fastest. But she's the most clever of the lot of you. She uses wile and she uses wit as much as muscle and speed. Get stronger," he said to Glenna. "Get faster."

For the first time he smiled. "And get a sword. We'll start on weapons."

By the end of the next hour, Glenna was dripping sweat. Her sword arm ached like a bad tooth from shoulder to wrist. The thrill of the work, of actually doing something tangible had long since faded into a bitter exhaustion.

"I thought I was in good shape," she complained to Moira. "All those hours of pilates, of yoga, of weights—and I might as well be speaking to you in tongues."

"You're doing well." And Moira herself felt weak and clumsy.

"I'm barely standing. I do regular exercise, hard physical training, and this is turning me into a wimp. And you look beat."

"It's been a very long, very hard day."

"That's putting it mildly."

"Ladies? If I could trouble you to join us. Or would you rather have a seat and discuss fashion?"

Glenna set down her water bottle. "It's nearly three in the morning," she said to Cian. "A dangerous time for sarcasm."

"And prime time for your enemy."

"That may be, but not all of us are on that same clock just yet. And Moira and Larkin have traveled a hell of a long way today and dealt with a very nasty welcome. We need to train, you're absolutely right. But if we don't rest we're not going to get strong, and we're sure as hell not going to get fast. Look at her," Glenna demanded. "She can barely stay upright."

"I'm fine," Moira said quickly.

Cian gave her a long look. "Then we can blame fatigue for your sloppy swordsmanship and poor form."

"I do well enough with a sword." When she reached for it, blood in her eye, Larkin stepped up. He slapped a hand on her shoulder, and squeezed.

"Well enough she does, so she proved earlier tonight. But the blade wouldn't be my cousin's weapon of choice."

"Oh?" A wealth of boredom was contained in the single syllable.

"She's a decent hand with a bow."

"She can give us a demonstration tomorrow, but for now—"

"I can do it tonight. Open the doors."

The tone of command had Cian's brow winging up. "You don't rule here, little queen."

"Nor do you." She strode over, picked up bow and quiver. "Will you open the doors, or will I?"

"You're not to go out."

"He's right, Moira," Glenna began.

"I won't have to. Larkin, if you would."

Larkin moved to the doors and threw them open to the wide terrace beyond. Moira notched an arrow as she moved to the threshold. "The oak, I think."

Cian moved to her side as the others crowded in. "Not much of a distance."

"She wouldn't be meaning the near one," Larkin said and gestured. "But that one there, just to the right of the stables."

"Lowest branch."

"I can barely see it," Glenna commented.

"Can you?" Moira demanded of Cian.

"Perfectly."

She lifted the bow, steadied, sighted. And let the arrow fly.

Glenna heard the whiz, then a faint thunk as the arrow hit home. "Wow. Got ourselves a Robin Hood."

"Nicely shot," Cian said in mild tones, then turned to walk away. He sensed the movement even before he heard his brother's sharp command.

When he turned, Moira had another arrow ready, and aimed at him.

He sensed King prepare to rush forward, and held up a hand to stop him. "Be sure to hit the heart," he advised Moira. "Otherwise you'll just annoy me. Let it be," he snapped to Hoyt. "It's her choice."

The bow trembled a moment, then Moira lowered it. Lowered her eyes as well. "I need sleep. I'm sorry, I need sleep."

"Of course you do." Glenna took the bow from her, set it aside. "I'll take you down, get you settled." Glenna aimed a look at Cian every bit as sharp as the arrow as she led Moira from the room.

"I'm sorry," Moira said again. "I'm ashamed."

"Don't be. You're overtired, overworked. Over everything. We all are. And it's barely begun. A few hours' sleep is what we all need."

"Do they? Do they sleep?"

Glenna understood what she meant. The vampires. Cian. "Yes, it seems they do."

"I wish it was morning so I could see the sun. They crawl back into their holes with the sun. I'm too tired to think."

"Then don't. Here, let's get you undressed."

"I lost my pack in the woods, I think. I don't have a night-dress."

"We'll figure that out tomorrow. You can sleep naked. Do you want me to sit with you awhile?"

"No. Thank you, no." Tears welled up and were willed back. "I'm being a child."

"No. Just an exhausted woman. You'll be better in the morning. Good night."

Glenna debated going back up, then simply turned toward her own room. She didn't give a damn if the men thought she was copping out, she wanted sleep.

The dreams chased her, through the tunnels of the vampire's cave where the screams of the tortured were like slashing knives in her mind, into her heart. Everywhere she turned in the labyrinth, each time she raced into the dark opening, like a mouth waiting to devour her, the screams followed.

And worse than the screams, even worse, was the laughter.

The dreams hunted her along the rocky shore of a boiling sea where red lightning hacked black sky, black sea. There the wind tore at her, there the rocks pierced up out of the ground to stab at her hands, her feet until both were bloody.

Into the dense woods that smelled of blood and death, where the shadows were so thick she could feel them brushing over her skin like cold fingers.

She could hear what craved her coming with the papery snap of wings, the slithery slide of snakes, the sly scrape of claw on earth.

She heard the wolf howl, and the sound was hunger.

They were everywhere she was, and she had nothing but her empty hands and pounding heart. Still she ran blindly, the scream trapped in her burning throat.

She burst out of the trees and onto a cliff above a raging sea. Below her, waves lashed at rocks that rose up, sharp as razors. Somehow in her terror she'd run in a circle, and was back above the cave that held something even death feared.

The wind whipped at her, and power sang in it. His power, the hot, clean power of the sorcerer. She reached for it, strained toward it. But it slipped through her shaking fingers and left her nothing but herself.

When she turned, Lilith stood, regal in red, her beauty luminous against the velvet black. At each side was a black wolf, quivering for the kill. Lilith stroked her hands over their backs, hands that glittered with rings.

And when she smiled, Glenna felt a terrible pull inside her own belly. A deep and terrible yearning.

"The devil or the deep blue." With a laugh, Lilith snapped her fingers for the wolves to sit. "The gods never give their servants decent choices, do they? I have better."

"You're death."

"No, no, no. I'm life. That's where they lie. They're death, flesh and bone moldering in the dirt. What do they give you these days? Seventy-five, eighty years? How small, how limiting."

"I'll take what I'm given."

"Then you'd be a fool. I think you're smarter than that, more practical. You know you can't win. You're already tired, already weary, already questioning. I'll offer you a way out, and more. So much more."

"To be like you? To hunt and kill? To drink blood?"

"Like champagne. Oh, the first taste of it. I envy you that. That first heady taste, that moment when everything falls away but the dark."

"I like the sun."

"With that complexion?" Lilith said with a gay laugh. "You'd fry like bacon after an hour on the beach. I'll show you the coolness. The cool, cool dark. It's inside you already, just waiting to be wakened. Can you feel it?"

Because she could, Glenna only shook her head.

"Liar. If you come to me, Glenna, you'll stand by my side. I'll give you life, eternal life. Eternal youth and beauty. Power so beyond what they've given you. You'll rule your own world. I would give you that, a world of your own."

"Why would you?"

"Why not? I'll have so many. And I'd enjoy the company of a woman such as yourself. What are men, really, but tools to us? If you want them, you'll take them. This is a great gift I offer you."

"It's damnation you offer me."

Her laugh was lilting and seductive. "Gods frighten children with talk of hell and damnation. They use it to keep you bound. Ask Cian if he would trade his existence, his eternity, his handsome youth and lithe body for the chains and traps of mortality. Never, I promise you. Come. Come with me, and I'll give you pleasure beyond pleasure."

When she stepped closer, Glenna held up both hands, drew what she could out of her chilled blood and struggled to cast a protective circle.

Lilith simply struck out a hand. The tender blue of her irises began to redden. "Do you think such puny magic will hold me? I've drunk the blood of sorcerers, feasted on witches. They're in me, as you will be. Come willing, and take life. Fight, and take death."

She moved closer, and the wolves rose to stalk.

Glenna felt the pull, mesmerizing, glorious and dark, a drawing up in the belly that was elemental. It seemed the beat of her blood answered that call. Eternity and power, beauty, youth. All for one moment.

She had only to reach for it.

Triumph lit Lilith's eyes, burned them to red. Fangs flashed as she smiled.

Tears slid down Glenna's cheeks as she turned, as she leaped toward the sea and the rocks. As she chose death.

There was a scream ripping through her head when she shot up in bed. But it wasn't her own, she knew it wasn't her own. It was Lilith's, a scream of fury.

With her breath sobbing, Glenna scrambled out of bed, dragging the blanket with her. She ran, trembling from terror and cold, her teeth chattering with them. She fled down the hallway as if the demons were still after her. Instinct took her to the one place, the only place, she felt safe.

Hoyt sprang out of a sound sleep to find his arms full of

naked, weeping woman. He could barely see her in the dim, predawn light, but he knew her scent, her shape.

"What? What's happened?" He started to shove her aside, to reach for the sword beside his bed. But she clung to him like ivy on an oak.

"Don't. Don't go. Hold on. Please, please, hold on."

"You're like ice." He dragged up the blanket, trying to find warmth for her, trying to find his wits. "Have you been outside? Bloody hell. Have you done some spell?"

"No, no, no." She burrowed into him. "She came. She came. Into my head, into my dream. Not a dream. It was real. It had to be real."

"Stop. Stop this." He took a firm grip on her shoulders. "Glenna!"

Her head jerked back, her breath came shuddering out. "Please. I'm so cold."

"Then hush now, hush." His tone and his touch gentled while he brushed tears from her cheeks. He wrapped her more fully in the blanket, then pulled her close. "It was a dream, a nightmare. Nothing more."

"It wasn't. Look at me." She tilted her head up so he could see her eyes. "It wasn't just a dream."

No, he realized. He could see it hadn't been only a dream. "Then tell me."

"She was inside my head. Or . . . she pulled some part of me outside myself. The way it was when you were in the woods, hurt, with wolves outside your circle. Just as real as that. You know that was real."

"Aye, it was real."

"I was running," she began, and told him all of it.

"She tried to lure you. Now think. Why would she do so unless she knew you were strong, unless she knew you could hurt her?"

"I died."

"You didn't, no, you didn't. You're here. Cold." He rubbed her arms, her back. Would he ever be able to warm her again? "But alive, and here. Safe."

"She was beautiful. Alluring. I don't go for women, if you understand, but I was drawn to her. And part of it was sexual. Even in fear, I wanted her. The idea of her touching me, taking me, was compelling."

"It's a kind of trance, nothing more. And you didn't allow it. You didn't listen, you didn't believe."

"But I did listen, Hoyt. And some part of me did believe. Some part of me wanted what she offered. So much wanted. To live forever, with all that power. I thought, inside me, I thought, yes, oh yes, why shouldn't I have it? And turning away from it—I nearly didn't—because turning away from it was the hardest thing I've ever done."

"Yet you did."

"This time."

"Every time."

"They were your cliffs. I felt you there. I felt you there, but I couldn't reach you. I was alone, more alone than I've ever been. Then I was falling, and I was even more alone."

"You're not alone. Here." He pressed his lips to her forehead. "You're not alone, are you?"

"I'm not a coward, but I'm afraid. And the dark . . ." She shuddered, looked around the room. "I'm afraid of the dark."

He cast his mind toward the bedside candle, toward the logs in the hearth, set them all burning. "Dawn's coming. Here, see." He gathered her into his arms, got out of bed with her to carry her to the window. "There now, look east. The sun's rising."

She saw the light of it, a gilding low in the sky. The cold ball inside her began to ease. "Morning," she murmured. "It's nearly morning."

"You won the night, and she lost it. Come, you need more sleep."

"I don't want to be alone."

"You won't be."

He took her back to bed, drew her against him. Because she still trembled, because he could, he passed his hand over her head. And sent her gently into slumber.

Chapter 10

She woke with sunlight sliding over her face, and she woke alone.

He'd snuffed the candles out, but left the fire burning low. Kind of him, she thought as she sat up, drawing the blanket over her shoulders. He'd been very kind and very gentle, and had given her exactly the comfort and security she'd needed.

Still, the wave of embarrassment came first. She'd run to him like a hysterical child fleeing from the monster in the closet. Sobbing, shaking and incoherent. She hadn't been able to handle it, and had looked for someone—for him—to save her. She prided herself on her courage and her wits, and she hadn't been able to stand up to her first showdown with Lilith.

No spine, she thought in disgust, and no real magic. Fear and temptation had smothered them. No, worse, she thought, fear and temptation had frozen them inside her, deep, where she hadn't been able to reach. Now, in the light of day, she could see how foolish she'd been, how stupid, how *easy*. She'd done nothing to protect herself before, during or after. She'd run through the caves, through the woods, on the cliffs because they'd wanted her to run, and she'd let terror block out everything but the desperate need to escape.

It wasn't a mistake she'd make again.

She wasn't going to sit here wallowing either, not over something that was done.

She got up, wrapped herself in the blanket, then peeked out into the corridor. She saw no one, heard nothing, and was grateful. She didn't want to talk to anyone until she'd put herself back together.

She showered, dressed, then took a great deal of care with her makeup. She hung amber drops at her ears for strength. And when she made the bed, she put amethyst and rosemary under her pillow. After choosing a candle from her supplies, she set it beside the bed. When she prepared for sleep that night, she would consecrate the candle with oil to repel Lilith and those like her from her dreams.

She would also make a stake, and get a sword from the weapons supply. She wouldn't be defenseless and open again.

Before she left the room she took a long look at herself in the mirror. She looked alert, she decided, and capable.

She would be strong.

Because she considered it the heart of any home, she went to the kitchen first. Someone had made coffee, and by process of elimination, she figured it had been King. There was evidence someone had eaten. She could smell bacon. But there was no one around, and no dishes in the sink.

It was some small comfort to know whoever had eaten— or at least whoever had cooked—had also tidied up. She didn't like to live in disorder, but neither would she care to be in charge of all things domestic.

She poured herself a cup from the pot, toyed with making some breakfast. But there was enough of the dream left in her that the sensation of being alone in the house was uncomfortable.

Her next choice was the library, which she thought of as the main artery of the heart. And there, with some relief, she found Moira.

Moira sat on the floor in front of the fire, surrounded by

books. Even now she was hunched over one like a student cramming for an exam. She wore a tunic the color of oatmeal with brown pants and her riding boots.

She looked up as Glenna entered, offered a shy smile. "Good morning to you."

"Good morning. Studying?"

"I am." The shyness faded so those gray eyes shined. "This is the most marvelous room, isn't it? We have a great library in the castle at home, but this rivals it."

Glenna crouched, tapped a finger on a book thick as a beam. Carved into its scrolled leather cover was a single word.

VAMPYRE.

"Boning up?" she asked. "Studying the enemy?"

"It's wise to know all you can about whatever you can. Not all the books I've read so far agree on all things, but there are some elements on which they do."

"You could ask Cian. I imagine he could tell you whatever you wanted to know."

"I like to read."

Glenna only nodded. "Where did you get the clothes?"

"Oh. I went out this morning, early, found my pack."

"Alone?"

"I was safe enough, as I kept to the bright path. They can't come out in the sunlight." She looked toward the windows. "There was nothing left of the ones that attacked us last night. Even the ash was gone."

"Where is everyone else?"

"Hoyt went up to his tower to work, and King said he would go into the town for supplies now that there are more of us. I've never seen a man so big. He cooked food for us, and there was juice from a fruit. Orange. It was wonderful. Do you think I could take some of the seeds of the orange when we go back to Geall?"

"I don't see why not. And the others?"

"Larkin, I imagine, is still sleeping. He tends to avoid the mornings as if they were the plague. The vampire is in his room, I would think." Moira rubbed her finger over the carved word on the book. "Why does he stand with us? I can find nothing in the books to explain it."

"Then I guess you can't find out everything from books. Is there anything else you need for now?"

"No. Thanks."

"I'm going to grab something to eat, then go up to work. I imagine whenever King gets back, we'll start whatever torture session he has in mind."

"Glenna . . . I wanted to thank you for last night. I was so tired, and upset. I feel so out of my place."

"I know." Glenna put her hand over Moira's. "I think in a way, we all do. Maybe that's part of the plan, taking us out of our place, putting us together so we find ourselves, what there is in us—individually and together—to fight this thing."

She rose. "Until it's time to move, we're going to have to make this our place."

She left Moira to the books and returned to the kitchen. There she found what was left of a loaf of brown bread and slathered butter on a slice. Damned if she'd worry about calories at this point. She nibbled on it as she climbed the stairs to the tower.

The door was closed. She nearly knocked before she reminded herself it was her work area, too, and no longer Hoyt's solitary domain. So she balanced the slice of bread on the mug of coffee, unlatched the door.

He wore a shirt the color of faded denim with black jeans and scarred boots, and still managed to look like a sorcerer. It wasn't just the rich and flowing black hair, she thought, or those intense blue eyes. It was the power that fit him more truly than the borrowed clothes.

Irritation crossed his face first when he glanced at her. She wondered if it was habitual, that quick annoyance at being interrupted or disturbed. Then it cleared, and she found herself being carefully studied.

"So, you're up then."

"Apparently."

He went back to work, pouring some port-colored liquid from a kind of beaker into a vial. "King went for provisions."

"So I'm told. I found Moira in the library, reading, from the looks of it, every book in there."

So, it was going to be awkward, she realized as he continued to work in silence. Better to get past that. "I was going to apologize for disturbing you last night, but that's just an indulgence on my part." She waited, one beat, then two before he stopped to look over at her. "So you could tell me not to worry about it, that of course it was all right. I was frightened and upset."

"That would be true enough."

"It would, and since we both know all that, indulgent. So I won't apologize. But I will thank you."

"It's of no matter."

"It is, for me, on several levels. You were there when I needed you, and you calmed me down. Made me feel safe. You showed me the sun." She set the mug down so her hands would be free as she crossed to him.

"I jumped into your bed in the middle of the night. Naked. I was vulnerable, hysterical. I was defenseless."

"I don't think the last is true."

"At that moment it was. It won't be again. You could have had me. We both know that."

There was a long beat of silence that acknowledged the simple truth more truly than any words. "And what manner of man would I be to have taken you at such a time? To have used your fear for my own needs?"

"A different one from what you are. I'm grateful to the one you are." She skirted the worktable, rose to her toes to kiss both of his cheeks. "Very. You gave me comfort, Hoyt, and you gave me sleep. And you left the fire burning. I won't forget it."

"You're better now."

"Yes. I'm better now. I was caught off-guard, and I won't be the next time. I wasn't prepared for her, and I will be the next time. I didn't take precautions, even the simplest ones because I was tired." She wandered to the fire he kept burning low. "Sloppy of me."

"Aye. It was."

She cocked her head, smiled at him. "Did you want me?"

He got busy again. "That's not the point."

"I'll take that as a yes, and promise the next time I jump into your bed, I won't be hysterical."

"The next time you jump into my bed, I won't give you sleep."

She choked out a laugh. "Well, just so we understand each other."

"I don't know that I understand you at all, but that doesn't stop the wanting of you."

"It's mutual, on both counts. But I think I'm beginning to understand you."

"Did you come here to work, or just to distract me?"

"Both, I guess. Since I've accomplished the latter, I'll ask what you're working on there."

"A shield."

Intrigued she moved closer. "More science than sorcery."

"They're not exclusive, but joined."

"Agreed." She sniffed at the beaker. "Some sage," she decided, "and clove. What have you used for binding?"

"Agate dust."

"Good choice. What sort of shield are you after?"

"Against the sun. For Cian."

She flicked her gaze to his, but he didn't meet it. "I see."

"We risk attack if we go out at night. He dies if he exposes himself to sunlight. But if he had a shield, we could work and train more efficiently. If he had a shield, we could hunt them by day."

She said nothing for a moment. Yes, she was beginning to understand him. This was a very good man, one who held himself to high standards. So he could be impatient, irritable, even autocratic.

And he loved his brother very much.

"Do you think he misses the sun?"

Hoyt sighed. "Wouldn't you?"

She touched a hand to his arm. A good man, she thought again. A very good man who would think of his brother. "What can I do to help?"

"Maybe I begin to understand you as well."

"Is that so?"

"You have an open heart." Now he looked at her. "An open

heart and a willing mind. They're difficult to resist."

She took the vial from him, set it down. "Kiss me, would you? We both want that, and it makes it hard to work. Kiss me, Hoyt, so we settle down."

There might have been amusement, just a sprinkle of it in his voice. "Kissing will settle us down?"

"Won't know unless we try." She laid her hands on his shoulders, let her fingers play with his hair. "But I know, right this minute, I can't think of anything else. So do me a favor. Kiss me."

"A favor then."

Her lips were soft, a yielding warmth under his. So he was gentle, holding her, tasting her the way he'd yearned to the night before. He stroked a hand down her hair, down the length of her back so the feel of her mingled in his senses with her flavor and her scent.

What was inside him opened, and eased.

She skimmed her fingers over the strong edge of his cheekbone and gave herself completely to the moment. To the comfort and the pleasure, and the shimmer of heat flowing under both.

When their lips parted, she pressed her cheek to his, held there a moment. "I feel better," she told him. "How about you?"

"I feel." He stepped back, then brought her hand to his lips. "And I suspect that I'll be needing to be settled again. For the good of the work."

She laughed, delighted. "Anything I can do for the cause."

They worked together for more than an hour, but each time they exposed the potion to sunlight, it boiled.

"A different incantation," Glenna suggested.

"No. We need his blood." He looked at her over the beaker. "For the potion itself, and to test it."

Glenna considered. "You ask him."

There was a thud at the door, then King pushed it open. He wore camo pants and an olive green T-shirt. He'd tied his dreadlocks back into a thick, fuzzy tail. And looked, Glenna thought, like an army all by himself.

"Magic hour's over. Fall in outside. Time to get physical."

If King hadn't been a drill sergeant in another life, karma was missing a step. Sweat dripped into Glenna's eyes as she attacked the dummy Larkin had fashioned out of straw and wrapped in cloth. She blocked with her forearm as she'd been taught, then plunged the stake into the straw.

But the dummy kept coming, flying on the pulley system King had rigged, and knocked her flat on her back.

"And you're dead," he announced.

"Oh, bullshit. I staked it."

"Missed the heart, Red." He stood over her, huge and pitiless. "How many chances you figure you're going to get? You can't get the one in front of you, how are you going to get the three coming at your back?"

"All right, okay." She got up, brushed herself off. "Do it again."

"That's the spirit."

She did it again, and again, until she despised the straw dummy as much as she had her tenth-grade history teacher. Disgusted, she swung around, picked up a sword with both hands, and hacked the thing to pieces.

When she was done, there was no sound but her own labored breathing and Larkin's muffled laugh.

"Okay." King rubbed his chin. "Guess he's pretty damn dead. Larkin, you want to put together another one? Let me ask you something, Red."

"Ask away."

"How come you didn't just tear into the dummy with magic?"

"Magic takes focus and concentration. I think I could use some in a fight—I think I could. But most of me is channelled into handling the sword or the stake, particularly since I'm not used to handling either. If I wasn't centered, I could just send my own weapon flying out of my hand, missing the mark. It's something I'll work on."

She glanced around to make sure Hoyt wasn't anywhere within earshot. "Generally, I need tools, chants, certain rituals.

I can do this." She opened her palm, focused, and brought out the ball of fire.

Curious, he poked at it. And snatched back his singed finger, sucked on it. "Hell of a trick."

"Fire is elemental, like air, earth, water. But if I pulled this out during a battle, tossed it at an enemy, it might hit one of us instead, or as well as."

He studied the shimmering ball with his odd eyes. "Like pointing a gun if you don't know how to shoot. Can't be sure who's going to get the bullet. Or if you'd just end up shooting yourself in your own damn foot."

"Something like that." She vanished the fire. "But it's nice to have it in reserve."

"You go ahead, take a break, Red, before you hurt somebody."

"No argument." She sailed into the house, intending to drink a gallon of water and put together some food. She nearly walked straight into Cian.

"Didn't know you were up and around."

He stood back from the sunlight that filtered through the windows, but she saw he had a full view of the outdoor activities.

"What do you think?" she asked him. "How are we doing?"

"If they came for you now, they'd snack on you like chicken at a picnic."

"I know. We're clumsy, and there's no sense of unity. But we'll get better."

"You'll need to."

"Well, you're full of cheer and encouragement this afternoon. We've been at it over two hours, and none of us is used to this kind of thing. Larkin's the closest King's got to a warrior, and he's green yet."

Cian merely glanced at her. "Ripen or die."

Fatigue was one thing, she thought, and she would deal with the sweat and the effort. But now she was flat-out insulted. "It's hard enough to do what we're doing without one of us being a complete asshole."

"Is that your term for realist?"

"Screw it, and you with it." She stalked around the kitchen, tossed some fruit, some bread, some bottled water into a basket. She hauled it out, ignoring Cian as she passed by.

Outside she dumped the basket on the table King had carried out to hold weapons.

"Food!" Larkin pounced like a starving man. "Bless you down to the soles of your feet, Glenna. I was wasting away here."

"Since it's been two hours for certain since you last stuffed your face," Moira put in.

"The master of doom doesn't think we're working hard enough, and equates us to chicken at a picnic for the vampires." Glenna took an apple for herself, bit in. "I say we show him different."

She took another bite, then whipped around toward the newly stuffed dummy. She focused in, visualized, then hurled the apple. It flew toward the dummy, and as it flew it became a stake. And that stake pierced cloth and straw.

"Oh, that was fine," Moira breathed. "That was brilliant."

"Sometimes temper gives the magic a boost."

The stake slid out again, and splatted as an apple to the ground. She sent Hoyt a look. "Something to work out."

"We need something to unify us, to hold us together," she told Hoyt later. She sat in the tower, rubbing balm into bruises while he pored through the pages of a spellbook. "Teams wear uniforms, or have fight songs."

"Songs? Now we should sing? Or maybe just find a bloody harper."

Sarcasm, she decided, was something the brothers shared as well as their looks. "We need something. Look at us, even now. You and I up here, Moira and Larkin off together. King and Cian in the training room, devising new miseries for us all. It's fine and good to have the whole of the team split into smaller teams, working on their own projects. But we haven't become a whole team yet."

"So we drag out the harp and sing? We've serious work to do, Glenna."

"You're not following me." Patience, she reminded herself. He'd worked as hard as she had today, and was just as tired. "It's about symbolism. We have the same foe, yes, but not the same purpose." She walked to the window, and saw how long the shadows had grown, and how low the sun hung in the sky.

"It'll be dark soon." Her fingers groped for her pendant. It struck her then, so simple, so obvious.

"You were looking for a shield for Cian, because he can't go out in the day. But what about us? We can't risk going out after sundown. And even inside, we know she can get to us, get inside us. What about *our* shield, Hoyt? What shields us against the vampire?"

"The light."

"Yes, yes, but what symbol? A cross. We need to make crosses, and we need to put magic into them. Not only shield, but weapon, Hoyt."

He thought of the crosses Morrigan had given him for his family. But even his powers, even combined with Glenna's, fell short of the gods.

Still . . .

"Silver," he mumbled. "Silver would be best."

"With red jasper, for night protection. We need some garlic, some sage." She began going through her case of dried herbs and roots. "I'll start on the potion." She grabbed one of her books, began flipping through. "Any idea where we can get our hands on the silver?"

"Aye."

He left her, went down to the first level of the house and into what was now the dining room. The furnishings were new—to him, at least. Tables of dark, heavy wood, chairs with high backs and ornate carving. The drapes that were pulled over the windows were a deep green, like forest shadows, and made of a thick and weighty silk.

There was art, all of them night scenes of forests and glades and cliffs. Even here, he thought, his brother shunned the light. Or did he prefer the dark, even in paintings?

Tall cupboards with doors of rippled glass held crystal and pottery in rich jewel tones. Possessions, he thought, of a man of wealth and position, who had an eternity of time to collect them.

Did any of the things mean anything to Cian? With so much, could any single thing matter?

On the larger server were two tall candlestands of silver, and Hoyt wondered if they did—or if they had, at least.

They had been his mother's.

He lifted one, and had the image of her—clear as lake water—sitting at her wheel and spinning, singing one of the old songs she loved while her foot tapped the time.

She wore a blue gown and veil, and there was ease and youth in her face, a quiet contentment that covered her like soft silk. Her body was heavy with child, he saw that now. No, he corrected, heavy with children. Himself and Cian.

And on the chest beneath her window stood the two candlestands.

"They were a gift from my father on the day of my wedding, and of all the gifts given, I prized them most. One will go to you one day, and one to Cian. And so this gift will be passed down, and the given remembered whenever the candle is lit."

He comforted himself that he needed no candle to remember her. But the stand weighed heavy in his hands as he took it up to the tower.

Glenna looked up from the cauldron where she mixed her herbs. "Oh, it's perfect. And beautiful. What a shame to melt it down." She left her work to get a closer look. "It's heavy. And old, I think."

"Aye, it's very old."

She understood then, and felt a little pang in her heart. "Your family's?"

His face, his voice, were carefully blank. "It was to come to me, and so it has."

She nearly told him to find something else, something that didn't mean so much to him. But she swallowed the words. She thought she understood why he had chosen as he had. It had to cost. Magic asked a price.

"The sacrifice you're making will strengthen the spell. Wait." She pulled a ring from the middle finger of her right hand. "It was my grandmother's."

"There's no need."

"Personal sacrifice, yours and mine. We're asking a great deal. I need some time to write out the spell. Nothing in my books is quite right, so we'll need to amend."

When Larkin came to the door they were both deep in books. He glanced around the room and kept to his side of the threshold. "I'm sent to fetch you. The sun's set, and we're going into evening training."

"Tell him we'll be there when we're done," Glenna said. "We're in the middle of something."

"I'll tell him, but I'm thinking he won't like it." He pulled the door shut and left them.

"I've nearly got it. I'm going to draw out what I think they should look like, then we'll both visualize. Hoyt?"

"It must be pure," he said to himself. "Conjured with faith as much as magic."

She left him to it and began to sketch. Simple, she thought, and with tradition. She glanced over, saw he was sitting, eyes closed. Gathering power, she assumed, and his thoughts.

Such a serious face, and one, she realized, she'd come to trust completely. It seemed she'd known that face forever, just as she knew the sound of his voice, the cadence of it.

Yet the time they'd had was short, just as the time they would have was no more than a handful of grains in the sand of an hourglass.

If they won—no when, when they won—he'd go back to his time, his life, his world. And she to hers. But nothing would ever be the same. And nothing would ever really fill the void he'd leave behind.

"Hoyt."

His eyes were different when they met hers. Deeper and darker. She pushed the sketch toward him. "Will this do?"

He lifted it, studied. "Yes, but for this."

He took the pencil from her, added lines on the long base of the Celtic cross she'd drawn.

"What is it?"

"It's ogham script. Old writing."

"I know what ogham is. What does it say?"

"It says light."

She smiled, nodded. "Then it's perfect. This is the spell. It feels right to me."

He took that in turn, then looked at her. "Rhymes?"

"It's how I work. Deal with it. And I want a circle. I'll feel better with one."

Because he agreed he rose, to cast it with her. She scribed fresh candles with her bolline, watched him light them.

"We'll make the fire together." He held out his hand for hers.

Power winged up her arm, struck the heart of her. And the fire, pure and white, shimmered an inch above the floor. He hefted the cauldron, set it on the flames.

"Silver old and silver bright." He set the candlestand in the cauldron. "Go to liquid in this light."

"As we stand in the sorcerer's tower," Glenna continued, adding the jasper, the herbs, "we charge this flame to free your power." She dropped in her grandmother's ring.

"Magicks from the sky and sea, from air and earth we call to thee. We your servants beg this blessing, shield us in this time of testing. We answer your charge with head, heart and hand to vanquish the darkness from the land. So we call you three times three to shield those who serve you faithfully.

"Let this cross shine light to night."

As they chanted the last line, three times three, silver smoke rose from the cauldron, and the white flames beneath it grew brighter.

It flooded her, light and smoke and heat, filled her as her voice rose with his. Through it, she saw his eyes, only his eyes locked on hers.

In her heart, in her belly, she felt it heat and grow. Stronger, more potent than anything she'd ever known. It swirled in her as with his free hand, he threw the last of the jasper dust into the cauldron.

"And each cross of silver a shield will be. As we will, so mote it be."

The room exploded with light, and the force of it shook

the walls, the floor. The cauldron tumbled over, spilling liquid silver into the flame.

The force nearly sent Glenna to the ground, but Hoyt's arms came around her. He spun his body around to shield hers from the sudden spurting flames and roaring wind.

Hoyt saw the door fly open. For an instant, Cian was framed in the doorway, drowned in that impossible light. Then he vanished.

"No! No!" Dragging Glenna with him, Hoyt broke the circle. The light shrank in on itself, swallowed itself and was gone with a crash like thunder. Through the ringing in his ears he thought he heard shouting.

Cian lay on the floor bleeding, his shirt half burned away and still smoking.

Hoyt dropped to his knees, his fingers reaching for a pulse before he remembered there would be none in any case. "My God, my God, what have I done?"

"He's badly burned. Get the shirt off of him." Glenna's voice was cool as water, and just as calm. "Gently."

"What happened? What the hell did you do?" King shoved Hoyt aside. "Son of a bitch. Cian. Jesus Christ."

"We were finishing a spell. He opened the door. There was light. It was no one's fault. Larkin," Glenna continued, "help King carry Cian to his room. I'll be right there. I have things that will help."

"He's not dead." Hoyt said it quietly, staring down at his brother. "It's not death."

"It's not death," Glenna repeated. "I can help him. I'm a good healer. It's one of my strengths."

"I'll help you." Moira stepped up, then eased her body toward the wall as King and Larkin lifted Cian. "I have some skill."

"Good. Go with them. I'll get my things. Hoyt. I can help him."

"What did we do?" Hoyt stared helplessly at his hands. Though they still vibrated from the spell, they felt empty and useless. "It was beyond all I've done."

"We'll talk about it later." She gripped his hand, pulled him into the tower room.

The circle was burned into the floor, scorched in a pure white ring. In its center glinted nine silver crosses with a circle of red jasper at the joining.

"Nine. Three times three. We'll think about all this later. I think we should let them stay there for now. I don't know, let them set."

Ignoring her, Hoyt crossed the circle, picked one up. "It's cool."

"Great. Good." Her mind was already on Cian, and what would have to be done to help him. She grabbed her case. "I have to get down, do what I can for him. It wasn't anyone's fault, Hoyt."

"Twice now. Twice I've nearly killed him."

"This is my doing as much as yours. Are you coming with me?"

"No."

She started to speak, then shook her head and rushed out.

In the lavish bedchamber, the vampire lay still on the wide bed. His face was that of an angel. A wicked one, Moira thought. She sent the men out for warm water, for bandages, and mostly to get them out from underfoot.

Now she was alone with the vampire, who lay on the wide bed. Still as death.

She would feel no heartbeat should she lay her hand on his chest. There would be no breath to fog a glass if she were to hold one to his lips. And he would have no reflection.

She'd read these things, and more.

Yet, he'd saved her life, and she owed him for that.

She moved to the side of the bed, and used what little magic she had to try to cool his burned flesh. Queasiness rose up and was fought down. She'd never seen flesh so scorched. How could anyone—anything—survive such wounds?

His eyes flashed open, searing blue. His hand clamped on her wrist. "What are you doing?"

"You're hurt." She hated to hear the tremor in her voice, but her fear of him—alone with him—was so huge. "An

accident. I'm waiting for Glenna. We'll help you. Lie still."
She saw the instant the pain woke in him, and some of her
fear died. "Lie quiet. I can cool it a little."

"Wouldn't you rather I burn in hell?"

"I don't know. But I know I don't want to be the one who
sends you. I wouldn't have shot you last night. I'm ashamed
I let you believe I would. I owe you my life."

"Go away, and we'll call it quits."

"Glenna's coming. Is it cooling a little?"

He simply closed his eyes; and his body trembled. "I
need blood."

"Well, you won't be having mine. I'm not that grateful."

She thought his lips curved, just the slightest bit. "Not
yours, though I'll bet it's tasty." He had to catch the breath
the pain stole. "In the case across the room. The black case
with the silver handle. I need blood to— I just need it."

She left him to open the case, then swallowed revulsion
when she saw the clear packs that held dark red liquid.

"Bring it over, toss it and run, whatever you want, but I
need it now."

She brought it quickly, then watched him struggle to sit
up, to tear the pack open with his burned hands. Saying nothing, she took the pack, opened it herself, spilling some.

"Sorry." She gathered her strength, then used an arm to
brace him, using her free hand to bring the pack to his lips.

He watched her as he drank, and she made herself look
back into his eyes without flinching.

When he'd drained it dry, she laid his head down again
before going into the bath for a cloth. With it she wiped his
mouth, his chin.

"Small but valiant, are you?"

She heard the edge in his tone, and some return of its
strength. "You haven't a choice because of what you are. I
haven't one because of what I am." She stepped back when
Glenna hurried into the room.

Chapter 11

"**D**o you want something for the pain?" Glenna coated thin cloth with balm.

"What have you got?"

"This and that." She laid the cloth gently on his chest. "I'm so sorry, Cian. We should have locked the door."

"A locked door wouldn't have stopped me from coming in, not in my own house. You might try a sign next time, something along the lines . . . Bugger it!"

"I know, sorry, I know. It'll be better in a minute. A sign?" she continued, her voice low and soothing as she worked. "Something like: Flammable Magicks. Keep out."

"Wouldn't hurt." He felt the burn not just on the flesh, but down into the bone, as if the fire had burst inside him as well as out. "What the hell were you doing in there?"

"More than either of us were expecting. Moira, coat more cloth, would you. Cian?"

"What?"

She simply looked at him, deeply, her hands hovering just above the worst of the burns. She felt the heat, but not the release. "It won't work unless you let it," she told him. "Unless you trust me and let go."

"A high price for a bit of relief, adding that you're part of what put me here."

"Why would she hurt you?" Moira continued to coat the cloth. "She needs you. We all do, like it or not."

"One minute," Glenna said. "Give me one minute. I want to help you; you need to believe that. Believe me. Look at me, into my eyes. Yes, that's right."

Now it came. Heat and release, heat and release. "There, that's better. A little better. Yes?"

She'd taken it in, he realized. Some of the burn, just for an instant, into herself. He wouldn't forget it. "Some. Yes, some. Thanks."

She applied more cloth, turned back to her case. "I'll just clean the cuts and treat the bruises, then give you something to help you rest."

"I'm not looking for rest."

She shifted back, eased down on the bed intending to clean the cuts on his face. Puzzled, she laid her fingers on his cheek, turned his head. "I thought these were worse."

"They were. I heal quickly from most things."

"Good for you. How's the vision?"

He turned those hot blue eyes on her. "I see you well enough, Red."

"Could have a concussion. Can you get concussions? I imagine so," she said before he could answer. "Are you burned anywhere else?" She started to lower the sheet, then flicked him a wicked glance. "Is it true what they say about vampires?"

It made him laugh, then hiss as the pain rippled back. "A myth. We're hung just as we were before the change. You're welcome to look for yourself, but I'm not hurt in that area. It caught me full on the chest."

"We'll preserve your modesty—and my illusions." When she took his hand the amusement faded from his face. "I thought we'd killed you. So did he. Now he's suffering."

"Oh, *he's* suffering, is he? Maybe he'd like to switch places with me."

"You know he would. However you feel or don't about him, he loves you. He can't turn that off, and he hasn't had all the time that you've had to step back from brotherhood."

"We stopped being brothers the night I died."

"No, you didn't. And you're deluding yourself if you believe that." She pushed off the bed. "You're as comfortable as I can make you. I'll come back in an hour and work on you some more."

She gathered her things. Moira slipped out of the room ahead of her, and waited. "What did that to him?"

"I'm not entirely sure."

"You need to be. It's a powerful weapon against his kind. We could use it."

"We weren't controlling it. I don't know that we can."

"If you could," Moira insisted.

Glenna opened the door to her room, carried her case inside. She wasn't ready to go back to the tower. "It controlled us, as far as I can tell. It was huge and powerful. Too powerful for either of us to handle. Even together—and we were linked as closely as I've been with anyone—we couldn't harness it. It was like being inside the sun."

"The sun's a weapon."

"If you don't know how to use a sword, you're just as likely to cut off your own hand as someone else's."

"So you learn."

Glenna lowered to the bed, then held out a hand. "I'm shaky," she said, watching it tremble. "There are places inside my body I didn't know I had shaking like my hand is."

"And I'm badgering you. I'm sorry. You seemed so steady, so calm when you were treating the vampire."

"He has a name. Cian. Start using it." Moira's head snapped back as if she'd been slapped, and her eyes widened at the whip in Glenna's tone. "I'm sorry about your mother. Sick and sorry, but he didn't kill her. If she'd been murdered by a blond man with blue eyes, would you go around hating all men with blond hair and blue eyes?"

"It's not the same, not nearly the same."

"Close enough, especially in our situation."

Sheer stubbornness hardened Moira's face. "I fed him blood, and gave what little I could to ease him. I helped you treat his burns. It should be enough."

"It's not. Wait," Glenna ordered as Moira spun around to leave. "Just wait. I *am* shaking, and short-tempered with it. Just wait. If I seemed calm before it's because that's the way it works for me. Handle the crisis, then fall apart. This is the falling apart portion of our program. But what I said goes, Moira.

"Just as what you said in there goes. We need him. You're going to have to start thinking of him, and treating him like a person instead of a thing."

"They tore her to pieces." Moira's eyes filled even as the defense of defiance crumbled. "No, he wasn't there, he had no part of it. He lifted his sword for me. I know it, but I can't feel it."

She slapped a hand on her heart. "I can't feel it. They didn't let me grieve. They didn't give me time to mourn my own mother. And now, now that I'm here it's all grief and all rage. All blood and death. I don't want this burden. Away from my people, from everything I know. Why are we here? Why are we charged with this? Why are there no answers?"

"I don't know, which is another non-answer. I'm sorry, so horribly sorry about your mother, Moira. But you're not the only one with grief and rage. Not the only one asking questions and wishing they were back in the life they knew."

"One day you will go back. I never can." She yanked open the door and fled.

"Perfect. Just perfect." Glenna dropped her head into her hands.

In the tower room, Hoyt laid each cross on a cloth of white linen. They were cool to the touch, and though the metal had dimmed somewhat, its light was bright enough to glare into his eyes.

He picked up Glenna's cauldron. It was scorched black. He doubted it could ever be used again—wondered if it was meant to be. The candles she'd scribed and lit were no more than puddles of wax on the floor now. It would need to be cleaned. The entire room should be cleansed before any other magic was done here.

The circle was etched into the floor now, a thin ring of pure white. And his brother's blood stained the floor and walls outside the door.

Sacrifice, he thought. There was always payment for power. His gift of his mother's candlestand, Glenna's of her grandmother's ring, hadn't been enough.

The light had burned so fierce and bright, so violently hot. Yet it hadn't scorched his skin. He held his hand up, examined it. Unmarked. Unsteady yet, he could admit. But unmarked.

The light had filled him, all but consumed him. It had twined him so truly with Glenna it had been almost as if they'd been one person, one power.

That power had been heady and fantastic.

And it had whirled out like the wrath of the gods at his brother. Struck down the other half of him while the sorcerer had ridden the lightning.

Now he was empty, hollowed out. What power that remained in him was like lead, heavy and cold, and the lead was coated thick with guilt.

Nothing to be done now, nothing to do but put order back into the room. He busied himself, calmed himself, with the basic tasks. When King rushed into the room, he stood still, arms at his side and took the blow he saw coming full in the face.

He had a moment to think it was like being hit by a battering ram as he was launched back against the wall. Then simply slid bonelessly to the floor.

"Get up. Get up, you son of a bitch."

Hoyt spat out blood. His vision wavered so he saw several black giants standing over him with ham-sized fists bunched. He braced a hand on the wall, dragged himself to his feet.

The battering ram struck again. This time his vision went red, black, shimmered sickly to gray. King's voice went tinny in his ears, but he struggled to follow the command to get back up.

There was a flash of color through the gray, a stream of heat through the iced pain.

Glenna flew into the tower. She didn't bother to shove at King, but rammed her elbow viciously into his midsection, then all but fell on Hoyt to shield him.

"Stop it! Get away from him. Stupid bastard. Oh Hoyt, your face."

"Get away." He could barely mumble the words, and his stomach pitched violently as he pushed at her and tried to rise again.

"Go ahead and throw one. Come on." King spread his arms, then tapped his chin. "I'll give you a free shot. Hell, I'll give you a couple of them, you miserable son of a bitch. It's more than you gave Cian."

"He's gone then. Get away from me." Hoyt shoved at Glenna. "Go ahead," he told King. "Finish it."

Though his fists remained bunched, King lowered them a fraction. The man was barely standing, and blood ran from his nose, his mouth. One eye was already swelling shut. And he just swayed there, waiting to take another hit.

"Is he stupid, or just crazy?"

"He's neither," Glenna snapped. "He thinks he's killed his brother so he'll stand here and let you beat him to death because he blames himself as much as you blame him. And you're both wrong. Cian's not dead. Hoyt, he's going to be fine. He's resting, that's all. He's resting."

"Not gone?"

"You didn't pull it off, and you won't get a second chance."

"Oh, for God's *sake*!" Glenna whirled to King. "Nobody tried to kill anyone."

"Just step away, Red." King jerked a thumb. "I'm not looking to hurt you."

"Why not? If he's responsible, so am I. We were working together. We were doing what we came here to do, *damn* it. Cian came in at the wrong time, it's as simple and as tragic as that. If Hoyt could, and would, hurt Cian like that purposely, do you think you'd be standing there? He'd cut you down with a thought. And I'd help him."

King's bi-colored eyes narrowed, his mouth went grim. But his fists stayed at his side. "Why don't you?"

"It's against everything we are. You couldn't possibly understand. But unless you're brick stupid you should understand that whatever affection and loyalty you feel for Cian, Hoyt feels it, too. And he's felt it since the day he was born. Now get out of here. Just go."

King unbunched his fists, rubbed them on his pants. "Maybe I was wrong."

"A lot of good that does."

"I'm going to check on Cian. If I'm not satisfied, I'm going to finish this."

Ignoring him as he strode out, Glenna turned to try to take some of Hoyt's weight. "Here now, you need to sit down."

"Would you get away from me?"

"No, I won't."

In response, Hoyt merely lowered to the floor.

Resigned, Glenna went for more cloth, poured water from a pitcher into a bowl. "It looks like I'm going to spend the evening mopping up blood."

She knelt beside him, dampening cloth, then gently cleaning blood from his face. "I lied. You are stupid, stupid to stand there and let him pound on you. Stupid to feel guilty. And cowardly, too."

His eyes, bloodied and swollen, shifted to hers. "Have a care."

"Cowardly," she repeated, her voice sharp because there were tears welling at the base of her throat. "To stay up here wallowing instead of coming down to help. Instead of coming down to see what shape your brother was in. Which isn't that much worse than you at this point."

"I'm not in the mood to have you jab at me with words, or flutter about me." He waved her hands away.

"Fine. Just fine." She tossed the cloth back in the bowl so water spewed up and lapped over onto the floor. "Tend to yourself then. I'm tired of every single one of you. Brooding, self-pitying, useless. If you ask me, your Morrigan screwed up royally picking this group."

"Brooding, self-pitying, useless. You forgot your part of the whole. Shrew."

She inclined her head. "That's a weak and old-fashioned term. Today, we just go with bitch."

"Your world, your word."

"That's right. While you're up here wallowing, you might take just a minute to consider this. We did something amazing here tonight." She gestured toward the silver crosses on the table. "Something beyond anything I've ever experienced. The fact that we did, that we could, should, in some way, bring this ridiculous group together. But instead we're all whining in our separate corners. So I guess the magic, and the moment was wasted."

She stormed out just as Larkin jogged up the steps. "Cian's getting up. He says we've wasted enough time and we'll be training an extra hour tonight."

"You can tell him to kiss my ass."

Larkin blinked, then craned his head around the curve of the stairs to watch her stride down. "Sure it's a fine one," he said, but very quietly.

He peeked into the tower room, saw Hoyt sitting on the floor, bleeding.

"Mother of Christ, did she do that?"

Hoyt scowled at him and decided his punishment for the night wasn't quite done. "No. For God's sake, do I look like I could be beaten by a woman?"

"She strikes me as formidable." Though he would have preferred keeping clear of magic areas, he could hardly leave the man sprawled there. So Larkin walked over to Hoyt, crouched. "Well, that's a mess, isn't it? You're coming up a pair of black eyes."

"Bollocks. Give me a hand up, will you?"

Agreeably, Larkin helped him up, gave him a shoulder to lean on. "I don't know what the bleeding hell's going on, but Glenna's steaming, and Moira's locked in her room. Cian looks like the wrath of all the gods, but he's out of bed and saying we're training. King's opened some whiskey and I'm thinking about joining him."

Hoyt touched fingers gingerly to his cheekbone, hissed as

the pain radiated to his face. "Not shattered, there's some fine luck. She might've done a bit more to help instead of pounding a lecture on my head."

"Words are a woman's sharpest weapon. From the looks of you, you could use some of that whiskey."

"I could." Hoyt braced a hand on the table, prayed he'd regain his balance in a moment. "Do what you can, would you, Larkin, to get the lot of them together in the training area. I'll be along."

"Taking my life in my hands, I'm thinking. But all right. I'll try sweetness and charm with the ladies. They'll either fall for it, or kick me in the balls."

They didn't kick him, but they didn't come happily. Moira sat cross-legged on a table, eyes, swollen from weeping, downcast. Glenna stood in a corner, sulking into a glass of wine. King stood in his own corner, rattling ice in a short glass of whiskey.

Cian sat, drumming his fingers on the arm of his chair. His face was white as bone, and the burns the loose white shirt didn't cover, livid.

"Music might be nice," Larkin said into the silence. "The sort you hear at funeral pyres and the like."

"We'll work on form and agility." Cian cast his glance around the room. "I haven't seen a great deal of that in any of you so far."

"Is there a point to you being insulting?" Moira asked wearily. "A point to any of this? Slapping swords and trading punches? You were burned worse than anyone I've ever seen, and here you are, an hour after, up again. If magic such as that can't take you down, keep you down, what will?"

"I take it you'd be happier if I'd gone to ash. I'm happy to disappoint you."

"That's not what she meant." Glenna shoved irritably at her hair.

"And you interpret for her now?"

"I don't need anyone to speak for me," Moira snapped right back. "And I don't need to be told what to do every bleeding hour of every bleeding day. I know what kills them, I've read the books."

"Oh, well then, you've read the books." Cian gestured toward the doors. "Then be my guest. Go right on out and take out a few vamps."

"It'd be better than tumbling about on the floor in here, like a circus," she shot back.

"I'm with Moira on this." Larkin rested a hand on the hilt of his knife. "We should hunt them down, take the offense. We haven't so much as posted a guard or sent out a scout."

"This isn't that kind of war, boy."

Larkin's eyes glittered. "I'm not a boy, and from what I can see it's no kind of war."

"You don't know what you're up against," Glenna put in.

"Don't I? I fought them, killed three with my own hands."

"Weak ones, young ones. She didn't waste her best on you." Cian rose. He moved stiffly and with obvious effort. "Added to that, you had help and were lucky. But if you came across one with some seasoning, with some skill, you'd be meat."

"I can hold my own."

"Hold it with me. Come at me."

"You're hurt. It wouldn't be fair."

"Fair is for women. If you take me down, I'll go out with you." Cian gestured toward the door. "We'll hunt tonight."

Interest brightened Larkin's eyes. "Your word on it?"

"My word. Take me down."

"All right then."

Larkin came in fast, then spun out of reach. He jabbed, feinted, spun again. Cian merely reached out, gripped Larkin around the throat and lifted him off his feet. "You don't want to dance with a vampire," he said and tossed Larkin halfway across the room.

"Bastard." Moira scrambled up, raced to her cousin's side. "You've half strangled him."

"The half's what counts."

"Was that really necessary?" Glenna got to her feet, moved to Larkin to lay her hands on his throat.

"Kid asked for it," King commented, and had her whipping her head around.

"You're nothing but a bully. The pair of you."

"I'm all right, I'm all right." Larkin coughed, cleared his throat. "It was a good move," he said to Cian. "I never saw it coming."

"Until you can, and do, you don't hunt." He eased back, lowered carefully into the chair. "Time to work."

"I'd ask you to wait." Hoyt came into the room.

Cian didn't bother to look at him. "We've waited long enough."

"A bit more. I have things to say. First to you. I was careless, but so were you. I should have barred the door, but you shouldn't have opened it."

"This is my house now. It hasn't been yours for centuries."

"That may be. But courtesy and caution should approach a closed door, particularly when magic is being done. Cian." He waited until his brother's eyes shifted to him. "I would not have had you hurt. That's for you to believe or not. But I would not have had you hurt."

"I don't know if I can say the same." Cian gestured with his chin toward Hoyt's face. "Did your magic do that?"

"It's another result of it."

"Looks painful."

"So it is."

"Well then, that balances the scales somewhat."

"And this is what we've come to, checks and balances." Hoyt turned to face the room, and the others. "Arguments and resentments. You were right," he said to Glenna. "A great deal of what you said was right, though I swear you talk too much."

"Oh, really?"

"We aren't united, and until we are, we're hopeless. We could be training and preparing every hour of every day of the time we have left, and never win. Because—this is what you said—we have a common enemy, but not a common purpose."

"The purpose is to fight them," Larkin interrupted. "To fight them, and kill them. Kill them all."

"Why?"

"Because they're demons."

"So is he." Hoyt laid a hand on the back of Cian's chair.

"But he fights with us. He doesn't threaten Geall."

"Geall. You think of Geall, and you," he said to Moira, "of your mother. King's here with us because he follows Cian, and in my way, so do I. Cian, why are you here?"

"Because I don't follow. You or her."

"Why are you here, Glenna?"

"I'm here because if I didn't fight, if I didn't try, everything we have and are and know, every one of us, could be lost. Because what's inside me demands that I be here. And above all, because good needs soldiers against evil."

Oh aye, this was a woman, he thought. She put shame to all of them. "The answer. The single one there is, and she's the only one who knew it. We're needed. Stronger than valor or vengeance, loyalty or pride. We're needed. Can we stand with each other and do this thing? Not in a thousand years and with a thousand more of us to fight. We're the six, the beginning of it. We can't be strangers any longer."

He stepped away from Cian's chair as he reached in his pocket. "Glenna said make a symbol and a shield, a sign of common purpose. That unity of purpose made the strongest magic I've ever known. Stronger than I could hold," he said with a glance at Cian. "I believe they can help protect us, if we remember a shield needs a sword, and we use both with one purpose."

He drew the crosses out so the silver glinted in the light. He stepped to King, offered one. "Will you wear it?"

King set his drink aside, took the cross and chain. He studied Hoyt's face as he looped it around his neck. "You could use some ice on that eye."

"I could use a great deal. And you?" He held a cross out to Moira.

"I'll work to be worthy of it." She sent Glenna a look of apology. "I've done poorly tonight."

"So have we all," Hoyt told her. "Larkin?"

"Not just of Geall," Larkin said as he took the cross. "Or no longer."

"And you." Hoyt started to hand Glenna a cross, then stepped closer, looked into her eyes as he put it around her neck himself. "I think tonight you put us all to shame."

"I'll try not to make a habit of it. Here." She took the last cross, put the chain over his head. Then gently, very gently touched her lips to his battered cheek.

At last, he turned and walked back to Cian.

"If you're about to ask if I'd wear one of those, you're wasting your breath."

"I know you can't. I know you're not what we are, and still I'm asking you to stand with us, for this purpose." He held out a pendant, in the shape of a pentagram much like Glenna's. "The stone in the center is jasper, like the ones in the crosses. I can't give you a shield, not yet. So I'm offering you a symbol. Will you take it?"

Saying nothing, Cian held out a hand. When Hoyt poured pendant and chain into it, Cian shook it lightly, as if checking the weight. "Metal and stone don't make an army."

"They make weapons."

"True enough." Cian slipped the chain over his head. "Now if the ceremony's finished, could we bloody well get to work?"

Chapter 12

Seeking solitude and occupation, Glenna poured a glass of wine, got out a pad of paper and a pencil, and sat down at the kitchen table.

An hour, she thought, of quiet, where she could settle down, make some lists. Then maybe she would sleep.

When she heard someone approaching, her back went up. In a house this size, couldn't everyone find some place else to be?

But King came in, and stood, shifting his weight, digging his hands into his pockets.

"Well?" was all she said.

"Ah, sorry about breaking on Hoyt's face."

"It's his face, you should apologize to him."

"We know where we stand. Just wanted to clear it with you." When she said nothing, he scratched the top of his head through his thick hair, and if a man of six six and two hundred and seventy pounds could squirm, King squirmed.

"Listen, I run up, and that light's blasting, and he's lying there bleeding and burning. Guy's my first sorcerer," King continued after another pause. I've only known him like a week. I've known Cian since . . . a really long time, and I owe him pretty much everything."

"So when you found him hurt, naturally, you assumed his brother tried to kill him."

"Yeah. Figured you had a part in it, too, but I couldn't beat hell out of you."

"I appreciate the chivalry."

The sting in her tone made him wince. "You sure got a way of cutting a man down to size."

"It would take a chain saw to cut you down to size. Oh, stop looking so pitiful and guilty." With a sigh, she scooped back her hair. "We screwed up, you screwed up, and we're all goddamn sorry about it. I suppose you want some wine now. Maybe a cookie."

He had to grin. "I'll take a beer." He opened the refrigerator, got one out. "I'll pass on the cookie. You're a butt-kicker, Red. Quality I admire in a woman—even if it's my butt getting the boot."

"I never used to be. I don't think."

She was also pretty and pale, and had to be dog tired. He'd worked her, all of them, damned hard that afternoon, and Cian had put them through the wringer tonight.

Sure she'd bitched a little, King thought now. But not nearly as much as he'd expected. And when it came down to it, Hoyt was right. She'd been the only one who'd known the answer to what the hell they were doing here.

"That stuff Hoyt was talking about, what you said, it makes a lot of sense. We don't straighten up, we're easy pickings." He popped the cap off the beer, swallowed half the bottle in one long gulp. "So I will if you will."

She looked at the enormous hand he held out, then placed hers in it. "I think Cian's lucky to have someone who'll fight for him. Who'd care enough to."

"He'd do the same for me. We go back."

"That kind of friendship usually takes time to form, to so-lidify. We're not going to have that kind of time."

"Guess we'd better take some shortcuts then. We cool now?"

"I'd say we're cool now."

He polished off the beer, then dumped the empty bottle in a can under the sink. "Heading up. You ought to do the same. Get some sleep."

"I will."

But when he left her alone, she was bruised and tired and restless, so Glenna sat alone in the kitchen with her glass of wine and the lights on full to beat back the dark. She didn't know the time and wondered if it mattered any longer.

They were all becoming vampires—sleeping through most of the day, working through most of the night.

She fingered the cross around her neck as she continued to write her list. And she felt the press of the night against her shoulder blades like cold hands.

She missed the city, she decided. No shame in admitting it. She missed the sounds of it, the colors, the constant thrum of traffic that was a heartbeat. She yearned for its complexity and simplicity. Life was just life there. And if there was death, if there was cruelty and violence, it was all so utterly human.

The image of the vampire on the subway flashed into her mind.

Or she'd once had the comfort of believing it was human.

Still, she wanted to get up in the morning and wander down to the deli for fresh bagels. She wanted to set her easel in the slash of morning light and paint, and have her strongest concern be how she was going to pay her Visa bill.

All of her life the magic had been in her, and she'd thought she'd valued and respected it. But it had been nothing to this, to know that it was in her for this reason, for this purpose.

That it could very well be the death of her.

She picked up her wine, then jolted when she saw Hoyt standing in the doorway.

"Not a good idea to go creeping around in the dark, considering the situation."

"I wasn't sure I should disturb you."

"Might as well. Just having my own private pity party. It'll pass," she said with a shrug. "I'm a little homesick. Small potatoes compared to how you must feel."

"I stand in the room I shared with Cian when we were boys and feel too much, and not enough."

She rose, got a second glass, poured wine. "Have a seat." She sat down again, set the wine on the table. "I have a brother," she told him. "He's a doctor, just starting. He has a whiff of magic, and he uses it to heal. He's a good doctor, a good man. He loves me, I know, but he doesn't understand me very well. It's hard not to be understood."

How could it be, he wondered, that there had never been a woman in his life other than family he could speak to about anything that truly mattered. And now, with Glenna, he knew he could, and would, talk with her of anything. And everything.

"It troubles me, the loss of him, of what we were to each other."

"Of course it does."

"His memories of me—Cian's—are faded and old while mine are fresh and strong." Hoyt lifted his glass. "Yes, it's difficult not to be understood."

"What I am, what's in me, I used to feel smug about it. Like it was a shiny prize I held in my hands, just for me. Oh, I was careful with it, grateful for it, but still smug. I don't think I ever will be again."

"With what we touched tonight, I'm doubting either of us could be smug again."

"Still, my family, my brother, didn't understand—not fully—that smugness or that prize. And they won't understand—not fully—the price I'm paying for it now. They can't."

She reached out, laid a hand over Hoyt's. "He can't. So, while our circumstances may be different, I understand the loss you're talking about. You look terrible," she said more lightly. "I can help ease that bruising a little more."

"You're tired. It can wait."

"You didn't deserve it."

"I let it take control. I let it fly out of me."

"No, it flew away from us. Who can say if it wasn't meant to." She'd bundled her hair up to train, to work, and now pulled out the pins so it fell, messily, just short of her shoulders.

"Look, we learned, didn't we? We're stronger together than either of us could have anticipated. What we're responsible for now is learning how to control it, channel it. And believe me, the rest of them will have more respect now, too."

He smiled a little. "That sounds a bit smug."

"Yeah, I guess it does."

He drank some wine and realized he was comfortable for the first time in hours. Just sitting in the bright kitchen with night trapped outside the glass, with Glenna to talk with.

Her scent was there, just on the edges of his senses. That earthy, female scent. Her eyes, so clear and green, showed some light bruising of fatigue on the delicate skin beneath them.

He nodded toward the paper. "Another spell?"

"No, something more pedestrian. Lists. I need more supplies. Herbs and so forth. And Moira and Larkin need clothes. Then we need to work out some basic household rules. So far it's been up to me and King for the most part. The cooking, that is. A household doesn't run itself, and even when you're preparing for war, you need food and clean towels."

"There are so many machines to do the work." He glanced around the kitchen. "It should be simple enough."

"You'd think."

"There used to be an herb garden. I haven't walked the land, not really." Put it off, he admitted. Put off seeing the changes, and what remained the same. "Cian might have had one planted. Or I could bring it back. The earth remembers."

"Well, that can go on the list for tomorrow. You know the woods around here. You should be able to tell me where to find the other things I need. I can go out in the morning and harvest."

"I knew them," he said half to himself.

"We need more weapons, Hoyt. And eventually more hands to wield them."

"There will be an army in Geall."

"We hope. I know a few like us, and Cian—it's likely he knows some like him. We may want to start enlisting."

"More vampires? Trusting Cian's been difficult enough.

As for more witches, we're still learning each other, as we learned tonight. We were to start with those we have. We've barely begun. But weapons. We can make them as we made the crosses."

She picked up her wine again, drank, breathed out slowly. "Okay. I'm game."

"We'll take them with us when we go to Geall."

"Speaking of. When and how?"

"How? Through the dance. When? I can't know. I have to believe we'll be told when it's time. That we'll know when it's time."

"Do you think we'll ever be able to get back? If we live? Do you think we'll be able to get back home?"

He looked over at her. She was sketching, her eyes on her pad, her hand steady. Her cheeks were pale, he noted, from fatigue and stress. Her hair was bright and bold, swinging forward as she dipped her head.

"Which disturbs you most?" he wondered. "Dying or not seeing your home again?"

"I'm not entirely sure. Death is inevitable. None of us get out of that one. And you hope—or I have—that when the time comes you'll have courage and curiosity, and so face it well."

Absently, she tucked her hair behind her ear with her left hand while her right continued to sketch. "But that's always been in the abstract. Until now. It's hard to think about dying, harder to think about it knowing I might not see home again, or my family. They won't understand what happened to me."

She glanced up. "And I'm preaching to the choir."

"I don't know how long they lived. How they died. How long they looked for me."

"It would help to know."

"Aye, it would." He shook it off, angled his head. "What do you draw there?"

She pursed her lips at the sketch. "It seems to be you." She turned it around, nudged it toward him.

"Is this how you see me?" His voice sounded puzzled, and not entirely pleased. "So stern."

"Not stern. Serious. You're a serious man. Hoyt McKenna." She printed the name on the sketch. "That's how it would be written and said today. I looked it up." She signed the sketch with a quick flourish. "And your serious nature is very attractive."

"Serious is for old men and politicians."

"And for warriors, for men of power. Knowing you, being attracted to you, makes me realize what I knew before you were boys. Apparently, I like much older men these days."

He sat, looking at her, with the sketch and the wine between them. With worlds between them, he told himself. And still he'd never felt closer to anyone. "To sit here like this with you, in the house that's mine, but not, in a world that's mine, but not, you're the single thing I want."

She rose, moved to him, put her arms around him. He rested his head just under her breasts, listened to her heart.

"Is it comfort?" she asked.

"Yes. But not only that. I have such a need for you. I don't know how to hold it inside me."

She lowered her head, closing her eyes as she rested her cheek on his hair. "Let's be human. For what's left of tonight, let's be human, because I don't want to be alone in the dark." She framed his face, lifted it to hers. "Take me to bed."

He took her hands as he got to his feet. "Such things haven't changed in a millennium, have they?"

She laughed. "Some things never change."

He kept her hand in his as they walked from the kitchen. "I haven't bedded many women—being a serious man."

"I haven't been bedded by many men—being a sensible woman." At the door to her room she turned to him with a quick, wicked smile. "But I think we'll manage."

"Wait." He brought her to him before she could open the door, and laid his lips on hers. She felt warmth, and an underlying shimmer of power.

Then he opened the door.

He'd lighted the candles, she saw. Every one of them, so the room was full of gilded light and soft scent. The fire burned as well, a low red simmer.

It touched a place in her heart even as it rippled anticipation over her skin.

"A very nice start. Thank you." She heard the click of the key in the lock, pressed a hand to her heart. "I'm nervous. All of a sudden. I've never been nervous about being with someone. Not even that first time. That smugness again."

He didn't mind her nerves. In fact, they added an edge to his own arousal. "Your mouth. This fullness here." He traced a fingertip over her bottom lip. "I can taste it in my sleep. You distract me, even when you're not with me."

"That annoys you." She reached up to link her arms around his neck. "I'm so glad."

She eased toward him, watching his gaze drop to her mouth, linger before it came back to hers. Felt his breath mix with her breath, and his heart beat against her heart. They held there, one endless moment, then their lips met. And they sank into each other.

Nerves fluttered in her belly again, a dozen velvet wings that swept against desire. And still that shimmer of power was like a hum in the air.

Then his hands were in her hair, sweeping it back from her face in a gesture of urgency that had her shuddering in anticipation of what was to come. And his mouth left hers to roam her face, to find that throbbing pulse in her throat.

She could drown him. He knew it even as he took more. This outrageous need for her could take him under, somewhere he'd never been. He knew, wherever that was, he would take her with him.

He molded the shape of her with his hands, steeped himself in it. She found his mouth again, avidly. He heard the shudder of her breath as she stepped back. The candlelight washed over her as she reached up, began to unbutton her shirt.

She wore something white and lacy beneath it that seemed to hold her breasts like an offering. There was more white lace when her pants slid down her hips, an alluring triangle that rode low on her belly, high on her legs.

"Women are the canniest creatures," he mused out loud, and reached out to skim a fingertip over the lace. When she trembled, he smiled. "I like these clothes. Are you always wearing these under the others?"

"No. It depends on my mood."

"I like this mood." He took his thumbs, brushed them up over the lace on her breasts.

Her head fell back. "Oh God."

"That pleasures you. What of this?" He did the same with the lace that sat snug below her belly, and watched the arousal slide over her face.

Soft skin, delicate and smooth. But there was muscle under it. Fascinating. "Just let me touch. Your body is beautiful. Just let me touch."

She reached back, gripped the bedpost. "Help yourself."

His fingers skimmed over her, made her skin quiver. Then pressed and made her moan. She could feel her own bones going to liquid, and her muscles to putty as he explored her. She gave herself to it, to the slow, enervating pleasure that was both triumph and surrender.

"Is this the fastener then?"

She opened heavy eyes as he fiddled with the front hook of her bra. But when she started to undo it, he brushed her hands aside.

"I'll figure it out on my own in a minute. Ah yes, there it is." As he unhooked it, her breasts spilled out and into his hands. "Clever. Beautiful." He lowered his head to them, tasted soft, warm flesh.

He wanted to savor; he wanted to rush.

"And the other part? Where is the fastener?" He ran his hands down her.

"They don't—" And over her. Her breath caught, a half cry as her fingers dug into his shoulders.

"Aye, look at me. Just like that." He skimmed his hands over the lace, under it. "Glenna Ward, who is mine tonight."

And she came where she stood, her body exploding and her eyes trapped by his.

Her head went limp on his shoulder as she shuddered, shuddered. "I want you on me, I want you in me." She dragged at the sweatshirt he wore, drawing it up and away. Now she found muscle and flesh with her hands, with her

lips. Now the power seeped back into her as she pulled him
with her onto the bed.

"Inside me. Inside me."

Her mouth crushed hungrily to his, hips arching and offering. He fought with the rest of his clothes, struggled to devour more of her as the heat pumped off them both.

When he plunged into her, the fire roared, and the candle
flames shot up like arrows.

Passion and power whipped through them, spurring them
on toward madness. Still she locked herself around him,
stared at him even as tears glazed her eyes.

A wind stirred her hair, bright as fire against the bed. He
felt her gather beneath him, tighten like a bow. When the
light burst through him, he could only breathe her name.

She felt alight, as if whatever they had ignited between them burned still. She wondered she didn't see
beams of its gilded light shooting out of her fingertips.

In the hearth, the fire had settled down to a quiet simmer;
another afterglow. But the heat that had bloomed from it,
and from them, dewed her skin. Even now her heart moved
at a gallop.

His head rested there, on her heart, and her hand on his
head.

"Have you ever . . ."

His lips brushed her breast, lightly. "No."

She combed her fingers through his hair. "Neither have I.
Maybe it was because it was the first time, or because some
of what we made earlier was still stored up."

We're stronger together. Her own words echoed in her
mind.

"Where do we go from here?"

When he lifted his head, she shook hers. "An expression,"
she explained. "And it doesn't matter now. Your bruises are
gone."

"I know. Thank you."

"I don't know that I did it."

"You did. You touched my face when we joined." He took

her hand, brought it to his lips. "There's magic in your hands, and in your heart. And still your eyes are troubled."

"Just tired."

"Do you want me to leave you?"

"No, I don't." And wasn't that the problem? "I want you to stay."

"Here then." He shifted, bringing her with him, tucking up sheet and blanket. "I have a question."

"Mmm."

"You have a brand, here." He traced his fingers over the small of her back. "A pentagram. Are witches marked so in this time?"

"No. It's a tattoo—my choice. I wanted to wear a symbol of what I am, even when I was skyclad."

"Ah. I mean no disrespect to your purpose, or your symbol, but I found it . . . alluring."

She smiled to herself. "Good. Then it performed its secondary purpose."

"I feel whole again," he said. "I feel myself again."

"So do I."

But tired, he thought. He could hear it in her voice. "We'll sleep awhile."

She tilted her head up so their eyes met. "You said when you took me to bed you wouldn't give me any sleep."

"This once."

She rested her head on his shoulder, but didn't close her eyes, even when he dimmed the candles. "Hoyt. Whatever happens, this was precious."

"For me as well. And for the first time, Glenna, I believe not only that we must win, but that we can. I believe that because you're with me."

Now she closed her eyes for just a moment, on the pang just under her heart. He spoke of war, she thought. And she'd spoken of love.

She woke to rain, and his warmth. Glenna lay, listening to the patter, absorbing the good, natural feel of a man's body beside hers.

She'd had to lecture herself during the night. What she had with Hoyt was a gift, one that should be treasured and appreciated. There was no point in cursing because it wasn't enough.

And what good did it do to question why it had happened? To wonder if whatever was driving them to the battleground had brought them together, had ignited that passion and need, and yes, love, because they were stronger with it?

It was enough to feel; she'd always believed that. And only doubted it now because she felt so much.

It was time to go back to being practical, to enjoy what she had when she had it. And to do the job at hand.

She eased away from him, started to get out of bed. His hand closed around her wrist.

"It's early, and raining. Come, stay in bed."

She looked over her shoulder. "How do you know it's early. There's no clock in here. Got a sundial in your head?"

"Sure a lot of good it would do as it's pouring rain. Your hair's like the sun. Come back to bed."

He didn't look so serious now, she noted, not with his eyes sleepy and his face shadowed by a night's growth of beard. What he looked was edible.

"You need a shave."

He rubbed a hand over his face, felt the stubble. Rubbed his hand over again, and the stubble was gone. "Is that better for you, *a stór*?"

She reached over, flicked a finger down his cheek. "Very smooth. You could use a decent haircut."

He frowned, scooped a hand through his hair. "What would be wrong with my hair?"

"It's gorgeous, but it could use a little shaping. I can take care of that for you."

"I think not."

"Oh, don't trust me?"

"Not with my hair."

She laughed and rolled over to straddle him. "You trust me with other, and more sensitive parts of you."

"A different matter entirely." His hands walked up and

cupped her breasts. "What's the name of the garment you wore over your lovely breasts last night?"

"It's called a bra, and don't change the subject."

"Sure I'm happier discussing your breasts than my hair."

"Aren't you cheerful this morning."

"You put a light in me."

"Sweet talker." She picked up a hank of his hair. "Snip, snip. You'll be a new man."

"You seem to like the man I am well enough."

Her lips curved as she lifted her hips. And lowered them to take him into her. The candles that had guttered out sparked. "Just a trim," she whispered, leaning over him to rub her lips to his. "After."

He learned the considerable pleasure of showering with a woman, then the fascinating pleasure of watching one dress.

She rubbed creams into her skin, and different ones over her face.

The bra, and what she called panties, were blue today. Like a robin's egg. Over these she pulled rough pants and the short, baggy tunic she called a sweatshirt. On it were words that spelled out WALKING IN A WICCAN WONDERLAND.

He thought the outer clothes made what she wore beneath a kind of marvelous secret.

He felt relaxed and very pleased with himself. And balked when she told him to sit on the lid of the toilet. She picked up scissors, snapped them together.

"Why would a man of sense allow a woman to come near him with a tool like that?"

"A big, tough sorcerer like you shouldn't be afraid of a little haircut. Besides, if you don't like it when I'm done, you can change it back."

"Why are women always after fiddling with a man?"

"It's our nature. Indulge me."

He sighed, and sat. And squirmed.

"Be still, and it'll be done before you know it. How do you suppose Cian deals with grooming?"

He rolled his eyes up, over, to try to see what she was doing to him. "I wouldn't know."

"No reflection must make it a chore. And he always looks
perfect."

Now Hoyt slid his eyes toward hers. "You like the way he
looks, do you?"

"You're almost mirror images, so it's obvious I do. He
has that slight cleft in his chin and you don't."

"Where the faeries pinched him. My mother used to say."

"Your face is a little leaner, and your eyebrows have more
of an arch. But your eyes, those mouths and cheekbones—
the same."

He watched hair fall into his lap, and inside the mighty
sorcerer, his belly trembled. "Jesus, woman, are you shear-
ing me bald?"

"Lucky for you I like long hair on a man. At least I do on
you." She dropped a kiss on the top of his head. "Yours is
like black silk, with just a little wave. You know, in some
cultures, when a woman cuts a man's hair it's a vow of marriage."

His head jerked, but she'd anticipated the reaction and
moved the scissors. Her laugh, full of fun and teasing,
echoed off the bathroom walls. "Joking. Boy, are you easy.
Almost done."

She straddled his legs, standing with hers apart, and her
breasts close to his face. He began to think a haircut wasn't
such a hardship after all.

"I liked the feel of a woman."

"Yes, I seem to recall that about you."

"No, what I'm meaning is I liked the feel of a woman
when I had one. I'm a man, have needs like any other. But it
never occupied so much of my mind as it does with you."

She set the scissors aside, then combed her fingers
through his damp hair. "I like occupying your mind. Here,
have a look."

He stood, studied himself in the mirror. His hair was
shorter, but not unreasonably. He supposed it fell in a more
pleasing shape—though it had seemed fine to him before
she'd gone after it.

Still, she hadn't sheared him like a sheep, and it pleased her.

"It's well enough, thank you."

"You're welcome."

He finished dressing, and when they went downstairs they found all but Cian in the kitchen.

Larkin was scooping up scrambled eggs. "Good morning to you. The man here has a magician's hands with eggs."

"And my shift at the stove's over," King announced. "So if you want breakfast, you're on your own."

"That's something I wanted to talk about." Glenna opened the refrigerator. "Shifts. Cooking, laundry, basic housekeeping. It needs to be spread out among all of us."

"I'm happy to help," Moira put in. "If you'll show me what to do and how to do it."

"All right, watch and learn. We'll stick with the bacon and eggs for this morning." She got to work on it with Moira watching her every move.

"I wouldn't mind more, while you're about it."

Moira glanced at Larkin. "He eats like two horses."

"Hmm. We're going to need regular supplies." She spoke to King now. "I'd say that falls to you or me, as these three can't drive. Both Larkin and Moira are going to need clothes that fit. If you draw me a map, I can make the next run."

"There's no sun today."

Glenna nodded at Hoyt. "I have protection, and it may clear up."

"The household needs to run, as you said, so you can draw up your plans. We'll follow them. But as to other matters, you have to follow. I think no one goes out alone, out of doors, into the village. No one goes out unarmed."

"Are we to be under siege then, held in by a shower of rain?" Larkin stabbed the air with his fork. "Isn't it time we showed them we won't let them set the terms?"

"He has a point," Glenna agreed. "Cautious but not cowed."

"And there's a horse in the stable," Moira added. "He needs to be tended."

The fact was Hoyt had intended to do so himself, while

the others were busy elsewhere. He wondered now if what he'd told himself was responsibility and leadership was just another lack of trust.

"Larkin and I will tend to the horse." He sat when Glenna put plates on the table. "Glenna needs herbs and so do I, so we'll deal with that as well. Cautious," he repeated. And began to devise how it could be done while he ate.

He strapped on a sword. The rain was a fine drizzle now, the sort he knew could last for days. He could change that. He and Glenna together could bring out sun bright enough to blast the sky.

But the earth needed rain.

He nodded to Larkin, opened the door.

They moved out together, splitting right and left, back-to-back to gauge the ground.

"Be a miserable watch in this weather if they just sit and wait," Larkin pointed out.

"We'll stay close together in any case."

They crossed the ground, searching for shadows and movement. But there was nothing but the rain, the smell of wet flowers and grass.

When they reached the stables, the work was routine for both of them. Mucking out, fresh straw, grain and grooming. Comforting, Hoyt thought, to be around the horse.

Larkin sang as he worked, a cheery air.

"I've a chestnut mare at home," he told Hoyt. "She's a beauty. It seemed we couldn't bring the horses through the dance."

"I was told to leave my own mare behind. Is it true about the legend? The sword and the stone, and the one who rules Geall? Like the legend of Arthur?"

"It is, and some say it was fashioned from it." As he spoke, Larkin poured fresh water in the trough. "After the death of the king or queen, the sword is placed back in the stone by a magician. On the day after the burial, the heirs then come, one by one, and try to take it out again. Only one will succeed, and rule all of Geall. The sword is kept in the great hall for all to see, until that ruler dies. And so it is repeated, generation after generation."

He wiped his brow. "Moira has no brothers, no sisters. She must rule."

Intrigued, Hoyt stopped to glance over. "If she fails, would it come to you?"

"Spare me from that," Larkin said with feeling. "I've no wish to rule. Bloody nuisance if you're asking me. Well, he's set, isn't he?" He rubbed the stallion's side. "You're a handsome devil, that's the truth. He needs exercise. One of us should ride him out."

"Not today, I think. But you're right in that. He needs a run. Still, he's Cian's, so it's for him to say."

They moved to the door, and as before, stepped out together. "That way." Hoyt gestured. "There was an herb garden, and may still be. I haven't walked that way as yet."

"Moira and I have. I didn't see one."

"We'll have a look."

It sprang off the roof of the stables, so quickly Hoyt had no chance to draw his sword. And the arrow struck it dead in the heart while it was still in the air.

Ash flew as a second leaped. And a second arrow shot home.

"Would you let us have one for the sport of it!" Larkin shouted to Moira.

She stood in the kitchen doorway, a third arrow already notched. "Then take the one coming from the left."

"For me," Larkin shouted at Hoyt.

It was twice his size, and Hoyt started to protest. But Larkin was already charging. Steel struck steel. It clashed and it rang. Twice he saw the thing step back when Larkin's cross glinted at him. But he had a reach, and a very long sword.

When Hoyt saw Larkin slip on the wet grass, he lunged forward. He swung the sword at the thing's neck—and met air.

Larkin leaped up, flipped the wooden stake up, caught it neatly. "I was just throwing him off balance."

"Nicely done."

"There may be more."

"There may be," Hoyt agreed. "But we'll do what we came to do."

"I've got your back then, if you've mine. God knows Moira's got them both. This hurt it," he added, touching the cross. "Gave it some trouble anyway."

"They may be able to kill us, but they won't be able to turn us while we wear them."

"Then I'd say that's a job well done."

Chapter 13

❖

There was no herb garden with its creeping thyme and fragrant rosemary. The pretty knot garden his mother had tended was now a gently rolling span of cropped green grass. It would be a sunny spot when the sky cleared, he knew. His mother had chosen it, though it hadn't been just outside the kitchen as was more convenient, so her herbs could bask in the light.

As a child he'd learned of them from her, of their uses and their beauty, while sitting by her as she weeded and clipped and harvested. She'd taught him their names and their needs. He'd learned to identify them by their scents and shapes of the leaves, by the flowers that bolted from them if she allowed it.

How many hours had he spent there with her, working the earth, talking or just sitting in silence to enjoy the butterflies, the hum of bees?

It had been their place, he thought, more than any other.

He'd grown to a man and had found his place on the cliff in what was now called Kerry. He'd built his stone cabin, and found the solitude he'd needed for his own harvest, for his magic.

But he'd always come back home. And had always found pleasure and solace with his mother here, in her herb garden.

Now, he stood over where it had been as he might have a grave, mourning and remembering. A flare of anger lit in him that his brother would let this go.

"This what you're looking for then?" Larkin studied the grass, then tracked his eyes through the rain, toward the trees. "Doesn't seem to be anything left of it."

Hoyt heard a sound, pivoted as Larkin did. Glenna walked toward them, a stake in one hand, a knife in the other. Rain beaded her hair like tiny jewels.

"You're to stay in the house. There could be more of them."

"If there are, there are three of us now." She jerked her head toward the house. "Five as Moira and King have us covered."

Hoyt looked over. Moira was in the near window, her arrow notched, her bow pointed downward. In the doorway to the left, King stood with a broadsword.

"That ought to do it." Larkin sent his cousin a cheeky grin. "Mind you don't shoot one of us in the arse."

"Only if I'm aiming for it," she called back.

Beside Hoyt, Glenna studied the ground. "Was it here? The garden?"

"It was. Will be."

Something was wrong, she thought, very wrong, to have put that hard look on his face. "I have a rejuvenation spell. I've had good luck with it, healing plants."

"I won't need it for this." He stabbed his sword in the ground to free his hands.

He could see it, just as it had been, and honed that image clear into his mind as he stretched out his arms, spread his hands. This, he knew, would come from his heart as much as from his art. This was tribute to the one who had given him life.

And because of it, would be painful.

"Seed to leaf, leaf to flower. Soil and sun and rain. Remember."

His eyes changed, and his face looked carved from stone.

Larkin started to speak, but Glenna tapped a finger to her lips to stop him. There should be no voice, no words now, she knew, but Hoyt's. Power was already thickening the air.

She couldn't help with the visualization as Hoyt hadn't described the garden to her. But she could focus on scent. Rosemary, lavender, sage.

He repeated the incantation three times, his eyes darkening further, his voice rising with each repetition. Beneath their feet, the ground shuddered lightly.

The wind began to lift, then swirl, then blow.

"Rise up! Return. Grow and bloom. Gift from the earth, from the gods. For the earth, for the gods. Airmed, oh ancient one, release your bounty. Airmed, of the *Tuatha de Danaan,* feed this earth. As once this was, let it return."

His face was pale as marble, his eyes dark as onyx. And the power flowed out of him onto, into, the trembling ground.

It opened.

Glenna heard Larkin suck in his breath, heard her own heartbeat rise up to drum in her ears. The plants rose up, leaves unfurling, blooms bursting. The thrill spun into her, released itself of a laugh of pure delight.

Silvery sage, glossy needles of rosemary, tumbling carpets of thyme and camomile, bay and rue, delicate spears of lavender, and more spread out of the ground and into the misting rain.

The garden formed a Celtic knot, she saw, with narrow loops and pathways to make harvesting easier.

As the wind died, as the earth stilled, Larkin blew out a long breath. "Well, that's some damn fine farming."

She laid a hand on Larkin's shoulder. "It's lovely, Hoyt. Some of the prettiest magic I've ever seen. Blessed be."

He pulled his sword out of the ground. The heart that had opened to make the magic was sore as a bruise. "Take what you need, but be quick. We've been out long enough."

She used her bolline, and worked with efficiency, though she wished she could linger, just enjoy the work.

The scents surrounded her. And what she harvested, she knew, would be only more powerful for the manner of their becoming.

The man who'd touched her in the night, who'd held her in the morning had more power than any she'd ever know. Any she'd ever imagined.

"This is something I miss in the city," she commented. "I do a lot of windowsill pots, but it's just not the same as real gardening."

Hoyt said nothing, simply watched her—bright hair sparkling with rain, slim white hands brushing through the green. It closed a fist over his heart, just one quick squeeze and release.

When she stood, her arms full, her eyes laughing with the wonder of it, that heart tipped in his breast and fell as if an arrow had pierced it.

Bewitched, he thought. She had bewitched him. A woman's magic always aimed first for the heart.

"I can get quite a bit done with these." She tossed her head to swing back her damp hair. "And have enough left to season a nice soup for dinner."

"Best take them in then. We've movement to the west." Larkin nodded toward the west edge of the woods. "Just watching for now."

Bewitched, Hoyt thought again as he turned. He'd forgotten his watch, spellbound by her.

"I count half a dozen," Larkin continued, his voice cool and steady. "Though there may be more hanging back. Hoping to lure us, I'm thinking, into going after them. So they'll be more, aye, more hanging back to cut us down as we come."

"We've done what we need for the morning," Hoyt began, then thought better of it. "But no point letting them think they've pushed us back inside. Moira," he said, lifting his voice enough to carry to her, "can you take one out at this distance?"

"Which one would you like?"

Amused, he lifted a shoulder. "Your choice. Let's give them a bit of something to think about."

He'd barely uttered the words when the arrow flew, and a second so quickly after he thought he imagined it. There were two screams, one melding into the next. And where

there had been six there were four—and those four rushed
back into the cover of the woods.

"Two would give them more than a bit to think about."
With a grim smile, Moira readied another arrow. "I can wing
a few back into the woods, drive them back more if you like."

"Don't waste your wood."

Cian stepped to the window behind her. He looked rumpled and mildly irritated. Moira automatically stepped aside.
"Wouldn't be wasted if they struck home."

"They'll move on for now. If they were here for more than
a nuisance, they'd have charged while they had the numbers."

He walked past her to the side door, and out.

"Past your bedtime, isn't it?" Glenna said.

"I'd like to know who could sleep through all this. Felt
like a bleeding earthquake." He studied the garden. "Your
work, I assume," he said to Hoyt.

"No." The bitterness from the wound inside him eked out.
"My mother's."

"Well, next time you've a bit of landscaping in mind, let
me know so I don't wonder if the house is coming down on
my ears. How many did you take out?"

"Five. Moira took four." Larkin sheathed his sword. "The
other was mine."

He glanced back toward the window. "The little queen's
racking up quite the score."

"We wanted to test the waters," Larkin told him, "and see
to your horse."

"I'm grateful for that."

"I'm thinking I could take him out for a run now and
again, if you wouldn't mind it."

"I wouldn't, and Vlad could use it."

"Vlad?" Glenna repeated.

"Just my little in joke. If the excitement's over, I'll be going back to bed."

"I need a word with you." Hoyt waited until Cian met his
eyes. "Privately."

"And would this private word require standing about in
the rain?"

"We'll walk."

"Suit yourself." Then he smiled at Glenna. "You look rosy this morning."

"And damp. There are plenty of dry, private places inside, Hoyt."

"I want the air."

There was a moment of humming silence. "He's a slow one. She's waiting to be kissed, so she'll worry less about you getting your throat ripped out because you want a walk in the rain."

"Go inside." Though he wasn't entirely comfortable with the public display, Hoyt took Glenna's chin in his hand, kissed her lightly on the lips. "I'll be fine enough."

Larkin drew his sword again, offered it to Cian. "Better armed than not."

"Words to live by." Then he leaned down, gave Glenna a quick, cocky kiss himself. "I'll be fine, as well."

They walked in silence, and with none of the camaraderie Hoyt remembered they'd shared. Times, he mused, they'd been able to know the other's mind without a word spoken. Now his brother's thoughts were barred to him, as he imagined his were to Cian.

"You kept the roses, but let the herb garden die. It was one of her greatest pleasures."

"The roses have been replaced, I can't count the times, since I acquired the place. The herbs? Gone before I bought the property."

"It's not property as the place you have in New York. It's home."

"It is to you." Hoyt's anger rolled off Cian's back like the rain. "If you expect more than I can or will give, you'll be in a constant state of disappointment. It's my money that bought the land and the house that sits on it, and mine that goes to maintaining both. I'd think you'd be in a better humor this morning, after romping with the pretty witch last night."

"Careful where you step," Hoyt said softly.

"I've good footing." And he couldn't resist treading on tender ground. "She's a prime piece, and no mistake. But I've had a few centuries more experience with women than you. There's more than lust in those striking green eyes of hers. She sees a future with them. And what, I wonder, will you do about that?"

"It's not your concern."

"Not in the least, no, but it's entertaining to speculate, particularly when I haven't a woman of my own to divert me at the moment. She's no round-heeled village girl happy with a roll in the hay and a trinket. She'll want and expect more of you, as women, particularly clever women, tend to."

Instinctively he glanced up, checking the cloud cover. Irish weather was tricky, he knew, and the sun could decide to spill out along with the rain. "Do you think if you survive these three months, satisfy your gods, to ask them for the right to take her back with you?"

"Why does it matter to you?"

"Not everyone asks a question because the answer matters. Can't you see her, tucked into your cottage on the cliffs in Kerry? No electricity, running water, no Saks around the corner. Cooking your dinner in a pot on the fire. Likely shorten her life expectancy by half given the lack of health care and nutrition, but well then, anything for love."

"What do you know of it?" Hoyt snapped. "You're not capable of love."

"Oh, you'd be wrong about that. My kind can love, deeply, even desperately. Certainly unwisely, which it appears we have in common. So you won't take her back, for that would be the selfish thing. You're much too holy, too pure for that. And enjoy the role of martyr too much as well. So you'll leave her here to pine for you. I might amuse myself by offering her some comfort, and seeing as we share a resemblance, I wager she'll take it. And me."

The blow knocked him back, but not down. He tasted blood, the gorgeous burn of it, then swiped a hand over his bleeding mouth. It had taken longer than he'd assumed it would to bait his brother.

"Well now, that's been a long time coming, for both of us." He tossed his sword aside as Hoyt had. "Let's have a go then."

Cian's fist moved so fast it was only a blur—a blur that had stars exploding in front of Hoyt's eyes. And his nose fountaining blood. Then they charged each other like rams.

Cian took one in the kidneys, and a second strike had his ears ringing. He'd forgotten Hoyt could fight like the devil when provoked. He ducked a jab and sent Hoyt down with a kick to the midsection. And found himself on his ass as his brother slashed out his legs and took his feet out from under him.

He could have been up in a fingersnap, ended it, but his blood was hot. And heated, preferred a grapple.

They rolled over the ground, punching, cursing while the rain soaked them through to the skin. Elbows and fists rammed into flesh, cracked against bone.

Then Cian reared back with a hiss and flash of fangs. Hoyt saw the burn sear into his brother's hand, in the shape of his cross.

"Fuck me," Cian muttered and sucked on burned flesh and welling blood. "I guess you need a weapon to best me."

"Aye, fuck you. I don't need anything but my own fists." Hoyt reached up, had nearly yanked off the chain. Then dropped his hand when he realized the utter stupidity of it.

"This is fine, isn't it?" He spat out the words, and some blood with it. "This is just fine. Brawling like a couple of street rats, and leaving ourselves open to anything that comes. If anything had been nearby, we'd be dead."

"Already am—and speak for yourself."

"This isn't what I want, trading blows with you." Though the fight was still on his face as he swiped blood from his mouth. "It serves nothing."

"Felt good though."

Hoyt's swollen lips twitched, and the leading edge of his temper dulled. "It did, that's the pure truth. Holy martyr, my ass."

"Knew that would get under your skin."

"Sure you always knew how to get there. If we can't be brothers, Cian, what are we?"

Cian sat as he was, absently rubbing at the grass and bloodstains on his shirt. "If you win, you'll be gone in a few months. Or I'll see you die. Do you know how many I've seen die?"

"If time's short, it should be more important."

"You know nothing of time." He got to his feet. "You want to walk? Come on then, and learn something of time."

He walked on through the drenching wet so that Hoyt was forced to fall in beside him.

"Is it all still in your hands? The land?"

"Most of it. Some was sold off a few centuries ago—and some was taken by the English during one of the wars, and given to some crony of Cromwell."

"Who is Cromwell?"

"Was. A right bastard, who spent considerable time and effort burning and raping Ireland for the British royals. Politics and wars—gods, humans and demons can't seem to get by without them. I convinced one of the man's sons, after he'd inherited, to sell it back to me. At quite a good price."

"Convinced him? You killed him."

"And what if I did?" Cian said wearily. "It was long ago."

"Is that how you came by your wealth? Killing?"

"I've had nine hundred years and more to fill the coffers, and have done so in a variety of ways. I like money, and I've always had a head for finance."

"Aye, you have."

"There were lean years in the beginning. Decades of them, but I came around. I traveled. It's a large and fascinating world, and I like having chunks of it. Which is why I don't care for the notion of Lilith pulling her own sort of Cromwell."

"Protecting your investment," Hoyt said.

"I am. I will. I earned what I have. I'm fluent in fifteen languages—a handy business asset."

"Fifteen?" It felt easier now, the walking, the talking. "You used to butcher even Latin."

"Nothing but time to learn, and more yet to enjoy the fruits. I enjoy them quite a bit."

"I don't understand you. She took your life, your humanity."

"And gave me eternity. While I may not be particularly grateful to her as it wasn't done for my benefit, I don't see the point in spending that eternity sulking about it. My existence is long, and this is what you and your kind have."

He gestured toward a graveyard. "A handful of years, then nothing but dirt and dust."

There was a stone ruin overcome by vines sharp with thorns and black with berries. The end wall remained and rose in a peak. Figures had been carved into it like a frame, and had been buffed nearly smooth again by time and weather.

Flowers, even small shrubs forced their way through the cracks with feathery purple heads drooping now, heavy from the rain.

"A chapel? Mother spoke of building one."

"And one was built," Cian confirmed. "This is what's left of it. And them, and the ones who came after. Stones and moss and weeds."

Hoyt only shook his head. Stones had been plunged into the ground or set upon it to mark the dead. Now he moved among them, over uneven ground where that ground had heaved, time and again, and the tall grass was slick with wet.

Like the carving on the ruin, the words etched into some of the stones were worn nearly smooth, and the stones bloomed with moss and lichen. Others he could read; names he didn't know. Michael Thomas McKenna, beloved husband of Alice. Departed this earth the sixth of May, eighteen hundred and twenty-five. And Alice, who'd joined him some six years after. Their children, one who'd left the world only days after coming into it, and three others.

They'd lived and died this Thomas, this Alice, centuries after he'd been born. And nearly two centuries before he stood here, reading their names.

Time was fluid, he thought, and those who passed through it so fragile.

Crosses rose up, and rounded stones tilted. Here and there weedy gardens grew over the graves as if they were tended by careless ghosts. And he felt them, those ghosts with every step he took.

A rose bush, heavy with rich red blooms grew lushly behind a stone no taller than his knees. Its petals were sheened like velvet. It was a quick strike to the heart, with the dull echoing pain behind it.

He knew he stood at his mother's grave.

"How did she die?"

"Her heart stopped. It's the usual way."

At his sides, Hoyt's fists bunched. "Can you be so cold, even here, even now?"

"Some said grief stopped it. Perhaps it did. He went first." Cian gestured to a second stone. "A fever took him around the equinox, the autumn after . . . I left. She followed three years after."

"Our sisters?"

"There, all there." He gestured at the grouping of stones. "And the generations that followed them—who remained in Clare, in any case. There was a famine, and it rotted the land. Scores died like flies, or fled to America, to Australia, to England, anywhere but here. There was suffering, pain, plague, pillage. Death."

"Nola?"

For a moment Cian said nothing, then he continued in a tone of deliberate carelessness. "She lived into her sixties—a good, long life for that era for a woman, a human. She had five children. Or it might've been six."

"Was she happy?"

"How could I say?" Cian said impatiently. "I never spoke to her again. I wasn't welcome in the house I now own. Why would I be?"

"She said I would come back."

"Well, you have, haven't you?"

Hoyt's blood was cool now, and ekeing toward cold. "There's no grave for me here. If I go back, will there be? Will it change what's here?"

"The paradox. Who's to say? In any case, you vanished, or so it's told. Depending on the version. You're a bit of a legend in these parts. Hoyt of Clare—though Kerry likes to claim you as well. Your song and story doesn't reach as high as a god, or even that of Merlin, but you've a notch in some guidebooks. The stone circle just to the north, the one you used? It's attributed to you now, and called Hoyt's Dance."

Hoyt didn't know whether to be embarrassed or flattered. "It's the Dance of the Gods, and it was here long before me."

"So goes truth, particularly when fantasy's shinier. The caves beneath the cliffs where you tossed me into the sea? It's said you lie there, deep beneath the rock, guarded by faeries, under the land where you would stand to call the lightning and the wind."

"Foolishness."

"An amusing claim to fame."

For a time they said nothing, just stood, two men of striking physical similarity, in a rainy world of the dead.

"If I'd gone with you that night, as you asked me, ridden out with you, to stop as you said at the pub in the village. A drink and a tumble . . ." Hoyt's throat went hot as he remembered it. "But I had work on my mind and didn't want company. Not even yours. I had only to go, and none of this would be."

Cian slicked back his dripping hair. "You take a lot on yourself, don't you? But then, you always did. If you'd gone, it's likely she'd have had us both—so it's true enough, none of this would be."

What he saw on Hoyt's face brought the fury rushing back into him. "Do I ask for your guilt? You weren't my keeper then or now. I stand here as I did centuries ago, and barring bad luck—or my own idiocy in letting you drag me into this thing and the serious risk of a stake through the heart, I'll stand here again centuries after. And you, Hoyt, food for the worms. So which of us has destiny smiled on?"

"What is my power if I can't change that one night, that one moment? I'd have gone with you. I'd have died for you."

Cian's head whipped up, and on his face was the same hot temper it had held in battle. "Don't put your death, or your regrets, on me."

But there was no answering anger in Hoyt. "And you would have died for me. For any one of them." He spread his arms to encompass the graves.

"Once."

"You are half of me. Nothing you are, nothing that was done changes that. You know it as I know it. Even more than blood, more than bone. We are, beneath all that, what we ever were."

"I can't *exist* in this world feeling this." Emotion swirled now, into his face, his voice. "I can't grieve for what I am, or for you. Or for them. And damn you, goddamn you for bringing me back to it."

"I love you. It's bound in me."

"What you love is gone."

No, Hoyt thought, he was looking at the heart of what he'd loved. He could see it in the roses his brother had planted over their mother's grave.

"You're standing here with me and the spirits of our family. You're not so changed, Cian, or you would not have done this." He touched the petals of a rose over his mother's grave. "You could not have done it."

Cian's eyes were suddenly ageless, filled with the torment of centuries. "I've seen death. Thousands upon thousands. Age and sickness, murder and war. I didn't see theirs. And this was all I could do for them."

When Hoyt moved his hand, the petals of an overblown rose spilled down and scattered on his mother's grave. "It was enough."

Cian looked down at the hand Hoyt held out to him. He sighed once, deeply. "Well, damn to us both then," he said and clasped hands with his brother. "We've been out long enough, no point in tempting fate any longer. And I want my bed."

They started back the way they'd come.

"Do you miss the sun?" Hoyt wondered. "Walking in it, feeling it on your face?"

"They've found it gives you cancer of the skin."

"Huh." Hoyt considered it. "Still, the warmth of it on a summer morning."

"I don't think about it. I like the night."

Perhaps it wasn't the time to ask Cian to allow him to do a little experimental bloodletting.

"What do you do in these businesses of yours? And with your leisure? Do you—"

"I do as I please. I like to work; it's satisfying. And makes play more appealing. And it's not possible to catch up on several centuries during a morning's walk in the rain, even if

I were inclined." He rested the sword on his shoulder. "But likely you'll catch your death from it, and spare me the questions in any case."

"I'm made of stronger stuff than that," Hoyt said, cheerfully now, "as I proved when I bashed your face not long ago. You've a fine bruise on your jaw."

"It'll be gone quicker than yours, unless the witch intervenes again. In any case, I was holding back."

"Bollocks to that."

The shadows that always fell on him when he visited that graveyard began to lift. "If I'd come at you full, we'd be digging your grave back there."

"Let's go again, then."

Cian slanted Hoyt a look. Memories, the pleasure of them so long suppressed, crept back on him. "Another time. And when I'm finished pounding you, you won't be up to romping with the redhead."

Hoyt grinned. "I've missed you."

Cian stared ahead as the house peeked through the trees. "The bloody hell of it is I've missed you, too."

Chapter 14

With a crossbow armed and ready by her side, Glenna kept watch from the tower window. She'd considered the fact that she'd had very little practice with that particular weapon, and that her aim could be called into serious question.

But she couldn't just sit up there, unarmed and wringing her hands like some helpless female. If the damn sun would come out, she wouldn't have to worry. More than that, she thought with a little hiss, if the McKenna boys hadn't wandered off—obviously to snarl at each other in private—she wouldn't have these images in her head of them being ripped to pieces by a pack of vampires.

Pack? Herd? Gang?

What did it matter? They still had fangs and a bad attitude.

Where had they *gone*? And why had they been out, exposed and vulnerable, so long?

Maybe the pack/herd/gang had already ripped them to shreds and dragged their mutilated bodies off to . . . And oh, God, she wished she could turn off the video in her head for five damn minutes.

Most women just worried about their man getting mugged or run over by a bus. But oh no, *she* had to get herself tangled up with a guy at war with blood-sucking fiends.

Why couldn't she have fallen for a nice accountant or stockbroker?

She had thought of using her skill and the crystal to look for them. But it seemed . . . intrusive, she decided. And rude.

But if they weren't back in ten minutes, she was going to say screw manners and find them.

She hadn't thought through, not completely, the emotional turmoil Hoyt was experiencing, what he missed, and what he risked. More than the rest of them, she decided. She was thousands of miles away from her family, but not hundreds of years. He was in the home where he'd grown up, but it was no longer his home. And every day, every hour, was another reminder of that.

Bringing back his mother's herb garden had hurt him. She should have thought of that, too. Kept her mouth shut about what she'd needed and wanted. Just made a damn list and gone out to find or buy supplies.

She glanced back at some of the herbs she'd already bundled and hung to dry. Small things, everyday things could cause the most pain.

Now he was out there somewhere, in the rain, with his brother. The vampire. She didn't believe Cian would attack Hoyt—or didn't want to believe it. But if Cian were angry enough, pushed hard enough, could he control what must be natural urges?

She didn't know the answer.

Added to that, no one could be sure more of Lilith's forces were out and about, just waiting for another chance.

It was probably silly to worry. They were two men of considerable power, men who knew the land. Neither of them were solely dependent on swords and daggers. Hoyt was armed, and he wore one of the crosses they'd conjured, so he was hardly defenseless.

And it proved a point, didn't it, the two of them being out, moving freely? It proved they wouldn't be held under siege.

No one else was worried, particularly. Moira was back in

the library, studying. Larkin and King were in the training area doing a weapon inventory. She was, undoubtedly, worked up about nothing.

Where the *hell* were they?

As she continued to scan, she spotted movement. Just shadows in the gloom. She grabbed the crossbow, ordered her fingers to stop shaking as she positioned it and herself in the narrow window.

"Just breathe," she told herself. "Just breathe. In and out, in and out."

That breath came out on a whoosh of relief when she saw Hoyt, Cian beside him. Trooping along, she noted, dripping wet, as if they had all the time in the world, and not a care in it.

Her brows drew together as they came closer. Was that blood on Hoyt's shirt, and a fresh bruise spreading under his right eye?

She leaned out, bumped the stone sill. And the arrow shot out of the bow with a deadly twang. She actually squealed. She'd hate herself for it later, but the purely female sound of shock and distress ripped out of her as the arrow sliced air and rain.

And landed, just a few inches short of the toe of Hoyt's boot.

Their swords were out, a blur of steel, as they pivoted back-to-back. Under other circumstances she would have admired the move, the sheer grace and rhythm of it, like a dance step. But at the moment, she was caught between mortification and horror.

"Sorry! Sorry!" She leaned out farther, waved her arm frantically as she shouted. "It was me. It got away from me. I was just . . ." Oh hell with it. "I'm coming down."

She left the weapon where it was, vowing to take a full hour of practice with it before she shot at anything but a target again. Before she set off in a run, she heard the unmistakable sound of male laughter. A quick glance showed her it was Cian, all but doubled over with it. Hoyt simply stood, staring up at the window.

As she swung down the stairs, Larkin came out of the training room. "Trouble?"

"No, no. Nothing. Everything's fine. It's nothing at all." She could actually feel the blood rise up to heat her cheeks as she dashed for the main floor.

They were coming in the front door, shaking themselves like wet dogs as she sprinted down the last steps.

"I'm sorry. I'm so sorry."

"Remind me not to piss you off, Red," Cian said easily. "You might aim for my heart and shoot me in the balls."

"I was just keeping watch for you, and I must've pulled the trigger by mistake. Which I wouldn't have done if the two of you hadn't been gone so damn long and had me so worried."

"That's what I love about women." Cian slapped his brother's shoulder. "They damn near kill you, but in the end it's your own fault. Good luck with that. I'm going to bed."

"I need to check your burns."

"Nag, nag, nag."

"And what happened? Were you attacked? Your mouth's bleeding—yours, too," she said to Hoyt. "And your eye's damn near swollen shut."

"No, we weren't attacked." There was a world of exasperation in his voice. "Until you nearly shot me in the foot."

"Your faces are all banged up, and your clothes are filthy—ripped. If you weren't . . ." It came to her, when she saw the expressions on their faces. She had a brother of her own, after all. "You punched each other? *Each other?*"

"He hit me first."

She gave Cian a look that would have withered stone. "Well, that's just fine, isn't it? Didn't we go through all this yesterday? Didn't we talk about in-fighting, how destructive and useless it is?"

"I guess we're going to bed without our supper."

"Don't get smart with me." She jabbed a finger into Cian's chest. "I'm here worried half sick, and the two of you are out there wrestling around like a couple of idiot puppies."

"You nearly put an arrow in my foot," Hoyt reminded her. "I think we're quits on foolish behavior for one day."

She only hissed out a breath. "Into the kitchen, both of you. I'll do something about those cuts and bruises. Again."

"I'm having my bed," Cian began.

"Both of you. Now. You don't want to mess with me at the moment."

As she sailed off, Cian rubbed a finger gently on his split lip. "It's been a long while, but I don't recall you having a particular fondness for bossy women."

"I didn't, previously. But I understand them well enough to know we might as well be after letting her have her way on this. And the fact is, my eye's paining me."

When they came in, Glenna was setting what she needed out on the table. She had the kettle on the boil, and her sleeves rolled up.

"Do you want blood?" she said to Cian, with enough frost in the words to have him clearing his throat.

It amazed him that he actually felt chagrined. It was a sensation he hadn't felt in . . . too long to remember. Obviously living so closely with humans was a bad influence.

"The tea you're making will do, thanks."

"Take off your shirt."

There was a smart comment on the tip of his tongue, she could all but see it. He proved himself a wise man by swallowing it.

He stripped it off, sat.

"I'd forgotten about the burns." Hoyt examined them now. There was no longer any blistering, and they'd gone down to a dull, ugly red. "If I'd remembered," he said as he sat across from Cian, "I'd have put more blows into your chest."

"Typical," Glenna said under her breath, and was ignored.

"You don't fight altogether the way you used to. You use your feet more, and elbows." And Hoyt could still feel the aching result of them. "Then there's that leaping off the ground."

"Martial arts. I have black belts in several of them. Master status," Cian explained. "You need to put more time into training."

Hoyt rubbed his sore ribs. "And so I will."

Weren't they chummy all of a sudden? Glenna thought. What was it about men that made them decide to be pals after they'd smashed their fists into each other's faces?

She poured hot water into the pot, and while it steeped came to the table with her salve.

"I would've said three weeks to heal with what I can do, considering the extent of the burns." She sat, slicked salve on her fingers. "I'm amending that to three days."

"We can be hurt, and seriously. But unless it's a killing blow, we heal—and quickly."

"Lucky for you, especially as you've got a mass of nice bruising to go with the burns. But you don't regenerate," she continued as she applied the salve. "If, say, we were to cut off one of their arms, it wouldn't grow back."

"There's a gruesome and interesting thought. No. I've never heard of anything like that happening."

"Then if we can't get to the heart or the head, we can go for a limb."

She went to the sink to wash the salve from her hands, and make cold packs for the bruising. "Here." She handed one to Hoyt. "Hold that on your eye."

He sniffed at it, then complied. "You shouldn't have worried."

Cian winced. "Bad tact. Wiser to say: 'Ah, my love, we're sorry we worried you. We were selfish and inconsiderate, should likely be flogged for it. We hope you'll forgive us.' Thicken the brogue a bit as well. Women are fools for brogues."

"Then kiss her feet, I suppose."

"Actually, you aim for the ass. Ass kissing is a tradition that never goes out of style. You'll need patience with him, Glenna. Hoyt's still working on the learning curve."

She brought the tea to the table, then surprised them both when she laid a hand on Cian's cheek. "And you're going to teach him how to deal with the modern woman?"

"Well, he's a bit pitiful, is all."

Her lips curved as she lowered her head, brushed them over Cian's. "You're forgiven. Drink your tea."

"Just that easy?" Hoyt complained. "He gets a pat on the cheek and a kiss with it? You didn't nearly put an arrow into him."

"Women are a constant mystery." Cian spoke quietly.

"And one of the wonders of the world. I'll take this up with me." He got to his feet. "I'm wanting some dry clothes."

"Drink all of it." Glenna spoke without turning as she took up another bottle. "It'll help."

"I will then. Let me know if he doesn't learn fast enough to suit you. I wouldn't quibble with being second choice."

"That's just his way," Hoyt told her when Cian left the room. "A kind of teasing."

"I know. So you made friends again while you were bloodying each other."

"It's true enough I hit him first. I spoke to him of our mother, and the garden, and he was cold. Even though I could see what was under that cold, I . . . well, I lashed out, and . . . After, he took me to where our family's buried. And there you have it."

She turned now, and all the pity in her heart swirled into her eyes. "It must've been hard for both of you to be there."

"It makes it real to me, that as I sit here now, they're gone. It didn't seem real before. Not solid and real."

She moved to him, dabbed her tincture on his facial bruises. "And for him, to have lived all this time with no family at all. Another cruelty of what was done to him. To all of them. We don't think of that do we, when we talk about war, and how to destroy them? They were people once, just like Cian."

"They mean to kill us, Glenna. Every one of us that has a heartbeat."

"I know. I know. Something drained them of humanity. But they were human once, Hoyt, with families, lovers, hopes. We don't think of that. Maybe we can't."

She brushed the hair back from his face. A nice account-ant, she thought again. A stockbroker. How ridiculous, how ordinary. She had, right here, the amazing.

"I think fate put Cian here, this way, so we understand there's a weight to what we're doing. So that we know, at the end of the day, we've done what we had to do. But not with-out cost."

She stepped back. "That'll have to do. Try to keep your face from walking into any more fists."

She started to turn, but he took her hand, rising as he drew her back to him. His lips took hers with utter tenderness.

"I think fate put you here, Glenna, to help me understand it's not just death and blood and violence. There's such beauty, such kindness in the world. And I have it." He wrapped his arms around here. "I have it here."

She indulged herself, letting her head rest on his shoulder. She wanted to ask what they'd have when it was over, but she knew it was important, even essential, to take each day as it came.

"We should work." She drew back. "I've got some ideas about creating a safe zone around the house. A protected area where we can move around more freely. And I think Larkin's right about sending out scouts. If we can get to the caves during the day, we might be able to find something out. Even set traps."

"Your mind's been busy."

"I need to keep it that way. I'm not as afraid if I'm thinking, if I'm doing."

"Then we work."

"Moira might be able to help once we have a start," Glenna added as they left the kitchen. "She's reading everything she can get her hands on, so she'd be our prime data source—information," she explained. "And she has some power. It's raw and untrained, but it's there."

While Glenna and Hoyt closed themselves in the tower and the house was quiet, Moira pored over a volume on demon lore in the library. It was fascinating, she thought. So many different theories and legends. She considered it her task to pick them apart for truth.

Cian would know it, or some of it, she concluded. Centuries of existence was plenty of time to learn. And anyone who filled such a room with books sought and respected knowledge. But she wasn't ready to ask him—wasn't sure she would ever be.

If he wasn't like the creatures she read of, those that sought human blood night after night—and thirsted not just for that blood, but the kill—what was he? Now he prepared to make war against what he was, and she didn't understand it.

She needed to learn more, about what they fought, about Cian, about all the others. How could you understand, and then trust, what you didn't know?

She made notes, copious notes, on the paper she'd found in one of the drawers of the big desk. She loved the paper, and the writing instrument. The pen, she corrected, that held the ink inside its tube. She wondered if she could smuggle some of the paper and pens back to Geall.

She closed her eyes. She missed home, and the missing was like a constant ache in her belly. She'd written down her wish, sealed the paper, and would leave it among her things for Larkin to find if it came to pass.

If she died on this side, she wanted her body taken back to Geall for burial.

She continued to write with thoughts circling in her head. There was one she kept coming back to, nibbling at. She would have to find a way to ask Glenna if it could be done—if the others would agree to it, if it could.

Was there a way to seal off the portal, to close the door to Geall?

With a sigh, she looked toward the window. Was it raining in Geall now, too, or was the sun shining on her mother's grave?

She heard footsteps approach, and danced her fingers over the hilt of her dagger. She let them fall away when King came in. For reasons she couldn't name, she felt easier with him than the others.

"Got something against chairs, Shorty?"

Her lips twitched. She liked the way words rumbled out of him, like rocks down a stony hill. "No, but I like sitting on the floor. It is time for more training?"

"Taking a break." He sat in a wide chair, a huge mug of coffee in his hand. "Larkin could go all damn day. Up there now, practicing some katas."

"I like the katas. It's like dancing."

"Just make sure you're doing the leading if you're dancing with a vampire."

Idly, she turned the page of a book. "Hoyt and Cian fought."

King took a drink. "Oh yeah? Who won?"

"I think neither. I saw them coming back, and from their faces and limps, it seemed to be a draw."

"How do you know they were fighting with each other? Maybe they were attacked."

"No." She traced her fingers over words. "I hear things."

"You got big ears, Shorty."

"So my mother always said. They made peace between them—Hoyt and his brother."

"That eliminates a complication—if it lasts." Given their personalities, King figured a full truce between the brothers had the life expectancy of a fruit fly. "What do you expect to find out in all these books?"

"Everything. Sooner or later. Do you know how the first vampire came to be? There are different versions in the books."

"Never thought about it."

"I did—do. One is like a love story. Long ago, when the world was young, demons were dying out. Before, long before that, there were more. Scores of them, walking the world. But man grew stronger and smarter, and the time of the demons was passing."

Because he was a man who enjoyed stories, he settled back. "Kind of an evolution."

"A change, yes. Many demons went beneath the world, to hide or to sleep. There was more magic then, because people didn't turn from it. Man and the faeries forged an alliance to wage war on the demons, to drive them under for once and all. There was one who was poisoned, and slowly dying. He loved a mortal woman, and this was forbidden even in the demon world."

"So man doesn't have a lock on bigotry. Keep going," he said when she paused.

"So the dying demon took the mortal woman from her home. He was obsessed with her, and his last wish was to mate with her before his end."

"Not so different from men in that area then."

"I think, perhaps, all living creatures crave love and pleasure. And this physical act that represents life."

"And guys want to get off."

She lost her rhythm. "Get off what?"

He nearly spewed coffee, choked instead. He waved a hand at her as his laugh rumbled out. "Don't mind me. Finish the story."

"Ah . . . Well, he took her deep into the forest and had his way with her, and she, like a woman under a spell, wanted his touch. To try to save his life, she offered her blood to him. So she was bitten, and drank his blood in turn, as this was another kind of mating. She died with him, but she did not cease to exist. She became the thing we call vampyre."

"A demon for love."

"Aye, I suppose. In vengeance against men, she hunted them, fed from them, changed them, to make more of her kind. And still she grieved for her demon lover, and killed herself with sunlight."

"Doesn't quite hit *Romeo and Juliet,* does it?"

"A play. I saw the book of it here, on the shelf. I haven't yet read it." It would take years to read all the books in such a room she thought as she toyed with the end of her braid.

"But I read another tale of the vampyre. It tells of a demon, mad and ill from a spell even more evil than it, thirsting wildly for human blood. He fed, and the more he fed, the more mad he became. He died after mixing his blood with a mortal, and the mortal became vampyre. The first of its kind."

"I guess you like the first version better."

"No, I like truth better, and I think the second is the truth. What mortal woman would love a demon?"

"Led a sheltered life back in your world, haven't you? Where I come from people fall for monsters—or what others consider monsters—all the time. Ain't no logic with love, Shorty. It just is."

She tossed her braid behind her back in a kind of shrug. "Well, if I love, I won't be stupid about it."

"Hope I'm around long enough to see you eat those words."

She closed the book, drew up her legs. "Do you love someone?"

"A woman? Been close a few times, and that's how I know I didn't make it all the way to the bull's-eye."

"How do you know?"

"When you hit the center, Shorty, you're down for the count. But it's fun shooting for it. Gonna take a special woman to get past this." He tapped a finger to his face.

"I like your face. It's so big and dark."

He laughed so hard he nearly spilled his coffee. "You got that one right."

"And you're strong. You speak well and you cook. You have loyalty to your friends."

That big dark face softened. "Want to apply for the position of love of my life?"

She smiled back at him, at ease. "I'm thinking I'm not your bull's-eye. If I'm to be queen, I must marry one day. Have children. I hope it won't be only duty, but that I find what my mother found in my father. What they found in each other. I'd want him to be strong, and loyal."

"And handsome."

She moved her shoulders, because she did hope that as well. "Do women here only look for beauty?"

"Couldn't say, but it don't hurt. Guy looks like Cian, for instance, he's got to beat them off with sticks."

"Then why is he lonely?"

He studied her over the rim of his mug. "Good question."

"How did you come to meet him?"

"He saved my life."

Moira wrapped her arms around her legs and settled in. There was little she liked more than a story. "How?"

"I was in the wrong place at the wrong time. Bad neighborhood in East L.A." He drank again, lifted a shoulder in a half shrug. "See, my old man took off before I was born, and my old lady had what we'll call a little problem with illegal substances. O.D.'d. Overdosed. Took too much of some bad shit."

"She died." Everything in her mourned for him. "I'm sorry."

"Bad choices, bad luck. You gotta figure some people come into the world set on tossing their life into the shitter. She was one of them. So I'm on the street, doing what I can to get by, and keep out of the system. I'm heading to this place I know. It's dark, steaming hot. I just wanted a place to sleep for the night."

"You had no home."

"I had the street. A couple of guys were hanging out on the stoop, probably waiting to make a score. I got my bad attitude on. Need to get by them to get where I want to go. Car rolls up, blasts at them. Drive-by," he said. "Like an ambush. I'm caught in it. Bullet grazes my head. More coming, and I know I'm going to be dead. Somebody grabs me, pulls me back. Things got blurry, but it felt like I was flying. Then I was someplace else."

"Where?"

"Fancy hotel room. I'd never seen anything like it outside of movies." He crossed his big, booted feet as he remembered. "Big-ass bed, big enough for ten people, and I'm lying on it. Head hurts like a mother, which is why I don't figure I'm dead and this is heaven. He comes out of the bathroom. Got his shirt off, and a fresh bandage on his shoulder. Got himself shot dragging me out of the cross fire."

"What did you do?"

"Nothing much, guess I was in shock. He sits down, studies me like I'm a frigging book. 'You're lucky,' he said, 'and stupid.' He's got that accent. I'm figuring he must be some rock star or something. The way he looks, the fancy voice, the fancy room. Truth is, I thought he was a perv, and he was going to want me to . . . Let's just say I was scared shitless. I was eight."

"You were a child?" Her eyes widened. "You were just a child?"

"I was eight," he repeated. "Grow up like I did, you aren't a kid long. He asks me what the hell I was doing out there, and I give him some sass. Trying to get some of my own back. He asks if I'm hungry, and I shoot back something like I ain't going to . . . perform any sexual favors for a goddamn meal. Orders a steak dinner, a bottle of wine, some soda pop.

And he tells me he isn't interested in buggering young boys. If I've got someplace I'd rather be, I should go there. Otherwise I can wait for the steak."

"You waited for the steak."

"Fucking A." He gave her a wink. "That was the start of it. He gave me food, and a choice. I could go back to where I'd been—no skin off his—or I could work for him. I took the job. Didn't know the job meant school. He gave me clothes, an education, self-respect."

"Did he tell you what he was?"

"Not then. Not long after though. I figured he was whacked, but I didn't much care. By the time I realized he was telling the truth, literal truth, I would've done anything for him. The man I was setting to be died on the street that night. He didn't turn me," King said quietly. "But he changed me."

"Why? Did you ever ask him why?"

"Yeah. That'd be for him to tell."

She nodded. The story itself was enough to think about.

"Break's about over," he announced. "We can get an hour's workout in. Toughen up that skinny ass of yours."

She grinned. "Or we could work with the bow. Improve that poor aim of yours."

"Come on, smart-ass." He frowned, glanced toward the doorway. "You hear something?"

"Like a knocking?" She shrugged, and because she tarried to straighten the books, was several paces behind him out of the room.

G lenna trotted down the steps. What little progress they were making she could leave to Hoyt for the time being. Someone had to see about the evening meal—and since she'd put her name on the list, she was elected. She could toss together a marinade for some chicken, then go back up for another hour.

A good meal would set the tone for a team meeting.

She'd just drop by the library, yank Moira away from the books for a cooking lesson while she was at it. Maybe it was sexist to put the only other woman next on the KP list, but she had to start somewhere.

The knock on the door made her jolt, then pass a nervous hand through her hair.

She nearly called up the stairs for Larkin or King, then shook her head. Talk about sexist. How was she going to fare in serious battle if she couldn't even open the door herself on a rainy afternoon?

It could be a neighbor, dropping by to pay a courtesy call. Or Cian's caretaker, stopping by to make sure they had everything they needed.

And a vampire couldn't enter the house, couldn't step over the threshold, unless she asked it in.

A highly unlikely event.

Still, she looked out the window first. She saw a young woman of about twenty—a pretty blonde in jeans and a bright red sweater. Her hair was pulled back into a tail that swung out of the back of a red cap. She was holding a map—seemed to be puzzling over it as she chewed on a thumbnail.

Someone's lost, Glenna thought, and the sooner she got her on her way and away from the house, the better for everyone.

The knock sounded again as she turned from the window.

She opened the door, careful to keep to her side of the threshold.

"Hello? Need some help?"

"Hello. Thank you, yes." There was relief, and a heavy dose of French in the woman's voice. "I am, ah, lost. *Excusez-moi,* my English, is not so good."

"That's okay. My French is fairly nonexistent. What can I do for you?"

"Ennis? *S'il vovs plaît?* May you tell me how the road it goes to Ennis?"

"I'm not sure. I'm not from around here myself. I can look at the map." Glenna watched the woman's eyes as she held out a hand for it—her fingertips on her side of the door. "I'm Glenna. *Je suis* Glenna."

"Ah, *oui. Je m'apelle* Lora. I am in holiday, a student."

"That's nice."

"The rain." Lora held out a hand so rain drops splattered it. "I am lost in it, I think."

"Could happen to anyone. Let's have a look at your map, Lora. Are you by yourself?"

"Pardon?"

"Alone? Are you alone?"

"Oui. Mes amies—my friends—I have friends in Ennis, but I turn bad. Wrong?"

Oh no, Glenna thought. I really don't think so. "I'm surprised you could see the house from the main road. We're so far back."

"Sorry?"

Glenna smiled brilliantly. "I bet you'd like to come in, have a nice cup of tea while we figure out your route." She saw the light come into the blonde's baby blue eyes. "But you can't, can you? Just can't step through the door."

"Je ne comprendrez pas."

"Bet you do, but in case my Spidey sense is off today, you need to go back to the main road, turn left. Left," she repeated and started to gesture.

King's shout behind her had her spinning around. Her hair swung, the tips of it going beyond the doorway. There was an explosion of pain as her hair was viciously yanked, as her body flew out of the house and hit the ground with a bone-wracking thud.

There were two more, and they came out of nowhere. Instinct had Glenna reaching for her cross with one hand, kicking out blindly with her feet. Movement was a blur, and she tasted blood in her mouth. She saw King slicing at one with a knife, holding it off while he shouted at her to get up, to get into the house.

She stumbled to her feet in time to see them surround him, closing in. She heard herself screaming, and thought— hoped—she heard answering shouts from the house. But they would be too late. The vampires were on King like dogs.

"French bitch," Glenna spat out, and charged the blonde. Her fist cracked bone, and there was satisfaction in that, and the sudden spurt of blood. Then she was once more hurdling back, and this time when she hit, her vision went gray.

She felt herself being dragged, struggled. It was Moira's voice buzzing in her ear.

"I have you. I have you. You're back inside. Lie still."

"No. King. They've got King."

Moira was already dashing out, dagger drawn. As Glenna pushed herself up, Larkin vaulted over her and through the door.

Glenna gained her knees, then swayed to her feet. Sickness burned its acrid taste at the base of her throat as she once more stumbled to the door.

So fast, she thought dully, how could anything move that fast? As Moira and Larkin gave chase, they bundled the still struggling King into a black van. They were gone before she got out of the house.

Larkin's body shimmered, shuddered, and became a cougar. The cat flashed after the van and out of sight.

Glenna went to her knees on the wet grass, and retched.

"Get inside." Hoyt grabbed her arm with his free hand. In his other was a sword. "Inside the house. Glenna, Moira, get inside."

"It's too late," Glenna cried, while tears of horror spilled out of her eyes. "They have King." She looked up, saw Cian standing behind Hoyt. "They took him. They took King."

Chapter 15

"**I**n the house," Hoyt repeated. As he started to drag Glenna inside, Cian shoved past him and flew toward the stables.

"Go with him." Glenna struggled past the tears and pain. "Oh, God, go with him. Hurry."

Leaving her, shaking and bleeding, was the hardest thing he'd ever done.

The door where the black machine sat was open. His brother tossed weapons carelessly inside.

"Will this catch them?" Hoyt demanded.

Cian barely spared him a glance with eyes rimmed red. "Stay with the women. I don't need you."

"Need or not, you have me. How the bloody hell do I get inside this thing?" He fought with the door, and when it opened, folded himself inside it.

Cian said nothing, only got behind the wheel. The machine let out a vicious roar, seemed to quiver like a stallion poised to run. And then they were flying. Stones and sod spewed into the air like missiles. Hoyt caught a glimpse of Glenna in the doorway, holding the arm he feared might be broken.

He prayed to all the gods he'd see her again.

She watched him go, and wondered if she'd sent her lover to his death. "Get all the weapons you can carry," she told Moira.

"You're hurt. Let me see to you."

"Get the weapons, Moira." She turned, her face fierce and bloodied. "Or do you intend for us to stay here like children while the men do the fighting?"

Moira nodded. "Do you want blade or bow?"

"Both."

Glenna went quickly to the kitchen, gathered bottles. Her arm was screaming, so she quickly did what she could to block the pain. This was Ireland, she thought grimly, and that should mean plenty of churches. In the churches would be holy water. She carried the bottles, along with a butcher knife and a bundle of garden stakes to the van.

"Glenna." With a longbow and crossbow slung over her shoulders, two swords in her hand, Moira crossed to the van. She put the weapons inside, then held up one of the silver crosses by its chain.

"This was up in the training room. I think it must be King's. He has no protection."

Glenna slammed the cargo door. "He has us."

Hedgerows and hills were no more than a blur through the gray curtain of rain. Hoyt saw other machines—cars, he reminded himself—traveling the wet road, and the edges of a village.

He saw cattle in fields, and sheep, and the ramble of stone fences. He saw nothing of Larkin, or the car that held King.

"Can you track them in this?" he asked Cian.

"No." He spun the wheel, sent up a flood of water. "They'll take him to Lilith. They'll keep him alive." He had to believe it. "And take him to Lilith."

"The caves?" Hoyt thought how long it had taken him to travel from his cliffs to Clare. But that had been on horseback, and he'd been wounded and feverish. Still the journey would take time. Too much time.

"Alive? Cian, why will they take him alive?"

"He'd be a prize to her. That's what he is, a prize. He's alive. She'd want the kill for herself. We can't be that far behind them. Can't be. And the Jag's faster than the bloody van they have him in."

"He won't be bitten. The cross will stop that."

"It won't stop a sword or an arrow. A fucking bullet. Guns and bows aren't the weapons of choice," he said almost to himself. "Too remote. We like close kills, and some tradition with it. We like to look in the eyes. She'll want to torture him first. Wouldn't want it to be quick." His hands tightened on the wheel enough to bruise the leather. "Should buy us some time."

"Night's coming."

What Hoyt didn't say, and they both knew, was there would be more of them at night.

Cian swung around a sedan at a speed that had the Jag fishtailing on the slick road, then the tires bit in and he shot forward again. A flash of headlights in his eyes blinded him, but didn't slow him down. He had a moment to think: bloody tourists as the oncoming car edged him over. Branches of hedgerows scraped and rattled over the side and windows of the Jag. Loose gravel spat out like stone bullets.

"We should've caught up with them by now. If they took another route, or she's got another hole . . ." Too many options, Cian thought, and pushed for more speed. "Can you do anything? A locator spell?"

"I haven't any . . ." He slapped a hand to the dash as Cian shot around another curve. "Wait." He gripped the cross he wore, pushed power into it. And bearing down, brought its light into his mind.

"Shield and symbol. Guide me. Give me sight."

He saw the cougar, running through the rain, the cross lashing like a silver whip around its throat.

"Larkin, he's close. Fallen behind us. Keeping to the fields. He's tiring." He searched, feeling with the light as if it were fingers. "Glenna—and Moira with her. They didn't stay in the house, they're moving. She's in pain."

"They can't help me. Where's King?"

"I can't find him. He's in the dark."

"Dead?"

"I don't know. I can't reach him."

Cian slammed on the brakes, wrenched the wheel. The Jag went into a sickening spin, revolving closer and closer to the black van that sat across the narrow road. There was a scream of tires and a dull thud as metal slapped metal.

Cian was out before the motion stopped, sword in hand. When he wrenched open the door of the van he found nothing. And no one.

"There's a woman here," Hoyt called out. "She's hurt."

Cursing, Cian rounded the van, yanked open the cargo doors. There was blood, he saw—human blood by its scent. But not enough for death.

"Cian, she's been bitten, but she's alive."

Cian glanced over his shoulder. He saw the woman lying on the road, blood seeping from the punctures in her neck. "Didn't drain her. Not enough time. Revive her. Bring her around," Cian ordered. "You can do it. Do it fast. They've taken her car, switched cars. Find out what she was driving."

"She needs help."

"Goddamn it, she'll live or she won't. Bring her around."

Hoyt laid his fingertips on the wounds, felt the burn. "Madam. Hear me. Wake and hear me."

She stirred, then her eyes flew open, the pupils big as moons. "Rory! Rory. Help me."

Roughly, Cian shoved Hoyt aside. He had some power of his own. "Look at me. Into me." He bent close until her eyes were fixed on him. "What happened here?"

"A woman, the van. Needed help, we thought. Rory stopped. He got out. He got out and they . . . Oh God, sweet God. Rory."

"They took your car. What kind of car was it?"

"Blue. BMW. Rory. They took him. They took him. No room for you. They said no room and threw me down. They laughed."

Cian straightened. "Help me get this van off the road. They were smart enough to take the keys."

"We can't leave her like this."

"Then stay with her, but help me move this bloody van."

Fury had Hoyt spinning around, and the van jumped three feet across the road.

"Nice work."

"She could die out here. She did nothing."

"She won't be the first or the last. It's war, isn't it?" Cian shot back. "She's what they call collateral damage. Good strategy this," he mumbled, and took stock. "Slow us down and switch to a faster car. I won't be catching them now before they reach the caves. If that's where they're going."

He turned toward his brother, considered. "I may need you now after all."

"I won't leave an injured woman on the side of the road like a sick dog."

Cian stepped back to his car, flipped open the center compartment and took out a mobile phone. He spoke into it briefly. "It's a communication device," he told Hoyt as he tossed the phone back into storage. "I've called for help—medical and the garda. All you'll do now by staying is get yourself hauled in, and asked questions you can't answer."

He popped the hood, took out a blanket and some flares. "Put that over her," he instructed. "I'll set these up. He's bait now," Cian added as he set the flares to light. "Bait as much as a prize. She knows we're coming. She wants us to."

"Then we won't disappoint her."

With no hope of cutting off the raiding party before they reached the caves, Cian drove more cautiously. "She was smarter. More aggressive, and more willing to lose troops. So she has the advantage."

"We'll be outnumbered, greatly."

"We always would have been. At this point, she may be willing to negotiate. To take a trade."

"One of us for King."

"You're all the same to her. A human's a human, so you have no particular value in this. You perhaps, because she respects and covets power. But she'd want me more."

"You're willing to trade your life for his?"

"She wouldn't kill me. At least not right away. She'd want to use her considerable talents first. She'd enjoy that."

"Torture."

"And persuasion. If she could bring me over to her side, it would be a coup."

"A man who trades his life for a friend doesn't turn and betray him. Why would she think otherwise?"

"Because we're fickle creatures. And she made me. That gives her quite a bit of pull."

"No, not you. I'd believe you'd trade yourself for King, but I don't think she'd believe it. You'll have to offer me," Hoyt said after a moment.

"Oh, will I?"

"I've been nothing to you for hundreds of years. He's more to you than me. She'd see that. A human for a sorcerer. A good exchange for her."

"And why should she think you'd give yourself for a man you've known for, what a week?"

"Because you'd have a knife to my throat."

Cian tapped his fingers on the steering wheel. "It could work."

The rain had passed into dreary moonlight by the time they reached the cliffs. They rose high above the road, jutted out to cast jagged shadows over the toiling sea.

There was only the sound of the water lashing rock, and the hum of the air that was like the breath of gods.

There was no sign of another car, of human or of creature.

Along the seaside of the road was a rail. Below it was rocks, water and the maze of caves.

"We lure her up." Cian nodded toward the edge. "If we go down to her, we're trapped, with the sea at our backs. We go up, make her come to us."

They started the climb, over slippery rocks and soggy grass. At the headland stood a lighthouse, its beam lancing out into the dark.

The both sensed the attack before the movement. The thing sprang out from behind the rocks, fangs bared. Cian merely pivoted, led with his shoulder, and sent it tumbling down to the road. For the second, he used the stake he'd hitched in his belt.

Then he straightened, turned to the third who appeared more cautious than his fellows.

"Tell your mistress Cian McKenna wants to speak with her."

Vicious teeth gleamed in the moonlight. "We'll drink your blood tonight."

"Or you'll die hungry, and by Lilith's hands because you failed to deliver a message."

The thing melted away, and down.

"There may be more waiting above," Hoyt commented.

"Unlikely. She'd be expecting us to charge the caves, not head to high ground for a hostage negotiation. She'll be intrigued, and she'll come."

So they climbed, then walked the slope to higher ground, and the point where Hoyt had once faced Lilith, and the thing she'd made of his brother.

"She'll appreciate the irony of the spot."

"It feels as it did." Hoyt tucked his cross out of sight under his shirt. "The air. The night. This was my place once, where I could stand and call power with a thought."

"You'd best hope you still can." Cian drew his knife. "Get on your knees." He flicked the point at Hoyt's throat, watched the dribble of blood from the thin slice. "Now."

"So, it comes to choices."

"It always comes to choices. You would have killed me here, if you could."

"I would have saved you here, if I could."

"Well, you did neither, did you?" He slid the knife from Hoyt's sheath, made a V with the blades to hold at his brother's throat. "Kneel."

With the cold edge of the blade on his flesh, Hoyt got to his knees.

"Well, what a handsome sight."

Lilith stepped into the moonlight. She wore emerald green robes with her hair long and loose to spill over her shoulders like sunbeams.

"Lilith. It's been a very long time."

"Too long." The silk rustled as she moved. "Did you come all this way to bring me a gift?"

"A trade," Cian corrected. "Call your dogs off," he said quietly. "Or I kill him, then them. And you have nothing."

"So forceful." She gestured with her hand toward the vampires creeping in at the sides. "You've seasoned. You were hardly more than a pretty puppy when I gave you the gift. Now look at you, a sleek wolf. I like it."

"And still your dog," Hoyt spat out.

"Ah, the mighty sorcerer brought low. I like that, too. You marked me." She opened her robes to show Hoyt the pentagram branded over her heart. "It gave me pain for more than a decade. And the scar never fades. I owe you for that. Tell me, Cian, how did you manage to bring him here?"

"He thinks I'm his brother. It makes it easy."

"She took your life. She's lies and death."

Over Hoyt's head, Cian smiled. "That's what I love about her. I'll give you this one for the human you took. He's useful to me, and loyal. I want him back."

"But he's so much bigger than this one. So much more to feast on."

"He has no power. He's an ordinary mortal. I give you a sorcerer."

"Yet you covet the human."

"As I said, he's of use to me. Do you know how much time and trouble it takes to train a human servant? I want him back. No one steals from me. Not you, not anyone."

"We'll discuss it. Bring him down. I've done quite a bit with the caves. We can be comfortable, have a little something to eat. I've a very Rubenesque exchange student on tap—Swiss. We can share. Oh, but wait." She let out a musical laugh. "I've heard you dine on pigs' blood these days."

"You can't trust everything you hear." Deliberately Cian lifted the knife he'd used to cut Hoyt, flicked his tongue over the bloodied blade.

That first taste of human after so long a fast reddened his eyes, churned his hunger. "But I haven't lived so long to be stupid. This is a one-time offer, Lilith. Bring the human to me, and take the sorcerer."

"How can I trust you, my darling boy? You kill our kind."

"I kill what I like when I like. As you do."

"You aligned yourself with them. With humans. Plotted against me."

"As long as it amused me. It's become boring, and costly. Give me the human, take this one. And, as a bonus, I'll invite you into my home. You can have a banquet on the others."

Hoyt's head jerked, and the blade bit. He cursed, in Gaelic now, with low and steady violence.

"Smell the power in that blood." Lilith crooned it. "Gorgeous."

"Another step, and I cut the jugular, waste it all."

"Would you?" She smiled, beautifully. "I wonder. Is that what you want?" She gestured.

At the edge of the cliff where the lighthouse stood, Cian could see King slumped between two vampires.

"He's alive," she said lightly. "Of course, you only have my word for it, as I have yours that you'd hand that one to me, like a pretty present all wrapped in shiny paper. Let's play a game."

She held her skirts out, twirled. "Kill him, and I give you the human. Kill your brother, but not with the knives. Kill him as you're meant to kill. Take his blood, drink him, and the human is yours."

"Bring me the human first."

She pouted, brushed fussily at her skirts. "Oh, very well." She lifted one arm high, then the other. Cian eased the knives from Hoyt's throat as they began to drag King forward.

They dropped him, and with a vicious kick sent him over the edge.

"Oops!" Lilith eyes's danced with merriment as she pressed a hand to her lips. "Butterfingers. I guess you'll have to pay me back now and kill that one."

With a wild roar, Cian charged forward. And she rose up, spreading her robe like wings. "Take them!" she shouted. "Bring them to me." And was gone.

Cian switched grips on the knives as Hoyt sprang up, yanking free the stakes shoved into the back of his belt.

Arrows flew, slicing through air and hearts. Before Cian could strike the first blow, a half a dozen vampires were dust, blown out to sea by the wind.

"More are coming." Moira shouted from the cover of trees. "We need to go. We need to go now. This way. Hurry!"

Retreat was bitter, a vile taste burning the back of the throat. But the choice was to swallow death. So they turned from battle.

When they reached the car, Hoyt reached for his brother's hand. "Cian—"

"Don't." He slammed in, watched the others leap into the van. "Just don't."

The long drive home was full of silence, of grief and of fury.

G lenna didn't weep. It went too deep for tears. She drove in a kind of trance, her body throbbing with pain and shock, her mind numb with it. And knowing it was cowardice, huddled there.

"It wasn't your fault."

She heard Moira's voice, but couldn't respond to it. She felt Larkin touch her shoulder, she supposed in comfort. But was too numb to react. And when Moira climbed in the back with Larkin to give her solitude, she knew only vague relief.

She turned into the woods, carefully maneuvered the narrow lane. In front of the house where the lights burned, she shut off the engine, the lights. Reached for the door.

It flew open, and she was wrenched out, held inches above the ground. Even then, she felt nothing, not even fear as she saw the thirst in Cian's eyes.

"Tell me why I shouldn't break your neck and be done with it."

"I can't."

Hoyt reached them first, and was flicked away with a careless backward swipe.

"Don't. He's not to blame. Don't," she said now to Hoyt before he could charge again. "Please don't." And to Larkin.

"Do you think that moves me?"

She looked into Cian's eyes again. "No. Why should it? He was yours. I killed him."

"It wasn't her doing." Moira shoved Cian's arm, but didn't budge him an inch. "She isn't to blame for this."

"Let her speak for herself."

"She can't. Can't you see how badly she's hurt? She wouldn't let me tend her before we followed you. We need to get inside. If we're attacked now, we all die."

"If you harm her," Hoyt said quietly. "I'll kill you myself."

"Is that all there is?" Glenna's words were a weary whisper. "Just death? Is that all there'll ever be again?"

"Give her to me." Hoyt cupped his arms, drew her out of Cian's grasp. He murmured to her in Gaelic as he carried her into the house.

"You'll come, and you'll listen." Moira closed a hand around Cian's arm. "He deserves that."

"Don't tell me what he deserves." He wrenched free of her with a force that knocked her back two steps. "You know nothing of it."

"I know more than you think." She left him to follow Hoyt into the house.

"I couldn't catch them." Larkin stared at the ground. "I wasn't fast enough, and I couldn't catch them." He yanked open the cargo doors, unloaded weapons. "I can't turn into one of these." He slammed the doors again. "It has to be alive, what I become. Even the cougar couldn't catch them."

Cian said nothing, and went inside.

They had Glenna on the sofa in the main parlor. Her eyes were closed, her face pale, her skin clammy. Against the pallor, the bruising along her jaw and cheek was livid. Blood had dried at the corner of her mouth.

Hoyt gently tested her arm. Not broken, he thought with relief. Badly wrenched, but not broken. Trying not to jar her, he removed her shirt to discover more bruising over her shoulder, her torso, running down to her hip.

"I know what to get," Moira said and dashed off.

"Not broken." Hoyt's hands hovered over her ribs. "It's good there's nothing broken."

"She's fortunate her head's still on her shoulders." Cian

went directly to a cabinet, took out whiskey. He drank straight from the bottle.

"Some of the injuries are inside her. She's badly injured."

"No less than she deserves for going out of the house."

"She didn't." Moira hurried back in, carrying Glenna's case. "Not the way you're meaning."

"You don't expect me to believe King went out, and she leaped to his defense?"

"He came out for me." Glenna opened eyes glassy from the pain. "And they took him."

"Quiet," Hoyt ordered. "Moira, I need you here."

"We'll use this." She selected a bottle. "Pour it on the bruising." After handing him the bottle, she knelt, rested her hands lightly on Glenna's torso.

"What power I can claim I call now to ease your pain. Warmth to heal and harm none, to take away the damage done." She looked entreatingly at Glenna. "Help me. I'm not very good."

Glenna laid her hand over Moira's, closed her eyes. When Hoyt laid his on top for a triad, Glenna sucked in a breath, let it out on a moan. But when Moira would have yanked her hand away, Glenna gripped it tight.

"Sometimes healing hurts," she managed. "Sometimes it has to. Say the chant again. Three times."

As Moria obeyed, sweat sprang onto Glenna's skin, but the bruising faded a little, going the sickly tones of healing.

"Yes, that's better. Thanks."

"We'll have some of that whiskey here," Moira snapped.

"No. I'd better not." Trying for steady breaths, Glenna pushed up. "Help me sit. I need to see how bad it is now."

"Let's see about this." Hoyt skimmed his fingers over her face. And she grabbed his hand. The tears came now, couldn't be stopped.

"I'm so sorry."

"You can't blame yourself, Glenna."

"Who else?" Cian countered, and Moira shoved up to her feet.

"He wasn't wearing the cross." She dug in her pocket, held it up. "He took it off upstairs and left it behind."

"He was showing me some moves. Wrestling," Larkin explained. "And it got in his way, he said. He must have forgotten about it."

"He never meant to go outside, did he? And wouldn't have but for her."

"He was mistaken." Moira laid the cross on the table. "Glenna, he needs to know the truth. The truth is less painful."

"He thought, he must have thought I was going to let her in, or step out. I wasn't. But I was being cocky, so what's the difference? Smug. He's dead because of it."

Cian took another drink. "Tell me why he's dead."

"She knocked on the door. I shouldn't have answered, but I saw it was a woman. A young woman with a map. I wasn't going out, or asking her in, I swear that to you. She said she was lost. She spoke with an accent, French. Charming, really, but I knew . . . I felt. And I couldn't resist toying with her. God, oh God," she said as more tears spilled. "How stupid. How vain."

She took a deep breath. "She said her name was Lora."

"Lora." Cian lowered the bottle. "Young, attractive, French accent?"

"Yes. You know her."

"I do." He drank again. "I do, yes."

"I could see what she was. I don't know how, but I knew. I should have just shut the door on her. But on the chance I was wrong, I thought I should give her directions and get her moving. I'd just started to when King shouted, and he came running down the hall. I turned around. I was startled, I was careless. She got some of my hair. She pulled me outside by it."

"It was so fast," Moira continued. "I was behind King. I barely saw her move—the vampyre. He went out after them, and there were more. Four, five more. It was like lightning strikes."

Moira poured herself a shot of whiskey, downed it to smooth the raw edge of her nerves. "They were on him, all of them, and he shouted for Glenna to get inside. But she got up instead, she got up and ran to help him. It knocked her back, the female of them, like she was a stone in a sling. She tried to help him, even though she was hurt. Maybe she was careless, but so was he."

Moira picked up the cross again. "And it's a terrible price he paid for it. A terrible price he paid for defending a friend."

With Hoyt's help, Glenna got to her feet. "I'm sorry isn't enough. I know what he meant to you."

"You couldn't possibly."

"I think I do, and I know what he meant to the rest of us. I know he's dead because of me. I'll live with that all of my life."

"So will I. And it's my bad luck that I'll live a great deal longer than you."

He took the whiskey bottle when he walked out.

Chapter 16

In the moment between wake and sleep, there was candlelight, and the bliss of nothing. Easy warmth and sheets scented with lavender, and floating on the comfort of nothing.

But the moment passed, and Glenna remembered.

King was dead, hurled into the sea by monsters with the same carelessness of a boy tossing a pebble into a lake.

She'd gone upstairs alone, by her own request, to seek the solitude and oblivion of sleep.

Watching the candle flicker, she wondered if she would ever be able to sleep in the dark again. If she would ever be able to see night coming and not think their time was coming with it. To walk in the moonlight without fear? Would she ever know that simplicity again? Or would even a rainy day forever send chills down her spine?

She turned her head on the pillow. And she saw him silhouetted by the silver light that slid through the window that overlooked his herb garden. Keeping watch in the night, she thought, over her. Over them all. Whatever burdens they all bore, his were heavier. And still he'd come to stand between her and the dark.

"Hoyt."

She sat up as he turned, and she held out her hands to him.

"I didn't want to wake you." He crossed to her, took her hands while studying her face in the dim light. "Are you in pain?"

"No. No, it's gone under, at least for now. I have you and Moira to thank for that."

"You helped yourself as much as we did. And sleep will help as well."

"Don't go. Please. Cian?"

"I don't know." He sent a troubled look toward the door. "Closed in his rooms with the whiskey." Looking at her, he brushed back her hair, turning her face to take a closer study at the bruising. "We're all using what we can tonight, so the pain goes under."

"She would never have let him go. She would never have released King. No matter what we'd done."

"No." He eased down to sit on the side of the bed. "Cian must have known that somewhere inside him, but he had to try. We had to try."

By pretending to be a bargaining chip, she thought, remembering Hoyt's explanation of what they'd seen on the cliffs.

"Now we all know there can be no bargaining in this," he continued. "Are you strong enough to hear what I have to say?"

"Yes."

"We've lost one of us. One of the six we were told we needed to fight this battle, to win this war. I don't know what it means."

"Our warrior. Maybe it means we all have to become warriors. Better ones. I killed tonight, Hoyt—more from luck than skill—but I destroyed what had once been human. I can and will do it again. But with more skill. Every day with more skill. She took one of us, and she thinks it'll make us weak and frightened. But she's wrong. We'll show her she's wrong."

"I'm to lead this battle. You have great skill in magicks. You'll work in the tower on weapons, shields, spells. A protective circle to—"

"Whoa, wait." She held up a hand. "Am I getting this? I'm consigned to the tower, what like Rapunzel?"

"I don't know this person."

"Just another helpless female waiting to be rescued. I'll work on the magicks, and I'll work harder and longer. Just like I'll train harder and longer. But what I won't do is sit up in the tower day and night with my cauldron and crystals, writing spells while the rest of you fight."

"You had your first battle today, and it nearly killed you."

"And gave me a lot more respect for what we're up against. I was called to this, just like the rest of us. I won't hide from it."

"Using your strengths isn't hiding. I was given the charge of this army—"

"Well, let me slap some bars on you and call you Colonel."

"Why are you so angry?"

"I don't want you to protect me. I want you to value me."

"Value you?" He shoved to his feet so the red shimmer from the fire washed over his face. "I value you almost more than I can bear. I've lost too much already. I've watched my brother, the one who shared the womb with me, taken. I've stood over the graves of my family. I won't see you cut down by these things—you, the single light for me in all of this. I won't risk your life again. I won't stand over your grave."

"But I can risk your life? I can stand over your grave?"

"I'm a man."

He said it so simply, the way an adult might tell a child the sky is blue, that she couldn't speak for ten full seconds. Then she plopped back against the pillows. "The only reason I'm not working on turning you into a braying jackass this very moment is I'm giving you some slack due to the fact you come from an unenlightened age."

"Un . . . unenlightened?"

"Let me clue you in to mine, Merlin. Women are equals. We work, we go into combat, we vote, and above all, we make our own decisions regarding our own lives, our own bodies, our own minds. Men don't rule here."

"I've never known a world where men rule," he muttered. "In physical strength, Glenna, you're not equal."

"We make up for it with other advantages."

"However keen your minds, your wiles, your bodies are more fragile. They're made to bear children."

"You just gave me a contradiction in terms. If men were responsible for childbearing, the world would've ended a long time ago, with no help from a bunch of glory-seeking vampires. And let me point out one little fact. The one causing this whole mess is a female."

"Somehow that should be my point."

"Well, it's just not. So forget it. And the one who brought us together is also female, so you're way outnumbered. And I have more ammo, but this ridiculous conversation is giving me a headache."

"You should rest. We'll talk more of this tomorrow."

"I'm not going to rest, and we're not going to talk about this tomorrow."

His single light? he thought. Sometimes she was a beam searing straight into his eyes. "You are a contrary and exasperating woman."

"Yes." Now she smiled, and once more held out her hands. "Sit down here, would you? You're worried about me, and for me. I understand that, appreciate that."

"If you would do this thing for me." He lifted her hands to his lips. "It would ease my mind. Make me a better leader."

"Oh, that's good." She drew her hands away to poke him gently in the chest. "Very good. Women aren't the only ones with wiles."

"Not wile, but truth."

"Ask me for something else, and I'll try to give it to you. But I can't give you this, Hoyt. I worry for you, too, and about you. For all of us. And I question what we can do, what we're capable of. And I wonder why in all the world—the worlds—we're the ones who have to do this thing. But none of that changes anything. We are the ones. And we've lost a very good man already."

"If I lose you . . . Glenna, there's a void in me at the very thought of it."

Sometimes, she knew, the woman had to be stronger. "There are so many worlds, and so many ways. I don't think we could ever lose each other now. What I have now is more than I've ever had before. I think it makes us better than we were. Maybe that's part of why we're here. To find each other."

She leaned into him, sighed when his arms encircled her. "Stay with me. Come lie with me. Love me."

"You need to heal."

"Yes." She drew him down with her, touched her lips to his. "I do."

He hoped he had the tenderness in him that she needed. He wanted to give her that, the magic of it.

"Slowly then." He brushed kisses over her cheek. "Quietly."

He used just his lips, skimming kisses over her mouth, her face, her throat. Warm and soothing. He brushed away the thin gown she wore to trace those easy kisses over her breasts, over her bruises. In comfort and with care.

Soft as birds' wings, lips and fingertips to ease her mind and her body, and to stir them.

And when their eyes met, he knew more than he'd ever known. Held more than he'd ever owned.

He lifted her up onto a pillow of air and silver light, making magic their bed. Around the room, the candles came to life with a sound like a sigh. And the light they shed was like melted gold.

"It's beautiful." She took his hands as they floated, closed her eyes on the sumptuous joy of it. "This is beautiful."

"I would give you all I have, and still it wouldn't be enough."

"You're wrong. It's everything."

More than pleasure, more than passion. Did he know what he made of her when he touched her like this? Nothing they faced, no terror or pain, no death or damnation could overcome this. The light inside her was like a beacon, and it would never be dark again.

Here was life at its sweetest and most generous. The taste of him was a balm to her soul even as his touch roused desires. Steeped in him, she lifted her arms, turned up her palms. Rose petals, white as snow, streamed down like rain.

She smiled when he slipped into her, when they moved together, silky and slow. Light and air, scent and sensation surrounded the rise and fall of bodies and hearts.

Once more their fingers meshed, once more their lips met. And as they drifted together, love healed them both.

I n the kitchen, Moira puzzled over a can of soup. No one had eaten, and she was determined to make some sort of meal should Glenna awake. She'd managed the tea, but she'd been shown how to conquer that.

She'd only watched King open one of the cylinders with the little machine that made the nasty noise. She'd tried and failed three times to make it work, and was seriously considering getting her sword and hacking the cylinder open.

She had a little kitchen magic—precious little, she admitted. Glancing around to be sure she was alone, she pulled what she had together, and visualized the can open.

It shimmied a bit on the counter, but remained stubbornly whole.

"All right, one more time then."

She bent down, studied the opener that was attached to the underside of the cupboard. With the proper tools she could take it apart, find out how it worked. She loved taking things apart. But if she had the proper tools, she could just open the bloody cylinder in the first place.

She straightened, shook her hair back, rolled her shoulders. Muttering to herself, she tried once again to do the deed. This time, when the machine whirled, the can revolved. She clasped her hands together in delight, then bent close again to watch it work.

It was so clever, she thought. So much here was clever. She wondered if she'd ever be allowed to drive the van. King had said he'd teach her how it was done.

Her lips trembled at the thought of it, of him, and she pressed them hard together. She prayed his death had been quick, and his suffering brief. In the morning, she would put up a stone for him in the graveyard she and Larkin had seen when they'd been walking.

And when she returned to Geall, she would erect another, and ask the harper to write a song for him.

She emptied the contents into a pot, and set in the burner, turning it on as Glenna had showed her.

They needed to eat. Grief and hunger would make them weak, and weakness would make them easier prey. Bread, she decided. They would have some bread. It would be a simple meal, but filling.

She turned toward the pantry, then stumbled back when she saw Cian in the doorway. He leaned against the wall, the nearly empty whiskey bottle dangling from his fingers.

"Midnight snack?" His teeth showed white with his smile. "I've a fondness for them myself."

"No one's eaten. I thought we should."

"Always thinking, aren't you, little queen? Mind's always going."

He was drunk, she could see that. Too much whiskey had dulled his eyes and thickened his voice. But she could also see the pain. "You should sit before you fall over."

"Thanks for the kind invitation, in my own bloody house. But I just came down for another bottle." He shook the one he held. "Someone appears to have made off with this one."

"Drink yourself sick if you want to be stupid about it. But you might as well eat something. I know you eat, I've seen you. I've gone to the trouble to make it."

He glanced at the counter, smirked. "You opened a tin."

"I didn't have time to kill the fatted calf. So you'll make do."

She turned around to busy herself, then went very still when she felt him behind her. His fingers skimmed the side of her throat, light as a moth's wings.

"I'd have thought you tasty once upon a time."

Drunk, angry, grieving, she thought. All of those made him dangerous. If she showed him her fear, he'd only be more so. "You're in my way."

"Not yet."

"I don't have time for drunkards. Maybe you don't want food, but Glenna needs it, for healing strength."

"I'd say she's feeling strong enough." Bitterness edged his tone as he glanced up. "Didn't you see the lights brighten a bit ago?"

"I did. I don't know what that has to do with Glenna."

"It means she and my brother are having a go at each other. Sex," he said when she looked blank. "A bit of naked, sweaty sex to top off the evening. Ah, she blushes." He laughed, moved closer. "All that pretty blood just under the skin. Delicious."

"Stop."

"I used to like when they trembled, the way you are. It makes the blood hotter, and it adds to the thrill. I'd nearly forgotten."

"You smell of the whiskey. This is hot enough now. Sit down, and I'll make a bowl for you."

"I don't want the fucking soup. Wouldn't mind that hot, sweaty sex, but likely I'm too drunk to manage it. Well then, I'll just get that fresh bottle, and finish the job."

"Cian. Cian, people turn to each other for comfort when death's come. It isn't disrespect, but need."

"You don't want to lecture me on sex. I know more of it than you could ever imagine. Of its pleasures and its pain and its purposes."

"People turn to drink as well, but it's not as healthy. I know what he was to you."

"You don't."

"He talked to me, more than the others, I think, because I like to listen. He told me how you found him, all those years ago, what you did for him."

"I amused myself."

"Stop it." The tone of command, bred into her bones, snapped into her voice. "Now it's disrespect you're showing for a man who was a friend to me. And he was a son to you. A friend and a brother. All of that. I want to put a stone up for him tomorrow. It could wait until sunset, until you could go out and—"

"What do I care for stones?" he said, and left her.

* * *

Glenna was so grateful for the sun she could have
wept. There were clouds, but they were thin and the
beams burst through them to toss light and shadows on the
ground.

She hurt still, heart and body. But she would deal with it.
For now, she took one of her cameras and she stepped outside to let the sun bathe her face. Charmed by the music of
it, she walked to the stream. Then just laid down on its bank
and basked.

Birds sang, pouring joy into air that was fragrant with
flowers. She could see foxglove dancing lightly in the
breeze. For a moment she felt the earth beneath her sigh and
whisper with the pleasure of a new day.

Grief would come and go, she knew. But today there was
light, and work. And there was still magic in the world.

When a shadow fell over her, she turned her head, smiled
at Moira.

"How are you this morning?"

"Better," Glenna told her. "I'm better. Sore and stiff,
maybe a little wobbly yet, but better."

She turned a bit more to study Moira's tunic and rough
pants. "We need to get you some clothes."

"These do well enough."

"Maybe we'll go into town, see what we can find."

"I have nothing to trade. I can't pay."

"That's what Visa's for. It'll be my treat." She lay flat,
closed her eyes again. "I didn't think anyone else was up."

"Larkin's taken the horse for a run. It should do both of
them good. I don't think he slept at all."

"I doubt any of us did, really. It doesn't seem real does it,
not in the light of day with the sun showering down and the
birds singing?"

"It seems more real to me," Moira said as she sat. "It shows
what we have to lose. I have a stone," she continued, brushing
her hand through the grass. "I thought when Larkin comes
back we could go to where the graves are, make one for King."

Glenna kept her eyes closed, but reached out a hand for
Moira's. "You have a good heart," she told her. "Yes, we'll
make a grave for King."

* * *

Her injuries prevented her from training, but it didn't stop Glenna from working. She spent the next two days preparing food, shopping for supplies, researching magic.

She took photographs.

More than busy work, she told herself. It was practical, and organizational. And the photos were—would be—a kind of documentation, a kind of tribute.

Most of all it helped keep her from feeling useless while the others worked up a sweat with swords and hand-to-hand.

She learned the roads, committing various routes to memory. Her driving skills were rusty, so she honed them, maneuvering the van on snaking roads, skimming the hedgerows on turns, zooming through roundabouts as her confidence built.

She pored through spell books, searching for offense and defense. For solutions. She couldn't bring King back, but she would do everything in her power to safeguard those who were left.

Then she got the bright idea that every member of the team should be able to handle the van. She started with Hoyt.

She sat beside him as he drove the van at a creeping pace up and down the lane.

"There are better uses for my time."

"That may be." And at this rate, she thought, they'd be a millennium before he got over five miles an hour. "But every one of us should be able to take the wheel if necessary."

"Why?"

"Because."

"Do you plan to take this machine into battle?"

"Not with you at the wheel. Practicalities, Hoyt. I'm the only one who can drive during the day. If something happens to me—"

"Don't. Don't tempt the gods." His hand closed over hers.

"We have to factor it. We're here, and where we are is remote. We need transportation. And, well, driving gives all of us a kind of independence, as well as another skill. We should be prepared for anything."

"We could get more horses."

The wistfulness in his voice had her giving him a bolstering pat on the shoulder. "You're doing fine. Maybe you could try going just a little bit faster."

He shot forward, spitting gravel from the tires. Glenna sucked in a breath and shouted: "Brake! Brake! Brake!"

More gravel flew when the van came to an abrupt halt.

"Here's a new word for your vocabulary," she said pleasantly. "Whiplash."

"You said to go faster. This is go." He gestured toward the gas pedal.

"Yeah. Well. Okay." She drew in a fresh breath. "There's the snail, and there's the rabbit. Let's try to find the animal in between. A dog, say. A nice, healthy golden retriever."

"Dogs chase rabbits," he pointed out, and made her laugh. "That's good. You've been sad. I've missed your smile."

"I'll give you a big, toothy one if we come through this lesson in one piece. We're going to take a big leap, go out on the road." She reached up and closed her hand briefly over the crystal she'd hung from the rearview. "Let's hope this works."

He did better than she'd expected, which meant no one was maimed or otherwise injured. Her heart got a serious workout from leaping into her throat, then dropping hard into her belly, but they stayed on the road—for the most part.

She liked watching him calculate the turns, his brows knit, his eyes intense, his long fingers gripping the wheel as though it were a lifeline in a storm-tossed sea.

Hedgerows closed them in, green tunnels dotted with blood-red drops of fuchsia, then the world would open up into rolling fields, and the dots were white sheep or lazy spotted cows.

The city girl in her was enchanted. Another time, she thought, another world, and she could have found a great deal to love about this place. The play of light and shadows on the green, the patchwork of fields, the sudden sparkle of water, the rise and tumble of rocks that formed ancient ruins.

It was good, she decided, to look beyond the house in the forest, to look and love the world they were fighting to save.

When he slowed, she glanced over. "You have to keep up your speed. It can be as dangerous to go too slow as too fast. Which applies, now that I think about it, to pretty much anything."

"I want to stop."

"You need to pull over to the shoulder—the side of the road. Put the signal on, like I showed you, and ease over." She checked the road herself. The shoulder was narrow, but there was no traffic. "Put it in park. That's all the way up. Good. So— What?" she said when he pushed his door open.

She pulled off her seat belt, grabbed the keys—and her camera as an afterthought—then hurried after him. But he was already halfway across a field, moving quickly toward what was left of an old stone tower.

"If you wanted to stretch your legs or empty your bladder, you just had to say so," she began, huffing a bit as she caught up to him.

The wind danced through her hair, blowing it back from her face. As she touched his arm, she felt the muscles there gone rigid. "What is it?"

"I know this place. People lived here. There were children. The oldest of my sisters married their second son. His name is Fearghus. They farmed this land. They . . . they walked this land. Lived."

He moved inside to what she saw now must have been a small keep. The roof was gone, as was one of the walls. The floor was grass and starry white flowers, the dung of sheep.

And the wind blew through, like ghosts chanting.

"They had a daughter, a pretty thing. Our families hoped we would . . ."

He laid his hand against a wall, left it there. "Just stone now," he said quietly. "Gone to ruin."

"But still here, Hoyt. Still here, a part of it. And you,

remembering them. What we're doing, what we have to do, won't it mean they had the very best chance to live a long, full life? To farm the land and walk it. To live."

"They came to my brother's wake." He dropped his hand. "I don't know how to feel."

"I can't imagine how hard this is for you. Every day of it. Hoyt." She laid her hands on his arms, waiting for his eyes to meet hers. "Part of it stands, what was yours. It stands in what's mine. I think that matters. I think we need to find the hope in that. The strength in it. Do you want some time here? I can go back, wait for you in the van."

"No. Every time I falter, or think I can't bear what's been asked of me, you're there." He bent, plucked one of the little white flowers. "These grew in my time." He twirled it once, then tucked it into her hair. "So, we'll carry hope."

"Yes, we will. Here." She lifted her camera. "It's a place that cries for pictures. And the light's gorgeous."

She moved off to choose her angles. She'd make him a present of one, she decided. Something of her to take with him. And she'd make a copy of the same shot for her loft.

Imagine him studying the photo while she studied hers. Each of them remembering standing there on a summer afternoon with wildflowers waving in a carpet of grass.

But the idea of it hurt more than it warmed.

So she turned the camera on him. "Just look at me," she told him. "You don't have to smile. In fact—" She clicked the shutter. "Nice, very nice."

Inspired, she lowered the camera. "I'm going to set it up on timer, take one of us together. She looked around for something to set the camera on, wished she'd thought to bring a tripod.

"Well, I'll have to mix a little something in." She framed him in. Man and stone and field. "Air be still and heed my will. Solid now beneath my hand, steady as rock upon the land. Hold here what I ask of thee. As I will, so mote it be."

She set the camera on the platter of air, engaged the timer. Then dashed to Hoyt. "Just look at the camera." She slipped an arm around his waist, pleased when he mirrored the gesture. "And if you can manage a little smile . . . one, two . . ."

She watched the light blink. "There we are. For posterity."

He walked with her when she retrieved the camera. "How do you know how it will look when you take it out of the box?"

"I don't, not a hundred percent. I guess you could say it's another kind of hope."

She looked back at the ruin. "Do you need more time?"

"No." Time, he thought, there would never be enough of it. "We should go back. There's other work to do."

"Did you love her?" Glenna asked as they started back across the field.

"Who?"

"The girl? The daughter of the family who lived here."

"I didn't, no. A great disappointment that was to my mother, but not—I think—to the girl. I didn't look for a woman in that way, for marriage and family. It seemed . . . It seemed to me that my gift, my work, required solitude. Wives require time and attention."

"They do. Theoretically, they also give it."

"I wanted to be alone. All of my life it seemed I never had enough of it, the solitude and the quiet. And now, now I'm afraid I may always have too much."

"That would be up to you." She stopped to look back at the ruins a last time. "What will you tell them when you go back?" Even saying it tore little pieces from her heart.

"I don't know." He took her hand so they stood together, looking at what was, imagining what had been. "I don't know. What will you tell your people when this is done?"

"I think I probably won't tell them anything. Let them think as I told them when I called before I left that I took an impulsive trip to Europe. Why should they have to live with the fear of what we know?" she said when he turned to her. "We know what goes bump in the night is real, we know that now, and it's a burden. So I'll tell them I love them, and leave it at that."

"Isn't that another kind of alone?"

"It's one I can handle."

This time she got behind the wheel. When he got in beside her, he took one last look at the ruin.

And, he thought, without Glenna, the alone might swallow him whole.

Chapter 17

It plagued him, the idea of going back to his world. Of dying in this one. Of never seeing his home again. Of living in it the rest of his life without the woman who'd given new meaning to it.

If there was a war to be fought with sword and lance, there was another raging inside him, battering the heart he'd never known could yearn for so much.

He watched her from the tower window as she took pictures of Larkin and Moira sparring, or posed them in less combative stances.

Her injuries had healed enough that she no longer moved stiffly, or tired as quickly. But he would always remember how she'd looked on the ground, bleeding.

Her manner of dress no longer seemed strange to him, but proper and so right for who she was. The way she moved in the dark pants and white shirt, her fiery hair pinned messily atop her head seemed the essence of grace to him.

In her face, he'd found beauty and life. In her mind, intelligence and curiosity. And in her heart both compassion and valor.

In her, he realized, he'd found everything he could want, without ever knowing he'd been lacking.

He had no right to her, of course. They had no right to each other beyond the time of the task. If they lived, if the worlds survived, he would go back to his while she remained in hers.

Even love couldn't span a thousand years.

Love. His heart ached at the word so that he pressed his hand to it. This was love then. The gnawing, the burning. The light and the dark.

Not just warm flesh and murmurs in the candlelight, but pain and awareness in the light of day. In the depths of the night. To feel so much for one person, it eclipsed all else.

And it was terrifying.

He was no coward, Hoyt reminded himself. He was a sorcerer by birth, a warrior by circumstance. He had held lightning in the palm of his hand and called the wind to launch it. He'd killed demons, and twice had faced their queen.

Surely, he could face love. Love couldn't maim him or kill him, or strip him of power. What level of cowardice was it then, for a man to shrink back from it?

He strode out of the room, down the stairs, moving with the rush of impulse. He heard music as he passed his brother's door—something low and brooding. He knew it as the music of grief.

And knew, too, if his brother was stirring, so might others of Cian's kind be stirring. Sunset was close.

He moved quickly through the house, into the kitchen where something simmered on the stove, and out the back.

Larkin was amusing himself, shimmering into a gold wolf while Glenna called out her delight and moved around him with the little machine that took the pictures. The camera, he reminded himself.

He shaped back into a man, and hefting his sword assumed a haughty pose.

"You look better as the wolf," Moira told him.

He raised his sword in mock attack and chased after her. Their shouts and laughter were so opposed to his brother's music, Hoyt could only stand in wonder.

There was still laughter in the world. Still time, and need, for play and fun. There was still light even as the darkness crept closer.

"Glenna."

She turned, the humor still dancing in her eyes. "Oh, perfect! Stand right there. Just there, with the house behind you."

"I want to—"

"Ssh. I'm going to lose the light soon. Yes, yes, just like that. All aloof and annoyed. It's wonderful! I wish there was time to go back in and get your cloak. You were made to wear one."

She changed angles, crouched down, shot up at him. "No, don't look at me. Look off, over my head, think deep thoughts. Look into the trees."

"Wherever it is I look, I still see nothing but you."

She lowered her camera for a moment, with pleasure blooming in her cheeks. "You're just trying to distract me. Give me that Hoyt look, just for a minute. Off into the trees, the serious sorcerer."

"I want to speak with you."

"Two minutes." She changed angles, kept shooting, then straightened. "I want a prop," she muttered, and studied the weapons on the table.

"Glenna. Would you go back with me?"

"Two minutes," she repeated, debating between long sword and dagger. "I need to go in and check the soup anyway."

"I don't mean back into the bloody kitchen. Will you go with me?"

She glanced over, automatically lifting her camera, framing his face and capturing the intensity of it. A good meal, she thought, another solid night's sleep, and she'd be ready for full training by the next morning.

"Where?"

"Home. To my home."

"What?" She lowered the camera, felt her heart do a quick, hard jump. "What?"

"When this is done." He kept his eyes on hers as he

closed the distance between them. "Will you come with me? Will you be with me? Belong to me?"

"Back with you? To the twelfth century?"

"Yes."

Slowly, carefully, she set the camera down. "Why do you want me?"

"Because all I see is you, all I want is you. I think if I have to live five minutes in a world without you in it, it would be eternity. I can't face eternity without seeing your face." He brushed his fingers over her cheek. "Without hearing your voice, without touching you. I think if I was sent here to fight this war, I was sent here to find you as well. Not just to fight with me. To open me. Glenna."

He gathered her hands in his, brought them to his lips. "In all this fear and grief and loss, I see you."

She kept her eyes on his as he spoke, searching. When the words were done, she touched a hand to his heart. "There's so much in there," she said quietly. "So much, and I'm so lucky to be part of it. I'll go with you. I'll go with you anywhere."

The joy of it spread inside him, warmed as he touched his fingertips to her cheek again. "You would give up your world, all you know? Why?"

"Because I've thought of living five minutes without you, and even that was eternity. I love you." She saw his eyes change. "Those are the strongest words in any magic. I love you. With that incantation, I already belong to you."

"Once I speak it, it's alive. Nothing can ever kill it." Now he framed her face. "Would you have me if I stayed here with you?"

"But you said—"

"Would you have me, Glenna?"

"Yes, of course, yes."

"Then we'll see which world is ours when this is done. Wherever, whenever it is, I will love you in it. You." He touched his lips to hers. "And only you."

"Hoyt." Her arms came hard around him. "If we have this, we can do anything."

"I haven't said it yet."

She laughed, rained kisses over his cheeks. "Close enough."

"Wait." He drew her back, just an inch. Those vivid blue eyes locked with hers. "I love you."

A single beam of light shot out of the sky, washed over them, centered them in a circle of white.

"So it's done," he murmured. "Through this life and all the ones to come, I'm yours. And you're mine. All that I am, Glenna."

"All that I'll be. I pledge that to you." She held close again, pressed her cheek to his. "Whatever happens, this is ours."

She tipped back her head so their lips could meet. "I knew it would be you," she said softly, "from the moment I walked into your dream."

They held each other in the circle of light, held close while it bathed them. When it faded, and twilight oozed over the day, they gathered the rest of the weapons, and took them into the house together.

Cian watched them from his bedroom window. Love had flashed and shimmered around them in a light that had all but burned his skin, seared his eyes.

And it had pressed against a heart that hadn't beat in nearly a thousand years.

So his brother had fallen, he thought, for the single blow against which there was no shield. Now they would live their short and painful lives within that light.

Perhaps it would be worth it.

Then he stepped back into the shadows of his room, and the cool dark.

When he came down, it was full dark, and she was in the kitchen alone. Singing at the sink, Cian noted, in an absent and happy voice. The sort, he decided, that a fanciful person would say had little pink hearts spilling out from between her lips with the tune.

She was loading the dishwasher—a homey chore. And the kitchen smelled of herbs and flowers. Her hair was bundled up, and now and then her hips moved with the rhythm of the song.

Would he have had a woman like that if he'd lived? he wondered. One who'd sing in the kitchen, or stand in the light, looking at him with her face alive with love?

He'd had women, of course. Scores of them. And some had loved him—to their loss, he supposed. But if their faces had been alive with that love, those faces were a blur to him now.

And love was a choice he had eliminated from his life.

Or had told himself he had. But the fact was he had loved King, as a father does a son, or a brother a brother. The little queen had been right about that, and damned her for it.

He had given his love and his trust to a human, and as humans were wont to do, it had died on him.

Saving this one, he thought now as Glenna set dishes in the rack. Another thing humans had a habit of doing was sacrificing themselves for other humans.

It was, or had been, a trait that had intrigued him often enough. Easier to understand, in his circumstances, their habit on the other side of the coin—of killing each other.

Then she turned, and jolted. The dish she held slipped out of her hands and shattered on the tiles.

"God. I'm sorry. You startled me."

She moved quickly—and jerkily, he noted, for a woman of easy grace. She took the broom and dustpan from the closet, and began to sweep the shards.

He hadn't spoken to her, nor to any of the others, since the night of King's death. He'd left them to train themselves, or do as they pleased.

"I didn't hear you come in. The others finished dinner. They—they went up to do some training. I had Hoyt out for an hour or so today. Um, driving lesson. I thought . . ." She dumped the shards, turned again. "Oh God, say *something*."

"Even if you live, you're from two different worlds. How will you resolve it?"

"Did Hoyt speak to you?"

"He didn't have to. I have eyes."

"I don't know how we'll resolve it." She put the broom away. "We'll find a way. Does it matter to you?"

"Not in the least. It's of interest to me." He got a bottle of wine from the counter rack, studied the label. "I've lived among you for a considerable amount of time. Without interest, I'd have died of boredom long ago."

She steadied herself. "Loving each other makes us stronger. I believe that. We need to be stronger. So far, we haven't done very well."

He opened the wine, got down a glass. "No, you haven't done very well, particularly."

"Cian," she said as he turned to go. "I know you blame me for King. You have every right to—to blame me and to hate me for it. But if we don't find a way to work together, to mesh, he won't just be the only one of us to die. He'll just be the first."

"I beat him to that by a few hundred years." He tipped the glass toward her in a kind of salute, then walked out with the bottle.

"Well, that was useless," Glenna muttered, and turned back to finish the dishes.

He would hate her, she thought, and likely hate Hoyt as well because Hoyt loved her. Their team was fractured even before it had a genuine chance to become a unit.

If they had time, nothing but time, she would let it lie, wait until Cian's resentment cooled, began to fade. But they didn't have that luxury of wasting any more of the precious little time they'd been given. She'd have to find a way to work around it, or him.

She dried her hands, flung the cloth down.

There was a thump outside the back door, as if something heavy had fallen. Instinctively she stepped back, reached for the sword braced against the counter, and one of the stakes lying on it.

"They can't get in," she whispered, and even the whisper shook. "If they want to spy on me while I'm cleaning up the kitchen, so what?"

But she wished she and Hoyt had had better luck devising a spell to create a protected area around the house.

Still, she couldn't let it frighten her, wouldn't let it. She certainly wasn't going to open the door again to have a chat with something that wanted to rip her throat out.

But there came a kind of scratching, low on the door. And a moan. And the hand gripping the sword went damp with sweat.

"Help me. Please."

The voice was weak, barely audible through the wood. But she thought . . .

"Let me in. Glenna? Glenna? In the name of God, let me in before they come."

"King?" The sword clattered on the floor as she leaped toward the door. Still, she held the stake in a firm grip.

Fool me once, she thought, and kept well out of reach as she opened the door.

He lay on the stones just outside, his clothes bloody and torn. More blood had dried on the side of his face, and his breathing was a thin wheeze.

Alive, was all she could think.

She started to crouch down, pull him inside, but Cian was beside her. He shoved her aside, lowered down himself. Laid a hand on King's battered cheek.

"We need to get him in. Hurry, Cian! I've got things that can help."

"They're close. Tracking me." He groped blindly for Cian's hand. "I didn't think I'd make it."

"You have. Come inside now." He gripped King under the arms, dragged him into the kitchen. "How did you get away?"

"Don't know." King sprawled on the floor, eyes closed. "Missed the rocks. Thought I'd drown, but . . . I got out, got out of the water. Hurt pretty bad. Passed out, don't know how long. Walked, walked all day. Hid at night. They come at night."

"Let me see what I can do for him," Glenna began.

"Close the door," Cian told her.

"Did everybody make it? Did everybody . . . thirsty."

"Aye, I know." Cian gripped his hand, looked into his eyes. "I know."

"We'll start with this." Glenna mixed something briskly in a cup. "Cian, if you'd go get the others. I could use Hoyt and Moira. We'll want to get King into bed, make him comfortable."

She bent to him as she spoke, and the cross around her neck dangled down, swung toward King's face.

He hissed like a snake, bared fangs and skuddled back.

Then to Glenna's horror, he got to his feet. And grinned.

"You never told me how it felt," he said to Cian.

"Words fall short. It needs to be experienced."

"No." Glenna could only shake her head. "Oh God, no."

"You could've taken me here a long time ago, but I'm glad you didn't. I'm glad it was now, when I'm in my prime."

King circled around as he spoke, blocking the door out of the kitchen. "They hurt me first. Lilith—she knows amazing ways to give pain. You know you don't stand a chance against her."

"I'm sorry," Glenna whispered. "I'm sorry."

"Don't be. She said I could have you. Eat you or change you. My choice."

"You don't want to hurt me, King."

"Oh yes, he does," Cian said easily. "He wants the pain in you nearly as much as he wants your blood in his throat. It's how he's made. Had she already given you the gift before they threw you off the cliff?"

"No. I was hurt though, hurt bad. Could hardly stand. They had a rope around me when they tossed me off. If I lived, she'd give me the gift. I lived. She'll take you back," he said to Cian.

"Yes, I know she will."

Glenna looked from one to the other. Trapped, she realized, between them. He'd known—she saw that now. Cian had known what King was before he'd let him in the house.

"Don't do this. How can you do this? To your brother."

"I can't have him," King told Cian. "Neither can you. She wants Hoyt herself. She wants to drink him, the sorcerer. With his blood, she'll ascend even higher. Every world there is will be ours."

The sword was too far away, and she no longer had the stake. She had nothing.

"We're to take Hoyt and the other female to her, alive. This one, and the boy? They're ours if we want them."

"I haven't drunk human blood for a very long time." Cian reached over, trailed a fingertip down the nape of Glenna's neck. "This one, I'd think, would be heady."

King licked his lips. "We can share her."

"Yes, why not?" He tightened his grip on Glenna, and when she fought, when she sucked in her breath, he laughed. "Oh aye, scream for help. Bring the others on down to save you. It'll save us the trip up."

"Rot in hell. I'm sorry for what happened to you," she said to King as he moved toward her. "Sorry for any part I played in it. But I won't make it easy for you."

She used Cian as a brace, swung up her legs and kicked out. She knocked King back a few steps, but he only laughed and moved toward her again.

"They let them run in the caves. So we can chase them. I like when they run. When they scream."

"I won't scream." She rammed back with her elbows, kicked out again.

She heard the rush of footsteps, and thought only, No! So screamed after all as she kicked and struggled.

"The cross. I can't get past the fucking cross. Knock her out!" King demanded. "Get it off her. I'm hungry!"

"I'll fix it." He tossed Glenna aside as the others rushed into the room.

And looking into King's eyes, drove the stake he'd had at his back into his friend's heart.

"It's all I could do for you," he told him, and tossed the stake aside.

"King. Not King." Moira dropped to her knees beside the dust. Then she laid her hands on it, spoke in a voice choked with tears. "Let what he was, the soul of him and the heart, be welcomed in a world again. The demon that took him is dead. Let him have light to find his way back."

"You won't raise a man from a pile of ash."

She looked up at Cian. "No, but maybe free his soul so it can be reborn. You didn't kill your friend, Cian."

"No. Lilith did."

"I thought . . ." Glenna still shook as Hoyt helped her to her feet.

"I know what you thought. Why shouldn't you?"

"Because I should have trusted you. I've said we aren't a unit, but I didn't understand I'm as much to blame for that as any. I didn't trust you. I thought you'd kill me, but you chose to save me."

"You're wrong. I chose to save him."

"Cian." She stepped toward him. "I caused this. I can't—"

"You didn't, no. You didn't kill him, you didn't change him. Lilith did. And sent him here to die once more. He was new, and not yet used to his skin. Injured as well. He couldn't have taken all of us, and she knew it."

"She knew what you would do." Hoyt moved to his brother's side, laid a hand on his shoulder. "And what it would cost you."

"In her way, she couldn't lose. So she'd think. I don't kill him, he takes at least one of you—maybe the lot if I turn. If I go the other way, destroy him, it costs me . . . oh quite a bit, quite a lot indeed."

"The death of a friend," Larkin began, "is a hard death. We all feel it."

"I believe you do." He looked down to where Moira still knelt on the floor. "But it comes to me first because he was mine first. She did this to him not because of you," he said to Glenna. "But because of me. I could've blamed you, and did, if she'd just killed him. Clean. But for this, it's not yours. It's hers and it's mine."

He walked over to pick up the stake he used, studied the killing point. "And when it comes time, when we face her, she's mine. If any of you step up to do the killing blow, I'll stop you. So you see, she miscalculated. I owe her for this, and I'll give her death for it."

Now, he picked up the sword. "We train tonight."

She trained, going one-on-one with Larkin, sword to sword. Cian had paired Moira with Hoyt, and stood back, or moved around them as steel clashed. He called out insults, which Glenna assumed was his style of motivation.

Her arm ached, and her still tender ribs throbbed. While sweat dribbled down her back, into her eyes, she continued to push. The pain, the effort, helped block out the image of King in the kitchen, moving toward her with fangs ready.

"Keep your arm up," Cian shouted at her. "If you can't hold a shagging sword properly you won't last five minutes. And stop dancing with her, for Christ's sake, Larkin. This isn't a bloody nightclub."

"She isn't fully healed," Larkin snapped back. "And what the hell's a nightclub?"

"I need to stop." Moira lowered her sword, wiped her sweaty brow with the back of her free hand. "Rest for a moment."

"You don't." Cian spun toward her. "Do you think you're doing her a favor, asking to rest? Do you think they'll be agreeable to a bloody time out just because your pal here needs to catch her breath?"

"I'm fine. There's no need to snap at her." Glenna struggled to catch her breath, to will some strength back into her legs. "I'm fine. Stop holding back," she told Larkin. "I don't need to be coddled."

"She needs to be looked at." Hoyt gestured Larkin back. "It's too soon for her to train like this."

"That isn't for you to say," Cian pointed out.

"I am saying it. She's exhausted, and she's in pain. And that's enough."

"I said I'm fine, and can speak for myself. Which, though he enjoys being a bastard, is what your brother pointed out. I don't need or want you to speak for me."

"Then you'll have to grow accustomed to it, because so I will when you need it."

"I know what I need and when I need it."

"Maybe the two of you will just talk the enemy to death," Cian said dryly.

Out of patience, Glenna thrust at Cian with her sword. "Come on. Come on then, you and me. You won't hold back."

"No." He tapped his blade to hers. "I won't."

"I said enough." Hoyt slashed his sword between them, and his fury sent a ripple of fire down the steel.

"Which one of us would you like to take on?" Now, Cian's tone was like silk. And his eyes darkened with a dangerous pleasure when Hoyt pivoted toward him.

"Should be interesting," Larkin said, but his cousin stepped in.

"Wait," she said. "Just wait. We're upset, all of us. Tired out, and overheated like horses at too long a gallop on top of it. It serves no purpose to hurt each other. If we won't rest, then at least, let's have the doors open. Have some air."

"You want the doors open?" Everything about him suddenly genial, Cian cocked his head. "A bit of air's what you're wanting? Sure we'll have ourselves some fresh air."

He strode to the terrace doors, threw them open. Then in a move fast as a fingersnap, reached out into the dark. "Come in, won't you?" he said and yanked a pair of vampires through the doorway.

"Plenty to eat here." He wandered to the table as both of them leapt up, drew swords. With the tip of his own he speared an apple from the bowl. Then leaned back against the wall, plucking it off to have a bite.

"Let's see what you can do with them," he suggested. "It's two against one, after all. You may just have a shot at surviving."

Hoyt pivoted, instinctively putting Glenna behind him. Larkin was already moving in, flashing his sword. His opponent blocked the slash easily, punched out with its free hand and sent Larkin flying halfway across the room.

It turned, rushed Moira. The first strike hit her sword, and the force knocked her down, sent her skidding over the floor. She groped desperately for her stake as it flew—seemed to fly—through the air toward her.

Glenna buried her terror, dug out her fury. She shot her power out—the first learned, the last lost—and brought the fire. The vampire burst into flames midair.

"Nicely done, Red," Cian commented, and watched his brother battle for his life.

"Help him. Help me."

"Why don't you?"

"They're too close to risk the fire."

"Try this." He tossed her a stake, took another bite of apple.

She didn't think, couldn't think, as she ran forward. As she plunged the stake into the back of the vampire who'd beaten Hoyt to his knees.

And missed the heart.

It howled, but there seemed to be more pleasure than pain in it. It turned, lifted its sword high. Both Moira and Larkin charged, but Glenna saw her death. They were too far away, and she had nothing left.

Then Hoyt sliced his sword through its neck. Blood splattered her face before there was dust.

"Fairly pitiful, but effective enough all in all." Cian wiped his hands. "Now pair off. Playtime's over."

"You knew they were out there." Moira's hand, still holding the stake, trembled. "You knew."

"Well, of course, I knew they were out there. If you'd use your brains, or at least some of your senses, you'd have known it as well."

"You'd have let them kill us."

"More to the point, you nearly let them kill you. You." He gestured at Moira. "Stood there, letting the fear soak you, scent you. You." And now Larkin. "You charged in without using your head, and nearly lost it for the trouble. As for you," he said to Hoyt. "Protecting the womenfolk may be chivalrous, but you'll both die—with your honor intact, of course. While Red, at least, used her head initially—and the power your bloody gods gave her—she then fell apart, and stood meekly waiting to be dead."

He stepped forward. "So, we'll work on your weaknesses. Which are legion."

"I've had enough." Glenna's voice was hardly more than a whisper. "Enough of blood and death, enough for one night. Enough." She dropped the stake and walked out.

"Leave her be." Cian waved a hand when Hoyt turned to follow. "For Christ's sake, an ounce of brain would tell you she wants only her own company—and a strong, dramatic exit like that deserves to stand. Let her have it."

"He's right." Moira spoke quickly. "As much as it pains

me to say it. She needs the quiet." She walked over to pick up the sword that had been knocked out of her hand. "Weaknesses." She nodded her head, faced Cian. "Very well then. Show me."

Chapter 18

Hoyt expected to find her in bed when he came in. He'd hoped she'd be sleeping, so that he could put her under more deeply and work on her injuries.

But she was standing by the window in the dark.

"Don't turn on the light," she said with her back to him. "Cian was right, there are more outside still. If you pay attention, you can sense them. They move like shadows, but there's movement—more a sense of movement. They'll go soon, I think. To whatever hole they burrow in during the day."

"You should rest."

"I know you say that because you're concerned, and I'm calm enough now not to take your head off for it. I know I behaved poorly upstairs. I don't really care."

"You're tired, as I am. I want to wash, and I want to sleep."

"You have your own room. And that was uncalled for," she continued before he could speak. Now she turned. Her face seemed very pale in the dark, pale against the dark robe she wore. "I'm not as calm as I thought. You had no right, no right, to stand in front of me up there."

"Every right. Love gives me the right. And even without that, if a man doesn't shield a woman from harm—"

"Stop right there." She held up a hand, palm out, as if to block his words. "This isn't about men and women. It's about humans. The seconds you took to think of me, to worry for me could have cost you your life. We can't spare it, neither of us. Any of us. If you don't trust that I can defend myself—that all of us can, we're nowhere."

That her words made sense didn't matter a whit as far as he was concerned. He could still see the way that monster had leaped on her. "And where would you be if I hadn't destroyed that thing?"

"Different. A different matter." She moved closer now so that he could scent her, the lotions she used on her skin. So utterly female.

"This is foolishness, and a waste of time."

"It's not foolish to me, so listen up. Fighting with and protecting fellow soldiers is one thing, a vital thing. We all have to be able to count on each other. But to brush me back from battle is another. You have to understand and accept the difference."

"How can I, when it's you, Glenna? If I lost you—"

"Hoyt." She gripped his arms, a kind of impatient comfort. "Any or all of us might die in this. I'm fighting to understand and accept that. But if you die, I won't live with the responsibility of knowing it was for me. I won't do it."

She sat on the side of the bed. "I killed tonight. I know how it feels to end something. To use my power to do that, something I never thought I'd do, need to do." She held out her hands to study them. "I did it to save another human being, and still it weighs on me. I know that if I'd done it with stake or sword I'd accept it more easily. But I used magic to destroy."

She lifted her face to his, and the sorrow was deep in her eyes. "This gift was always so bright, and now there's a darkness in it. I have to understand and accept that, too. And you have to let me."

"I accept your power, Glenna, and what you can and will do with it. I think all of us would be better served by it if you worked solely on the magicks."

"And left the bloody work to you? Off the front line, out of harm's way, stirring my cauldron?"

"Twice this night I nearly lost you. So you'll do as I say."

It took a moment to find her voice. "Well, in a pig's eye. Twice this night I faced death, and I survived."

"We'll discuss this further tomorrow."

"Oh no, oh no, we won't." She flicked out a hand, slammed the door to the bathroom inches before he reached it.

He whirled back, a man obviously at the end of his tether. "Don't slap your power out at me."

"Don't slap your manhood out at me. And that didn't come out the way I meant it." Because there was laughter tickling the back of her throat right along with the temper, she took a breath. "I won't snap to, Hoyt, when you order it, any more than I expect you will for me. You were frightened for me, and oh boy, do I understand that, because I was frightened for me. And for you, for all of us. But we have to get past it."

"How?" he demanded. "How is that done? This love is new for me, this need and this terror that goes with it. When we were called for this, I thought it would be the hardest thing I'd ever done. But I was wrong. Loving you is harder, loving you and knowing I could lose you."

All of her life, she thought, she'd waited to be loved like this. What human didn't? "I never knew I could feel so completely for anyone. This is new for me, too, hard and scary and new. And I wish I could say you won't lose me. I wish I could. But I know the stronger I am, the better chance I have of staying alive. The stronger each one of us is, the better chance we have of surviving this. Of winning."

She stood again. "I looked at King tonight, a man I'd come to like quite a lot. I looked at what they'd made of him. What they made of him wanted my blood, my death, would have rejoiced in it. Seeing that, knowing that, hurt beyond the believing of it. He was a friend. He became a friend so quickly."

Her voice trembled, so that she had to turn away, move back to the window and the dark. "There was a part of me, even as I tried to save myself, that saw what he had been—the man who'd cooked with me, sat with me, laughed with me. I couldn't use my powers against him, couldn't pull it out of me to do that. If Cian hadn't . . ." She turned back now, straight and slim.

"I won't be weak again. I won't hesitate a second time. You have to trust me for that."

"You called out for me to run. Would you say that was putting yourself in front of me in battle?"

She opened her mouth, closed it again. Cleared her throat. "Seemed like the thing to do at the time. All right, all right. Point made and taken. We'll both work on it. And I've some ideas on weaponry that might be helpful. But before we put this, and ourselves to bed, I want to cover one more thing."

"I don't find myself at all surprised."

"Fighting with your brother over me isn't something I appreciate or consider flattering."

"It wasn't only about you."

"I know that. But I was the catalyst. And I'm going to have a word with Moira about it, too. Of course, her idea of distracting Cian from us changed the entire scope of things."

"It was madness for him to bring those things into the house. His own temper and arrogance could have cost us lives."

"No." She spoke quietly now, and with absolute certainty. "He was right to do it."

Stunned, he gaped at her. "How can you say so? How can you defend him?"

"He made a very big and illuminating point, one we won't be able to forget. We won't always know when they'll come, and we have to be ready to kill or be killed every minute, every day. We weren't, not really. Even after King, we weren't. If there'd been more of them, the odds more even, it might've been a very different story."

"He stood by, did nothing."

"Yes, he did. Another point. He's the strongest of us, and the smartest in these circumstances. It's up to us to work toward closing that gap. I have some ideas, at least for the two of us."

She came to him, rising on her toes to brush her lips over his cheek. "Go ahead, wash up. I want to sleep on it. I want to sleep with you."

She dreamed of the goddess, of walking through a world of gardens, where birds were bright as the flowers, and the flowers like jewels.

From a high black cliff, water the color of liquid sapphire tumbled down to strike a pool clear as glass where gold and ruby fish darted.

The air was warm and heavy with fragrance.

Beyond the gardens was a silver sickle of beach where the turquoise water lapped its edges gently as a lover. There were children building sparkling castles of sand, or splashing in the foamy surf. Their laughter carried on the air like the birdsong.

Rising from the beach were steps of shimmering white with diamonds of ruby red along their edges. High above them were houses, painted in dreamy pastels, skirted with yet more flowers, with trees that dripped blossoms.

She could hear music drifting down from the tall hill, the harps and flutes singing of joy.

"Where are we?"

"There are many worlds," Morrigan told her as they walked. "This is just another. I thought you should see that you fight for more than yours, or his, or the world of your friends."

"It's beautiful. It feels . . . happy."

"Some are, some are not. Some demand a hard life, full of pain and effort. But it is still life. This world is old," the goddess said, her robes flowing as she opened her arms. "It earned this beauty, this peace, through that pain and that effort."

"You could stop what's coming. Stop her."

Her bright hair dancing in the wind, she turned to Glenna. "I have done what I can to stop it. I have chosen you."

"It's not enough. Already we've lost one of us. He was a good man."

"Many are."

"Is this how fate and destiny work? The higher powers? So coldly?"

"The higher powers bring laughter to those children, they bring the flowers and the sun. Love and pleasures. And yes, death and pain. It must be so."

"Why?"

Morrigan turned, smiled. "Or it would all mean so little. You are a gifted child. But the gift has weight."

"I used that gift to destroy. All of my life I've believed, been taught, I *knew* what I had, what I was, could never harm. But I used it to harm."

Morrigan touched Glenna's hair. "This is the weight, and it must be carried. You were charged to strike at evil with it."

"I won't be the same again," Glenna stated, looking out to sea.

"No, not the same. And you're not ready. None of you. You're not yet whole."

"We lost King."

"He isn't lost. He's only moved to a different world."

"We're not gods, and we grieve for the death of a friend. The cruelty of it."

"There will be more death, more grieving."

Glenna closed her eyes. It was harder, even harder, to speak of death when she looked at such beauty. "We're just full of good news today. I want to go back."

"Yes, you should be there. She'll bring blood, and another kind of power."

"Who will?" Fear had Glenna jerking back. "Lilith? Is she coming?"

"Look there." Morrigan pointed to the west. "When the lightning strikes."

The sky went black, and the lightning arrowed out of the sky to strike the heart of the sea.

When she whimpered, turned, Hoyt's arms came around her.

"It's dark."

"Nearly dawn." He touched his lips to her hair.

"A storm's coming. She's coming with it."

"Did you dream?"

"Morrigan took me." She pressed closer. He was warm. He was real. "Some place beautiful. Perfect and beautiful. Then the dark came, and the lightning struck the water. I heard them growling in the dark."

"You're here now. Safe."

"None of us are." Her mouth lifted, met his desperately. "Hoyt."

She rose above him, slim and fragrant. White skin against pearled shadows. She took his hands, pressed them to her breasts. Felt his fingers cup her.

Real and warm.

As her heartbeat quickened, the candles around the room began to flicker. In the hearth, the fire woke to simmer.

"There's a power in us." She lowered to him, her lips racing over his face, down his throat. "See it. Feel it. What we make together."

Life, was all she could think. Here was life, hot and human. Here was a power that could strike back the icy fingers of death.

She rose up again, taking him into her, strong and deep. Then bowing back as the thrill washed through her like wine.

He wrapped around her, coming to her so his mouth could take her breast, so he could taste the pounding of her heart. Life, he thought as well. Here was life.

"All that I am." Already breathless, he feasted on her. "This is more. From the first moment, for the rest of time."

She took his face, watched herself in his eyes. "In any world. In all of them."

It poured through her, so fast, so hot, she cried out.

Dawn broke quietly while their passion raged.

"It's the fire," Glenna told him.

They were in the tower, sitting over coffee and scones. She had the door firmly locked, and had added a charm to make certain no one and nothing entered until she was finished.

"It's exciting." His eyes were still sleepy, his body relaxed.

Sex, Glenna thought, could work wonders. She was feeling pretty damn good herself.

"Wake-up sex agrees with you, but I'm not talking about that kind of fire. Or not exclusively. Fire's a weapon, a big one, against what we're fighting."

"You killed one with it last night." He poured more coffee. He was, he realized, developing quite a taste for it. "Effective, and quick, but also—"

"A little unpredictable, yes. If the aim's off, or one of our own is too close—or steps or is shoved in the line, it would be extremely tragic. But . . ." She tapped her fingers against her cup. "We learn to control it, to channel it. That's what we do, after all. Practice, practice. And more, we can use it to enhance the other weapons. The way you did last night, with the fire on the sword."

"I'm sorry?"

"The fire on your sword when you clashed with Cian." She lifted her eyebrows at his blank expression. "You didn't call it, it just came. Passion—in that case anger. Passion, when we're making love. A flame shot down your sword last night, just for an instant. A flaming sword."

She pushed up from the table to pace around the room. "We haven't been able to do anything about creating a protected zone around the house."

"We may yet find the way."

"Tricky, since we have a vampire on the premises. We can't set down a spell to repel vampires without repelling Cian. But yes, in time—if we have the time—we may find a way around that. In the meantime, the fire's not only effective, it's beautifully symbolic. And you bet your gorgeous ass, it'll put the fear of the gods into the enemy."

"Fire takes focus and concentration. A little difficult when you're fighting for your life."

"We'll work on it until it isn't so difficult. You wanted me to work more on magic, and in this case I'm willing. It's time to make ourselves a serious arsenal."

She came back, sat on the table. "When it's time to take this war to Geall, we're going loaded."

She spent the day at it, with him and without him. She buried herself in her own books, and the ones she dragged up from Cian's library.

When the sun set, she lit candles for work light and ignored Cian's banging on the door. She closed her ears to his curses, and his shouts that it was bloody well time for training.

She *was* training.

And she'd come out when she was damn good and ready.

The woman was young, and fresh. And very, very alone.

Lora watched from the shadows, gleefully pleased with her luck. To think she'd been annoyed when Lilith had sent her out with a trio of foot soldiers on a simple scouting mission. She'd wanted to hit one of the outlying pubs, have some fun, have a feast. How long did Lilith expect them to keep to the caves, lying low, picking off the occasional tourist?

The most fun she'd had in *weeks* had been smacking that witch around, and stealing the black man right from under the noses of that tedious, holy brigade.

She wished they could have based somewhere, *anywhere* but in this dreary place. Somewhere like Paris or Prague. Somewhere so full of people she could pluck them like plums. Somewhere full of sound and heartbeats, and the smell of flesh.

She would swear there were more cows and sheep than people in this stupid country.

It was boring.

But now, there was this interesting possibility.

So pretty. So unfortunate.

This one would be a good candidate for the change as well as a quick snack. It would be fun to have a new companion, a woman particularly. One she could train, and play with.

A new toy, she decided, to stave off this endless ennui, at least until the real fun began.

Where, she wondered, had the pretty thing been going after dark in her little car? Such bad luck to have a puncture on this quiet country road.

Nice coat, too, Lora thought as she watched the woman haul out the jack and spare. They were close enough to the same size that she could have the coat as well as what was in it.

All that lovely warm blood.

"Bring her to me." She gestured at the three who stood with her.

"Lilith said we weren't to feed until—"

She whirled, fangs glinting, eyes burning red. And the vampire who'd once been a man of two hundred and twenty pounds of muscle when alive, backed off hurriedly.

"You question me?"

"No." She was here, after all—and he could smell her hunger. Lilith was not.

"Bring her to me," Lora repeated, tapping him on the chest, then wagging that finger playfully in front of his face. "And no tasting. I want her alive. It's time I had a new playmate." Her lips moved over her fangs in a pretty pout. "And try not to damage the coat. I like it."

They moved out of the shadows and onto the road, three males who'd been ordinary in life.

They scented human. And female.

Their hunger, always waiting, woke—and only the fear of Lora's reprisal prevented them from charging like wolves.

She glanced over as they approached. She smiled, quick and friendly as she straightened from her crouch at the side of the car, and raked a hand through short, dark hair that left her throat and neck exposed in the gloomy light.

"I was hoping someone would come along."

"Must be your lucky night." The one Lora had chastised grinned.

"I'll say. Dark, deserted road like this, middle of nowhere. Whew. It's a little scary."

"It can get scarier."

They spread out in a triangle to close her in with the car at her back. She took a step back, eyes going wide, and they growled low in the throat.

"Oh God. Are you going to hurt me? I don't have much money, but—"

"Money's not what we're after, but we'll take that, too."

She still held the tire iron, and when she lifted it, the one closest to her laughed. "Stay back. Just keep away from me."

"Metal's not a big problem for us."

He charged toward her, hands lifted toward her throat. And exploded into dust.

"No, but the pointy end of this is." She wagged the stake she'd held behind her back.

She lunged, kicking one aside with a flashing foot to the belly, blocking a blow with her forearm then leading with the stake. She let the last one come to her, let the momentum of his rage and hunger rush him forward. She swung the tire iron full at his face. She was on him in an instant when he landed on the road.

"Metal's a little problem after all," she said. "But we'll finish up with this."

She staked him, rose. Dusted off her coat. "Damn vampires."

She started back to her car, then stopped, her head lifting like a dog scenting the air.

She spread her legs, shifted her grip on the tire iron, on the stake. "Don't you want to come out and play?" she called out. "I can smell you out there. These three didn't give me much action, and I'm revved."

The scent began to fade. In moments, the air was clear again. She watched, and waited, then with a shrug hooked the stake into the sheath on her belt. When she finished changing the tire, she glanced up at the sky.

Clouds had rolled over the moon, and in the west thunder grumbled. "Storm's coming, she murmured.

I n the training room, Hoyt landed hard on his back. He felt every bone in his body rattle. Larkin pounced, then brought the blunted stake down to tap Hoyt's heart.

"I've killed you six times already tonight. You're off your game." He cursed lightly when he felt the blade at his throat.

Moira eased it back, then leaned over him to give him an upsidedown smile. "He'd be dust, that's certain, but you'd be bleeding all over what's left."

"Well, if you're going to come at a man from behind—"

"They will," Cian reminded him, giving Moira one of his rare nods of approval. "And more than one. You make your kill, you move on. Quick, fast and in a bloody hurry."

He vised his hands on Moira's head, feigned giving it a twist. "Now the three of you are dead because you spend too much time talking. You need to handle multiple opponents, whether it's sword, stake or bare hands."

Hoyt stood, shook himself off. "Why don't you demonstrate for us?"

Cian lifted his brows at the irritable challenge. "All right then. All of you, on me. I'll try not to hurt you more than is necessary."

"Bragging. That would be talking, wouldn't it?" Larkin crouched into fighting stance.

"It would be, in this case, stating the obvious." He picked up the blunted stake, tossed it to Moira. "What you want to do here is anticipate each other's moves, as well as mine. Then . . . So you decided to join the party."

"I've been working on something. Making progress." Glenna touched the hilt of the dagger she'd strapped to her waist. "I needed to step away from it awhile. What's the drill here?"

"We're going to kick Cian's arse," Larkin told her.

"Oh. I'll play. Weapons?"

"Your choice." Cian nodded toward the dagger. "You seem to have yours."

"No, not for this." She moved over, selected another blunted stake. "Rules?"

In answer, Cian shot over, flipped Larkin and sent him tumbling to a pad. "Win. That's the only rule."

When Hoyt moved on him, Cian took the blow, let the momentum of it carry him into the air. He kicked off the wall, revolved, and used his body to knock Hoyt into Moira. And took them both down.

"Anticipate," he repeated, and kicked back almost idly to send Larkin into the air.

Glenna grabbed a cross, held it out as she stepped forward.

"Ah, smart." His eyes went red, just at the rims. Outside the doors, thunder began to grumble. "Shield and weapon, put the enemy in retreat. Except . . ." He lashed out, forearm to forearm and knocked the cross away. But when he spun to dispatch the stake, Glenna dived, going under him.

"Now this one's clever." Cian nodded approval, and for a moment, his face was illuminated by a ripple of lightning against the glass. "She uses her head, her instincts—at least when the stakes—haha—are low."

They circled him now, which he considered a small improvement in their strategy. Not quite a team, not yet an oiled machine, but an improvement.

As they closed in, he could see the need to pounce in Larkin's eyes.

Cian chose what he considered the weakest link, pivoted, and using one hand simply lifted Moira off her feet. When he tossed her, Larkin instinctively shifted to catch her. All Cian needed to do was sweep out a leg, take Larkin off his feet, and both of them went down in a tangle of limbs.

He spun to block his brother, gripped Hoyt's shirt. The solid head-butt had Hoyt stumbling back, giving Cian the instant he needed to wrench the stake from Glenna.

He had her back against him, his arm hooked tight around her neck.

"What now?" he asked the rest of them. "I've got your girl here. Do you back off, leave her to me? Do you come in, risk me snapping her in half? It's a problem."

"Or do they let me take care of myself?" Glenna gripped the chain around her neck, swung the cross back toward Cian's face.

He released her, vaulted clear to the ceiling. He clung there a moment, a dangerous fly, then dropped lightly to his feet.

"Not bad. And still, the four of you have yet to put me down. And if I were to—" There was a burst of lightning as his hand shot out, snatched the flying stake an inch from his own heart. The end was honed to killing point.

"We'd call that cheating," he said mildly.

"Back away from him."

They turned to see the woman step through the terrace doors as another flash of lightning ripped the sky behind her. She was slim in a black leather coat that hit her at the knees. Her dark hair was cut short, showcasing a high forehead and enormous eyes of vivid blue.

She dumped the large sack she carried on the floor, and with another stake in one hand, a two-edged knife in the other, she moved farther into the light.

"Who the hell are you?" Larkin demanded.

"Murphy. Blair Murphy. And I'll be saving your lives to-night. How the hell'd you let one of them in the house?"

"It happens I own it," Cian told her. "This is my place."

"Nice. Your heirs should be celebrating really soon. I said keep back from him," she snapped as both Larkin and Hoyt moved in front of Cian.

"I'd be his heir, as this is my brother."

"He's one of us," Larkin said.

"No. He's really not."

"But he is." Moira held up her hands to show they were empty, and moved slowly toward the intruder. "We can't let you hurt him."

"Looked to me like you were doing a piss-poor job of try-ing to hurt him when I came in."

"We were training. He's chosen to help us."

"A vampire helping humans?" Those big eyes narrowed in interest, and what might have been humor. "Well, there's always something new." Slowly Blair lowered the stake.

Cian pushed his shields aside. "What are you doing here? How did you come here?"

"How? Aer Lingus. What? Killing as many of your kind as I can manage. Present company, temporarily, excluded."

"How do you know about his kind?" Larkin asked her.

"Long story." She paused to scan the room, eyebrows lifting

thoughtfully at the stockpile of weapons. "Nice stash. There's something about a battle-ax that warms my heart."

"Morrigan. Morrigan said she'd come with the lightning." Glenna touched a hand to Hoyt's arm, then walked to Blair. "Morrigan sent you."

"She said there'd be five. She didn't mention any undead in the crew." After a moment, she sheathed the knife, tucked the stake into her belt. "But that's a god for you. Just gotta be cryptic. Look, it's been a long trip." She picked up her bag, slung the strap over her shoulder. "Got anything to eat around here?"

Chapter 19

"**W**ell I have a lot of questions."

Blair nodded at Glenna as she sampled stew. "Bet you do, and right back at you. This is good." She took another spoonful. "Thanks, and compliments to the chef and all that."

"You're welcome. I'm going to start, if that's okay." Glenna scanned the faces of the rest of the group. "Where did you come from?"

"Lately? Chicago."

"The Chicago in the here and now?"

A smile tugged at Blair's wide mouth. She reached for the hunk of bread Glenna had set out, ripped it in two with nails painted a deep candy pink. "That's the one. In the heartland, Planet Earth. You?"

"New York. This is Moira, and her cousin Larkin. They're from Geall."

"Get out." Blair studied them as she ate. "I always figured that for a myth."

"You don't seem particularly surprised it's not."

"Nothing much surprises me, less now after the visit from the goddess. Heavy stuff."

"This is Hoyt. He's a sorcerer from Ireland. Twelfth-century Ireland."

Blair watched as Glenna reached behind her for Hoyt's hand, the way their fingers smoothly intertwined. "You two paired up?"

"You could say that."

Now she lifted her wine, took a small sip. "That's taking going for older men to a new level, but who could blame you?"

"Your host is his brother, Cian, who was made a vampire."

"Twelfth century?" Blair leaned back, took a good, long look at him, with all the interest but none of the amusement she'd shown when studying Hoyt. "You've got nearly a thousand years? I've never met a vamp who lasted that long. The oldest I ever came across was a couple decades shy of five hundred."

"Clean living," Cian said.

"Yeah, that'll be the day."

"He doesn't drink humans." Since it was there, Larkin got another bowl, spooned up stew for himself. "He fights with us. We're an army."

"An army? Talk about delusions of grandeur. What are you?" she asked Glenna.

"Witch."

"So, we've got a witch, a sorcerer, a couple of refugees from Geall and a vampire. Some army."

"A powerful witch." Hoyt spoke for the first time. "A scholar of remarkable skill and courage, a shape-shifter, and a centuries-old vampire who was made by the reining queen."

"Lilith?" Now Blair set down her spoon. "She made you?"

Cian leaned back against the counter, crossed his ankles. "I was young and foolish."

"And had really bad luck."

"What are you?" Larkin demanded.

"Me? Demon hunter." She picked up her spoon to resume

eating. "I've spent most of my life tracking and dusting his kind."

Glenna angled her head. "What, like Buffy?"

With a laugh, Blair swallowed stew. "No. First, I'm not the only, just the best."

"There are more of you." At that point, Larkin decided he could use some wine as well.

"It's a family thing, has been for centuries. Not all of us, but every generation one or two more of us. My father's one, and my aunt. His uncle was—and like that. I have two cousins on the job now. We fight the fight."

"And Morrigan sent you here," Glenna put in. "Only you."

"I'd have to say yes, since I'm the only one here. Okay, so the last couple of weeks, things have been weird. More un-dead activity than usual, like they're getting some brass ones. And I'm having these dreams. Portentous dreams go with the package, but I'm having them every time I close my eyes. And sometimes when I'm wide awake. Disturbing."

"Lilith?" Glenna asked.

"She made some appearances—cameos we'll say. Up till then, I figured she was another myth. Anyway, in the dream, I thought I was over here—Ireland. It looked like here any-way. I've been to Ireland before, another family tradition. But I'm on this rise. Barren place, rough ground, deep chasms, wicked rocks."

"The Valley of Silence," Moira interrupted.

"That's what she called it. Morrigan. She said I was needed." Blair hesitated, looked around. "I probably don't have to fill in all the details since you're all here. Big battle, possible apocalypse. Vampire queen forming an army to eliminate humankind. There would be five waiting for me, gathered together. We'd have until Samhain to prepare. Not a lot of time considering, you know—goddess, eternity. But that's how it's laid out."

"So you came," Glenna said. "Just like that?"

"Didn't you?" Blair shrugged. "I was born for this. I've dreamed of that place before, as long as I can remember. Me standing on that rise, watching it rage below. The moon, the fog, the screams. I always knew I'd end up there."

Always assumed she would die there.

"I just expected a little more backup."

"In three weeks we've killed more than a dozen," Larkin said with some annoyance.

"Good for you. I don't keep a tally of kills since I had my first thirteen years ago. But I took out three tonight on the road, on the way here."

"Three?" He held up his spoon. "Alone?"

"There was another. It stayed back. Chasing it down didn't seem like a good way to stay alive, which is the first rule in the family handbook. There might have been more of them, but I only scented the one. You've got more stationed around the perimeter of this place. I had to slip through them to get inside."

She pushed her empty bowl away. "That was really good. Thanks again."

"You're welcome again." Glenna took the bowl to the sink. "Hoyt, can I have a word with you? Excuse us, just for a minute."

She drew him out of the kitchen, toward the front of the house. "Hoyt, she's—"

"The warrior," he finished. "Yes, she's the last of the six."

"It was never King." She pressed her fingers to her mouth as she turned away. "He was never one of the six, and what happened to him—"

"Happened." Hoyt took her shoulders, turned her to face him. "Can't be changed. She's the warrior, and completes the circle."

"We have to trust her. I don't know how we begin to do that. She damned near killed your brother before she bothered to say hello."

"And we have only her word she's who she says she is."

"Well, she's not a vampire. She walked right into the house. Added to that, Cian would know."

"Vampires can have human servants."

"So how do we know? Do we take what she says she is on faith? If she is what she says, she's the last of us."

"We have to be sure."

"It's not like we can check her ID."

He shook his head, not bothering to ask her meaning. "She has to be tested. Upstairs, I think, in the tower. We'll make the circle, and we'll be sure."

When they were gathered upstairs, Blair looked around. "Close quarters. I like things roomier. You're going to want to keep your distance," she warned Cian. "I might stake you, just knee-jerk."

"You can try."

She tapped her fingers on the stake in her belt. There was a ring, a ridged band of silver, on her right thumb. "So, what's all this about?"

"We had no sign you were coming," Glenna began. "Not you specifically."

"So, you're thinking Trojan Horse?"

"It's a possibility we can't dismiss without proof."

"No," Blair agreed, "you'd be stupid just to take my word. And I feel better, actually, knowing you're not stupid. What do you want? My demon hunter's license?"

"You actually have—"

"No." She planted her feet, very like a warrior bracing for battle. "But if you're toying with doing some kind of witchcraft that involves my blood or other bodily fluid, you're out of luck. Line drawn on that."

"Nothing like that. Well, witchcraft, but nothing that requires blood. We're linked, the five of us. By fate, by necessity. And some, yes, by blood. We are the circle. We are the chosen. If you're the last link of that circle, we'll know."

"Otherwise?"

"We can't harm you." Hoyt laid a hand on Glenna's shoulder. "It's against all we are to use power against a human being."

Blair glanced toward the broadsword leaning against the tower wall. "Anything in the rule book about sharp, pointy objects?"

"We won't harm you. If you're Lilith's servant, we'll make you our prisoner."

She smiled, one corner of her mouth rising, then the other. "Good luck with that. All right, let's do it. Like I said, if you'd swallowed everything without a *hmmm,* I'd be more worried about what I'd walked into here. You guys around this white circle, me in it?"

"You know witchcraft?" Glenna asked her.

"I know something about it." She stepped into the circle.

"One of us at each point," Glenna instructed, "to form a pentagram. Hoyt will do the search."

"Search?"

"Of your mind," he assured Blair.

"There are some private things in there, too." Uncomfortable, she moved her shoulders, frowned at Hoyt. "Am I supposed to think of you as my witch doctor?"

"I'm not a witch. It will go more quickly, and without discomfort if you open to this." He lifted his hands, and lit the candles. "Glenna?"

"This is the circle of light and knowledge, formed by like minds, like hearts. Within this circle of light and knowledge no harm will we impart. We seek to link so we may know, within this ring only truth bestow. With mind to mind in destiny, as we will, so mote it be."

The air rippled, and still the candle flames rose straight as arrows. Hoyt held out his hands toward Blair.

"No harm, no pain. Only thoughts within thoughts. Your mind to my mind, your mind to our minds."

Her eyes looked deeply into his, had something flickering in his head. Then they went black, and he saw.

They all saw.

A young girl fighting a monster nearly twice her size. There was blood on her face, and her shirt was torn. They could hear each drawing of her labored breath. A man stood off to the side, and watched the battle.

She was struck to the ground with a vicious backhanded blow, and sprang up. Struck down again. When the thing leaped, she rolled. And stabbed it through the back, into the heart, with a stake.

Slow, the man said. *Sloppy, even for a first kill. You'll need to do better.*

She didn't speak, but the mind inside her mind thought, *I'll do better. I'll do better than anyone.*

Now she was older, and fought beside the man. Ferociously, savagely. The odds were five to two, but it was done quickly. And when it was done, the man shook his head. *More control, less passion. Passion will kill you.*

She was naked, in bed with a young man, moving with him in the low light of the lamp. She smiled as she arched to him, nipped his lip. A diamond winked madly on her finger. Her mind was full of passion, of love, of joy.

And of despair and misery as she sat on the floor in the dark, alone, weeping out the shards of a broken heart. Her finger was bare.

She stood on the rise above the battleground, with the goddess a white shadow beside her.

You were the first to be called, and the last, Morrigan told her. *They're waiting for you. The worlds are in your hands. Take theirs, and fight.*

She thought, *I've been coming toward this all my life. Will it be the end of it?*

Hoyt lowered his hands, brought her slowly back, as he closed the circle. Her eyes cleared, blinked.

"So? Did I pass the audition?"

Glenna smiled at her, then walked to the table, lifted one of the crosses. "This is yours now."

Blair took it, let it dangle. "It's nice. Beautiful craftsmanship, and I appreciate the gesture. But I have my own." She tugged the chain from under her shirt. "Family thing again. Like an heirloom."

"It's lovely, but if you'd—"

"Wait." Hoyt snatched at the cross, stared at it as it lay in his palm. "Where did you get this? Where did it come from?"

"I told you, family. We have seven of them. They've been passed down. You're going to want to let go of that."

When he looked up into her eyes again she narrowed hers. "What's the problem?"

"There were seven, the goddess gave me, on the night she charged me to come here. I asked for protection for my family, the family she ordered me to leave behind. And these were what she gave me."

"That was what, nine hundred years back? It doesn't mean—"

"It's Nola's." He looked over her head to Cian. "I can feel it. This is Nola's cross."

"Nola?"

"Our sister. The youngest." His voice thickened as Cian moved closer to see for himself. "And here, on the back, I inscribed it with her name. She said I'd see her again. And by the gods, I am. She's in this woman. Blood to blood. Our blood."

"There's no question?" Cian said quietly.

"I put this around her neck myself. Look at her, Cian."

"Aye. Well." He looked away again, then moved to the window.

"Forged in the fire of the gods, given by the hand of a sorcerer." Blair breathed deep. "Family legend. My middle name is Nola. Blair Nola Bridgit Murphy."

"Hoyt." Glenna touched his arm. "She's your family."

"I guess you'd be my uncle, a thousand times removed or however it works." She glanced over toward Cian. "And isn't it a kick in the ass? I'm related to a vampire."

In the morning, under a weak and fitful sunlight, Glenna stood with Hoyt in the family graveyard. The storm had soaked the grass, and rain still dripped from the petals of the roses that climbed over his mother's grave.

"I don't know how to comfort you."

He took her hand. "You're here. I never thought I would need anyone to be with me, not the way I need you. It's all so fast, all of this. Loss and gain, discovery, questions. Life and death."

"Tell me about your sister. About Nola."

"She was bright and fair, and gifted. She had sight. She loved animals—had, I think, a special affinity for them. Before I left, there were puppies born to my father's wolfhound. Nola would spend hours in the stables playing with them. And while the world turned, she grew to a woman, had children."

He turned, rested his brow against Glenna's. "I see her in this woman, this warrior who's with us now. And inside of me is another war."

"Will you bring her here? Blair?"

"It would be right."

"You do what's right." She tipped up her head so her lips brushed his. "It's why I love you."

"If we were to marry—"

She took one quick, jerky step back. "Marry?"

"Sure that hasn't changed over the centuries. A man and a woman love, they take vows, make promises. Marriage or handfasting, a tie to bind them to each other."

"I know what marriage is."

"And it disturbs you?"

"Not disturbs, and don't smile at me that way, as if I'm being endearingly stupid. Give me just a minute here." She looked over the stones, toward the sparkling hills beyond. "Yes, people still marry, if they like. Some live together without the ritual."

"You and I, Glenna Ward, we're creatures of ritual."

She looked back at him, felt her stomach jitter. "Yes, we are."

"If we were to marry, would you live here with me?"

It was a second jolt. "Here? In this place, in *this* world?"

"In this place, in this world."

"But . . . don't you want to go back? Need to?"

"I don't think I can go back. Magically, aye, I think it's possible," he said before she could speak. "I don't think I can go back, to what was. To what was home. Not knowing when they'll die. Knowing that Cian is here—that other half of me. I don't think I could go back knowing you would go with me, and pine for what you left here."

"I said I would go."

"Without hesitation," he agreed. "Yet you hesitate at the rite of marriage."

"You caught me off guard. And you didn't actually ask

me," she said with some annoyance. "You more posed a hypothesis."

"If we were to marry," he said a third time, and the humor in his voice had her fighting her own, "would you live with me here?"

"In Ireland?"

"Aye, here. And in this place. It would be a kind of melding of our worlds, our needs. I would ask Cian to let us live in the house, to tend it. It needs people, family, the children we'd make together."

"Leaps and bounds," she murmured. Then took a moment to settle herself, to search herself. Her time, his place, she thought. Yes, it was a loving compromise, could be—would be—a melding of spirits.

"I've always been a confident sort, even as a child. Know what you want, work to get it, then value it once you have it. I've tried not to take anything in my life for granted, or not too much. My family, my gift, my lifestyle."

Reaching out, she brushed her fingers over one of his mother's roses. Simple beauty. Miraculous life.

"But I've learned that I took the world for granted, that it would always be—and that it would roll along, pretty much without my help. I learned otherwise, and that's given me something else to work for, to value."

"Is that a way of saying this isn't the time to speak of marriage and children?"

"No. It's a way of saying I understand the little things—and the big ones—the normal things, life, become only more important when it's all on the line. So . . . Hoyt the Sorcerer."

She touched her lips to his cheek, then the other. "If we were to marry, I would live here with you, and tend this house with you, and make children with you. And I'd work very hard to value all of it."

Watching her, he held up a hand, palm to her. When hers met it, their fingers linked, firm and strong. Light spilled out of their clasped hands.

"Will you marry me, Glenna?"

"Yes."

He cupped the back of her neck, drawing her to him. The kiss spun out, full of promise and possibilities. Full of hope. When her arms came around him, she knew she'd found the strongest part of her destiny.

"We have more to fight for now." He turned his face into her hair. "More to be now."

"Then we will be. Come with me. I'll show you what I'm working on."

She took him with her closer to the house where there were targets set up for archery training. The sound of hoof-beats had her looking over, just in time to see Larkin ride the stallion into the trees.

"I wish he wouldn't ride in the woods. There are so many shadows."

"I doubt they could catch him, if they were lying in wait. But if you asked him," Hoyt said, running a hand down Glenna hair, "he'd keep to the fields."

Her brows lifted in puzzlement. "If I asked?"

"If he knew you worried, he'd give that to you. He's grateful for what you do for him. You feed him," Hoyt said when she frowned.

"Oh. Well, he certainly likes to eat." Glenna looked toward the house. Moira, she imagined, was having her morning session with the books, and Cian would be sleeping. As for Blair, it would take a little time before Glenna learned the newcomer's routine.

"I think we'll have lasagna for dinner. Don't worry." She patted his hand. "You'll like it—and it occurs to me that I'm already tending the house, and the family in it. I never thought of myself as particularly domestic. The things you learn. And now."

She drew her dagger, moving she realized, with complete ease from cookery to weaponry.

The things you learn.

"I worked on this yesterday."

"On the dagger," Hoyt prompted.

"On charming the dagger. I thought I should start small, eventually work up to a sword. We talked about doing something about weapons, but with one thing and the other, we haven't really gotten down to it. Then I thought of this."

He took it from her, skimmed a finger up the edge. "Charmed in what way?"

"Think fire." His gaze moved back to hers. "No, literally," she said as she stepped back a pace. "Think fire. Visualize it, skimming over the blade."

He turned the dagger in his hand, then shifted to a fighting grip. He imagined fire, pictured it coating the steel. But the blade remained cool.

"Are there words to be said?" he asked her.

"No, you just have to want it, to see it. Try it again."

He focused, and got nothing.

"All right, maybe it only works for me—for now. I can refine it." She took it back from him, drew out the image, and pointed the dagger toward the target.

There wasn't so much as a spurt.

"Damn it, it worked yesterday." She took a closer look to make certain she hadn't grabbed the wrong weapon that morning. "This is the right one, I inscribed a pentagram on the hilt. See?"

"Yes, I see it. Perhaps the charm is limited. It wore off."

"I don't see how. I should have to break the charm, and I didn't. I put a lot of time and energy into this, so—"

"What's going on?" Blair strolled out, one hand tucked in the front pocket of her jeans, the other holding a steaming cup of coffee. There was a knife in a sheath at her hip, and the glimmer of moonstones dangling from her ears. "Knife-throwing practice?"

"No. Good morning."

She lifted an eyebrow at the irritation in Glenna's voice. "For some of us anyway. Nice dagger."

"It's not working."

"Let's see." Blair snatched it from Glenna, tested the weight. And sipping coffee, threw it toward the target. It stabbed the bull's-eye. "Works for me."

"Great, so it's got a pointy end, and you've got excellent aim." Glenna stomped toward the target, wrenched out the dagger. "What happened to the magic?"

"Search me. It's a knife, a nice one. It stabs, it hacks, it slices. Does the job. You start counting on magic, you can get sloppy. Then somebody puts that pointy end into you."

"You have magic in your blood," Hoyt pointed out to her. "You should have respect for it."

"Didn't say otherwise. I'm just more comfortable with sharp implements than voodoo."

"Voodoo is a different matter entirely," Glenna snapped. "Just because you can throw a knife doesn't mean you don't need what Hoyt and I can give you."

"No offense—seriously. But I count on myself first. And if you can't fight with that, you should leave the combat to the ones who can."

"You think I can't hit that stupid target?"

Blair sipped more coffee. "I don't know. Can you?"

Riding on insult, Glenna turned, and with curses running through her head flung the knife.

It hit the outer circle. And burst into flame.

"Excellent." Blair lowered her coffee. "I mean your aim's for shit, but the fire show is very cool." She gestured with the mug. "Probably going to need a new target though."

"I was pissed off," Glenna mumbled. "Anger." She turned her excited face to Hoyt's. "Adrenaline. We weren't angry before. I was happy. She pissed me off."

"Always happy to help."

"It's a fine charm, a good weapon." He laid a hand on Glenna's shoulder as the target burned. "How long will the flame last?"

"Oh! Wait." She stepped away, centered herself. Calmed, she put out the fire in her mind. The flame flickered out to smoke.

"It needs work. Obviously, but . . ." She went back to the target, gingerly tested the dagger's hilt. It was warm, but not too hot to touch. "It could give us a real edge."

"Damn straight," Blair agreed. "Sorry about the voodoo crack."

"Accepted." Glenna sheathed the dagger. "I'm going to ask you for a favor, Blair."

"Ask away."

"Hoyt and I need to get to work on this now, but later today . . . Could you teach me to throw a knife like you do?"

"Maybe not like me." Blair grinned. "But I can teach you to throw it better than you do, less like you're shooing pigeons."

"There's more," Hoyt said. "Cian takes charge of the training after sunset."

"A vampire training humans to kill vampires." Blair shook her head. "There's some sort of strange logic in there. Okay, so?"

"We train in the day as well—a few hours. Outside if the sun holds."

"From what I saw last night, you can use all you can get. And don't take insult," Blair added. "I work on it a couple hours a day myself."

"The one in charge of our daylight training . . . we lost him. Lilith."

"Rough. I'm sorry, it's always rough."

"I think you'd be the best to lead that training now."

"Give you guys orders, make you sweat?" Sheer pleasure shone on her face. "Sounds like fun. Just remember you asked when you start to hate me. Where are the others anyway? Daylight shouldn't be wasted."

"I imagine Moira's in the library," Glenna told her. "Larkin took the horse out a little while ago. Cian—"

"I got that part. Okay, I'm going to do a little scouting around, get the lay a little better. We'll get the party started when I get back."

"The trees are thick." Glenna nodded toward the curve of the forest. "You shouldn't go too far in, even during the day."

"Don't worry."

Chapter 20

Blair liked the woods. She liked the smell of them, the look of the big-trunked trees, the play of light and shadow that, for her, made a kind of visual music. The forest floor was carpeted with leaves that had fallen over countless years, and the fairy green of moss. The stream that ran glinting through it only added to that fairy-tale quality. It was slender and curvy, making more music with the water singing over rock.

She'd been to Clare before, had wandered field and forest and hill, and wondered how she'd missed this place if it truly was her beginnings. She supposed she hadn't been meant to find it before, to walk here. To know.

It was now, with these people, in this place.

The witch and the wizard, she mused. They were so full of love, all shiny and new, they all but glistened with it.

Advantage or disadvantage—she'd have to wait and see.

But she knew one thing. She wanted Glenna to make her a fire dagger.

The witch was okay. Great hair, too, and an urban sense of style that showed through even with simple pants and shirts. Lot of smarts going on in there, if Blair was any judge. And she was. She'd gone out of her way to be welcoming, it seemed, the night before. Fixing food, fluffing up the room she'd assigned to Blair.

It was a lot more than she was used to. And it was nice.

The wizard seemed to be on the intense side. Did a lot of watching, didn't have a lot to say. She could respect that. Just as she could, and did, respect the power he wore like skin.

As for the vampire, she was in a holding pattern there. He would be a formidable ally, or foe—and to date, she'd never considered a vamp any kind of ally. Still, she'd seen something in his face when his brother had spoken of Nola. It had been pain.

The other woman was quiet as a mouse. Watchful, oh yeah, and a little on the soft side yet. She hadn't made up her mind about Blair any more than Blair had about her.

And the guy? Larkin. Some serious eye-candy. He had a good, athletic build that should make him an asset in a fight. Boiling with energy, too, she thought. The shape-shifting deal could come in handy, if he was any good at it. She'd have to ask for a demo.

It was a lot—they were a lot—to whip into shape in a very short time. She'd have to be up to it if any of them were going to make it out of this alive.

But for now, it was nice to take a morning stroll through the trees, listening to the water sing, watching the light dance.

She skirted around a rock, cocked her head at what was curled sleeping under its shadow.

"This is your morning wake-up call," she said, and pulled the trigger on the crossbow she carried.

The vampire barely had time to open its eyes.

She retrieved the arrow, set it again.

She took out three more, disturbing another who sprinted off down the path, dodging beams of thin sunlight. Without a clear shot, and unwilling to waste an arrow, she took off after him.

The horse leaped onto the path, a gleaming black beast,

with the gilded god on its back. Larkin sliced down with his sword, and beheaded the fleeing vampire.

"Nice job," she called out.

Through streams of sunlight, Larkin trotted the horse toward her. "What are you doing out here?"

"Killing vampires. You?"

"The horse needed a run. You shouldn't be out here alone, so far from the house."

"You are."

"They couldn't catch this one." He patted Vlad on the neck. "He's the wind. So then, how many have you seen?"

"The four I killed, and yours makes five. There are probably more."

"Four others, you say? Aren't you the busy one. Do you want to hunt them now?"

He looked up to it, but she couldn't be sure. Working with an unknown partner was a good way to die, even if that partner showed a wicked skill with a sword. "That should do it for now. One of them, at least, will run back to Mommy and report we're taking them out of their nests during the day. Should tick her off."

"Tick?"

"Annoy her."

"Ah. Aye, there's that."

"Anyway, we need to do some training so I can see what you're made of."

"You can see?"

"I'm your new sergeant." She could see he wasn't thrilled with that news—and who could blame him? But she held up a hand. "How about a lift, cowboy?"

He reached down, and with a clasp of hands to forearms, she vaulted up behind him.

"How fast will this guy move?" she asked.

"You'd best hold on, and tight."

A tap of his heels sent the horse flying.

Glenna rubbed her thumb and finger together over the cauldron to add another pinch of sulfur to the mix.

"A little at a time," she said absently to Hoyt. "We don't want to overdo it and end up—"

She jerked back as the liquid flashed.

"Mind your hair," Hoyt warned.

She grabbed some pins, bundled it hastily on top of her head. "How's it coming there?"

Inside the metal trough, the dagger continued to burn. "The fire's still unstable. We have to tame it or we'll burn ourselves as well as vampires."

"It's going to work." She took a sword, slid it into the liquid. Stepping back, she held her hands in the smoke and began her chant.

He stopped what he was doing to watch her, to study the beauty that came into her with the magic. What had his life been before she'd come into it? With no one with whom he could fully share what he was, not even Cian? With no one to look into his eyes in a way that made his heart shine?

Fire licked at the edges of the cauldron, shimmied up the sword, and still she stood, in the smoke and the flame. Her voice like music, her power like dance.

When the flames died, she removed the sword with tongs, set it aside to cure and cool.

"Each has to be done separately. I know it's going to take time, days, but in the end . . . what?" she said when she caught him staring at her. "Have I got magic soot all over my face?"

"No. You're beautiful. When will you marry me?"

She blinked in surprise. "I thought after, when it's over."

"No, I don't want to wait. Every day is a day less, and every day is precious. I want us to be married here, in this house. Before long, we'll travel to Geall, and then . . . It should be here, Glenna, in the home we'll make."

"Of course it should. I know your family can't be here, except for Cian and Blair. Neither can mine. But when it's over, Hoyt. When everyone's safe again, I'd like another ritual here, I'd like my family here then."

"A handfasting now, a wedding ceremony after. Would that suit?"

"Perfect. I'd—now? As in *now*? I can't be ready now. I have to . . . do things first. I need a dress."

"I thought you preferred your rituals skyclad."

"Very funny. A few days. Say the coming full moon."

"The end of the first month." He nodded. "It seems right. I want to—what is all that shouting?"

They walked to the window to see Blair going toe-to-toe with Larkin. Moira stood, hands fisted on her hips.

"Speaking of rituals," Glenna commented. "Looks like the head-butting portion of the daily training's started without us. We'd better get down there."

"She's slow and she's sloppy, and slow and sloppy get you dead."

"She's neither," Larkin shot back at Blair. "But her strengths lie in her bow and in her mind."

"Great, she can think a vamp to death. Let me know how that works out. As for the bow, yeah, eye like an eagle, but you can't always kill at a distance."

"I can speak for myself well enough, Larkin. And you—" Moira jabbed a finger at Blair. "I don't care to be spoken to as if I were addle-brained."

"I've got no problem with your brain, but I've got a big one with your sword arm. You fight like a girl."

"So I am."

"Not during training, not during battle. Then you're a soldier, and the enemy doesn't give a rat's ass about your plumbing."

"King had her working on her strengths."

"King's dead."

There was a moment of utter silence that couldn't have been sliced through with Cian's battle-ax. Then Blair sighed. That, she could admit, had been unnecessarily harsh.

"Look, what happened to your pal is terrible. I sure as hell don't want it to happen to me. If you don't want it to happen to you, you'll work on your weaknesses—and you've got plenty. You can play with your strengths on your own time."

She planted her feet as Hoyt and Glenna came to join them. "Did you put me in charge of this?" Blair demanded.

"I did," Hoyt affirmed.

"And we've nothing to say about it?" Fury tightened Larkin's face. "Nothing at all?"

"You don't, no. She's the best for it."

"Because she's your blood."

Blair rounded on Larkin. "Because I can put you on your ass in five seconds flat."

"Sure of that, are you?" He shimmered and changed, and the wolf he became crouched and snarled.

"Excellent," Blair said under her breath, with temper smothered by pure admiration.

"Oh, Larkin, leave off, would you?" Obviously out of patience, Moira slapped a hand at him. "He's only angry because you were rude to me. And you've no cause to be so insulting. It happens I agree with you about working on the weaknesses." And Cian had said the same, Moira recalled. "I'm willing to practice, but I won't be after standing and being berated while I'm about it."

"More flies with honey than vinegar?" Blair said. "I always wondered why the hell anyone would want to catch flies. Look, you and I can paint our toenails and talk about boys when we're off the clock. While I'm training you, I'm the bitch because I want you alive. Does it hurt when you do that?" Blair asked Larkin when he changed back. "Shifting bones and organs and so on?"

"Some actually." He couldn't recall anyone ever asking him. His temper cooled as quickly as it had flared. "But it's fun, so I don't mind so much."

He slung his arm around Moira's shoulder, gave her arm a little rub as he spoke to Hoyt and Glenna. "Your girl here took out four of them in the forest. I took a fifth myself."

"This morning? Five?" Glenna stared at Blair. "How close to the house?"

"Close enough." Blair glanced toward the woods. "Lookouts, I figure, and not very good ones. Caught them napping. Lilith's going to get word of it. She's going to be unhappy."

* * *

It wasn't a matter of killing the messenger; not in Lilith's long-standing opinion. It was a matter of killing it as painfully as possible.

The young vampire who'd foolishly gone back to the nest after Blair's morning foray was now on a slow roast, belly-down, over a simmering fire. The smell wasn't particularly pleasant, but Lilith understood command required certain sacrifices.

She circled him now, careful to keep the hem of her red gown away from the lick of flames. "Why don't we go over this again?" Her voice was melodious, somewhat like a devoted teacher speaking to a favored student. "The human—female—destroyed everyone I'd posted, save you."

"The man." Pain turned the words to guttural rasps. "The horse."

"Yes, yes. I keep forgetting the man and the horse." She stopped to study the rings she wore. "The one who came along after she'd already cut down—what was it now—four of you?"

She crouched down, a spider of stunning beauty, to stare into his red, wheeling eyes. "And she was able to do this because? Wait, wait, I remember. Because you were *sleeping*?"

"They were. The others. I was at post, Majesty. I swear it."

"At post, and yet, this single female human lives. Lives because—do I have this detail correct? Because you ran?"

"Came back . . . to report." Its sweat dripped into the fire, and sizzled. "The others, they ran away. They ran. I came to you."

"So you did." She tapped him playfully on the nose with each word, then rose. "I suppose I should reward your loyalty."

"Mercy. Majesty, mercy."

She turned around with a silky rustle of skirts to smile at the boy who sat cross-legged on the floor of the cave, systematically ripping the heads off a pile of *Star Wars* action figures.

"Davey, if you break all your toys, what will you have to play with?"

His lips moved to pout as he beheaded Anikin Skywalker. "They're boring."

"Yes, I know." She ran a loving hand over his sunny hair. "And you've been cooped up too long, haven't you?"

"Can we go outside now?" He bounced, and his eyes went round and wide at the prospect of a promised treat. "Can we go outside and play? *Please!*"

"Not quite yet. Now don't sulk." She tipped his chin up to peck a kiss on his lips. "What if your face froze like that? Here now, my sweet boy, what if I gave you a brand-new toy?"

Round cheeks bright with temper, he snapped Han Solo in two. "I'm tired of toys."

"But this will be a new one. Something you've never had before." She turned her head, and with her finger still on his chin, turned his until they both looked at the vampire over the fire pit.

And on the spit, seeing their eyes, it began to struggle and thrash. And weep.

"For me?" Davey said brightly.

"All for you, my own dumpling. But you must promise Mama not to get too close to the fire. I don't want you burned, my precious one." She kissed his little fingers before she rose.

"Majesty, I beg you! Majesty, I came back to you."

"I dislike failure. Be a good boy, Davey. Oh, and don't spoil your dinner." She gestured to Lora, who stood quietly by the door.

The screams began before it was closed behind them. And locked.

"The Hunter," Lora began. "It had to be. None of the other women have the skill to—"

A single look from Lilith silenced her. "I haven't given you leave to speak. My fondness for you is all there is between you and the pit. And my affections only go so far."

Lora bowed her head in deference and followed Lilith into the adjoining chamber. "You lost three of my good men. What can you say to that?"

"I have no excuse."

With a nod, Lilith roamed the chamber, idly picking a ruby necklace from the top of a chest. The single thing she

missed of life was mirrors. She longed, even after two millennia, to see herself reflected. To be wooed by her own
beauty. She had hired—and fed on—countless sorcerers,
witches and magicians over the centuries to make it so.

It was her greatest failure.

"You're wise not to offer one. I'm a patient woman, Lora.
I've waited more than a thousand years for what's coming.
But I won't be insulted. I dislike having these *people* pick
and pluck us off like flies."

She threw herself into a chair, tapped her long red nails
on its arms. "Speak, then. Tell me about this new one. This
Hunter."

"As the seers prophesied, my lady. The warrior of old
blood. One of the hunters who has plagued our kind for centuries."

"And you know this because?"

"She was too fast to be a mere human. Too strong. She
knew what they were before they moved on her that night,
and she was ready. She completes their number. The first
stage is set."

"My scholars said the black man was their warrior."

"They were wrong."

"Then what good are they?" Lilith heaved the necklace
she still toyed with across the room. "How can I rule when
I'm surrounded by incompetence? I want what's due me. I
want blood and death and beautiful chaos. Is it too much to
ask that those who serve me be accurate on the details?"

For nearly four hundred years Lora had been by Lilith's
side. Friend, lover, servant. No one, she was sure, knew the
queen better. She poured a glass of wine, carried it to the
chair.

"Lilith." She said it gently, offering both it and a kiss.
"We've lost nothing important."

"Face."

"No, not even that. They only believe what they've done in
these past weeks matters. It's good they do, because it makes
them overconfident. And we killed Cian's boy, didn't we?"

"We did." Lilith pouted another moment, then sipped.
"There was satisfaction in that."

"And sending him to them only demonstrated your brilliance, and your strength. Let them take dozens of the meaningless foot soldiers. We cut their heart."

"You're a comfort to me, Lora." Drinking her wine, Lilith stroked Lora's hand. "And you're right, of course, you're right. I'm disappointed, I admit. I so wanted to break their number, to foil the prophecy."

"But it's better this way, isn't it? And it'll be the sweeter when you take them all."

"Better, yes, better. And yet . . . I think we need to make a statement. It would improve my mood, and morale as well. I have an idea. I'll think it through a bit." She watched the wine swirl in her glass. "One day, one day soon, this will be the sorcerer's blood. I'll drink it from a silver cup, and nibble on sugar plums between sips. All that he is will be in me, and all that I am will make even the gods tremble.

"Leave me now. I need to plan."

As Lora rose to go to the door, Lilith tapped on her glass. "Oh, and this irritating business has made me hungry. Bring me someone to eat, will you?"

"Right away."

"Make sure it's fresh." Alone she closed her eyes and began to plot. While she plotted, the screams and squeals from the next chamber battered the cave walls.

Her lips curved. Who could be blue, she thought, with a child's laughter ringing in the air?

oira sat cross-legged on Glenna's bed and watched Glenna work on the magic little machine she called a laptop. Moira was desperate to get her hands on it. There were worlds of knowledge inside, and so far she'd only been allowed a few peeks.

She'd been promised a lesson, but just at the moment, Glenna seemed so absorbed—and they only had an hour free.

So she cleared her throat.

"What do you think of this one?" Glenna asked and tapped the image of a woman wearing a long white dress.

Angling her head for a better view, Moira studied the screen. "She's very lovely. I was wondering—"

"No, not the model, the dress." Glenna scooted around on the chair. "I need a dress."

"Oh, did something happen to yours?"

"No." With a little laugh Glenna twisted the pendant around her neck. "I need a very special dress. A wedding dress. Moira, Hoyt and I are going to be married. Hand-fasted. We decided on handfasting, with a wedding cere-mony later. After."

"You're betrothed to Hoyt? I didn't know."

"It just happened. I know it might seem rushed, and the timing of it—"

"Oh, but this is wonderful!" Moira sprang up, and in a burst of enthusiasm, threw her arms around Glenna. "I'm so happy for you. For all of us."

"Thanks. For all of us?"

"Weddings, they're bright, aren't they? Bright and happy and human. Oh, I wish we were home so I could have a feast made. You can't make your own wedding feast, and I'm still not very good at the cooking."

"We won't worry about that, not yet. Weddings *are* bright—and happy and human. And I'm human enough to want the perfect dress."

"Well, of course. Why would you want less?"

Glenna let out a long, happy sigh. "Thank God. I've been feeling a little shallow. I should've known all I needed was another girl. Help me, will you? I have a few picked out, and I need to narrow it down."

"I'd love to." Gently, curiously, she tapped the side of the screen. "But . . . how do you get the dress out of the box?"

"We'll get to that, too. I'm going to have to take a few shortcuts. But later, I'll show you how to shop online the conventional way. I want something—I think—along these lines."

While they were huddled, Blair gave the doorjamb a knuckle rack. "Sorry. You got a minute, Glenna? I wanted to talk to you about requisitions and supplies. Figured you were the go-to. Hey. Nice toy."

"One of my favorites. Cian and I are the only ones linked up, so if you need to use—"

"Brought my own, but thanks. Shopping? Nieman's," she said as she moved close enough to see the screen. "Pretty fancy duds for wartime."

"Hoyt and I are getting married."

"No kidding? That's great." She gave Glenna a friendly punch on the shoulder. "Congratulations. So when's the big day?"

"Tomorrow night." When Blair only blinked, Glenna hurried on. "I know how it must seem, but—"

"I think it's terrific. I think it's excellent. Life can't stop. We can't let it. We can't let them make it stop; that's the whole point. Plus, it's great, seriously great, that the two of you found what you've got when everything's so extreme. It's one of the things we're fighting for, right?"

"Yes. Yes, it is."

"Wedding dress?"

"A potential. Blair, thank you."

Blair put a hand on Glenna's shoulder in a gesture that might have been woman-to-woman or soldier-to-soldier. Glenna supposed it was now one and the same.

"I've been fighting for thirteen years. I know better than anyone you need some real, you need things that matter, and that warm you up inside, or you lose the mission. I'll let you get back to it."

"Want to help us shop?"

"Really?" Blair did a little shuffle dance. "Are vampires blood-sucking fiends? I'm so in. One thing, not to put the damper, but how are you going to get the dress here by to-morrow?"

"I've got my ways. And I'd better get started. Would you mind closing the door? I don't want Hoyt coming in while I'm trying them on."

"Trying . . . Sure." Blair obliged while Glenna set several crystals on and around the laptop. She lit candles, then stood back, held her arms out to the side.

"Mother Goddess I ask your grace to bring this garment to this place. Through the air, from there to here, in the light unto my sight a symbol of my destiny. As I will so mote it be."

With a shimmer and flash, Glenna's jeans and T-shirt were replaced by the white gown.

"Wow. A whole new level of shoplifting."

"I'm not stealing it." Glenna's scowled at Blair. "I'd never use my powers that way. I'm trying it on, and when I find the one, I've got another spell to work the sale. It's just to save time, which I don't have."

"Don't get bent. I was just kidding." Sort of. "Will that work for weapons if we need more?"

"I suppose it would."

"Good to know. Anyway, great dress."

"It's lovely," Moira agreed. "Just lovely."

Glenna turned, studied her reflection in the antique cheval glass. "Thank God Cian didn't strip all the mirrors out of this place. It's beautiful, isn't it? I love the lines. But . . ."

"It's not the one," Blair finished, and settled down on the bed with Moira to watch the show.

"Why do you say that?"

"It doesn't light you up. That light, in the gut, in the heart, that just spreads out right to your fingertips. You put on your wedding dress, take one look at yourself in it and you know. The others are just practice."

So it had gotten that far, Glenna thought, remembering the vision of Blair and the engagement ring on her finger. And the image of her weeping in the dark, her hand bare.

She started to comment, then said nothing. A tender area like that required more than camaraderie. It needed true friendship, and they weren't there yet.

"You're right, it's not the one. I've got four more picked out. So we'll try number two."

She hit it on the third, and felt that light glowing. Heard it in Moira's long, wistful sigh.

"And we have a winner." Blair circled her finger. "Do the turn. Oh, yeah, that one's yours."

It was romantic, and simple, Glenna thought. Just as she'd hoped. There was a little float in the long skirt, and the soft sweetheart neckline was framed by two thin straps that left her shoulders bare then ran down her shoulder blades to spotlight her back.

"It's so exactly right." She glanced at the price again, winced. "Well, maxing out my credit card doesn't seem that big a deal considering the possible apocalypse."

"Seize the day," Blair agreed. "You doing a veil, a head-piece?"

"Traditional Celtic handfastings call for a veil, but in this case . . . Just flowers, I think."

"Even better. Soft, earthy, romantic and sexy all rolled into one. Do the deal."

"Moira?" Glenna looked over, saw Moira's eyes were damp and dreamy. "I can see it has your vote, too."

"I think you'll be the most beautiful of brides."

"Well, this was serious fun." Blair got to her feet. "And I agree with the brain trust here—you look outstanding. But you need to wrap it up." She tapped her watch. "The two of you are due in training. You need some major hand-to-hand practice. Why don't you come with me now?" she said to Moira. "We can get started."

"I'll only be a few minutes," Glenna told them, then turned back to study herself in the glass.

From wedding dresses to combat, she thought. Her life had become a very strange ride.

Because he heard the music playing inside, Hoyt knocked on Cian's door a little before sundown. There'd been a time, he remembered, he wouldn't have thought of knocking, when asking permission to enter his brother's chambers wouldn't have been necessary.

A time, he thought, he wouldn't have needed to ask his brother if he could live with his wife in his own home.

Locks clicked and snicked. Cian wore only loose pants and a sleepy expression when he opened the door. "A bit early for me, for visiting."

"I need a private word with you."

"Which, of course, can't wait on my convenience. Come in then."

Hoyt stepped into a room that was pitch black. "Must we speak in the dark?"

"I can see well enough." But Cian switched on a low light beside a wide bed. The covers on the bed gleamed jewel-like in that light, and the sheets carried the sheen of silk. Cian moved to a cold box, took out a packet of blood. "I haven't had breakfast." He tossed the packet into the microwave sitting on top of the box. "What do you want?"

"When this is done, what do you intend to do?"

"As I choose, as always."

"To live here?"

"I think not," Cian said with a half laugh, and took a crystal glass from a shelf.

"Tomorrow night . . . Glenna and I are to be handfasted."

There was a slight hesitation in his rhythm, then Cian set the glass down. "Isn't that interesting? I suppose congratulations are in order. And you intend to take her back, introduce her to the family. Ma, Da, this is my bride. A little witch I picked up a few centuries from now."

"Cian."

"Sorry. The absurdity of it amuses me." He took the package out, broke it open and poured the warmed contents in the glass. "Well, anyway. *Sláinte.*"

"I can't go back."

After the first sip, the first long stare over the rim, Cian lowered the glass. "More and more interesting."

"It's no longer my place, knowing what I know. Waiting for the day to come when I know they'll die. If you could go back, would you?"

Cian frowned into his glass, then sat. "No. For thousands of reasons. But that would be one of them. But that aside, you brought this war to me. Now you take time from it to handfast?"

"Human needs don't stop. They're only keener, it seems, when the end of days threaten."

"It happens that's true. I've seen it countless times. It also happens war brides don't always make reliable wives."

"That's for me and for Glenna."

"It certainly is." He raised his glass, drank some more. "Well then, good luck to you."

"We want to live here, in this house."

"In my house?"

"In the house that was ours. Setting aside my rights, and our kinship, you're a businessman. You pay a caretaker when you're not in residence. You'd no longer have that expense. Glenna and I would tend this place and the land, at no cost to you."

"And how do you propose to make a living? There isn't much demand for sorcerer's these days. Wait, I take it back." Cian laughed, finished off the blood. "You could make a goddamn fortune on television, on the Internet. Get yourself an eight-hundred number, a web site, and off you go. Not your style though."

"I'll find my way."

Cian set the glass aside, looked off into the shadows. "Maybe I hope you do, providing you live, of course. I've no problem with you staying in the house."

"Thanks for that."

Cian shrugged. "It's a complicated life you've chosen for yourself."

"And I intend to live it. I'll let you get dressed."

A complicated life, Cian thought again when he was alone. And it stunned and annoyed him that he could envy it.

Chapter 21

Glenna figured most brides were a little stressed and very busy on their weddings days. But most brides didn't have to fit in sword practice and spells between their facials and pedicures.

At least the pace cut down on the time for the nerves she'd had no idea she'd have. She couldn't squeeze in much of an anxiety attack when she was worried about flower arrangements, romantic lighting and the proper form for be-heading a vampire.

"Try this." Blair started to toss the weapon, then obviously changed her mind when Glenna's mouth dropped open. She walked it over. "Battle-ax. More heft than a sword, which would work better for you, I think. You got pretty decent upper body strength, but you'd cut through easier with this than a sword. You need to get used to its weight and its balance. Here."

She walked back, picked up her own sword. "Block me with it."

"I'm not used to it. I could miss, hurt you."

"Believe me, you won't hurt me. Block!" She thrust out,

and more from instinct than obedience, Glenna clanged the axe to the sword.

"Now see, I'd just stab you cheerfully in the back while you're fumbling to turn."

"It's top heavy," Glenna complained.

"It's not. Spread out your grip more for now. Okay, stay forward after the first strike. Come down on the sword, back up at me. Slow. One," she said and thrust. "Two. Again, keep it coming. You want to counter my moves, sure, but what you want is to throw me off balance, to make me counter yours, force me to follow your moves. Think of it as a dance routine where you not only want to lead, but you also really want to kill your partner."

Blair held up a hand, stepped back. "Let me show you. Hey, Larkin. Come be the practice dummy." She tossed him her sword, hilt up, then took the battle-ax. "Take it slow," she told him. "This is a demo."

She nodded. "Attack."

As he moved on her, she called out the steps. "Strike, strike, turn. Thrust up, across, strike. He's good, see?" she said, still calling out to Glenna. "So he's pushing at me while I push at him. So you ad lib as necessary. Turn, kick, strike, strike, pivot. Slice!"

She flipped the dagger strapped to her wrist and swiped it an inch from Larkin's belly. "When his guts are spilling out, you—"

And dodged back from the swipe of what looked like a very large bear claw.

"Wow." She rested the head of her axe on the floor, leaned on the handle. Only his arm had changed shape. "You can do that? Just pieces of you?"

"If I like."

"I bet the girls back home can't get enough of you."

It took him a moment—she'd already turned to go back to Glenna—then he burst into delighted laughter. "Sure that's the truth. But not due to what you're meaning. I prefer my own shape for that kind of sport."

"Bet. Square off with Larkin. I'm going to work with Shorty for a while."

"Don't call me that," Moira snapped.

"Lighten up. I didn't mean anything by it."

Moira opened her mouth, then shook her head. "I'm sorry. That was rude."

"King called her that," Glenna said quietly.

"Oh. Got it. Moira. Resistance training. We're going to pump you up."

"I'm sorry I spoke to you that way."

"Look. We're going to irritate each other a lot before this is done. I don't bruise easily—literally or figuratively. You're going to have to toughen up yourself. Five-pound free weights. You're going to be cut by the time I'm done with you."

Moira narrowed her eyes. "I may be sorry I lashed at you, but I'm not going to let you cut me."

"No, it's an expression. It means . . ." And every other term Blair could think of would be just as confusing. Instead she curled her arm, flexed her biceps.

"Ah." A smile glimmered in Moira's eyes. "Sure I'd like that. All right then, you can cut me."

They worked a full morning. When Blair paused to gulp water from a bottle she nodded at Glenna. "You're coming right along. Ballet lessons?"

"Eight years. Never thought I'd pirouette with a battle-ax, but life's full of surprises."

"Can you do a triple?"

"Not so far."

"Look." Still holding the bottle, Blair whipped her body around three times then shot her leg out to the side, up at a forty-five-degree angle. "That kind of momentum puts a good solid punch in a kick. You need solid to knock one of these things back. Practice. You've got it in you. So." She took another swig. "Where's the groom?"

"Hoyt? In the tower. There are things that need to be done. As important as what we're doing here, Blair," she added when she sensed disapproval.

"Maybe. Okay, maybe. If you come up with more stuff like the fire dagger."

"We've fire charmed a number of the weapons." She

walked to another section of the room, took down a sword to bring it back. "Those that are charmed we've marked. See?"

On the blade near the hilt was a flame, etched into steel.

"Nice. Really. Can I try it?"

"Better take it outside."

"Good point. Okay, we should break for an hour anyway. Grab something to eat. Cross- and longbows, boys and girls, after lunch."

"I'll come with you," Glenna told her. "In case."

Blair used the terrace doors, jogged down to ground level. She glanced at the straw dummy Larkin had hung from a post. You had to give it to the guy, she mused. He had a sense of humor. He'd drawn fangs on the stuffed face and a bright red heart on the chest.

It would be fun to test the fire sword out on it—and a waste of good material. No point burning up Vampire Dummy.

So she began in a fighting stance, her arm arched behind her head, the sword pointing out.

"It's important to control it," Glenna began. "To pull the fire when you need it. If you're just slapping the burning sword around, you could burn yourself, or one of us."

"Don't worry."

Glenna started to speak again, then shrugged. There was nothing and no one to hurt but the air.

Then she watched as Blair began to move, slowly, fluid as water, the sword like an extension of her arm. Yes, a kind of ballet, she thought, a lethal one. But nonetheless compelling. The blade shimmered when the sun struck its edge, but remained cool. Just as Glenna began to assume Blair needed coaching on how to use it, the woman thrust out, and the blade erupted.

"And you're toast. God, I *love* this thing. Will you make me one, out of one of my personal weapons?"

"Absolutely." Glenna lifted her brows as Blair swished the sword through the air and the fire died. "You learn fast."

"Yeah, I do." She frowned, scanning the sky. "Clouds boiling up in the west. Guess we're in for more rain."

"Good thing I planned an indoor wedding."

"Good thing. Let's go eat."

Hoyt didn't come down until late afternoon, and by that time Glenna had given herself permission to take time for herself. She didn't want to do a quick glamour to look her best. She wanted to pamper herself, just a bit.

And she needed flowers to make the circlet for her hair, to make a bouquet. She'd made the facial cream herself, from herbs, so dabbed it on generously as she studied the sky from the bedroom window.

The clouds were moving in now. If she was going to get flowers, she had to get them before the sun was lost and the rain came. But when she opened the door to dash out, Moira and Larkin stood on the other side. He made some sound as his eyes widened, reminding her of the soft green goo on her face.

"It's a female thing, just deal with it. I'm running behind. I haven't got the flowers for my hair yet."

"We . . . Well." Moira brought her hand from behind her back and offered the circlet of white rosebuds with red ribbon braided through it. "I hope it's all right, that it's what you wanted. I know something red's traditional for a handfasting. Larkin and I wanted to give you something, and we don't have anything really, so we did this. But if you'd rather—"

"Oh, it's perfect. It's perfectly beautiful. Oh, *thank* you!" She grabbed Moira in a crushing hug, then turned a beaming smile up to Larkin.

"I've thought it wouldn't be a hardship to have you kiss me," he began, "but just at the moment . . ."

"Don't worry. I'll catch you later."

"There's this as well." He handed her a nosegay of multi-colored roses twined with more red ribbon. "To carry, Moira says."

"Oh God, this is the sweetest thing." Tears dribbled through the cream. "I thought this would be hard without family here. But I have family here, after all. Thank you. Thank you both."

She bathed, scented her hair, creamed her skin. White candles burned as she performed the female ritual of preparing herself for a man. For her wedding, and her wedding night.

She was in her robe, brushing her fingers over the skirt of the dress that hung outside the wardrobe when someone knocked.

"Yes, come in. Unless you're Hoyt."

"Not Hoyt." Blair came in carrying a bottle of champagne nestled in an ice bucket. Behind her, Moira brought in three flutes.

"Compliments of our host," Blair told her. "I gotta say, he's got some class for a vampire. This is prime bubbly we got here."

"Cian sent champagne?"

"Yep. And I'm going to get down to popping this cork before we suit you up."

"I have a wedding party. Oh, you should have dresses. I should've thought of it."

"We're fine. Tonight's all about you."

"I've never had champagne. Blair says I'll like it."

"Guaranteed." Blair gave Moira a quick wink then popped the cork. "Oh, I got something for you. It's not much, seeing as I don't have your style with on-line shopping, but anyway." She dug into her pocket. "I didn't have a box either."

She put the pin in Glenna's hand. "It's a claddaugh. Traditional Irish symbol. Friendship, love, loyalty. I'd've gone for the toaster or salad bowl, but time was limited. And I didn't know where you'd registered."

Another circle, Glenna thought. Another symbol. "It's beautiful. Thank you." She turned, pinned it to the ribbon trailing from her bouquet. "Now I'll carry both of your gifts with me."

"I love sentiment. Especially with champagne." Blair poured three glasses, passed them around. "To the bride."

"And her happiness," Moira added.

"And to the continuity represented by what we do tonight. To the promise of the future it represents. I'm going to get all the teary stuff out before I do my make-up."

"Good plan," Blair agreed.

"I know what I found with Hoyt is right, is mine. I know what we're promising each other tonight is right, is ours. But having you here with me, that's right, too. And it's special. I want you to know it's very special to me, having you share this."

They touched glasses and drank. Moira closed her eyes. "Blair was right. I do like it."

"Told ya. Okay, Moira, let's you and me make ourselves a bride."

Outside the rain splashed down and fog billowed. But in the house was candlelight and the scent of flowers.

Glenna stepped back from the mirror. "Well?"

"You look like a dream," Moira stated. "Like a goddess in a dream."

"My knees are shaking. I bet goddesses don't get shaky knees."

"Take a couple of deep breaths. We'll go down, make sure everything's set up. Including the lucky guy. You're going to blow his socks off."

"Why would she—"

"You know, sweetie," Blair said to Moira as they started for the door. "You're too literal. Start studying contemporary slang while you're buried in books." She pulled open the door, stopped short when she saw Cian. "This is girl territory."

"I'd like a moment with my . . . future sister-in-law."

"It's all right, Blair. Cian. Please come in."

He stepped inside, sent Blair a mild look over his shoulder, then shut the door in her face. Then he turned and took a long look at Glenna. "Well now, you're a vision, aren't you? Truly. My brother's fortune leaps and bounds."

"You probably think this is foolish."

"You'd be wrong. While it may be something I think of as particularly human, it's not one of the things I think of as foolish. Though there are many of those."

"I love your brother."

"Yes, a blind man could see that."

"Thank you for the champagne. For thinking of it."

"My pleasure. Hoyt's ready for you."

"Oh boy." She pressed a hand to her jumpy belly. "I hope so."

Cian smiled at that, stepped closer. "I have something for you. A wedding gift. I thought to put it in your hand as I assume, at least for now, you'd be in charge of the paperwork."

"Paperwork?"

He handed her a thin leather portfolio. After opening it, she sent him a puzzled look. "I don't understand."

"It should be clear enough. It's the deed to this house, the land. It's yours."

"Oh, but we can't. When he asked if we could stay, he only meant—"

"Glenna, I only make grand gestures once every few decades, if the whim happens to strike me. Take it when it's offered. It's more to him than it could ever be to me."

Her throat had filled so she had to wait to speak. "I know what it means to me. It will mean a great deal more to him. I wish you'd give it to him yourself."

"Take it," was all he said, then turned to the door.

"Cian." She set the folder aside, picked up her bouquet. "Would you walk me down? Would you take me to Hoyt?"

He hesitated, then opened the door. Then held out a hand to her.

She heard music as they started down.

"Your handmaidens have been busy. I expected it of the little queen—a lot of sentiment there. But the hunter surprised me."

"Am I shaking? I feel like I'm shaking."

"No." He tucked her hand into his arm. "You're steady as a rock."

And when she stepped into the room filled with candles and flowers, when she saw Hoyt standing in front of the low, gold flames of the fire, she felt steady.

They crossed the room to each other. "I've waited for you," Hoyt whispered.

"And I for you."

She took his hand, scanned the room. It was, as was traditional, madly decked with flowers. The circle had been formed, and the candles lighted, but for the ones they would light during the ritual. The willow wand lay on the table that served as altar.

"I made this for you." He showed her a thick ring of silver, deeply etched.

"One mind," she said, and drew the one she'd made him from her thumb.

They joined hands, walked to the altar. Touched fingers to the candles to light them. After slipping their rings onto the willow wand, they turned to face the others.

"We ask you to be our witnesses at this sacred rite," Hoyt began.

"To be our family as we become one."

"May this place be consecrated for the gods. We are gathered here in a ritual of love."

"Beings of the Air be with us here, and with your clever fingers tie closely the bonds between us." Glenna looked into his eyes as she spoke the words.

"Beings of the Fire be with us here . . ."

And they continued through Water, through Earth, the blessed goddess and laughing god. Her face was luminous as they spoke, as they lit incense, then a red candle. They sipped wine, scattered salt.

She and Hoyt held the wand with the rings gleaming on it between them.

The light grew warmer, brighter as they spoke to each other, the rings under their hands sparkling wildly.

"It is my wish to become one with this man." She slipped the ring from the wand and onto his finger.

"It is my wish to become one with this woman." He mirrored her gesture.

They took the cord from the altar, draped it over their joined hands.

"And so the binding is made," they said together. "Then, as the goddess and the god and the old ones—"

A scream from outside shattered the moment like a rock through glass.

Blair leaped to a window, yanked back the drape. Even her nerves jolted at the vampire's face only inches away behind the glass. But it wasn't that which turned her blood cold; it was what she saw beyond it.

She looked over her shoulders at the others, and said: "Oh, shit."

There were at least fifty, probably more, still in the forest or hidden nearby. Three cages sat on the grass, their occupants bloodied and shackled—and screaming now as they were dragged out.

Glenna shoved her way by to see, then groped behind her for Hoyt's hand. "The blonde one. That's the one who came to the door. When King—"

"Lora," Cian said. "One of Lilith's favorites. I had an . . . incident with her once." He laughed when Lora hoisted a white flag. "And if you believe that, I've all manner of bridges you can buy."

"They have people out there," Moira added. "Injured people."

"Weapons," Blair began.

"Best wait—and see how best to use them." Cian stepped away, and walked to the front door. Wind and rain sliced in when he opened it. "Lora," he called out, almost conversationally. "Why you're good and soaked, aren't you now? I'd ask you and your friends in, but I still have my sanity and my standards."

"Cian, it's been too long. Did you like my present, by the way? I didn't have time to wrap him."

"Taking credit for Lilith's work? That's just sad. And you should tell her she'll pay dearly for it."

"Tell her yourself. You and your humans have ten minutes to surrender."

"Oh? All of ten?"

"In ten minutes, we'll kill the first of these." She grabbed one of the prisoners by the hair. "Pretty, isn't she? Only sixteen. Old enough to know better than to go walking along dark roads."

"Please." The girl wept, and the blood on her neck showed

that something had already tasted her. "Please, God."

"They're always calling for God." With a laugh, Lora threw the girl facedown on the sodden grass. "He never comes. Ten minutes."

"Close the door," Blair said quietly from behind him. "Close it. Okay, give me a minute. One minute to think."

"They'll kill them regardless," Cian pointed out. "Bait is all they are."

"That's not the issue," Glenna snapped. "We have to do something."

"We fight." Larkin drew one of the swords they'd stocked in an umbrella stand near the door.

"Hold your water," Blair ordered.

"We don't surrender, not to the likes of them."

"We fight," Hoyt agreed. "But not on their terms. Glenna, the shackles."

"Yes, I can work that. I'm sure I can."

"We need more weapons from upstairs," Hoyt began.

"I said hold it." Blair grabbed his arm. "You've been in a couple of skirmishes with vampires. That doesn't prepare you. We're not just charging out there and getting cut down like meat. You can work the shackles?"

Glenna drew a breath. "Yes."

"Good. Moira, you're upstairs, bows. Cian, they've probably got guards around the house. Pick a door, start taking them out, quiet as you can manage. Hoyt's with you."

"Wait."

"I know how to do this," she told Glenna. "Are you ready to use that axe?"

"I guess we'll find out."

"Get it. You're up with Moira. They'll have archers too, and they see a hell of lot better in the dark than we do. Larkin, you and me, we're going to create a diversion. Moira, you don't start picking them off until you get the signal."

"What signal?"

"You'll know it. One more thing. Those three out there, they're already gone. All we can do is make a statement. You have to accept that chances are slim to none when it comes to saving any of them."

"We have to try," Moira insisted.

"Yeah, well, that's what we're here for. Let's go."

"Is that one of your trick swords?" Cian asked Hoyt as they approached the east door.

"It is."

"Then keep it well away from me." He touched his finger to his lips, eased open the door. For a moment, there was no sound, no movement but the rain. Then Cian was out, a blur of dark in the dark.

Even as Hoyt stepped out to follow, he saw Cian snap two necks and behead a third. "On your left," Cian said quietly.

Hoyt pivoted and met what came at him with steel, and with fire.

Upstairs, Glenna knelt within the circle she'd cast and chanted. The silver around her throat, on her finger glowed brighter with every heartbeat. Moira crouched to the side of the open doorway, a quiver at her back, a bow in her hand.

Moira glanced back at her. "The shackles."

"No, that was for something else. I'll start that now."

"What was it . . . Oh." Moira looked back into the dark, but now thanks to Glenna, with the vision of a cat. "Oh aye, that's a right good one. They've archers back in the trees. I only see six. I can take six."

"Don't go outside. Don't go out until I'm done here." Glenna fought to clear her mind, calm her heart, and call the magic.

Out of the dark, like vengeance, came a gold horse. And the rider on its back wielded death.

With Larkin at a gallop, Blair swung the torch, striking three that burst into flames and took two more into the blaze with them. Then she heaved it, spinning destruction through the air, and flashed a fiery sword.

"It's now, Glenna!" Moira let the first arrow fly. "It's now!"

"Yes, I've got it. I've got it." She grabbed the ax, and a dagger, at a run.

Moira's arrows were winging as they both sprinted into the rain. And the things that were waiting rushed them.

Glenna didn't think, only acted, only felt. She let her

body move into that dance of life and death, striking, block-ing, thrusting. Fire rippled over the blades as she swung.

There were screams, such horrible screams. Human, vampire, how could she tell? She smelled blood, tasted it; knew some of it was her own. Her heart beat, a war drum in her chest so she barely registered the arrow that whizzed by her head as she plunged fire into what leaped at her.

"They've hit Larkin. They've hit him."

At Moira's shout, Glenna saw the arrow in the foreleg of the horse. But it ran still like a demon with Blair raging de-struction from its back.

Then she saw Hoyt fighting fang and sword to get to one of the prisoners.

"I have to go help. Moira, there are too many down there."

"Go. I've got this. I'll lower the odds, I promise you."

She charged down, screaming to draw some away from Hoyt and Cian.

She thought it would be a blur, just madness rushing over her, and through her. But it was clear in every detail. The faces, the sounds, the scents, the feel of warm blood and cold rain running over her. The red eyes, the terrible hunger in them. And the horrible flash and screaming when fire took them.

She saw Cian break off the end of an arrow that had found his thigh, and plunge it into the heart of an enemy. She saw the ring she'd put on Hoyt's finger burn like another fire as he took two with one blow.

"Get them inside," he shouted to her. "Try to get them in-side."

She rolled over the wet grass toward the girl Lora had tor-mented. She half expected to find her dead. Instead she found her showing fangs in a grin.

"Oh God."

"Didn't you hear her? He doesn't come."

She pounced, knocking Glenna onto her back, then threw back her head with the joy of the kill. Blair's sword cut it off.

"You'd be surprised," Glenna returned.

"Inside," Blair shouted. "Back in. That's enough of a god-damn statement." She reached down to help Glenna mount behind her.

They left the field flaming, and covered with dust.

"How many did we kill?" Larkin demanded as he collapsed on the floor. Blood ran down his leg to puddle on the wood.

"At least thirty—damn good ratio. You've got some speed, Golden Boy." Blair looked straight into his eyes. "Winged you a little."

"It's not altogether too bad. It just—" He didn't scream when she yanked the arrow out. He didn't have the breath to scream. When he got it back, all he could manage was a stream of shaky curses.

"You next," she said to Cian, nodding at the broken arrow protruding from his thigh.

He simply reached down, yanked it out himself. "Thanks all the same."

"I'll get supplies. Your leg's bleeding," Glenna told Blair.

"We're all banged up some. But we're not dead. Well." She sent Cian a cocky grin. "Most of us."

"That never gets tired, does it?" Cian speculated and went for the brandy.

"They weren't human. In the cages." Moira held her shoulder where the tip of an arrow had grazed it.

"No. I couldn't tell from in here. Too many of them to separate the scents. It was smart." Blair nodded, a grim acknowledgment. "A good way to engage us and not waste any of their food supply. Bitch has a brain."

"We didn't get Lora." With his breath still heaving out of his lungs, Hoyt eased down. He had a gash on his side, another on his arm. "I saw her when we were fighting our way back into the house. We didn't get her."

"She's going to be mine. My very special friend." Blair pursed her lips when Cian offered her a brandy. "Thanks."

Standing in the center of them on shaky knees, Glenna took stock. "Blair, get Larkin's tunic off. I need to see the wound. Moira, how bad is your wound?"

"More a scratch, really."

"Then get some blankets from upstairs, some towels. Hoyt." Glenna moved to him, knelt, then just took his hands and buried her face in them. However much she wanted to fall apart, it wasn't time. Not time yet. "I felt you with me. I felt you with me every moment."

"I know. You were with me. *A ghrá*." He lifted her head, pressed his lips to hers.

"I wasn't scared, not while it was happening. I couldn't think to be scared. Then I reached that girl, that young girl and saw what she was. I couldn't even move."

"It's done. For tonight it's done. And we proved a match for them." He kissed her again, long, deep. "You were magnificent."

She laid a hand over the wound on his side. "I'd say we all were. And we proved more than being able to hold our own. We're a unit now."

"The circle is cast."

She let out a long sigh. "Well, it wasn't the handfasting celebration I was looking for." She struggled to smile. "But at least we . . . No, no, damn it, we didn't. We didn't finish. Just hold everything." She shoved at her dripping hair. "I will not let those monsters ruin this for us." She gripped his hand as Moira rushed down with arms loaded with towels and blankets. "Are you all listening? You're still witnesses."

"We got it," Blair said as she cleansed Larkin's wound.

"Your head's bleeding." Cian passed Moira a damp cloth. "Go right ahead," he told Glenna.

"But Glenna, your dress."

She only smiled at Moira. "It doesn't matter. Only this matters. She clasped hands with Hoyt, locked her eyes with his. "As the goddess and the god and the old ones . . ."

Hoyt's voice joined hers. "Are witness to this rite. We now proclaim we're husband and wife."

He reached down, took her face in his hands. "I will love you beyond the end of days."

Now, she thought, now, the circle was truly cast, strong and bright.

And the light glowed warmer, a wash of gold when their lips met, when their lips clung in hope and promise, and in love.

* * *

"So," the old man said, "with the handfasting complete, they tended to their wounds and began the healing. They drank a toast to the love, the true magic, that had come out of dark and out of death."

"Inside the house while the rain fell, the brave rested and prepared for the next battle."

He sat back, picking up the fresh tea a servant had sat beside him. "That is all of the story for today."

The protests were immediate, and passionate. But the old man only chuckled and shook his head.

"There'll be more tomorrow, I promise you, for the story's not finished. Only this beginning. But for now, the sun is out, and so should you be. Haven't you learned from the beginning of the tale that light is to be treasured? Go. When I finish my tea, I'll come out to watch you."

Alone, he drank his tea, watched his fire. And thought of the tale he would tell on the morrow.

Glossary of Irish Words, Characters and Places

◈

a chroi, (ah-REE) Gaelic term of endearment meaning "my heart," "my heart's beloved," "my darling"

a ghrá, (ah-GHRA) Gaelic term of endearment meaning "my love," "dear"

a stór, (ah-STOR) Gaelic term of endearment meaning "my darling"

Aideen, (Ae-DEEN) Moira's young cousin

Alice McKenna, descendant of Cian and Hoyt Mac Cionaoith

An Clar (Ahn-CLAR) modern-day County Clare

Ballycloon (ba-LU-klun)

Blair Nola Bridgitt Murphy, one of the circle of six, the "warrior"; a demon hunter, a descendant of Nola Mac Cionaoith (Cian and Hoyt's younger sister)

Bridget's Well, cemetery in County Clare, named after St. Bridget

Burren, the, a Karst limestone region in County Clare, which features caves and underground streams *cara*, (karu) Gaelic for "friend, relative"

Ceara, one of the village women

Cian (KEY-an) **Mac Cionaoith/McKenna**, Hoyt's twin brother, a vampire, Lord of Oiche, one of the circle of six "the one who is lost"

Cirio, Lilith's human lover

ciunas, (CYOON-as) Gaelic for "silence"; the battle takes place in the Valley of Ciunas—the Valley of Silence

claddaugh, the Celtic symbol of love, friendship, loyalty

Cliffs of Mohr (also Moher), the name given to the ruin of forts in the South of Ireland, on a cliff near Hag's Head "Moher O'Ruan"

Conn, Larkin's childhood puppy

Dance of the Gods, the Dance, the place in which the circle of six passes through from the real world to the fantasy world of Geall

Davey, Lilith, the Vampire Queen's "son," a child vampire

Deirdre (DAIR-dhra) **Riddock**, Larkin's mother

Dervil, (DAR-vel) one of the village women

Eire (AIR-reh), Gaelic for Ireland

Eogan, (O-en) Ceara's husband

Eoin, (OAN) Hoyt's brother-in-law

Eternity, the name of Cian's nightclub, located in New York City

Faerie Falls, imaginary place in Geall

fàilte à Geall, (FALL-che ah GY-al) Gaelic for "Welcome to Geall"

Fearghus, (FARE-gus) Hoyt's brother-in-law

Gaillimh (GALL-yuv) modern-day Galway, the capital of the West of Ireland

Geall, (GY-al), in Gaelic means "promise"; the city in which Moira and Larkin come; the city which Moira will someday rule

Glenna Ward, one of the circle of six, the "witch"; lives in modern-day New York City

Hoyt Mac Cionaoith/McKenna, (mac KHEE-nee) one of the circle of six, the "sorcerer"

Isleen, (Is-LEEN) a servant at Castle Geall

Jarl, (Yarl) Lilith's sire, the vampire who turned her into a vampire

Jeremy Hilton, Blair Murphy's ex-fiance

King, the name of Cian's best friend, whom Cian befriended when King was a child; the manager of Eternity

Larkin Riddock, one of the circle of six, the "shifter of shapes," a cousin of Moira, Queen of Geall

Lilith, the Vampire Queen, aka Queen of the Demons; leader of the war against humankind; Cian's sire, the vampire who turned Cian from human to vampire

Lora, a vampire; Lilith's lover

Lucius Lora's male vampire lover

Malvin villager, soldier in Geallian army

Manhattan, city in New York; where both Cian McKenna and Glenna Ward live

mathair, (maahir) Gaelic word for mother

Michael Thomas McKenna, descendant of Cian and Hoyt Mac Cionaoith

Mick Murphy, Blair Murphy's younger brother

Midir, (mee-DEER) vampire wizard to Lilith, Queen of the Vampires

miurnin, (also sp. miurneach [mornukh]) Gaelic for sweet-heart, term of endearment

Moira, (MWA-ra) one of the circle of six, the "scholar"; a princess, future queen of Geall

Morrigan, (Mo-ree-ghan) Goddess of the Battle

Niall, (Nile) a warrior in the Geallian army

Nola Mac Cionaoith Hoyt and Cian's youngest sister,

ogham, (ä-gem) (also spelled ogam) (ä-gem): fifth/sixth century Irish alphabet

oiche (EE-heh) Gaelic for night

Oran (O-ren) Riddock's youngest son, Larkin's younger brother

Phelan, (FA-len) Larkin's brother-in-law

Prince Riddock, Larkin's father, acting king of Geall, Moira's maternal uncle

Region of Chiarrai (kee-U-ree), modern-day Kerry, situated in the extreme southwest of Ireland, sometimes referred to as "the Kingdom"

Samhain, (SAM-en) summer's end, (Celtic festival), the battle takes place on the Feast of Samhain; the feast celebrating the end of summer

Sean Murphy, (Shawn) Blair Murphy's father, a vampire hunter

Shop Street, cultural center of Galway

Sinann, (shih-NAWN) Larkin's sister

sláinte, (slawn-che) Gaelic term for "cheers!"

slán agat, (shlahn u-gut) Gaelic for "good-bye," which is said to person staying

slán leat, (shlahn ly-aht) Gaelic for "good-bye," which is said to the person leaving

Tuatha de Danaan, (TOO-aha dai DON-nan) Welsh Gods

Tynan, (Ti-nin) guard at Castle Geall

Vlad, Cian's stallion